KEEPER
LOST CITIES
OF THE

FLASHBACK

SHANNON MESSENGER

Aladdin
New York   London   Toronto   Sydney   New Delhi

ALADDIN

An imprint of Simon & Schuster Children's Publishing Division

First Aladdin paperback edition October 2019

Text copyright © 2018 by Shannon Messenger

Cover illustration copyright © 2018 by Jason Chan

Also available in an Aladdin hardcover edition.

All rights reserved, including the right of reproduction in whole or in part in any form.

ALADDIN and related logo are registered trademarks of Simon & Schuster, Inc.

For information about special discounts for bulk purchases, please contact Simon & Schuster Special Sales at 1-866-506-1949 or business@simonandschuster.com.

The Simon & Schuster Speakers Bureau can bring authors to your live event. For more information or to book an event contact the Simon & Schuster Speakers Bureau at 1-866-248-3049 or visit our website at www.simonspeakers.com.

Cover designed by Karin Paprocki

Interior designed by Mike Rosamilia

The text of this book was set in Scala.

Manufactured in the United States of America 0819 OFF

6 8 10 9 7

Library of Congress Control Number 2018957531

ISBN 9781481497435 (hc)

ISBN 9781481497442 (pbk)

ISBN 9781481497459 (eBook)

For Mara Anastas, for believing from the beginning.
For Jon Anderson, for throwing down the gauntlet.
And for the rest of my incredible team at
Simon & Schuster, for rising to the challenge.

PREFACE

THIS TIME WE WIN.

It was Sophie's only thought, even as the world around her fell into shadow and chaos.

Even as the Neverseen revealed their next move—their next twist in this deadly game.

A game Sophie had lost over and over again.

But this time she was ready.

This time she'd trained—and so had her friends.

This time, they knew how to fight back.

So Sophie's hand didn't shake as she reached for one of the throwing stars she'd learned to carry.

And she knew exactly where to aim.

No hesitation.

No fear.

But . . . things weren't always as they appeared.

And as everything flickered and faded, as her friends shouted and struggled to understand . . .

Sophie knew.

Illusion was her enemy's new secret weapon.

ONE

S O IS IT STRANGE COMING HERE AND *not* being the one on trial?" Keefe asked, checking his expertly styled blond hair in a shiny facet on one of the jeweled walls before he followed Sophie into Tribunal Hall. "Because I'd be happy to help you break a few laws if you're feeling left out."

"Me too!" Ro—Keefe's bodyguard—jumped in. Her pierced nose crinkled as she surveyed the empty auditorium, which was built entirely out of emeralds. "Ugh, you guys have really out-sparkled yourselves with this place. It's basically begging me to smash something."

"No one will be smashing anything," Sandor—Sophie's bodyguard—warned. "Or causing any other problems!"

The threat didn't sound all that terrifying, thanks to Sandor's squeaky voice. But he backed it up by being a seven-foot-tall goblin warrior—and by folding his gray arms across his bare chest and flexing some seriously impressive muscles.

Ro flashed a pointy-toothed smile and patted the rows of daggers—a recent addition to her ogre arsenal—strapped to her toned thighs. "I'd like to see you try to stop us."

"Believe me, I'd enjoy every second," Sandor growled, gripping the hilt of his giant black sword. "I still can't believe the Council is allowing you into these proceedings."

Neither could Sophie.

Then again, she hadn't expected to be invited either.

The Tribunal was supposed to be restricted to members of the Vacker family, since it was only a sentencing hearing—and mostly a formality. Alvar was already being held in the secret prison the Black Swan had designed specifically for him. The Council was simply deciding how many years he'd have to stay there.

But Alden had stopped by Havenfield that morning and explained that he'd gotten permission for Sophie to attend. And when she'd light leaped to Eternalia, she'd found Keefe and Ro already waiting.

Keefe looked dressier than usual, in a starched white shirt with a fitted black jerkin and an embroidered gray cape—and Sophie was relieved to see it, since she'd decided to show her support with a dusty-rose gown that was much more Biana's fancy style than hers. She'd also used the gold-flecked eyeliner Biana had been telling her would bring out the glints in her brown eyes—even though she hated drawing more attention to their unique-for-an-elf color.

"What?" Sophie asked, wiping under her lashes when she noticed Keefe staring. "Did I smudge it?"

"No, Foster. You look . . . perfect."

She blushed at the slight catch in his voice—and then wished she hadn't when he flashed his trademark smirk.

"Did Alden tell you he wanted you to be here for moral support too?" she asked, stopping in the center of the hall as she realized she didn't know which of the hundreds of seats were theirs.

His smile faded. "Yeah. He said Fitz was going to need a friend today."

"He said a lot more than that," Ro muttered.

"Relax, Foster," Keefe said, shooting Ro a glare before he pointed to the crease that had formed between Sophie's eyebrows. "No need to get all crinkly on me. Nothing's going on. Alden's just . . . worried about how Fitz is going to handle this."

"So am I," Sophie admitted.

Anger was often Fitz's crutch in emotionally fraught situations—and nothing brought out his fury more than his traitorous older brother.

"Yeah, well, now I'm stuck listening to a bunch of stuffy, know-it-all elves arguing with each other," Ro groused as she twisted one of her choppy pigtails, which she'd recently dyed the same vivid pink she'd painted her claws. "It almost makes me wish I were still bedridden. Seriously, who thought having *twelve* Councillors was a good idea?"

Sophie was tempted to point out that the system was much more balanced than having a single power-hungry king. But since Ro was the daughter of the ogres' fear-inspiring leader—and the elves' alliance with King Dimitar had become rather shaky after the Neverseen almost killed Ro during their attack on Atlantis—she decided it was smart to avoid that particular conversation. Especially since the elvin Council was far from perfect.

She turned toward the twelve jeweled thrones that filled a large platform at the front of the glinting green room. Each had been ornamented to reflect the style and taste of the Councillor whose name was displayed along the top: Clarette, Velia, Alina, Terik, Liora, Emery, Oralie, Ramira, Darek, Noland, Zarina, and Bronte.

Sophie knew some of them better than others, and there were a couple she'd even grown to trust. But she would never stop wishing that there was still a simple, sturdy throne for Councillor Kenric.

Kenric had been kind. And funny. And one of Sophie's most loyal supporters.

And he'd still be alive if it weren't for her.

She tried not to let herself think about it, because the guilt might shatter her sanity. But she could still feel the stinging heat of the flames—still hear the crunches and crackles and screams as the jeweled tower melted around them. And she'd never forget Fintan's taunt as he'd ignited the Everblaze to prevent her from retrieving his memories.

Sophie had only been in Oblivimyre that night because of a direct order from the Council. But if she'd been stronger, faster, smarter than Fintan . . .

"You okay?" Keefe asked, flicking a strand of her blond hair to get her attention. "And before you answer, remember: You're talking to an Empath. Plus, you've already pulled out two eyelashes since we got here, and I can tell you're dying to go for a third."

She was.

Her eyelashes itched whenever she felt anxious, and tugging on them was *such* a relief. But she kept trying to break the habit, so she held her hands at her sides and forced herself to meet Keefe's ice blue eyes. "I'm fine."

When he raised one eyebrow, she added, "I'm just frustrated. I wish the Council was holding a Tribunal for Fintan, not Alvar."

Keefe leaned slightly closer. "I wouldn't let the Fitzster hear you say that."

"I know. Or Biana."

The younger Vacker siblings had been counting down the days to Alvar's sentencing—and Sophie didn't blame them for wanting everything settled with their older brother.

But . . .

She glanced over her shoulder, grateful the auditorium was still empty, so she could ask the question she'd been trying not to say.

"Doesn't this feel like a waste of time?"

"Because Alvar can't remember anything?" Keefe asked.

Sophie nodded.

Alvar had been a longtime member of the Neverseen, involved in many of their cruelest schemes before Sophie and her friends found him drugged, bleeding, and trapped in a cell in an abandoned hideout. And when he'd finally regained consciousness, he couldn't even remember his own name.

He didn't seem to be faking, either. Sophie had checked. So had Fitz. And Alden. And Mr. Forkle. And Quinlin. And Councillor Emery—along with every other Telepath the Council trusted. None of them could find a single memory in Alvar's head, no matter how deeply they searched. The Black Swan had even brought in Damel—a trained Washer—who'd told them that Alvar's past had been scrubbed cleaner than he'd realized was possible. And Sophie had tried using her unique telepathic abilities to perform a mental healing, but it hadn't made a difference. Neither had any of the elixirs a team of physicians had given him.

Alvar's mind wasn't broken or damaged.

It was . . . blank.

Sophie had never felt anything like it—and she'd experienced some pretty bizarre mental landscapes over the last few years. There was no cold, suffocating darkness. No sharp, fragmented images. Just soft, fuzzy gray space.

"I don't understand why the Council is focusing on someone with amnesia," she whispered to Keefe, "when they have Fintan in custody and they're doing *nothing*."

The former leader of the Neverseen had been captured during the raid on Nightfall. But Fintan had cut a deal with the Council for his cooperation. So he was currently being held in a prison built specifically for him, in exchange for sharing the location of a small supply of the antidote to soporidine—a dangerous sedative the Neverseen had developed for some still-undetermined purpose. He'd also demanded that all Telepaths be kept far away, to ensure that no one could mess with his memories. And while the Council did at least make him agree to help them gain access to his old cache—a small, marble-size gadget that contained dangerous memories called Forgotten Secrets—either Fintan was sabotaging the process, or caches were flawed inventions, because weeks had passed and they hadn't recovered a single piece of information.

"You think he's planning something," Keefe guessed.

"Don't you?"

Fintan had already proven that he was the master of long, intricate schemes. He'd destroyed Lumenaria—and freed Vespera from the castle's dungeon—with a plan that required key members of the Neverseen to allow themselves to be imprisoned. He could be pulling a similar trick again—and Sophie knew she could find out if the Council would just let her meet with him.

But all of her requests for a visit had been denied. And when she'd asked the Black Swan's Collective for help, they'd told her the Council wasn't giving them access either.

"Why is Fintan still calling the shots?" she murmured. "He already gave us the antidote."

"I don't know." Keefe seemed to debate with himself before he added, "But he's never going to cooperate. So do you *really* want to do another memory break on him? After what happened with Alden—and Kenric . . ."

Sophie stared at her hands, tracing her finger along one of the thumb rings peeking through her lacy gloves. The engraved bands had been a gift from Fitz, to identify the two of them as Cognates—and the rare telepathic connection made them far more powerful together than they'd been the last time they'd taken on Fintan. She'd also manifested as an Enhancer, which meant she could boost Fitz's mental strength with a single touch of her fingertips. So she had no doubt that they *would* get past Fintan's blocking and find whatever he was hiding.

But . . . memory breaks were horrible, brutal things—even when they were necessary.

"I don't see any other choice," she admitted. "Even if he's not part of some bigger scheme, Fintan has to at least know what Vespera's planning."

"But he won't know what my mom's up to," Keefe reminded her. "And she's the one running things now."

Sophie wasn't entirely convinced that was true.

Lady Gisela *had* seized control of the Neverseen when she'd tried to destroy Atlantis. But Vespera only allied with her because Keefe's mom trapped her in a force field and threatened to leave her there until the Council arrived to arrest her. And Vespera didn't seem like the type who'd cooperate for long—especially since she'd insisted that she and Lady Gisela had opposite visions.

Then again, Keefe's mom had already clawed her way back to power once, so she must be taking precautions to make sure no one could overthrow her again.

"We have too many villains," Sophie said through a sigh.

Keefe snorted. "You're not wrong."

She wasn't even counting the other members of the Neverseen. Or the ogres who'd defected from King Dimitar. Or the dwarves who'd disappeared months ago, presumably to join the rebellion. Or—

"Hey," Keefe said, fanning the air the way he always did when her emotions started to spiral. "We've got this, okay? I know it doesn't feel like it—"

"It doesn't," Sophie agreed.

They'd been trying to come up with a plan for weeks and still had nothing. And whenever the Neverseen kept them stumped like that, people got hurt.

Sophie had even risked using Keefe's old Imparter, which his mom had rigged with a secret way to contact her. But Lady Gisela was either ignoring them, or she'd severed the connection. And the Black Swan had confiscated the gadget in case anyone could use it to monitor them.

Keefe grinned. "You're so adorable when you worry. I've told you that, right?"

Sophie gave him her best glare, and his smile only widened.

He stepped closer, reaching for her hands. "Let's just get through today, okay? Then no one will be distracted by Alvar anymore, and we'll be able to focus."

"Yeah. I guess."

"Hmm." He traced his thumb over the sliver of skin between her glove and the edge of her beaded sleeve. "There's something you're not saying right now. I can feel it."

There was.

The *other* question she'd been trying not to ask, because she was pretty sure she knew what her friends would say.

"Come on, Foster. It's me. You know you can trust me. And you already know all of my worst secrets, so . . ."

It was the sincerity in his eyes that made her glance over her shoulder again, making sure the room was still empty before she whispered, "Do you think it's weird to punish someone for crimes they don't remember committing?"

"Weird?" Keefe asked. "Or *wrong*?"

"Both, I guess."

He nodded and stepped back, running a hand down his face. "Well . . . everything about this is weird. But, just because Alvar doesn't remember the creepy things he did, it doesn't mean they didn't happen."

"True."

Sophie knew better than anyone what Alvar was capable of. And yet . . . the few times she'd seen him since he lost his memory, he'd seemed *different*.

He wasn't slick, or arrogant, or angry.

He was terrified. And desperate. And he'd spent the whole time begging everyone to realize he wasn't the person they thought he was.

"He could still get his memories back," Keefe reminded her. "Just because we haven't found the right trigger yet doesn't mean the Neverseen didn't plan for one."

That was another reason Sophie wanted a chance to poke around Fintan's head. They'd recovered Alvar months before Fintan was arrested, so he had to know why Alvar ended up in that cell.

But since the Council wasn't cooperating, Sophie had convinced Mr. Forkle to bring Alvar to places from his past, like the apartment he'd been living in and the destroyed Neverseen hideouts they'd found. They'd also spent days exposing Alvar to random images and sounds and smells—even tastes—trying to trigger a hint of familiarity.

None of it had caused even the tiniest flashback.

And she was starting to think that nothing ever would.

"I'm not saying I trust Alvar," she said, turning to stare at the hundreds of empty seats. "But I also know how terrifying it is to stand in this room and face the Council, and I can't imagine going through it without even remembering why I'm on trial. I mean . . . Alvar's future is being decided by a past he doesn't believe is his."

"But it *is* his," Keefe argued. "It's not like we're making this up. He helped kidnap you and Dex, and he helped the Neverseen grab Wylie and torture him, and he helped abduct your human family—and that's only the stuff we know about. I saw what he was like when I was pretending to join the Neverseen. He was *all in*. One-hundred-percent committed to their cause, no matter what they asked him to do. And he'd still be just as dedicated if they hadn't gotten rid of him—if that's really what happened. Do you want to let him off the hook just because they wiped his mind to keep him from telling us their secrets?"

"No. But keeping him locked up in that miserable cell still feels . . . unfair, somehow."

"Ugh, you elves overthink everything," Ro grumbled. "It's simple: A traitor's a traitor, and they need to be punished so everyone understands there are consequences for treason. If you're not willing to end him, lock him up and destroy the key. Or better yet, leave it hanging in his line of sight so he has to stare at it forever, knowing he'll never be able to reach it."

"For once the ogre princess and I agree," Sandor added.

Sophie sighed. "Well, I guess it's a good thing I don't have to make the decision."

"It is," Keefe agreed. "'Cause I'm pretty sure Fitz is going to have a meltdown if the Council gives Alvar anything less than a life sentence."

The idea made Sophie cringe.

The elves called their life span "indefinite," because so far no one had ever died of old age. So if Fitz got his wish, Alvar would be spending thousands of years locked away—maybe even millions. And his cell wasn't just cramped and stuffy. It was buried in the middle of a putrid bog and smelled worse than imp breath.

Keefe moved back to her side, leaning in to whisper. "I do get what you're saying, Foster. Punishing the bad guys is supposed to be easier than this—and way more fun."

"Yeah," Sophie said quietly. "I've been angry at Alvar for so long, I never thought I'd end up feeling sorry for him."

"Aaaaaaaaaaaaaaaaand this is why we're going to be stuck here for hours," Ro whined.

"Nah, I'm sure the Council already made their decision," Keefe told her. "They're just putting on a good show for the Vackers."

"Wanna bet?" Ro's grin looked dangerous when she added, "I say we'll be here until sunset—and if I'm right, you have to wear ogre armor to school, instead of your uniform."

Keefe smirked. "No big deal. I would rock that metal diaper. But *I* say that this hearing will be done in an hour—and if I'm right, you have to call me Lord Hunkyhair from now on."

Sophie shook her head. "You guys are terrible."

"That's why you love us!" Keefe draped his arm around her shoulders. "You should get in on this, Foster. I'm sure that devious mind of yours can come up with some particularly humiliating ways to punish us if we're wrong."

She probably could. But no way was she risking having to wear a metal breastplate to Foxfire. Ro's looked like a medieval corset paired with spiked metal bikini bottoms.

"Hard pass," she told him.

Keefe heaved a dramatic sigh. "Fiiiiiiiiiine. I guess I can't blame you, since I already owe you a favor. Any thoughts on what my penance is going to be, by the way? Don't think I haven't noticed how long you've been stalling."

"I'm not *stalling*," Sophie insisted. "I just . . . haven't figured out what I want."

"Yeah, I know." The teasing tone faded from his voice, replaced with something that made Sophie very aware of how close they were standing. "Take your time," he told her, the words mostly a whisper. "Just . . . let me know when you figure it out. Because I—"

The doors to the hall burst open, cutting off whatever else he was going to say.

"Oh good. Here comes the elf parade," Ro muttered.

"The *Vacker* parade," Keefe corrected. "And get ready for it. They're the sparkliest of us all."

They really were.

Sophie's jaw even dropped a little as she watched the legendary family filing into the hall in their elaborate gowns and perfectly tailored jerkins and jeweled capes. She'd thought she was used to the extreme wealth and ageless beauty of the elves. But the Vackers *demanded* attention in a way she didn't know how to explain. There was something striking about each and every one of them—which was extra impressive considering how different they all looked from each other. She spotted every hair color, skin color, feature shape, and body type. It probably shouldn't have caught her by surprise—the family line went back thousands of years, and elves didn't separate themselves by appearance the way humans often did. But she was so used to how closely Fitz, Biana, and Alvar resembled their parents that she'd foolishly imagined all their relatives with similar dark hair and pale coloring.

She studied everyone as they passed, hoping she'd catch a glimpse of Fallon Vacker—Fitz and Biana's great-great-great-great-great-great-great-great-great-great-great-great-great-great-great-great-great-great-grandfather. She'd been trying to meet with him for months, hoping he could tell her more about why he'd sentenced Vespera to the Lumenaria dungeon. But he'd been annoyingly uncooperative.

There were quite a few males with pointy ears—the trademark

of the Ancients—but Sophie didn't know any other details about Fallon's appearance to help her narrow it down. And she couldn't ask Keefe—the hall was *way* too quiet. No one said a word as they climbed the auditorium's stairs and took their seats.

And yet, somehow, the silence grew thicker when the doors opened again and Alden and Della strode into the hall, followed by Fitz and Biana and their goblin bodyguards, Grizel and Woltzer.

Sophie had seen her friends shattered by grief, shaking with anger, sobbing with hysterics—even battered and bloody and half dead. But she'd never seen them looking so . . . timid. Their clothes were dark and boring, and they kept their teal eyes focused on the floor. Biana even disappeared for longer between her steps than her vanishing ability usually caused.

So did Della, who'd worn her long hair pulled back into a simple knot, along with a gown and cape that were dull gray, without any frills.

Alden's cape and jerkin were equally plain.

Not that any of it helped them draw less attention.

The air in the room shifted, turning hotter and heavier with each stare sent their way—a blast of searing judgment aimed at the family of Vackers who'd brought scorn upon the name. And Fitz and Biana seemed to shrink under the weight of it, ducking their chins and picking up their pace as angry murmurs began to swell—starting as a low rustle and growing into a pounding thrum.

Sophie tried to think of something to say as they drew closer, but her mind wasn't cooperating—and for once Keefe didn't seem to have a joke ready. So she was forced to go with the less-than-inspiring "Hey."

Biana's head snapped up. "Whoa, what are you guys doing here?"

"Your dad didn't tell you he got us in?" Keefe asked, dropping his arm from Sophie's shoulders when he noticed Fitz staring at them.

"I wanted it to be a surprise," Alden explained. "I hope that's okay."

"Of course it is!" Biana practically tackled Sophie with her hug—but Sophie hugged her back as gently as she could.

Biana kept claiming that she'd recovered from the brutal injuries she'd suffered in Nightfall, but Sophie had noticed that Biana always wore long sleeves now and chose gowns and tunics that covered her neck and shoulders.

"By the way, you look awesome," Biana said, pulling away to admire Sophie's dress. "Now I'm wishing I braided my hair or something."

"Oh please, you look amazing," Sophie assured her. "Like always."

It wasn't a lie.

Even in a hall full of Vackers, Biana managed to shine.

So did Fitz—though Sophie was trying not to notice.

"Hey, Fitzy," Keefe said, elbowing Fitz's side. "Wanna join our bet on how long this Tribunal is going to last? You get to name your terms—oh, but if you lose, you'll have to wear a metal diaper to school and call me Lord Hunkyhair from now on."

"Uh . . . yeah, *no*," Fitz said as Biana asked, "Hunkyhair?"

"*Lord* Hunkyhair," Keefe corrected. "What? It's accurate." He tossed his head like he was in a shampoo commercial. "I think we need to make it a thing either way—don't you, Foster?"

"I think you're ridiculous," Sophie told him.

Then again, Biana was giggling. And Fitz's lips were twitching with the beginning of a smile. Even Alden and Della had relaxed a little.

But everyone turned serious as Alden motioned for them to follow him toward a narrow silver staircase that led up to a platform with a row of chairs facing the Councillors' thrones.

Fitz offered Sophie his arm, and she tried to ignore the way her insides fluttered at the gesture. He was probably only doing it because everyone knew that climbing things without tripping wasn't one of her strengths—particularly when she was wearing heels. But her face still grew warm as she hooked her elbow around his.

It got even warmer when he told her, "I'm glad you're here."

"So am I."

She meant it, even though the buzz in the room was shifting tone—and she caught enough scattered words to know many were now talking about her.

"Raised by humans."

"Genetically altered."

"Project Moonlark."

There were also a few mentions of "matchmaking" in the mix, and Sophie decided she did *not* want to know what they were saying. Especially when she noticed Keefe's smirk.

Fitz guided her to a chair on the far left of the platform and took the seat next to her, with Keefe sitting on his other side, followed by Biana, Della, and Alden. All the bodyguards took up positions behind them.

"Where's Alvar going to be?" Sophie whispered, noticing that there were no empty seats.

Alden pointed to a portion of the floor that had a square pattern. "That platform will rise once he's standing on it."

"He has to face the Council alone," Della added quietly.

"And it looks like our time starts *now*," Keefe told Ro, as two dozen heavily armed goblins marched into the hall and took up positions around the Councillors' thrones.

"They call *that* security?" Ro huffed. "I could take them down without even drawing a dagger."

Fanfare drowned out Sandor's reply—which was probably for the best. And Sophie's insides squished together as all twelve Councillors shimmered onto the platform in their gleaming silver cloaks and twinkling circlets.

Ro snorted. "Wow. Do the jewels in their crowns *seriously* match their thrones?"

"I suppose you'd rather we ink our adornments to our skin?" Councillor Emery called back.

His deep, velvety voice bounced off the emerald walls—but Ro didn't look the least bit intimidated as she reached up and traced one of her pink claws over the tattoos swirling across her forehead.

"I doubt you guys could handle the pain," she told him.

"I think you'd be surprised what we can bear," Councillor Emery responded.

His skin was usually a shade similar to his long dark hair—but whatever memories inspired his statement had turned him slightly ashen.

"But that's not what we're here to discuss," he added, taking a seat in his sapphire-encrusted throne, which matched both his circlet and his eyes. "I know many in this hall have important assignments to return to. So let's not waste time."

"Did you hear that?" Keefe asked Ro as the other Councillors sat in their respective thrones. "They're *not* going to waste time."

"Psh—like that's going to last," Ro argued.

"Bring in the accused!" Emery commanded, and four additional goblin warriors marched into the hall, flanking a hooded figure who blinked in and out of sight with every step, just like his mother and sister.

Alvar had never been as effortlessly attractive as his younger siblings, but he'd always made up for it with immaculate clothes, perfectly gelled hair, and a build that looked like he'd spent hours working out every day. He would've been horrified by the scrawny, battered person he'd become. His loose gray cloak seemed to swallow him, and greasy strands of his dark hair hung in his pale blue eyes.

But worst of all were the curved red scars marring his gaunt face.

"The Council better get this right," Fitz whispered as the platform raised Alvar to the Councillors' height.

"State your name for the record," Councillor Emery ordered.

Alvar gave a wobbly bow and drew back his hood. "I'm told it's Alvar Soren Vacker."

"You sound as if you don't believe that to be the case," Emery noted.

"I don't know what I believe," Alvar told him. "Like I keep telling you, I have no memory of my past."

Fitz reached for Sophie's hand when Councillor Emery closed his eyes. As spokesperson for the Council, Emery's job was to telepathically mediate all arguments, to ensure the Councillors presented a unified front for the audience.

Several long seconds passed—and Ro's grin widened with each one—before Emery asked Alvar, "Do you understand why we've brought you before us today?"

Alvar bowed again. "I understand that certain charges have been raised against me. But I have no way to verify them."

"Are you implying that we're liars?" a sharp voice barked.

All eyes shifted to Councillor Bronte, the oldest member of the Council—with the pointy ears to prove it, along with the piercing stare of an elf who could inflict pain on anyone he wished with a simple glance.

Alvar shrank back a step. "Of course not. I'm just . . . emphasizing my predicament. You keep outlining my crimes—but I feel no connection to any of it. Just like I feel no connection to anyone in this room, even though I'm told you're my family." He glanced behind him, studying the intimidating crowd before his eyes settled on Alden and Della. "I wish I could remember you. I wish I could remember *anything*. But since I can't, all I'll say is . . . whoever did these horrible things that you've accused me of—that's not me. Maybe it used to be. And if that's the case, I'm truly sorry. But I promise I'm not that person anymore."

"Right," Fitz muttered, loud enough for the word to echo off the walls.

"I understand your skepticism," Councillor Emery told him. "We have doubts as well."

"Then let me prove myself!" Alvar begged. "I realize the chance of regaining my freedom is slim. But if you *did* decide to grant it—"

"We'd be endangering the lives of everyone in the Lost Cities," Councillor Emery finished for him. "Whether you remember your past or not, your connection to the Neverseen poses a threat we cannot ignore."

Alvar's shoulders slumped.

"*But,*" Emery added, and the whole room seemed to suck in a breath, "your current imprisonment also creates quite the conundrum."

Fitz's hand shook and Sophie tightened her hold, twining her gloved fingers with his as Councillor Emery closed his eyes and rubbed his temples.

Ro leaned down and whispered to Keefe, "Settle in for a long debate, Betting Boy. And get ready to prance around school in our tiniest armor."

Keefe shrugged.

But Emery stood, pacing twice along the platform before pausing to face Alvar. "I'll admit, none of us are entirely comfortable with what I'm about to say—but we're also not willing to issue a sentence while there are so many uncertain variables."

"WHAT?" Fitz blurted, jumping to his feet.

"We understand that this is an emotionally challenging situation for you," Emery told Fitz. "That's why I'm tolerating your interruptions. But surely you can agree that the primary goal of any punishment must be to prevent further crimes from being committed. And we cannot determine what's necessary for your brother in that regard until we discover who he is *now*. We need to witness how he interacts with others and study how he behaves in ordinary situations—which cannot happen in his isolated cell. But since we can't trust him either, we must move him to an environment where we can keep him constantly monitored and separated from our larger world while still providing ample opportunities for us to take his measure."

Sophie noticed the total lack of surprise on Alden's and Della's faces the same moment she realized that *this* was why she'd been invited for moral support.

A quick glance at Keefe told her he'd come to the same conclusion.

So neither of them gasped with the rest of the crowd when Emery announced the Council's decision. But she still felt a sour wave of dread wash through her when he said, "For the next six months, Alvar will be returning to Everglen."

TWO

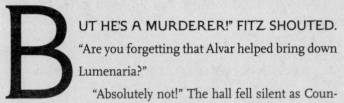

BUT HE'S A MURDERER!" FITZ SHOUTED. "Are you forgetting that Alvar helped bring down Lumenaria?"

"Absolutely not!" The hall fell silent as Councillor Terik rose from his emerald-encrusted throne.

Sophie hadn't seen him since the devastating Peace Summit, when the majestic castle had crumbled around them—and he actually looked better than she'd been imagining, given his injuries. His pale skin showed no sign of any scars, and his cobalt blue eyes were bright and clear. But when he stepped forward . . .

His right leg moved smoothly, but his left leg was much stiffer and slower. If it weren't for the silver cane he pulled from the folds of his cloak, he would've toppled over.

"As you can see, I'm still adjusting." He tapped his left leg with his cane, filling the hall with a soft clanking that confirmed what was hidden underneath the thick fabric of his clothes.

Elvin physicians were light-years ahead of human medicine, but even they couldn't regrow a severed limb. Instead, a team of Technopaths had built Terik a custom prosthesis.

But metal would never work exactly the same as muscle and bone.

In fact, when Terik took another wobbly step, he couldn't hide his grimace—which was probably why he told Fitz, "I understand your fury better than anyone. But . . . we must not let our anger make us overlook potential."

The last word rippled through the room as his meaning sank in.

"Yes," he said, tucking a loose piece of his wavy brown hair back under his emerald circlet. "I performed a new reading on Alvar."

Terik was the Lost Cities' only Descryer, which meant he could sense the potential of anyone he tested. But he rarely put the ability to use, claiming it caused too many problems.

He turned to study Alvar. "I told myself that if the results were the same as my prior reading, I'd push for a life sentence. But something's changed."

Alvar sucked in a breath. "What does that mean?"

"Truthfully? I have no idea," Terik admitted. "Readings can be difficult to interpret."

"Then how do you know he's not worse?" Fitz countered.

"I don't. Potential is a tricky thing. We have to live up to it in order for it to matter. But it shouldn't be ignored either— especially in a situation like this. We're all born with certain qualities. Certain limitations and abilities. But our experiences are what truly shape us. Everything we see and learn and do makes us who we are. And in Alvar's case, all of that has been wiped away. So we can't presume to know anything about him. Nor can we assume that he'll make the same choices he once did."

"Which is why we're giving you these six months," Emery told Alvar. "Prove yourself worthy, and we'll take it into consideration during your final sentencing. Fail to impress, and we'll make sure you never see daylight again."

"And don't expect any leniency," Councillor Alina—Sophie's least favorite Councillor—added. She tossed her long dark hair, which gleamed with caramel-colored highlights as she rose from her peridot-covered throne. "The smallest mistake will end your trial period immediately. And you'll be sharing your apartment with two of our most trusted goblin warriors, who'll make sure we know everything you do."

Biana frowned. "What apartment?"

"A team of gnomes is building a separate residence for Alvar on our property," Alden explained. "Your mother and I figured that would be easier than having him in the main house."

Fitz whipped around. "So then you guys knew this was happening."

"Fitz," Della tried.

He shook his head, turning to Sophie and Keefe. "Did you know too? Is that why you're here?"

"They're here because I asked them to come," Alden jumped in. "I didn't tell them why. But yes, your mother and I found out this morning, when Councillor Terik stopped by to make sure the Council had our permission to move Alvar to our private property."

"And you gave it?" Biana asked, moving to Fitz's side, as if an invisible line had just been drawn between them and their parents.

Della sighed. "I know this isn't what either of you want to hear. But Alvar's our son—and your brother. We owe it to him to—"

"We don't owe him *anything*!" Fitz interrupted. "He betrayed us! And if you think he won't do it again, you're—"

"I'd think twice before resorting to insults," Councillor Emery warned. "This is the *Council's* decision."

Fitz clenched his jaw so tight, a muscle twitched along his chin.

Alden cleared his throat. "I know you're angry, Fitz. And I won't tell you not to be. But try not to make this a bigger deal than it is. It's six months of your life."

"A lot can happen in six months," a voice called from the hall's entrance, with the same crisp accent that Fitz, Biana, and Alden all shared.

Whispers rustled through the crowd as a blond male wearing a pristine white cloak stepped the rest of the way through the doors. His face was all lines and angles, and his ears had the highest points Sophie had ever seen, so she wasn't completely surprised when Bronte said, "It's good to see you, Fallon. I wasn't expecting you to join us today."

"I wasn't expecting to be here," Fallon admitted, glancing behind him like he was tempted to turn and flee.

Sophie craned her neck to get a better view of the notoriously reclusive Vacker—and for the first time, she understood why people often paired the word "handsome" with "devastating." His white-blond hair grew to a dramatic widow's peak, adding a severity to his perfectly chiseled features. But it was his eyes that demanded the most attention. Dark as a midnight sky and shining with an intensity that could only come from millennia of wisdom.

"Well . . . we're glad you could make it," Emery said as all twelve Councillors gave a slight dip of their heads. The gesture wasn't a bow, but Sophie suspected it was meant to acknowledge the fact that Fallon wasn't just a former Councillor. He'd been one of the three founding members, serving for nearly a thousand years before he resigned to marry Fitz and Biana's great-great-great-great-great-great-great-great-great-great-great-great-great-great-great-great-great-great-great-grandmother.

Councillors weren't allowed to have husbands or wives or children in case it biased their decisions.

Fallon wrung his hands as he gazed around the room. "Forgive my tardiness. I prefer the solace of home. It's the only place where my mind doesn't struggle to separate what *is* from what used to be. I don't know how you bear it, Bronte."

"It helps to stay immersed," Bronte told him. "Keep myself fully in the present."

"I suppose." Fallon's eyes glazed over as he stared at some distant point. "But the world has grown . . . exhausting."

Silence followed, until Emery said—with the slightest hint of irritation—"I assume you have a reason for interrupting our proceedings."

Fallon blinked hard, dropping his hands back to his sides. "I do. Or . . . I did. I think I lost track of it. What did I say again?"

"This guy's my new favorite," Ro whispered as she grabbed Keefe's shoulders and gave him a rough shake. "Get ready to show off those skinny legs at school."

"They're not skinny," Keefe muttered before he called to Fallon, "You said, 'A lot can happen in six months.'"

"Ah. Yes. That does sound familiar. And a lot *can* happen." Fallon stared at his fingers, twisting them around each other. "But there was something else I was going to add . . . and I seem to have lost my hold on it."

Ro snickered through another long stretch of silence, and Sophie tried not to smile at the way Keefe squirmed.

Eventually Emery said, "Well, you're welcome to visit our offices whenever you remember. But for now, we must get back to the matter at hand." He turned to Alvar. "We'll move you to Everglen as soon as—"

"Everglen!" Fallon repeated. "That's what it was!" He stepped closer, into the shadow of the Council's thrones. "You don't think it's imprudent to send him home?"

"Why would it be?" Emery asked.

"I can think of two reasons," Fallon told him. "For one, Everglen is an Ancient property. In fact, I believe some of the original structure still stands."

"One room does, yes," Alden agreed. "The space I use for my personal office has been there since the beginning. Why does that matter?"

"I can't say for certain." Fallon's eyes shifted to Bronte. "But things from our past are often more than they seem."

Sophie's heart paused at that, and her mind ran through a list of the lies she'd already helped uncover.

The Four Seasons Tree. Nightfall. Even the reason the elves sank Atlantis and severed all ties with humans.

All of those had turned out to be very different from what their Mentors taught in elvin history—if the stories had been mentioned at all.

The Lost Cities wasn't a bad place. But it wasn't the ideal world everyone wanted it to be either. And it had a *lot* of buried secrets.

"Is there anything weird about Everglen?" she asked Alden.

"Not that I'm aware of," he told her. "When I inherited the property, I made extensive renovations. But it's always been used as a private residence. Do you know something that I don't, Fallon?"

"Not necessarily," Fallon said, staring into the distance once again. "But everyone in this room knows that Vackers never do anything arbitrarily. That property was chosen for a reason."

"Yes. I liked the view," a gorgeous female with pointed ears jutting from her shiny black hair said as she rose from her seat. Her angled, clear blue eyes were lined with deep purple— the same shade as her long, silky gown. And her bronze skin shimmered with flecks of amethyst glitter. "The lake was so serene at night, the way it reflected the stars. It was the perfect place to let my mind rest after a long day of bending the sun."

"Who's that?" Sophie leaned in and whispered to Keefe.

He tilted his head. "Pretty sure that's Luzia Vacker. She's a super-famous Flasher."

"Not the *most* famous, though," Luzia clarified, and Sophie flushed, wondering how Luzia could've heard them. "That would be my son."

"Orem," Keefe whispered, pointing to an elf a few seats over from Luzia, with neatly cropped hair and his mother's coloring.

Orem was one of the few Vackers that Sophie had heard of. She'd even been to the famous light show that he put on during the Celestial Festival.

"Don't be so modest, Sister," Fallon told Luzia, and Sophie's eyebrows shot up at the label. "We'd all be living underground without your work."

"Luzia helped create many of the illusions that keep our cities hidden," Alden explained.

"Wait," Sophie said, sitting up straighter. "Does that mean she worked with Vespera?"

"Occasionally," Luzia admitted, smoothing the waistline on her gown. "Many of her ideas were my starting point. But we had very little contact. I always found her *unsettling*—and I certainly never invited her to my home, in case anyone is now wondering. Sorry, Brother, you're on the wrong track with this."

Several other Vackers echoed Luzia's sentiments. And Sophie wanted to believe them.

But she also remembered what Alvar had told Biana when he'd finally revealed that he was part of the Neverseen.

You'll understand, someday, when you see the Vacker legacy for what it is.

"Don't you think we should check before we move Alvar back to Everglen?" Sophie asked, loud enough to address the Council. "To make sure we haven't missed something?"

"There's nothing to miss," Luzia insisted. "The property was my personal refuge, nothing more."

"Then why did you let it go?" Fallon asked. "I would never part with Mistmead, and I'm sure all of us feel that way about our homes."

"Yes, well, I've learned to keep free from such silly sentiments," Luzia told him.

Fallon narrowed his eyes. "I don't believe you. You may be

able to fool others with your nonchalance. But I'm your brother."

Luzia laughed. "My brother who hasn't bothered to visit me in centuries. Yes, you're right. You do know me so well."

"I know you better than you think," Fallon insisted. "We both know you've played a role in as many secrets as any Councillor. The only difference is, your secrets never get erased."

"That's because they don't need to be!" Luzia snapped. "And I have nothing more to say on this matter."

"Neither do we," Emery added. "Except to assure everyone here that we'll be performing a thorough inspection of Everglen's grounds as soon as the apartment is complete."

"And we'll be making numerous other enhancements to the property's security," Bronte added.

"Let's also not forget," Alina said, "that we're talking about Alvar's family home. It's not like he's never had access to the property before now."

"Yeah, but my dad changed the security at the gates once we found out Alvar was with the Neverseen," Biana warned. "What if Alvar hid something there and hasn't been able to get to it?"

"If that's the case, why would the Neverseen erase his memory of it?" Alina countered.

"Because memories can come back!" Fitz snapped. "All it takes is the right trigger."

"Which is why he'll have guards with him constantly," Emery reminded him.

Fallon sighed and rubbed his forehead. "It's quite tragic to think how often crucial choices come down to our best guess."

"This is hardly a guess," Emery argued.

"Yes, I remember telling myself the same thing when I served," Fallon told him. "But like it or not, that's the truth of it. We gather what information we can and let it guide our decision. But only time reveals whether it was the right one. And if it wasn't . . ."

He threw out his hands as if to say, *What can you do?*

"May I say something?" Alvar asked.

Fallon ignored him. "It's also the predictability that bothers me. Surely these rebels—these *Neverseen*, as they've chosen to call themselves—assumed we would send him home to his family in his condition. Is it such a stretch to think that it could also be their wish?"

"We considered the possibility," Emery admitted. "And that's another reason we're posting guards. But in the past, those the Neverseen planted into specific positions were also well aware of the roles they had to play."

"I'm sure they were," Fallon agreed. "But as has already been pointed out: Memories can return. Or . . . perhaps the rebels felt an unwitting accomplice would be harder for us to detect."

Alina snorted. "You think the Neverseen are such masters of manipulation that they could guide Alvar through some intricate scheme without him realizing it?"

"It doesn't have to be intricate in order to be effective," Fallon corrected. "Generally, the most powerful plans are also the simplest."

"Seriously—will you please let me say something?" Alvar asked again. "You're acting like I don't have any control in this. I *do*. Even if my memories come back and I *am* part of some conspiracy, I'm giving you my word that I won't let myself play any part in it. In fact, I'll be doing everything in my power to make sure their plans fail. But honestly? I don't think their goals have anything to do with me. Would they have given me these if they wanted my loyalty?"

He pulled back his sleeves, revealing more curved red scars like the ones on his neck and face—but these looked much longer and deeper, as if the weapon had cut all the way to the bone.

The gashes had been made with a shamkniv, a special kind of ogre blade meant to mark someone who failed at their assignment—which did support the theory that the Neverseen were done with him.

"They left me to die," Alvar said. "And they're going to wish I had, because my new goal is to make them pay for everything they've done. I know you don't trust me enough to let me join the resistance—and given what I've heard about my past, I can't blame you for that. But I *will* find a way to help take them down."

"But if they're intending for you to be an *unwitting* accomplice," Fallon warned, "you'd be assisting them without any knowledge of what you're doing. And I know you're going to claim that's far too challenging of a feat for the Neverseen to achieve," he told Alina. "But who among us ever thought they could bring down Lumenaria? Or flood Atlantis? Or burn the glittering city we're standing in? Underestimating our opponents has not fared us well."

"Neither has giving the rebels more credit than they deserve," Alina argued. "When we think of them as these ridiculous supervillains, we end up second-guessing ourselves and hesitating—which has *also* cost us greatly."

"But if we . . ." Fallon's voice trailed off, and he tilted his head, studying her. "I had a counterpoint to your argument, but I keep hearing music when I look at you, and it's breaking my concentration. Do you know why that is?"

Alina rolled her eyes. "Absolutely no idea."

Fallon hummed a few bars of a soft melody, and Sophie wondered if he realized he was losing credibility with every note. "That doesn't sound familiar?"

"Can't say that it does," Alina told him.

He hummed a few more beats, rocking back on his heels. "I believe it's from a wedding. I can see the gown so clearly. It looked like . . . spun sunlight. And I think there was some sort of commotion. Wait! You were the one who interrupted!"

Alina's face turned tomato red. So did Alden's. And Della's.

It was no secret that Alina had once dated Alden and then tried to stop him from marrying Della. But clearly none of them appreciated the reminder.

"Well," Alina rasped, smoothing her hair, "that was a long

time ago, and it worked out in the end." She pointed to her peridot circlet.

"Serving on the Council is a tremendous honor," Fallon told her. "But it shouldn't be your *life*. I gave the same advice to another, once. Sadly, I don't believe she listened either."

He could've been referring to anyone, of course, but . . .

Councillor Oralie's cheeks had turned the same shade of pink as the tourmalines on her throne. Her azure eyes also looked glassy with unshed tears—which broke Sophie's heart. She'd long suspected that Oralie had resisted her feelings for Kenric in order to remain on the Council. And now Kenric was gone.

"Okay," Emery said, clapping his hands to get everyone's attention. "We've gotten *way* off track."

"We *have*," a new voice agreed as yet another Vacker stood— a female with vivid red hair and small points to her ears. "And no one has asked the most important question. How do you think people are going to react when they hear that a notorious criminal is living back home with his family instead of being locked away? And don't tell me they won't find out. This kind of gossip never stays quiet."

"Interesting word choice, Norene," Alina said with a chilly smile. "Tell me, is it public unease you're worried about? Or public outcry against your family?"

Norene raised her chin, her indigo eyes flashing. "I won't deny that I'd hoped today's proceedings would put an end to at least *some* of the rumors currently tarnishing our hard-earned reputation. But as an Emissary—with centuries more experience than you, I might add—my only concern is ensuring the safety of our world. People are frightened. They need to see their Council taking action. And this—"

"Is our way of reminding everyone that our job is to ensure justice—not vengeance," Bronte finished for her. "We do not act out of fear or anger, nor do we pursue revenge. And we do not hand out a life sentence without ensuring that it is absolutely necessary!"

"But if he escapes—" Norene argued.

"We'll make sure he doesn't," Emery jumped in. "Not only will he have the guards we've already mentioned, and additional security at the property, but we've also arranged for a rather unique means of monitoring his every move." He craned his neck, focusing on something toward the back of the hall as he commanded, "Please come forward!"

A hush fell over the room as another goblin marched toward the Council—a female warrior who Sophie recognized immediately. And she knew the strawberry blond boy trailing behind even better.

"Dex?" she asked, watching her best friend step onto another section of the floor, which then rose and connected to Alvar's platform. "What's going on?"

"Whatever it is, make it quick," Keefe added. "Some of us are running out of time."

Ro snickered.

"This *will* be quick," Emery assured him. "Mr. Dizznee is here to deliver a gadget he's designed per our specifications."

Unease swirled in Sophie's stomach as Dex pulled a small metal box from his cape pocket and held it out. He was one of the Lost Cities' most talented and innovative Technopaths and had created all kinds of brilliant gadgets—like her Sucker Punch bracelet. But one time he'd gotten a little too reckless with a circlet he invented, and the Council had forced her to wear it. She'd never forget the brutal headaches that the ability restrictor had caused, or the hopelessness she'd felt having her talents stripped away.

"Don't worry—this will *only* work on Alvar," Dex promised, his periwinkle eyes locking with hers as he removed a wide golden cuff from the box. "It's keyed to his DNA. I call it the Warden, because I got the idea from a human movie I saw, where the criminal had to wear a tracker around his ankle. The Warden will report every move Alvar makes, and every word he says. It'll also monitor his heart rate, so we'll be able to tell if he's nervous or lying. *And* it'll make sure he can't go anywhere without permission." He turned to Alvar and pointed to a silver circle in the center of the cuff. "This piece is like a reverse nexus. If you try to leap without the Council's approval, you'll scatter and fade, no matter how strong your concentration is."

Alvar blanched. "Is that safe?"

"As long as you don't try to escape." Dex unhinged the cuff and crouched. "Take off your left boot."

Alvar did as he was told, and Dex snapped the cuff around his ankle with a loud *click*.

"That's . . . a little tight," Alvar told him.

Dex nodded. "It has to fit under your boot. Plus, it's not supposed to be comfortable. It's supposed to remind you that we're tracking every single thing you do. I wouldn't recommend trying to take it off, either. It'll shock you if it senses you tampering with the latch—and I don't mean a little sting. You'll need a physician to treat the burns with a gross balm made out of yeti pee. And if you try to leave Everglen any way besides leaping, I've programmed it to zap you harder than a melder. It'll knock you out for a couple of days."

Keefe whistled. "Remind me never to get on your bad side, Dizznee."

Dex didn't smile. His eyes narrowed on Alvar. "I know you don't remember me. But I remember every single thing you did—and I have a scar to prove it. That's why I have this."

He held out his wrist, pointing to a narrow gold cuff with a black jewel set into the center. "The Warden sends alerts to me if you do anything suspicious. All I have to do is press this button, and you'll *wish* you were back in that stinky cell. Got it?"

Alvar swallowed hard as he nodded—and Dex looked pretty proud of himself. But his dimpled grin faded when Biana said, "So . . . if you had time to make the Warden, then you knew this was happening—and didn't tell us."

"I didn't know for sure," Dex mumbled. "The Council told me they were considering it and wanted to know if I could make something, just in case. But it wasn't a done deal."

"How long ago was that?" Fitz demanded.

"A week," Councillor Emery jumped in. "And we made it clear that the project was classified, so do not blame Mr. Dizznee for his silence. He was following our orders—and we expect you to as well." He turned back to Dex. "Thank you. You're dismissed."

"I was just trying to help," Dex told Fitz and Biana as his platform lowered back to ground level. "I figured this way we'd have some control, you know?"

Neither of them nodded.

Dex's eyes shifted to Sophie, and she gave him as much of a smile as she could. She knew he'd been in an impossible position. But he was still going to have to give Fitz and Biana time to cool off.

"Before we're interrupted by any further outbursts," Emery said as Dex slunk toward the exit, "I want to make it clear that this decision is *final*. As soon as the security at Everglen is ready, Alvar *will* be moved to his new apartment, where he'll remain for the next six months—unless he gives us any reason to remove him earlier. And while he's there, we'll be providing weekly lists of tasks to test his behavior. All observations will be taken into account during his final sentencing."

"I won't disappoint you," Alvar promised, dipping his shakiest bow yet before bending to put his boot back on.

"I hope you don't," Terik told him. "I also hope you realize how lucky you are to have this opportunity."

"I do," Alvar said, tears welling in his eyes as he turned to Alden and Della. "I'm . . . looking forward to getting to know you."

"So are we," Della whispered, wiping her cheeks.

"This is your last chance," Alden warned.

Fitz shook his head, his face twisted with disgust, and Sophie noticed similar expressions among many in the crowd.

"Wait!" Ro said as Emery ordered the guards to take Alvar back to his cell. "That's it?"

"What more were you expecting?" Emery asked.

"I don't know. Some of you didn't even talk. Like you, red guy!" She pointed to the rubies in Councillor Darek's circlet. "Don't you have anything you want to add to the conversation? Or you, with the weird animal faces all over your throne. Anything you want to say?"

"We had our say earlier," Councillor Clarette told her.

"Just like I told you they would," Keefe said, folding his hands behind his head and giving Ro an unbearably smug smirk.

"And that concludes our proceedings," Emery told the crowd as the rest of the Council stood. "We'll notify you when the date is set for the final sentencing. For now, you're dismissed."

Fanfare shook the walls as the Councillors glittered away,

followed by steady stomping as their goblin bodyguards marched out of the hall.

The rest of the Vackers followed, their voices echoing as they argued among themselves. Sophie couldn't understand much, but she was pretty sure she heard several say, "They're ruining our family." And no one so much as glanced Alden and Della's way.

Keefe tried to break the tension, pumping his fist and shouting, "LORD HUNKYHAIR LIVES! Say it now, Ro. *Say it!*"

Ro said it, all right. Along with several ogre words that weren't very nice.

Sophie wanted to laugh, but Biana was clutching her stomach like she was going to throw up—and Fitz's fists were squeezed so tight, his knuckles looked bloodless.

Alden cleared his throat. "I know we have lots more to discuss. But—"

"Don't pretend like you actually care how we feel about this," Fitz interrupted.

"We do," Della promised.

"Then why didn't you talk to us before you gave the Council permission?" Biana asked. "We have to live with him too."

"And we have to deal with the drama," Fitz added. "If you think this is bad"—he pointed to the last few Vackers grumbling their way out of the hall—"wait until we're back at school. You should hear the things people are saying about us."

Sadly, he wasn't exaggerating. Foxfire had been back in session for a couple of weeks, and everywhere Fitz and Biana went, Sophie heard very unpleasant whispers.

"It'll quiet down soon," Della promised.

"I doubt it," Biana mumbled.

"Well, even if you're right," Alden said, "this is hardly the first time we've had anyone gossip about our family. You didn't care when Fitz was sneaking off to the Forbidden Cities to find Sophie and people were wondering where he was disappearing to. And neither of you thought twice about running off to join the Black Swan, even though you knew you'd be banished."

"But this time the people gossiping about us are right!" Fitz snapped. "You're making us live with a murderer!"

"You won't be living *with* him," Alden corrected. "You'll be living *near* him. And you'll be able to control whether you have any contact."

"Like that makes a difference," Fitz muttered.

"It does a little," Biana conceded. "But you should've warned us about this before we got here."

Della wrung her hands. "You're right. I'm sorry."

"We thought it'd be easier for you to hear it from the Council," Alden explained.

"No, you thought it'd be easier for *you*," Fitz argued. "You didn't want us to know that it was happening until it was too late to stop it."

"You couldn't have stopped it," Alden assured him. "The

Council had already made up their minds. If we didn't let them use Everglen, they would've found somewhere else."

"Fine by me!" Fitz shouted.

"I dunno," Keefe jumped in. "Wouldn't you rather be able to keep an eye on Alvar?"

Fitz reeled on him. "You're on *their* side? Is that why you just sat there and talked about your stupid hair?"

"Okay, first? We both know my hair is awesome," Keefe said with his hugest smirk yet. "And second: It's not like they're setting your brother free. Were you listening to Dizznee? I'm pretty sure if Alvar breathes too hard, Dex'll zap him."

"Don't even get me started on Dex," Fitz muttered.

"I know," Biana said quietly. "I can't believe he knew for a week and didn't tell us."

Sophie opened her mouth to defend Dex but swallowed back the words. She could tell Fitz and Biana weren't ready to hear them.

Fitz must've noticed, though, because he reeled toward her. "Don't tell me you're okay with this."

"'Okay' isn't the right word," she mumbled. "I think . . . it's a hard call."

"A hard call," Fitz repeated. "That's it? I thought for *this*, of all things, we'd be on the same side."

"We are," Sophie promised, reaching for him.

He jerked away. "No, we're—"

Keefe stepped between them, placing a hand on Fitz's shoulder. "Okay, as your best friend I have to stop you right there. Otherwise you're going to go all rage-monster like you always do and say a bunch of things it's going to be super hard to take back. And we both know you don't want to do that again. Especially to Foster."

Sophie wasn't sure what to make of the last part—or of the glance Keefe and Alden exchanged—but she *was* relieved when it seemed to work. She hadn't seen Fitz that angry since the dark days when Alden's mind had shattered, and it'd taken their friendship a while to recover.

"I think . . . we all need to cool off," Della said to break the silence. "Why don't we go home and—"

"No."

Fitz's voice was so cold, it made Sophie's skin prickle.

Alden sighed. "Fine. Take some time to process. We'll be waiting at Everglen whenever you're ready."

"Well, you'll be waiting a while." Fitz straightened up until he was nearly as tall as his father and reached under the neckline of his tunic.

"Uh . . . whatever you're doing," Keefe said as Fitz pulled out his home crystal, "I'm pretty sure it's a bad idea. Like, epic-level bad. Me-running-off-to-join-the-Neverseen bad."

"I don't care." Fitz yanked the chain and snapped one of the links before he tossed the crystal to Alden. "You guys made your decision. Now I'm making mine. If Alvar's moving back to Everglen, I'm moving out."

THREE

I HAD A FEELING I'D FIND YOU OUT HERE,"
Sophie said, striding up behind Fitz as he hurled a goblin
throwing star toward a wooden dummy about a hundred
feet away.

SHHHHHHHICK!

The sliver weapon blurred through the air and splintered
into the dummy's arm.

Awkward silence followed, until Sophie told him, "Nice
shot."

"Not really," Grizel jumped in. "He was supposed to hit it
between the eyes."

She grabbed Fitz's wrist and swung his arm through the
throw's range of motion. "You let go here"—she lined Fitz's

palm up with his shoulder—"and you need to let go *here*." She adjusted his arm. "Feel the difference?"

"Not really," he grumbled.

In his defense, both positions did look *really* similar.

"Then you're not concentrating hard enough," Grizel said, dragging his arm through both positions again. "Now do you feel it?"

"Maybe?" Fitz hedged.

Grizel sighed and rotated his arm through the throw again. Then again.

And again.

And again.

"Practice is about building muscle memory," she told him. "But it won't do you any good if you're building the *wrong* muscle memory. You need to learn precision. Every throw should go like this."

She pulled three throwing stars from the pockets of her sleek black jumpsuit and hurled them one after another.

SHHHHHHHICK!

SHHHHHHHICK!

SHHHHHHHICK!

All three struck side by side in the center of the dummy's forehead.

"See?" Grizel sauntered over to the target to retrieve the weapons, somehow managing not to leave a single footprint in the reddish sand. She wasn't as burly as other goblins, but she made up for it with an uncanny grace that allowed her to sneak up on pretty much anyone. And she'd been putting Fitz through goblin military training for the last few weeks to help him work off his Alvar frustrations. That was how Sophie knew where to look after Fitz had stormed out of Tribunal Hall—and why she'd taken a few minutes to stop by her house and change from her gown and heels into slouchy boots, black leggings, and a loose white tunic. Grizel had set up their secret training arena in the middle of a rust-colored desert surrounded by rocky caverns. Apparently, the dusty landscape was the ideal place to train for strength, skill, and stealth—and also far enough out of the way that no one would find them.

All Sophie knew was that it was *hot*.

She'd only been there a couple of minutes and could already feel sweat trickling down her back—though that might've also been from the scowl Fitz was giving her.

She smiled back, refusing to let him chase her away.

"Let's try this again," Grizel said, tossing her long braid over her shoulder as she handed Fitz one of the throwing stars she'd retrieved. "Aim for the center of the forehead—and make sure you let go at the point I just showed you."

Fitz squinted at the target as he raised his arm, then let the star fly.

SHHHHHHHHICK!

"The chest is closer," Grizel told him. "But we're not stopping until you hit the mark."

His next throw struck the dummy's ear, and the one after that hit the chest again.

Grizel sighed. "You're not concentrating."

"Yes I am—why does it matter if I hit the forehead? Any of those throws would've taken someone down."

"*Down* isn't the same as *dead*," Grizel argued as she handed him another weapon. "And that's the kind of distinction that could cost you your life—just like your sloppy throws could cost someone theirs. What if your enemy's holding a hostage?"

She spun around and pulled Sophie into a headlock. "If the Neverseen had Sophie pinned like this, what happens if your aim goes low?"

Sandor drew his sword. "Something we'll never need to worry about, because *I* will be there. And anyone who touches my charge will end up dead."

"Not if they're faster than you." Grizel kept her stranglehold on Sophie as she drew her own weapon and knocked his away.

"If this were a real threat, I would've cut down your knees already," Sandor growled.

"Yes, but *I* would've sliced off your sword hand before you could," Grizel corrected.

"Is that so?" Sandor tossed his sword to his left hand and swung, striking Grizel's blade with a *clang!* "Good thing I can fight just as skillfully with either."

Grizel laughed and released Sophie, then spun around with a move that managed to look both elegant *and* lethal, and ended with the edge of her sword pressed against Sandor's throat. "You're so cute when you think you can beat me."

"I *can* beat you," Sandor insisted.

"No, you can't." Grizel spun away, blocking his next swipe with a clash so loud it made Sophie's teeth sing. "But we *are* an even match. So you can keep wasting time trying to prove you're better than me—or you can admit that no matter how good either of us is, we've been assigned charges that have a gift for sneaking away to do really dangerous things. Which is why they should be training—and I mean *seriously* training," she added, turning to Sophie and Fitz, "not just working off a few frustrations. In fact, all of your friends should complete our full military regimen. And *you*"—she pointed at Sandor— "should be helping me guide them through the program."

It wasn't the first time Grizel had made the suggestion, and it wasn't a horrible idea, considering how many attacks Sophie and her friends had barely survived. Even Ro agreed— though of course she'd argued that the focus should be *ogre* training.

But . . . the thought of all the slicing and slashing turned Sophie's stomach squirmy. She was stunned Fitz could handle it—though maybe he got that from his mom.

Della had a flair for physical defense, blending her ability as a Vanisher with clever sneak attacks. She'd even taught Sophie and her friends some basic moves back when they were living with the Black Swan in Alluveterre.

But *defending* and *attacking* were two different things—especially when weapons were involved. And these weren't weapons that stunned, like the melders they'd occasionally carried for protection. These were cold metal blades with sharp points and even sharper edges. And yes, there'd been times when Sophie had been given goblin throwing stars to carry in case of emergency—but she hadn't necessarily been thrilled about that. Plus, Grizel and Ro wanted them to master swords and knives and all kinds of other stabby things. *And* they wanted them to study hand-to-hand combat, with moves that went way beyond punching and kicking.

And the thing was: Elves weren't naturally violent creatures.

Killing could shatter their sanity, stirring up too much guilt for their sensitive minds to process. That was why the Ancients had secured peace treaties with the other intelligent species and relied on them for protection. And even when the Council ordered everyone to attend special lessons with the Exillium Coaches to hone their mental defensive skills, no one had excelled, and eventually the program had petered out.

Plus, Sophie was an Inflictor, and *that* was where she'd been focusing her training—trying to learn how to constrain her power and target exactly who she wanted to take down, instead of causing everyone around her to writhe in pain.

But so far, she hadn't made any progress.

Councillor Bronte, her inflicting Mentor, kept assuring her that she'd get there with time and practice—but she could tell that he was a little surprised by her lack of control. And so was she. All of her other abilities worked so effortlessly, she didn't understand why this one was such a struggle.

"Well, as long as you're here, Sophie," Grizel said as she sheathed her sword, "you should take a few turns. See if we can improve your aim."

"She's not here to train," Fitz jumped in. "She's here to talk me into going back to Everglen—and it's not going to happen."

Sophie fought off her smile as Fitz kicked the sand, stirring up a coppery cloud. He was so determined to be angry that it was honestly kind of adorable.

"Actually, throwing things sounds pretty good right now," she told him, taking the star Grizel offered.

She swung her arm around a few times to loosen up, then kept her eye on the target as she let the weapon fly, and . . .

THHHHHHWACK!

"Your throw was a little soft," Grizel informed her. "That's why it sounded different. And obviously it was too low."

"I was aiming for the leg," Sophie insisted, deciding not to mention that she'd been aiming for the *other* leg.

Grizel handed her a new throwing star. "Okay, then try aiming for the forehead this time."

Sophie stared at the dummy, telling herself it was just a faceless, weathered hunk of wood shaped like a body. But her queasy stomach didn't get the message.

"I get it," Grizel told her. "This isn't your thing. But like I just reminded Fitz: If someone's trying to kill you, an injury isn't going to stop them."

"I know." But the thought of throwing a weapon into someone's skull—someone's *brain* . . .

She could imagine the sound it would make.

The way things would splatter.

"Your enemies aren't going to show you any mercy," Grizel warned. "They don't deserve yours."

"I know," Sophie repeated.

But she couldn't help worrying that this was exactly what the Neverseen wanted—why Vespera had spent years experimenting on humans before she ended up imprisoned, and why she'd abducted Sophie's human parents and used them to lure Sophie to Nightfall for a brutal test. Vespera believed that if the elves didn't learn to be ruthless, it was only a matter of time before their treaties collapsed and one of the more violent species overthrew them. And Keefe's mom was just as bad. She'd exposed Ro to a fatal dose of soporidine right before she'd had Ruy use his ability as a Psionipath to breach the force field around Atlantis—all to teach Sophie and Keefe that they needed to learn to make hard choices.

And here Sophie was, deciding how violent she was willing to be.

"Battle skills are simply another tool," Grizel reminded her. "Adding them to your arsenal doesn't mean you have to *use* them. But if you need them, you'll be glad you're prepared."

"I guess." But Sophie's arm still shook as she tried to line up a deadly aim.

"It helps me to picture the Neverseen's faces," Fitz told her. "That way I'm only thinking about hurting people who *deserve* it."

"That helps me, too," Sandor agreed. "I focus on the look in my enemies' eyes to remind myself that they wouldn't hesitate to end me."

"*You* struggle with this?" Sophie had to ask.

Sandor was always so quick to draw his weapon, it seemed like he'd been born with a sword in his hand.

But he nodded. "Killing will always feel a little wrong—and in some ways, that's a good thing. It helps us know where to draw the line. But it could also cost someone's life, so I've trained my mind to focus on the reasons I'm fighting, rather than the fight itself."

"I guess that makes sense," Sophie mumbled, closing her eyes as she raised her arm.

She let her photographic memory paint every tiny detail of Vespera's face, right down to the cold glint in her azure eyes and the sharp curve of her cruel mouth, reminding herself that Vespera wasn't just a murderer—she was the elvin world's darkest secret. Her crimes had been so indescribably awful that the Council was still covering them up, afraid the truth would fracture their world.

And she'd done some of those terrible things to Sophie's human parents.

THHHHHHHHWACK!

She nailed the dummy smack in the middle of the forehead.

"Still too soft a throw," Grizel told her. "But otherwise that was awesome."

Fitz cracked a smile. "Should've known you'd make me look bad."

Sophie's cheeks flushed. "I'm sure it's just beginner's luck."

"Let's see, shall we?" Grizel handed her another star, and this time Sophie pictured the jagged pieces of glass she'd seen jutting from Biana's skin after they'd found her passed out in a pool of her own blood.

Biana had risked everything to save her friends. And Vespera had sounded almost gleeful when she'd told Sophie: *I made sure their Vanisher will never be the same.*

SHHHHHHICK!

The star stuck right beside the other, embedding deep into the splintered wood.

"Perfect!" Grizel shouted. "You're a natural!"

Sophie smiled. But the words kept crashing around her mind, sharpening every time they hit. And when her next two throws struck the same mark—without her even trying—she realized why the idea felt so prickly.

There'd been a moment in Nightfall when Vespera had told Sophie's friends: *I suspect the moonlark could tear these halls down stone by stone if she truly unleashed herself.*

She'd been taunting Sophie at the time—trying to make her

lose her temper—and Sophie had refused to give in. But . . .

Could Grizel and Vespera both be right?

Sophie already knew she was part of a genetic experiment.

And she'd been raised in the much more violent world of humans.

And now she seemed to have a talent for lethal throws.

Could all of that be connected—and if it was, did that mean . . .

Had Project Moonlark made her a *natural killer*?

FOUR

"OU OKAY?" FITZ ASKED, WAVING a hand in front of Sophie's eyes and snapping her back to the present.

"Yeah," she mumbled, swiping away the strands of hair sticking to her sweaty forehead. "Sorry. I was just . . . thinking."

"About?" he pressed.

Sophie considered telling him the truth—it certainly wouldn't have been the worst fear she'd ever admitted to him. And if Fitz hadn't run away screaming when he found out her genetics had been modeled off alicorn DNA, this probably wouldn't even faze him.

But . . . she was tired of making her friends give her pep

talks—especially when she already knew what he would say: No matter what the Black Swan had in mind when they created her, she still had a choice in the matter.

She wasn't a robot. Or a puppet.

She was a girl with strange abilities and a different way of looking at the world. What she decided to do with those things was up to her.

And she didn't want to be a killer. So . . . she wouldn't be.

Even if she was a *natural*.

Plus, maybe it really was just beginner's luck.

Either way, she decided she was done practicing her aim.

"Sorry," she repeated, "I realized I was showing off."

"So?" Fitz asked as she handed him her last throwing star. "If my throws were as perfect as yours, you'd never hear the end of it."

"They're *nearly* perfect," Sandor corrected. "She's still holding the weapon by the wrong blade. You both are."

Grizel threw her hands up. "Here we go."

"Yes, here we go," Sandor agreed. "If you want me to train them, I'm going to teach *proper* technique."

Fitz squinted at the four twisted blades of the throwing star in his hand. "Aren't they all the same?"

"YES!" Grizel told him, the same time Sandor said, "Absolutely not!"

"Our weapons are handmade," Sandor argued. "Of *course* there are variations. One blade is always slightly lighter than the others, and one is always slightly heavier, and whichever you choose to throw with makes a difference, both in how the weapon spins, and how it slices through the air."

"I know he *sounds* logical," Grizel told them. "But he's talking fractions of an ounce."

"Fractions of an inch are the difference between a true aim and a miss, aren't they?" Sandor countered.

He handed Sophie another throwing star and asked her to pick the lightest blade.

"Don't feel bad," Grizel told her when she guessed wrong. "*No one* can feel what he's talking about."

"Those with proper training can," Sandor insisted. "When I was in charge of a squadron, I made them spend hours every day cleaning the blades to learn their feel. And my soldiers had the highest accuracy rate in the entire regiment."

"That's because you also made them *practice* for hours every day!" Grizel argued.

"You did the same with your squadron, and *their* performance was never as precise as mine," Sandor reminded her. "So either your teaching skills are lacking, or I'm right about the weight of the blades. Actually, both seem likely."

Grizel narrowed her eyes. "It's a good thing I love you, or I'd be kicking you in the teeth right now. And that comment just cost you another night of dancing—don't think I've forgotten about the one you still owe me!"

Sophie started to smile—but then Grizel's words caught up with her. "Wait, did you say *love?*"

She'd known Sandor and Grizel were dating.

But *love?*

A huge, goofy grin spread across her lips as both Sandor and Grizel flushed bright pink. "Oh my goodness—that's the sweetest thing EVER!"

Sandor groaned. "As if they don't tease us about our relationship enough already!"

"I'm not going to tease you," Sophie promised.

"But Keefe will," Fitz jumped in. "And I'm sure he's going to be here any second, so—"

"Actually, Keefe said he wasn't getting anywhere near you and a bunch of weapons right now," Sophie told him.

She'd been surprised, since Keefe usually insisted on tagging along for *everything*. But he'd told her that Fitz would be way more likely to listen if she went there on her own. And before she could argue—or figure out why Ro seemed so annoyed with him—Alden had agreed, and somehow that settled it.

"Huh," Fitz said, flinging his throwing star—and hitting the dummy's stomach. "He must be afraid I'll ask if I can stay with him."

"Is that your plan?" Sophie asked. "You want to live at the Shores of Solace? With *Lord Cassius?*"

"It's better than living with Alvar."

"Uh, I doubt that."

Keefe's father wasn't physically abusive, but he was still a horrible person who'd crushed his son through years of criticism and belittling insults. The only reason Keefe was living with him again was because of Sophie—and she hated that. She'd tried to talk him out of it, but his father was withholding crucial information in the search for her human parents, and Keefe was the kind of guy who was always willing to take the hit if he thought it would help a friend, regardless of how much it was going to hurt him.

"Fine, maybe I'll ask Tiergan if I can stay with him," Fitz said, grabbing another star. "He's already letting Tam and Linh live there."

"True," Sophie agreed, wishing the idea didn't put a sour taste in her mouth.

Linh was her friend. She refused to be jealous of the way Fitz always seemed so wowed by her talent—especially since Linh deserved every bit of that praise. But Linh was so sweet and pretty and was always doing supercool water tricks. And if Fitz were living in the same place, and they were seeing each other every day . . .

"You're really not going back to Everglen?" she asked, focusing on the larger issue at stake.

"Nope. And I know you think I'm throwing a tantrum—"

"I don't think that." She stepped in front of him so he'd have to look at her. "I get why you don't want to live with him."

"*But?*" he added, and the question had a definite snap. "Go on. We both know there's more to that sentence."

Sophie stared at the sky, watching the sun sink behind the flat-topped mountains like a pat of melting butter. "I know you hate what he did—"

"No, I hate *him*. And I hate my parents for falling for his 'I'm a changed elf' act."

"I don't think they've fallen for anything," Sophie said gently.

"Yes they have. First thing my dad did after he found out Alvar was with the Neverseen was make sure Alvar couldn't get inside Everglen again. He blocked him from the gates—and changed the locks on the door to his office, just in case—and he told Grizel to use lethal force against him if she needed to. And now he's letting him move back in?"

"I think your parents just . . . *want* to believe. He's their son, you know?"

"Yeah, well, so am I. And while they're busy trying to get back their perfect happy family, they're putting all of us in danger."

"Then why not stay at Everglen to make sure nothing happens?" Sophie asked.

"Because he's a Vanisher. He can sneak around as much as he wants."

"Not with that gadget Dex made him—"

"Let's not talk about what Dex did," Fitz warned, stepping around her to fling his throwing star—and missing the target completely.

Grizel snorted. "You know what that means, Pretty Boy: fifty dead drops to work off your temper!"

Fitz scowled—and before Sophie could ask what a dead drop was, he'd flipped himself into a handstand and began lowering his arms until his elbows were bent at right angles, then straightening them again, like the world's most impossible push-up.

"You're making him do *fifty* of those?" Sophie asked as Fitz counted them off. She was pretty sure she'd have a heart attack after ten.

Okay, fine—after five.

Actually, she'd probably face-plant into the sand just trying to get into position.

Grizel grinned. "I usually make him do a hundred."

She must not have been exaggerating, because Fitz made it through without collapsing—though his face was red and his clothes were so sweaty they'd suctioned onto his skin.

"Cooled off now?" Grizel asked as he flipped back to his feet. "Or do you want a few more?"

His answer was to whip off his soggy jerkin and throw it at her head—but Grizel was too fast, drawing her sword and shredding the fabric to bits.

She scooped up a ragged piece with the tip of her blade and held it under his nose. "Don't make me tie you up and leave you in one of those caverns. You know I will."

The threat triggered a flashback, and Sophie closed her

eyes, trying to squeeze out her memories of black cloaked figures jumping out of the shadows, grabbing her and Dex, and shoving drugged cloths over their faces. The Neverseen had ambushed them in one of the rocky caves along the beach near her house before dragging them away to be interrogated. Her wrists still stung sometimes, remembering the searing pain from her burns.

"Alvar was there for that," Fitz said, making her jump. "And no, I didn't sneak past your mental blocking. I know you well enough to know what you're thinking right now—or . . . I thought I did."

Sophie fidgeted with the star she still hadn't thrown. "You *do* know me, Fitz."

"Then how can you be okay with this?" His voice cracked, and he cleared his throat and turned to Sandor. "And how can you be okay with Alvar having another chance to come after Sophie?"

"My calm doesn't mean I agree with the Council's decision," Sandor corrected. "It means I have confidence in my ability to protect my charge."

"Really? Because you couldn't stop him before," Fitz argued. "None of us could."

"Maybe not," Sophie jumped in. "But now we know what we're dealing with."

"Do we? You heard Fallon today. He asked all kinds of stuff that none of us had thought of."

"So you think he's right about Everglen?" Sophie asked. "You think there's something important hidden at the property?"

"I have no idea," Fitz admitted. "It's hard to know what to think of anything Fallon says."

"Yeah, he's . . . strange."

Fitz snorted. "That's putting it nicely."

He reached up and wiped a stream of sweat trickling down the side of his face with the sleeve of his undershirt. "But he was right that people usually hold on to their properties. I never thought about how weird it is that Luzia gave Everglen to my dad."

"Do you know how long ago that happened?" Sophie asked.

"It's been a few decades. I think she offered it to him when he became an Emissary. And she's the one who told my dad to add the gates. She said that if he was working for the Council, he should protect his privacy. I think she might've even *made* the gates. I know a Flasher did something to the metal to make it absorb light, so no one can light leap in."

Sophie had always wondered exactly what the massive glowing fence that surrounded the property was meant to keep out—especially since the elves claimed the Lost Cities were such a safe place.

"Do you really think she picked Everglen because of the view?" she asked.

Fitz shook his head. "There are tons of lakes that are way prettier than ours."

Sophie had thought the same thing. Not that Everglen wasn't

gorgeous—it was one of the most beautiful places she'd ever been. But that was mostly because the house was a shimmering crystal palace with jeweled mosaics and twinkling chandeliers and fountains everywhere. The lake . . . was just a lake.

And Everglen was *huge*. Way bigger than Havenfield, which was saying a lot, since Havenfield's grounds were used for an animal preserve. Sophie had spent hours running around the property when she'd played base quest with Fitz, Biana, and Keefe, and she still hadn't explored the whole place.

"Have you ever seen pictures of what the original house looked like?" she asked.

"No. But my dad said it was small and boring. That's why he tore it down. He'd met my mom and wanted to impress her."

"So he built her a palace?" Grizel asked, glancing at Sandor. "Sounds like I should have Alden give you some pointers."

Sandor crossed his arms. "My home is more than adequate."

"Oh, 'more than adequate.' Now *there's* an epic love poem if I've ever heard one," Grizel retorted, but she had to be teasing. Sophie had stayed at Sandor's house after the ogre attack at Havenfield, and it was huge—and built almost entirely of gold.

"Did your dad ever say why he kept Everglen's office and tore down everything else?" Sophie asked Fitz.

"I think it was because of the aquarium. It goes way deeper than it looks, and they would've had to move all the creatures living down there."

"Is it normal to have something like that in a house?"

"I want to say yes—but I'm basing that mostly on some of my relatives' houses, so who knows?"

"And Vackers never do anything arbitrarily," Sophie murmured, remembering what Fallon had said. "What do you know about Luzia?"

"Not much more than you do. She's a famous Flasher, but she's mostly known for being Orem's mom."

"And Fallon's sister," Sophie added. "I wasn't expecting that."

Fitz grinned. "Probably because they don't look like each other."

"Yeah, not at all." Fallon's skin was so pale he was almost translucent, while Luzia looked like some sort of Egyptian goddess.

Fitz leaned closer and whispered, "It's because they have different dads."

Sophie shouldn't have gasped, since stepfamilies were super common among humans. But death was incredibly rare in the Lost Cities—and divorce seemed to be even rarer—so she had to ask, "What happened?"

"I don't actually know. It's one of those Ancient scandals my relatives like to pretend never happened. Just like I'm sure they want to do with Alvar." He kicked the sand again. "Did you hear them today? They hate us."

"I don't think they hate *you*. But even if they do . . . do you really care?"

"Why wouldn't I?"

Sophie shrugged. "It's not like you see them very often."

"No, but they're still my family. And they're not the only ones bothered by my brother. You've seen what it's been like at school—and this is going to make it a million times worse. I know I shouldn't care, but . . ."

His gaze dropped to his feet as he kicked the side of his shoe. "The thing is . . . I *like* being a Vacker—or I did until all of this happened. I know you're probably going to think I'm a jerk for admitting that, but . . . I like knowing I'm part of a huge legacy—and not whatever creepy legacy Alvar was talking about that has Biana all freaked out. The name's always felt like proof that I'd do something important someday. But now I'm pretty sure the only thing anyone's going to remember about me is that I'm the brother of a murderer."

"That's not true. I'll always remember that you found me and brought me to the Lost Cities and showed me where I really belong. And that you came when I called for help and saved me from fading away. And that you left everything behind to go with me when I joined the Black Swan. Need me to keep going? Because I can."

His smile really was a beautiful thing.

But it didn't last.

"None of that's like . . . world changing, though," he mumbled, staring at the orangey clouds.

It had been for her—but saying that felt too sappy. And he obviously didn't care. So she told him, "It will be when we take down the Neverseen. You're still with me on that, right?"

"Of course."

"Then we need a plan—and Fallon gave me an idea. I think we should search Everglen ourselves, to make sure the Council doesn't miss anything. I know Luzia said Vespera never went to the house, but I don't like that they knew each other. And I couldn't help feeling like she was hiding something, you know?" When Fitz agreed, she added, "Of course . . . it's going to be a lot harder to search the property if you're refusing to go back there."

"Ha—you walked right into that one," Grizel told him.

"I'm not trying to trick you," Sophie promised. "If you don't want to go back until Alvar's gone, that's your call."

"He's never going to *be* gone!" he snapped, kicking up another cloud of red dust. "They're building him an apartment! And you already heard the garbage Alvar's spewing out, about how he wants to help the rebellion and prove himself worthy." He mimed gagging. "We both know how this is going to end. In six months, the Council's going to sentence him to stay there permanently, and we're all going to be expected to act like nothing ever happened."

"You may be right," Sophie had to admit. "But if you are . . . don't you think there's a reason people say 'keep your friends close and your enemies closer'?"

Fitz closed his eyes. "Probably. But I don't know if I can stomach watching my parents fall for his 'I'm so innocent' act.

I bet you anything, by the Celestial Festival he'll be back living in the main house."

"How soon is that?" Keeping track of dates in the Lost Cities was impossible. Plus, the festival only happened on total lunar eclipses.

"A little less than three months. So, basically half of Alvar's little testing period. I guarantee that's all it'll take for him to win everyone over—even Biana. And I just . . . I can't even think about it without wanting to punch everyone."

"I get that. And I promise, I'm not trying to talk you into going back home or doing anything you don't think you can handle. Just . . . please don't get mad at me if I go back without you, okay? Searching Everglen's the first lead we've gotten since Keefe's mom disappeared with Vespera—and it may end up being nothing. But at least it's *something* worth looking into."

Fitz turned back to face her. "I'm not going to get mad at you, Sophie—especially over my jerk of a brother. And . . . if you're going to search my house, I'll be right there with you."

"Just to visit?" Grizel jumped in. "Because even though you haven't asked my opinion—a foolish oversight, by the way—I'm also in camp It's Smarter to Keep an Eye on Your Creepy Brother. Alvar won't get away with *anything* on my watch. But I can't be there to supervise if you're off sulking."

Fitz dragged out a sigh as he scraped his toe across the sand. "I guess I can *try* staying there and see how it goes—but if I do . . . I'm going to need your help with something," he told Sophie.

"Anything," she promised.

He stepped closer, a new intensity brightening his eyes. "I don't believe Alvar's memories are gone. Memories don't just disappear."

"Sometimes they do," she reminded him. "Damel was able to permanently erase me from my human parents' minds."

"Only because you were there to enhance him. Plus, humans don't shield their thoughts the way we do."

"True." Sophie had suffered horrible headaches from the moment she'd manifested as a Telepath. "But we've checked Alvar's mind. You and I tried for *hours*, remember?"

"I know." Fitz lowered his eyes, twisting the verdigris thumb rings that matched the pair he'd given her. "But, we haven't kept up with our training, you know? And I'm not blaming you for that—we've had a ton of stuff to deal with. But now that things have calmed down . . . we need to get back to it. It might be the only way to find anything hidden in Alvar's head."

Sophie wanted to argue so badly.

But he had a point—and it made her eyelashes itch like crazy. Because Cognate training was about so much more than practicing telepathy.

Cognates weren't supposed to keep secrets from each other. *Any* secrets.

Which meant Cognate training involved *lots* of trust exercises.

And that was a problem, since Sophie had one secret she really, really, really, really, really didn't want to share.

"You said we'd start training again once we found your human parents," Fitz reminded her gently. "And . . . you said this time we wouldn't hold anything back."

"You remember that, huh?" she asked, trying to smile. "I'd been hoping you wouldn't."

She'd made the promise while reeling from the discovery that Mr. Forkle had spent his entire life lying to everyone about the fact that he had an identical twin brother, because multiple births were looked down upon in the Lost Cities. In that moment, secrets had felt exhausting and pointless—and confessing her crush on him hadn't seemed nearly so scary.

But afterward she'd definitely wondered what she'd been thinking.

"I figured," Fitz told her. "That's why I haven't brought it up. But . . . I need to know that I've tried everything I can to stop what's happening with my brother—because I *know* something's happening. And I can't do this without you."

Sophie took a slow, deep breath, letting the words settle into her head. They had a weight to them. A truth—bigger than any embarrassment or hurt feelings her secret might cause.

"Okay," she whispered. "We'll train as much as we can."

Fitz's shoulders sagged with relief. "When?"

She could tell he wanted the answer to be very, very soon.

But she needed a little time to mentally prepare for that conversation.

"A couple of days?" she tried.

"How about tomorrow?" he countered.

She closed her eyes, wondering if her stomach was turning inside out. But stalling was probably only going to prolong her misery.

"Tomorrow," she agreed, barely managing to choke out the word.

Fitz's answering smile was full movie-star mode, which somehow made her feel better *and* worse. Same thing happened when he reached for her hands.

"It's not going to be scary," he promised. "There's nothing you can tell me that's going to change *anything* between us, okay?"

She nodded.

Her voice was gone at that point—her brain was too busy trying to imagine how he was going to react.

Would he cringe?

Laugh?

Run away screaming?

Most likely he'd just get super fidgety and mumble about how he'd always thought of her like a little sister. And if he did . . . she was going to have to find a way to live with that.

If Dex could get past the way she'd rejected him, surely she could put any hurt aside too.

And yet . . . a tiny part of her brain couldn't help reminding her about all the sweet gifts Fitz had given her over the last few months, and those moments under Calla's Panakes tree, where it almost felt like maybe Fitz was going to—

"That's weird," Fitz said, interrupting all of those silly, silly thoughts.

He pointed to her shadow, which was . . . moving.

So was his.

And Sandor's.

And Grizel's.

Each of the four dark shapes kept stretching longer and longer and longer.

"What's happening?" Sophie asked as they stumbled back.

"You can't guess?" a sickeningly familiar voice said behind them—a voice Sophie hadn't heard since the Lumenaria dungeon.

Gethen.

She whipped around right as Sandor and Grizel charged toward three figures striding out of one of the caverns in black hooded cloaks with the white eye symbol of the Neverseen on their sleeves.

Then the world went dark.

FIVE

OPHIE WASN'T UNCONSCIOUS.

There were no sweet sedatives burning her nose.

No fuzzy thoughts or foggy dreams.

But everything was black—and when she reached to remove whatever cover must've been thrown over her face, all she felt was her own skin.

"Still haven't figured it out?" Gethen asked, his tone dripping with icy amusement. "How unfortunate."

Sandor snarled.

"Are you sure you want to do that?" Gethen asked as Sophie raised her arm to fling the throwing star she was still holding. "You might hit something you'll regret—though it'd be entertaining to watch."

It sounded like Gethen's vision wasn't impaired, which meant the darkness was somehow selective—and with that realization, Sophie finally pieced together what must be happening.

Keefe had told her that the Neverseen had a freakishly powerful Shade among their ranks—a female called Umber, who must be flooding their minds with shadows.

Which meant there was only one way to get them out of this.

Sorry, brace yourselves, she transmitted to Sandor, Grizel, and Fitz—letting her fear and fury crackle through her veins as her knotted emotions unraveled. Mental energy fueled the storm until hints of red lit the edges of her darkened vision, and a primal scream slipped through her lips as she blasted the force from her mind.

Rage spiraled like a hurricane, tearing down everything in its path. But when the tempest faded, Sophie could hear the soft clicking of a tongue.

"Such a pity," Gethen said. "You have so much potential, Sophie. But you rely on the same predictable defenses— though it does make our job easier. Look at how well you've handled your mighty guards."

The sound of snapping fingers brought back her vision, leaving Sophie squinting through tear-blurred eyes at where Sandor, Grizel, and Fitz had collapsed in the sand, limbs thrashing and faces scrunched with agony.

All three members of the Neverseen were perfectly fine.

"We came prepared," Gethen explained, tossing back his hood and pointing to the fitted hat made of shimmering chain mail that covered most of his blond hair. "You know how well these block your little mind tricks. And in case you've manifested something we don't know about, let's get you more contained, shall we? Though I'm pretty sure the only ability you're hiding has to do with those gloves."

Sophie was so thrown by the fact that he seemed to know about her enhancing ability that it took her a second to catch his threat—and another to realize she was still holding a throwing star. By then, the figure on Gethen's left had raised his arms and trapped her in a glowing white force field.

Panic bubbled up her throat as three more domes of energy appeared, imprisoning Sandor, Fitz, and Grizel. But she choked it down, knowing the best thing she could do was feign confidence. Make them wonder why she wasn't freaking out.

"I guess I'm not the only predictable one," she said, taking a steadying breath as she stared down the cloaked figure that had to be Ruy. "How many times have you played the force field card now?"

"Why stop if you keep falling for it?" Ruy countered, his voice every bit as familiar as it was nauseating.

She shrugged, trying to channel Keefe's snark—which was easier than she'd expected. All she had to do was look at the crooked line of Gethen's nose and remember how good it had felt to deck him with the full strength of her Sucker Punch.

"I like it in here," she told him. "It means I don't have to smell you guys while you give your boring speech. That's what you're here for, right? If you didn't want to talk, you would've drugged me by now. So let's get on with it, okay?"

Gethen's piercing blue eyes twinkled. "This is why I enjoy our little chats. It's always so adorable watching you play tough while you try to trick information out of me. You're attempting to break into my head right now, aren't you? Slamming that strange telepathy of yours against the force field, hoping you'll be able to sneak into my mind and dig out all of our secrets? But even if I took my hat off, you're not strong enough without the Vacker boy, are you?" He nudged his chin toward Fitz— who, thankfully, looked less pained than he had a few seconds earlier. "And you'd both need your little Shade to help. Pity he's not here."

Unfortunately, he was right.

Tam's shadows were the only thing that had ever broken through Ruy's force fields.

Well . . . unless Sophie wanted to use the trick that Biana had discovered when they'd first clashed with Ruy in the Neutral Territories. The monocle pendants that the Black Swan gave them when they swore fealty had a special lens set into the curve of dark metal. And when Biana hurled hers into the force field that Ruy had been hiding behind, the energy hit the glass and exploded, covering Ruy in white flames.

If Sophie tried the same method now, she'd be the one

showered with fire. *And* she'd have to take out three members of the Neverseen by herself with only one throwing star.

She'd call that plan B.

Not that plan A sounded a whole lot better.

Her panic-switch ring was carefully hidden under her glove, and if she pressed the center stone, it would send Dex an alert and allow him to track her. She hated using it, because it meant asking him to risk his life—but she knew he'd tell her that that's what he'd designed it for.

And he'd have his bodyguard with him.

But . . . Dex and Lovise would still be outnumbered—and totally unprepared, since the ring didn't let her warn them about what they'd be facing. She'd have to suggest that as an upgrade.

Assuming they survived . . .

"You've gone quiet," Gethen noted. "Beginning to grasp the gravity of your situation? Or are you still trying to think of a way out? Or maybe you're realizing that if you'd used the weapon you're holding when you first saw us, you would've had a better chance than you did with your pathetic inflicting."

"Actually, I'm waiting for you to tell me what you want," she said, pressing the center of her ring before she could change her mind.

There was no way to know if the signal was strong enough to transmit through the force field, but she had to believe that it would—and she had to try to stall until Dex and Lovise got there.

"Or, wait, am I supposed to guess?" she asked. "Let's see. . . ."

She closed her eyes, pressing two fingers against one of her temples and pretending to read his mind. "You're here because you've finally realized that your cause is totally creepy, and that you're never going to win, so you're hoping to cut a deal for your cooperation. Not a bad move, honestly. But you're forgetting that the Council holds a grudge."

"Do they?" Gethen asked. "Seems to me like they've gotten rather lenient lately."

His smile made it clear that he was well aware of Alvar's sentence—and she refused to rise to his bait.

She polished the blades of her throwing star with the edge of her tunic. "Don't worry, when your time comes I have a *long* list of suggestions for how they can punish you. My favorites involve flesh-eating bacteria."

"Ugh, now I get why Keefe was always going on about this one," the figure on Gethen's right grumbled. "They both think they're so clever."

Her voice was soft and raspy, like curls of smoke. And the shadow at her feet seemed darker than the others.

"You're Umber, right?" Sophie asked.

"To some people." She crossed her arms, pulling back her sleeves and drawing attention to her black-painted fingernails. "I only give that name to those I don't trust."

"Huh," Sophie said. "Seems like you could've come up with something cooler. Like Dusk—or Midnight! Midnight would've been so much more mysterious. Plus, Umber sounds like a noise your stomach makes when you eat something too spicy."

"Careful, Sophie," Gethen warned as Umber's fingernails grew, and Sophie realized the black that coated them wasn't polish—it was shadows. Thick, sludgy darkness that seemed to pour out of her and curl into long claws.

"You have no idea who you're dealing with," Umber told her.

"You're right," Sophie agreed, "because you're still wearing that ugly cloak. Aren't you guys supposed to be done with that? Isn't that why Lady Gisela told everyone in Atlantis that you weren't hiding anymore? I know she was still covered up when she said it, but I figured that was because you slashed her up before handing her over to King Dimitar. Think she's still angry about that, by the way? She seems pretty vain."

"She knows that was Fintan's decision," Gethen assured her.

"Right, but you still let it happen. Well, not *you*," she corrected, stopping herself from thinking about where Gethen had been or what he'd been preparing for during that time. She had to keep her cool—even if rage was slithering down her spine. "But you guys," she added, pointing her throwing star at Ruy and Umber and wishing she had a way to fling it through the force field. "Don't you worry that Lady Gisela's planning some sort of payback? You let Fintan torture her. And you didn't even try to rescue her. *And* you kept working with Fintan after he took over."

"She knows we had our reasons," Umber insisted.

"You'd better hope that's true. Otherwise you'll be the next bodies left sliced up and drugged in an abandoned cell."

"Is this your attempt to trick us into revealing why Alvar was cast out of our order?" Gethen asked. "Because you really needn't bother. He was simply no longer useful."

"You expect us to believe that?" Fitz shouted, and Sophie's knees nearly collapsed with relief as she watched him struggle to his feet. He looked sweaty and pale, but his legs held steady and his eyes were clear and focused.

Sandor and Grizel had recovered as well and were busy trying to tunnel out of their force fields—but the energy kept stretching with the shifting sand, keeping them sealed inside.

Sophie pressed her panic switch again, trying not to worry about why Dex was taking so long to get there.

"I don't really expect anything from *you*," Gethen told Fitz. "But I'm telling the truth—and I erased your brother's mind personally, so I would know. I'm sure you've both seen how *thorough* I was."

"That doesn't mean his memories won't trigger," Fitz snapped back.

"Actually, it does. My washing skills are the reason I was recruited to the order. Do you think we would've released him if there was any chance you could learn something?"

"Why release him at all?" Fitz countered. "If you're really done with him, why not just kill him?"

"You sound as if that's what you would've preferred." He smiled when Fitz didn't deny it. "Clearly no love lost between the Vacker brothers—though I suppose that was always the problem, wasn't it? Families are so gloriously complicated. Which also makes them predictable. I knew you'd envision some grand conspiracy for your brother after my success in Lumenaria—but if you think Alvar could ever muster the discipline, determination, and endurance he would need to pull off a feat like that, you're even more foolish than I thought."

The pride in Gethen's voice was equal parts disgusting and terrifying.

It took a special kind of evil to brag about murder.

"How's the Black Swan faring without their bloated leader, by the way?" Gethen asked, as if he knew what Sophie had been thinking.

But he didn't know that there used to be two Mr. Forkles gobbling up ruckleberries to disguise themselves for that role—or that one of the twin brothers lived on. And it was Sophie's job to make sure it stayed that way.

So she let her shoulders slump and curled one arm around herself, looking every bit the grief-broken girl she knew Gethen wanted her to be.

He rewarded her performance with another smile.

"I still have the sword," he said, pulling aside the thick fabric of his cloak to reveal the familiar diamond-encrusted hilt protruding from a gleaming silver sheath. "I'm sure I'll find another use for it eventually."

His voice sounded flat and bored, as if he were talking about a pair of shoes instead of an ancient weapon he'd pulled from a stone in Lumenaria and used to steal a life. But there was a wild gleam in his eyes, a hint of whatever damage the murder had done to his mind—and now was not the time to let that madness take over.

"The Black Swan is . . . adjusting," Sophie told him. "Mr. Forkle had a plan in place for his death."

"I'm sure he did," Gethen said, "but it's not working very well, now, is it? All these weeks since Atlantis, and what has your Collective done—besides waste time investigating a worthless prisoner with no memories? Though I suppose that isn't all that unusual for them. Aside from creating you, what *has* the Black Swan done, other than lie to you and risk your life—and the lives of everyone you care about—while we succeed over and over and over? And now here you are, trapped like the helpless little bird you were designed to be. Does it bother you knowing you'll always be weak because your creators were too afraid to make you strong?"

"You and I have different definitions of weak," Sophie snapped, pressing her panic switch a third time and promising herself that if Dex didn't get there in the next five minutes, she'd switch to plan B—and make sure Gethen burned right along with her. "I can get out of this cage anytime I want. But I'm still waiting for you to tell me why you're here. I'm assuming you're planning to trade me for somebody. I just can't decide if you want Fintan or Alvar."

"I told you: Alvar is worthless. And Fintan has no place with us any longer."

"Then it must be the caches," Sophie realized.

Keefe had stolen Fintan's cache—and the cache that used to belong to Councillor Kenric—when he'd abandoned his plan to infiltrate their order.

Ruy snorted. "Wow, I thought you guys would've figured that out by now."

"I know!" Umber's laugh was verging on a cackle when she told Sophie, "The caches you have are fake."

"Fintan knew Keefe would be dumb enough to go after them," Ruy added, "so he had our Technopath make a couple of replicas."

Sophie opened her mouth to call them liars, but . . .

It would explain why Fintan hadn't been able to retrieve any of the secrets from his cache. And why all of Dex's efforts had been thwarted—even when she was enhancing him.

"Yes, Sophie," Gethen told her, "you should feel shaken. We really are *that* many steps ahead. Any victories you think you've had are only because we've let you believe. And lest you forget, we haven't yet brought our ogre allies into play. Or our dwarves. And we have so many other plans in the works— things you can't even begin to imagine. That's why I came here to deliver a message. It's time for you to understand that the fact that you're alive at this moment and generally free to do as you wish has nothing to do with your sloppy abilities, or the Council's paltry protection, or the Black Swan and their ridiculous methods, or your absurdly loyal bodyguard, or your father's tedious Mesmer tricks, or your obnoxious friends. We can find you anytime we want, anywhere we want, and if we wanted you dead—or in our custody—you would be. The only reason we haven't taken you out is because Lady Gisela is still clinging to her hope that you'll prove yourself useful— especially with her son. But her patience will only last so much longer. In fact, she's already preparing your replacement."

Bile turned Sophie's mouth sour, but she swallowed it down and asked, "Is that supposed to scare me?"

"No," Umber told her. "This is."

She circled her hands, bending all the nearby shadows into a spear—then thrust her arms toward Sandor and sent the darkness slicing through his force field.

A strangled sound tore from Sophie's chest as the spear hit Sandor's face, smashing his nose and splattering red as the dome sealed any gaps, keeping him caged.

"And this," Umber added, launching another shadow spear at Grizel, nailing her in the stomach hard enough to make her vomit.

"Stop!" Sophie screamed as yet another shadow spear smashed into Fitz's legs, knocking him into his force field and making his body twitch and flail as the white energy zapped him with a thousand bolts of lightning.

She grabbed her monocle pendant, ready to put plan B into

action—and hoping her aim with her throwing star was as deadly as possible—but Umber's next shadow spear blasted toward her, smashing the monocle into needle-sharp splinters that tore through her skin.

The pain nearly knocked Sophie over, and as the throwing star slipped from her grasp, Umber's shadows snatched the weapon and dragged it back to her waiting hand.

"Had enough?" Umber asked, holding up her new trophy.

"Let's hope so," Gethen said as he strode to the edge of Sophie's force field. He tilted his head, watching her wrap her bleeding fingers with her tunic, staining the white fabric red. "Ugh, that looks gruesome. You with me, Sophie? Your eyes seem a little glazed."

They probably were. All the throbbing and bleeding was making it hard to concentrate.

"You need to get yourself, and your friends, to a physician," he told her. "But first you need to prove that you understand the importance of cooperation. So I'm going to give you a little test—and I'll be kind enough to make it easy. All I need you to do is tell me where Wylie's hiding."

The name dragged Sophie out of her daze.

Wylie had barely escaped the Neverseen after they'd tortured him for information about his mom. Cyrah had been a Flasher, and Lady Gisela had blackmailed her into making special starstones—and then Fintan had Cyrah killed in order to make sure she couldn't tell anyone. But she hadn't delivered the final starstone, and now the Neverseen were trying to find it—or that was one of the prevailing theories. Wylie had also met with Gethen a few weeks earlier, trying to keep him distracted while Sophie and her friends snuck into Nightfall, and Gethen had seemed much more interested in learning about Wylie's recently recovered father, Prentice.

But whatever they wanted, Sophie would *never* put Wylie at risk, no matter what they threatened.

"There's no need to look so defensive," Gethen told her. "I just want to have a little heart-to-heart with him—and since he called the last meeting, it's my turn to extend the invitation."

Sophie straightened up, pressing her hand against her stomach to keep pressure on the wounds. "If you can find anyone, anytime, why would you need me to tell you where he is?"

Gethen sighed. "I didn't say we can find anyone. I said we can find *you*."

"And that was the wrong answer," Umber added, whipping her hands again.

Sophie tried to dodge, but there were two spears this time, one smashing into her right shoulder as the other nailed her injured hand again, this time cracking bone. And instead of dissipating, the shadows sank under her skin, shredding muscle and nerve with a million icy tentacles.

"Let's hope you're ready to tell me now," Gethen said as Sophie dropped to her knees, gritting her teeth to silence her screams. "Otherwise this is going to get messy."

Tears blurred Sophie's eyes as she used her good hand to retrieve the Panakes blossoms tucked inside her pockets.

"That won't help as much as you think it will," Gethen warned as she swallowed the pinkish, purplish, bluish petals.

"It won't," Umber agreed, twisting her fingers and making the darkness slice into Sophie's bones. "If you think that hurts, imagine how it will feel when I tell the shadows to expand."

"I doubt she cares," Ruy warned.

"Oh, I'm sure she does." Umber smiled, and Sophie closed her eyes, bracing for pain—but nothing could prepare her for the agony that followed.

There was a crackling pop—almost like a firework—and a stomach-heaving pressure as jagged bone punched through her skin and her knuckle just . . . collapsed. Then another and another—though by then Sophie had lost feeling, her senses too overloaded to process the horror.

"Had enough?" Umber asked. "Or shall I keep going? There are still *plenty* of little bones left—it's one of my favorite things about the hand."

"You won't break her that way," Ruy insisted. "You have to threaten her bodyguard."

"Is that the trick?" Umber asked, taking out another of Sophie's knuckles. "Look at me!" she ordered. *"Look at me, Sophie!"*

Pain had made the world hazy—but it snapped into focus

when Umber turned toward Fitz and asked, "Would it be better if I try this on your little boyfriend?"

"DON'T!" Sophie gritted out—which was a mistake.

Umber laughed and stalked to where Fitz lay collapsed on the sand. His eyes were closed and he wasn't moving.

"I've always wanted to break a Vacker," she said, gathering a fresh batch of shadows.

"Please," Sophie begged, "he has nothing to do with this."

"Of course he does," Umber insisted. "He's with you, isn't he?"

"NO!" Sophie screamed, the sound shredding her throat. But it didn't stop the darkness from slamming into Fitz's injured leg with a gut-wrenching crunch—followed by a deeper, wetter crackle that had her spitting bile on the sand.

Even Gethen looked green as he told her, "End this, Sophie. Where. Is. Wylie?"

"Right here!" a new voice shouted—and for a second Sophie thought she must be hallucinating.

But Gethen spun toward the sound as well, facing a tall, muscular guy with dark skin and hate in his deep blue eyes. And he was flanked on either side by a strawberry blond boy and a battle-poised goblin.

Dex and Lovise had finally arrived.

And somehow, they'd brought Wylie.

SIX

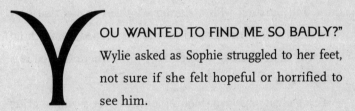

OU WANTED TO FIND ME SO BADLY?" Wylie asked as Sophie struggled to her feet, not sure if she felt hopeful or horrified to see him.

He stretched out his arms as a challenge while Dex and Lovise fanned out and charged toward the Neverseen. "Come and get me!"

"Gladly," Umber said, hurling a shadow spear straight for his face.

Wylie dropped into a crouch to dodge, and as soon as he was down, Ruy tried to trap him in a force field. But Wylie somersaulted away before the energy could lock into place.

Lovise snarled, and a blur of metal streaked toward Ruy's

chest, but he shielded himself in time to block the spinning blades.

"Hiding in your bubble already?" Wylie asked, jumping back to his feet, and Sophie tried to spot where Dex and Lovise had disappeared to. But a flash of green caught her attention, and she watched Wylie shape the light into a vivid sphere that looked almost solid as it hovered over his palm—before he whipped it at Gethen's head.

Gethen ducked in time, collapsing to his knees as Umber swung a beam of darkness like a baseball bat and knocked the squishy ball of light toward Lovise as she charged forward. But the orb whizzed over Lovise's head, smashing into a nearby dune and bursting with a shower of green sparks that only seemed to speed Lovise's sprint. And Dex leaped from behind a nearby dune, tossing a silver cube right where Gethen was still kneeling.

The gadget exploded, blotting out the world with a gritty red fog.

But when the dust settled, Gethen, Ruy, and Umber were safely shielded inside a glowing white dome.

Now it was a standoff, Sophie realized.

And the Neverseen looked way too happy about it.

"Cowards," Wylie muttered. "If you want a fight—let's *fight*!"

Gethen's smile widened, and he took his time shaking the red powder out of his hair. "You do seem like you've been practicing. But I only came here to talk. And I must say, this is certainly a surprise. If Sophie didn't look so stunned to see you, I'd almost think this was proof that she'd decided to cooperate. Pity for her that it isn't."

Wylie stole a glance at Sophie, swallowing hard when he looked at her ruined hand. "I wouldn't have blamed you if you told them where I was."

"*I* would've blamed me." Her words were a rasp, her throat still hoarse from all the screaming.

Gethen sighed. "Stubborn, foolish child. You can't protect him any more than you can protect yourself."

"I don't need her to!" Wylie snapped. "You think I haven't been waiting for you guys to come after me?"

He flashed another orb—yellow this time, and even squishier-looking than the green one—and pitched it toward the Never-seen like a curveball.

Sophie braced for an explosion. But the golden blob deflated the second it touched the white energy, spluttering around like a wild balloon before winking out with a shower of glitter.

Ruy laughed. "You'll have to do better than that."

"How about this?" Dex shouted, and Sophie pivoted to watch him throw what looked like a handful of Hershey's Kisses. But these were no candy—the small silver blobs latched onto the force field and unleashed some sort of sonic pulse that made the white energy ripple and spark.

"Eh," Ruy said, waving his arms to thicken their shield. "You would've been better off bringing along your Shade."

"Nah, he'd be no match for me," Umber argued. "He lacks proper training."

Ruy shrugged. "He's still the only one they have with any real potential."

"Then why do you keep coming after *me*?" Wylie asked, pressing his hands together and forming a beam of light that was the same deep blue as his eyes.

He slashed it like a sword, and Sophie's heart swelled with hope as it sliced through the force field like butter, making the white energy blink away with a crackle of static.

But the second the shield disappeared, Ruy had another one in place. "You realize I can do this all day, right?"

Wylie sliced the new dome with another blue beam. "So can I!"

Sophie wanted to believe him—but sweat was pouring down the strained lines on his face. And the next gadget Dex hurled only kicked up a little dust.

"I'm done with this!" Umber shouted, launching shadow spears at both of them.

Lovise tackled Dex to save him from being hit, and they both tumbled across the dunes, rolling out of sight as Wylie formed a red orb around himself—and this time the light held strong when the shadows landed.

"Interesting," Gethen said, adjusting his ugly hat. "Weren't you just calling us cowards for shielding ourselves?"

"You lower yours, I'll drop mine," Wylie offered, forming a green orb with each of his hands. "We'll settle this right here."

"And you'll lose," Gethen warned. "Your little tricks will never be strong enough—no matter how hard you've been practicing. Look at the state of your friend, if you don't believe me."

Wylie's eyes shifted to Sophie's hand, and fear, fury, and pity flickered across his face.

"Same goes for you, boy," Gethen added, his voice projected toward wherever Dex was currently hiding. "Technology will never beat natural ability."

Wylie's jaw clenched. "If you're so sure about that, prove it."

Umber sighed. "If you insist."

She whispered something Sophie couldn't understand, and her shadowy claws expanded, the darkness pouring out of her fingers and twisting into a short, thin strand that looked blacker than anything else Umber had formed.

Sophie realized it was an arrow the same moment Wylie dropped to his stomach to dodge—and it was a good thing he did, because his shield unraveled the second the darkness hit.

"That's the problem with light," Umber said as Wylie struggled to shield himself inside a purple orb. "It will *always* be weaker than shadows. No matter what you try."

"It's one of the great flaws of our world," Gethen agreed. "We built everything around the lesser force because we were fooled by the shimmer and shine. But if we want to harness true power, we're going to need to embrace darkness."

"Like this," Umber said, weaving another arrow from her shadow claws. She threw back her arm, aiming it toward Wylie, but halfway through the throw she pivoted and launched it at Fitz.

Sophie's scream sounded like a death rattle as she watched the darkness slice through his force field and pierce his chest—then liquify and sink into his heart.

Dex's shout sounded just as guttural. But then he was charging toward Umber and tossing another handful of his silver blobs—but not at her.

At Sandor's force field.

Ruy spun to reinforce the bodyguard's cage—which meant he wasn't ready for Wylie to swipe a long blue beam toward Grizel and unravel her force field. Lovise lunged out of the dunes beside her, and together they sprinted for the Neverseen, while Wylie hacked at their shield and Dex hit it with silver gadgets.

But the female warriors only made it a few steps before a massive bolt of darkness blasted them both backward, sending them tumbling across the sand until they both fell very, very still.

Sandor roared.

Umber pumped her fist. "Two down—though I guess it's three, since there's no way the Vacker boy is going anywhere now that my shadows have seeped in."

More darkness poured from the ends of her fingers, and she wove it into another eerie arrow. "Who's next? How about you?"

It looked like she was aiming at Dex—and Wylie made another purple shield to cover him.

But the arrow blasted into Sophie's mangled hand.

A sob broke free when the darkness sank into her veins, tearing up her arm like frozen fire, blazing past her elbow, over her shoulder, up her neck.

Flashes and shouts raged all around. But Sophie lost track of the battle. She lost track of herself as the shadows seared into her head and sank into her brain.

"Hang on!" Dex shouted.

She didn't want to listen—she wanted to hide in the soft little nook in her mind where it was quiet and safe and far, far away from the pain.

But she sucked in a long breath, trying to slow her pulse as she shoved another Panakes blossom into her mouth and dragged her throbbing body back to her feet. Her head spun and her eyes watered, and when the world came into focus she found Dex and Wylie standing side by side in the center of a massive, blobby-green bubble. Both still looked strong and steady, but Wylie had a deep gash above his right eyebrow, and Dex's left arm was twisted at an odd angle.

The Neverseen, meanwhile, were hiding behind yet another force field.

But at least they'd taken some hits. Ruy's cloak was now missing a sleeve, and his exposed skin was covered in blisters. And Umber seemed to be favoring one of her legs.

Gethen's lips were even swollen and bleeding as he shouted, "Enough! I don't think you realize the predicament you're in."

He pointed to Fitz, whose face was now a terrifying shade of blue—the same shade that Sophie's wounded right hand was turning.

"Those shadows you're fighting are different," Umber warned. "The longer they mix with your blood, the more they take over. You have about thirty minutes before you lose your arm—and half that before the Vacker boy's dead. And don't even get me started on what's happening to that special little brain of yours."

"Your goblins aren't looking so good either," Ruy noted.

They weren't.

Sandor was at least on his feet, pacing around his glowing cage. But he was bloody and pale. And Grizel and Lovise still hadn't moved.

Sophie stared at her blue-tinted fingers, feeling the truth in Umber's words. This pain was different than the blood and the breaks—deeper and more defining, like everything the shadows touched was changing.

And they kept spreading with every heartbeat—the Panakes blossoms didn't feel like they were helping.

"You have a choice to make," Gethen said, flashing a smile streaked with red as he turned to Wylie. "Surrender now and leave with me while your Technopath brings the others to a physician. Or you can have your friends' losses on your conscience while we drag you away."

"Don't do it!" Dex shouted, and Sophie tried to say the same. But the panic and pain choked off the words.

"How do I know you won't hurt us?" Wylie asked.

Umber laughed. "We already have. Far more than you realize—or maybe Sophie does. You can feel the shift, can't you? The way the darkness is slowly remaking you?"

"You're running out of time," Gethen agreed. "And you're in no position to bargain. But since I find these sorts of standoffs to be rather tedious, let me be clear: I wanted to locate Wylie—and I have. So I have no more need for anyone else." His eyes fixed on Wylie's. "I'm willing to let your friends go *if* you come peacefully. And all I need from you is information. Once I have it, you'll be free to go as well."

"Right," Dex snorted. "After you torture him."

"Telepaths have no reason to resort to such dramatics," Gethen argued. "I can find the memory I need in a matter of minutes."

"What memory?" Wylie demanded. "I already told you—I wasn't there when my mom made her final leap!"

Gethen wiped his bloody chin. "Yes, I know. I *was* there."

Wylie flinched at the words. And even with the shadows dimming her brain, Sophie realized . . .

He was facing his mother's murderer.

If the story Lady Gisela told her was true, Fintan sent Gethen to do some sort of mind trick to break Cyrah's concentration as she tried to leap home, causing her to fade away—right in front of her son.

Wylie's hands crackled with threads of light as he stalked to the edge of his green bubble. "If you knew I wasn't there, why did you keep calling me a liar during my interrogation?"

Gethen sighed. "*I* didn't. That's the problem with compartmentalizing information. Fintan and Brant only had certain pieces of the story, because they weren't supposed to be focusing on your mother at that point. But Fintan adjusted the timeline when he took over—and I wasn't around to fill him in on the many ways he was mistaken. So now I'm trying to get us back on track—and adjust for Vespera's additions. Which means I need to know what your mother hid from us—and before you claim that she never told you, ask yourself this: Have you ever noticed any gaps in your memories? Any details that seem a little fuzzy?"

Wylie pressed his lips together.

"That's what I thought. Cyrah was no fool. She knew anything she told you would put you in danger. But she also knew that something might happen to her if she chose to cross us, and then the information would be lost. If she'd written it down, I would've found it by now. So she must've had one of her Telepath friends hide her secrets deep in your head."

"That's all just a theory!" Sophie managed to grit out as she turned to Wylie. "If he can't find what he's looking for, he'll do a memory break."

"I'm not wrong," Gethen insisted calmly, "and if Wylie cooperates, I won't need to resort to anything so extreme. But that's a risk he's going to have to take—and you're wasting precious seconds. Is the Vacker boy even still breathing?"

Sophie couldn't tell. But Fitz's skin was turning from blue to gray, and the shadows in her head were latching on like they were permanently part of her brain—which made the selfish, terrified part of her want to beg Wylie to do whatever he could to save them.

Instead, she forced herself to remind him, "Whatever your mom hid, she did it to keep it away from them."

"I know that," he said quietly. "But . . . they're never going to stop coming after me until they get what they want. At least this way we get something out of it too."

"Such refreshing wisdom," Gethen said, flashing another bloodstained smile. "See the beauty of cooperation? I hope you'll remember this, Sophie, the next time we pay you a visit. Especially since I think it might be time to bring a few of our ogre friends along—or maybe some dwarves. But we'll save that fun for later. For the moment, I'm going to need everyone that's still conscious to raise your hands above your head—except you, Sophie. Given your condition, I'll settle for just your good arm."

She had to let go of her injured hand to obey, and the pain left her doubled over.

"Very good," Gethen said, narrowing his eyes at Sandor before he turned back to Wylie. "Now I want you to unravel your shield on the count of three—and if you so much as *think* about reaching for one of your little trinkets, Dex, I'll have Umber send her shadows somewhere I suspect you'll find *very* unpleasant."

"Just do what he says," Wylie ordered when Dex didn't agree. "I know what I'm doing, okay?"

"Everybody ready?" Gethen asked.

He waited until Dex nodded, then counted to three, and Wylie snapped his fingers, making their green shield dissolve into the sand.

"Now, walk slowly over to me," Gethen ordered. "And everyone else, keep those hands where I can see them."

Sobs shook Sophie's body, and she forced her eyes to stay focused—forced herself to watch as Wylie handed himself over to the enemy to save her.

But when he was only halfway to Gethen, he threw out his hands and shouted, "GET DOWN!" as a beam of rainbow-streaked light swirled from his fingers.

"Fool," Umber snarled, waving her arms and creating a long spear of black woven from threads of both kinds of shadows—those she gathered, and that strange darkness that poured from her hands.

Thunder clapped and lightning flashed when the light and darkness collided, hurling both Wylie and Umber backward as the force exploded.

Sophie tried to cover her head, her vision dimming from a fresh surge of pain. But she could still see the waves of shadowy light whip in every direction, spinning into a cyclone and spreading wider and wider until it burst with a blinding flash that somehow blacked out the sky.

More crackles and flashes followed. And when the air finally calmed, all of the force fields were gone.

All of them.

Sandor must've realized the same thing, because he raised his sword and charged.

And when Ruy tried forming a new force field, the energy flickered and dissipated.

So did Umber's shadows.

"Well," Gethen said, frowning as Sandor closed in, "looks like we'll have to finish this another time."

He reached into his cloak, pulling out a cobalt blue crystal and holding it up to the sky. Ruy and Umber did the same, calling, "See you soon," before they stepped into the light.

The last thing Sophie heard was Dex telling her to hold on. Then someone lifted her off the sand, and her consciousness slipped away.

SEVEN

OICES FADED IN AND OUT. SOME
Sophie recognized. Some she couldn't
place. And most of the words were lost in
the layers of black.

The pain was only a memory now.

Gone but not forgotten.

Another thing to carry—and she would.

But the fear . . .

This was not the kind of terror she'd battled before.

This was solid.

Tangible.

A monster in the dark.

Prowling into the prickliest places. Feasting on what'd been hidden away.

Growing stronger. Fiercer. Dragging her down.

"Sophie," a voice whispered. Wrapping around her heart and pulling her closer. "Sophie, please wake up."

She tried.

But the monster was too strong.

And the bright light of reality was too full of horrifying possibilities.

Neither was safe.

Panic coiled tight, and the voice seemed to understand.

"Okay," it told her. "Just sleep."

She didn't know how—not with the monster down below, waiting. It would hurt her this time. Somehow she knew that. And she wasn't ready—not yet.

But then a soft blue breeze trickled through her mind, scattering the shadows like dandelion seeds. Slowing her racing thoughts. Steadying her breath.

Until there was only silence.

And rest.

Hours passed—or maybe it was minutes.

It might've even been days.

Then the darkness thinned and there were voices again. Two of them. Calling her name louder and louder until she forced her eyes open, groaning as a blast of light burned into her brain.

The world shifted into focus, and she realized she was staring at the ceiling of the Healing Center, with a bruised, weary Dex leaning over her and a boy next to him with black hair and silver-tipped bangs.

"It's about time," Tam said, then winked one of his silver-flecked blue eyes. "Leave it to you to find a completely new way to almost die."

"Sadly, he's not exaggerating," Elwin agreed as he leaned in between Dex and Tam. His dark, wild hair was even more rumpled than usual, and his eyes looked bloodshot behind the huge iridescent spectacles he always wore while treating patients. "Bullhorn screamed his head off when he saw you, and then he insisted on lying by your side—which pretty much gave me a meltdown, just so you know. Especially when you wouldn't respond to any of the elixirs I gave you. But when Tam called the shadows out of your blood, your system finally started cooperating, and Bullhorn scurried back to his favorite spot under my desk."

"Wow," Sophie mumbled, the word sour and broken.

Elwin's pet banshee only acted like that if someone was almost out of time.

"Yeah, it's not a moment I want to live again anytime soon," Elwin admitted, snapping his fingers and forming an orange orb around her torso. "Those shadows were like poison. If Tam hadn't rushed over when I hailed him . . ."

"It's a good thing I actually had my Imparter with me," Tam added quietly.

He and Linh had spent years on their own after the Council banished them from the Lost Cities because Linh's untrained ability had earned her the nickname "the Girl of Many Floods." So staying in contact wasn't really a habit for them.

"Well . . . thank you," Sophie told him. "All of you," she added, taking a careful sip from the bottle of Youth Elwin pressed against her lips and wondering if it would ever not feel awkward to thank people for saving her life.

It was the kind of moment that deserved some sort of deep, impassioned speech. But everything still felt too shattered.

"How long have I been here?" she whispered.

Elwin made her take two more swallows of the cool, sweet water before he told her, "Not that long—about eighteen hours."

That was shorter than she'd expected. But still plenty of time for horrible, life-changing things.

She could almost feel that monster of fear stirring.

Biting her lip and bracing for the worst, she forced herself to ask, "How's Fitz?"

"Heavily sedated at the moment—but he's going to be fine." He pointed across the room to where Fitz must've been sleeping.

She couldn't see him from her current position—and lifting her head didn't feel possible yet—but she was familiar enough with the layout of the Healing Center to picture it.

The space was divided into three rooms: Elwin's personal office, an alchemy area where he made his medicines, and the treatment space they were in, with a row of cots and lots of shelves filled with bottles of colorful elixirs and tiny pots of balms and poultices and salves.

"How bad were his injuries?" she whispered as Elwin waved the orange light away and pressed another vial against her lips.

He poured a thick, floral-tasting syrup into her mouth and waited for her to swallow it before he told her, "Pretty bad. Bull-horn ran to him before he went to you. And Tam had to fight hard to get those shadows away from his heart."

Tam looked slightly green as he nodded. "I've never felt anything like that before. I don't know who their Shade is, but—"

"She calls herself Umber," Sophie told him. "But that's all we know."

"Well, whoever she is, she's doing some *dark* stuff—which I know sounds obvious, since she's a Shade. But . . . those weren't normal shadows."

"They weren't," Sophie agreed. "She said they were different. And they kind of poured out of her hands, like they came from somewhere inside her."

Tam shivered. "I don't know how that's possible. But those creepy things wouldn't obey *any* of my commands. I had to wrap my shadowvapor around them and control *that*—and when I finally pulled them free, they wouldn't fade. They just . . . slithered away."

"Seriously, it was one of the freakiest things I've ever seen," Dex said with a shudder.

"Yeah, my Shade Mentor and I have a *lot* to talk about," Tam mumbled.

Sophie glanced at Elwin. "Fitz won't have any permanent damage, will he?"

"It's a little too early to tell about scars," he admitted, pouring a second dose of the floral medicine into her mouth, "but I have everything else covered. We talked before I put him under, and he sounded good. Exhausted and weak, of course—and super worried about you. But his mind was sharp and his vitals were strong. He even convinced his mom and sister to go home and rest, so that should tell you something."

Sophie closed her eyes, repeating the words until they felt real. "Then why did you sedate him?"

"I want to keep his pulse slow and steady for a bit, so I can run some tests on his heart—just to double-check a few things. *Not* because he's in any danger. Plus, I needed to set his broken leg."

"Is it a bad break?" She could still hear the horrible *crack*.

"Unfortunately, yes. The bone split in three different places." He let out a sigh. "But they were clean breaks, so the marrow regenerator should seal them pretty fast. Same goes for his cracked ribs. Then it's just all the nerve and tissue damage from the force field, and—"

"Uh, I don't think this is making her feel better," Dex warned. And he was right.

Every word was making it harder and harder to breathe.

"He's not in *any* pain," Elwin assured her. "And by the time he wakes up, most of his injuries will be taken care of. The broken bones will take a few days, but everything else is easy, okay? I could put you out too, so you'd just sleep through—"

"No sedatives," she told him.

"I figured you were going to say that. You even fought me when I tried to knock you out before I worked on your hand and arm—and you weren't even conscious. That's quite a talent."

She tried to smile, but . . .

She couldn't move her right arm.

Or feel it at all.

"It's in there," Elwin assured her when she scraped together the strength to lift her head enough to find a massive cocoon of silver bandages completely encasing her shoulder, arm, and hand. "And don't worry, it'll be good as new by the time I'm done. But . . . it's going to be a process—way more involved than what I had to do for Keefe after his sparring match with King Dimitar. What the Neverseen did to you . . ."

His voice choked off, and his eyes turned shiny behind his glasses. And Dex and Tam both started blinking really hard.

"That bad, huh?" she asked, forcing her lips into a wobbly smile.

Elwin nodded. "Some of the breaks were clean. But some . . ."

She squeezed her eyes shut, wishing it could block the memories of her knuckles shattering.

"Can you really fix that?" she whispered.

"I can," he promised. "And I *will*. The Neverseen might be stepping up their game, but I can step up mine, too."

His tone had such a strange mix of anger, confidence, and exhaustion that it made her reach for him with her good hand.

"Thank you," she said, her voice thick and squeaky. "I don't know where I'd be without you."

But she did know.

She'd be dead.

And so would Fitz.

Elwin cleared his throat, squeezing her fingers back. "And to think, the first time you met me, you were afraid of me."

She had been—though it wasn't because of anything he did. Several traumatic hospital stays during her years living with humans had left her terrified of doctors—and the needles and pain and scary beeping machines that always seemed to go with them.

But Elwin was different—and not just because his treatments were gentle and he always wore funny glasses and silly tunics covered in colorful animals.

After everything they'd been through together, Elwin . . . felt like family.

"Well," she told him, "now you're my favorite."

"You're mine, too. And it's a good thing. Because we're going to be spending *lots* of time together. I set your bones as much as I could, but the shattered parts have a lot of missing pieces, which means a lot more marrow regenerator—and you can't move any part of your arm or hand until everything's sealed. That's why I have you wrapped up like that. And even after the bandages come off, you won't be able to light leap for at least a couple more days, because breaking your body down would undo some of the recovery. So I told your parents to plan on at least a week before we can move you to Havenfield—that's why they're not here right now, in case you were wondering. They were by your side the whole time Tam and I were treating you. But since you didn't seem to want to wake up, Edaline went to pack up your stuff. She figured you'd probably want something better to wear—though I think you look awesome."

That was when she realized she was wearing one of his tunics, with the right sleeve chopped off to accommodate her bandage. The blue fabric was decorated with eurypterids, but Sophie was far less disturbed by the idea of wearing sea scorpions than she was by the thought that someone had to have changed her into it, and she decided she didn't want to know the who or when or where or how.

She knew the why, and the rest was better left unanswered.

"Edaline should be back pretty soon," Elwin added. "And Sandor, Grady, and Alden went to talk to Magnate Leto about how to adjust the campus's security while you're staying here."

"Wait, I'm staying at *Foxfire*?" Sophie asked—then wanted to kick herself for focusing on such an unimportant detail when there was a much better question. "Sandor's okay?"

"Yep to both," Elwin said, making her swallow a third dose of the floral medicine. "It's going to be a Foxfire slumber party! And Sandor's fine—he wasn't exposed to the kind of shadows that you and Fitz were, so he just had a broken nose and some cuts and bruises."

"And a *lot* of rage," Tam added. "Even Ro looked scared of him."

"Ro was here?"

Actually, now that Sophie was thinking about it, she remembered a blue breeze swishing through her head and helping her sleep. "Was Keefe here too?"

They'd discovered that if Keefe held her hand when she wasn't wearing gloves, her enhancing allowed him to send rushes of energy into her mind that could affect her moods.

"I'm sure he's still around somewhere," Elwin said, stopping her from sitting up to look and reminding her that she wasn't supposed to move.

Tam grinned. "Elwin made him wait out in the hall—and he was *not* happy about it."

"It was either that or strap him down to one of the cots so he'd stop all the frantic pacing," Elwin explained, adjusting her pillow to prop her head up a little more.

"I would've voted for that," Tam noted.

Sophie sighed.

Tam and Keefe had been feuding since the moment they'd met—even though they were so similar it was kind of hilarious.

"I think Ro went with the others to talk to Magnate Leto," Dex added.

"Are Grizel and Lovise with them too?" Sophie wondered, wishing she'd thought to ask about them sooner.

"I don't think so—but they're both okay," Dex promised.

"I wouldn't say they're *okay*," Elwin argued. "They both have broken ribs, and Grizel has a few other hairline fractures. But instead of letting me treat them, Lovise gave her some sort of goblin battlefield remedy that's supposed to boost her strength. They're both refusing to rest until the security's reorganized. Sandor's even less happy about it than I am. He threatened to call their queen and ask her to order them back to Gildingham, but Grizel said if he did that, she'd cover all of his weapons in Ro's flesh-eating bacteria."

"And it's not like Sandor's letting you treat him, either," Tam added. "He didn't even wipe the blood off his face."

"I know," Dex said. "I can't imagine being that tough."

"Um, you already are." Sophie pointed to the giant bruise on his cheek, then to his left arm, which she could now see was supported by a golden sling.

He tried to shrug—then winced. "It's just a sprained shoulder."

"There's no 'just' about that, Dex," she said, reaching for him with her good hand.

Tears blurred the room as her gloved fingers tangled with his.

"If you hadn't answered when I pressed my panic switch— or made it for me in the first place . . ."

Dex cleared his throat. "I'm just glad you used it. Thank you for trusting me."

"Thank you for saving us."

He tightened his grip. And as the last fragments of space vanished between them, so did any lingering wisps of the awkwardness that had rattled their friendship after their epic fail of a kiss.

"Uh . . . should I leave you guys alone?" Tam asked.

Dex laughed, his dimples making a quick appearance. "Nope. We're good."

And the best part was: They really were.

They were also *safe*—and Sophie clung to that word as hard as she clung to Dex. But then she realized . . .

"Where's Wylie?" She hated herself for not asking about him sooner.

After everything Wylie had risked and how hard he'd fought, and—

"He went home to protect his dad," Dex told her.

"*WHAT?* Did the Neverseen—"

"He's just being cautious," Elwin assured her. "In case Gethen searched his mind during the attack and found out where he's living."

Her heart stumbled. "I . . . didn't even think about that."

"Don't worry—the Black Swan's on it," Dex promised. "Blur and Wraith both went as backup, and Granite's setting up somewhere for them to move to. In fact, I bet they're already in their new place."

"I'm sure they are," Tam agreed. "Granite doesn't mess around when it comes to Wylie. Or Prentice."

He definitely didn't.

Granite had adopted Wylie after Cyrah was killed, while Prentice was locked away in Exile—and didn't seem to mind sharing fatherly responsibilities now that Prentice had been healed.

But Sophie still felt ill. "How bad were Wylie's injuries?"

"Not bad at all," Elwin insisted. "Just some gashes and scrapes and bruises."

"How is that possible?" she asked. "He got flung across the desert in that explosion—and what *was* that, by the way?"

"No idea," Tam admitted. "I'm guessing it has something to do with those weird shadows."

"Probably," Sophie agreed. "I saw Umber swirl them with normal shadows before she attacked."

Tam tugged on his bangs, pulling them lower across his eyes. "Well. I need to talk to my Shade Mentor about it—which isn't going to be fun, by the way. Lady Zillah is *intense*."

Elwin flashed a blue sphere around Sophie's body. "That she is."

"You know her?" Tam asked.

"I've *met* her," Elwin corrected. "And let's just say it was *memorable*. But she knows her stuff. In fact, would you mind sharing what she tells you? It might explain the anomalies I'm seeing—which aren't serious," he added before Sophie could ask. "If I was worried, I'd be tracking down every Shade I could find and dragging them here. Everything's good. I just don't understand why certain places look different."

"Different how?"

Elwin sighed, rubbing his chin. "I don't really know how to describe it. Usually, when I wrap something in light, it sharpens through my lenses. But right now, certain spots are . . . murky. I'm not worried, since it's not affecting your vitals in *any* way. But I'd still love to understand it."

Sophie would too. "Which places is it affecting?"

He pointed to her bandaged hand. Then to her forehead. Then to Fitz's chest.

All places that Umber's creepy shadows had touched.

But not *everywhere* they touched.

"It's not like that in my arm or shoulder?" Sophie verified, since she'd felt the darkness tear through both.

"Nope. Just those three spots."

"And there are definitely no shadows there," Tam promised, closing his eyes and waving his hand back and forth. "I'd be able to feel them."

"Which is why it's not a big deal," Elwin added.

Sophie wanted to believe him. But . . .

"Umber made it sound like the shadows were changing us," she whispered.

"Yeah, but she said that when they were trying to scare Wylie into turning himself in," Dex reminded her, fidgeting with the strap of his sling. "I really thought he was going to."

"So did I." And she had a feeling Wylie would have if the final attack he'd tried hadn't worked. "Why was he with you?"

"Total coincidence. I was at his house when the panic switch went off, and he insisted on helping. Then we got there and you were screaming and Gethen said Wylie's name and . . . well . . . you know the rest."

She did.

And she was trying hard not to relive it.

"Why were you with Wylie in the first place?" Tam asked. "Linh had hailed him earlier to see if he wanted to meet up, and he said he was busy doing memory exercises with his dad."

"That's what he was doing when I got there. I didn't tell him I was coming. I just wanted to see what he thought of some of the stuff Luzia Vacker said at the Tribunal, since he's a Flasher too."

"Luzia Vacker," Elwin repeated, scratching one of his cheeks. "Now, *there's* a name I rarely hear. What'd she say?"

"Nothing major. It just felt like she was giving really weak excuses for why she used to live at Everglen—like how she needed somewhere peaceful after a long day of bending the sun and stuff."

"That's not as weak as it sounds," Elwin told him. "Light has a weight to it—I never felt it until I manifested. And if I don't take breaks from it, the constant pressure can really drag me down."

"That's what Wylie said too," Dex admitted. "But that still doesn't explain why she picked Everglen specifically. It gets dark everywhere, you know?"

"But not always the same way," Elwin corrected. "Some parts of the world have longer nights than others. And anywhere close to a human city gets a hint of their light pollution."

"It's a thing," Sophie agreed when she saw Tam and Dex's confusion. "There are places where you can barely see the stars."

"So you didn't think it seemed like Luzia was hiding something?" Dex asked her.

"No, I totally did. Especially since she knew Vespera. Fitz and I were planning to search Everglen ourselves, to make sure the Council doesn't miss anything. But . . ." She glanced at her bandage cocoon.

"I can do it," Tam offered. "I'm sure Biana would let me into the property. She'd probably even want help."

"Oh, let me know when you're going," Dex told him. "I want to look around too. Maybe I can even find somewhere to hide one of my stashes. Might be a good thing to have handy in case Alvar's up to something."

"Since when do you have stashes?" Sophie had to ask.

"Since Atlantis. I thought it might be good to make some gadgets that counteract the tricks we know the Neverseen always use, and I've been trying to hide them places we might need to use them."

"Smart," Sophie said, feeling equal parts impressed and ashamed.

She'd spent weeks stressing about how little they were accomplishing, and Dex had used that same time to build secret weapon stashes?

"The only problem is, unless I hide a stash *everywhere*, it takes too long to leap to one and find all the stuff I hid," he admitted. "That's why it took me so long to get to you. Well, that and I wasted time trying to talk Wylie out of coming. If we'd gotten there sooner . . ."

Sophie shook her head. "Don't do that. You came as fast as you could. And you got us out of there alive—that's all that matters."

"I agree," a familiar voice said from the direction of the doorway. "You kids did exactly the right thing."

Sophie craned her neck, expecting to see Mr. Forkle shuffling toward her. Instead, it was Magnate Leto—which was the same thing, of course. But his heavily gelled black hair and sharper features always made him seem more intimidating than his pudgy alter ego.

Alden was right behind him, along with . . .

"Grady." She could barely sneak the word past all the emotions closing off her throat as her adoptive father closed the distance between them and pulled her into a hug.

"Hey, kiddo," he whispered, his voice as thick and crackly as hers. "How are you feeling?"

"I'm okay," she promised. "You know . . . all things considered."

He kissed her cheek and leaned back to study her, and her heart cracked a little when she saw the shadows around his blue eyes. Worry lines creased his handsome features, and his blond hair looked like he'd spent hours tearing his hands through it.

"I'm sorry for worrying you," she whispered.

He shook his head and kissed her cheek again. "*You* have nothing to apologize for."

"We're the ones who should be apologizing," Alden added as he crossed to the other side of the room, and Sophie had to work up the courage to let her gaze follow.

Until that moment, she hadn't actually *seen* Fitz's injuries. But now . . .

Well.

At least he looked peaceful.

His eyes were closed. Features relaxed. But his skin looked clammy and pale. And his whole torso was wrapped in thick silver bandages. His arms were peppered with dark purple bruises. And his left leg was propped up on a mountain of pillows and cocooned in more silver bandages from the middle of his thigh to the tips of his toes.

"I never should've let you go after him alone, Sophie," Alden murmured, brushing the hair off Fitz's forehead.

"She wasn't alone," Sandor growled from the doorway.

He stomped into the room, and Sophie couldn't help wincing when she saw the dried blood still crusting his lips and cheeks. His usually flat nose had swollen into a mound that reminded her of cauliflower, and his chest and arms were scratched and bruised. But it was the sorrow in his eyes that cracked her chest wide open.

"This wasn't your fault—"

"Yes, it was, Miss Foster. You're *my* charge. *My* responsibility—"

"But *I'm* the one who knocked you out with my inflicting," she argued. "I didn't even think to use the throwing star I was holding—"

"It never should've fallen on you to protect us! *I* let them get close enough to obscure our sight with their shadows. *I* failed to detect their presence."

"Grizel didn't sense them either," Grady reminded him gently. "And despite what Ro kept claiming, there's no guarantee that she could've scented them any earlier."

"She might have," Sandor mumbled.

The fact that he would acknowledge even the slightest possibility that an ogre could do anything superior to him worried Sophie way more than the brownish red crusting his skin.

She wondered if Magnate Leto was feeling the same way, because he removed a handkerchief from his cape pocket and grabbed an elixir from one of the shelves, soaking the cloth in the green liquid before he handed it to Sandor.

"I realize there's nothing I can say to convince you not to hold yourself accountable," he said quietly. "And in many ways, that dedication is what makes you an excellent bodyguard. But if you let them get in your head, you're helping them accomplish what they intended today. The Neverseen want us scrambling and afraid, doubting ourselves and changing all of our protocols—"

"We should be changing our protocols!" Sandor growled. "We should be changing everything!"

"I'm not saying adjustments won't need to be made," Magnate Leto clarified. "But don't let that make you forget that today was a victory. Not a perfect one, no. But in the end, the Neverseen still fled empty-handed, and everyone they attacked will make a full recovery."

"And you're the reason they fled," Sophie reminded Sandor. "They saw you charging for them and knew they'd be dead if Ruy couldn't shield them."

Sandor squeezed the cloth so hard, green drops splattered his feet. "Letting them get away only means I've given them a chance to come after you again!"

"But you'll be better prepared when they do," Magnate Leto assured him. "We all will."

Sandor shook his head, and his gray eyes were brimming with tears as he made his way to Sophie's side and studied her bandages. "I'm sorry I failed you, Miss Foster."

"You didn't—"

"Yes, I did. But"—he took a long, heaving breath—"it's never going to happen again."

"It won't," Magnate Leto agreed. "We're going to learn from

this attack and be ready for whatever the Neverseen might be planning next."

"I'm sure you will," Sandor told him, his voice squeakier than ever. "But . . . that's not what I meant."

The tears in his eyes finally spilled over, carving trails through the dried blood as he turned back to Sophie. "I meant that you need a bodyguard who's capable of protecting you. So I'm going to ask Queen Hylda to reassign me."

EIGHT

O!" SOPHIE LUNGED TO GRAB Sandor's arm with her unbandaged hand, ignoring the pain that tore through her wounded shoulder in the process. "I don't want another bodyguard. I want *you*."

Her fingers only wrapped about a quarter of the way around his massive forearm, so he could've easily pulled away. But thankfully, he stayed.

"I appreciate the sentiment," he said quietly, staring at where her fingers rested on his skin. "But 'want' should never be a factor in these kinds of matters. What you *need* is someone who hasn't failed you—time and again."

"No, what I need is someone I trust," Sophie argued.

His gaze shifted to her cast, and he pulled his arm free of her grasp. "Your trust is misplaced."

"You don't get to decide that! *I* do. And I know you did everything you could possibly do to protect me. *Everything*."

"Exactly," he said, finally using the handkerchief to clean the blood off his face—scrubbing so hard it looked painful. "My methods failed. I was useless to you, and Fitz and . . . everyone else."

The tiny hesitation made her wonder if he'd been about to say "Grizel." And if he had been, maybe that's what this was really about.

Maybe watching the female he loved get brutally attacked was enough to make him want a safer assignment.

"If guarding me is too dangerous," she said, "I get it. I want you and Grizel to be happy."

"Grizel has nothing to do with this," Sandor insisted. "As far I know, she has no plans to leave her position. And she currently has no idea I'll be requesting reassignment. It's not a decision that involves her."

"Pretty sure she'd disagree with you on that," Grady warned.

"I'm sure she would," Sandor agreed. "But the point I was trying to make is that I would never put any personal attachment ahead of my responsibilities. I simply want what's best for Miss Foster."

"Then stay," Sophie told him. "Please."

She hadn't asked for a bodyguard—and she hadn't always

enjoyed having an overprotective goblin following her everywhere.

But she couldn't imagine it being anyone other than Sandor.

"Please," she said again, not caring how desperate she sounded. "I can't do this without you."

Sandor sighed, staring at the handkerchief now soaked with his blood. "The oath I swore promises to place the needs of my charge above anything else. And that includes putting your need for safety above our friendship."

"But I *am* safe with you."

"If that were true, you wouldn't be bruised and broken and facing a very lengthy recovery after barely surviving the latest attempt on your life." He turned to Grady. "Surely you agree that your daughter deserves better."

"She does," Grady said, holding up his hands to stop Sophie from shouting at him. "She deserves to not have a group of villains constantly trying to kill her. She deserves to feel safe regardless of where she is or who she's with. But since neither of those are possible at the moment, she deserves a bodyguard who's fearless and loyal, someone she trusts with her life. And that's you."

"See?" Sophie said. "No one's blaming you for what happened."

"You should be!"

"But we're not," Sophie insisted. "So please don't blame yourself. And please don't leave. You can make any other changes you want to my security. Just . . . not that. I promise, I'll follow any rules you want me to. I'll even promise I won't sneak off without you."

Alden huffed a small laugh. "You should take that deal, Sandor. It's the bargain of the century."

"Seriously," Grady agreed. "Can I get in on that?"

Sophie shook her head. "It's just for Sandor—and it doesn't apply to any replacement bodyguards. In fact, I'll go out of my way to make their job impossible."

"No, you won't," Sandor told her. "You're much too smart to resort to such reckless behavior."

Sophie's eyebrows shot up. "You sure about that? You've seen how much time I spend with Keefe."

"I'll give her some pointers, too," Tam volunteered. "I picked up *lots* of tricks at Exillium."

"And I have lots of prank elixirs," Dex added.

"How many weeks do you think the new guard would last before they'd run screaming back to Gildingham?" Tam wondered.

"I doubt they'd last *days*," Sophie told him. "Especially if Keefe and Ro join in the torment."

Sandor's sigh had a definite snarl. "I'm trying to help—can't you see that? You need someone with a fresh approach to your security—someone with different strengths and new ideas and—"

"Okay," Sophie jumped in. "If that's what I need, then . . . bring them in too."

"You mean you'd have two bodyguards," Magnate Leto clarified.

Sophie nodded.

The thought of *two* overprotective goblins shadowing her

every move made her want to shout *Never mind—just kidding!*

But . . .

"If it'd make Sandor stay, it'd be worth it," she said, before she could change her mind. She glanced at Sandor. "What do you think?"

"I'm sure your queen would be more than willing to provide you with a backup, considering the circumstances," Magnate Leto added when Sandor didn't respond.

Sandor pinched the bridge of his swollen nose.

"You know it's a good idea," Sophie pressed. "I can see it in your eyes. You just don't want to admit it."

"No, I want to make sure it would actually be beneficial," he argued. "*More* doesn't always mean *better*."

"If anyone could arrange an effective security team," Magnate Leto said, "it's you. And I can see *many* advantages."

"So can I," Alden agreed. "I'm sure Fitz would even understand if you wanted it to be Grizel—"

"I wouldn't," Sandor interrupted. "Grizel is . . . distracting."

"Then ask for anyone you want," Sophie told him. "Make it someone you hate—I don't care."

He looked away, and she could *feel* the rejection coming.

"Please," she whispered. "Don't let the Neverseen take away another person I care about."

Sandor's eyes welled up again. "I care about you too, Miss Foster. More than I should. That's why I can't trust myself to make this decision."

"Then talk to your team," Grady told him. "Sophie's safe here. Why don't you go find Grizel and Lovise? See what they think."

"But I wouldn't recommend telling Grizel you were planning to request reassignment without consulting her," Alden warned.

"Or that you find her distracting," Grady added. "I'm sure she'd have some thoughts about that."

"Very loud ones," Alden agreed.

"And more punishments," Sandor muttered under his breath. "But I suppose it would be wise to get their insights. You're sure—"

"No one's getting anywhere near Sophie right now," Grady assured him. "Take as long as you need."

"But you have to promise you won't go to Queen Hylda without telling me," Sophie added as he headed for the door and she realized he could choose to never come back, and there'd be nothing she could do to stop him.

Sandor glanced at her over his shoulder, and she watched his gaze trace over her bandaged arm again. "I would never leave without saying goodbye, Miss Foster."

It wasn't the vow she'd been looking for.

But it was all he said before he was gone.

"Think we convinced him?" Sophie asked.

"I hope so, kiddo." Grady brushed a hand down her cheek, smudging away a tear she hadn't realized was there. "But it's hard to say. Guilt makes us do funny things."

"It does indeed," Magnate Leto said quietly.

His eyes glazed, and there was such sorrow in his features that Sophie had a feeling he was thinking of a lonely Wanderling growing on a hillside in Norway. But when he blinked, he was back to being Foxfire's principal.

"If you're up for it," he told Sophie, "I'd love to hear your account of the attack, so I can better determine how to arrange campus security."

"Take this first," Elwin told her, pressing yet another vial against her lips.

She'd expected it to be the same floral medicine he'd been giving her. But this was thicker and slimier and tasted like burnt toast.

"That's to undo any damage you might've caused when you lunged for Sandor like that," he explained.

"Sorry," Sophie mumbled. "I couldn't let him walk away."

"I know. But you're at a *really* crucial stage right now. So no more moving, okay?"

Sophie promised, and he helped her get better situated against her pillows before he told Magnate Leto, "She's all yours. But try to keep it quick."

Magnate Leto sat on the empty cot next to Sophie's. "It will be. Sandor already filled me in on everything he remembered about the attack—as did Wylie. I'm just hoping Miss Foster can fill in any final gaps."

"While they talk," Grady said to Elwin, "I have a few questions about Sophie's treatment. Is it okay if we discuss them out in the hall?"

Sophie was about to argue that anything they were going to say about her should be said in *front* of her, when she realized that Grady was probably trying to get Elwin out of the room so Magnate Leto could talk more freely. Elwin didn't know that Magnate Leto was one of Mr. Forkle's alternate identities, and he might guess the secret if he heard Sophie telling him too much— or if he saw Magnate Leto searching her memories, since only Mr. Forkle and Fitz could sneak past her mental blocking.

Sure enough, as soon as Grady and Elwin had left the room, Magnate Leto asked permission to slip into her consciousness.

"Is it okay if I watch what you show him?" Alden asked.

"Sure, but . . . some of it isn't pretty," Sophie warned.

Alden took a long look at his son. "I have no doubt of that."

He reached for Magnate Leto's temples, and Magnate Leto reached for Sophie's, and both of them closed their eyes as Sophie replayed the attack. Halfway through, their hands were shaking. Then their breathing turned ragged. And when they finally pulled away, their eyes were wet.

Alden stumbled away, and Sophie figured he was heading back to his son. Instead he threw his arms around Dex, and Sophie wanted to laugh at the stunned look on Dex's face. But it felt a lot less funny when Alden kept whispering, "Thank you for saving my son."

He pulled Tam into the hug too.

"Well," Magnate Leto said, clearing the catch from his throat, "obviously there is much to say. This was . . . a far closer call than I realized. But for now, it's probably best if we try to focus on what we can learn. For instance, it appears they know you're an Enhancer—or they suspect it, anyway. I'm surprised Gethen didn't pry your gloves off and test his theory."

"That could mean he's assuming the ability is something else," Alden suggested, finally letting Tam and Dex go. "He might think she's an Empath."

"How many Empaths wear gloves?" Dex countered.

"All I know is, I do *not* want to find out what Umber can do with a Sophie boost," Tam said quietly—and everyone shuddered.

"Agreed," Magnate Leto said. "Clearly we need to find a way to give Miss Foster more control over the ability. Weren't you working on a gadget along those lines, Mr. Dizznee?"

Dex looked anywhere but at Sophie when he mumbled, "I made a prototype. But the concept . . . wasn't right."

Tam narrowed his eyes. "Why are you blushing?"

"I'm not," Dex argued—too loud and too fast.

"So are you," Tam said to Sophie.

She turned her face away. "Like Dex said. The concept wasn't right."

The gadgets themselves had worked pretty well: two tiny microtransmitters that put nonreactive force fields around her hands. But . . . he'd chosen to camouflage them with crush cuffs, and it had led to the most awkward conversation in the history of the world.

"I'll try something else," Dex promised.

"Make it your top priority," Magnate Leto told him.

"Even over the caches?" Dex asked.

"Definitely," Alden said, running a hand down his face. "Apparently the caches are fake."

Tam's eyebrows shot up.

"How could they . . . ?" Dex said, sinking onto one of the empty cots. "Actually? That explains a *lot*."

"I know," Sophie admitted, not sure what made her sicker: thinking about how many months they'd wasted trying to learn something useful from the fakes, or the fact that they'd been counting on the caches to become a huge lead.

"It's okay to hate me," Keefe said from the doorway.

He looked rumpled and pale and like he couldn't decide if he wanted to cry or punch someone.

Or maybe he really wanted to punch himself.

He tore his hands through his hair, destroying what was left of his careful style. "That was the one thing I thought I did right. But I guess I messed it up—and don't try to make me feel better, Foster. You know I don't deserve it."

"Oh joy, it's going to be a long night of sulky-boy angst," Ro groaned as she shoved Keefe aside and stomped into the room. "Quick, who wants to trade jobs with me?"

Keefe ignored her, tilting his head back and staring at the ceiling. "Fintan's good. His emotions always felt normal when I asked about the caches. A little nervous. A little suspicious. Exactly the way he would've felt if they were real."

"You're not the only one he fooled," Magnate Leto reminded him. "Bronte's been working with Fintan on the caches for weeks, and he hasn't noticed anything strange."

"Neither have I," Dex admitted.

"Wait," Sophie said, wishing she could sit up more. Her lounge-y position wasn't great for thinking, especially after taking so much medicine.

"Since Fintan knew the caches weren't real when he made that bargain with the Council," she said slowly, "that voids their agreement, right?"

Magnate Leto frowned. "There isn't any sort of official contract—and telling Fintan we've discovered his lie will only give him a good laugh."

Sophie was sure it would.

"But the Council's been going along with all of his demands because they thought he was cooperating, right?" she asked. "So now they can move him somewhere miserable and make him meet with as many Telepaths as it takes to find out what he's hiding."

"I suppose it's worth considering," Magnate Leto told her. "But . . . I also fear it may cause the Council to ask about Kenric's cache. And as I'm sure you know, if they discover *that's* fake, there will be consequences."

There definitely would be.

Sophie had sworn to protect Kenric's cache with her life.

"No need to look so nervous," he assured her. "These kinds

of challenges can always be managed. But part of that involves risk assessment. And speaking with Fintan doesn't seem worth the risk of cluing the Council in to our deception about Kenric's cache—for all the reasons that you and I have discussed many times, and for the added fact that if the Councillors *did* agree to the meeting, the best Telepaths for the job are currently confined to this room for at least a week, with bed rest at home to follow—"

"Whoa, back it up there," Ro jumped in. "Did you just say that Sophie and the pretty boy are staying *here* for a week? *Together?*"

"He did," Elwin said, striding back into the room along with Grady. "Neither of them can light leap until their bones are completely healed. So they're stuck with me."

Tam grinned at Sophie. "I'm guessing that's news to you?"

It really was.

She probably should've assumed that Fitz wouldn't be able to go anywhere with his leg wrapped up. But her mind hadn't made the connection. And now that it had . . .

A week was a very long time.

And the room was a very small space.

Ro elbowed Keefe. "Nothing you want to say about this, Lord Hunkyhair?"

Any other time, Keefe would've already made five different Fitzphie jokes. But he didn't respond—even when Ro told him she was going to start calling him "Lord Funkyhair."

"Seriously, Keefe," Sophie told him. "Don't beat yourself up about the caches. We'll figure something out."

"We will," Magnate Leto agreed.

"Tomorrow," Elwin clarified, snapping his fingers and forming another orange orb around Sophie's arm. "Right now, I need to give Sophie a dose of a much stronger marrow regenerator, and it's going to make her pretty sleepy."

"Then there's one more thing we need to discuss first," Magnate Leto told him, placing a hand on Sophie's good shoulder to help her focus. "Gethen claimed the Neverseen can find you anytime, anywhere. That implies they have some sort of tracking device. Any idea what it could be?"

She traced a gloved finger along her choker-style necklace. "Could they have hacked my registry feed?"

Grady shook his head. "Your feed is being scrambled. Same as all of your friends. The Council agreed to let us, after Atlantis. We thought it'd prevent something like this from happening. But clearly we were wrong—*and* it made it so we couldn't track any of you after Dex and Wylie left."

"Has anyone given you anything that you keep with you all the time?" Magnate Leto asked.

"Not unless you count my Cognate rings."

"It couldn't be them," Alden jumped in. "I've known the jeweler Fitz bought them from for decades."

"Yeah, well I was planning a wedding for Brant and Jolie," Grady reminded him, "so sometimes people aren't who we think they are."

Sophie wished he were standing closer so she could hug him.

"I suppose you're right, my friend," Alden said quietly. "Much as I hate to turn paranoid, past experience has proven that trust can be misguided. We should test Sophie's rings before we rule them out."

Keefe sighed. "Don't waste your time."

"Why not?" Sophie asked.

"Because Fitz never makes those kinds of mistakes. That's *my* specialty."

"I think we're going to need a little more explanation than that," Magnate Leto told him.

"I know. It's just . . ." Keefe's eyes shifted to Sophie, and he looked like the Most Miserable Boy in the Universe. "If you didn't hate me before, you're definitely going to hate me for this."

"Will you please stop worrying about that?" she asked. "I'm never going to hate you."

"You should." He trudged over and snatched the chain for the ruined monocle pendant she hadn't realized she was still wearing.

He pulled hard, snapping the clasp and holding it out to Magnate Leto. "Test this. I bet anything you'll find it's a tracker."

NINE

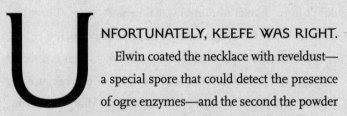

UNFORTUNATELY, KEEFE WAS RIGHT.

Elwin coated the necklace with reveldust—a special spore that could detect the presence of ogre enzymes—and the second the powder touched the dark metal, the pendant glowed bright pink.

So did Keefe's hand.

And parts of Sophie's chest, neck, and glove.

Elwin even spotted pin-size holes along the pendant's edge, housing microscopic colonies of whichever bacteria secreted the enzyme.

"I thought something was only a tracker if it glowed red," Dex argued.

Keefe shook his head. "Red means aromark, which doubles

as a tracker because it's a homing device for ogre weaponry. Green would be a basic tracker. Pink is . . . I don't know—but if it's there, it can't be good."

He kicked the nearest cot so hard it made everyone wince.

Ro rumpled his hair. "Listen to my little elf boy, sounding all knowledgeable about microbiology and stuff! I've never been so proud."

Keefe didn't bother to respond.

"So what does pink mean?" Magnate Leto asked.

"And please tell me there's a way to remove it without having to melt off my skin," Sophie added.

That was the only way to remove aromark. The process didn't hurt, thanks to numbing balms and elixirs. But it was still one of the freakiest things she'd ever endured.

"Pink means it's ethreium," Ro told her, "which is another enzyme for tracking. We don't use it as often, because it's weaker. But it's also odorless. That's why I didn't detect it." Her eyes dropped to her feet as she added, "Sorry about that."

"You don't need to apologize," Sophie promised.

"I kinda do. I trained with some of the ogres who've defected, and one of them . . . This is the kind of trick he'd pull. I should've realized he wouldn't have betrayed my father unless he was *all in*. Cad always wanted to be a leader."

"Cad?" Sophie repeated.

Ro nodded. "His full name is Cadfael. He was a Mercadir, and he always resented that the title didn't give him any actual power. I'm sure that's why he defected—taking his chance to prove he should be in charge without having to openly challenge my father in a spar."

"Sounds like you knew him well," Alden noted.

"Like I said, we trained together. And since we had similar strengths, we were often paired up." She reached for her forehead, trailing a claw across her tattoos—then seemed to realize everyone was watching her. "I'll have no problem killing him, if that's what you're worried about. A traitor's a traitor. And with Cad . . . I almost hope I face him before this is all over."

"Can you think of anything else he might help them plan?" Grady asked.

"It all depends on what resources he has access to."

"I think it's safe to assume the Neverseen will acquire anything he needs," Magnate Leto told her.

"Probably. Cad was always a bragger. I'm sure he's convinced them he's an expert on everything. I'll have to talk to my father—and I'll tell him to send over some voracillius when I do. That's how you get rid of ethreium." She pointed to the pink glow on Sophie's chest, which was already fading. "Mind you, I think an epic round of skin melting sounds like something we could all use right now. But if you're not with me on that, all you need to do is spread some voracillius on there and let them gobble up the ethreium like candy. Then you just wash it away."

"We should probably sweep the campus," Magnate Leto added. "Make sure the ethreium hasn't spread."

"I'll ask Lady Cadence to send over more reveldust," Elwin said, heading for his office.

"Have her send enough to cover Havenfield, too," Grady called after him.

"And Everglen," Alden added. "And we should probably dust everywhere Sophie's recently been."

Tam barked a sharp laugh. "Then add my parents' house to the list! We went to Choralmere after we found Alvar—and my dad is going to *freak* when he finds out you're going to sprinkle ogre spores all over his precious stuff. Can I please be there when you do it?"

His smile was downright wicked—and Sophie didn't blame him one bit.

Quan and Mai Song weren't as horrible as Keefe's parents— but they ran a close second. They'd chosen to protect their reputations instead of standing up to the Council when they banished Linh for causing so many floods. And even before that, they'd tried to force Tam and Linh to lie about their ages to hide the fact that they were twins.

"Wait," Dex said, fishing his own monocle pendant out from under his tunic. "Does this mean all of our necklaces are contaminated?"

Sophie shook her head. "No. Mine is . . . different."

"You don't have to cover for me," Keefe told her before turning to Magnate Leto. "That's my pendant. Alvar ripped hers off her neck and gave it to Brant, who tried to make me burn her with it—"

"And you didn't," Sophie reminded him. "You helped me escape."

"This was the day he stole Kenric's cache and used it to join the Neverseen?" Grady verified.

Keefe kicked the cot again. "Yep. They took my pendant too. And I thought I was being all smooth by stealing it back and giving it to Foster when I snuck into Foxfire."

"You're talking about the day you followed the Neverseen's order to set off a shock wave in Magnate Leto's office—and left Sophie curled up in a ball on the floor, covered in broken glass?" Grady asked.

"He gave me his cloak to protect me," Sophie reminded him. But she had a feeling Grady would be going back to calling Keefe *That Boy*, like he had the whole time Keefe was playing double agent with the Neverseen.

"You don't have to tell me I'm a jerk," Keefe mumbled. "I already know."

"Keefe—"

"Save your pep talk, Foster. Grady's right to be mad. This is my fault. *I* ran off, thinking I could fix everything myself. *I* stole your cache—and then brought back a fake instead. *I* gave you the tracker they used to find you. And *my mom* sent them there to mess you up. Oh, and let's not forget that she did it to scare you into cooperating, because she wants you to be useful *to me*—and then I wasn't even there to help you fight, because I promised Alden . . ."

"Promised Alden what?" Sophie asked, glancing between the two of them.

Keefe shook his head. "It doesn't matter."

"Kinda sounds like it does," she pressed.

But Alden was staring at his injured son, and Keefe was kicking the cot harder and harder and harder, so she decided to let it go—for the moment. Instead she reminded Keefe, "If you'd been there, the only thing that'd be different right now is that Elwin would have another patient."

"And there's no guarantee I would've saved you," Tam added with a smirk.

"I wouldn't blame you if you hadn't," Keefe muttered.

"Stop," Sophie told him. "Seriously."

"I *am* serious! Don't you get it? I'm as toxic as Umber's freaky shadows. *That's* my legacy."

The last word felt huge, like the letters were slowly squeezing all the air out of the room.

It was the word Lady Gisela used to hint at whatever creepy plans she had for Keefe's future—and every reckless decision he'd made over the last year was all part of his desperate attempt to relieve the shame and fear that were eating him up inside. That was the problem with guilt. If it didn't fracture his sanity, it could send him spiraling down a very dangerous path, and Sophie refused to let either disaster happen.

"Hey," she said, offering him her gloved left hand.

When he didn't take it, she turned to Magnate Leto. "Can we have a few minutes?"

"On it," Ro jumped in. "Everybody out! Lord Funkyhair needs a pep talk."

"No, I don't," Keefe snapped back.

Ro rolled her eyes and hauled him over to the cot next to Sophie's, muttering about moody boys as she forced him to sit. Then she herded Magnate Leto and Alden out of the Healing Center and went back for Tam and Dex.

"I forgot to say," Keefe called after them, "thanks. For helping her. And Fitz."

Dex shrugged with his good shoulder. "Wylie did most of it."

"He wouldn't have been there without you," Keefe reminded him before his eyes shifted to Tam. "And if you hadn't rushed over . . ."

"Well," Tam said, fidgeting with his cape. "I guess that's why we're a team. We each have our part."

"Too bad I'm stuck being the designated loser," Keefe said under his breath.

"Ugh—this is why you need a pep talk," Ro grumbled as she shoved the other boys out of the room.

Elwin locked his knees when she came after him. "Hang on. Sophie *really* needs to take her medicine now."

"I'll give you *three* seconds," Ro told him, dragging Grady out instead.

"Yeah, well I'm going to need a few more than that," Elwin

argued as he grabbed a bottle of orange liquid and held it to Sophie's lips. "Try to down this in one go—and plug your nose."

Sophie did as he asked. But she still got a taste of something that reminded her way too much of the way sasquatches smelled.

"Ugh, what's *in* that? Actually, never mind. I don't think I want to know."

"You don't. Here, this will help." He handed her what looked like a hard candy wrapped in silver paper—but the thing inside was black and squishy and looked frighteningly like a dead bug.

"Just trust me," Elwin told her.

That would've been a whole lot easier to do if Elwin hadn't been notorious for picking revolting flavors for the DNA panels on the Foxfire lockers. But even bug guts would probably still be better than liquid sasquatch, so she took a tiny bite and . . .

"Oh! It's like a snickerdoodle."

"Okay, I don't know what a snickerdoodle is or why anyone would want to eat something called that," Ro said, hooking her arm around Elwin's elbow and hauling him toward the door, "but she took her medicine and your three seconds are up. So out with you! My boy needs a good, long talking-to."

"Better talk fast then, Sophie," Elwin called over his shoulder. "The drowsiness will set in pretty soon."

Ro looked like she wished she could carry Fitz out too, even though he was still sedated. Instead, she told Keefe, "It's time to listen to your girl. No arguing—she's smarter than you. And remember what you and I have talked about."

"What have you and Ro talked about?" Sophie asked as Ro closed the Healing Center door.

"It doesn't matter," he told his feet.

Sophie sighed, wondering how many things he was hiding from her.

"Look at me, Keefe."

She had to repeat the command two more times before he turned to face her—and when their eyes met, she caught a glimpse of the terrified, broken boy he always tried to hide behind bravado and pranks.

"Do you trust me?" she asked.

"Of course I do—*that's* not the problem."

"Yes, it is. If you trusted me, you'd know I'd never hold something like this against you."

"You should." He pointed to her cocoon of bandages.

"Um, are you living a double life as a creepy Shade? Because that's who messed me up."

Keefe stood, turning his back to her so he could kick the cot again. "Umber wouldn't have been able to find you if I hadn't given you that pendant. Just like the day the Neverseen broke Silveny's wing because of the Sencen crest I was wearing."

"And you know what both of those things have in common?" Sophie asked. "You had no idea that the Neverseen were manipulating you."

"Yeah, well I should've figured it out. Or I should've—"

"Don't go down that road, Keefe. It doesn't lead anywhere

good. Trust me, I know. If I let myself take that journey, I'd be sitting here thinking about the fact that if I hadn't hit my panic switch, Dex's arm wouldn't be in a sling. And if you'd been the one to go talk to Fitz after the Tribunal instead of me, he wouldn't have a broken leg and cracked ribs. And if I hadn't let you guys come with me to Nightfall, Biana wouldn't—"

"Uh, you didn't *let* us come," he reminded her. "We *chose* to. Just like Dex chose to make you that panic switch—and he wouldn't have done that if he didn't want you to use it. And trust me, you were the only one Fitz wanted going after him yesterday."

She highly doubted that, but . . .

"Even if you're right, nothing will change the fact that if Fitz hadn't found me that day in the Natural History Museum— or if he'd decided my weird eyes meant I couldn't be an elf and leaped away—all of the bad things from the last few years wouldn't have happened. Kenric. Calla. Mr. For—"

"That's not true. The Black Swan wanted Fitz to find you. They sent Alden that newspaper article, didn't they? If that hadn't worked, they would've found another way to get you to the Lost Cities. You're their moonlark."

"Exactly. I'm the moonlark. You realize what that means, right?" She hugged herself with her free arm and sank deeper into her pillows. "Everything about this mess comes back to me. Good or bad—right or wrong—I'm a part of it. And no matter how hard I try to protect the people I care about, someone always seems to get hurt."

Including herself. But that was easier to live with.

"So . . . I'm learning to focus on the things I *can* control," she told him quietly. "Like who I blame. And who I trust. And who I want by my side—even if it means asking those people to risk their lives."

Like she'd just done with Sandor.

Part of her couldn't believe she'd done that—especially while he was standing there battered and bloody. She should've let him move on to a safer assignment. But . . . she couldn't let him go.

"The Neverseen don't get to control who I care about," she told Keefe. "And neither do you. Even when you make mistakes, that doesn't change how I feel about you—and you're an Empath. You know I'm not just saying that."

Keefe's laugh sounded more like a sigh. "Trust me, Foster, if I could understand your feelings, life would be way easier."

"Okay, then remember this: Your mom's trying to get in your head. She wants you to feel like nothing you do will ever be good enough so you'll finally give up and decide to cooperate."

"Psh—she doesn't need me to cooperate. I fall for her tricks every time."

"We *all* fall for her tricks," she argued, the words blurred by a yawn.

Elwin's medicine must've been starting to kick in, but she shook her head to clear it.

"The Neverseen are good at what they do," she told him.

"They're going to beat us sometimes. But that's when we have to rally."

Keefe fidgeted with a fraying thread on the sleeve of his tunic. "You know what scares me? I . . . can't picture us winning anymore. I used to be able to. I used to imagine the moment where we'd finally take them out. But now . . ."

He sank back onto the cot and rested his head against the wall—right beneath the framed pictures of him and her in their embarrassing Opening Ceremonies costumes. Elwin had hung them as a joke, to commemorate their record-breaking number of emergency Healing Center visits.

Some days it didn't feel so funny.

"You almost died," Keefe whispered. "So did Fitz—and I mean *really* almost died. I've never seen it that close. Bullhorn was watching every breath you guys took, and Elwin was *begging* Tam to rush over. And all I could do was sit there, trying to figure out how I'd make the Neverseen pay. But I couldn't think of anything. Even now . . ."

"Well," Sophie said, forcing a smile, "maybe that's progress. At least you didn't race off to Ravagog and challenge King Dimitar to another sparring match. Then again, if you had, you could be joining in the Foxfire slumber party. Now Fitz and I get to have all the fun without you."

She waited for him to laugh, or tease her, or . . . *anything*.

But he just thumped the back of his head against the wall and tugged on the fraying string until it snapped off in his hand.

"How did you know I was here?" she asked.

"Dex hailed Elwin and told him you'd hit your panic switch, so he should head to the Healing Center and be ready. Elwin hailed the rest of us so we'd know what was going on. Then we all got to sit here imagining all kinds of horrible things. Oh, and brainstorming ways to punish Dex for not telling anyone where he was going. His mom had some particularly brutal ideas. Remind me never to get on Juline's bad side."

"Dex's parents were here?"

"Only his mom. His dad stayed home with Rex, Bex, and Lex, probably so they couldn't break everything."

"Good call."

Dex's triplet siblings could cause more chaos in five minutes than a pack of saber-toothed tigers.

"How long were you guys waiting here?" she asked.

"I don't know. It felt . . . endless. And then Wylie showed up first, and he had Fitz. And Sandor stumbled in with Grizel and Lovise. And there was still no sign of you or Dex, and blood was everywhere, and Bullhorn was screaming, and for a second I thought . . ."

He twisted the loose thread around his finger, pulling tighter, tighter, tighter.

"I'm okay," Sophie reminded him.

"For *now*. Umber's smart. She wouldn't have wrecked your pendant unless they had other ways of tracking you. Probably something else that's going to turn out to be my fault."

"*Please* stop saying that. But you might have a point about other trackers." The last word was swallowed by another yawn, and she had to blink to fight the fresh wave of drowsiness. "Maybe Grady should test all of my stuff with reveldust. And if that doesn't work, maybe we can convince the Council to let us—"

"Please don't say 'talk to Fintan,'" Keefe interrupted. "Sorry—I know you think he's the answer to everything. But . . . come on, Foster—have we *ever* gotten anything useful from him? In fact, have we ever gotten anything useful from *anyone* in the Neverseen? I mean . . . I lived with them for *months*, and I can't even tell you Umber's real name or what Ruy looks like!"

"You can't?" Sophie asked. "Ruy . . ."

She closed her eyes, searching for the words to describe him. But . . .

"I don't know what he looks like either." Which didn't make any sense. She'd helped *capture* him. There was no way she wouldn't have pulled back his hood and seen his face—and she had a photographic memory, so . . .

"He wears an addler," Keefe explained. "Like Alvar wore the day you saw the Boy Who Disappeared. Though his doesn't look like an addler, so no one can tell he's wearing it. He bragged about it. A *lot*."

Addlers were gadgets that made it impossible to focus on someone's face.

"Well," Sophie said, struggling to wrap her weary mind

around that. "That's . . . weird. But we know his full name is Ruy Ignis, so we just have to look up his registry file—"

"Won't help. He told me he had their Technopath wipe any records of his appearance. Don't ask me why he cares, but . . . yeah. And you know what else we don't know? Who their Technopath is. The only other member of the Neverseen I met is Trix—and the only things I know about him are that he's a Guster and Trix isn't actually his name. See what I mean? All this time—all our planning and scheming and searching. All the risks we've taken. All the times we've almost died. And we still don't know *anything* about our enemies or what they're planning or what they want. We don't even know who's actually in charge right now! And we've never figured out what the Lodestar Initiative is—or maybe I should say *was*, since we also don't know if they're still going by it. Just like we don't know why Fintan was keeping a list called Criterion, or why they made all those barrels of soporidine, or what the Nightfall facility my mom built was supposed to be used for, or why Vespera and Fintan abandoned it and moved to the facility under Atlantis—we couldn't even find my mom's stupid Archetype, remember?"

Sophie definitely hadn't forgotten.

The last time they'd seen the thick book that supposedly outlined all of Lady Gisela's plans, Vespera had been holding it in Nightfall—and Sophie had been sure they'd find it when they went back and searched the facility. But the Black Swan had scoured every nook and cranny, and there'd been no sign of it.

No sign of anything, except broken mirrors and empty halls and the last remaining gorgodon—the hybridized creature Keefe's mom had created to be her guard beast. It was huge and ugly, with giant claws and fangs and a scorpion-like tail—and it could fly, breathe underwater, and climb walls. So caring for it was an *adventure*—even with it being kept in a *very* secure, *very* isolated pasture.

And yet, somehow the deadly behemoth was the least of their problems.

"I'm with you, Foster," Keefe said, gesturing to her frown. "It's like . . . could we fail any harder?"

"Hey—we've done *some* things," she argued. "We saved Atlantis. And we caught Fintan and Alvar. And Mr. Forkle killed Brant. And we have the key to your mom's Archetype—and even figured out the trick to piece it together. And . . ."

Wow.

Was that *really* all they'd done?

There had to be more. . . .

"I know we've done stuff, Foster. But it's not even close to enough. And the scariest part is how little we know. I mean . . . I can't even tell you if I've gotten back all the memories my mom erased. Meanwhile they know *everything* about us: where we live, where we go to school, what our abilities are, who our friends and family are, how to find us—do you need me to keep going? Because we both know I can."

"No . . . I get it," she mumbled, wishing she could come up

with a single argument against what he was saying.

But Keefe was right. They were hopelessly and gloriously out of their depth. Far more than she'd ever let herself admit.

"So what are you saying?" she asked. "You want to give up?"

"Of course not. I just . . . don't know how to beat them. Everything I try only makes it worse—even when I think I've been so careful, it turns out I played right into their scheme."

"That's because they think we're predictable," Sophie informed him. "And they're right. We always do what they expect. We have to break the cycle somehow. We have to . . ."

Nope.

She had no end to that sentence.

And as the seconds dragged by, she realized there was freedom in admitting that. Power in letting her heart sink to that absolute low.

Maybe hitting the bottom gave her something new to stand on.

Or maybe the medicine was seriously starting to mess with her head.

Either way, something was stirring inside her—something that went against everything she'd been telling herself to resist.

"I'm tired of being weak," she whispered, remembering Gethen's taunts in the desert. "I want to fight back—and I mean *really* fight."

"Like . . . with weapons?" Keefe asked.

She nodded, waiting for the queasiness to hit.

When it didn't, she told him, "Yeah. With whatever it takes."

TEN

RIZEL'S BEEN TELLING ME FOR weeks that I should be learning goblin battle tactics," Sophie explained, "but I've been focusing on inflicting—and that's exactly what the Neverseen expected. They showed up prepared to block me, knowing I'd take Sandor down in the process. And if I'd used the throwing star I'd been holding, I could've taken one of them out."

"Okay, but . . . that still would've left two more, right?" Keefe asked.

"Maybe not. They fled the second they realized Ruy's force fields weren't working. So they probably would've done the same thing if one of them went down."

Keefe narrowed his eyes as he studied her. "And you'd be okay ending someone like that?"

Sophie forced herself to picture what it would be like before she answered. "Yeah. I think I would. Is that terrible?"

"No. But I'm probably not the right person to ask."

"Why?"

He sighed. "Ugh, I shouldn't tell you this, since it'll just make you think I'm even more messed up than you already do—"

"I don't think you're messed up," Sophie interrupted. "But go on."

He sank back onto one of the cots and closed his eyes as he said, "I feel like . . . fighting comes easier for me. I used to think I was just angry about some of the stuff that's happened. But sometimes I wonder if it's part of my *legacy*. Maybe that's why my mom let my dad be so hard on me—maybe she was trying to desensitize me. Or maybe she did other stuff I don't remember. All I know is, weapons and blood don't bother me the way they bother other people, so . . . yeah. Feel free to think I'm super creepy—"

"I don't," Sophie promised. "I'm serious! In fact . . . I've actually been thinking that Project Moonlark might've done the same thing to me. Grizel said she thought I was a natural when we saw how good my aim is—and at first it freaked me out. But after what just happened? I don't know. . . . I think it might be a good thing. I mean, *someone* has to fight the Neverseen, right?"

She did a quick gut check and still couldn't feel any hint of queasiness.

"And honestly, if you *really* think about it," she added, "most of our group pushes the limits. Fitz has been training with Grizel for weeks. Dex is always making things that explode. Biana charged after Vespera all by herself without hesitating. Linh took out half of Ravagog with a tidal wave. Tam knows how to break through force fields. Even Wylie looked ready to stomp the Neverseen into the ground. I don't know if that's our way of responding to all the scary, dangerous stuff we've been through, or if it's something we just naturally have in common and that's why we ended up friends. But . . . I think it's time we all push ourselves to see how far we can go with it. It might turn out to be the best asset we have."

"You sound like you really believe that," Keefe noted.

"You don't?"

"I don't know." He tilted his head back and stared at the ceiling. "I mean . . . even if we trained all day every day, it's not like we could ever hold our own against an ogre. They have two hundred pounds of muscle on us—and claws and fangs. And they train from, like, birth."

"True. I'm guessing that's why the Council's always put so much focus on our abilities . . . and I think we need to get *way* better with those, too. I'm supposed to be this power-ful moonlark thing, and Umber *crushed* me. And I'm sure if I'd thought to use any of my skills, the Neverseen would've beaten me at those, too. Didn't you say they had you train every day?"

"Yeah, an hour on skills and at least an hour on abilities."

"Then we should be doing the same thing . . . and weapons and combat training, too, and Grizel could teach us goblin tricks, and Ro could cover ogre stuff, and . . . hopefully the Exillium Coaches would be willing to work on our skills . . . and then we could ask our ability Mentors to push us harder in our sessions, and maybe Dex should make us stashes . . . but I think we should carry them with us to save time, so . . . we'll need pockets. Why do clothes never have enough pockets? There should always be lots of pockets . . . the more pockets the better!"

"Easy there, Foster," Keefe said. "I think you're sleep-scheming. Your eyes aren't even open right now and you keep trailing off. Plus, you're talking a lot about pockets."

"Am I?" She blinked hard, smacking one of her cheeks a few times to wake herself up. "Okay, but what I said makes sense, right?"

"It does. Especially the part about the pockets." He winked. "But, you realize all that stuff takes a long time to make a difference, right? The Neverseen are *years* ahead of us."

"I know. But we're never going to catch up if we don't even try. Plus . . . if they're doing two hours a day and we do eight, that has to start closing the gap, right?"

"You want to do *eight* hours of training every day?"

"That'd be the ideal—two hours for each part of the program. But . . . the real goal would just be to train every day, for every minute we possibly can. I'm sure progress will be slow. But I still think it's the smartest plan, since it's the last thing the Neverseen will expect. You know what they're thinking right now? They're waiting for us to do what we always do— spend every waking minute trying to figure out what they're up to. They think we'll search Wylie's memories until we learn everything we can about Prentice and Cyrah, and then hunt down the missing starstone—and I bet you *anything* they're planning to ambush us the second we get close and take it for themselves. They want us either wasting our time or doing their dirty work—or both. And . . . I'm done with that. I'm done scrambling to get ahead and then ending up even more behind. I'm done trying to beat them at their own game. I'm done . . . focusing on *them*. I want to focus on *us*—on getting strong. Learning to fight . . . Doing whatever it takes to be ready . . . for the next time they show up."

"Okay, your eyes are closed and you're trailing off again, so I have to make sure this isn't delirium talking: Are you *actually* saying you don't want to keep trying to figure out what my mom and Vespera are planning?"

Sophie gave her cheek another smack—much harder this time—and tried leaning her head forward to fight the pull of the medicine. "I'm saying I don't want to waste any more time. It's not like we have any solid leads. The caches are fake. Odds are we won't find anything at Everglen. And like you said: Talking to Fintan's probably a waste. Wylie and Prentice are already working on memory exercises together, so they can keep doing that to see if they learn anything—and if they do, we'll change gears. But until we have something to go on, doesn't training sound better than having the Black Swan tell us to go read a bunch of boring books?"

"Actually, I was thinking it'd be smart to spend some time learning everything we can about the history of ogre weaponry."

"Seriously?"

He cracked a smile. "Nah. Just wanted to make sure you were still awake."

"So, you agree with the plan?"

"I do!" Fitz called from across the room—and just like that she was wide awake. "Bring on the training!"

Sophie turned toward him, so relieved to see his beautiful eyes staring at her that she didn't care that he'd been eavesdropping. "You don't think I'm losing my mind?"

His jaw set. "No, I think you're angry. And I'm right there with you."

"So am I," Biana said, appearing in a shadowy corner.

"Vanishers," Keefe grumbled. "How long have you been there?"

"Not *that* long." Biana blinked in and out of sight as she moved closer. "I snuck off with my dad when he went with Sandor and Grady to talk to Magnate Leto about security. But I stayed for this, because I wanted to make sure you guys didn't decide something without me, since you've been super overprotective lately."

"We have?" Sophie asked.

"Not *you*. But Fitz refused to let me go to Grizel's training sessions. And Woltzer won't teach me either."

"That's because Woltzer doesn't like you," Fitz informed her. "You're always sneaking off and getting him in trouble for losing his charge. Like right now."

Biana grinned. "It's not *my* fault he can't keep up with me. And all I'm saying is, I'm sick of being treated like I'm some broken doll because of what Vespera did—and you know that's what you've been doing."

"We found you passed out in a puddle of your own blood!" Fitz argued.

"You don't have to remind me!" Biana snapped back, rolling up one of her sleeves and revealing the scars that Sophie knew she'd been hiding.

Most of the jagged lines had faded to white—but each mark still told a clear story of pain. And it looked like that story extended to Biana's shoulder, back, and neck, too.

"The next time I take on Vespera, I want to win," Biana said, tracing her finger down the thickest scar, which curled across her biceps in a long, raised arc. "And I'm sure Tam, Dex, and Linh will want to get in on this. Probably Marella, too. Maybe even Wylie. We should ask them."

"You guys realize you're forgetting one huge detail, right?" Keefe asked.

"You mean the fact that Fitz and I are on bed rest and Dex's arm is in a sling?" Sophie guessed.

"Seems at least worth mentioning," Keefe agreed.

Sophie glared at her bandages. "I know. But the rest of you guys can get started without us, and we'll join in as soon as we can. Plus, we can work on skills like telekinesis and outward channeling—even night vision and body temperature regulation."

"And don't forget about Cognate training!" Fitz added. "It's actually kind of perfect that we have to stay here together. Bring on the marathon training sessions!"

Sophie tried to make her smile look at least a little bit genuine.

But the only thing worse than confessing her crush to Fitz would be having to confess it in a tiny space neither of them could get away from.

"You okay there, Foster?" Keefe asked. "Your mood just shifted."

"I'm fine."

Or, she would be. Because Fitz was right. They needed to put this time to the best use possible, and Cognate training should absolutely be a part of it—even if it was going to be ten thousand kinds of awkward.

"I think you need to rest first, though," Biana jumped in.

"Let the medicine do its job." Her eyes drifted from Sophie's bandages to her brother's, turning slightly glassy. "You guys need to get better, okay?"

"We will," Sophie promised. "Elwin's on it."

"Yeah, don't worry about us," Fitz told her. "We're safe in here. You guys are the ones the Neverseen might come after."

Biana pulled down her sleeve. "I guess that's another reason why we should be training. I'll talk to the others and see if we can come up with a schedule."

"Wait," Sophie said as Biana led Keefe toward the door. "Keefe still hasn't said if he's with us."

Keefe's smile looked sad but determined as he stepped back and took Sophie's hand. "I'm always with you, Foster. Whatever you want, I'm in. Now get some sleep—it sounds like you're going to need it!"

The monster had been waiting for her.

Lurking in the mental shadows, ready to pounce the second Sophie's consciousness was left unguarded—the moment she stepped from the thick haze of deep sleep and let her mind drift into dreams.

It dragged her down, trapped her in the hidden, chilly abyss where everything was a darker shade of black and thought had no meaning.

That was where the pain lived. Stretching and straining against the edges. Feeding off every awful memory.

Sophie tried to scream—tried to fight.

But the monster roared. And the sound . . .

It was Gethen's voice.

See you soon, he told her.

Over and over and over—each repetition a blade, slicing slow and deep into her still-healing wounds.

It felt like torture.

It felt like *madness.*

And then . . .

"Sophie."

The soft, familiar voice seeped through the shadows, sending Gethen's words scattering and the monster scurrying away as Sophie followed the trail of warmth up, up, up. Back into the searing light.

"It's okay," Edaline whispered, swiping sweaty hair off Sophie's forehead. "Try not to thrash anymore. It was only a nightmare."

"A nightmare," Sophie rasped, latching onto the word.

Nightmares she could handle.

Nightmares were far less scary than monsters.

Everything looked blobby and indistinct as the room came into focus—a splotch of alabaster, a smear of amber, hints of turquoise—until the colors sharpened into the lovely face of her adoptive mother, who was lying next to her on a cot that had been pushed right up against hers.

"Sorry," Sophie whispered, forcing herself to still as Elwin swooped in, adjusting pillows and untangling blankets before he carefully twisted her body back into the stiff position she'd been in the day before.

She opened her mouth to say more, but . . . she didn't want to talk about the dream.

Didn't want to give it words and make it stick around. She wanted it to flicker and fade, the way figments of her imagination tended to do.

But the pain . . .

The pain lingered on.

Gethen's sharp words had sliced into her head, stabbed into her hand—and now those same places ached.

But she knew that was actually backward.

Dreams were just her subconscious playing games. Weaving thoughts with reality. So her medicine must've worn off, and her mind must've dragged the pain into her nightmare— no different than when she dreamed of waterfalls and streaming fountains when her bladder wanted her to wake up.

"You okay?" Edaline asked, brushing smooth fingers down Sophie's cheeks.

Sophie hadn't realized her face was damp—with tears or sweat, she couldn't tell. But either way, it explained the pinched shapes that had taken over Edaline's usually soft features.

She nodded, trying not to wince from the headache. "Just a nightmare."

Edaline scooted closer, her turquoise eyes studying Sophie

as if she were looking for some deeper answer. "We'll get through this."

"We will," Elwin agreed. "And it might help if—"

"No sedatives," Sophie told him.

She didn't mean to be stubborn. But triggers were stubborn things, and sedatives brought her mind back to too many dark, drugged days.

Elwin sighed. "Can't blame a physician for trying. But I get it." He snapped his fingers, forming an orange orb around her arm. "Let's see how you're doing."

He adjusted his glasses the way he always did. Tilted his head from side to side. But this time he breathed out, "Darn."

"Well . . . that's not what we want to hear," Edaline said, forcing a tight smile as she sat up and swept her wavy amber hair behind her narrow shoulders.

"It's not," Elwin agreed, running a hand down his face. "Sorry. It looks like the thrashing set us back a day. I can try giving Sophie a double dose of marrow regenerator tonight to see if it gets us back on track. Unless . . ."

"Unless . . . ," Edaline prompted.

"Just wondering if I have something better." He moved to the shelves of medicine, squinting at the colorful vials and tracing his fingers over several before snatching one that was a deep, earthy red. "Perfect! I wasn't sure if I had any left. But it looks like I have one dose—which is more than enough. I made this for Sandor after he got thrown off a mountain—remember that?"

Sophie shivered, wondering how long it'd be before this latest attack would be discussed so casually.

Remember when the Neverseen tried to kill us with creepy shadows?

"He had so many broken bones," Elwin continued, "that I had to tweak my usual formula. So this should make up for the lost time—maybe even get ahead. Just plug your nose when you take it because this stuff is *potent*. Bullhorn wouldn't come near me for three days after I brewed it."

"Great," Sophie mumbled. But she still reached for the vial.

"Oh, you can't take it now," Elwin told her, tucking the vial into the satchel slung across his shoulders. "We'll have to wait until right before bed so you can sleep through the worst of the queasiness. This is tough stuff. Like I said, I made it for Sandor, and I'm sure you've noticed that he's a *little* bigger than you. You're in for kind of a rough night. But it'll be worth it to get your bones strong again, I promise. I may check with Livvy, too, and see if she has any suggestions. She usually comes at things differently than I do, so she might think of something I'm missing."

Livvy was the Black Swan's physician—though she usually called herself Physic when she played that role—and she'd been part of Project Moonlark, so she understood Sophie's unique genetics even better than Elwin.

Edaline reached for Sophie's good hand, tracing her thumb back and forth over Sophie's glove. "Don't worry, I'll be right here the whole time."

"You will?"

Edaline nodded. "Unless you don't want me to stay."

She did.

She *really* did.

But she didn't want to seem like some wimpy little girl who couldn't function without her mommy.

"Is Della going to stay too?" she asked.

"I don't think so. They have a lot going on over at Everglen. And Fitz is still sedated."

"He is?" She tried to turn to see him, and her brain did not appreciate it.

"What's wrong?" Elwin asked when she sucked in a breath.

"Just a headache."

He frowned and snapped his fingers, flashing a purple orb around her face. "What kind of headache?"

"I don't know. The normal kind? I woke up with it, and it's just sort of there. Throbbing behind my eyes."

His frown lines deepened.

"Everything okay?" Edaline asked.

"It is," Elwin said slowly, switching from purple light to pink. "*That's* what I don't get. I can usually see headaches. They glow right where the pain is centered. But . . ." He tried green, red, yellow, orange, and blue light too, shaking his head after each one. "Nothing. And I know you're not making it up, Sophie."

She wished she were.

That would've been a whole lot less painful.

But it made her wonder . . .

"What do you see when you look at my hand?" she asked. "The broken one."

Elwin waited until he'd flashed through every color on the spectrum before he said, "I'm hoping this is a trick question, because I'm not seeing anything. Well . . . I'm seeing the breaks and all the other damage I still have to get to. But the nerves still look dulled from the medicine. Why? Is it hurting?"

She thought about denying it.

But her hand was killing her.

And what was the point?

"It feels like something's stabbing my fingers," she admitted. "I woke up with that, too."

And dreamed about it—but *that* part she decided to leave out.

"What does that mean?" Edaline asked as Elwin flashed through the spectrum again.

"Well . . . first it means we need to get this girl some more pain medicine," he said, fishing a pale elixir out of his satchel and handing it to Sophie.

Edaline had to help her pull off the lid, since having only one hand was incredibly annoying—especially since it was her left hand. But it was worth the struggle when the tart elixir tingled through her veins, dulling the throb in her fingers.

"Better?" Elwin asked, draping a cool silver cloth across her forehead.

"*So* much better," she breathed as the headache faded. "Thank you."

"That's what I'm here for. I wish you'd told me you were in pain earlier."

"Sorry. I guess I'm used to you knowing what I need without me ever having to ask for it."

"So am I," Elwin mumbled, snapping his fingers and flashing various colored orbs around her head and hand again.

"Do they look different now?" Edaline asked.

Elwin blew out a breath. "No. And I really don't get it. They're both spots where my light's a little murky right now for some reason, so that *might* explain why—but I'm still seeing enough that I should notice *something* flickering off as the medicine does its job."

He flashed a color Sophie had never seen him try before: a murky brown that looked like glowing smog. But that didn't seem to help either.

"You know what?" he said, pulling an Imparter from his pocket. "I'm going to have Tam do another check for shadows, just to be safe."

He tapped the flat silver square a few times, then shoved it back in his pocket. "There. Magnate Leto said he'll bring Tam here as soon as study hall's over."

"Study hall?" Sophie repeated, scanning what little she could see of the room. The crystal walls had no windows to give her any cues about the time. "How long was I asleep?"

"A little more than a day," Edaline told her.

"A *day*?"

Elwin nodded. "You need the rest. If I had my way, I'd keep you knocked out like your cuddly friend over there, but—"

"Cuddly?" Sophie interrupted, skipping right over the sedative part of that conversation.

"See for yourself," Elwin told her, helping her scoot up a little so she could see where Fitz was sleeping with his arms wrapped around a sparkly red stuffed dragon.

Elwin had given him Mr. Snuggles during the dark months after Alden's mind shattered, and Keefe had teased him relentlessly when he found out—until everything happened with Keefe's mom. Then Elwin and Sophie gave Keefe a stuffed green gulon, which Elwin had named Mrs. Stinkbottom—and now both boys were as attached to their sleeping buddies as Sophie was to her Ella.

"She's right here," Edaline said, leaning down to scoop up the bright blue, Hawaiian-shirt-wearing stuffed elephant from the floor. "You knocked her off when you were thrashing."

"Stinky's hanging with us too," Elwin told her, retrieving something fluffy and peach from his personal office.

He'd told her once that he couldn't sleep without his stuffed stegosaurus, but she'd forgotten all about it until right then. And Stinky looked very well loved. His feathers were faded and missing in several places, and his body was extra lumpy, like the stuffing had shifted around during all the years of hugging.

"All the cool kids sleep with stuffed animals," Elwin told her. "It's why I gave Biana Betty-the-Yeti while I treated her injuries from Nightfall—though she insisted on renaming her Lady Sassyfur." He glanced around the room. "Good. Looks like Biana finally went to session. *Vanishers.* I've found her hiding in the corner three times today, even though I promised I'd give you her message once you finally woke up."

"What message?" Sophie asked.

Edaline's smile was hard to read. The corners said *happy news*, but the curve said *you're busted*.

Which made sense when she told Sophie: "Biana wanted you to know that everyone's in for your weapon-training program, and—"

"She told you?" Sophie interrupted, hugging Ella tighter and trying to figure out why Biana would do that.

Battle training obviously wasn't something they'd be able to keep secret—especially now that she couldn't sneak off anywhere without breaking her promise to Sandor. But she'd been planning to wait until the attack wasn't so fresh.

Grady and Edaline had come a *long* way since the day when they'd canceled her adoption because they were too overwhelmed by all of her near-death experiences. But this was still the kind of news that needed to be handled *delicately*.

"I know it sounds—"

"Hang on," Edaline interrupted, holding out her hands like stop signs. "Before you try to explain, I want you to know one thing, okay?"

She waited for Sophie to nod.

Then Edaline smiled and told her, "I think battle training's a good idea. And so does Grady."

Elwin cracked up. "Didn't see that one coming, did you?"

"Not really," Sophie admitted, studying Edaline's face, looking for any sign that this was a trick. "You're not going to tell me it's too violent?"

"I'm not," Edaline agreed, tracing a finger down Sophie's cocoon of bandages. "I wish our world was the safe, peaceful place I used to believe it was. But . . . there's ugliness here. And it's coming for you and your friends—coming for all of us, really—whether we want it to or not. So you need to protect yourselves any way you possibly can, even if that means crossing a few careful lines. Why do you think I've learned to handle certain weapons myself?"

Sophie considered that. "I guess I figured you wanted to be prepared in case one of the animals got out of control in the pastures."

"That's part of it," Edaline agreed, standing up and smoothing her silky tunic. "But I'd never use something like this"—she snapped her fingers and conjured a short, braided whip—"on an animal. Even the gorgodon—though sometimes I'm tempted."

She jumped and spun, cracking the whip in the same fluid motion and striking a nearby pillow, sending bits of feather and fluff scattering as she leaped into a backflip and cracked the whip against the floor.

Sometimes Sophie forgot that while Edaline might seem

timid and sweet, with her pink cheeks and frilly clothes, but she also spent most of her days lassoing woolly mammoths or riding dinosaurs or wrangling giant prehistoric bugs.

"Does the thought of violence ever get to you?" Sophie asked, toying with the hem on Ella's Hawaiian shirt.

"I don't *like* it," Edaline admitted as she coiled her whip into a tight bundle. "Neither does Grady. And we're both hoping that things never come to another battle. But . . . if they do, knowing how to wield certain weapons might be the only thing that keeps the people we love safe. So we've made our peace with that. And we've made our peace with you and your friends learning to protect yourselves as well, so long as you're responsible with your training, working with instructors who will teach you proper techniques and make sure you're considering the risks to both yourselves and others—which it sounded like you'd be doing. Biana also mentioned that you'll be stepping up your ability lessons, so Grady wanted me to remind you to stick to your limits."

"Yeah, he gave me a whole big speech a while back about what happened with his Mesmer training," Sophie told her.

And she'd been trying to keep it in mind ever since, making sure she didn't push too hard during her inflicting lessons so she wouldn't lose control.

But that could also be why she wasn't progressing with the ability.

"Just . . . try to ask yourself every day, 'How is this training affecting me?'" Edaline suggested, snapping to make the whip disappear back to wherever she'd conjured it from. "And make sure you're really honest with your answer. Never be afraid to say, 'I don't think I can handle this.' And if you ever need to talk, you can always come to me—or Grady."

"But let's not forget that you're not allowed to join your friends in whatever program they're planning until I give you the all clear," Elwin said, pulling the silky cloth off Sophie's forehead. "Same goes for Fitz. And I'll be honest—that's probably going to take several weeks."

"I know," Sophie told him. "We're going to focus on skill and Cognate training until then—well . . . once Fitz isn't sedated anymore. Do you know how much longer that's going to be?"

"Not exactly," Elwin admitted. "His bones are healing slower than I expected, and I think it's because there's so much nerve damage from when he got shocked by the force field. So now I'm treating him for both at the same time—which is a pretty rough elixir combination. Even harder on the stomach than the medicine you'll be taking. So I'll probably keep him knocked out until he's past that, which should be at least a couple more days. Plus, I think I want to run a few more tests on his heart. There's still nothing wrong," he added quickly. "I just want to check one more time to make sure I'm not missing something—especially now that I couldn't see your headache. And I want Tam to check him when he gets here, which should be pretty soon. I would've had Magnate Leto pull him out early, but we're trying to keep our little slumber party a secret. That's why there's not a huge crowd in here, in case you're wondering. I've had to chase all your friends away—and Keefe's been even worse than Biana. I swear, it's a good thing that boy didn't manifest as a Vanisher—the world would've dissolved into chaos. But I digress. This slumber party is closed to visitors unless the Council says otherwise. They don't want anyone knowing what happened until you and Fitz are fully recovered."

Sophie shouldn't have been surprised, considering how much the Council was already hiding. And she didn't totally blame them for trying to prevent panic. But the more secrets and lies they piled on top of each other, the bigger the mess would be when it came crashing down.

"Aren't people going to notice that we're not at school?" she asked. "Or wonder why Dex's arm is in a sling?"

"Dex stayed home today—and he'll stay home tomorrow, too. And then he'll be out of the sling and back to normal. And I've put Keefe and Biana in charge of making sure everyone thinks you're all busy with some mysterious assignment for the Black Swan. Though, from what I've heard, everyone's mostly gossiping about the Council's verdict for Alvar."

Sophie glanced at Fitz, glad he was at least getting to sleep through some of that. "You said there's a lot going on at Everglen," she reminded Edaline. "Does that mean the Council moved Alvar in?"

"Actually, that's been stalled. Grizel's redoing all the security, and the Council agreed to wait until she's finished—and also until she's had time to go back to Gildingham and get treated for her injuries. So it'll be a few more days at least."

Another sliver of good news.

But it also reminded Sophie that her own security situation was very much still up in the air. And she couldn't help noticing that there was definitely *not* a seven-foot-tall goblin anywhere in the Healing Center.

"So . . . ," she said, pulling Ella tighter to her chest. "Has anyone heard from Sandor?"

"We have," Edaline told her, and Sophie couldn't breathe—until Edaline's lips stretched into the hugest smile ever. "He's not going anywhere! He wanted to tell you the good news himself, but again, we're trying not to draw too much attention to the Healing Center. So I promised I'd let you know—and Grizel wanted me to inform you that you're allowed to come up with one punishment for him for what he put you through."

Sophie laughed. "I don't need to punish him."

"You might want to put a pin in that thought," Elwin told her, "because if you think he was overbearing before . . ."

"It's worth it," Sophie insisted. "And hey, he's leaving me here without a guard, right?"

"Oh, you have guards," Elwin told her. "Queen Hylda assigned fifty goblins to Foxfire."

"*Fifty*? As in five-zero? Not fifteen?"

"Fifty," Edaline confirmed.

"That's . . . a lot of goblins."

"That's what we want," Edaline agreed. "The Neverseen need to understand that if they try to get anywhere near you, they're going to face an army."

Sophie pressed her nose between Ella's ears, wishing any part of that sentence actually made her feel safer. "So did Sandor say who the backup bodyguard's going to be?"

"He did," Edaline agreed.

"Uh-oh. You just wrung your fingers," Sophie noted. "Nothing good ever happens when adults do that."

Elwin snorted. "She has a point."

"It isn't bad news," Edaline insisted. "Just . . . try to keep an open mind—and remember that this is the reason Sandor decided to stay."

"Now you're *really* scaring me," Sophie mumbled.

"It's not scary," Edaline promised, sitting back down beside her. "It's just . . . odd."

"*That's* putting it mildly," Elwin chuckled. "Remember that thought I told you to put a pin in? Pretty sure you're going to want to use that punishment at some point."

"Okay, will you tell me already, so I stop imagining horrible things?" Sophie begged.

"All right," Edaline said, dropping her hands to her lap to stop herself from wringing them. "Sandor decided that adding an extra goblin to your team wasn't going to fix the problem. He thinks you need someone with a different skill set, different senses, a different approach to everything."

"Okay, so . . . he wants my backup bodyguard to be an *ogre*?" Sophie guessed. "Will they be able to work together without killing each other?"

Edaline shrugged. "Sandor's convinced the Council that he can handle it. And King Dimitar agreed to send one of his Mercadirs. So, I guess we'll see. . . ."

"Why did you think that would freak me out?"

In a way, it felt a little inspiring to know that the two hostile species would be setting aside their prejudices to protect her.

But Edaline and Elwin shared a look that definitely couldn't be good.

"Well . . . while everyone was discussing the advantages of bringing in an ogre," Edaline said carefully, "Sandor realized that each of the intelligent species had something unique and essential they could offer if they were willing to serve."

It took Sophie another second to process what that meant.

"Please tell me I'm not going to be stuck with four bodyguards."

Edaline shook her head. "Five."

"*FIVE?*" Sophie repeated. "What does that even mean? I'll have Sandor, an ogre, a dwarf, a troll, and . . ."

"A gnome," Edaline finished for her.

Sophie didn't know where to begin.

Or, maybe she did. "Gnomes aren't fighters."

The child-size creatures were much more plantlike than

animal, drawing nourishment from the sun and requiring almost no sleep. Their efficiency was legendary, and the produce they grew surpassed anything Sophie had ever tasted, but . . . gnomes spent most of their time singing to trees. They definitely weren't warriors. In fact, they lived in the Lost Cities because the ogres starved them out of their homeland.

"Elves aren't fighters either," Elwin reminded her.

"Yeah, but—"

"It was Flori's idea," Edaline jumped in. "And she was *very* determined."

"Flori?" Sophie repeated, wishing she'd misheard.

The tiny female gnome was one of Sophie's favorites.

But . . . she was Calla's great-great-grandniece.

Sophie should be protecting *her*.

"Flori volunteered when she overheard Sandor and Grady discussing your security," Edaline explained. "She also gave quite a memorable demonstration of the methods she'd use to defend you. From what I hear, don't ever upset her when you're near any tree roots."

Sophie had to smile at that.

But it faded as soon as she tried to imagine sweet, green-toothed Flori leaving her peaceful spot in the shade of Calla's Panakes tree and facing down the Neverseen. Calla had sacrificed herself to save the rest of her species from a deadly plague. Sophie doubted she'd want her favorite niece to put herself in so much danger.

Also: Having a gnome and an ogre serving together was a recipe for every possible kind of disaster.

"Does Flori realize she'll be working side by side with one of King Dimitar's Mercadirs?" Sophie asked.

"She does. And she said that if the ogre's willing to risk their life to protect you, she's willing to fight at their side. Sandor also made it clear to King Dimitar that whoever he sends needs to view a goblin as a leader and a gnome as an equal—along with a dwarf and a troll."

"You okay?" Elwin asked, waving a hand in front of Sophie's face after a stretch of silence.

"Yeah. I'm just . . . trying to picture it."

She could see herself with Sandor and Flori—and it wasn't *that* hard to imagine a dwarf and an ogre standing there too.

But a troll?

She'd only seen trolls three times since she'd arrived in the Lost Cities, and each time they'd been drastically different creatures.

At Kenric's planting, the trolls had wet, grayish-green skin and stood peacefully among the crowd in the Wanderling Woods. But in someone's memory, she'd watched a much larger, much more rabid troll disembowel two human teenagers. And at the ogre Peace Summit, she'd been introduced to Empress Pernille, who reminded her of a tiny Muppet with a potbelly, fuzzy skin, and an upturned nose.

Apparently, trolls aged in reverse, which must explain the

discrepancies. But it didn't make a whole lot of sense.

"It really won't be as weird as you're thinking," Edaline promised.

"I'm pretty sure it'll be worse. I mean . . . everyone's barely gotten used to Ro, and now I'm going to show up with a troll? How's the Council going to explain that? I thought they didn't want people to know I was attacked."

"By the time you're out in public with your new security team, people will know that *something* happened. And Sandor will be training the guards to keep a lower profile. They're supposed to arrive at Havenfield tomorrow. That way he'll be able to organize them before you get there."

Sophie wasn't sure what to say.

Edaline scooted closer. "I'm sure this feels like a lot—and it *is*. But Sandor's convinced it's going to keep you safe. And I've never seen him so determined. He's checked every single thing you own for any sign of trackers or ogre enzymes—and swept every inch of Havenfield with reveldust. Good news: He didn't find any traces of ethreium—or any other ogre enzymes. Same goes for Magnate Leto's sweep of Foxfire."

Which of course meant the bad news was: They had no idea if the Neverseen had another way of tracking her.

"And King Dimitar sent over the voracillius we needed to get rid of the ethreium on your skin," Elwin jumped in. "I already brushed it on, so all you have to do is wash it off. I have a basin and some sponges ready to go whenever you want them—and there's a curtain that lowers around your cot to give you some privacy."

"I brought fresh clothes, too." Edaline added. "I couldn't find any tunics that would fit over your bandages, but the gnomes helped me make some adjustments to a few that I'm hoping weren't your favorites. So let me know when you're ready and I'll help you get undressed."

Sophie had thought nothing could be more embarrassing than the sparkly green dragon costume she'd had to dance around in—and all the slithery choreography—during the Foxfire Opening Ceremonies a few weeks earlier.

But this was definitely worse.

"I know it's hard having people take care of you," Edaline said gently. "But . . . that's what family's for."

She had a point.

Sophie might not remember to call Edaline and Grady "Mom" and "Dad" very often—but that wasn't because she didn't think of them that way. It just came from the strangeness of being born and raised by humans, then moved to a new world and adopted by elves, all while knowing that somewhere out there were two more "parents" who'd donated their DNA to Project Moonlark but didn't want her to know who they were.

She could never let herself forget how lucky she was to have ended up in such a loving, supportive home despite all of that insanity.

"I can help with the bath, too," Edaline offered, "since it's going to be difficult with only one arm."

"Uh . . . is this a bad time?" Tam asked from the doorway, his silver-blue eyes darting around the room like he wasn't sure where to look. "Elwin said to head here straight after study hall, but . . ."

"It's fine!" Sophie said, pulling her covers up higher, even though there was absolutely no reason to. "We were just . . ."

She glanced at Edaline, who stood up to give her some space.

"Never mind, it doesn't matter," Sophie told Tam. "You're here! Let's talk about Shade stuff!"

Linh peeked her head over his shoulder. "This is fun! I never get to see Tam blush!"

She pinched her brother's cheeks, and Tam rolled his eyes and stalked into the Healing Center, with Linh giggling right behind him.

The similarities between the twins were always super noticeable—same silver-blue eyes and silver-tipped black hair and dramatic features. And their matching green Level Four uniforms definitely added to the resemblance. But so did the way Linh carried herself ever since she'd saved Atlantis. She was no longer the shy, quiet girl fighting a constant battle against her power. Now she moved with a confidence that looked a whole lot like swagger—though her pink cheeks paled when she got a look at Sophie's bandaged arm.

"It looks worse than it is," Sophie promised.

"I hope so," Linh whispered. Her chin trembled when she noticed Fitz's broken leg. "Now I know why Biana's ready to start stabbing things."

"Yeah, bring on the weapons," Tam agreed.

"*You* shouldn't waste your talent on such ordinary defenses," a statuesque female told him as she strode into the room, trailed by Magnate Leto. Her gown and cape were the whitest white Sophie had ever seen—almost glowing against her warm brown skin, and her height alone would've made her intimidating. But paired with the angled crop of her shiny black hair and the way her eyes somehow changed from light to dark blue as she moved, Sophie found herself fighting an inner war between wanting to stare and wanting to shrink away.

"This is Lady Zillah," Tam explained. "My Shade Mentor."

"Forgive me," Lady Zillah said in a soft, breathy voice that didn't match her piercing stare. "I realize I wasn't invited to this meeting. But ever since Tam described the attack, I've been longing to test my theory."

"What theory?" Tam asked.

"Patience," she told him as she stretched out her hands.

Her fingers had long curved nails—but they weren't black, thankfully. They looked like they'd been dipped in gold.

And as she squinted at Sophie with her strange, shifting eyes, Sophie definitely understood why Tam had described her as "intense." She fought the urge to fidget—or tug on her itchy eyelashes—and was nearly ready to give in when Lady Zillah clapped her hands and shouted, "I knew it!"

"I'm assuming you're going to explain?" Magnate Leto said when Lady Zillah moved to Sophie's side and waved her hand over Sophie's bandaged arm.

"I can feel the echoes so clearly," she whispered. *"Here"*— she pointed to Sophie's right hand. "And *here*"—she moved her finger toward Sophie's forehead.

Sophie, Elwin, and Edaline all exchanged a look.

"Echoes?" Elwin repeated. "Is that the reason for the anomalies I'm seeing?"

"I'm sure it is." She moved closer, reaching out as if she were going to touch Sophie's forehead, but before her fingers made contact she whipped her hand away. "They're strong. *Very strong.*"

"Don't look at me," Tam said. "I have no idea what any of this means."

"Of course you don't," Lady Zillah told him. "You're too new to your studies."

"Then would you care to enlighten us?" Magnate Leto asked.

"*Light* has nothing to do with this," she argued, waving her fingers back and forth over Sophie's hand. "The echoes are a remnant. A souvenir from an extraordinary encounter. Proof that this girl's been touched by shadowflux."

ELEVEN

OPHIE WAS ONE HUNDRED PERCENT
certain that she wasn't going to like the answer.
But she still made herself ask, "What's shadowflux?"

"And why have I never heard of it?" Elwin added.

"Because Flashers prefer to pretend it doesn't exist," Lady
Zillah told him. "It shatters your naive pretensions about
the illustriousness of light—though, to be fair, many Shades
choose to avoid the subject as well. It's easier to focus on
shadowvapor because we understand it on instinct. It lives
within us and never ignores our commands. Whereas shadowflux is something else entirely."

"But these shadows poured out of Umber," Sophie argued.

"I'm sure they did. Because she put them there—which is no small feat. Shadowflux doesn't like to obey."

"That's why I had to fight so hard to remove it," Tam confirmed.

His Mentor nodded. "We'll discuss that in a moment. First, I'm curious: Tam said there was some sort of eruption at the end of the attack. Was the light used for that final strike more than one color?"

Sophie closed her eyes, reliving the memory. "Yeah. It looked like a swirling rainbow."

Lady Zillah smiled. "I've always wondered what would happen if shadowflux were pitted against the full spectrum. Fascinating that it hindered the Psionipath's ability in the end—though I suppose I shouldn't be surprised. There are always consequences for playing with the elements."

"You're saying this is a sixth element?" Magnate Leto clarified. "Earth, wind, water, fire, quintessence, and . . . shadowflux?"

"The building blocks of everything we know," Lady Zillah agreed. "No one wants to see it that way. No one wants to be *made* of darkness—not with the warped views we hold of it. Everyone would rather sweep the knowledge away, bury it with the other bits and pieces that don't fit within the neat box we use to define our world. But that won't stop it from existing. Just like it won't stop a few brave souls from reaching for the sky, calling for that pure, raw darkness. I know I've tried. But it resists me. Even now"—she waved her hand over Sophie's bandaged palm—"the echoes skitter away. But they embrace my prodigy."

She motioned for Tam to come closer and grabbed his wrist, holding his hand over Sophie's forehead. "Tell me what you feel."

Tam closed his eyes. ". . . Nothing."

"Don't reach for shadows—reach for darkness," she demanded, pushing his fingers closer, until they were just a hairsbreadth away from touching Sophie's forehead.

His eyebrows crushed together.

"I still don't . . . Wait."

A shiver rocked up his arm.

"I remember that chill from earlier," he said, with a slight chatter to his teeth as he jerked his arm away.

"Remarkable," Lady Zillah breathed. "I knew your power was immense. But *commanding shadowflux!*"

"I didn't command it," Tam argued. "I just said I felt something cold."

"I'm not talking about the echoes. I'm talking about what you did to spare your friends after they were exposed. Commanding *those* shadows."

"Technically I didn't command them," Tam corrected. "I wrapped them in shadowvapor and commanded *that*."

"Yes, but the shadowflux still allowed itself to be contained," Lady Zillah insisted. "It respects you. Sees you as an equal."

Elwin snorted. "You make it sound like it's alive."

"In a way, it is. Just as fire hungers and wind breathes and water roars and earth waits. I've never been near quintessence, but I hear it pulses. And shadowflux *dreams*—hovering high above, waiting for something to capture its interest."

Tam glanced at Sophie. "Like I said. She's *intense*."

"It's hard not to be intense when discussing elemental energy," Lady Zillah told him. "Your sister understands. So do Gusters. And Pyrokinetics."

Linh trailed her fingers through the air, creating swirls of mist. "But Tam doesn't feel a steady pull the way I do—or do you?" she asked her brother.

Tam shook his head.

"You have water around you constantly," Lady Zillah reminded Linh. "Shadowflux is distant. It has to be called for and convinced that it wants to respond—and even then, it's always ready to rebel. I can teach you the basic commands," she told Tam. "The rest will be up to you. Training will be tricky, since it resists me, but I'm sure we can figure it out."

Tam tugged his bangs lower across his eyes. "I think I'll pass. That stuff feels way too creepy."

"It feels as it was made to feel—nothing more, nothing less. Shadowflux is neither good nor bad. Safe nor deadly. It is all things, waiting to discover how it will be wielded. What you do with it is entirely up to you."

"Yeah, well, I'm pretty sure no one should be messing with it."

"But they are," Magnate Leto reminded him. "And if the Neverseen are using shadowflux, it would be wise for us to learn as much about it as possible."

Tam sighed. "Okay, but . . . isn't there someone with more training who should do that? I've only been at Foxfire a few months."

"And you've shown more potential in our sessions than any Shade I've ever worked with," Lady Zillah insisted. "And with the right discipline—"

"See, that's the thing, though: I'm *bad* with discipline. Ask my Exillium Coaches. They *hated* me."

"From what I've heard about the conditions you endured in that struggling program, I'd say any defiance you demonstrated was both deserved and necessary," Magnate Leto assured him.

"Maybe," Tam conceded. "But . . . I still don't think I'm the right guy for this. I've seen what Linh deals with—and I know you're saying it won't be as bad as that. But the thing is: She's also *way* more determined than I am."

Lady Zillah stepped closer, cupping his cheeks the way a grandmother would. "This isn't doubt I'm hearing. This is fear. And you should never fear your power, Tam. Or yourself. I know our world makes it hard not to. Very few value our talent the way they should. But darkness is vital—and *not* because it teaches us to appreciate the light. It's part of everything we know, and we've only begun to harness its potential. And if shadowflux respects you, that is *significant*. I won't call it a gift, because it may very well end up a burden, as is so often the case when it comes to immense power. But it's important—and if

I had any worries about your ability to handle it, I would never offer to teach you."

Tam pulled away, blowing out a breath hard enough to ruffle his bangs. "This is how you feel all the time, huh?" he asked Sophie.

"If you mean the sense that you're about to agree to something that'll probably change everything, and part of you is excited while the other part is terrified that you're going to ruin all the stuff you care about—yep. Why do you think I tug on my eyelashes?"

Tam's smile looked grim.

"For what it's worth," Sophie added, "one thing I've realized is that nothing can change *me* unless I let it. And I have to believe I'm strong enough to *not* let it. Plus, I have awesome friends and family who always have my back."

"So do you," Linh said, spinning her brother around to face her and resting her hands on his shoulders. "You stood by my side all the years I fought with my ability. I'll stand by yours through whatever comes—whether you open yourself to this darkness or choose to keep it far away. And I *know* you can handle it."

Tam gave Linh's shoulders a gentle squeeze before he stepped away.

He glanced at Sophie. Then Fitz. Then Magnate Leto. And finally back to his Mentor. "Fine. I guess we can give it a try."

Lady Zillah's smile had a gleam to it. "I look forward to tomorrow's session."

"Wait!" Edaline said as Lady Zillah turned to leave the Healing Center. "Aren't you forgetting something?"

When Lady Zillah frowned, she pointed to Sophie's hand and forehead. "You need to remove the rest of the shadows. Or teach Tam how to if they won't respond to you."

Lady Zillah shook her head. "There are no shadows. All that remains are the echoes."

"I don't understand what that means," Edaline told her.

"I'd wager none of you do. No one bothers learning about Shades. You'd rather banish us like criminals."

Sophie wished she could argue. But while the elves didn't discriminate because of money or skin color—like many humans did—they had plenty of their own prejudices. The Talentless suffered the brunt of the inequality, but certain abilities were also valued above others. And some—like Shades and Pyrokinetics—were scorned or forbidden. She'd even heard some of her friends talk about Shades as if the ability made them harder to trust—though that was before they'd really gotten to know Tam.

"For what it's worth," Magnate Leto said carefully, "I'm incredibly grateful you accepted my offer to mentor Mr. Tam, just as I was extremely happy when Mr. Tam agreed to attend Foxfire—and I'm thrilled you'll be exploring this new facet of his power. I've always believed that Shades have a tremendous amount to offer."

"We do," Lady Zillah agreed, turning back to Edaline. "But

even the greatest among us could not do what you're asking. Echoes cannot be removed. They are a whisper of memory. The body's story of its encounter with the kind of force that changes everything it touches. They will likely fade with time. But they are the girl's burden to bear. And the boy's."

"Fitz has an echo?" Linh asked, beating Sophie to the question.

"Only one," Lady Zillah said, and Sophie already knew where it had to be.

Still, it felt like someone kicked her in the stomach when Lady Zillah pointed to Fitz's heart and said, "Here." She moved to Fitz's side, closing her eyes and waving her hands over his chest. "His is much softer, though. Less angry."

"How can an echo hold emotion?" Magnate Leto wondered.

"Shadowflux transmits the will of the one commanding it— and the echo is a reflection of that transmission. So in the girl's case—"

"Her name is *Sophie*," Edaline interrupted. "I realize you find this all fascinating, but you're talking about my daughter."

Lady Zillah ducked her chin. "You're right. I did not mean to seem insensitive."

She made her way back to Sophie's side, tapping one finger against Sophie's forehead before whipping her hand back like she'd been burned. "The shadowflux that struck your daughter was filled with rage. And now that rage has left an echo."

"I still don't know what that means," Edaline told her.

"Honestly, neither do I," Lady Zillah admitted. "At least not completely. There are no rules for such things. Only discovery. But I'd wager Sophie is being haunted by ghosts of pain. And nightmares. Both of which will slow her recovery."

Sophie hesitated before she nodded.

"Does that mean Fitz is having nightmares too?" she asked, hoping the sedatives weren't trapping him in some mental horrorscape.

"No, his echo is in his heart," Lady Zillah reminded her. "It will likely affect his pulse. And perhaps certain feelings—and those will slow *his* recovery. But as I said, the shadowflux that touched him was far less angry. There's a strange sort of triumph mixed in. Was he harmed to punish you?"

"And to convince me to cooperate," Sophie added.

"That makes sense. The triumph tempers the rage, making the echo far more tolerable. His will fade faster than yours."

"But they *will* fade," Edaline verified in that voice parents often get when they're trying to sound calm—and failing completely.

"Mostly, yes. Some tiny remnant will always remain. Think of it like scar tissue."

"But scars are harmless," Elwin noted.

"When the echoes fade to that point, they will be," Lady Zillah promised.

"And in the meantime?" Edaline asked. "Isn't there anything you can do?"

"I'm sorry," Lady Zillah said.

Sophie reached for Edaline's hand. "It's fine. I'm a pro with nightmares."

"I'm sure you are," Lady Zillah told her. "I feel tremendous strength in your shadowvapor."

"Forgive my ignorance," Magnate Leto jumped in, "but I'm trying to understand. If the echoes will eventually fade, it seems like there must be something that would speed that process along. Some trick of light—"

"Light is not the answer," Lady Zillah interrupted. "It rarely is."

Elwin huffed a laugh. "Getting a little tired of your slams against my ability."

"I'm sure you are. Now you know how I feel every day of my life."

Elwin had the wisdom not to argue.

Magnate Leto cleared his throat. "What about a trick of shadows, then? Darkness can be soothing and restful—and you said these echoes reflect emotion. So perhaps a new wave of shadows could calm the anger somehow."

"I suppose it's possible," Lady Zillah admitted. "But that would be up to my prodigy to try. The echoes do not respond to me."

All eyes turned to Tam.

"I have no idea how to do anything you guys are talking about," he warned.

"That's where instincts come in," Lady Zillah reminded him.

Tam glanced at Sophie. "Do you seriously want me to try this?"

She shrugged her good shoulder. "I don't know. It sounds weird and convoluted—which is how most of the stuff I've done tends to sound too, and it usually works."

His eyes narrowed, studying her for a long second before he reached up and swept his bangs off his forehead. "I don't even know where I'd begin."

"How about by relaxing?" Linh suggested, guiding him over to the empty cot next to Sophie and forcing him to sit. "You didn't know how to lift veils of shadowvapor until you tried it."

"Yeah, and that caused a whole lot of screaming," Tam argued.

"This may as well," Lady Zillah warned. "You're managing a trauma. And traumas can be ugly things. But it's no different than treating physical injuries. I assume it wasn't pleasant when Elwin set her fractures. But it was necessary. And now it's aiding Sophie's recovery."

"Why does this scare you so much?" Linh whispered when Tam just sat there staring into space.

"I don't know. I just . . . I hated those shadows. I hated how cold they were. And how they didn't listen to me. And I hate that I haven't been able to stop thinking about them since I felt them."

"Then you don't have to do this," Sophie told him. "Seriously."

He tugged his bangs over his eyes. "No. I guess I'll just . . .

send my shadow into your head, and if my instincts don't kick in, I'll try to send some happy shadow thoughts or something to see if it makes the echo less angry."

Linh grinned. "I think I need to get *Happy Shadow Thoughts* embroidered on a tunic for you—with a bunch of smiley faces."

"I definitely think I need to see him wear that," Sophie agreed. "Especially if it's pink."

"Hot pink," Linh decided. "With sparkly letters."

"And it should say *Angry echoes—beware!* on the back!" Sophie added.

"You're distracting him," Lady Zillah warned—but Sophie was pretty sure that was Linh's intention. And it seemed to be helping.

Tam looked much more like his usual snarky self as he asked Sophie, "You ready?"

She nodded, smiling so he'd know she meant it. "Bring on the happy shadows!"

Darkness flooded Sophie's mind. But it was softer somehow.

Peaceful.

A sliver of shade on a scorching day.

The first wisps of a long, quiet night.

The shadow of a perfect hiding space.

Her consciousness curled up, snuggled in, folded the layers over like blankets, and sank into the sweet, soothing black.

Seeking shelter.

Craving rest.

Feeling safe.

Dreams beckoned, and she let them guide her to that hazy line between present and past. Thought and memory.

And slowly, her mind crossed over.

But that was a mistake.

That was when the darkness shifted.

Tightened.

Grabbed hold and dragged her down, down, down. To that cold, lonely abyss.

Where the monster was waiting.

She thrashed and flailed. Screamed for help. But the beast was already roaring—Gethen's voice again. Each taunt scraping away scabs and tearing open wounds.

Predictable.

Weak.

Preparing your replacement.

We can find you.

See you soon.

And the monster was only getting started.

Its claws dug in, scraping bottom.

Unearthing what was hidden underneath.

Then the roars shifted tone and cadence—morphing into other ghosts. Other voices.

Older, deeper pains.

Their Vanisher will never be the same.

This is my swan song.

You can't fix me.

Everyone will pay.

Damaged.

What are they hiding in that impenetrable little brain?

Sophie, please—stop!

Each cry came with flashbacks. The memories shredding and slicing and stabbing. Blending old wounds with new— except the last one.

The last phrase stayed detached.

A nameless, faceless haunt—the voice familiar but impossible to place.

And the monster fixated. Roaring over and over and over.

Sophie, please—stop!

And for a fraction of a second, her thoughts flickered to a pair of terrified green eyes.

Recognition hit.

But she wasn't alone anymore. There were new voices— stronger than the ghosts.

Calling her name.

She lunged toward the sound and the sound lunged for her—and when they met, the shadows crumbled, burying the monster as she kicked free and crawled up and out.

Back to the light.

Not caring that her head was pounding and her hand was aching or that something strong and heavy was holding her down.

Because two silver-flecked eyes were staring into hers, filled with such horror and anguish it stole the air from her lungs.

"What happened?" Tam whispered, reaching a shaky hand up to tug on his sweat-soaked bangs. Linh tightened her grip on his shoulders, but it didn't ease his trembling. "One second you were there. And then you just . . . weren't. And I didn't know how to wake you up."

She swallowed hard, trying to find her voice. "I know. I'm sorry."

"But what happened?" Tam repeated. "What did I do wrong?"

She shook her head, wincing from the headache. "It wasn't you. I had the same nightmare before."

And that's all it was, she told herself.

Just a nightmare.

Not even the scariest one she'd ever had.

But Magnate Leto said, "That was more than a nightmare."

And she couldn't bring herself to ask.

Edaline did it for her. "What was it?"

He turned, staring at the shimmering walls and trailing a hand over his greasy hair. "I have no idea."

Definitely not what Sophie wanted to hear.

The weight pinning her shoulders lifted, and Elwin stepped from behind her, snapping his fingers and forming a strange sphere of light around her whole body—thicker than the others, layered with rings of every color.

And he did not look happy.

"I'm sorry," Tam mumbled, pulling away from Linh and

stalking to the corner of the room, hiding in the shadows. "I knew this was a bad idea."

"It wasn't you," Sophie repeated, forcing herself to stay calm. "It was the thrashing, right?" she asked Elwin. "I set my recovery back again?"

She really needed that to be the reason.

But Elwin pulled his glasses off, cleaning the lenses on his tunic before squinting at her again. "You didn't thrash. I pinned you as soon as I saw you move. So everything should be the same. But . . . your progress *has* regressed. Not as much as last time—but there shouldn't be *any* change. And I'm assuming you have another headache? And more pain in your hand?"

She forced herself to nod. "I take it that means you still can't see it with your glasses?"

"Of course he can't," Lady Zillah jumped in. "The pain isn't real. It's just an echo."

"Uh, it *feels* pretty real," Sophie argued.

"And it responds to medicine," Edaline added.

"Right—sorry." Elwin scrambled to hand her another vial of the same elixir she'd taken earlier.

He also placed a fresh silver cloth over her forehead, and Sophie closed her eyes, trying to focus on how quickly both remedies made a difference.

Whatever this was couldn't be *that* big of a deal. Not if Elwin could fix it that quickly.

"May I try something?" Lady Zillah asked.

"I don't think that's a good idea," Edaline told her.

"I understand your concern. But I'm not going anywhere near your daughter's mind. Only her hand—and the echoes don't respond to me anyway. I just want to see what my shadow can sense. She won't feel a thing."

"If *anything* starts to happen . . . ," Edaline warned.

"It won't. But if it does, I'll stop."

"I still don't think—"

"It's fine," Sophie interrupted, meeting Edaline's eyes. "I'm fine."

She needed the words to be true.

And Lady Zillah seemed to be the only one who had any idea what might be happening. So Sophie held still as a shadow crawled down her arm and sank into her bandages.

She waited for chills or tingles—or worse things she didn't want to imagine. But Lady Zillah was right.

Nothing happened.

Seconds dragged by, and Magnate Leto must've been feeling just as restless, because he used the time to transmit, *I saw your nightmare.*

"That was not my doing," Lady Zillah informed Edaline when Sophie jumped.

"It was mine," Sophie agreed. "Sorry."

She took a steadying breath before she transmitted back, *I thought you said it wasn't a nightmare.*

I said it was MORE than a nightmare. And it was. Your sub-

conscious wasn't in control in that moment. I couldn't see what took over, but it almost felt like your memories were under attack.

His description was close enough to the truth that Sophie had to ask, *You couldn't see the monster?*

Monster?

It sounded so ridiculous when he said it.

Never mind. Forget I—

No, Sophie. Tell me about the monster.

She was too tired to argue. And honestly? It felt good to say it. Like she was grabbing some small bit of control.

So . . . I'm guessing you think I'm losing my mind, she said when she'd finished.

She shaped the words into a tease. Masking the fear tangled around them.

Hiding the nagging worry that wondered if this time the Neverseen really had broken her.

No, Magnate Leto said with the kind of absolute conviction that made her meet his gaze. *That's not madness, Sophie. That's your subconscious trying to make sense of the echoes—assigning a word to what you're experiencing to help you wrap your head around it. But the monster isn't real.*

Really?

She'd known that, of course—but it felt so, so good to hear it.

Tell me this: Can you actually see the monster? Can you describe what it looks like?

She couldn't.

It had no shape. No detail.

That's what I thought. It's a monster by name alone.

I don't understand what that means.

It means it's a monster because you say it's a monster, and that's how your brain is choosing to understand it. But in reality, it's simply an echo of whatever trauma the shadowflux caused.

Well . . .

That *almost* made sense.

Assuming we can trust Lady Zillah about this shadowflux stuff, she reminded him. *You've really never heard of it?*

I haven't. But I have heard claims that certain Shades have access to a greater reserve of power. And truthfully, I don't know as much about the ability as I should. Once I ruled it out for Project Moonlark, I stopped researching it.

Why did you rule it out?

Not for the reason you're fearing. As someone whose entire life has been shaped by the ridiculous prejudices of our world, I do my best to resist their influence. We were simply trying to pick abilities that brought something unique to your skill set—and many of the feats that Shades accomplish are in a similar vein to your telepathy and inflicting. But if you should end up manifesting the ability as a natural result of your genetics—like you did with enhancing—I wouldn't give it a moment's pause.

Wait. I thought you knew what all of my abilities are.

Definitely not. I've mapped out your genetic code, but there's plenty I've been unable to translate or predict. Like when you sud-

denly found yourself able to jump off cliffs and teleport.

That *had* been a pretty big surprise.

So . . . does that mean I might still manifest another ability?

He hesitated a second too long before he told her, *It's hard to say.*

That sounds like a yes.

At best, it's a "maybe." Most elves manifest before they turn fifteen, so you're outside of that window. But . . . you've never been like most elves. You've also had your abilities reset—twice—

Twice? Sophie interrupted. *When was the other time?*

She only remembered the day she'd flown with Keefe and Silveny to one of the Black Swan's hideouts and trusted their dangerous cure to fix her broken abilities. And given that she'd nearly died in the process—and had a small, star-shaped scar on her hand as a souvenir—she was pretty sure she wouldn't have forgotten if it had happened another time.

Unless . . .

You said you saw my nightmares, she transmitted quietly. *What . . . did you see?*

Something we probably shouldn't discuss with this large of an audience.

Which was confirmation enough.

And he was right. It definitely wasn't the right time.

But that didn't stop the terrified green eyes from filling her mind again.

Amy's eyes.

The name alone made her shiver. But the real chills came from the blank space surrounding the memory.

Sophie knew what that space meant.

She'd been begging the Black Swan for years to tell her why she'd woken up in the hospital when she was nine years old with no memory of how she'd gotten there and no explanation, other than the doctor's diagnosis of a severe reaction to some unknown allergen. And the whole thing had become much more mysterious after she discovered that she was allergic to limbium—an *elvin* substance, which she shouldn't have had access to while living with humans. She'd also discovered that her sister had the same blank spot in her past, so whatever had happened had affected both of them.

And Magnate Leto's slip now made it clear they'd given her limbium that day to reset her abilities.

But the rest of the memory was still missing, still stolen away—except for one piece.

One piece the monster unearthed from the darkest shadows of her mind. And in that tiny, fractured flashback, her sister had stared at her like *she* was the monster.

Screaming, *Sophie, please—stop!*

TWELVE

THIS IS NOT MY DOING EITHER," Lady Zillah assured everyone when Sophie's headache spiked, sharp enough to make her gasp.

"How do you know?" Edaline demanded, gently massaging the back of Sophie's neck—which helped a little. "You're the only one trying anything right now."

"I suspect that's not true," Lady Zillah said with a glance in Magnate Leto's direction that would've made Sophie wonder how much she knew about who he was—if her brain didn't currently feel like the gorgodon was chewing on it.

Lady Zillah's strange eyes turned darker as she tilted her head to study her. "What were you thinking about just now?"

"A gorgodon eating my brain," Sophie told her.

She knew it wasn't the answer Lady Zillah wanted. But her head hurt and her hand hurt and everyone was staring at her like she was some fragile vase with a huge crack in the middle—and she was starting to worry that they were right.

And somehow it made her feel better being just a little bit difficult.

She wondered if that was Keefe's motivation.

"Okay," Lady Zillah said through a drawn-out sigh. "What about before the headache flared?"

"Why does it matter?" Sophie countered.

"Because I think I might understand what's happening. But if you don't feel like cooperating—"

Sophie sighed. "I was thinking about . . . one of my nightmares."

"The same nightmare you had while Tam was attempting to quiet your echoes?" Lady Zillah clarified.

Sophie nodded—and even though she tried to block it, Amy's voice screamed through her brain again, each word a fresh stab.

"Then it's what I suspected," Lady Zillah murmured. "The echoes have built a bridge between fear and pain."

"Am I supposed to know what that means?" Sophie asked.

"I'd hoped you would—but I suppose it *is* an abstract concept. And it's possible I'm not choosing the best metaphor. But for now, let's go with it." She turned to pace, her white cape billowing behind her as she slowly crossed the Healing Center. "You were afraid during the attack, weren't you? I'm sure we all would be. And the shadowflux fed on that fear. It also caused you a significant amount of pain as it carried out the orders it was given. So now, as far as the echoes are concerned, fear and pain are one and the same. And when something frightens you—like a nightmare—the echoes react and cause pain everywhere they touch. But it's a different kind of pain. A shadow of the trauma you experienced. Which is why you can't see it," she told Elwin. "This pain is grounded in darkness. You've probably even noticed that it looks dimmer where the echoes reside."

"Murkier," Elwin agreed, placing a fresh silver cloth over Sophie's forehead. "But I thought you said the pain wasn't real."

"I was wrong. It *shouldn't* be real—and if the echoes were simply echoes, it *wouldn't* be. But shadowflux can cause change. And in Sophie's case, that change gives the echoes more power— enough to drag her fears to a place where they become actual physical pain. Maybe that's a better metaphor. Not a bridge, but a bully, preying on her trauma."

"Sounds a bit like a monster," Magnate Leto noted, with a meaningful glance at Sophie. "But the question is: How do we tame it?"

Lady Zillah shook her head. "We don't. I can do nothing. And the echoes resisted Tam's attempts to soothe them."

"And I'm not trying again," Tam added from the shadows.

"You shouldn't," Lady Zillah agreed. "Not until you've

overcome your own trepidation. The echoes won't respond to someone timid—someone doubting themselves. They want someone confident. Relentless. The person who commanded the shadowflux."

"But I *didn't* command it!"

"You did. You showed it you were more determined, more resourceful than it could ever be, and it bent to your will in response. You must find that part of yourself again for the training we have ahead—and I'm not letting you back out of that, in case that's what you're thinking. If anything, the strength of these echoes proves how vital this power may someday be. There's greatness in you, Tam. But it will never amount to anything unless you embrace it."

Tam looked away.

Linh crossed the room to stand beside him, whispering something in his ear.

"Okay," Edaline said, breaking the silence. "So . . . how do we fix this?"

"We wait for the echoes to fade," Lady Zillah told her. "That's all we can do."

Something inside Sophie shriveled, and Edaline sounded just as deflated when she said, "And in the meantime, every nightmare's going to cause Sophie pain and slow her recovery?"

"I doubt it will happen with *every* nightmare," Lady Zillah said quietly. "But you're right that she'll need to be careful. She'll need to focus on positive thoughts while she's awake. And when it's time to sleep, I'm sure Elwin has plenty of sedatives."

And there it was.

Something that shouldn't be a huge thing. It wasn't like Sophie hadn't occasionally taken sedatives over the last few years.

But . . . it felt like another victory for the Neverseen.

They might as well have been there, pressing a drugged cloth over her nose.

"We could try somnalene," Edaline suggested. "That helped you after Oblivimyre."

"Maybe," Sophie mumbled.

Somehow she doubted the shimmering eye drops would keep the monster at bay.

"Is Fitz going to have this same problem?" Linh asked—and shame twisted Sophie's insides.

She should've been the one to ask that question.

Should've been thinking about someone besides herself.

"His echo is weaker," Lady Zillah reminded them. "And it isn't near his mind."

"No, it's near his *heart*," Sophie argued.

"It is," Lady Zillah agreed, moving to Fitz's side and waving her hand over his chest. "I wish I could tell you how that's going to affect him. But I truly don't know. My best advice would be to keep him sedated until the echo fades."

Elwin sighed. "I was thinking the same thing."

"I'll do some research on shadowflux as well," Magnate Leto told them, which seemed to end the conversation.

The others were soon gone, and Sophie spent the rest of the afternoon focusing on one task at a time: letting Edaline help her bathe and change. Slurping down a bowl of bland broth. Chugging a dozen different elixirs, including the marrow regenerator Elwin had made for Sandor—which tasted like liquefied dead things mixed with rotten bananas.

She was on her second bottle of lushberry juice, still trying to wash the taste away, when Elwin set one more vial in her lap.

A hot pink elixir that Sophie remembered taking once before.

"You need happy dreams, right?" he asked. "You won't get happier than that."

She wouldn't.

She'd be in for a long night of sparkles and rainbows and dancing animals.

"But it *is* a sedative," Elwin added gently, "so if you'd rather not, we can try somnalene first."

"No pressure," Edaline added. "It's *your* call."

Sophie glanced at Fitz, still curled up peacefully with Mr. Snuggles nestled under his chin, totally oblivious to shadowflux and echoes.

And she thought about the monster.

And her sister's panicked screams.

And all the other voices haunting her nightmares.

And she took the sedative.

THIRTEEN

ELL, I THINK IT'S SAFE TO
say that the Fitzphie slumber party
is a total snoozefest," Keefe said,
plopping dramatically onto the
empty cot next to Sophie. "And I mean that literally."

He pointed across the room, to where Fitz was still curled
up with Mr. Snuggles, looking far more peaceful than Sophie
felt at the moment.

Ro was watching Fitz like a hawk, like she suspected him of
eavesdropping again. But every time she poked his shoulder,
Fitz let out a snuffly snore.

Keefe smirked. "Epic Fitzphie fail."

Sophie rolled her eyes, wanting to be annoyed. But . . . it was nice to see him acting more like his old self.

Honestly, it was nice to see him at all.

Her other friends had been checking in every day, thanks to the Imparter that Edaline had brought her. But she hadn't spoken to Keefe. She only knew he wasn't running off and adding to his list of regrets because Biana had told her he was faithfully attending the basic sword-technique lessons that she'd arranged with Woltzer.

She almost asked him why he hadn't reached out, but decided to keep their conversation on safer trails. "How'd you convince Elwin to let you in today?"

"You know I never reveal my secrets."

"He had a pass from Magnate Leto," Elwin called from his office.

Keefe scowled. "Yeah—but that doesn't explain how I convinced him to give it to me!"

"Edaline told him to!" Elwin countered.

"Really?" Sophie hadn't seen Edaline since that morning when they'd had . . . words.

And she hadn't meant to lash out and tell Edaline to go back to Havenfield. But the Healing Center's walls were crowding closer every minute, and there wasn't enough space to fit all the worried glances anymore.

Keefe tilted his head, his eyes lingering on the braid that Edaline had woven into Sophie's hair the night before, after she'd helped her through yet another awkward sponge bath.

"She's worried about you," he said.

"I know." Her itchy eyelashes called to her, but she kept her hand in her lap. "But I'm fine."

"Yeah. She said you'd say that." He crossed his arms. "She also told me about the echoes."

Sophie pulled her blanket tighter around herself.

She hadn't mentioned the echoes to any of her friends, figuring they probably already knew, since Tam and Linh had been there, and all the Vackers had been told why Fitz was still sedated.

And it was so much easier to pretend she wasn't that weak little girl that Gethen—

Nope.

She shut the memory down before it could wake the monster.

She'd been having to do that a lot.

Constant mental self-editing.

So now the Neverseen even got to control her thoughts.

"I gotta say," Keefe said, settling back against his cot's pillows, "the explanation didn't make a whole lot of sense. Something about bridges and bullies—"

"I thought it was about monsters," Ro interrupted.

"Yeah, there was something about those too," Keefe agreed. "But it was mostly about boring Shade stuff and . . ." He faked a huge, loud yawn.

"Still . . . I'm guessing it's kind of a big deal," he added gently, "if you're chugging those every night."

He pointed to the vials of bright pink elixir lined up next to her cot, making her cheeks turn a similar color. And there was nothing she could say.

"Okay," Keefe said, leaning closer, "I'm pretty sure I'm not going to get an honest answer to this question, but I'm going to start there anyway: How are you holding up?"

"I'm fine."

He raised one eyebrow.

"I am! The treatments are working now. I'm getting a little better every day. No more setbacks. No more nightmares."

"Cool. Now how about you try that again with the truth?"

"That *is* the truth."

It just wasn't the whole story.

But she was supposed to be staying positive, which meant she couldn't think about the fact that she'd been stuck in the same position in the same cot, staring at the same four walls for over a week. And she *definitely* couldn't think about the fact that Elwin had no idea how much longer it was going to take before she could leave—or how many weeks after that she'd still be on bed rest or having to baby her stupid right hand, or taking sedatives every night to keep her dreams from straying anywhere she couldn't handle. He'd even brought Livvy in, and they came up with a whole new approach to her treatment. But so far it hadn't made any noticeable difference—except that it meant downing dozens and dozens of disgusting elixirs.

"Okay, new plan!" Keefe said, jumping to his feet. "As soon

as Leto goes home for the night we're busting you out of this room—and before you tell me you're not allowed to move, don't worry. Ro will be *super* careful as she carries you."

"NOPE!" Elwin called out.

"You can't stop me!" Ro shouted back. "And don't worry—I can be gentle when I want to be. I was thinking we'd go spike a few DNA panels with some of my favorite amoebas. Make sure all the brats who tried to harass me when I first got to this place know I haven't forgotten them."

"And then we'll raid the *secret* cafeteria where they hide all the fancy desserts for the Mentors," Keefe added.

Sophie's stomach growled, and she gave herself three seconds to imagine it—to picture what it would be like to creep through the shimmering halls when they were empty and quiet and dark and see all the hidden places Keefe had discovered.

But . . .

"Don't you go shaking that adorable little head at me, Foster," he said before she could get a word out. "Clearly you need my help. You've had this campus to yourself all night every night, and you haven't caused even a tiny bit of chaos. Don't you realize you have the chance to top the Great Gulon Incident—or *try*, at least, since nothing will *ever* top that kind of genius?"

It said something that she was too tired to ask him about his infamous prank.

"Believe me," she told him. "No one wants out of here more than I do. But I'm not going to risk undoing the progress I've made on my arm—not after everything I've gone through to get this far."

His eyes met hers—some sort of staring contest.

And she didn't blink.

"Ugh. Fine, we can hold off the late-night exploring—for now. But I'm still super disappointed in you, Foster. You've got the Fitzster passed out cold right there. And you *know* Elwin would be down with sneaking him a few funky elixirs. You could be giving him hairy feet and purple freckles and pretty pink ringlets. But what have you been doing instead?"

He snatched the knotted piece of extra bandage from her lap and held it up by the corner, like it was some icky dead thing. "Do I want to know why I found you staring at this like it holds the secrets of the universe?"

"It's called trying to improve my telekinesis," she grumbled, reaching for the scrap—but of course Keefe raised his arm and dangled it just out of her reach. And he was too far away to punch.

"Why would *you* need to improve that?" he asked. "Need I remind you that you're the Ultimate Splotching Champion? Also the Girl Who Dropped Bronte on His Grumpy Butt—which you should be bragging about more, by the way. Why isn't that embroidered across all of your Foxfire uniforms?"

"It's not that kind of telekinesis," she argued. "I'm trying to learn how to untie the knot with my mind."

And she'd been squinting at the scrap of fabric for days and hadn't done anything except spin it around—which was extra disappointing since she was stuck relying on her clumsy left hand. She'd tried working on some of the makeup schoolwork that Magnate Leto had sent over, and it'd been a debacle. She couldn't hold a book and turn a page at the same time. Couldn't take notes. Couldn't even write her name.

"Can I have my knot back, please?" she asked, holding out her good hand.

A glint flashed in Keefe's eyes. "Nooooo, I think you're going to have to take it from me."

Sophie locked her jaw. "I'm *really* not in the mood."

"I know—that's what makes it extra fun. Go on." He tossed the knot up in the air and caught it with his mind. "Pretend it's a splotcher and show me how you beat the Great Fitzy at his favorite game."

"I didn't beat him—I knocked him backward against a wall and knocked myself out in the process."

"Oooh, that sounds fun!" Ro jumped in. "Let's try that again!"

"I'm game," Keefe said. "But Foster looks a little scared, doesn't she?"

He raised that smug eyebrow again, and it was *so* on.

But wow, was his mind faster than Sophie expected.

She tried sneak attacks and desperate flailing snatches and everything in between. And every time, the fabric zipped easily out of her reach.

"Okay, how were you not in the final round of the Splotching Championship?" she demanded. "Did you let Fitz win?"

"Psh, like I'd *ever* do that!"

"I don't know . . . ," Ro told him—and he sent her a death glare.

"That's different," he insisted.

"Not really," she grumbled. "But it's your call."

"It *is*," he agreed, dodging Sophie's latest mental lunge, despite his distraction.

"Seriously, how are you so good at this?" she asked.

He grinned and lowered the knot, dangling it under her nose the same way she used to taunt her cat with a strip of ribbon. "Let's just say I've been practicing."

She gathered her energy for an all-out pounce, determined to beat him, when she realized what he probably meant.

"You're talking about the training you did with the Neverseen, aren't you?"

Keefe's smile fell.

So did the knotted bandage, which plopped into her lap with a muffled thud.

"Some of the training's from Foxfire," he said slowly, "but . . ."

"It's okay," she told him. "It doesn't matter who taught you."

And she meant it.

In fact, she couldn't believe she hadn't thought of this earlier.

"Did they teach you any tricks?" she asked. "Or was it just all the practice that made you better?"

"Both," he said, looking squirmy.

But that was the answer she'd been hoping for.

She might be stuck in a cramped bed in a cramped room with a wounded arm and a sedated Cognate and no access to visitors and ten zillion other limitations that were making her want to shred her blankets into itty-bitty pieces.

But she could do *this*.

"Teach me what they taught you," she begged.

"It wasn't anything exciting, if that's what you're hoping for," Keefe warned. "I wish it was—believe me. I pushed myself harder in their boring lessons than I ever have at anything before. I thought if they saw me as Captain Committed, they'd teach me something good. But it was always the same stuff we did at Exillium, just with a few different tips."

"Tips are good," Sophie promised. "Tips are better than sitting here, staring at this until I go cross-eyed."

She held up the knotted scrap of bandage.

"Please," she added when it looked like he was going to argue. "I'm *so* sick of being useless."

"You're not—"

"Yes, I am. Biana, Tam, and Dex have searched Everglen—*twice*. And you guys have all started training—even Wylie and Marella. Meanwhile I spent the morning having my mommy dress me like some stupid doll."

She wasn't being fair to how hard Edaline was working to take care of her. But . . . it was all so absurd. Sitting there with braided hair, wearing one of the jeweled tunics that had been altered to fit around her bandage. The sleeves were gone, leaving her arms and shoulders bare, and the neckline had been altered to tie like a halter—which did make getting dressed way easier. But it also made her feel like Healing Center Barbie.

"Embrace the sparkles, Foster," Keefe told her. "They look good on you."

Any other day she might've blushed.

Instead, she stared at her one working hand and whispered, "I can't even take my medicine without needing someone to open the vials for me."

His smile faded and he leaned against the side of her cot. "That still doesn't make you useless. But . . . I do know the feeling. I got to spend a whole week in bed while you guys went to Nightfall without me, remember?"

"And you should've heard the whining!" Ro chimed in. "And the sniveling. And the moronic escape plans. It's amazing he made it through without me bashing his pretty face."

"Aw, did you hear that? Ro thinks I'm pretty! I mean—I usually go for more of a roguish handsome, but . . ." He tossed his hair and fluttered his eyelashes.

Sophie's lips curled into a smile—without her permission. "I'm serious, Keefe. I need to train or I'm going to go out of my mind. If you won't teach me—"

"I will," he promised. "Sorry. I was just . . . stalling."

"Why?"

He tugged at the edge of her blanket, smoothing out the wrinkles. "The thing is . . . I'm not exactly proud of that time period, you know? Whenever I think about it, I want to slam my head into the wall."

"You ever need help with that, I'm your girl," Ro told him with a wink.

Keefe ignored her. "I guess I just wish I could pretend it never happened. But . . . we might as well try to get something out of it. The training wasn't fancy, but it was solid—and it did make me stronger. Probably because Alvar handled most of it, and he was one of few who actually liked having me there. He *wanted* me on their side—and not because he was playing head games like Fintan, or because of my mom and her creepy legacy. He seriously believed in the cause, and for some reason he wanted me to believe in it too. That's why I hope his memories really are gone and not just tucked away somewhere. Because if he ever remembers why he joined, I *know* he'll go back."

"You really think so?" Sophie had to ask. "You don't think he'll look at his scars and be too angry—like he said at the Tribunal?"

Keefe shook his head. "For one thing: We don't know who gave him those scars. Might not have been the Neverseen."

Well . . . *that* was something she hadn't thought of.

"Who else would've done it?" she whispered.

"No idea. All I know is it's possible. But even if it *was* the Neverseen, I just don't see Alvar turning his back on them— not after everything he's already given up. I mean, think about it: He wasn't like Fintan or Brant, where his ability was banned—or Ruy, who was banished. He was a *Vacker*. He had all the power and prestige he could ever want. And he passed it up for the Neverseen."

She wasn't a fan of how much sense he was making.

"I'm assuming he never told you why he joined?" she asked.

"Nope. Just lots of 'you'll see someday.' But one time he did give me this speech about how history only has two sides—the right side and the wrong side—and how we were both exactly where we should be. And that kind of conviction doesn't go away. He may have forgotten about it. But if he ever remembers . . ."

Every word made Sophie more desperate to sprint across the room, shake Fitz awake, and get started on Cognate training. She didn't care about the echoes, or any pending humiliation. Because her mind was spinning new ways—new directions. And it was making her piece together a whole new set of questions.

Questions she should've been asking herself from the moment she'd woken up in the Healing Center, instead of lying there feeling sorry for herself:

What if the Neverseen's attack wasn't a warning to get her to cooperate—or their way of trying to find Wylie?

What if all of that had been a distraction?

What if this was really about taking her and Fitz out of commission?

After all, Umber had focused her attacks on *them*. And

Gethen had clearly known about the Council's verdict for Alvar.

What if they wanted to make sure the Black Swan's most valuable Telepaths weren't available when they needed them?

"Relax, Foster," Keefe said, squeezing her good hand and lacing their fingers together.

A gentle breeze swept across her consciousness, and she realized he must've also peeled off her glove. The wind was a swirl of purples and blues—a whisper of mental twilight, brushing away the darkness gathering in her mind.

Calming the monster before it could stir.

She closed her eyes, letting her breathing match the flow of the breeze as her pulse slowly steadied.

"You okay there?" he whispered.

She nodded, not quite ready to use her voice.

Not ready to let go of his hand, either.

It had been close.

Too close.

She'd felt the headache rolling in like fog, but the wind had knocked it back.

"Sorry," Keefe said, tightening his fingers with hers. "I shouldn't have brought up any of those worries. Edaline warned me that you need to stay calm right now."

"But that might be what they want! What if—"

"Can I say something before you let that powerful imagination run wild again?" he asked, filling her head with another soft, trickling breeze. "I've been doing my own tests on Everglen's security all week—that's why I haven't had time to check in—"

"And I did an actual *useful* search," Ro added, "with my senses."

"It took us days," Keefe continued. "We searched both inside and outside the fence. And I'm not exaggerating when I tell you that Everglen's a fortress. Seriously, Foster. No one's getting in or out unless they go through the main gate—and the Council has guards posted there around the clock. Dex also added a few extra fail-safes to the Warden just in case. So there's no way Alvar's going anywhere."

"I hope you're right," she said, taking a long, slow breath. "But that doesn't mean the Neverseen don't still want me trapped in this bed. What if—"

"That's absolutely what they want," Ro interrupted. "Isn't that obvious? I mean . . . they exploded your bones—and filled you with those echo things, and—"

"Uh, we're supposed to be keeping her *calm*, remember?" Keefe cut in.

"Fine," Ro huffed. "My point is, of *course* they want you out of commission. Some of them would probably even prefer to have you dead, but they're keeping you alive for the same reason they want you out of their way. You're the moonlark! You're this mysterious, untested thing. As far as they're concerned, you're the single biggest threat they're facing—and maybe the biggest advantage if they could find a way to turn you. I'm sure half their plans revolve around trying to scare you, stop you, or recruit you—and all your little friends and allies, too."

"Which means your job right now, Foster," Keefe said, tightening his grip on Sophie's hand, "is to keep doing exactly what you've been doing. Rest. Recover. Take whatever medicine and time you need to get strong again. And trust the rest of us to cover anything that comes up while you're down."

"But you're not Telepaths," she argued. "That could be what this is about."

"If it is, we have Forkle. And Granite. And Alden. And Quinlin. And technically even Prentice. I know they can't do as many fancy tricks as you—and they're definitely not as good at staring into each other's eyes as you and the Fitzster. But I think they can cover for you guys while you get back on your feet. So just take care of *you*. You're the only one who can really do that."

She blew out a breath. "It's really annoying when you're right."

"Don't worry," Ro told her. "It doesn't happen very often."

Keefe smirked. "So . . . you okay? I don't have to let go yet if you still need the boost."

"One second," she said, closing her eyes and imagining herself stuffing her scariest questions into thick mental boxes and marking them *Deal with Later*.

But she needed one more piece of information before she could seal everything shut: "Has the Council set the date for when they're moving Alvar to Everglen? Biana hasn't said anything, and I haven't wanted to bring it up."

"Yeah, I haven't wanted to bring it up either," Keefe admitted. "But Dex said Lovise and Grizel are due back from Gildingham within the next few days. So I'm assuming it won't be long after that."

"Great," Sophie mumbled. "He'll be home before I am."

"Maybe not. You said it yourself: You're getting better every day. Right?"

"She is," Elwin answered for her. "And yes, I *have* been listening this whole time," he added as he strode over from his office. "And part of me definitely wanted to charge in here when I heard Sophie start to lose control. But it sounded like you had it covered."

"I did," Keefe agreed.

Elwin slipped on his spectacles. "Let's see, shall we?"

He snapped his fingers, flashing through each color of the spectrum, nodding with each one.

"Does that mean I didn't do any damage?" Sophie whispered as Keefe helped her pull her glove back on.

"It does," Elwin said, and the last hidden worry evaporated from Sophie's mind. "And that's why I'm going to allow you two to go ahead with those plans you were discussing, despite the way this spiraled. As long as you're careful, I'll let you train together every day. You can even get started now, if you want."

"You still up for it, Foster?" Keefe asked.

"Pick something quick and easy," Elwin said when Sophie nodded. "She's going to need to rest soon."

"Done and done! I was already planning to have us start with telekinesis, since that's what got Foster all swoony about my skills in the first place."

"I didn't get *swoony*," Sophie felt the need to point out.

"Keep telling yourself that, Foster. Keeeeeeeeeep telling yourself that."

Sophie glanced at Elwin. "I'm going to regret asking him to teach me, aren't I?"

"Oh, that's a given," he said, chuckling. "I'll leave you to it—but remember, quick and easy."

"On it!" Keefe said as Elwin ducked back into his office. "Let's do this!"

He floated the scrap of knotted bandage into the space between them and clapped his hands. "Okay, pay attention to what I do."

The bandage started to spin, moving in wider and wider circles, and he stretched out his arms and spun around with it, whipping the bandage so fast it became nothing more than a blur.

"Figure out the secret yet?" he asked, leaning on the nearest cot like he'd made himself dizzy.

"Um. Not really," Sophie admitted.

Ro snorted. "Wow. You're a *horrible* teacher."

"Psh, I'm the best," Keefe insisted. "No boring lectures. And Foster'll get it this time—you'll see."

He floated the scrap of bandage back toward himself, then set it back down. "You know what? It'll be easier to notice with something bigger. Hmmmmmm . . . Oh! I know!"

He lunged and thrust his arms toward Ro—who yelped as she launched toward the ceiling.

"Put. Me. Down!"

"Aw, is the big, tough ogre princess scared of a little elf-y mind trick?" Keefe asked.

"You realize I can end you with one dagger, right?" Ro asked, drawing one from the sheath around her thigh. "And there's no way you'd be fast enough to stop it."

"Probably not," Keefe agreed. "But I could do this." He let her plummet, then blasted her back up with a big enough jolt to knock her weapon from her grasp.

"Uh, I'm pretty sure she's going to murder you in your sleep tonight," Sophie warned.

"Oh, I'm planning something *much* more painful than that," Ro snarled.

"See, and I thought you'd be honored to be part of this important moment, when Foster shows us how much she's learned from my brilliant demonstration. Go ahead," he told Sophie. "Tell Ro the secret."

She shook her head.

All that was missing was the sound of a cricket chirping.

His smile faded. "Okay, maybe I *am* bad at teaching. Weren't you watching my feet?"

"Why would I be?"

"Because I told you to pay attention." He waited until she'd leaned over enough to see the floor, then stepped forward and thrust his arms, launching Ro higher. "See? It's all about the foot energy."

"Foot . . . energy . . . ," Sophie repeated.

"Yep! Alvar called it 'full body momentum,' but that's boring and confusing because all it means is: You want some extra oomph, move your feet. See?"

He shifted his weight onto his other foot at the same time he waved his hands forward, and Ro shot backward, nearly crashing into the wall.

"It's a small thing," he said. "But that's the point. Everyone forgets their feet with telekinesis. They focus on their hands and their arms and pulling energy from their core. And it doesn't have to be a big movement. The tiniest step makes a huge difference. Try it."

"I'm not allowed to get out of bed," Sophie reminded him.

"And yet, you're moving your feet right now." He pointed to where her feet were, in fact, fidgeting under the covers.

"Wow—remind me again: Why do so many people think you guys are so special?" Ro wondered.

"No idea," Sophie told her.

"Don't let her fool you, Ro. If Foster used foot energy, she could smash you through the ceiling."

"So? It's all still a party trick. You try something like this in a battle and you'll end up with a dagger through the forehead."

"Not Foster. Foster could catch that dagger and whip it back at you. Even with only one hand."

"Pretty sure I couldn't," Sophie argued.

"I *know* you couldn't," Ro corrected.

"See, and I *know* she could," Keefe insisted. "Especially with a little foot energy."

"Then prove it," Ro said. "*Not* with a dagger," she added for Elwin, who was already on his feet. "With that." She pointed to one of the empty sedative vials near Sophie's cot. "I'll fling that toward her head—and don't worry, I'll make sure it will miss her—and we'll see if she knocks it back at me or if it shatters a few inches from her ear."

"Works for me," Keefe told her, setting Ro back on the floor. "But I think we should put a wager on it."

"Guys," Sophie said.

Ro's grin was equal parts gleeful and vicious. "How about if I'm right, I get to shave your head?"

"Keefe," Sophie warned.

He smirked. "Okay. And if Foster knocks the vial back at you, you have to get a tattoo that says *Sparkles Rule!* It can be tiny. But it has to be somewhere we can see it."

"GUYS!" Sophie shouted as they both said, "Deal!"

"Uh, hello—I never agreed to this!" she reminded them.

Ro shrugged. "This isn't about you anymore. *We* have a deal. It's your job to settle it."

"She's right," Keefe agreed. "And don't look so nervous, Foster. Trust the foot energy!"

"I've never used foot energy!"

"Eh, you've always been a fast learner."

Elwin joined them from his office.

"You're going to tell us we can't do this, right?" she asked. "Because it'll hurt my recovery?"

"Nah. I just want to see what happens," he said.

Keefe pumped his fist. "WOO, we have Elwin approval! That makes this official. This. Is. Happening!"

"Ready?" Ro asked, snatching an empty vial and raising her arm.

"No!" Sophie said as Keefe said, "Yep!"

"I'm going to throw this whether you play along or not," Ro told her. "So you can either give your boy a *chance*. Or forfeit. You have three seconds to decide. One . . ."

On "two" Sophie reached deep into her core, gathering every drop of energy she could find and mixing it with her mental reserves—reminding herself that Keefe got himself into this mess, so it wouldn't be her fault if it ended badly.

And his hair would grow back eventually. . . .

"Three!" Ro said, and Keefe shouted, "Team Foster-Keefe for the win!" as Ro whipped the vial toward Sophie's head.

Sophie threw out her left hand and kicked her feet as much as she could, and her fingers tingled as the energy poured out of her, hurtling toward the tiny bottle like a tidal wave.

Glass shattered and someone screamed—it might've been Sophie—as the broken pieces changed direction, slamming into Ro's breastplate like a stampeding woolly mammoth, sending her toppling head over feet and crashing into the wall of medicine.

Shelves collapsed and shouts echoed as hundreds and hundreds of vials plummeted—and Sophie whipped her hand and feet again, reaching to save anything she could.

All that medicine—all of Elwin's hard work.

She couldn't let it go to waste because of their silly game. So she imagined herself with thousands of hands, grasping in every possible direction and . . .

A beat of silence followed.

"So that's why the moonlark's special," Ro breathed as she stared at the vials hovering around her like tiny glass satellites.

Not a single one had hit the floor.

"You okay, Sophie?" Elwin asked. "No headache? No pain?"

"None," she promised.

And she knew then, beyond any of the doubts waiting to roar at her from the shadows.

She might be broken.

She might be healing.

But she was *strong*.

FOURTEEN

I T TOOK ELWIN MOST OF THE NIGHT TO clean up after the Foster Foot Energy Triumph—as Keefe had named it—so Sophie was stunned when he still let Keefe and Ro into the Healing Center the next afternoon.

She also couldn't believe that Ro already had a new tattoo inked to the underside of her right wrist.

Bold, impossible-to-ignore letters declaring, *Sparkles Rule!*

"Did it myself this morning," Ro said when she caught Sophie staring. "A bet's a bet. I figure this is my reminder to never side against the moonlark."

"Always the best way to go," Keefe agreed, his eyes trailing over Sophie's bandages. "No setbacks from yesterday?"

"Nope!"

According to Elwin's numerous tests, her echoes hadn't stirred at all. So physical strain didn't seem to bother them. Only emotional turmoil.

Whether that was good news or bad news was yet to be determined.

"And I see Fitzy's *still* snoozing," Keefe noted, moving to his best friend's side and waving a hand in front of his face. "Since he's also cuddling with his sparkly dragon buddy and looking all rosy cheeked and peaceful, I'm guessing we don't need to be worried about that?"

"You don't," Elwin agreed. "The sedatives are just a precaution."

"But how much longer are you going to keep him knocked out?" Sophie had to ask.

It'd already been over a week.

"Hopefully until his echo fades," Elwin told her. "But I guess it depends on how long that takes. Right now it's one day at a time."

She couldn't help her sigh.

One day at a time.

One problem at a time.

It was the plan they always fell back on, no matter how hard they tried to widen their focus.

And it never seemed to get them anywhere.

"Is Edaline here?" Keefe asked, turning to scan the rest of the Healing Center.

Sophie shook her head. "She hailed me this morning and said the Council put Grady on assignment for the next few days—something to do with the dwarves, I think. So she's going to stay at Havenfield to take care of the gorgodon and help Sandor with everything he's got going on with my new bodyguards."

The excuse made perfect sense—but Sophie was also 90 percent certain that Edaline was trying to give her some space. And while she felt a little bit bad for chasing her away, she couldn't deny how nice it'd been to not be fussed over all morning.

Then again, she'd also had to get dressed all by herself, and *that* had been an adventure. Even with the altered tunics, she'd still had to twist her body in all kinds of unnatural ways as she fought to wriggle out of one shirt and tie on another without moving her right arm.

"That's right—I heard you were going to be part of a multi-speciesial bodyguarding experiment," Keefe said. "Please tell me you're going to make them wear glittery armor that says *Fearsome Foster Five!*"

Sophie rolled her eyes. "Ha-ha."

"I'm serious! What's the point of having your own army if you can't make them wear embarrassing uniforms? Feel free to draw inspiration from this." He cringed as he waved his hands in front of his Level Six uniform.

It was the same half cape, plus jerkin, plus pants combo as all the other grade levels—but it looked significantly worse in solid white, with a yeti pin at the base of his neck.

"They're not an army," she argued, because denial was becoming her new best friend.

Keefe smirked. "If you say so, Foster. Did Edaline tell you anything about them?"

"Not much. All I know is it's going to be Sandor and Flori, plus a dwarf named Nubiti, a troll named Tarina, and an ogre named Botros."

The last name made Ro unleash an impressive string of ogre curses.

"I take it that means you know the guy?" Keefe asked.

Sophie could see every one of Ro's pointed teeth when she said, "I do."

"And?" Keefe pressed.

"It's none of your business," Ro snapped back.

"Pretty sure it is, since Foster's supposed to trust him with her life," Keefe argued.

Ro muttered a few more creative words under her breath. "Bo's a loyal Mercadir. That's not the issue."

"You call him *Bo*?" Keefe noted as Sophie asked, "Then what's the issue?"

Ro ignored both of them.

"Stay here," she told Keefe, "and don't even think about leaving until I return."

"Where are you going?" Elwin called as she headed for the exit.

"To throttle my father."

The door slammed hard enough to shake the walls, and Sophie, Keefe, and Elwin all shared a look.

"Yeah . . . we definitely need to get the story on Bo and Ro," Keefe decided.

Sophie nodded. "Do you think they dated?"

"Ohhhhhhhh, now I do! And I've been trying to get dirt like that on Ro since she got here!" He cracked his knuckles. "Okay, this is going to call for some epic-level snooping—and if that doesn't work, I guess I know what my next bet will be!"

"No more betting," Elwin warned. "At least not on my watch. And today's lesson better be chaos-free or I'm nixing these little sessions."

"Aw, we can't have that. Foster would miss me too much. Who knew the way to her heart was my mad teaching skills?"

"Or I'm just bored," Sophie countered.

"Nah, you're realizing I'm the total package. Beauty *and* brains—"

"And super modest," she noted.

"Exactly! *And*, because my amazingness knows no bounds, I even come bearing presents!" He pulled a box of Prattles from his cape pocket with a dramatic flourish. "Today you're getting my brilliant lesson *and* candy!"

He tore open the box and fished out the tiny satchel, dumping the collectible pin into his hand.

"*Cool*—the Prattles kraken! I've always wanted one of those!" He held up the tiny replica of the giant sea monster. "Remember when the Black Swan had us leap under the ocean and that kraken wanted to eat us?"

"Kinda hard to forget," Sophie told him. "And you can keep the pin."

"Uh-uh, it's yours."

"But you want it."

"And I want *you* to have it! So how about we call him *ours*? We'll name him Krakie, and he can live right here." He pointed to the bandage covering her right hand. "That way Krakie can protect you from the echo—not that you *need* protection. He'll just be your backup."

Sophie wasn't sure why her voice sounded so thick when she said, "It's good to have backup."

"It is." His smile softened into something that made Sophie's cheeks warm. And her heart seemed to trip over itself as he leaned close and carefully pinned Krakie to the back of her hand, right in the center.

His palm rested over hers when he finished, and she got the sense that there was something he wasn't saying. But then his eyes skipped past her, landing on Fitz for a beat before he shifted his focus to Elwin.

"Any chance you could get us a bucket of ice water for today's lesson?" he asked, straightening up and clearing his throat. "I promise *not* to dump it on Foster's head—unless she wants me to."

Elwin sighed as he headed for the alchemy section of the Healing Center. "Why do I have a feeling I'm going to regret this?"

"You won't!" Keefe assured him. "We're working on body temperature regulation."

Sophie groaned.

The day they'd practiced that skill at Exillium had been long, hot, and very, very sweaty. And given the large silver basin of freezing water that Elwin set on the cot next to hers, it looked like a lot of shivering would soon be in her future.

"You sure you don't want to work on something else?" she tried.

"I'm sure. I know it seems like a pointless skill when you first think about it—like, 'Why can't I just put on a heavier cape or roll up my sleeves?' But I bet if we'd all mastered it before the ambush on Everest, my mom wouldn't have gotten away. And Alvar told me it's the only reason he didn't die when Brant trapped him in a room full of flames to punish him. That's why he made me practice it for a few minutes every day, along with appetite suppression, breathing control, and darkness vision. He called them our 'survival instincts.'"

They both stared at the basin, watching the ice swirl, until Keefe whispered the words they were both thinking.

"I should've taught you this stuff a while ago."

"I should've asked you to," she said, accepting her half of the blame.

They'd *both* wanted to put Keefe's time with the Neverseen behind them. And they'd both been mourning the loss of one of the Forkles, and trying to find her human parents, and battling a million other distractions.

All that mattered was, "You're teaching me now."

"Yeah, I guess." He helped her prop herself up with a few extra pillows and scooted the basin close enough to her left side to make the chill seep through her blankets.

"I thought we'd start with cold temperatures because it's a little less miserable than training for heat," he explained as he pulled off her glove. "Though you're probably still going to want to punch me when you dunk your arm in."

"My whole arm? Not just my hand?"

"Yep. The colder you are, the more it'll trigger your instincts."

"Of course."

Condensation was dribbling down the sides of the metal basin, and even touching the rim made her fingers sting. So she steeled herself for a serious shock of cold—but the reality was a thousand times more miserable.

"Aw, those little shrieking sounds you're making are super adorable," Keefe told her. "Ready to punch me yet?"

"S-splashing y-you s-sounds b-better," she said through chattering teeth.

"I suppose. But we both know I'll splash you back—and then you'll retaliate, because you may look all sweet and innocent, but you have a feisty streak. And then it'll be an ice-water war, and Elwin will ban me from the Healing Center and you'll be lost without my visits, and I'd rather not make you suffer like that. So how about I teach you Alvar's trick to make it not feel so cold?"

"You c-c-could've o-offered th-that f-five m-minutes a-ago!"

"Ah, but then you wouldn't have been as freezing as I needed you to be. See how well I distracted you?"

She was *very* tempted to dunk his head.

"W-WHAT'S THE TR-TRICK?"

"This." He raised his hand and snapped his fingers.

"Th-that d-does n-nothing," she argued, copying the gesture over and over.

"Oh, but it does. It creates friction. And if you let your brain amplify the heat from that friction, you'd be warm and toasty right now. But you're still concentrating on the cold. Come on, Foster. Think warm thoughts and snap again."

She gave him her surliest glare before she closed her eyes and tried to make her mind home in on the subtle hints of warmth drifting around the basin—like the water immediately around her arm, which had absorbed her body heat. And the water near the surface, where air from the room had tempered the chill.

It wasn't much, but it was *something*, and she willed her cells to embrace that warmth, to soak it up and *really* feel it. Then she snapped her fingers, imagining it like striking a match in a room full of kindling.

"Oh wow," she breathed as the temperature shifted—or her sense of it, at least.

Suddenly the basin felt like a swimming pool, or a tepid bath. Even the ice cubes felt like nothing more than floating squares.

But the warmth faded just as fast. And when the cold rushed back, it felt harsher than before, stabbing her skin with icy needles.

"Holding on to the feeling's the hard part," Keefe said, wrapping her arm in a soft towel as she yanked it out of the water. "That's why Alvar had me practice every day. He said if I kept at it, the instinct would become second nature. Guess I should probably get back in the habit."

"We could practice together," Sophie offered.

"Is that your way of making sure I suffer with you?"

She gave him half a shrug—and a full smile. "You in or not?"

He grinned. "Oh, I am *so* in."

The next day they both lasted ten minutes with their arms in the icy basin—though some of that might've been thanks to the extra body heat in the water.

But still, it was progress—which was more than Sophie could say for the lesson afterward, which turned out to be on appetite suppression.

"Get ready to hate me," Keefe said as he set a tray in her lap filled with mouthwatering candy and desserts and then told her she couldn't eat any of it.

Ro and Elwin were zero help—both munching happily on trays of their own.

"I know, appetite suppression's rough," Keefe told her. "And sadly there's no real trick except distraction—unless you can convince yourself that you're not hungry. You're not, right? You don't want this butterblast, do you?"

He took a huge bite of a round, golden pastry topped with giant sugar crystals.

If it weren't for her injuries, she would've leaped out of bed and wrestled it away from him.

"Don't worry, I'll save you a bite. But first you need to go one solid hour without your stomach growling. So ignore me"— he took another giant bite of the butterblast—"and focus on Krakie. *Or* you can focus on Krakie's new buddies."

He set three Prattles pins on her tray—a jaculus, a kelpie, and a sasquatch. "Meet Bitey, Scaley Butt, and The Stink—your new bandage buddies! We need to figure out the perfect place to put them. I think Scaley Butt should be near Krakie so it looks like they're swimming together. And then Bitey could be close to The Stink so it looks like he's trying to chomp him."

"You're a very strange person, you know that?" she asked as he pinned the new creatures in place.

"I think the word you're looking for is 'awesome.' I'm an *awesome* person—who stopped you from thinking about how hungry you are for, like, five minutes."

"And then reminded me," Sophie noted with a stomach growl.

"Oops. Well . . . okay, your new hour starts now!"

It was a very long afternoon.

But it was worth it when Keefe gave her the last bite of butterblast, which was chewy like a doughnut but tasted like pancakes hot off the griddle and was filled with some sort of thick, maple-y cream. It was quite possibly the most amazing thing she'd ever put in her mouth—and that was saying something, considering she lived in a world with mallowmelt and custard bursts and ripplefluffs and pudding puffs.

"If you want another," Keefe told her, "you're going to have to let Ro carry you with me into the secret cafeteria."

"Not happening," Elwin warned.

Keefe smirked. "Keep telling yourself that."

The next day was a little easier. Sophie and Keefe both lasted fifteen minutes in the ice basin before the shivering took over. And Sophie nailed the breath control trick on the first try.

It helped that breath control had been one of the skills she'd excelled at while they attended Exillium. But Alvar's trick of wiggling her toes did make it easier to distract herself.

And when she made it twenty minutes in the ice basin the next afternoon, she was feeling pretty proud of herself.

But the skill of the day was darkness vision—a skill she'd failed at when she tried it at Exillium. Too many nightmares had lurked in the shadows—and that was before they had claws and teeth.

Keefe cut the lesson off as soon as he felt the spike of fear.

Sophie didn't argue.

She could feel the monster stirring—hear the whispers that would roar if she let the memories take over.

"Remember, Krakie's got your back," Keefe told her as she

lay still, letting Elwin check for signs of setbacks. "And so does Fluffy," he added, pinning a Prattles T. rex next to the kraken on her bandaged hand.

"Dude, enough with the cutesy pin names," Ro told him.

"Never!" Keefe said, adding a verminion he called Cheeky. "You've got this, Foster."

But she didn't.

They'd stopped the lesson in time to block any pain or damage. But they'd also proven the monster was alive and well.

Even with all the progress her shattered bones had made.

All the strength Sophie had discovered during her lessons.

All the waiting.

All the elixirs and blurry sedatives.

All the distractions.

The echoes hadn't faded. Not even a little.

"They will," Keefe promised.

Elwin said the same thing.

So did Edaline when she checked on Sophie the next morning.

Biana told her that too, when she hailed with her next round of updates. Apparently the rest of her friends were adding daggers into their training now. And Woltzer was planning to work in some hand-to-hand combat soon.

Meanwhile Sophie was still stuck in the same place.

She knew it wasn't her friends' fault. But . . . she hated everything.

And even though it was the most counterproductive thing ever, she skipped her lesson with Keefe that day. She just . . . couldn't.

She told him she needed to rest.

They both knew she needed to sulk.

And sulk she did—a long day of glaring and pouting and generally feeling sorry for herself.

Which seemed extra childish every time her eyes drifted to Fitz. At least she wasn't going to get pulled from a drugged stupor and find out she'd lost days and days and days.

And really, how much longer were they going to wait?

"One day at a time" could mean weeks—months—*years* before the echoes faded.

Terrifying as that thought was, they couldn't keep ignoring it. Otherwise, what? Were they just going to leave Fitz unconscious indefinitely?

Shouldn't they at least wake him up and tell him what was going on, see how the echoes actually affected him, and let him decide if he wanted more sedatives?

Then again, wasn't it better that he was getting to sleep through all the angst and frustration she was currently living with?

She studied the relaxed lines of his features. The soft flutter of his long, dark eyelashes. The adorable way his arms cradled Mr. Snuggles against his bandaged chest.

I don't know what to do.

She hadn't meant to transmit the words, but . . . it felt good to say them. And it wasn't like he could hear her. He hadn't flinched. His breathing hadn't changed rhythm.

So she told him, *I really wish you were awake.*

He let out a snuffly snore, which gave her the courage to ask, *What if I just want you to wake up because I'm tired of fighting the echoes all by myself?*

That wasn't the right question, though.

What if I want you to wake up because I miss you?

She'd been trying to stay busy, trying not to look at the beautiful boy sleeping over in the corner—the boy Umber had attacked in order to make *her* cooperate.

But she hated having him so close and still so far away.

She watched his eyelids flutter a second longer. Then forced her gaze elsewhere, realizing she'd taken wallowing to a whole new level. And it was time to get back on track.

Tomorrow she'd return to her routine. More medicine. More lessons. More—

A sharp intake of breath sliced through her planning.

And when she turned back to Fitz, his eyes were more than fluttering.

One blink.

Two.

Three.

And then . . . they stayed open.

FIFTEEN

OW LONG HAVE I BEEN ASLEEP?"
Fitz asked, his voice crackly from all the days
without use.

His expression was still sleepy and clueless—
hair tousled, eyes blinky, lips stretching into wide yawns—and
Sophie hated to strip away that innocence.

But she scraped together the courage.

"It's been—"

"We'll get to that question in a minute," Elwin interrupted
as he rushed to Fitz's side and slipped on his special glasses.
"First I need to check a few things to make sure you're really
up for that conversation."

"Why wouldn't I be?" Fitz aimed the question at Sophie. "What aren't you telling me?"

"A lot," she admitted as Elwin snapped his fingers and flashed one of those layered light bubbles around Fitz's chest.

Time crawled by—forty-three endless seconds—before Elwin stepped back, scratched his forehead, and said, "Well, it's probably safe to tell him about the echoes."

"Probably?" Sophie said in the same breath that Fitz asked, "Echoes?"

Elwin shrugged. "No guarantees when it comes to any of this. And yes," he told Fitz. "You're going to hear a lot about echoes. And something called shadowflux. But I'll admit, I don't really know how to explain it."

He gave Sophie a *Care-to-take-it-from-here?* look.

She pulled Ella from her tangled blankets, needing something to hold on to.

"It's weird and confusing," she warned, then chose each word carefully, trying to soften the blow while still making the situation clear. The only part she glossed over was the monster, since that was *her* battle. And she tried to focus on how strong his vitals were.

But Fitz still looked shadowed and pale when she'd finished.

"So . . . ," he said, tracing a finger over the bandages covering his chest, "there's something wrong with my heart."

"Not necessarily," Elwin corrected. "All we know is that the shadowflux left an echo there. We don't know what that means, or when it will fade—that's why we kept you sedated."

Fitz swallowed hard. "And how long have I been out?"

Elwin and Sophie shared a look.

"About two weeks," Elwin said.

"TWO WEEKS? WHY—oh."

He clutched his chest and rolled onto his side as much as his bandaged leg allowed.

"What's wrong?" Sophie asked as a strangled groan poured from Fitz's lips and Elwin flashed a purple orb around him.

"No idea," Elwin admitted, flickering through several more colors before he told Fitz, "I need you to talk to me. I can't see this kind of pain, so you're going to have to tell me what you're feeling."

"It's not pain," Fitz gritted out, his hands curling into fists. "It's more like . . . pressure. Like my heart is pushing against my ribs."

"Your pulse is also racing," Elwin noted. "So let's try deep breaths. Like this."

He sucked in a long breath and slowly let it go.

Again.

Again.

Sophie joined them, trying to keep her own panic from digging its claws in.

Another breath.

Another.

And Fitz unclenched his fists, reaching to wipe his sweaty brow. "I think it's easing up," he rasped, and Sophie blinked hard, fighting the tears of relief gathering in her eyes.

"Good. Then just keep breathing," Elwin said as he moved to his wall of medicine and studied the newly reorganized shelves.

He grabbed two vials and headed back, flashing an opalescent bubble of light around Fitz and squinting through his spectacles. "I would *highly* recommend taking this," he said, holding up a midnight blue serum.

"I'm assuming it's a sedative," Fitz guessed.

Elwin nodded.

"Then forget it."

"Fitz," Sophie tried.

"FORGET IT! I'm not—oh. Wow. Okay, it's not good to get angry." He curled up again, hugging Mr. Snuggles as tightly as he could.

He would've looked adorable if his features weren't twisted and sweaty.

"Remember to breathe," Elwin told him.

Inhale.

Exhale.

Repeat.

When Fitz's grip on his sparkly dragon relaxed, Elwin told him, "I figured you were going to say that. It's why I also grabbed this." He held up a forest green elixir. "I designed this medicine for Caprise Redek, trying to help her steady her moods. It sadly wasn't strong enough, thanks to the complexities of her injuries. And I have no idea if it's the right approach for you. But your emotions seem to affect the echo, so—"

"I'll take it," Fitz told him, holding out his hand.

A million arguments raged in Sophie's head as she watched him swallow the elixir, but she kept them there, knowing she would've made the same choice.

"How does that feel?" Elwin asked, flashing a blue orb around him.

"I can't really tell," Fitz admitted.

But after several more seconds he rolled onto his back, staring at the ceiling. "Okay, I think that's better. My chest just feels a little tight now. And sore."

Sophie slumped against her pillow, relief warm and tingly in her head.

"Is that how it is for you?" Fitz asked her.

"Sort of. It hits me just as fast—and my emotions definitely trigger it. But I get a headache. And if I'm asleep, the nightmares are . . ." She stopped herself before she could relive any of them. "I also get pain in my hand, and it can affect how my bones are healing."

"Unfortunately, it looks like your ribs might have the same issue," Elwin warned Fitz. "That's why you're feeling sore."

He switched to a red orb around Fitz's torso and placed his hand on the left side of Fitz's chest. "The cracks over here were sealed the last time I checked, and now a couple look like they've refractured. I suppose it's possible the little bit of flailing you did played a part in that—but I have a feeling it was mostly the echo. Don't worry—I can fix it. I can fix all of this."

"Except the echoes," Fitz mumbled.

"Those do seem to be beyond my control," Elwin admitted. "The most I can do is keep you sedated so you don't make yourself worse."

Fitz shook his head. "No more sedatives."

"Are you *sure*?" Sophie had to ask.

"Seriously? *You're* asking me that?"

"I am." She pointed to the pink vials lined up beside her cot. "I take one every night before bed."

"Wow," he whispered. "I can't believe you agreed to that."

"I had to. Otherwise . . . it's bad. I don't like it, but . . . the Neverseen got us good this time."

"Yeah. I guess." He hugged Mr. Snuggles again. "But, you still only take sedatives at night, so why can't I—"

"You can," Elwin jumped in. "And you should. But it might not be enough. Honestly, it's not always enough for Sophie. She's had a few close calls. But her echoes are also in her head, so her dreams seem to be the biggest threat."

"That's why the sedative I'm taking makes me dream about glitter and dancing animals," Sophie added. "I'm pretty sure my brain would explode if I never gave it a break from that."

Fitz sighed. "I hear what you guys are saying, but . . . I don't want to lose any more time. I *can't*. At least not without trying to manage it. I'll take any elixirs you want. I'll keep my moods even. . . ."

"We can give it a try," Elwin told him. "But you need to understand the risks. If you get bad news, or something stressful happens, you likely won't be able to control your reaction. And considering the challenges your family is enduring right now—"

"Why would you bring that up?" Sophie asked as Fitz sucked in a sharp breath.

"Because he needs to consider it when he makes this decision. He needs to remember exactly how much turmoil his life is in right now."

Fitz gritted his teeth, falling back into the slow, steady breathing pattern as he strangled Mr. Snuggles.

Five seconds passed.

Then another five.

But after a few more, the crease between his eyebrows faded.

"I can handle what's going on with my brother," he promised. "I won't let him affect me like that. And if you don't believe me, tell me what's going on with him and I'll show you I can get through it. I should know anyway."

"I'm not sure that's a good idea," Sophie warned.

"Why not? If the echo doesn't freak out, it proves I can handle it. If it does . . . I guess I'll have to consider more sedatives."

"It *might* be a good measure," Elwin admitted after a second.

"Not necessarily," Sophie argued. "Everything with Alvar's pretty much the same right now. The Council's been waiting to move him to Everglen until Grizel is healed."

Some of the tension faded from Fitz's shoulders. "How much longer will that be?"

"Probably pretty soon," Sophie reluctantly admitted. "Keefe heard that Grizel's due back from Gildingham any day now."

"Okay," Fitz said, taking lots of long, slow breaths. "Okay. See? I can handle it. What else have I missed?"

"Might as well tell him," Elwin told her. "He's taking this all much better than I would've expected."

"Of course I am!" Fitz said. "Mr. Snuggles has my back!"

He held up the sparkly dragon like it was the ultimate champion.

His smile was so bright—so genuine—that Sophie decided to trust it, and shared what Biana had told her about searching Everglen with Tam and Dex. She also told him that Keefe and Ro had done their own investigation.

"Did any of them search my dad's office?" Fitz asked.

"I'm not sure," Sophie admitted. "I forgot to ask."

"See?" he said. "This is why you need me."

"I never said we didn't," she reminded him. "I just—"

"I know," he interrupted, his eyes softening as they met hers. "I'll be careful, I promise. But I know I can make this work."

She hoped so.

"Do you want me to hail Biana so you can ask about your dad's office?" she offered. "She's going to be so relieved you're awake. Your parents too."

"Alden's been hailing me every day for updates," Elwin agreed.

"He has?" Sophie asked, unable to hide her relief.

"I take it that means my parents haven't been visiting?" Fitz guessed. "Too busy preparing for the murderer's homecoming?"

"You were also asleep," Sophie reminded him.

"Pretty sure that wouldn't have mattered."

"It would have," Elwin insisted. "They've been a mess, Fitz. And I'm sure they'll rush right over the second I tell them you're awake."

"Then can we wait?" Fitz asked as Elwin took out his Imparter. "I don't think I'm up for a visit yet. I haven't really talked to them since the Tribunal, you know? So it's going to be . . . intense. I should probably mentally prepare."

Elwin sighed. "I suppose that's smart. But I can't keep this news from them. So how about I tell them you're awake but that I'm not allowing you to talk to anyone or have any visitors until I've figured out how much your emotions can handle?"

"That works," Fitz agreed. "Thanks."

Elwin nodded, then headed for his office to hail Alden and Della—but not without strongly suggesting they try to get some rest.

Fitz was done resting, though.

He had two weeks to catch up on. And he wanted to know *everything*.

So Sophie told him what she knew about Biana's training program.

And about her five multispeciesial bodyguards.

And about Ro's bizarre reaction to Bo—which they still hadn't gotten the details on. Keefe had tried everything he could think of to pry the secret out of her. He'd even been tormenting her with an epic poem he'd written—*The Ballad of Bo and Ro*. But the princess still hadn't cracked.

She also told Fitz about the skill training she'd been working on with Keefe—though she left out the part about how most of the tips had actually come from Alvar. And she showed him Krakie and Fluffy and Cheeky and Bitey and Scaley Butt and The Stink—and he agreed that Keefe won the prize for strangest sense of humor.

And because Fitz insisted, she also gave him a few more details about her own battle with the echoes.

"That's not everything, though—is it?" he asked when she'd finished.

"No," she admitted.

She still hadn't told him about the monster.

"The nightmares . . . if I talk about them . . . if I even *think* about some of them . . ."

"Then don't," he told her. "I get it. I'm sure there's probably going to be stuff I can't talk about either."

"Probably," she agreed.

He slumped back against his pillows, letting out the kind of sigh that sounded more like deflating. "Well . . . I guess that means no Cognate training, huh?"

She wanted to deny it, but . . . "Yeah. At least until the echoes fade."

The words killed her a little. She still hadn't given up on her theory that they'd been attacked to hinder their telepathy.

But there were too many risks at the moment.

"I'm sure Keefe won't mind letting you join our skill lessons, though," she suggested.

Fitz snorted. "Great."

"Aw, it's not so bad. I know, it sounds like it'd be a disaster. But . . . the lessons have actually been pretty awesome. I think I might've had a meltdown without them—but don't ever tell him I said that, okay? He'll start wearing tunics that say *Foster's Hero* or something."

"Sounds about right," Fitz mumbled.

His eyes drifted to her hands and she realized she was fidgeting with the pins Keefe had given her.

"Well . . . I'm glad he's been there for you," he said quietly.

"Me too."

The conversation seemed to die there, and Sophie hoped that meant he was going to get some rest.

But after a few minutes, he whispered, "I heard you, you know."

"Heard what?"

"When I was still out of it, I heard your voice in my head—I think it's why I woke up."

Her face tried its best to burst into flames. "Sorry, I—"

"Don't be," he interrupted. "I'm *glad* I'm awake."

"So am I," she admitted. "But . . . you have to be super careful, okay?"

"I will if you will," he made her promise.

He waited for her to meet his eyes, and when she did, he gave her the sweetest smile she'd ever seen.

"By the way," he murmured, pressing Mr. Snuggles against his heart. "I missed you too."

"I've got it!" Fitz shouted, and from the way his cot creaked, Sophie was pretty sure there'd been a fist pump along with the words.

"It?" she asked, feeling like she'd missed the first part of the conversation—because she had.

She'd been asleep.

In fact, her head was still full of ballerina bunnies and punk-rock leopards and somersaulting orcas.

"Sorry," Fitz said as she rubbed her blurry eyes, trying to smear away the lingering rainbows. "My sedative wore off about an hour ago—and that stuff is horrible, by the way. It felt like my brain was barfing glitter."

"I know. I'm surprised Keefe's never slipped any to Ro."

"Maybe he's saving it for a special occasion," Fitz suggested.

"Or he's worried the sparkle overload will break her. But I think I sidetracked us. You said you found something?"

"No—I figured something out!" He paused, almost like he was waiting for a drumroll before he said, "I know how we can still do some Cognate training!"

"Oh. Wow. That's . . . great."

Her excitement definitely needed some work.

"I don't mean a trust exercise," he promised. "I know those are still off the table. But I realized we've been forgetting the basics. Remember when we first started training? Tiergan said Cognates need trust and *balance*—and he had us do stuff to try to get my telepathy closer to your level. But your ability still runs circles around mine. *And* you're an Enhancer now, which I'm sure changes things. So I think we should make that our project—working on basic telepathy skills, both with *and* without your enhancing, trying to get our ability levels more even. I know that'll benefit me more than it'll benefit you, but . . . it gives us something to do, right? And it's all simple stuff that won't be too exhausting, so I doubt Elwin will freak out about it."

"I wouldn't count on that!" Elwin called from his office.

"Aw, come on!" Fitz shouted back. "The first thing I want us to try is something Sophie's already doing anyway!"

"I am?" she asked.

"I think so. Don't you check on Silveny and Greyfell every day?"

Shame prickled her cheeks. "I'm . . . supposed to."

Not only were the alicorns her close friends, but they were arguably the most important creatures on the planet, thanks to the Timeline to Extinction. And Sophie had promised the Council she'd make sure that both of the incredibly rare creatures were safe and that Silveny's pregnancy was going okay.

But with everything that had happened, she'd . . . forgotten.

And even before that, Silveny had gotten *way* more difficult to track down. Half the time, Sophie had been pretty sure the stubborn alicorn was ignoring her. And the few times Silveny did respond, she spent the whole conversation refusing to come for a visit.

For some reason, she seemed super paranoid about letting elvin physicians check on her baby, and nothing Sophie could say would change her mind. So maybe having Fitz reach out with her would catch Silveny's attention.

"I guess we could give it a try," Sophie said—and before she'd even finished the sentence, Fitz was propping himself up to face her.

She did the same, wincing as she waited for her head rush to pass.

"You okay?" Fitz asked.

"Yeah, just give me a second. The stupid sedative is still getting out of my system."

Three deep breaths got her pulse steady again, and she stretched, feeling her spine pop in several places. She curled her legs to her side and opened her eyes—to find Fitz staring at her with his eyebrows practically launching off his forehead.

She glanced down, realizing how ridiculous her tunic must look now that she wasn't covered by blankets.

It was very red.

And very fitted.

And *very* sparkly.

And between her hair being pulled back into a messy ponytail and the tunic's missing sleeves, it also didn't feel like nearly enough fabric.

"I know, I look ridiculous," she mumbled. "Edaline had the gnomes alter some of the tunics I don't like so they'd fit over my bandages."

"Why would she pick tunics you don't like?"

"Because they had to ruin them," she said, running her hand over her bare shoulder.

Fitz cleared his throat. "I . . . wouldn't call that ruined."

He didn't say what he *would* call it, though, and it made her wish her Polyglot ability worked for translating Cute Boy so she could figure out if that was supposed to be a compliment.

It kinda felt like one.

But she was also rumpled and tangled—and it'd been at least two days since her last sponge bath—so she was pretty sure if she stepped in front of her spectral mirror, Vertina would take one look at her and short-circuit.

"Anyway," she said, pulling Ella into her lap to hide behind, "how do you want to do this?"

"Hang on!" Elwin told them, barging into the room and stationing himself between them. "No telepathy exercises until you've both had checkups and taken your morning round of medicine. And then plan on me watching you guys to make sure you don't overdo it."

There was no point arguing.

Though Sophie couldn't help a small protest when he brought over their trays of elixirs and one of the vials was very yellow and very . . . chunky.

"Don't ask," he told her. "Just chug it and don't think about it. And plan on lots of interesting remedies over the next few days. Livvy and I talked last night, and we're stepping up our strategy—and I'll be honest: It's *not* going to taste good. But I think we're onto something this time."

The words would've been a lot more encouraging if the new elixir hadn't tasted like chewy sneeze. But they both managed to choke it down—and passed Elwin's quick exam.

"Okay," Sophie said, turning back to face Fitz. "*Now* how do you want to do this?"

"I guess just give me permission to enter your mind and then I'll follow your lead?" he suggested.

"Works for me!"

He closed his eyes, and barely a second later his crisp, accented voice whisked across her consciousness. *Feels like old times, huh?*

Sophie smiled. *It does. Someday you're going to have to tell me what you say to make my mind let you in so fast.*

Her usually impenetrable blocking had a point of trust built into it—a place where someone who knew how to find it could transmit something like a password and convince her mind to pull them past her barricades.

Fitz grinned. *How about I tell you when you finally share the secret you keep holding back from me?*

Walked right into that one, didn't I?

You totally did—but don't worry, I know we can't get into any of that now.

They definitely couldn't. Not if Fitz's echo reacted to emotions.

Okay, she said, *I'm going to try reaching out to Silveny. Brace yourself—I basically have to scream to get her to pay attention to me.*

Does that mean she's somewhere far away?

I think it's mostly that she's avoiding me. She doesn't want me trying to make her come in and have Vika examine her.

Can't blame her for that.

I know.

Sophie had no idea what that exam would entail, but she imagined it would be very . . . *personal.*

And Vika Heks was the kind of snobby, rude person who deserved to have smelly stuff flung at her head. But she was also the leading expert on unicorn breeding. And since there'd never been a pregnant alicorn before, that made her the most qualified.

How far is Silveny into her pregnancy now? Fitz asked.

I keep trying to figure that out. I think she's about halfway—

which is why I NEED to get her to come in for a checkup. I can't believe it's been this long and she's never had one.

Don't worry, Fitz told her. *We've got this.*

I hope so. You ready?

She waited until he nodded before she sent a blaring *SILVENY!* into the world.

Fitz whistled. *I can't believe you can transmit that loud without anyone enhancing you.*

She smiled. *I guess the Black Swan designed me to be annoying.*

Nothing annoying about that.

Ah, but see, we've only just begun. Brace yourself. . . .

SILVENY! PLEASE! IT'S SOPHIE!

And Fitz! he added—then cringed. *Wow. That was pathetic.*

No it wasn't.

He laughed. *You forget I can hear your thoughts right now, so I know you agree with me.*

Her cheeks burned. *Well . . . this is why we're training. Try it again with a little more energy.*

She sent him a boost from her own mental reserves, and Fitz pressed his hands against his temples, letting his concentration build.

SILVENY! IT'S FITZ!

Much better! Sophie told him.

But it still wasn't enough to convince Silveny to respond.

Do you think something happened? Sophie asked, hating to give the question a voice.

I doubt it. Silveny would've called for you.

I guess—unless she did and I was sedated . . .

That worry was sharper than the others—the words shaping into claws.

You okay? Fitz asked as she scrambled to bury the monster.

I might need to take a break, she admitted, hating herself for the weakness.

Is this who she was now?

Someone who crumbled at the tiniest obstacle?

You're not being fair to yourself, Fitz told her. *Just relax and breathe. Let your mind shut down if you need to. I'm going to try one more thing, but I can do it by myself, no worries.*

What are you going to try?

I think it's time to let Silveny worry as much as she's worrying you.

I'm not sure if that's a good idea, she warned.

But Fitz was already gathering his concentration.

SILVENY! he transmitted. *PLEASE! SOPHIE NEEDS HELP!*

Still no reply.

Um . . . now I'm really starting to panic, Sophie admitted as the monster stirred in the shadows. *Maybe we—*

Her thought was cut short by a terrified mental blast.

SOPHIE OKAY? SOPHIE OKAY? SOPHIE OKAY?

SIXTEEN

I'M OKAY! SOPHIE PROMISED.

But cold waves of Silveny's panic crashed into her mind anyway, and she locked her jaw, fighting to remind her brain that the emotion wasn't hers.

I just needed to know you're safe, she added, repeating the last word until relief flared like mental sunshine, sending the monster scattering.

Too bad Silveny wasn't so easily subdued.

She shoved her consciousness into Sophie's memories, and when she got to the parts with black cloaks . . .

I'm okay, Sophie insisted as a fresh wave of emotion slammed into her head—this time a mix of rage and horror and disgust.

She fought back with images of herself in the Healing Center: drinking medicine and smiling at Keefe and Fitz and generally looking much healthier than she really was.

Elwin's taking care of me—see?

But Silveny's thoughts fixated on Sophie's bandages. *NOT OKAY! NOT OKAY! NOT OKAY!*

And with each repetition, she filled Sophie's mind with images of silver-tipped hooves kicking and stomping the black cloaked figures into the ground.

Dude, Fitz transmitted. *Remind me to never make an alicorn angry.*

I know.

Silveny had always been an overprotective mother hen. But now she'd gone full-on mama bear—her anger twisting into something much darker and colder, until it shaped into a word Sophie had never heard her use before.

HATE!

I know, Sophie told her. *I hate what happened too.*

NO! HATE BAD PEOPLE!

Oh, Sophie said, cringing away as Silveny's thoughts added in lots of snapping and biting.

BAD PEOPLE! Silveny repeated. *HATE! HATE! HATE!*

Hey, Sophie said, sending peaceful, calming images: endless starry skies, perfect for midnight flying. Verdant meadows perfect for galloping. Glistening streams perfect for splashing—or taking a long, slow drink. *It's going to be okay.*

NOT OKAY! NOT OKAY! NOT OKAY!

Silveny's mind circled back to the attack, fixating on the moment Umber's darker shadows sank in and spread, and it was clear the furious alicorn somehow understood the significance of that moment.

Tears pricked Sophie's eyes and she shut down the replay. *I'll make her pay for that—don't worry.*

WHEN? WHEN? WHEN?

Soon, Fitz jumped in, sending Silveny images of the training Biana and the others were doing—all imaginary, of course. And Sophie's eyes burned again when he imagined her and him joining the others.

SOPHIE . . . FIGHT? Silveny asked.

Yes, Sophie told her. *We're going to make sure they never hurt us again.*

Silveny sorted through the words, trying to make sense of them as she replayed Fitz's training scenes.

HELP! she decided. *HELP! SOPHIE! FIGHT!*

No way, Sophie transmitted. *That would be much too dangerous.*

But Silveny's mind had latched onto the idea.

HELP! SOPHIE! FIGHT!

HELP! SOPHIE! FIGHT!

HELP! SOPHIE! FIGHT!

Sophie rubbed the space between her eyebrows, gathering the mental strength to transmit *STOP!*

You have to protect your baby, she reminded her.

The last word poured down like a rainstorm, washing all of Silveny's other thoughts away.

That's right, Sophie told her, transmitting what she imagined baby Silveny was going to look like—all gangly legs and sparkly fur and fluttering wings.

Okay, that might be the cutest thing ever, Fitz transmitted.

Silveny seemed just as affected, clinging to the image as her mind shifted from utter bliss to pure joy to bubbling hope to . . . worry.

Why are you worried? Sophie asked, her heart screeching to a halt. *Is the baby—*

BABY OKAY! BABY OKAY!

But Sophie could still feel a cloud of worry casting a shadow of doubt in Silveny's mind.

What aren't you telling me?

BABY OKAY! BABY OKAY!

Then why—

A stream of new images cut off the question—nonsensical things: tiny alicorn hooves, rivers and grassy fields, windy skies, piles of food, Silveny and Greyfell, then more tiny alicorn hooves, and it all piled up in her head until it felt a lot like responsibility.

And then it clicked, and Sophie could breathe again.

You're going to be a great mom, Sophie promised. *And Greyfell's going to be a great dad.*

She sent images of both alicorns nuzzling their baby.

HOPE! Silveny told Sophie. *HOPE! HOPE! HOPE!*

You know what will make you a good mom? Sophie asked, waiting for Silveny's *YES! YES! YES!* before she told her: *Keeping your family safe.*

BUT SOPHIE FAMILY!

A lump lodged in Sophie's throat. *You're my family too— that's why I want YOU to stay safe.*

SAFE! SAFE! SAFE!

Silveny filled Sophie's head with white dunes covered in thick stalks of beach grass and frothy waves in the background. The place was a bit starker than some of the other spots the alicorns had chosen to hide, but it was quiet and empty, with plenty of food for them to graze.

SAFE, Silveny repeated. *KEEP FAMILY SAFE.*

It took Sophie a second to realize the words were an invitation.

That's very sweet, she told her, sending an image of herself stroking Silveny's velvety nose. *I'm sure you and Greyfell would keep me out of trouble. But I can't leave Havenfield.*

She couldn't even leave the Healing Center at the moment, but she decided not to remind Silveny of that.

Silveny wasn't surprised by the answer—but her thoughts still faded to a dull gray. And Sophie grabbed the opportunity.

You could come visit me. Havenfield is safer now than it's ever been, and—

NO! VISIT! NO!

Sophie sighed. *Why don't you trust me anymore?*

TRUST! TRUST! TRUST!

If that were true, you wouldn't ignore my calls—and don't even try to tell me you haven't been. The only reason you responded today is because Fitz made you worry.

BUSY! Silveny told her. *BUSY! BUSY!*

Somehow Sophie doubted that a sparkly flying horse had all that hectic of a schedule.

Please, she transmitted, *I can't fix the problem if you won't tell me what it is.*

NO PROBLEM! NO PROBLEM! NO PROBLEM!

Yes, there is. You never used to avoid me. Or cut our chats short. I miss you.

MISS! Silveny agreed.

Then what's keeping you away? Sophie asked. *Is it Vika?*

Silveny's mind shuddered. *NO VIKA! NO VIKA! NO VIKA!*

She's not going to hurt you—I won't let her.

NO VIKA! NO VIKA! NO VIKA!

Okay, Sophie said as a warm rush trickled into her brain, giving her a much needed boost.

She realized Fitz had sent the energy and smiled her thanks before she told Silveny, *If you really don't want Vika, maybe Edaline can check on you instead—*

NO CHECK! NO CHECK! NO CHECK!

Someone HAS to check on the baby, Silveny.

NO CHECK! NO CHECK! NO CHECK!

Why not?

BABY OKAY! BABY OKAY!

You don't know that for sure.

BABY OKAY! BABY OKAY!

Sophie gritted her teeth. *I don't understand why you're being so stubborn about this.*

Or . . . maybe she did.

I know doctors can be scary, she tried. *I used to be terrified of them. But they also save lives.*

Silveny ignored her, repeating, *BABY OKAY! BABY OKAY!* and *NO CHECK! NO CHECK! NO CHECK!* as her mental walls thickened, slowly shutting Sophie out.

Fitz must've sensed it too, because he jumped in, transmitting, *OKAY—NO CHECK!* He held up his hand to silence Sophie before she could remind him that the Council wasn't going to let him keep that promise.

NO CHECK RIGHT NOW, he clarified. *Not while Sophie needs you.*

NEEDS? Silveny asked as Sophie mouthed the same word.

NEEDS! Fitz repeated. *Sophie probably doesn't want me to tell you this, because she doesn't want you to worry. But . . . ever since the attack, she's had to take sedatives to block all the nightmares.*

Sophie wasn't sure how much of that Silveny understood. But the alicorn caught at least two words.

SOPHIE NIGHTMARES?

Yes, Fitz agreed as Sophie fought to block the voices that kept haunting her. *And you used to help her sleep, didn't you?*

HELP! SOPHIE! SLEEP! Silveny agreed, sending a blast

of warmth along with a memory of the two of them soaring together in the sky.

I can't right now! Sophie told her, shaking her head to clear it. *I just woke up.*

But tonight, Fitz jumped in. *Will you help Sophie sleep tonight?*

TONIGHT! TONIGHT! TONIGHT! HELP! SOPHIE! SLEEP!

Fitz flashed a triumphant smile, and Sophie grinned right back at him. It didn't solve the baby checkup conundrum—but at least Silveny was cooperating. And hopefully once they were in regular contact, she could figure out what was really keeping the stubborn alicorn away.

And hey—maybe Silveny's help would save her from taking so many sedatives.

Thank you, she transmitted more to Fitz than to Silveny, smiling wider when Silveny said, *SOPHIE! TALK! SOON!*

Soon, Sophie agreed.

Silveny severed the connection, and Fitz's grin shifted into movie-star mode.

Team Fitzphie for the win!

"Keefe's right," Elwin said, making them both jump. "You two do stare into each other's eyes a lot."

"It's how we concentrate," Sophie argued, becoming very interested in smoothing her disaster of a ponytail.

"I'm sure that's what it is," he teased. "And I take it those triumphant smiles you had a few seconds ago mean Silveny finally agreed to come in for a checkup?"

"Not yet. But she will," Fitz said, with a confidence Sophie wished she could feel. "But we *did* get her to agree to help Sophie with her dreams. So now Sophie can skip the freaky sedative."

Elwin shuffled his feet. "I'm not sure that's the best idea. The system we have right now is working."

"But you're changing up all our other medicines anyway," Fitz reminded him.

"I'm only changing the ones that aren't doing their job," Elwin argued. "And the sedative isn't one of those. Plus, the tricky thing about nightmares is, by the time I know they're happening, Sophie's thrashing and screaming and the echo's already done its damage."

"True," Sophie admitted, letting any excitement she'd felt fizzle away.

"But Silveny's helped you with nightmares tons of times before, hasn't she?" Fitz pressed. "And you *hate* sedatives."

"I know. But it's fine."

She gave him her most reassuring smile—which must not have been very convincing, because Fitz reached up and ran a hand down his face.

"Okay," he said after a second, "what if I monitor your dreams tonight? That way I'll know the first second they start to shift—*if* they start to shift—and can wake you up and make you take the sedative instead?"

"You can't stay up all night," Sophie argued.

"Yes I can. I just slept for two weeks. I'm good."

"It doesn't work that way," Elwin informed him. "Our bodies don't store sleep in reserve."

"Fine, then I'll nap today," Fitz countered. "And tomorrow if I need it. It's not like I have a lot on my schedule."

"Uh, you're busy trying to recover from almost dying," Sophie reminded him. "And sleep's a pretty important part of that. Seriously, Fitz. It's super sweet of you to offer, but—"

"Please," he interrupted, leaning toward her. "I can't make the echoes fade, or get us out of these cots, or stop my creepy brother from moving back home. I can't work on any of the training we should be focusing on. But I can do *this*. Please don't make me lie here tonight feeling useless instead."

The words sounded a whole lot like the desperate plea she'd given Keefe when she'd begged him to give her skill lessons. And the intensity in Fitz's eyes made her heart ache *and* want to flutter away.

Elwin sighed. "If you *really* want to try this, I guess I can't stop you."

"We do," Fitz agreed—then seemed to realize he was speaking for Sophie. "Don't we?"

Her itchy eyelashes told her there was a very good reason why giving Fitz access to her dreams was a seriously bad idea. And the thought of him seeing the monster made her want to bury her head under her pillow.

But . . . she kept hearing him call himself useless.

And she'd definitely love to break free from the sedatives.

"If you're really up for it," she said, needing to make sure.

"I am," he promised, and his lips curled into his meltiest grin.

"Fine," Elwin said, the sound more of a groan than a word. "But as soon as Alden and Della leave, I want you doing some serious napping!"

"My parents are coming?" Fitz asked.

"No keeping them away," Elwin agreed. "Should be here within the hour. Don't worry—I told them it'd have to be a short visit and that they couldn't get emotional."

"Right, like *that's* going to happen," Fitz muttered.

His parents tried—they really did.

Considering they hadn't seen their son awake in more than two weeks, there were shockingly few tears. But there were a whole lot of choked apologies and weepy voices and lots and lots of blinking.

And hugs. So many hugs.

Elwin finally had to warn them about Fitz's cracked ribs.

Sophie wished she could give them privacy for their family reunion and told herself not to eavesdrop. And she'd been doing a pretty good job—until Fitz started asking about Alvar.

"We still don't know the exact day he'll arrive," Della told him, reaching for the hand Fitz had pulled out of her grasp.

"But it'll be soon," Fitz pressed.

Alden nodded. "The house is ready. It's passed every possible security protocol."

"What about the emergency override?" Fitz asked.

"I removed your brother's DNA from the gates the first night I learned he was with the Neverseen," Alden told him. "You know that."

"Yeah, but he still knows where the override is," Fitz argued, and Sophie had to bite her tongue to stop herself from asking, *What's the override?*

"He doesn't, actually," Alden corrected. "His memories are gone, Fitz."

"For now," Fitz snapped back.

Alden pinched the bridge of his nose. "If your brother went anywhere near the override, we'd know. And if he tried to turn off the gates, Dex's gadget would render him unconscious before he could leap away. He also doesn't have the code to activate the panel. But if it would make you feel better, I can station one of the goblins there."

"*Two,*" Fitz countered.

"Fine," Alden promised. "Feel better now?"

Sophie did. But Fitz ignored the question.

"What about your office?" he asked. "Why haven't you let anyone search there?"

"Because I'm an Emissary for the Council and ninety percent of my records are highly classified. I can't have your sister and her friends rifling through them because you're trying to punish me!"

"If we were trying to punish you, we'd trash the house," Fitz argued, sucking in a long, calming breath. "We want to check your office because we're trying to stop whatever the Neverseen are planning."

"I can assure you, son, if the answers were in there, I would've found them. *I've* searched my office."

"Since the Tribunal?" Fitz verified.

"Yes. Twice, actually. There's nothing but books and papers and some creatures swimming behind glass. But even if there were something more interesting than that, my office is also locked—very thoroughly. No one has access but me."

"Alvar won't even have access to the main house," Della added quietly.

"Until you let him in for the big Welcome Home Dinner," Fitz grumbled.

"I'm not planning a dinner, Fitz."

"You will."

"Please don't do this," Della begged. "Let's not use what little time we have to argue. Especially since it puts you at risk." She placed her hand over his bandaged chest, like she was trying to feel the echo. "We've been so worried."

"Yeah, I'm sure. Sophie told me how much time you spent here, waiting for me to wake up."

Sophie would've traded all of her abilities to be a Vanisher right then—or for a nice tall cliff to jump off and teleport away.

Instead she had to settle for slinking farther under her covers.

"That's not fair," Della told him. "They didn't want us drawing attention to the Healing Center."

Fitz rolled his eyes. "Yeah, and it's not like you can turn invisible or anything!"

"Careful," Elwin warned.

"I'm fine," Fitz promised, placing a hand over his chest and taking another deep breath.

"You were sedated," Alden reminded him.

"And you were busy getting everything ready for a murderer," Fitz said through gritted teeth. "And you know what my favorite part is? I bet neither of you have thought at all about the fact that if the Neverseen hadn't dumped him, Alvar would've been right there with them when they attacked me and Sophie."

There was no way to know if that was true.

But no way to deny it either.

And the silence said more than enough.

"I'm tired," Fitz told them. "And I'm not allowed to lose my temper. So . . . I think you should go."

His parents didn't argue.

Alden just patted him on the shoulder and Della hugged him again, whispering something in his ear as she kissed his cheek.

She left without another word, and Sophie tried to blend in with her pillows as Alden turned to leave. But his teal eyes still met hers, and she couldn't help thinking how much they looked like his son's—or how watery they were.

"I wish the circumstances were different," he told her quietly, "but I'm glad you're here together."

He was gone before Sophie could figure out how to respond.

SEVENTEEN

I'M FINE," FITZ PROMISED, EVEN AS MR. Snuggles went flying across the room and crashed into the door his parents had just exited through.

Sophie didn't see how that could possibly be true.

But Fitz wasn't acting like he was in pain.

And Elwin didn't see any signs that his echo had stirred.

Fitz also agreed to take more of the mood elixir just to be safe.

So . . . there really wasn't much she could do—except have Elwin tell Keefe she needed to skip the day's skill lesson, since Keefe's teasing and Fitz's fragile mood would surely be a disastrous combination.

She'd also asked Fitz if he wanted to talk.

He did *not*—though he'd at least been willing to answer her questions about the override.

Apparently it was a way to deactivate Everglen's gates in case they ever malfunctioned—which made Sophie very glad that he'd convinced his father to station guards nearby. It also made her wonder why guards hadn't been assigned there in the first place.

What other vulnerabilities were they missing?

She kept the question to herself, letting Fitz nap for the remainder of the day. And even though he seemed much calmer when he woke up, she tried talking him out of monitoring her dreams again.

"You need the rest," she told him.

But he shook his head. "I need a *distraction*. Please, Sophie. Let me help you with this."

It was impossible to say no when his eyes got all puppyish.

Even Elwin caved and pushed Fitz's cot next to hers.

There was still at least a foot of space between the two narrow beds. But after two weeks of having Fitz all the way across the room, that gap felt *very* tiny.

"Awwww, look at you guys, all snuggly with your little stuffed animals!" a familiar voice called from the doorway, and they both turned to find Livvy grinning at them.

The pink jewels woven through her tiny braids glinted as she made her way closer, as did the matching gems flecked across her dark skin. But all that shimmer and sparkle couldn't hide the way her eyes clouded over when she got a better look at Sophie's and Fitz's bandages.

"I'd been hoping Elwin was exaggerating," she said, placing her palm on Sophie's broken hand. "But don't worry, we have a brilliant new plan."

She rattled the overstuffed satchel slung over her shoulders, and the sound of hundreds of clinking vials filled the room.

"You found everything?" Elwin asked as he joined them.

Livvy nodded. "Took me three stops to find all the right feces."

"They better not be for our new medicines," Fitz warned, and Sophie definitely echoed that sentiment.

"Don't worry—they only go in the topical stuff," Livvy promised, handing her satchel to Elwin. "Though I did also bring congealed selkie skin. And hollowthistles—remember those, Fitz?"

The tinge of green to Fitz's skin made it clear that he absolutely remembered them—and the week of misery he'd endured, thanks to hollowthistle tea.

"Relax," Elwin told them. "It won't be as bad as you're thinking."

Translation: It definitely *would* be bad.

"The lab's this way," Elwin said, leading Livvy toward the alchemy section of the Healing Center. "We should probably get started. Some of these elixirs are going to take a few hours to brew."

"Isn't it convenient," Livvy asked Sophie and Fitz, "how Elwin just happened to have an all-night project the same time you're doing your little dream experiment?"

"It's called multitasking," Elwin argued.

"And spying," Livvy added.

"Making sure I'm up if they need anything," Elwin corrected.

"So wait—I'm going to be the only one sleeping?" Sophie clarified. "Great, because that doesn't make me feel weird at all."

"You shouldn't," Elwin told her.

"Well, you should a little," Livvy argued, "since I'm betting the Pretty Boy's going to spend most of the night staring at you as he listens to your dreams."

"What else am I supposed to stare at?" Fitz wondered.

Elwin laughed and winked at Sophie. "You know where to find us."

They left them alone then, and the room was suddenly very, very quiet.

"You don't want to do this anymore, do you?" Fitz asked as Sophie tugged out an itchy eyelash.

Not even a little bit.

"I'll stare at the wall," he offered. "Or the floor."

Before Sophie could decide, an exuberant voice blared inside her head—*SOPHIE! FRIEND! HELP!*—and she learned that there was simply no turning down the assistance of an over-protective mama alicorn.

"It won't be weird," Fitz promised as Sophie settled back against her pillows. "Trust me."

Oh, it would definitely be weird.

But she *did* trust him.

And Silveny was already flooding her mind with vivid scenes

of the two of them soaring through a sunset sky. So she closed her eyes and focused on the rush tingling under her skin as Silveny imagined them flipping and diving and somersaulting through a sea of soft pink clouds.

Higher and higher they went, until the ground was nothing more than a memory. And still, they kept climbing.

Away from reality.

Away from monsters.

Away from anything that would ever try to catch them.

The next thing she knew, it was morning and she'd slept twelve straight hours.

Fitz grinned. "Another victory for Team Fitzphie!"

The new congealed selkie skin medicine tasted like eating a stale gummy bear that had spent a few days chilling in a dirty litter box—but choking it down turned out to be the *least* disgusting part of Sophie and Fitz's morning.

The real prize for Ickiest Way to Start the Day went to the moment Elwin announced that he needed to change out their bandages to give their treatment a fresh start. Even Livvy didn't stick around when Elwin sliced into the cocoons and unleashed a musky plume—and she kept a running top ten list of the grossest things she'd done.

There were no words to describe the odor, or the grayish-green ooze that splashed everywhere, which was some sort of by-product of the marrow regenerator. But Fitz's face turned a color similar to the shade of his eyes, and Sophie had been very glad she'd only had a couple bites of her breakfast.

And that was before she got a glimpse of her swollen hand.

"Try not to move your fingers," Elwin warned.

She couldn't have even if she'd tried. Her hand felt stiff and numb, as if she'd left it out in the cold too long. And her fingers were currently the size of raw sausages—and just as pale and squishy and gross.

"I know it's hard to believe me when I say this," Elwin told her, flashing a glowing orange orb around her hand, "but this is actually much better than Livvy and I were expecting. The echo wasn't letting me get a clear picture of your progress, and it looks like the bones have set far more than I thought—enough that I can finally start treating some of the nerve and tissue damage too. So the next time you see this hand, it'll look almost normal."

Sophie tried not to focus on the "almost" in that sentence.

Or the *potent* smell of the blackish, reddish, bluish goop he smeared across her palm.

"I'm guessing I don't want to know what that stuff is," she said as Elwin started wrapping her fingers mummy-style in strips of thin white bandage.

"Yeah, you guys aren't going to want to know about pretty much anything I do to you for the next few days," Elwin admitted. "But I promise, it *will* be worth it. I'm betting we'll have you home by the end of the week."

Fitz didn't look very excited about that prospect, but given the tension between him and his parents, Sophie couldn't blame him.

"Hold your hand a little higher," Elwin instructed, draping something that looked like golden chain mail over Sophie's fresh cocoon of bandages and binding it every few inches with thin black bands. "This is for compression, so it's supposed to feel tight. But let me know if it feels *too* tight, okay?"

It felt like when someone had too firm of a handshake: not painful—just annoying.

"I still need you to try not to move," he added as he set her arm back on its nest of pillows—and Sophie doubted she could have, even if she'd wanted to. The chain mail was *heavy*. "But hopefully that'll be changing soon."

Fitz's leg got the same treatment. So did his ribs—and he did not look happy when Elwin strapped him into some sort of chain-mail vest.

He looked even grumpier when Elwin set a tray of medicine in his lap.

It had to have at least thirty elixirs on it.

Sophie was all set to tease him, until Elwin brought over her tray, and it probably had forty. Her mouth watered just looking at it all—and not in the "I'm hungry" kind of way.

In the "vomiting is probably in my immediate future" way.

"This is actually only half of it," Elwin warned. "But I don't want to overwhelm your stomachs. So you'll take the rest tonight."

"Can't wait," Sophie mumbled—but it sounded like "hant ate" because she was trying to use her teeth to open the first dose.

"Here," Fitz said, leaning over and taking the vial before she spilled it all over herself.

At some point during the night, their cots had gotten scooched even closer together. Only a few inches separated them now.

She'd expected him to hand her the opened vial, but he scooted even closer and pressed the glass against her lips—something Elwin had done for her dozens and dozens of times.

But it was a *very* different experience with Fitz.

Especially when his finger accidentally grazed the edge of her lips. Not that he seemed to notice.

He didn't blush the tiniest bit—which was *extra* annoying, since she was certain her cheeks were neon red.

"You're helping me so you don't have to take your own medicine, huh?" Sophie teased, ordering her head and heart to get their act together.

This was one friend helping another—nothing more.

Fitz confirmed it when he winked and added, "Also letting you test them all, so I know which ones are the grossest. Want this one next?" He pointed to a thick brown elixir. "I'm guessing it's all kinds of wrong."

"Actually, that's one of the good ones," Elwin corrected. "It's the shimmery pink one you should be afraid of. In fact, you're probably going to need a chaser for that."

He reached into his pocket and pulled a handful of the silver-wrapped squishy candies he'd given Sophie before, setting them on the tray next to the vial in question.

The elixir looked like melting sugar swirled with strawberry syrup—but when Fitz twisted off the lid, it smelled like a bathroom after someone had eaten a whole lot of asparagus.

"Drink it *fast*," Elwin recommended. "And hold your breath."

Sophie nodded, using her free hand to plug her nose as Fitz counted to three and tipped the medicine into her mouth—but her taste buds still immediately tried to convince her that she should spit the rotten sludge back out as fast as she possibly could.

Her eyes watered and her stomach contracted, even after Fitz helped her take a bite of the black squishy candy.

"You okay?" he asked, offering her the other half.

"No."

She took the bite anyway, trying to focus on the snickerdoodle flavor.

It sort of helped.

"That was seriously the worst thing I've ever put in my mouth," she told Elwin.

"I know. And believe it or not, it's nectar from these tiny pink flowers called sugarbelles. But I promise, it's worth the bad taste. That's one of the most important medicines that Livvy and I came up with."

"Then I'm glad I kept it down."

"So am I," Fitz teased. "For a second I thought it was going to be like the day we found out you're allergic to limbium."

Sophie groaned. "Great, I'm so glad you still remember that."

"It's kinda hard to forget," he admitted. "But it was . . ."

"Super gross?" she guessed when he couldn't seem to figure out where he was going with that sentence.

"Well. Yeah. *But*"—he reached up to wipe a crumb off her lips, and she forgot how to breathe for a second—"I'm still glad I was there. If I hadn't been . . ."

He didn't finish. But he didn't need to.

And she was glad he'd been there too.

She just wished she could've lived *and* not thrown up all over him.

"Ready for more?" he asked, right around the time her lungs decided to remind her that air was a pretty important thing.

"Yeah," she said, mentally smacking herself to try to get it together.

Seriously, what was it about cute boys that made it so hard to function?

"Probably smart to get the teal one over with next," Elwin suggested.

Fitz held up the vial in question, squinting at the ocean-colored liquid as it sloshed around the tiny bottle. "Hmm. Hopefully this doesn't ruin your favorite color for you."

"It won't." She ordered herself not to meet his eyes. The last thing she needed was him guessing *why* the color was her favorite.

But she couldn't help a quick glance, and . . .

Breathing became impossible again—which turned out to

be a good thing when he poured the medicine into her mouth and the taste of old broccoli and boiled cabbage hit her hard.

"Here," he said, placing another candy on her tongue. "Better?"

"Kinda."

The second bite did the trick—until Keefe's voice called from the doorway, "Dude, are you guys feeding each other?"

"No—we were just . . ." Sophie stopped when she realized there was no good way to explain the last few minutes.

Keefe clutched his stomach and pretended to hurl all over his Level Six uniform. "Wow. You guys have really out-Fitzphie'd yourselves—and don't even get me started on how close your cots are now. How'd you get Elwin to agree to *that*?"

"Easy," Fitz said. "I stayed up all night, monitoring Sophie's dreams."

"Yeah . . . that doesn't sound creepy at *all*," Keefe told him. He opened his mouth to say something else, then shut it. "Never mind. Elwin said I'm not supposed to tease you."

"We'll see how long *that* lasts," Ro said, shoving her way into the Healing Center. Her eyes scanned Fitz up and down. "So . . . you're awake."

Fitz nodded. "I am."

"And you're okay now?" Keefe asked.

"Mostly," Fitz admitted.

"Good. Because you were out for a pretty long time, and *some* people were starting to worry—I mean, not *me*. I figured you were just playing it up for sympathy, but . . ." He cleared his throat. "Ugh, this is really hard if I can't make fun of you."

Fitz laughed. "That almost makes it worth it."

"Oh, I'll find a way," Keefe promised.

"I'm sure you will," Fitz told him, taking the dark red elixir that Sophie had been struggling to open and unscrewing the lid.

"Looks like things are about to get interesting here in sparkle town," Ro said as Fitz held the vial to Sophie's lips.

"Why's that?" Fitz wondered, blocking Sophie from snatching the vial away.

"Because now you can help me write *The Ballad of Bo and Ro!*" Keefe jumped in. "Did Foster tell you how much they looooooooooooooooooove each other? Step aside, Sandor and Grizel—Bo and Ro are vying for cutest bodyguard couple. And their names rhyme!"

"Keep it up," Ro said, sharpening one of her claws. "I'm going to make you pay for every single joke."

Keefe smirked. "You can try, but . . ."

His words trailed off as Fitz poured the elixir into Sophie's mouth, and she shook her head, wondering if the sour flavor could make the glands near her ears explode.

"Here," Keefe said, pulling a fresh box of Prattles from his cape pocket. "Wash it down with this."

"We're good," Fitz told him, giving Sophie another piece of the snickerdoodle candy.

"Wow," Ro said, elbowing Keefe. "Nothing you want to say about that, Hunkyhair?"

"Nope!" But his smile faded when he noticed Sophie's chain-mail-covered hand.

"Don't worry, Krakie's safe with me," Sophie promised. "So are all his friends." She scooped up the tiny metal animals she'd piled in her lap. "Be glad you weren't around when Elwin cut through the fabric."

"I'm pretty sure I'm going to have nightmares about the ooze," Fitz added.

Keefe reeled toward Elwin. *"You did something oozy without me?"*

"And me?" Ro added.

Elwin laughed. "Don't worry, there'll be *lots* more ooze tomorrow."

"There will?" Sophie whined as Ro stalked forward, poking Elwin in the chest.

"You'd better wait until I'm here," she told him.

"Yeah, what time should we arrive to catch the Great Fitzphie Ooze Fest?" Keefe asked.

"We're not calling it that," Sophie told him.

"Oh, I think we are. And don't worry, Foster," Keefe added, patting her on the head. "I'll still love you when you're oozy. Maybe I should get you a tunic that says *Oozemaster*."

"Please don't," she begged.

He grinned, taking the tray of medicine from her lap and setting it aside. "You can have Fitzy feed you the rest of these when I'm gone—otherwise *I'm* going to puke. Right now, we need to find Krakie a new home."

He grabbed a roll of wide gauze from one of the shelves and wrapped it carefully around her left wrist to form a loose-fitting cuff. Then carefully attached each of the pins.

"Is that a *K*?" Fitz asked, tilting his head to study the new arrangement.

Keefe nodded. "Best letter in the whole alphabet! But don't worry, Foster, this isn't like when Dizznee gave you those bracelets."

"What bracelets?" Fitz asked.

Keefe had the wisdom to look sheepish.

"They were . . . a prototype," Sophie told Fitz. "Dex has been trying to design a gadget to help me control my enhancing, and he needed something to camouflage what they were, so he used some bracelets he'd bought."

Fitz's eyebrows shot up. "*Cloth* bracelets?"

She was pretty sure he already knew the answer. But even if he did, she'd promised Dex she wouldn't tell anyone what had happened between them.

"It doesn't matter," she said quietly. "They . . . didn't work."

"In more ways than one," Keefe said under his breath—but Fitz still must've heard him.

His eyes narrowed. "How do you know so much about it?"

Keefe shrugged. "I'm the reigning president of the Foster Fan Club. It's my job to know these things. But don't worry, Fitzy, you're still the runner-up."

If he'd been standing any closer, Sophie would've smacked him. But he was *just* out of her reach.

"I thought you weren't supposed to be teasing Fitz," Sophie reminded him instead.

"I'm not, but . . . he makes it so *easy*."

Fitz rolled his eyes. "Sometimes I can't remember why we're friends."

"Pretty sure everyone wonders that at some point," Ro pointed out.

Keefe flashed the smuggest of smiles. "It's because I make everything better."

"Like giving Sophie the pendant that helped the Neverseen find her?" Fitz snapped back.

The question was like a record scratch, leaving the room agonizingly silent.

"Sorry," Fitz mumbled, tearing a hand through his hair. "I shouldn't—"

"No, you're right," Keefe interrupted. "And no need for the cyclone of worry you're hitting me with, Foster. I'm done freaking out. In fact, that's why I'm here. Now that Fitz is awake, I thought we could move on from our skill lessons, because I've been thinking about what you said—about how the Neverseen think we're predictable, and how they guess what we're going to do ahead of time and use that against us. That's what my mom's been doing with me every time she mentions my *legacy*. She wants me afraid—that way I won't ask my powerful telepathic friends to dig into my past and find whatever memories she erased. Then she can trigger them on *her* timeline. Maximum manipulation. And I'm over it."

"So what are you saying?" Fitz asked.

"I'm saying . . . if you guys are up for it, I want the full Fitzphie experience! Dig around my head, stare into each other's eyes—whatever you need to do to figure out what Mommy Dearest is hiding from me."

"I'm in," Fitz agreed immediately. "When do you want to start?"

"Hang on," Sophie said, holding up her good hand like a stop sign and waiting for Keefe to look at her. "Let's skip the whole 'are you sure you can handle that' conversation for a second because, uh . . . you realize Fitz and I have no idea how to trigger erased memories, right?"

"You guys can figure it out. I believe in the all-powerful Fitzphie! Actually, you know what? We should call this one Sophitz, since—let's face it—Foster's the real talent when it comes to this kind of thing."

Fitz didn't argue, but Sophie sighed. "Keefe—"

"Hear that, Ro?" he interrupted. "She's giving me her *serious* voice."

"And that pout she does, with the big eyes and the little

crease between her eyebrows," Ro noted. "She's definitely figured out how to use her cuteness against you."

Sophie scowled at both of them, wishing her echoes came with a "no teasing" requirement like Fitz's. "No, I'm just trying to make sure you've thought this through."

"Oh, are we already back to the 'can you handle this' conversation?" Keefe asked, stretching out on the empty cot on Sophie's other side and propping his hands behind his head. "That was fast! And yes, Foster. I *have* thought this through. And I *can* handle it. I know my track record hasn't been great when it comes to this stuff, but—"

"It's been horrible," Sophie corrected.

"Fair enough. But that's because I wasn't ready. Now I am."

"Are you?"

"Uh—the Neverseen just tried to kill my best friend, and . . . you." He rolled onto his side to face her. "Isn't that why you're so eager to start battle training?"

"Right, but—"

"This is *my* fight," he interrupted again, standing up to pace with a twitchy sort of energy. "And the good news is, we can work on this while you guys are still recovering. Isn't that what you wanted, Foster? To use that powerful telepathy as much as you can, in case the Neverseen were trying to stop you?"

She did want that—sort of. She mostly wanted another chance in Alvar's head. But more important . . .

"That's not what I meant," she said, trying to figure out how to make him understand the minefield he wanted to charge full speed into. "You realize if we do this, we're going to have to dig through *all* your memories, right? Remember what happened when I tried to help you in Alluveterre?"

Keefe stopped moving.

"What happened?" Fitz asked.

Sophie shrugged, leaving it up to Keefe to decide whether or not to answer.

He held her gaze for a long second, then spun to face Fitz. "She saw a bunch of stuff from my past that I hadn't been planning to let her see, like the time my parents left me in Atlantis all day because they forgot about me. And the day my dad destroyed one of my sketchbooks to punish me for doodling during my sessions. And the night I wet the bed when I was way too old to be doing something like that. What?" he asked Sophie. "You thought I wouldn't tell him?"

"I wasn't sure," she admitted.

He glanced back at Fitz, who didn't seem to know where to look anymore.

"You're going to see some dark stuff in my past," Keefe warned him. "Both of you are. But . . . it doesn't have to be an issue—as long as you guys agree to one thing: no feeling sorry for me."

"I won't," Fitz promised.

"I *don't*," Sophie added.

Keefe nodded. "Does that mean I passed your little test?"

"It wasn't a test. I just wanted to make sure you're really thinking about what it will be like if we do this."

"I *am*. I know it's going to be rough. But . . . I can deal."

She studied his face, searching for any trace of the scared, broken boy hidden underneath. But all she found was steely determination.

"I can handle it," he promised.

Sophie glanced at Fitz. "What about you? I'm pretty sure some of the stuff we find will make us angry."

Or Keefe would get defensive and take his teasing too far—but bringing that up would only increase the chance of it happening.

"If I made it through that fun little chat with my parents," Fitz told her, "I'm sure I can make it through this. What about you—will it give you nightmares, or will Silveny take care of that?"

"Aw, is Glitter Butt helping you sleep again, Foster?" Keefe jumped in.

"We tested it out last night," Sophie confirmed. "And it was way better than sedatives."

"So *that's* why the Fitzster played creepy dream stalker. I guess that's fair. How's she doing? Still telling everyone I'm her favorite?"

"Still being weirdly stubborn," Sophie corrected. "I'm worried she's hiding something. But I'm hoping I can wear her down."

Keefe laughed. "Sounds like what I'm always saying about you."

"Oh—that was a good one!" Ro said, raising her hand for a high five.

"It was," Sophie had to admit.

"So . . . does that mean Operation: Privacy Invasion is a go?" Keefe asked when the conversation dissolved into silence.

"I don't know—you're still assuming Fitz and I will be able to figure out how to trigger the memories."

"True. But, I mean . . . it's you guys. I know I make a lot of Fitzphie jokes—but that doesn't mean I don't get the hype. I was there when you snuck past Forkle's blocking. Shoot—I watched you guys slip into Dimitar's head and find out all that stuff about the cure for the plague."

"I still can't believe you were able to breach my father's mind," Ro muttered. "Or that he let you live."

"He didn't *let* us live," Fitz argued. "We—"

He stopped himself, like he'd realized it probably wasn't the best idea to remind Ro about their dramatic escape, given the death and destruction they'd left in their wake. There'd been bigger, darker forces at play that day—and Ro seemed to understand that. But it was still the kind of subject that needed to be handled *delicately*.

"I'll let that go," Ro told him, "if you tell me what it was like in my father's head."

Fitz let out a relieved breath. "Fluffy."

"Like sinking into a giant marshmallow covered in feathers," Sophie agreed.

Ro choked on her laugh. "Okay, I need to figure out how to blackmail him with that."

"Maybe you can get him to reassign Bo," Sophie suggested.

"Yeah, that's never going to happen. Once my father gets an idea in his head, he can't let it go."

"What kind of idea?" Keefe asked. "The kind that involves smooching and weddings and little baby prince and princess BoRos?"

"Dude, she is seriously going to stab you," Fitz warned.

"No, I'm thinking I'll tunnel us deep underground and leave him in a dark little hole for a few days," Ro corrected. "Just him and some of my favorite bacteria."

"Sounds like the *perfect* place to add more verses to *The Ballad of Bo and Ro*," Keefe noted.

"He really doesn't know when to quit, does he?" Ro asked Sophie.

"I'm pretty sure it's a disease," Fitz told her.

"Coping mechanism," Keefe argued. "Which you'd already know if you'd agree to Operation: Privacy Invasion."

"I already said I'm in," Fitz reminded him.

All eyes turned to Sophie—and she could think of a hundred ways this could go very, very wrong.

But Keefe's eyes held the same plea that Fitz's had when he'd begged her to let him monitor her dreams—the same desperation hers surely showed when she'd asked Keefe to give her skill lessons.

"I guess we can try."

"WOO-HOO!" Keefe clapped his hands together, rubbing his palms back and forth. "So how do you want to do this? Should I sit between you guys, so it's like a Sophitz sandwich? Or will that make it too hard for all the staring into each other's eyes?"

"You want to start now?" Sophie asked.

"Why not? You're awake. The Fitzster's awake. I'm ready for a huge pile of humiliation. What more do we need?"

"Uh, a plan?"

"Eh. You guys are best when you make it up as you go along."

"We kind of are," Fitz agreed.

"See? This is why you're my best friend! Let's do this!"

"Not today," Magnate Leto informed them as he marched into the Healing Center.

Keefe heaved a huge sigh. "Do adults have some sort of sixth sense that tells them when they should show up and stop us from doing something that's actually productive?"

"No, but we *do* know when reckless decisions are being made—and I'm not saying that what I just overheard isn't a potentially valuable course of action," Magnate Leto told him. "But triggering memories is not a process that should be taken lightly—and it's *definitely* not a process that two relatively untrained Telepaths who are still battling the unknown effects of shadowflux echoes should embark upon without consulting a Mentor. I'm going to insist that you speak with Sir Tiergan before you attempt this—and since I'm well aware of how limited your patience is, I'll make sure he pays the Healing Center a visit tomorrow."

And I'd like to weigh in as well, he transmitted to Sophie. *But we can discuss that later.*

Out loud, he added, "In the meantime, I need you to return to your session, Mr. Sencen. I realize elvin history isn't your favorite subject, but it's crucial that you attend, both for a better understanding of our world, and to prove you're committed to your education."

Keefe snorted. "We all know *that's* not true."

Magnate Leto ignored him. "I've spoken to Lady Sanja, and she'll have an exam ready for you when you arrive, covering the lectures you've missed recently."

"Please, like I need to be tested." Keefe tapped the side of his head. "I skimmed through the reading material on the first day. Photographic memories are so handy that way."

"I'm glad to hear it. But it won't help you with the notes I expect you to take during the lecture Lady Sanja will give once you've completed the exam. I'll be checking them in this afternoon's study hall."

"Aw, come on, Leto," Ro whined. "I can't take another speech on how the world would be lost if you guys hadn't started bossing everyone around. I swear, for such a scrawny species, your egos are out of control!"

"Nonetheless," Magnate Leto said, reaching up to rub his temples, "elvin history is an important segment of Mr. Sencen's education. And his recent lack of attendance has drawn the notice of his father, who hailed me today to discuss his son's absence records."

"You're going to let him bully you?" Keefe asked.

"I'd rather him bully me than bully you," Magnate Leto said gently.

"I can handle him—"

"I'm sure you can. But I'd prefer you didn't have to. Especially since—in this instance—he's not completely wrong. I realize that traditional learning is not your favorite pastime. But being a Foxfire prodigy is not only an honor—it's an advantage. One that not everyone receives. Even fewer are accepted to the elite levels, which you'll be tested for at the end of the year."

"Aaaaaaaaaaaaaaaaaaand that's what this is really about. Father of the Year is worried I'm going to embarrass him by not being accepted, so now he's got you hassling me—"

"Quite the contrary. My involvement stems entirely from my desire to see you succeed. You would be a valuable asset to the nobility *if* you could learn to exercise a modicum of discipline—"

"Not exactly the best sales pitch," Keefe interrupted.

"Perhaps not. But deny it all you want—we both know you care about our world's future. Why else would you spend so much time helping Miss Foster's causes?"

"Uh . . . you've seen how cute she is, right?" Keefe asked.

Sophie flung a pillow at his head.

Or, she tried to.

Throwing with her left arm was much harder than she'd expected, and . . .

She ended up nailing Magnate Leto in the face.

Keefe doubled over, clutching his sides and gasping between choking laughs: "THAT . . . WAS . . . THE . . . GREATEST . . . THING . . . I'VE . . . EVER . . . SEEN!"

"IT WAS!" Ro agreed, nearly collapsing to the floor in a fit of giggles.

Fitz and Elwin were cracking up too—though they at least *tried* to cover it with coughs.

Sophie slunk down under her covers. "Sorry."

"It's all right, Miss Foster," Magnate Leto said, handing her back her pillow. "It's good to see you regaining some strength."

Keefe wiped the tears streaming down his cheeks. "You realize I'm going to call you Principal Pillowhead from now on, right?"

Magnate Leto's smile was equal parts rueful and patient. "I'm sure you will. But getting back to our *important* conversation. I want to make sure you're keeping in mind that Level Six is a turning point year. I'd hate to see you damage your future because of the Neverseen."

"Is Fitz damaging *his* future by being here?" Keefe countered. "Or Foster?"

"They have no choice. They'll also have an extensive amount of makeup work to tackle during the midterm break—and no, that option is not available to you, so don't ask and don't test my patience. I can become *very* creative with my punishments if you force me to."

"See, but now you've got me curious," Keefe told him.

"Uh-uh," Ro jumped in. "*I* have to suffer through this stuff with you."

"You do," Magnate Leto agreed. "And I found an entire room filled with recordings of speeches from the Ancient Councillors that I think you'll find particularly enjoyable."

Ro grabbed Keefe's arm and hauled him toward the door. "We're going to your session, and you're acing that test and taking lots of notes or I will hang a banner in the middle of this campus—and we both know what I will have that banner say!"

"Bo and Ro 4 Eva?" Keefe guessed, because he clearly had a death wish.

"That's it!" Ro picked him up, hefting him over her shoulder and trudging toward the door. "We'll be back after study hall."

"You'll be back *tomorrow*," Magnate Leto corrected. "Lord Cassius is expecting you both to be home immediately after school—and I wouldn't recommend disobeying."

"Why not?" Sophie asked.

"He was in . . . a mood."

"Goody! Raise your hand if you're jealous of my life!" Keefe said, twisting in Ro's grasp to survey the room. "No takers?"

"Don't worry," Ro told him, patting his back as she carried him into the hall. "I'll sneak your dad some amoebas tonight."

"I guess I'd better make up a batch of my strongest stomach

remedy," Elwin said as the Healing Center's doors slammed shut behind them.

"Are you sure it's safe to let Keefe go home?" Sophie asked Magnate Leto.

"Of course. Lord Cassius and I have had many lengthy discussions recently about ways to *properly* motivate his son. He sounded desperate enough to actually try some of them."

"Then why do you look so worried?" She pointed to his forehead, where deep creases were pressed into his skin.

"I'm not worried. I'm . . . vacillating."

"On what?"

"On how to advise you on an unexpected development."

"Is it with my brother?" Fitz asked, sitting up straighter.

"No. As far as I know, there's been no news in that regard." He moved to pace, his steps heavier than they should be—as if his body was used to bearing the extra weight he carried when he was Mr. Forkle. "First, I want you to promise me that you will not make this decision hastily. In fact, I don't want to hear any sort of answer until tomorrow—at minimum. Take the night to think about it, regardless of whether or not you feel you've made up your minds—and make sure you're being *very* honest with yourselves about your limitations."

He waited for them to agree, giving Sophie a chance to come up with a long list of theories.

But she definitely did not expect him to say, "Fintan has demanded a meeting."

EIGHTEEN

ITH BOTH OF US?" FITZ asked, his brain processing the news way faster than Sophie's.

She was too stuck on the irony.

After weeks of her begging for a meeting, Fintan was dropping one in her lap right when she'd decided that talking to him would waste time and mess with her head—not to mention the fact that she was currently stuck on bed rest.

"Yes," Magnate Leto told him. "In fact, he requested each of you by name. He also asked that you come alone—but *that* won't happen. Given the attack, and the possibility that the Neverseen still have a means of tracking you, there's no way you're going anywhere near Fintan without your bodyguards.

The Council *is* hoping that Sandor would be willing to exclude the other members of your security detail to keep things simpler. But we'll figure that out if you decide to commit to the meeting."

"Why wouldn't we?" Fitz asked, glancing at Sophie.

But her mind was focused on a different question: "Why now?"

"That was my first thought as well," Magnate Leto told her. "And sadly, the answer is: We don't know."

"Do you think it has something to do with the attack?" she wondered.

"I asked the Council the same thing. Apparently he's made no mention of it. And, I'm honestly not sure how he would know. His only contact is with his guards—and none of them have been told that the attack occurred."

"Unless the Neverseen planned the attack before Fintan was arrested," Sophie reminded him.

If they really had targeted her and Fitz because of their telepathy, the Neverseen could've been planning the assault from the moment they put Alvar in that cell.

"I could totally see them doing that," Fitz agreed.

"So could I," Elwin added. "Sorry, should I not have been listening?"

"If I didn't want you to hear us, I would've asked you to leave," Magnate Leto assured him. "You've already proven yourself more than trustworthy with my secrets."

Elwin grinned. "*So* many things make sense now."

"Wait—does that mean Elwin knows . . . ?" Sophie asked, stopping there in case she was wrong.

But Magnate Leto nodded. "Given my need to remain in this form while you're here, I decided it was time to clue him in to one of the other roles I play."

"There's more than one?" Elwin asked. "How do you keep it all straight?"

"Not as well as I used to." The catch in his voice broke Sophie's heart.

She wanted to ask how he was handling all the challenges and grief that came with losing his twin. But it sounded like Elwin didn't know that detail. And honestly, that was the kind of question that had no real answer.

"But getting back to what we were discussing," Magnate Leto said, clearing the thickness from his throat. "I think it's important to remember that while the attack feels fresh to us because of your current condition, it has also been more than two weeks since it happened. So there may be no connection. Fintan could simply be growing tired of his confinement and hoping to strike a new bargain."

Fitz's eyes narrowed. "Or he's done the math. He knows how long it's been since he gave the Council the antidote to soporidine, and I'm sure he figured we'd give some to my brother. He also knows how long it takes the Council to sentence someone—and I bet he could guess that Alvar would be sent back to Everglen. So this meeting could be the next step in whatever they're planning with my brother."

"Also a viable theory," Magnate Leto admitted. "But the Council said he hasn't asked his guard about Alvar even once."

"All that means is, he's good at keeping his secrets," Fitz argued.

"We could keep guessing like this all day," Sophie said quietly. "The only way to know what Fintan *actually* wants is to talk to him."

"Yes," Magnate Leto agreed. "But the question you must ask yourself is: Do you *care* what he has to say? I know you've now begun to question whether this kind of meeting will offer any actual value—and I think that's an important instinct. That's why I want you to take the night and think about this before you make your decision."

"Sounds like you don't think we should do it," Sophie noted.

"I'm of two minds on the matter. The security where he's being kept is incredibly effective, so there's little physical risk. But Fintan has a gift for games—and both of you are especially vulnerable, given your past experiences with him, and the toll emotion and nightmares take on the two of you at the moment."

Sophie hated that word.

Vulnerable.

Even if it was true.

"There's still a chance we could learn something important," Fitz argued.

"There is," Magnate Leto agreed. "And that is why I'm of two minds. As were your families when I spoke to them."

"Our parents know?" Sophie was surprised Grady hadn't rushed over and ordered her to stay away from Fintan—or demanded to go with her if she did meet with him.

He must still be away on assignment.

"I hailed them before I came to speak to you," Magnate Leto explained. "Not for their *permission*, since I believe you've earned the right to make this choice without restrictions—but out of respect for the fact that they deserve to know what's going on with their children. And you should know that both of your families are willing to support whatever you choose— provided that you keep them informed and promise not to fight any efforts for your security if you decide to agree to the meeting. The Council has told me essentially the same thing. So this truly comes down to you—though there is also the matter of your recovery to consider."

"I was just going to say," Elwin jumped in, "they won't be physically ready for something like this for at least a couple of weeks."

"I assumed as much," Magnate Leto added. "So take your time. Remember that your primary focus still needs to be on your recovery. And make sure you finish taking your medicine."

He pointed to their trays, which still had *way* more vials than Sophie's stomach wanted.

"And just to be incredibly clear," he added, "in case Mr. Sencen manages to sneak back in later—*please* don't attempt to recover his memories until you speak to Sir Tiergan."

Didn't you say you wanted to weigh in too? Sophie transmitted as he headed for the door.

I do. But my advice is rather brief, since Tiergan will cover all of the specifics. I simply want to make sure that you realize the dynamic between you, Mr. Vacker, and Mr. Sencen is . . . complicated.

What does that mean?

That's up to you to figure out.

"Why did he wink at you before he left?" Fitz asked as soon as Magnate Leto was gone.

"Because adults are annoying," Sophie mumbled, focusing on choking down the rest of her medicine.

Fitz still helped her with the vials, but there was a new kind of silence between them—not an awkward quiet so much as a heavy thoughtfulness.

A mental standoff, as they each waited for the other to plunge into the murky waters of the Fintan conversation.

Fitz dived in first. "So . . . do you *really* think we should pass on the meeting?"

"I don't know. If we agree to it, we're basically telling him he can still boss us around. And the thought of listening to another one of his speeches?" She shoved her empty vials away a little harder than she needed to, enjoying the satisfying clatter. "Plus, he's not going to tell us anything until we agree to do something for him."

"What do you think he'll want?"

"No idea. He's a prisoner, so the obvious ask would be for freedom—but he has to know we're not powerful enough to make that happen."

"So maybe he's after information," Fitz suggested.

"Then why ask for *us*? Why not demand to meet with the Council? Or someone in the Black Swan? Especially since he's made such a point to keep Telepaths away—why demand to meet with two *Cognates*?"

"Yeah, that doesn't make sense. Unless . . ."

He sat up straighter, setting his own empty tray aside. "Do you think it's because we're the ones who healed him? He interrupted you last time so he could escape—what if that left a little bit of damage? Or maybe all the creepy stuff he's done has gotten to him and he wants us to seal some cracks."

"If it is," Sophie whispered, closing her eyes and trying to smother any bad memories before they could wake the monster, "then going to meet with him would be pointless. I'm never healing him again. Not after what he did to Kenric."

"You don't think it'd be worth it for the chance to poke around his head? We're stronger now—"

"Not strong enough, Fitz. Look at how badly we lost to Gethen—and that was before we had echoes to deal with."

"We'd have a few weeks to train," Fitz countered. "And I know we can't do full-on trust exercises. But . . . that doesn't mean we can't work on our connection. There are shades of trust, you know? Maybe we can't get into any bigger secrets right now, but . . . we could dig into some of the small stuff we hold back."

"Like what?"

He stared at his hands, twisting the Cognate rings round and round before he transmitted, *Like all the stuff you tell Keefe and don't tell me.*

She reached for Ella, deciding it was easier to continue this conversation with her face mostly hidden behind blue floppy ears. *I don't—*

Yes, you do.

The words didn't sound angry, but he still took a long, slow breath, like he was fighting to keep his emotions under control when he added, *You both tell each other stuff you don't tell anybody else. It's, like . . . a thing.*

A thing, Sophie repeated—hearing Magnate Leto's voice in her head.

Complicated, he'd said.

But it *wasn't* complicated.

I tell Keefe that stuff because it's been the only way to get him to open up to me, she explained. *He's super secretive.*

He's not the only one.

The accusation was impossible to miss. But . . . he wasn't wrong.

I've had to keep secrets my whole life, she reminded him. *It's a hard habit to break.*

I get that. But if you can tell Keefe, why can't you tell me?

I never said I can't, she argued.

Maybe not. But you don't.

Sophie sighed. *I really don't tell him as much as you're thinking I do.*

Uh, I can think of a bunch of stuff that he knows.

Like what? she found herself asking again—and regretted it long before he said, *He knows about the bracelets Dex gave you.*

She reached up, tugging on an itchy eyelash. *That's . . . different. Keefe guessed most of the story on his own, and I couldn't deny it because Empaths are annoyingly impossible to lie to.*

Telepaths are supposed to be the same way. Especially your Cognate.

But I'm not lying to you. I'm just . . . trying to keep my promise to Dex. He didn't want me telling anyone what happened.

So if I guessed, you'd tell me?

I don't know. It doesn't seem right to betray Dex after he saved our lives.

True, he thought, fidgeting with his Cognate rings again, sliding them halfway off and then shoving them back down. *I guess you're right. I just . . . hate that it's a secret between us— and not because I want the gossip. It damages our connection, you know? And especially now, with all the limits we're trying to work around, thanks to the echoes, it's just . . . a drag that there has to be one more thing.*

She wanted him to be wrong.

Wanted to argue that it shouldn't—didn't—matter.

But like he'd said, there were shades of trust—and her Cognate should probably hold all the brightest, clearest spaces.

So she squeezed Ella tighter, trying to find some sort of line she could walk between all of her loyalties.

What if, she thought slowly, *I told you I'm pretty sure you already guessed most of what happened? Would that be enough?*

It . . . might be.

His mind blinked to an image: two periwinkle cloth bracelets stitched with the words *Sophie Foster + Dex Dizznee.*

He'd guessed the color wrong, but . . .

Yeah.

The thought was softer than a whisper, but the way Fitz sucked in a breath made it clear he'd heard her—and she didn't dare glance over to see whatever expression was on his face.

Instead, she forced herself to add, *The fact that I'm not wearing them should tell you the rest.*

She could almost hear the pieces click into place.

Okay, he transmitted slowly, *I have one more question, and then I swear I'll drop it forever.*

Forever? Sophie verified, really, really, really, really hoping the question wouldn't have anything to do with kissing.

Forever, he agreed, his mind shuffling through hundreds of words she couldn't catch until he settled on, *So, the reason you're not wearing the cuffs—is that because they're a matchmaking thing and you're still deciding if you're okay with that? Or is it . . . a different reason?*

Gah, that was almost worse than the kissing question.

But she'd promised to answer, so she closed her eyes and transmitted, *Dex is awesome, but . . . he's just a friend. And I think he actually agreed with me about that by the time we were done with everything. It was still messy for a while, but it seems like we're past that now—so PLEASE don't tell him you know. It'd make everything awkward again and—*

I won't, he promised. *You can trust me.*

I know. I DO trust you, Fitz. It's just . . . this kind of stuff is so extra complicated, you know?

It is, he agreed. *I'm pretty sure that's why the Council came up with matchmaking.*

She snorted a laugh. *Right, because matchmaking's not complicated at all. It's not super messy having strangers give you a list of people you're allowed to marry. Nope.*

Fitz looked away. *Sounds like you're leaning toward not registering. . . .*

I'm not leaning toward anything, she promised. *I seriously have no idea what to do.*

She couldn't deny that a small part of her desperately wanted to find out who would end up on her match lists—the same part that had a feeling the Winnowing Galas would be . . . kind of amazing. She was sure they'd be awkward and embarrassing, too, but . . . it'd be like going to prom—only a million times prettier and cooler and fancier because that's how the elves rolled.

But at the same time, the whole matchmaking process sounded so . . . unnatural.

She understood why the elves had created the system, given that their indefinite life span and ageless appearance made the chance of distant relatives accidentally ending up together a really gross possibility. And they were also trying to match people on a genetic level, so that their kids would have the best shot at manifesting powerful abilities, and so the elvin gene pool would be as strong and diverse as possible.

But none of that was very romantic, and she *really* didn't like the idea of having that part of her life controlled. And sometimes the process was super unfair. Dex and his siblings had been looked down on their whole lives because their dad was Talentless, and that made him a bad match. And Brant had joined the Neverseen because he and Jolie were a bad match too, since pyrokinesis was forbidden.

You're overthinking it, Fitz told her, and her heart jumped into her throat as she realized he'd probably overheard that entire mental monologue. *But I get it—it's a big decision.*

It IS, Sophie agreed. *I'm super glad I'm only a Level Four and have another year before I have to deal with it.*

Yeah . . .

What? she asked, because it hadn't been an "I'm agreeing with you" kind of "yeah."

It was the kind of "yeah" that usually got followed with something like "So, funny story . . ."

It's nothing, Fitz told her.

But it was definitely something. *Weren't you the one who was just getting on me for holding little things back?*

Fitz sighed, reaching up to run a hand through his hair.

Okay—don't freak out, he said, which of course had her freaking out even before he added, *but . . . matchmaking technically goes by age. You have to be fifteen in order to pick up your packet, sixteen to turn it in, and seventeen to get your first list. And since those ages kinda match the Levels at Foxfire, it became a tradition to say, "Register after the Level Five midterms, turn the packet in at the end of the year, and get your first list at the end of Level Six." But it doesn't have to be that way. Once you turn fifteen . . .*

He didn't finish the sentence—but he didn't have to.

Just like he didn't have to remind her that *she* was fifteen.

So . . . she could register *now.*

I thought elves didn't pay attention to age, Sophie argued, grasping for any loophole that would save her from what Fitz was saying.

But it was also a valid point. Ever since she'd moved to the Lost Cities, Sophie had been struggling to keep track of exactly how old she—or anyone else—was. The elves didn't acknowledge birthdays, counting age by something they called their "inception date" instead—but then they barely paid attention to that. No one ever mentioned when they turned a year older, and half the time it seemed like they weren't even sure how old they were—especially the Ancients.

The system had felt strange at first. But Sophie had grown to understand why the elves didn't feel the need to mark every year when they were going to live for *thousands* of them.

The match is different, Fitz explained. *They want us to have our lists as early as possible, so we have lots of time to consider everyone on them—and probably so we don't get too attached to anyone before we know who we're matched with. But also not so young that we haven't manifested our abilities, since that's one of the big deciding factors.*

Sophie was pretty sure her human parents would've told her that the ages Fitz was talking about were still *way* too young for dating of any kind—much less *matchmaking*. Actually, they'd probably have a *lot* to say about the whole system.

But . . . she wasn't living with humans anymore.

She was an elf in the Lost Cities.

She was supposed to be doing things *their* way.

And, for better or worse, the elvin way involved matchmaking—which she qualified for *right now*.

But you said I had time to think about it, she reminded him. *When we were sitting under Calla's Panakes tree.*

She remembered that conversation *very* clearly, mostly because it was the same conversation where he'd told her he was hoping she'd decide to register. And even though there was a decent chance he'd only said that part because he was trying to protect her from all the problems she'd face if she ended up in a bad match, her silly, hopeful brain sometimes liked to imagine there'd been another reason.

You do have time, he told her. *Fifteen's the minimum age, but there's no maximum. It's not like I went the first day I was old enough or anything.*

Yeah. True.

Fitz smiled. *Do you realize you look like a cornered gremlin whenever you have to talk about this?*

Gee, thanks.

What? Gremlins are cute.

She tuned out the part of her brain that was suddenly wondering if Fitz had just called her cute and tried to find something to make him understand where she was coming from. *I know matchmaking's normal for you,* she tried. *It's just . . . not for me.*

I know. And I would NEVER want you to think I'm trying to pressure you. I just don't want you to make it a bigger deal than it is and end up with all kinds of stress and drama for no reason. I mean, even if you register, you haven't committed to anything. You could choose to never pick up any of your lists—or you could pick them up and choose to ignore them.

I guess. But . . . won't I show up on other people's lists—even if I don't get mine?

Yeah, but it's not like you'd be obligated to date anyone.

No, but it'd be super strange knowing there are people out there being told we'd make a good match.

Well . . . what if you liked some of them, though? Wouldn't that end up being a good thing?

YES! the silly, hopeful part of her brain wanted to scream. But she forced that part to be quiet.

All the match lists mean is we're genetically compatible, right? she asked.

Nope. Genetics are the starting point. But you'll see when you pick up your match packet—well . . . IF you pick it up—the questions make you think about things you never would've thought about before. It's hard to explain until you work through it, but it's actually pretty brilliant. You should at least pick up your packet and read the questions. You don't have to turn it in.

Sophie sighed. *Maybe. It's just . . . every time I think about doing that, I think about the people the system's hurt.*

It's definitely not perfect, Fitz agreed. *But . . . that doesn't mean it's ALL bad.*

I know.

The smart thing would've been to stop there—back far, far away from the dangerous territory they'd wandered into.

But Sophie must not have been feeling very smart.

What would you do if you didn't like any of your matches? she asked, blurting out the words in a messy burst.

Fitz shifted his weight. *I have no idea. I mean . . . being a bad match is a mess for anyone. But for a Vacker?*

Has anyone in your family ever—

Nope. Some have never gotten married—but that's different. If I ended up in a bad match, it'd be this huge thing that EVERYONE would talk about. I'd never, ever stop hearing about it. My parents and sister would never, ever stop hearing about it. And . . . I don't know if I could handle that.

She couldn't fault him for not wanting to live through that kind of drama.

But he'd also shone a big, glaring spotlight on something she hadn't let herself think about. She'd been so worried about confessing her crush and wondering whether or not he might ever like her that way that she'd never realized . . .

Even if he *did*, it might not matter.

Not if her name wasn't on one of his match lists.

NINETEEN

KAY," SOPHIE SAID, CLOSING HER
eyes and taking a second to shove all
matchmaking-related worries into another
mental box marked *Deal with Much, Much,
Much, Much, Much Later*. "Somehow we got sidetracked.
We're supposed to be figuring out what to do about meeting
with Fintan."

"Right," Fitz agreed, sitting up straighter. "So . . . maybe we
should test where we're at. We could count to three and each
say which way we're leaning. See if it syncs up."

"Worth a shot," she said, even though she was pretty sure
she knew exactly how that was going to go.

Sure enough, when they got to "three," Fitz said, "I think we have to do it," at the same time she said, "I'm worried it's not worth the risk."

Fitz blew out a breath. "Well, *that* didn't help."

"I know," she agreed, half wondering if they'd be better off leaving it up to rock, paper, scissors. But they probably needed to put a *little* more thought into it than that.

"Maybe we should try a speed round," she suggested, "and each give *one* sentence about why we think we should or shouldn't meet with Fintan."

"All right," Fitz said, brushing his hair off his forehead. "I . . . want to find out if he knows anything about what's going on with my brother."

"And I'm worried he'll only tell us things that mess with our heads—or our echoes," she told him.

Fitz nodded slowly. "So . . . how does that help us figure this out?"

Sophie wasn't sure.

"Well . . . I guess it shows we're coming at this from different places," she realized after a few seconds. "You have an agenda. And I'm . . . afraid."

"Is one better or worse?" Fitz asked.

"I don't know. Trying to get anything from the Neverseen usually leads to disappointment. But . . . fear's a terrible reason to decide anything. It's like letting them win without even making them earn it."

"Okay, so, where does that leave us?"

"Between a rock and a hard place," Sophie grumbled. "But . . . if there's no obvious right choice, maybe it's better to go with the option that at least *tries*."

"Meaning . . . we meet with Fintan?" Fitz verified.

"As long as we do everything we can to prepare for whatever head games he's going to play, yeah. We can't let him set us back any more than Umber's attacks already have."

Fitz nodded. "Does that mean we've decided?"

"I think so."

"Should we hail Magnate Leto, then?" he asked, a hint of excitement leaking into the words. Sophie was sure Fitz's brain was already imagining how the meeting would go—all the questions they'd ask and all the things they'd learn.

"He said to wait until morning," Sophie reminded Fitz, bracing for a long day of stressing and second-guessing—and an even longer night.

But Silveny broke the worry cycle when she reached out a few hours later.

The motherly alicorn insisted on sorting through Sophie's recent memories, catching every single one of the doubts and worries that Sophie was trying to bury. And instead of the usual flying dreams, she filled Sophie's head with images of them galloping through the white-capped rapids of a surging river— cold water crashing into them. The currents tried to drag them under, but they kept their legs moving, kept their heads above the surface because they were stronger and faster and more powerful than anything the river could throw at them.

For a sparkly winged horse, Silveny gave a pretty awesome pep talk.

And when Fitz held up his Imparter the next morning and asked, "Should we tell Magnate Leto?" she didn't hesitate to agree.

Magnate Leto took the news better than she'd expected. No lecture. No questions. No noticeable reaction, really. He'd simply nodded and told them, "I'll let the Council know to start making arrangements," before his image flashed away.

"Arrangements for what?" Keefe asked, striding through the doors to the Healing Center.

"And please tell me it involves extra ooze!" Ro added.

Fitz groaned. "I forgot about the next Ooze Fest."

Ro grinned. "Good thing we didn't!"

"But getting back to my question," Keefe said, stopping at the foot of their cots and putting his hands on his hips. He studied both of them for a beat before his eyes settled on Sophie. "What arrangements is Leto making—and why does the Fitzster look way more excited about it than you do?"

She wasn't sure if they were allowed to tell him—but it was so much easier than arguing.

He took the news about as well as she'd expected.

"You're wasting your time," he warned.

"Maybe," Fitz said. "But if your mom was demanding a meeting, would you turn her down?"

"Of course not! But you're kinda scraping bottom if you're using *me* as the model of good decisions. Especially decisions concerning my parents."

"That's right—how'd it go with your dad yesterday?" Sophie asked.

"Pitiful attempt at a subject change, Foster. Tell me more about this Fintan meeting. I take it you guys are planning on going all Mega-Cognate on him?"

"Yes, but we're going to be smart about it," Sophie promised. "Now back to your dad. What did he want yesterday?"

Keefe shrugged. "Oh, you know, typical father-son bonding time."

"Which means?" Sophie pushed.

He ran a hand through his hair, messing up the style a little. "He thinks my empathy Mentor isn't pushing me hard enough. So he wants me to start training with *him*—because nothing says 'good idea' like combining me, my dad, and a bunch of emotion exercises. What could possibly go wrong?"

"Uh, you told him no, right?" Sophie asked.

"Not this time." His eyes dropped to his feet and his shoulders curved slightly inward—which happened sometimes when he was dealing with his dad. All the fight and energy drained out of him, leaving a muted Keefe shell. "No need to fling so many worries at me, Foster," he said.

"Then tell me how he's forcing you to do this," she countered.

He shrugged, raising one defiant eyebrow as he glanced

up to face her. "You're looking at it the wrong way. My dad *sooooooooo* hasn't thought this one through. Do you have any idea how miserable I can make him?"

"Probably about as miserable as he can make you," Sophie noted.

"Nah—he also has me," Ro jumped in. "And *I* have parasites."

"Speaking of which," Elwin said, clattering into the room carrying the silver basin they'd been using for their skill lessons and a tray of colorful balms, "I'm surprised Lord Cassius hasn't hailed me about another round of stomach issues. Does that mean you decided to go easy on him?"

Ro batted her eyelashes. "Give it a few more hours."

Elwin grimaced. "Are you going to at least tell me what you gave him this time?"

"Now, where would the fun be in that?" Ro asked. "Besides, it's good training! The traitors who defected from my father might use this stuff against you someday. Better learn how to recognize it."

"Unfortunately, I suppose that's true," Elwin said, setting the basin on the floor between Sophie's and Fitz's cots.

"Is it ooze time, is it ooze time, is it ooze time?" Ro asked, bouncing on the balls of her feet and clapping her hands.

Elwin nodded, turning to Fitz and Sophie. "Who wants to go first?"

"Foster volunteers!" Keefe said, with a smirk that *so* deserved a pillow to the head.

"You good with that?" Elwin asked her.

"Wouldn't you rather do it *not* knowing what's about to happen?" Keefe added—which was an excellent point.

Sophie shot Fitz an apologetic glance as she told Elwin, "Yep, I'll go."

Elwin set the tray of balms in her lap. "I'd recommend plugging your noses," he told all of them as he lifted her bad arm and held it over the basin.

"Psh, I want to bask in this!" Ro sucked in a long breath as Elwin untied the bands securing Sophie's chain mail and unleashed a plume of something Sophie could only describe as weaponized morning breath.

The strips of bandage underneath had gone from white to brownish yellow, and they made a horrible squish as Elwin slowly cut through them with narrow scissors.

"Here we go!" Ro said, clapping as Elwin pulled the cocoon apart and . . .

Keefe coughed. "Okay. That might even be too gross for me."

Sophie couldn't decide which was worse: the way the ooze fizzled and foamed the second it hit the air, or the way it clung to her skin, dangling off her arm in long snotty threads instead of dripping into the basin.

"Any chance I can get a bottle of that stuff?" Keefe asked. "I think my dad really needs to smell it."

"Nope. This is all going to Livvy," Elwin told him.

"Uh, if she's going to use it for an elixir, I'm never taking one of her medicines ever again," Fitz jumped in.

"Me neither!" Sophie agreed.

Elwin laughed. "It's only for tests. She wants to study how the shadowflux affected your cells. And let's see . . ."

He used a tiny squeegeelike device to swipe the slime into the basin in long, gloopy strips. Her skin was pink and shriveled underneath—like when she soaked in a hot bath for too long. And her fingers were *finally* the size they were supposed to be.

"I told you your hand would be almost back to normal," Elwin said as Sophie gently touched each of her knuckles, grateful to feel solid bone in all the places that had collapsed during the attack.

"What about the numbness?" she asked.

"That's where the 'almost' comes in," Elwin admitted. "It's going to take me at least a couple more days to fix all the nerve damage. And it'll be even longer before you get back your strength. Can you try moving your fingers for me? Go one at a time, like this."

He showed her the back and forth motion he wanted, and Sophie tried to copy him. But halfway through, her arm was shaking and she was breathing like she'd just run a marathon.

"I know this probably doesn't seem very encouraging," he said when she had to admit that she couldn't finish, "but this is exactly how it's supposed to be. Your hand is mostly new right now—new bone, new muscle, new flesh. So you're going to have to teach it how to work again. Fitz is going to face a similar struggle with his leg."

"I am?" Fitz asked.

Elwin nodded. "I'm sure you're going to need crutches for a week or two. Don't let it freak you out. We'll get you there, okay? Both of you."

He smeared a poultice over Sophie's arm that looked like regurgitated spinach and wrapped it in a layer of gauze. Then they got to endure the ooze all over again—much to Ro's delight—as he repeated the process with Fitz's leg. Fitz's ribs also got a bandage change, along with a thick layer of bright orange balm that smelled very, *very* fermented. And for the finale, they each got trays filled with dozens of elixirs.

Sophie wasn't sure how she'd find the will to choke them down—until Elwin told her, "This next round should get you out of those cots. I'm betting by tomorrow night you'll be able to move around a little. And if all goes to plan, you should be able to leap home in two to three days."

"Glad to hear it," a familiar voice said behind them, and they all turned to find Sir Tiergan watching them from the doorway, shaking his pale blond hair out of his deep blue eyes.

"That's right," Elwin said. "I forgot Magnate Leto said you'd be stopping by this morning. Don't worry, we're almost done."

"You just missed the Fitzphie Ooze Fest," Keefe informed him.

Tiergan stole a glance at the slime-filled basin, and his olive-toned skin took on a greenish tinge. "That explains the smell."

"Yeah, sorry about that," Elwin told him. "I'll take care of it as soon as I get this packed up."

Tiergan looked like he wished he'd arrived ten minutes later—or had waited in the hall—as Sophie and Fitz gagged their way through their medicine and Elwin wrapped up all the foamy ooze.

"So, what brings you to our smelly little corner of the school?" Sophie asked when she'd finished her last elixir.

"That hurts, Foster," Keefe jumped in. "Have you already forgotten about Operation: Privacy Invasion?"

She had, actually. And a different kind of queasiness settled in.

"Do you really think we'll be able to trigger Keefe's erased memories?" she asked Tiergan.

"Ordinarily, I'd be skeptical," he said, smoothing the edges of his simple gray cloak. "But you've always had a gift for making the impossible possible, so I guess we'll find out— assuming you're still up for it."

"We are," Keefe said, glancing at Fitz and Sophie. "Right?"

"I'm in," Fitz immediately agreed.

"I can handle it," Keefe promised yet again when Sophie hesitated.

She had a horrible feeling he couldn't. But she still asked Tiergan, "Okay, how do we do this?"

TWENTY

THE FIRST STEP," TIERGAN SAID, turning to Keefe, "is that I need you to prom- ise me you'll stop after every breakthrough, no matter how insignificant that breakthrough may be, and give your mind time to adjust—and I'm not talk- ing about emotional adjustment. You're going to need time for that as well, but I'm speaking from a much more practical standpoint. Everything you learn will cause mental ripples as your mind makes space to fit the new information in among everything else. So you need time to let any revelations settle, and let your brain work through the small ramifications of each new memory—not just for your sanity, but because it may lead to further discovery."

"And you two," Elwin jumped in, "need to be careful. I know I don't need to remind you about the echoes—but keep in mind how close you both are to being able to go home, and remember that pushing too hard could set you back."

"This is a gradual process," Tiergan told them. "Even if you were at the peak of your strength, there's no way you're going to uncover everything you're looking for in one go. So plan on pacing yourselves. The most effective way to search memories is by sifting, not digging, so subtlety should be the theme of your approach."

"Okay, are we done with all the 'be careful' speeches?" Keefe asked. "Because I don't know about you guys, but I'm super ready for some heart-crushing humiliation. And for lots of Fitzphie eye staring."

"I'm still not sure what Fitzphie is supposed to mean," Tiergan said, "and I don't want to know," he added when Ro opened her mouth to tell him. "But there's no need for this process to be embarrassing. You can mask any memories you don't want anyone seeing."

"Won't that kind of mess with the whole 'finding my mom's dirty secrets' process?" Keefe asked.

"Why would it?" Tiergan countered. "You're searching for things you *don't* remember—not things you *do*. And the memories will still be there either way. You'll just be flagging them, so to speak, marking them to make it clear you'd prefer they stay away."

"So . . . it's kind of like putting a big sign on anything super embarrassing that says, *HEY GUYS—OVER HERE, BUT ALSO DON'T LOOK, OKAY?*" Keefe clarified.

Tiergan sighed. "I suppose that's one way of looking at it. Yes, it does require any Telepaths to respect the boundary you've set. But since Sophie and Fitz are your friends, I'm assuming they won't have a problem respecting your boundaries."

"Of course not," Sophie promised.

Fitz shrugged. "Pretty sure I'm better off not knowing what you're hiding."

Keefe smirked. "Yeah . . . probably. But is this going to be some huge process that requires weeks of practice and reading boring books and—"

"It's a simple visualization exercise," Tiergan interrupted. "It should only take a few minutes, and it'll hold for at least a couple of days."

"Then what happens?" Fitz asked.

"Then the masking fades, the same way time always dulls our memories. But by then I'll have showed him how to do it, and he can prepare his mind anytime he wants."

"Question," Ro said. "Does this mean I'm going to have to stand here while you stare at each other and do boring elf-y mind things? Because I'm already kind of maxed out, just from this conversation."

Elwin laughed. "How about instead you leave them to work

and help me make the serum Sophie will soak her arm in tomorrow? It has pooka pus."

"Now we're talking!" Ro said.

Sophie scowled. "I swear, I'm starting to hate elvin medicine almost as much as human medicine."

"Well, I'm loving it," Ro told her, hooking her arm through Elwin's and leading him toward his office. "Bring on the pus!"

"On *that* note," Tiergan said, turning to Keefe, "ready to learn how to mask your memories?"

"Bring it on." But he flinched as Tiergan reached for his temples. "Right. Sorry. I always forget how grabby you Telepaths are."

Tiergan placed two fingers against each of Keefe's temples. "I'm going to say the instructions out loud. That way Sophie and Fitz will know how to walk you through this if you need a refresher. And now I want you to close your eyes and imagine that you've just discovered an empty box hidden in the center of your mind. Picture it any size and shape—but it must have a color. And it usually works best if you give it a color you're connected to in some way. Don't tell me what color you pick—"

"Can't you see it?" Keefe asked.

"I'm not reading your mind. Why do you think I haven't asked your permission to enter your consciousness?"

"I guess that's a good question," Keefe told him. "But a better one might be: Then why are you touching my face?"

"To make the process feel more tangible for you. Can you see the box?"

"Yeah. It's a big square box. And it's—"

"Don't tell me the color!" Tiergan reminded him. "We'll use that to determine if the masking worked. But before we do that, I need you to imagine yourself dragging all the memories you'd rather keep hidden into that mental box—and really make yourself believe those moments are truly solid pieces you're picking up and putting into that designated space."

Keefe's eyebrows crunched together. "Not gonna lie. This feels *super* pointless."

"It's hard to understand the workings of an ability that's not your own," Tiergan told him.

"Uh, I can feel Foster's confusion wafting my way, so I'm not the only one."

"Well, you'll all see soon enough. Trust the process—and let me know when you're ready."

His eyebrows pressed even closer together. "Okay. I guess the imaginary pieces of memory are all in the imaginary box now, and it totally feels like I actually did a thing and not just stood here feeling ridiculous."

Tiergan smiled. "Excellent. Now picture yourself sealing that box as tight as you can."

Keefe nodded. "Now what?"

"That's it."

"That's it?" Keefe repeated as Tiergan dropped his hands and stepped back.

"Should be—but we still have to test it." Tiergan steered

Keefe into the narrow space between Fitz's and Sophie's cots. "Do they have permission to enter your mind?"

"Um . . . sure." But he still flinched when Fitz sat up and reached for his forehead. "Sorry. Reflex."

Sophie kept her good hand in her lap. "It's probably better not to bring enhancing into this, right?"

"Agreed," Tiergan said.

She closed her eyes.

"So . . . are they just supposed to stay away from the big box o' secrets?" Keefe asked.

"It was never about the box, Keefe," Tiergan told him.

"Oh!" Sophie breathed. "It was about the color!"

"The box was gold, wasn't it?" Fitz asked.

Keefe nodded. "Do I want to know why you guys are grinning like that?"

"Because some of your memories are gilded now," Sophie told him. "It's like . . . standing in the middle of thousands of holographs, and some of them have been tinted gold."

"Exactly," Tiergan said. "And now you and Fitz know to look past all of those."

"Dude, you masked a *lot* of memories," Fitz noted.

"Well, it's also deceptive," Tiergan warned, "because he's brought everything he'd like to keep private to the forefront of his mind. So you're seeing them all in one mental space— which is another advantage to this process. Once you push deeper into his consciousness, you'll see very little gold."

"So . . . should we do that?" Sophie asked.

"I don't see why not."

"Me neither," Keefe said.

But his voice sounded fragile somehow. And when Sophie peeked at his expression, he had everything squeezed tight, like he was bracing for impact.

"We don't have to—"

"Yes, Foster," he interrupted. "We do. You know we do."

"Okay," she said slowly. "But then I need you to do one thing."

She held out her left arm, shaking her makeshift bracelet covered in pins. "Take Krakie for backup."

Something flickered across his expression—an emotion Sophie doubted even an Empath could translate. And he nodded, unpinning the tiny kraken and fastening it to his cape.

"Okay," he told her, clearing his throat and squaring his shoulders. "For real this time. Let's find what my mom hid."

TWENTY-ONE

THE GILDED MEMORIES CALLED TO Sophie, like warm sunlight streaming through wide-open windows, daring her to see where they led—and that was before she saw a fleeting glimpse of herself.

She hadn't meant to peek—and only caught the briefest flash as she struggled to disregard anything with a golden sheen. But it was enough to tell her the memory was recent.

In fact, she was pretty sure it was from the day she'd opened her Level Three finals presents and found the incredible drawings Keefe had done for her. But she'd lived that moment with him—so why didn't he want her to see his memory of it?

It's hard to ignore the gold, huh? Fitz transmitted, his crisp voice saving her from taking a longer look.

Yeah, she admitted, feeling shame burn across her consciousness.

Keefe deserved as much privacy as they could give him.

But that didn't stop the curiosity from itching, itching, itching.

I always forget how vivid his mind is, she thought, forcing herself to focus on the broader mental landscape—a dense whirl of flashing memories, laced with a soundtrack of blaring voices. Keefe's photographic memory retained every detail, sound, and thought, forming a storm of color and noise. *It's . . . disorienting.*

It is, Fitz agreed. *Though it's still way less intense than yours.*

Her heart stalled at that.

She'd never given any thought to what her headspace must look or feel like, since it wasn't something she could experience.

So do my memories look like this? she asked, imagining a similar whirlwind churning with all of her secrets.

Sorta. Everything's dimmed because of your blocking. And the memories flicker way faster, so I can't tell what I'm looking at unless I'm focusing really hard—and even then, you keep a bunch of mental paths closed off.

He didn't say "from me." But she could feel those unsaid words.

Your memories spread out more too, he added. *It's like . . . staring at the horizon. I can't actually see where your consciousness ends—and I seriously don't get how you have that much information in your head.*

Photographic memory, she reminded him. *Plus seven years of hearing the thoughts of everyone around me.*

True. And all the stuff the Black Swan planted.

She squirmed at the reminder.

It'd been so long since she'd had any of those extra memories trigger that she sometimes forgot Mr. Forkle had spent years filling her head with facts and secrets while she slept, in order to prepare her for her role as the moonlark.

In some ways, it was a relief not having to constantly analyze whether a scrap of memory was *hers,* or if she'd pulled a crucial detail from those murky reserves. But it also meant that the current struggle had strayed so far from anything the Black Swan had anticipated that she was pretty much on her own.

So how should we do this? Fitz asked. *I'm guessing we'll want to focus on memories with Keefe's mom in them.*

Yeah, we probably should've told Keefe to think about her before we dived in, so those would already be at the front of his mind.

I can do that now if you want, Keefe offered, nearly giving them each a heart attack.

You can hear us? Fitz asked.

Yep. AND feel what you're feeling. So we're all learning fun new stuff about each other today!

Great. Fitz had heaped plenty of sarcasm onto that transmission.

Can you try concentrating on your mom? Sophie asked, attempting to keep the conversation on track.

The scenery shifted, with some memories shuffling back and others rolling forward until they were surrounded by nothing but flickers of Lady Gisela's face.

I'm going to have nightmares about this forever, Fitz thought with a shudder.

Sophie nodded. *Same.*

Lady Gisela had blond hair like her son, and there were definite similarities between their features. But she was so cold and stern and immaculate that she looked like she might crack if she flashed a real smile or let a hair slip from her intricate updos.

Good old Mom, Keefe thought as Lady Gisela's sharp voice echoed around them. The words mostly blurred together, but Sophie caught a few:

"Legacy."

"Disappointment."

"Stubborn."

"Foolish."

"Waste."

Ready to take a journey into my awesome childhood? Keefe asked as more memories flooded in, piling on top of each other and forming a tunnel that spiraled down, down, down into the dark.

Are you? Sophie countered.

YEP! Like I said, it's gonna be a party! Just don't make it a pity party, okay?

Is that why some of these memories are gold? Fitz asked, trying to keep his concentration away from a gilded flicker right below them. *You think they'll make us feel sorry for you?*

No. Those ones are just . . . distracting.

Sophie wasn't sure what that was supposed to mean, but she could've sworn she'd caught a glimpse of her face again and shifted her focus to the nearest memory so she wouldn't be tempted.

Her stomach soured as she took in the scene replaying around her: Keefe's mom wearing a stiff green gown—the color the elves wore when they were going to their version of a funeral.

Lady Gisela stood beside Keefe's enormous canopy bed, watching as he tried to muffle his sobs with his pillow—and she didn't once try to hug him or take his hand or provide any sort of comfort.

Eventually, Keefe wiped his nose and choked out, "What do you want?"

And she smiled—*smiled*—and told him she needed him to take a sedative so his crying wouldn't bother his father.

I mean it, Foster, Keefe said as Sophie sucked in a breath. *I can feel that rising sympathy—and I appreciate it. But I don't need it.*

Sympathy's not pity, she argued.

It's close enough. So how about you focus on all that fury I can feel boiling underneath? It's always fun when you get feisty.

When she didn't agree he added, *That memory happened after your planting—think about that. My mom knew you were still alive as she watched me break down like that.*

Anger burned through Sophie's veins, but it cooled just as quickly, tempered by sorrow that came with knowing he'd been crying because of *her.*

But then she remembered something Lady Gisela had told her during one of the horrible conversations they'd had through Keefe's old Imparter: She'd made Keefe take that sedative not to silence his sobbing, but because she needed to steal some of his blood.

THERE'S the rage I was looking for, Keefe said as Sophie's whole body shook. *Hold tight to that!*

She tried.

But the more memories she studied, the more her heart broke for him.

She skimmed as much as she could, but some flashes demanded attention. Like the loud argument in Keefe's too-fancy bedroom, where Lord Cassius loomed over a younger, scrawnier version of his son and shouted, "Alden is not your father!"

"I wish he was!" Keefe snapped back, tearing off his blue Level Two cape and flinging it across the room.

"Well," Lord Cassius said, smoothing his slicked blond hair

and glancing at Keefe's mother, who stood off to the side study-ing her son through narrowed eyes. "I suppose that makes us even, since I much prefer Alden's sons. But since I'm stuck with this"—he gestured to Keefe from head to toe and crinkled his nose—"I'm not going to let you ruin our family!"

Keefe smirked, and Sophie could feel something inside him shift as he said, "Good luck with that."

It was as if he'd decided right then and there that he was going to do everything in his power to humiliate his father. And Lord Cassius must've felt that resolve, because he hurled the goblet he'd been holding, splattering Keefe's feet with fizzleberry wine as it shattered against the floor.

"Clean that up!" Lord Cassius ordered. "And plan on spend-ing your entire break making up for your lack of dedication. I'll have your first study assignments sent to you in the morning."

"Running off to Atlantis again?" Lady Gisela asked as Lord Cassius stalked toward the staircase.

"Don't start with me," he told her. "And don't wait up."

Her eyes flashed and she lifted her chin, keeping her head high until he was gone

"Well," she told Keefe. "Sounds like you have some work to do."

She was halfway down the stairs when she glanced over her shoulder.

"Keefe?" she said, waiting for him to look at her. "Someday, you'll be glad you're not a Vacker."

What was that supposed to mean? Fitz asked, and Sophie winced.

She'd forgotten she wasn't the only one watching that memory.

No idea, Keefe told him. *My mom was already working with Alvar back then, so maybe she meant all the gossip you're dealing with now that everyone knows he's with the Neverseen?*

But she was leading *the Neverseen,* Fitz argued, *so she knew all that drama would be coming for you, too.*

True. Well, maybe it's something with the mysterious Vacker legacy, then. And wait a minute—I just realized we're Legacy Buddies! We should get matching tunics that say, My Legacy Is Creepier Than Yours! *Or* I tried to discover my legacy and all I got was this ugly tunic!

Sophie wanted to laugh, but she couldn't quite get there. Not when her mind kept replaying the way Keefe's father had shattered that glass.

When did that happen? she asked.

After the Level Two midterms. My dad wasn't happy with two of my scores.

Uh, weren't your lowest scores still in the nineties? Fitz asked.

Ninety-eight and ninety-nine. But Dear Old Daddio expected me to get a perfect one hundred on everything. Apparently, that's what HE got when HE was at Foxfire.

Okay, but did he skip Level One like you did? Sophie wondered.

Nope. But he also doesn't have a photographic memory, so he said being the top of my Level should be a given. Imagine how excited he was when he found out I came in second!

Fitz shuffled his feet. *I . . . came in first.*

Oh, I know. Had to go and make the rest of us look bad, didn't you, Fitzy?

I didn't—

Relax, I'm kidding. But it's a good thing I like you, 'cause it's not exactly easy being your friend.

The thought was meant to be teasing. But Sophie could feel a glimmer of truth behind it.

Fitz must've felt it too, because he told him, *I'm sorry.*

Don't be. It's seriously not a big deal.

Then why didn't you say anything?

Uh, our friendship wasn't really at the "sharing" stage back then. I sat at your table at lunch sometimes—not really enough to be all, "Let me unload all my daddy drama." Plus, it wasn't your fault Lady Delmira thought my elixir was too frothy and Sir Bubu snuck in a trick question on me.

His name is Sir Bubu? Sophie had to ask.

Yep! I had a LOT of fun with that during the second half of the year. And that's the thing: This made me realize I was never going to be who my dad wanted me to be, so I might as well have some fun. In fact, that was the night I first came up with the Great Gulon Incident.

She could almost hear his smirk—and when a new memory flashed to the front of his mind, she wondered if he was finally going to show her the story.

But Fitz interrupted.

Why was your dad talking about my dad anyway?

Keefe sighed. *I was hoping you weren't going to ask that. Guess it's probably easier to show you.*

His memories shuffled again, flashing to the Level Two atrium at Foxfire all decked out in tinsel and filled with big bubbles floating with candy and treats in the center. Everywhere Keefe looked, parents were hugging their kids and celebrating.

But his mom hadn't bothered to come. And his dad had his wrist in a death grip as he dragged him away from his locker, forcing him to leave behind his presents.

"Wait," Alden called, rushing to catch up to them in the hall. "You're not leaving already, are you, Cassius?"

"*Lord* Cassius," Keefe's father corrected. "And yes. Keefe needs to study."

"Tonight?" Alden asked. "I think he's earned a night off, don't you? To test so high—and at his age—"

"Yes, well, I've never felt youth should be an excuse," Keefe's father interrupted.

Alden's jaw tightened, and the quick glance he stole at Lord Cassius's hand made Sophie wonder if he realized how hard Keefe's father was squeezing.

"Why don't you come to Everglen tonight?" Alden suggested. "Della's been planning quite the celebration, and—"

"Perhaps another time." Lord Cassius turned to pull Keefe away.

But Alden grabbed Keefe's shoulder and leaned down to whisper, "I'm *very* proud of you, Keefe. I want you to know that."

Oh wow, Sophie thought as Keefe's head erupted with a hundred different emotions.

Yeah, Keefe said quietly. *No one had ever told me that before, so . . .*

And your dad felt it, she realized. *Since he had his hand wrapped around your wrist.*

Pretty much. And you saw how happy he was about it.

Fitz muttered something under his breath that didn't sound like a very nice word—and Sophie felt like doing the same.

You okay over there, Fitzy? Keefe asked. *Your moods keep shifting on me.*

I'm fine. I'm just . . . trying to understand why you never told me about any of this once we became best friends. You could've said something.

I know. Keefe shifted his weight. *The thing is . . . talking about it made it real. And I didn't want it to be real. I wanted to pretend my life was as perfect as yours.*

My life isn't perfect, Fitz argued.

Maybe not. But it's pretty close, dude. I mean, yeah, Alvar's a creep—but you still have your dad. And your mom. And Biana. And you're still the top of our class. And you're Foster's Cognate and . . . even without all of that, you're still a Vacker. You're always going to be the golden boy everyone expects greatness from. And I'll always be the mess.

You're not a mess, Sophie promised.

Oh, I am, Foster. The more we do this, the more you'll see. And that's fine. I can't pretend everything's normal anymore. Too much has happened.

Then why still hide some of your memories? Fitz asked.

Keefe snorted. *Because I'd like to actually keep you guys as friends.*

Sophie had no idea what that meant—but it didn't matter. *I'm always going to be your friend.*

So am I, Fitz added.

You sure about that? Keefe asked, making his memories shift again, this time to a flashback Sophie had already seen several months earlier—but Fitz hadn't.

This was the first memory I got back, Keefe explained.

Why is it all crackly and distorted? Fitz asked.

Keefe shrugged. *I guess it got a little damaged by the Washer.*

He was just a kid in the memory, following his mom's voice up to the roof in the middle of the night, where he found her talking to two figures in hooded black cloaks. *Now* Sophie knew the figures were Brant and Alvar, and that they'd been discussing Alvar's failed efforts to find where the Black Swan hid Sophie among humans. But in that moment, the only thing Keefe understood was that his mom implied that she was going to encourage him to become friends with Fitz so that he could keep an eye on Fitz's search for Sophie.

So? Fitz asked. *You think that's the only reason we're friends?*

No—but I'm sure it was a big part of it, Keefe told him.

Couldn't have been that *big,* Fitz argued, *since we didn't start really hanging out until years later, when we were both at Foxfire.*

I guess, Keefe mumbled.

Besides, Fitz said, *my dad . . . kinda did the same thing. After those same midterms, he started asking me about you all the time, telling me I should invite you over. I figured he just wanted us to hang out since we were ranked one and two or whatever. But now I'm pretty sure he was worried about you, and wanted to give you somewhere else to go after school.*

Huh, Keefe said—and Sophie recognized his jumbled feelings.

Alden had done something similar with Biana, encouraging her to befriend the strange new girl who'd been living with humans.

He was a master of well-meaning meddling.

The thing is, she told Keefe, *it doesn't matter WHY we all became friends. Just that we did.*

Exactly, Fitz said.

Yeah, I guess. Keefe cleared his throat. *But I gotta say— heartwarming as all of this is, it's noooooooooot what I'm looking for. Where are the fancy Telepath tricks to dredge up all my mom's secrets? Do you guys need to stare into each other's eyes more or something?*

Sophie let out a long sigh. *I told you—we have no idea how to trigger memories.*

Then hit me with all the Fitzphie pizzazz and see what happens.

The Fitzphie pizzazz, Sophie repeated. *There's no such thing.*

Not with that attitude, there isn't! Keefe told her.

I guess we could try probing, Fitz suggested after a few seconds.

Sophie's brain automatically flashed through the various "probing" scenes she'd seen in human sci-fi movies, and Fitz cracked up. *No wonder you got so freaked out when we took you to Atlantis to have Quinlin try a probe on you.*

It's a super weird word! she argued.

With you on that one, Foster, Keefe told her. *But I'm up for a Fitzphie probe-athon. Commence all the probing!*

We have to stop calling it that, Sophie noted.

Probably, Fitz agreed. *But don't you think it might work?*

I don't know. I don't know how to probe.

"You don't know how to probe?" he said out loud, turning to where Tiergan stood watching them. "You never taught her?"

"Why would I?" Tiergan asked. "Her mind uses a better method instinctively."

"Okay, will someone please tell me what 'probing' is?" Sophie begged.

"It's a way of pushing through someone's mental blocking," Tiergan told her.

"Then why do you think that will help us find Keefe's missing memories?" Sophie asked Fitz.

"Because when you probe, you transmit different words until you get a reaction, and then you keep transmitting that same word over and over until it breaks through."

"I . . . still don't understand how that helps with this. Keefe's not blocking us from the memories. They were erased."

"No, they were *washed*," Tiergan corrected. "And washing is mostly about knocking memories loose and burying them out of reach—usually under the person's deepest fears, since they instinctively avoid that section of their mind. So probing might be a useful solution—assuming you can find the right word. It would need to be something that specifically connects to those memories."

"I guess we could try saying 'Neverseen,'" Fitz suggested.

"Isn't that too vague?" Sophie wondered.

"The Neverseen are in *tons* of my memories," Keefe agreed. "But Washers aren't—and I'm betting there's a moment in all of my erased memories where my mom tells someone to call for one."

Tiergan nodded. "'Washer' could work."

"Of course it could—I'm a genius. We ready to do this?"

"All we do is transmit the word?" Sophie clarified.

"Think of it more like giving a command," Tiergan told her. "Put as much energy behind it as you can."

Sophie closed her eyes, digging deep into her mental reserves until her thoughts felt warm and tingly.

"On three?" Fitz asked.

Keefe counted for them—and when he called out, "Three!" they both transmitted *WASHER* with every bit of authority they could channel.

"Did I do something wrong?" Sophie asked when nothing happened.

"It usually takes a few tries," Fitz told her. "Let's go again."

WASHER!

WASHER!

WASHER!

WASHER!

Still nothing.

"Are you getting a headache?" Tiergan asked as Sophie reached up to rub her temples.

"I'm fine. Just running low on mental energy."

"Then you should quit for the day," Tiergan told her. "Get some rest and pick up where you left off tomorrow. The last thing you want to do is push yourself too hard."

"Or," Sophie countered, "we could see what happens if we add enhancing to the mix. That usually gives Fitz a huge surge of energy, and he can share some with me."

Tiergan sighed. "I suppose you could give it a try. But then I'm going to insist you stop."

"Deal," Sophie agreed, using her teeth to pull off her glove and then holding out her bare hand to Fitz.

"Ready?" he asked Keefe.

"*So* ready. Give me all the Fitzphie probing pizzazz!"

Fitz pressed his palm against Sophie's, and a blast of warmth surged between them—a richer, rawer kind of power that left trails of tingling sparks shooting from the tips of her fingers to the top of her head.

"I swear this gets stronger every time," Fitz murmured.

"It does," Sophie agreed, tightening her grip and soaking up the energy he shared with her, letting it build and build and build until her brain felt ready to burst from the pressure.

"Count us down," he told Keefe.

And when he got to "one" . . .

WASHER!

The word was more than a command. It was a blade, slicing through Keefe's consciousness and striking somewhere deep, turning everything cold and dark.

For a second Sophie worried they'd miscalculated.

Then Keefe whispered, "I think we found something."

TWENTY-TWO

KEEFE SANK ONTO THE NEAREST cot as a memory flashed to the front of his mind—a scene so distorted that Sophie couldn't tell what she was supposed to be seeing.

Some parts were too dim and others were too bright, and there were strange flickering gaps, like trying to watch a really old, scratched-up piece of film with some of the frames missing. Even the soundtrack was warped, with voices fading in and out.

But then the images sharpened, and she realized she was watching Lady Gisela lean down and talk to a slightly younger version of Keefe, both of them standing in front of a wall of bookshelves.

How old are you here? Sophie transmitted.

Keefe looked skinnier than she was used to, and his chin and cheeks were rounder.

Eleven, I think? Or maybe ten?

You don't know? Fitz asked.

Not yet. I can't figure out where the memory's supposed to fit. I guess that's what Tiergan meant when he was rambling about "mental ripples."

You're at Candleshade, though, right? Sophie recognized the study area in Keefe's bedroom.

Yep. I keep trying to see what books are on my shelves, since that'll tell me when this was. But the background's too blurry.

Yeah, what's up with that? Fitz asked.

No idea. This one's way more damaged than the other memory. Think another burst of energy will fix it?

Worth a shot, Fitz said, tightening his grip on Sophie's hand and pouring all the warmth that pooled between them into Keefe's mind.

But the tingly energy didn't change a thing.

"I need you to do me a favor," Lady Gisela said in the memory—or that's what Sophie assumed. All they could hear was, "I need . . . do . . . favor."

She handed Young Keefe something white and blurry, and Sophie was pretty sure it was a sealed envelope. "Deliver . . . man . . . green door."

Uh, did she just say "man"? Fitz asked, beating Sophie to the question. *Not "elf"?*

Looks like it, Keefe thought as they watched Lady Gisela hand his younger self something small and cobalt blue—a leaping crystal to the Forbidden Cities.

"Yes," his mom said when Young Keefe's mouth fell open, and for a moment the memory sharpened, letting them hear her clearly when she told him, "I need you to go right now."

Young Keefe's eyes glittered with excitement, and Sophie expected him to hold the facet up to the light and zip away.

But he glanced back at his mom. "Why?"

"Because I'm telling you to."

"Yeah, but *why*?"

She reached up to pinch the bridge of her nose. "Does Fitz question his father when Alden sends him off on their little errands?"

"I don't know—like I've told you a zillion times, Fitz doesn't tell me anything about that. But I'm pretty sure he knows where he's going and why he's going there."

"Yes, well, all you need to know is that the message you're holding needs to be delivered discreetly. And since no one's watching your registry feed, you can sneak away far easier than I can."

The memory distorted again, warping most of Keefe's response. But they caught the part where he insisted, "Tell me what's in the letter."

"You're not in a position to bargain," Lady Gisela warned.

"Funny—it sounds like *you're* the one who isn't in a position to bargain," he countered.

Looks like you were old enough to be driving your parents crazy, Fitz noted. *And it sounds like we were friends.*

Yeah, Keefe said. *So I was probably eleven.*

"That kind of information is earned," Lady Gisela told him in the memory. "And you can prove you're ready by delivering that message without any further argument."

Young Keefe's attention snagged on the gleaming splotch of gold in the center of the envelope. It looked like wax or putty, and it was stamped with a symbol that Sophie had never seen before: two crescents forming a loose circle around a glowing star.

Do you think that symbol has anything to do with her facility? Fitz asked. *Didn't the runes on the door say, "The star only rises at Nightfall"?*

I thought that was a reference to the Lodestar Initiative, Sophie reminded him, *which had a different symbol.*

True, Fitz said. *And Vespera's symbol was more of a swirly shooting star, wasn't it?*

Keefe sighed. *Anyone else getting super sick of symbols?*

Sophie definitely was. But they were still going to need to figure out what the new symbol meant, unless the memory would just tell them—but she highly doubted *that* was going to happen. Especially since Young Keefe didn't seem particularly interested in the symbol. He was much more focused on whatever was inside—he even held the letter up to the light and squinted at the note's silhouette.

"You won't be able to read it," his mom told him. "Think of where you're going."

Young Keefe's eyebrows shot up. "It's in *human*?"

"There is no *human* language—honestly, what is that school teaching you? Humans insist on dividing themselves into different groups, which I've always found strange. If they united, they'd likely have progressed much further as a species—but I suppose it's better for us that they haven't. And to answer your question: My letter isn't written in the Enlightened Language. So it would be pointless for you to open it."

"Then tell me what it says," Keefe demanded. "Or deliver it yourself."

She grabbed his shoulder. "Did I give you the impression that this was optional?"

The memory shifted speed then, skipping through what looked like a vicious argument and not slowing until Keefe wrenched his arm free and stalked away.

But the door he'd been heading for banged shut in his face, as if his mom had closed it with her telekinesis.

"Fine," she said through gritted teeth. "That crystal leaps to a city called London, near a house with a green door. The person who lives there might be useful—we'll see. That's why I need you to slide this letter through the metal slot on the door and then leave without being seen. You should be gone less than five minutes—but I'll give you ten, since you might have to slip down an alley before you can leap home. Don't speak to anyone, and if anyone tries to speak to you, just look confused. It shouldn't be hard since you won't understand a word they're saying. Understood?"

His reply was lost to a crackle of static. Then the scene blurred again, jumping to when Lady Gisela removed his cape and examined the rest of his outfit: a black tunic and gray pants, which weren't human-style by any means, but were at least boring enough to blend in.

"You're running . . . time," she told him. "I need . . . back before . . . father . . . errand."

The memory sharpened as Young Keefe held the crystal up to the light. But he just stood there staring at the deep blue beam.

"I didn't want to play this card," his mom snapped. "But let's not forget that your father was ready to send you to Exillium after that stunt you pulled last week. *I* talked him out of it. And I can change his mind again."

"You're threatening me?" he asked.

"Not if you cooperate." Her smile was cold. Calculated. Leaving no doubt that she would make good on that threat.

Young Keefe must've decided the same thing, because he closed his eyes and stepped into the light—and Sophie held her breath as the warm rush tickled his skin and the light whisked him away and . . .

The memory ended.

"COME ON!" Keefe shouted, smacking the palm of his

hand against his forehead, as if he could knock the rest of the scene loose.

"What's wrong?" Tiergan asked.

Keefe reeled toward Sophie and Fitz. "Whatever you did before—do it again!"

They both nodded, and Fitz twisted his fingers even tighter with Sophie's.

Warmth surged between them, building and building and building, and they blasted it from their minds with another transmission. But the blade of energy vanished into the shadows of Keefe's mind.

"Try again," Keefe said.

"Absolutely not," Tiergan jumped in. "You promised to pause between revelations."

"This wasn't a revelation!" Keefe argued. "It was half a revelation. Not even half, if you consider how many parts were damaged."

"Damaged?" Tiergan repeated.

"Some parts were missing or distorted," Sophie explained.

"Can I take a look?" Tiergan asked, reaching for Keefe's temples.

Keefe nodded and Tiergan closed his eyes, and the creases on his forehead grew deeper and deeper until he murmured, "A recovered memory shouldn't look like that. Once a memory triggers, it should be every bit as clear as it was before it was washed—especially for someone with a photographic memory."

"But my other memories are like that too," Keefe argued.

"Only one of them," Sophie reminded him. "The memory of your mom taking you to Nightfall was flawless."

"Okay," Keefe agreed. "So why are two damaged and one's fine?"

"Because the damaged memories weren't washed," Tiergan said quietly. "They were shattered."

TWENTY-THREE

HEN YOU SAY 'SHATTERED,'"
Fitz said, "do you mean what hap-
pened to my dad's memories when
his mind broke?"

"Yes and no," Tiergan told him. "In your father's case—
and Prentice's as well—it was their sanity that shattered, and
the mental breakdown caused everything else to fracture. But
in Keefe's case, the damage is limited to targeted memories.
Whoever did this is incredibly talented."

"Gethen told me his washing skills were the reason the
Neverseen recruited him," Sophie said quietly. "I'm assuming
this is what he meant. But why were some memories shattered
and some washed?"

"I can only speculate, of course," Tiergan told her. "But I'm assuming there are certain moments that will eventually need to be triggered in order for Keefe to understand the full scope of his alleged legacy. Those memories would've been washed. But then there could've been other instances where Keefe discovered something they hadn't meant for him to learn, and those were shattered to prevent him from remembering."

"That makes sense," Fitz agreed. "Wasn't the first damaged memory something you saw by accident?" he asked Keefe. "And your mom seemed kind of desperate in this new one, so maybe she had to involve you in something she didn't want you to know about."

"But she didn't tell me anything!" Keefe argued. "So unless you want to search the entire city of London for a house with a green door . . ."

"We saw the seal on the envelope," Sophie reminded him. "Maybe it's important—like how the Lodestar symbol was a map."

"Anyone else *really* hoping that's not true?" Keefe asked. "I mean, I know I wasn't around when you guys figured out what all the dashes and circles meant, but that process had to be worse than back-to-back history lectures."

"It kind of was," Sophie admitted. "But this symbol's much simpler, so it should be easier to figure out."

Then again, maybe it was *too* simple. A single star surrounded by two crescent moons wasn't much to go on.

"I bet the important stuff's in the part of the memory we're still missing," Fitz said quietly. "Keefe probably talked to every single person he saw, or found a way to read the letter—or both."

"Sounds like me," Keefe agreed. "So how do we find the missing piece?"

"We may not be able to," Tiergan warned. "Think of it like smashing a piece of glass. Gethen would've aimed his blow at the most critical spot, and that section would shatter far more than the outlying area. So there's a very good chance that this is all that remains—at least beyond fragments too small and scattered to piece together."

"Okay, but we have Foster, remember?" Keefe said. "Can't she just heal the memory, the same way she healed Alden and Prentice?"

"Sophie healed their *sanity*," Tiergan corrected, "and our sanity is a much more tangible thing. Memories are nothing more than wisps of thought. That's why Prentice is currently living a normal, happy life, but still recalls almost nothing from the days before his sanity shattered."

"But my dad got his memories back," Fitz reminded them.

"Yes, because his sanity was only fractured for a few weeks," Tiergan countered. "The damage had far less opportunity to spread. And honestly? I'm sure your father *has* lost some of his memories. You saw what he was like after the breakdown. Do you really think that level of trauma wouldn't cause at least some permanent damage?"

Fitz frowned. "But . . . he seems normal."

"No, he seems like *himself*—because he *is* himself. Just like all of you remain true to yourselves despite the traumas you've endured. It's a coping mechanism we all have, a way of recentering and regrouping as we recover. But it doesn't mean we aren't also altered. Sometimes the changes are noticeable. Sometimes they're hidden. Either way, I promise you, no one fractures the way your father did and escapes unscathed. Let's not forget that there's now a Wanderling that bears the name Alden Vacker and grows with his DNA. He's done a brilliant job of returning to life as though nothing happened—but that will never change the fact that something *did* happen. I would tell you to ask him about it, but your father's a proud elf, and I know in many ways he feels like he failed you when he let himself fracture. I doubt he's eager to admit the incident has had any lasting effects."

Sophie wanted to argue with what Tiergan was saying—wanted to keep believing she'd fixed Alden 100 percent. But . . . as someone who *also* had a Wanderling bearing her name and was still haunted by the nightmares that came with it, she probably should've realized that Alden would be waging his own battles.

You okay? she asked Fitz when she noticed him rubbing his chest. *Your echo—*

It's fine! he transmitted, closing his eyes and taking a long breath.

Then another.

And another.

You're worrying me, Sophie admitted.

I know. I'm sorry. I never realized my dad might be dealing with that.

Just try to remember—he's still acting like himself. So whatever he lost can't be important.

Somehow I doubt that. My dad's been an Emissary for decades. Do you have any idea how many secrets he's protecting?

I'm sure he kept records.

Fitz shook his head. *Maybe for the stuff he did* officially. *But he had tons of* unofficial *projects too—like when he was trying to find you. I know he wouldn't have left any evidence of that stuff, in case the Council ever investigated him. So if those memories are gone, they're GONE.*

Well . . . if that's true, the good news is the memories have been gone for months and it hasn't been a problem, Sophie reminded him.

Yet, Fitz added, sucking in another long breath as the word just sort of hung there taunting them.

Keefe cleared his throat, jolting them back to the present. "If you guys are talking about me—"

"We're not," Sophie promised. "We were talking about Alden."

"Is that why Fitz looks so pale?" Tiergan wondered.

"I'm fine," Fitz assured him.

But Elwin had already rushed in from his office and flashed

an orb of layered light around his chest. "Your ribs still look okay . . . but the murkiness looks thicker, so I'm guessing that means the echo stirred."

"A little," Fitz admitted. "But I know how to breathe through it."

"I'm glad," Elwin told him. "But I still want you to rest now. You too, Sophie."

"That's fine," Tiergan agreed. "Keefe needs to let the revelation settle too."

"I told you: That wasn't a revelation," Keefe argued as he made his way over to the shelves of medicine. "Do you have any fathomlethes around here?"

"I hope you're not talking about the weird river-pearl thing you took in Alluveterre that made you cover your walls in scraps of paper like a serial killer," Sophie told him.

"Oh I am—and I know you're not going to like it, Foster. But I remembered a ton of stuff last time. So how about I promise to let you help me sort through the notes again? Remember that? Such a classic Keephie moment!"

"Keephie?" Tiergan asked. "Never mind. Best if I don't know. And I hate to break it to you, Keefe, but fathomlethes are overwhelming at best and unreliable at worst—and an incredibly poor substitute for proper telepathic exercises. They're what some rely on when they don't have access to the tremendous resources that you have."

"And they are an adorable resource, aren't they?" Keefe

asked, smirking at Sophie and Fitz. "But they need to rest—and I am *so* not ready to sleep, so . . ." He crouched to study the lowest shelf.

"You won't find any," Elwin told him. "I keep them locked up."

"Fine, then I'll swing by Slurps and Burps and pick some up on my way home."

"Don't let him," Sophie begged Ro. "Not unless you want him pacing around the room all night, covering every surface with scribbled questions."

Ro shrugged. "Pretty sure he's going to be up freaking out anyway. It'll be way more entertaining if he's all loopy."

"Best bodyguard ever!" Keefe said, pulling a pathfinder out of his cape pocket.

Tiergan placed a hand on his shoulder. "Okay, counteroffer: Why don't you stay with me tonight? Tam and Linh's suites have an extra bed, and I can walk you through a couple of mental exercises before you go to sleep that might help your subconscious target the shattered memories as you dream."

"*Might* help," Keefe repeated, tilting his head to study him. "Is this that thing adults do where they make you think they're giving you what you want but really they're just wasting your time?"

"No, Keefe," Tiergan said. "I don't have time I can afford to waste. Mind you, I can't guarantee that the mental exercises will help. But they'll still be far more useful than fathomlethes."

Keefe glanced at Sophie and let out a sigh. "Fiiiiiiiiiiiiine. I guess it's worth a try if it'll get rid of that crinkle between Foster's eyebrows. And who knows? Maybe I can talk Bangs Boy into doing the shadowvapor-veil-lifting thing while I'm there, see if it brightens up some of the darker spots in the memory."

"Hang on—you're *volunteering* to let Tam send shadows into your head?" Fitz verified.

"Sadly, yes—and I'm sure I'm going to want to punch him in the bangs after about thirty seconds," Keefe told him. "But . . . if it helps me figure out how much damage I did when I was playing Mommy's Little Messenger—"

"*You* didn't do any damage," Sophie assured him.

"Uh, whatever was in that letter I delivered couldn't have been good news," he argued.

"You might not have delivered it," Sophie reminded him. "And even if you did, you aren't responsible for things your mom made you do. We all saw her threaten you—"

"Relax, I don't need another Foster pep talk."

"Yes, you do," Sophie insisted. "And you need to promise me you won't do anything reckless."

Keefe smirked. "Now, what makes you think I'd do that?"

She shook her head. "I mean it, Keefe. Work with Tiergan or Tam as much as you want. But promise me you won't do anything else without me, okay?"

"It's going to be fine," he told her. "Get some rest. I'll see you tomorrow."

Sophie didn't realize until after he'd left that he never made her that promise.

TWENTY-FOUR

HO'S READY TO GET OUT of those cots?" Elwin asked as he strode into the room, carrying their morning trays of medicine.

"I am!" Sophie and Fitz both shouted, already throwing back their blankets.

"Hmm, I guess I should've phrased that differently," Elwin realized. "What I meant is, who wants to be out of those cots *by this evening*? You still need one more treatment, but if all goes according to plan, you should be back on your feet—or in Fitz's case, on crutches—by the end of the day and taking a late-night stroll through Foxfire. You guys up for it?"

"Are you kidding?" Sophie and Fitz asked, once again in perfect unison.

Elwin chuckled. "I'm sure if Keefe were here, he'd have a *lot* to say about how in sync you two are getting."

"Just more proof that Fitzphie's the best," Fitz told him, with a wink that shouldn't have made Sophie's heart flutter. But hearts could be foolish things.

"Have you heard from Keefe?" she asked as Elwin handed over her tray of elixirs.

Elwin shook his head. "No, but it's early, and I'm betting he was up half the night working through whatever exercises Tiergan taught him."

"I'm betting he was up the *whole* night," Fitz corrected, taking his tray from Elwin.

"Probably," Elwin admitted, helping Sophie remove the lids from her vials. "But don't worry, Tiergan will keep him in line. So why don't you two tackle your medicine while I prepare your mineral baths? We're getting you out of those beds!"

He ducked back into his office, and Sophie was too excited to care how thick and chunky the medicines were, or how many times they made her gag—though her brain was a bit stuck on the word "baths."

Fortunately, when Elwin returned he was carrying two silver basins that definitely weren't big enough to take the Healing Center to a whole new realm of awkward.

Unfortunately, they were filled with some sort of noxious

yellow-green slime that made the room smell like rotting onions.

"You're going to love this," Elwin promised as he set one basin on each of their cots.

Sophie doubted "love" would be the word she'd use, but as long as the stinky slime got her out of the Healing Center, she could handle it.

"I'm guessing we don't want to know what this is?" Fitz asked, dipping a finger tentatively into the slime.

Elwin nodded. "Same goes for your activating serums."

He held up a small bottle filled with some sort of thick, milky liquid, shaking it a few times before pouring it into Sophie's basin and making the slime fizzle and froth.

"Time to soak some strength into those bones," he told her, unwrapping her gauzy bandages and wiping her arm clean of any remaining poultice before gently lowering it into the surprisingly warm goo, and . . .

"Wow," she whispered, letting out what was probably an embarrassing moan. "That's . . . wow."

"What does it feel like?" Fitz asked.

Sophie shook her head, unable to find words to properly describe it. The closest she could come up with was, "It's like . . . soaking in sunshine."

"Told you you'd love it!" Elwin said smugly. "All the treatments I've put you through were to get you to this point—and it only gets better from here. Can you make a fist for me, Sophie?"

Her fingers easily obeyed, curling into her palm as her thumb wrapped around them.

"Good. Now uncurl your fingers until you feel a stretch across your palm. Does that hurt at all?"

"Nope!"

"Perfect! Then I want you to *try* for a hundred sets of that: *Curl, uncurl.* But don't be afraid to stop if your hand tells you it's too much. I'm picking that number arbitrarily. *You* know your limits."

Sophie set to work as Elwin poured a sludgy brown serum into Fitz's bath, making the slime crackle like Pop Rocks as he helped Fitz lower his leg into the basin.

The groany sound Fitz made might've been the most adorable thing Sophie had ever heard.

"Amazing, right?" she asked.

His response was some sort of garbled sigh.

"Don't go relaxing too much," Elwin warned. "You have strength exercises to work through too. But first . . ."

He helped Fitz sit up and removed the bandages around his ribs, then wrapped his chest in a long cloth soaked with slime from the basin. A fitted tunic made from some sort of liquid-resistant material prevented the gloop from spreading anywhere else—though there was a little splashing as Elwin showed Fitz the kicking motions he wanted him to make.

"Remember, you can stop anytime," Elwin told him as Fitz slowly worked through the exercises. "The last thing I want either of you doing is pushing too hard."

Sophie stopped at eighty-one, when her fingers started twitching. And Fitz made it to seventy-five before his knee got shaky.

"Excellent," Elwin said as he gathered up all the discarded bandages and vials. "Honestly, I wasn't sure if you'd make it past fifty, so this is tremendous progress! And now, just try to lie still and let the serums soak in. Holler if you need anything."

Sophie closed her eyes after he left, trailing her fingers through the fizzy slime just because she could.

Hey, you okay? Fitz transmitted. *You look like you're crying.*

Was she?

She blinked, and sure enough, a handful of tears streamed down her cheeks.

I'm fine, she promised. *It's just . . . really nice to feel my hand, you know? I knew Elwin kept promising he'd fix it, but . . .*

It was hard to believe sometimes, he finished for her.

She nodded and another tear broke free. *Sorry. After all the things I've been through, I don't know why I'm being such a baby.*

You're not being a baby. I heard what Umber said about losing your arm—I would've been freaked out too. And don't even get me started on the creepy echo things.

Yeah.

Her mind flashed to the monster, but the beast didn't stir, as if the warm bubbles tingling across her skin had lulled it to sleep.

Anyway, she said, swiping the final tears off her skin, *it's just really nice to not be sitting here with a numb arm bound in thick bandages, you know?*

I do. I can't believe I'm going to get to walk tonight! Well, I guess I should probably say "hobble."

Do you mind that you'll be on crutches?

He sighed. *A little? I mean, it's better than being bedridden. But I have a feeling I'm going to be super clumsy with them and Keefe's never going to let me hear the end of it.*

Sounds about right, Sophie admitted, smiling as she imagined it. But her smile faded when she realized at least another hour had slipped away. *You don't think it's bad that we haven't heard from him yet? I feel like there's at least a fifty-fifty chance he and Tam will strangle each other.*

Fitz laughed. *You're not wrong. But Tiergan will stop any attempts at murder—and Linh will dump water on their heads until they cool off.*

True.

But another hour slipped away. Then another. And another. And several more. And when she finally caved and asked Elwin for her Imparter, Keefe ignored her—which of course made her brain imagine all kinds of terrifying scenarios.

What if Keefe had found a way to contact his mom?

Or Gethen?

Or what if he'd snuck off and taken a bunch of fathomlethes?

That's it—I'm tracking him down, she told Fitz, not caring if she was going to seem naggy or obnoxious.

Need help? he offered.

Hopefully not—but if he ignores me, we're going full Cognate power on him.

Fitz laughed. *You really are adorable when you worry.*

Any other time, she might've latched onto the compliment, but she was too busy rallying her concentration.

KEEFE! she called, counting to five before repeating the transmission, each time stretching her consciousness farther and farther. *KEEFE! KEEFE! KEEFE!*

Aw, you sound just like Silveny, he told her as his mind *finally* connected with hers.

YOU DON'T GET TO MAKE JOKES AFTER WORRYING ME ALL DAY!

"Did you reach him?" Fitz asked, probably noticing the way she was grinding her teeth.

"I did! And I'm starting to wonder if enhancing would let me mentally strangle him."

Fitz grinned. "I'm game for trying."

"I might be too." She switched her focus back to Keefe. *WHY HAVEN'T YOU CHECKED IN?*

Relax, Fos—

DON'T TELL ME TO RELAX! she interrupted. *You ignored me when I hailed you. And we all know how reckless you get when it comes to your mom!*

I know, he told her. *But I'm fine. I'm still at Tiergan's, and I'm not doing anything you wouldn't want me to be doing. We've been working through a bunch more memory exercises—and it feels like we're getting close to another breakthrough.*

She sat up straighter. *Really?*

Yeah. That's why I haven't checked in. I didn't want to break Tiergan's concentration. But then SOMEONE got all demanding, so . . .

I'm not going to apologize for worrying, she told him.

I wouldn't want you to. It's fun having proof that the Mysterious Miss F cares. BUT . . . if I PROMISE I'll check in tomorrow, can I get back to what we were working on?

She sighed. *Fine. But if you forget to reach out, I swear Fitz and I will find a way to smack you with our brains.*

Fear the almighty Fitzphie—got it.

And do you promise you'll be careful—and tell me everything you learn?

He didn't answer, and it took her a second to figure out that he'd already shut down the connection between them.

"Everything okay?" Fitz asked, making her realize that both of her hands were currently squeezed into very tight fists.

She forced them to unclench as she told him what little Keefe had shared.

"Huh," he breathed. "I guess I shouldn't be surprised that Tiergan's helping, since he's our telepathy Mentor for a reason, but . . ."

"I know, it feels like we should be there—"

"But you shouldn't," Elwin jumped in as he made his way over with a huge heap of towels. "You should be right here, taking care of yourselves, just like you've been doing. And let's see how well it worked, shall we?"

He used one of the towels to lift Sophie's arm out of her

basin, then surrounded it with a vivid purple orb and made her move each of her fingers. He did the same thing to Fitz's leg and chest, once he'd wiped away all the slime.

Without a word, he disappeared into his office and retrieved two more trays of elixirs, waiting until they'd each downed the doses of sour sludge before he retreated back to his office, returning with his hands full yet again.

But this time he held a silver arm brace in one hand and two silver crutches in the other.

"Okay," he said with a huge grin. "*Now* who's ready to get out of those cots?"

Walking was always a bit of a challenge for Sophie. But walking after weeks of bed rest brought new meaning to the word "clumsy." Her legs wobbled like a newborn fawn, and she managed to crash into two cots, one wall, and the door all within the first ten seconds. But after a couple of minutes, she found a shaky rhythm.

And she had it easy compared to Fitz. The sling made her right arm basically useless and threw off her center of balance a little—but if she'd been the one stuck on crutches, she probably would've broken a few bones.

Because the thing about elves and crutches?

The elves didn't just stick crutches under their arms and swing their bodies forward step-by-step like humans did.

They added levitation to the mix.

The advantage, of course, was that Fitz could move farther with every step, with way less strain on his arms and shoulders—and it would make stairs much more manageable for him.

But levitation also didn't allow nearly as much control as human movies loved to imagine it did. There was no traction in the air. No easy way to stop or pivot directions. Which meant Fitz spent most of their walk flailing and bumping into things.

And that was with the dark halls quiet and empty. Sophie could only imagine how much worse it would be once they were surrounded by prodigies.

"On a scale of one to ten," Fitz began as he barely managed to dodge the jagged branches of the crystal trees scattered around the Level Four atrium, "how weird do you think it would look if I had Grizel carry me everywhere until I could put weight on my leg?"

"Do you think she's even up for that?" Sophie wondered. "I know she's back from Gildingham, but Biana didn't say if she's made a full recovery or if she's still regaining her strength."

Fitz sank back to the floor, catching his weight with his crutches to keep pressure off his bad leg. "Wow, I'm a terrible person. I haven't even asked how she's doing."

"You're *not* a terrible person. You've had a lot going on."

"So do you, and you've still checked on Sandor." He tried reaching up to tear a hand through his hair and nearly lost his balance when his crutches shifted.

"Seriously," Sophie said as she helped him steady himself. "Grizel wouldn't want you worrying about her."

"I know. But . . . I still should."

"Well . . . if you feel bad, you could always get her a present."

"True. But what do you get a goblin warrior?"

"No idea," Sophie admitted. "I'm sure you'll think of something, though. You give the best gifts."

"You think?"

"They're always my favorite." She didn't realize how mushy that sounded until the words were already out of her lips.

But Fitz just smiled, his white teeth glowing in the dim light.

And something about the look in his eyes made her very aware of how close they were standing—and how very quiet and empty the atrium was.

How quiet and empty the entire campus was.

Elwin had let them wander just the two of them, so long as they promised to take it easy and be back within thirty minutes. And the guards patrolling the halls were keeping their distance.

So they were alone.

In a moonlit room.

Surrounded by lockers, Sophie reminded herself. *And a giant statue of a dragon that looked like it wanted to eat them.*

Not exactly romantic—which was good since now *so* wasn't the time to talk about crushes.

With her luck, the confession would set off Fitz's echo and

she'd have to explain to Elwin how her silly feelings literally tried to kill him.

She looked away and stepped back, studying the atrium. "This place looks so different at night."

Foxfire's walls were made of stained glass, each wing the same color as the corresponding grade level, so everything should've had a soft emerald green glow. But the moonlight had bleached out most of the color, leaving the room gray and shadowy.

It felt a bit ominous if she really thought about it.

So many dark corners and crannies.

So many places someone could hide.

Fitz cleared his throat and shifted his weight, making her wonder if he was noticing the same thing.

"Think we should head back?" he asked, his voice almost a whisper.

She nodded, reminding herself that Sandor never would've left her unguarded if the campus wasn't completely secure. "It's probably getting close to thirty minutes," she said, "and I doubt we're going to find the Mentors' cafeteria without Keefe."

They'd set off from the Healing Center in search of celebratory butterblasts. But Foxfire was *huge*—and the cafeteria could be anywhere. Plus, she doubted it would have a sign saying, ····· ·· ··· ···· ·· ···· ·· ···· ·· ·······•

"How about we loop back the opposite way?" Fitz suggested. "That way we're at least covering new ground?"

"Works for me," she said, letting him take the lead, partially because his levitating made him faster—when he wasn't crashing into the walls or ceiling, at least. But mostly because the campus still felt like a maze to her.

Sophie had been attending Foxfire off and on for more than two years and still barely managed to find her sessions. The halls were too twisted and tangled for her to figure out the flow of them. And there were so many—for every path she'd explored there were hundreds she'd never wandered.

So she wasn't the least bit surprised that nothing along their route back to the Healing Center looked familiar. The banners dangling from the ceiling all bore a saber-toothed tiger, so they had to be in the Level Five wing. But the winding halls were just row after row of silent, unmarked doors.

Some were metal. Some were glass. Some were old, weathered wood.

Nothing ominous about them.

And yet, Sophie could feel the tiny hairs on the back of her neck getting pricklier and pricklier with each turn.

"Is it me, or does this place give you the creeps?" she whispered, picking up her pace to keep closer to Fitz.

"It does," he admitted. "And I can't figure out why. I know this hall. I had multispeciesial studies right there last year." He pointed to one of the doors, made from intricately faceted crystal. "But . . . does it feel colder here?"

Now that he mentioned it, the hall did have a noticeable chill.

It also felt drafty, as if there was a fan nearby.

Or an open window . . .

"Maybe it's the high ceilings," she suggested, glancing up at the arched skylights—and the millions of twinkling stars beyond.

It was a breathtaking view.

Far too pretty to feel scary.

She'd almost convinced herself. And then . . . there was a boom.

"You heard that, right?" Fitz whispered, scooting even closer to Sophie.

She nodded. "Think it was one of the guards?"

"That's probably it," Fitz decided. "They must've closed a door or something."

"That makes sense," Sophie agreed. "I'm sure they do all kinds of routine checks."

"Right," Fitz said, like they'd settled it.

They listened for another beat and found only silence—which should've been comforting, but . . .

"Want to walk faster?" they both asked in unison.

And their hurried pace was smoother than how they'd been moving earlier, as if the adrenaline was steadying their motions. Fitz didn't crash into a single wall. And Sophie easily kept up with him, her sling bumping softly against her chest as they rounded the next corner, and the next and the next.

"I didn't realize we'd walked this far," Sophie said, her words punctuated by gasping breaths.

"Me neither." Fitz paused to study the hallway. "Ugh! Because we didn't. I led us the wrong way."

He turned to backtrack and they picked up their pace again, shoes hammering the floor, Fitz's crutches clanging with every hit.

But even with all the noise, Sophie still heard it.

She even stopped to make sure.

Voices.

"Wait!" Fitz said, grabbing her good arm as she turned to flee. "Don't you recognize them?"

She didn't, but that might've been because her pulse was pounding, pounding, pounding and her brain was screaming, *RUN! RUN! RUN!*

"I think they're this way," Fitz said, turning down a new hall to their right. And even though it went against all her instincts, Sophie followed.

Fitz knows them, she told herself as she willed her heart to slow and strained her ears, trying to hear what he'd heard.

For several endless beats there was nothing—long enough that she started to wonder if they'd imagined the whole thing.

Then the voices spoke again, sounding much closer that time.

And she recognized them a second before she rounded the corner and found the speakers in the flesh.

Tam, Linh, and Lady Zillah, standing in a round room under an open skylight, surrounded by threads of inky black shadowflux.

TWENTY-FIVE

ON'T LET GO!" LADY ZILLAH shouted as the shadowflux twisted and thrashed, fighting to break free of Tam's hold.

He spun his hands, dragging the darkness closer—each thread so much blacker than the other shadows filling the round alcove.

So much more solid and wild.

So terrifyingly familiar.

And with that thought, the monster in Sophie's mind stirred.

Stretched its legs.

Sharpened its claws.

But Sophie refused to let the nightmares take control.

She stumbled back, pressing her shoulders against the nearest wall to keep her balance as she stared at the stars through the open skylight, imagining herself soaring toward the moon with Silveny—racing for the light.

Leaving the shadows far behind.

And with every slow, deep breath, she caged the monster in.

"You okay?" Fitz whispered.

She glanced his way, realizing he was slumped against the wall, both hands pressed over his heart, crutches balanced precariously against his shoulder.

She nodded. "Are you?"

"I think so. But maybe we should—"

"Fitz?" Linh called. "Sophie?" Her face broke into an enormous grin as she raced toward them. "I can't believe you guys are here!"

"Me neither," Tam said, dropping his arms and releasing whatever hold he'd had on the threads of darkness.

Lady Zillah shook her head as the shadowflux curled back into the night. "Every time you let it win," she told Tam, "you'll have to fight that much harder to earn its respect."

"I didn't *let* it win," Tam argued. "I sent it away, so it couldn't hurt anyone."

"It can't hurt anyone unless you tell it to," Lady Zillah corrected.

"I don't know," Linh said, her eyes darting from Fitz to Sophie and back again, taking in his crutches and her sling before studying each of their faces. "You guys look a little pale. Is it the echoes?"

Fitz nodded.

"But we're fine," Sophie promised when Tam backed farther away, as if he was afraid that standing too close would make them worse. "We're both getting pretty good at stopping the attacks."

"The echoes shouldn't have been affected by anything we were doing," Lady Zillah insisted as she strode over to them, her white cape billowing behind her like a ghost.

She waved her palm over Fitz's chest, then over Sophie's hand and head, and her lips pulled into a deep frown. "Well . . . I suppose seeing the shadowflux could've triggered flashbacks of the attack, and *those* might've stirred the echoes."

Tam turned away, tugging hard on his bangs. "If I'd known you'd be in the halls, I would've warned you we'd be training."

"It's fine," Fitz told him. "We didn't know we'd be in the halls either until about an hour ago. This is our first time out of bed since the attack."

"Really?" Linh asked, studying them again, and Sophie became very aware of how horrifying she must look.

She could feel at least half her hair falling out of her ponytail and couldn't remember how many days it had been since the last time she'd done a quick sponge bath. She probably also smelled like onions, thanks to her mineral soak. *And* she was still wearing one of her sparkly halter-style tunics. So she was basically a walking disaster—which felt extra awesome standing next to Fitz, who somehow managed to look even more adorable all rumpled and bed-heady.

And she wasn't even going to *think* about how sleek and shiny Linh looked, with her hair swept back into two jeweled barrettes and her silky gray tunic bringing out the silver in her eyes. But Sophie's chest still tightened when Linh leaned to help Fitz adjust positions on his crutches—especially when he gave Linh his perfect smile. And she was so busy telling herself not to care that she missed the question Linh asked and had to make her repeat it.

"I asked if this means you're going home," Linh told her.

"Oh! I wish," Sophie said, tucking a greasy strand of hair behind her ear. "I have a feeling Elwin's going to make us wait at least another day before he'll let us light leap."

"As well he should," Lady Zillah agreed. "Honestly, I'm amazed it's still our main method of transport. You'd think we'd have found a better way to move around—one that doesn't require breaking down our bodies and putting them back together. But once again, we've focused all our attention on light."

"Ugh, not another 'light is weak and shadows are strong' lecture," Tam grumbled.

"Why not?" Lady Zillah countered. "You clearly need it. Look at you, cowering over there, still afraid of your power."

"She's not wrong," Linh told her brother.

Tam scowled at everyone.

Linh snorted a laugh. "I swear, if I was this sulky while I adjusted to my power, I kind of don't blame the Council for banishing me."

"I'm not sulking," Tam argued. "And I'm not *adjusting to my power*—I'm messing with creepy shadows we probably shouldn't be messing with. But I'm still here practicing every night, aren't I?"

"*Every* night?" Sophie verified.

"He has a lot to learn," Lady Zillah agreed.

"Do Shades always train here at night?" Fitz asked.

"No—not that there are many that are actually allowed to attend Foxfire," Lady Zillah said under her breath. "Our regular sessions are in a dark room. But shadowflux is easier to feel when there's starlight, so Magnate Leto arranged for Tam and me to access the campus after hours for these more specialized lessons."

"And I've been tagging along," Linh added, "to make sure Tam doesn't need any cheering up—"

"Which mostly means finding ways to annoy me," Tam noted.

"Exactly," Linh agreed, flicking her wrist and splashing Tam's face with a mini wave of water. "Best part of my job as his sister."

Tam glared.

Linh winked.

Lady Zillah sighed.

"I thought about sneaking over to the Healing Center to

check on you guys," Linh added, turning back to Sophie and Fitz, "but I figured you'd probably be sleeping. Oh—but since you're here, I can give you your present! Hang on!"

"On *that* note," Lady Zillah said as Linh took off down the hall, "we should get back to our lesson."

"I'm not calling down any more shadowflux while Fitz and Sophie are here," Tam told her.

"I never said you should," Lady Zillah huffed. "And I doubt it would respond to you anyway, after the way you just dismissed it. But we can work with the echo in your hand."

"*You* have an echo?" Sophie asked, tasting bile when Tam nodded.

"How?" Fitz demanded.

"It's nothing like what you're experiencing," Lady Zillah assured them. "There was no pain or anger to Tam's encounter— nothing negative at all. He simply let the shadowflux sink under his skin and leave a gentle echo, so that we can begin to understand some of their most basic effects."

"It's not a big deal," Tam added. "I wouldn't have done it if it was."

Sophie sighed. "Still, I—"

"*There* you are!" Elwin interrupted, stomping down the hall behind them. "I told you thirty minutes, and it's been—"

He stopped short when he spotted Tam and Lady Zillah. "Well . . . I guess this explains the delay."

"You didn't know they're training here at night?" Fitz asked.

Elwin shook his head. "I haven't left the Healing Center much myself."

"That's true," Sophie said quietly. "You're probably even more eager for us to go home than we are."

"Nah—it's been fun having the company," Elwin assured her. "But our Foxfire slumber party really is coming to an end. I'm betting Fitz will be ready to head home tomorrow, and you'll be ready the day after."

"Why not at the same time?" Tam wondered.

"Sophie had a lot more breaks than Fitz did," Elwin explained, "so she needs a little more time to let all the new bone harden."

"Well, I'm not leaving until Sophie does," Fitz decided.

"You don't have to do that," Sophie told him.

"I know I don't *have* to," he said, with a smile that made her breath catch a little. "I *want* to."

She was saved from having to come up with a nonmushy response by Linh racing back into the alcove and handing Sophie a soft, hot pink tunic.

Elwin cracked up when he saw the embroidery.

So did Sophie.

Dozens of smiley faces surrounded silver glittery letters that said, *Happy Shadow Thoughts.* And on the back, more glittery letters said, *Angry echoes—beware!*

"I know it's silly," Linh mumbled. "But I made one for Tam, and I thought it might help with the echoes somehow. Don't worry, you don't have to wear it."

"Are you kidding?" Sophie asked, pulling Linh into a one-armed hug. "It's amazing! I'm changing into this as soon as I'm back in the Healing Center!"

And she did.

Sophie couldn't look at it without smiling—and neither could Fitz once she'd explained the joke.

Just like Sophie couldn't stop wiggling her bandage-free fingers or reminding herself that she could get out of her cot anytime she wanted. And very, very soon, she'd be home again.

Her mood was on such a high that she wasn't sure she'd need Silveny's dreams to chase away any nightmares.

And it was a good thing she didn't.

Because that night, Silveny didn't check in.

SORRY! SORRY! SORRY! Silveny kept repeating when Sophie and Fitz finally managed to make contact the next morning.

Apparently, Silveny had been so exhausted that she'd slept through all of Sophie's and Fitz's attempts to make contact.

And Sophie knew it wasn't necessarily strange for someone to be tired during pregnancy, but it still made her more determined than ever to convince Silveny to come in for a checkup.

BABY OKAY! BABY OKAY! Silveny insisted.

I hope you're right, Sophie told her. *But what about you? You have to take care of yourself, too.*

TAKING CARE! Silveny insisted, sending images of the lush meadow she'd been grazing in that morning.

It's not just about eating, Sophie argued. *You might need some extra vitamins or fluids or . . .*

Okay, she knew nothing about what a pregnant flying horse needed—or what *anyone* who was pregnant needed. Which proved even more why Silveny should be examined by someone with actual medical knowledge.

But every time Sophie suggested it, Silveny flooded her head with *NO VISIT! NO VISIT! NO VISIT!*

Sophie's probably going home tomorrow, Fitz jumped in, triggering a loud swell of *SOPHIE HOME! SOPHIE HOME! SOPHIE HOME!*

Right, he agreed. *She's just as excited as you are. So why don't you meet her there? You guys could celebrate together.*

Sophie could feel that Silveny was tempted. But she still went back to repeating, *NO VISIT!*

WHY? Sophie shouted over Silveny's next few chants.

BABY OKAY! BABY OKAY!

And round and round they went.

"This feels like banging our heads into a wall, doesn't it?" Sophie asked Fitz, out loud so Silveny couldn't hear them.

"She's definitely the most stubborn creature I've ever met," Fitz agreed. "And I live with Biana."

"Excuse me?" Biana asked, blinking into sight in the middle of the Healing Center—and startling Sophie and Fitz so badly that Silveny blasted their heads with a bunch of *SOPHIE OKAY? FITZ OKAY?*

We're fine! Sophie promised. *Biana just surprised us.*

"You *had* to manifest as a Vanisher," Fitz grumbled to his sister.

"Jealous?" Biana asked, disappearing again and reappearing next to Fitz's cot. She flicked the tip of his nose before vanishing again and reappearing with a smirk on the other side of the room.

"I'm allowed to get out of this bed now," Fitz warned, reaching for his crutches, "and these don't slow me down as much as you'd think."

"I know. Linh told me she saw you guys last night—thanks for hailing me to let me know," she deadpanned.

"Thanks for all the visits," Fitz countered, his tone trying for sarcastic teasing but his eyes not really selling it.

"Hey—Elwin kept shooing me away!" Biana argued.

"Yeah, and you never sneak around orders like that."

Biana sighed. "You're right. I just . . . didn't want to upset you. I figured if I came here, you'd want to know what's going on with Alvar and—"

"What *is* going on with Alvar?" Fitz interrupted.

She shot him a look and pointed to where he'd pressed his hand over his chest. "See? That's what I mean! I knew you'd ask all kinds of questions you don't really want to know the answers to, and it'd mess with that echo thing and set back your recovery. So I figured it'd be better if I just checked in with Sophie and left you alone until you were better."

Fitz blew out a breath. "Well . . . I guess that's a better excuse than Mom and Dad's."

"It's killing them, you know," Biana said quietly. "Knowing you're here, still recovering, and don't want to see them. I catch Mom crying all the time."

"Good," Fitz said.

"Don't be like that," she told him.

"And don't tell me you're on their side now!" Fitz snapped back, taking a long breath and rubbing his chest. "I'm fine," he told Sophie when he caught her staring at him.

"Want me to leave you guys alone to talk?" Sophie offered.

"No," Biana told her. "He'll be on better behavior if you're here."

Fitz rolled his eyes and Biana slumped against one of the cots.

"I'm still mad at them," she told him. "And I hate a lot of what they're doing. But they still love us, Fitz. And they've been worried sick about you. They're *trying*. It's all just . . . a mess."

"It is," Fitz agreed.

Silence followed, and Sophie couldn't decide if she should be the one to break it.

"Do you want me to go?" Biana eventually asked.

Fitz shook his head. "Not until you tell me what's going on with Alvar. I know there has to be something—and it's fine, I can handle it. I'll tell you to stop if I need you to."

Biana's eyes dropped to her hands and she fussed with the

beaded sash on her tunic—which made Sophie realize it must not be a school day, since Biana wasn't in her Foxfire uniform. But more important . . .

"You didn't cover your scars." She regretted the words when Biana's cheeks turned as pink as the fabric. "Sorry. I shouldn't—"

"No, it's fine," Biana interrupted, holding out her arm and letting the light play off the jagged white lines. "It feels a little weird. But . . . these scars are part of me now, and I decided I'm done pretending they're not. Maybe it's good if people see them. Especially today."

"What's today?" Sophie and Fitz asked in unison.

Biana chewed her lip, still fidgeting with her sash. "I guess I should've said tonight, since it's happening after sunset. But . . . tonight, Alvar's moving back to Everglen."

TWENTY-SIX

HY ARE THEY WAITING until after sunset?" Sophie asked as Fitz curled his shaky hands into fists and pressed them against his heart.

"It's a security thing," Biana explained, glancing warily at her brother. "Um. Should we be worried about him?"

"I'm fine," Fitz gritted out. "I just need a second."

But Elwin still emerged from his office and flashed a layered bubble of light around Fitz's torso.

"What kind of security thing?" Sophie asked Biana.

"Luzia made some changes to the gate so that it will react if Alvar gets too close, and I guess that means they have to disable everything to bring him through. Apparently that's easier to do at night when there isn't as much light fueling the mechanisms? I don't know—none of it really makes sense to me, but . . ." She shrugged.

"They're *disabling the gate?*" Fitz's fists curled tighter when Biana nodded. "Great, so once Alvar's in, he's never leaving—but I guess we already knew that."

But Sophie was much more interested in the fact that Luzia had gotten involved. "Did she admit there's something weird about the property?"

"No, she claims the only reason she made an adjustment is to prevent Alvar from escaping. And she was there for, like, two minutes, so I don't think the change is that big a deal. She seriously showed up, stood outside the gate, did some weird flashy things, and left. She wouldn't even come inside."

"I still don't like it," Sophie decided.

"Neither do I," Biana admitted. "But I've searched and searched and searched, and I can't find anything weird about our house or the grounds. And Grizel and Woltzer swear they have it covered."

"How's Grizel doing?" Fitz asked.

"Pretty good, actually. She still moves a little stiffly sometimes, but it doesn't slow her down. She totally overhauled Woltzer's training regimen when she got back, and it's kicking all of our butts. But I think she's eager to have someone to guard again." Her eyes dropped to her hands. "When are you coming home?"

"Tomorrow, I think," Fitz said, taking another long breath.

"Oh." Biana traced a finger over one of her scars. "Linh said you might be ready to go today."

"He is," Elwin said, snapping his fingers and flashing a green orb around Fitz's body. "His bones are strong enough to handle a leap now. But he'll still need the crutches for a few more days."

Fitz shook his head. "I'm not leaving until Sophie does."

"You don't have to—" Sophie tried, but he cut her off.

"We're leaving here together."

Biana nodded slowly. "That's fine."

But Sophie knew it wasn't.

Can you give us a minute? she transmitted to Elwin and Biana.

They both made loud, forced excuses to look at poultices that might help Biana's scars and ducked into Elwin's office, closing the door.

Subtle, they were not.

But Sophie was pretty sure Fitz was already onto her.

"I'm not leaving early," he said, reaching for Mr. Snuggles and squeezing the sparkly dragon so hard, the stuffing bulged.

"Okay . . ."

She could tell this conversation was going to be like crossing a frozen lake, and she tried her best to tread carefully. "Is that because you don't think you can handle being there when Alvar arrives, without triggering your echo?"

Fitz snorted. "No. It's because I'm not going to start living my life around my jerk of a brother. If my parents want me there, they can wait one lousy day until I'm home. But they won't. So I'm not rushing back to make it easy for them."

"They might be thinking they're protecting you by doing it before you're there," she reminded him.

"Uh, if they were worried about me, they wouldn't be doing this—period. This is about Alvar. He's probably been whining to everyone about how miserable his little cell is, and my parents are rushing to get him out."

"Or it's the Council's decision," Sophie countered.

"Nah, it's my parents' private property—the Council doesn't get to drop a prisoner off without their permission."

"Okay, but . . ."

She hesitated a second, hoping she wasn't about to cross a line—then decided it might be best to switch to transmitting, in case they had anyone eavesdropping.

The thing is, she started again, *Biana needs you. You know that's why she's here, right? I mean, yeah, I'm sure she also thought you should know what's going on—but if that's all it was, she would've left as soon as she finished telling you. But she's still here, probably hoping you'll decide to go home with her so she isn't alone when she has to watch your parents let your brother in. And honestly? I don't blame her for that.*

I don't either. He let out a breath, and it sounded a lot like he was deflating. *Ugh, I hate this.*

I know.

I mean, I REALLY hate it.

I know.

This is how it's going to be from here on out. Everything's going to revolve around Alvar. First they drag me home early because they couldn't be bothered to wait one day. And next it'll be, "We can't have anyone over right now—it's a security risk." Not that anyone will want to come over knowing there's a murderer at my house.

I will, Sophie promised. *And I'm sure Keefe will—and Tam and Linh and Dex. Probably even Marella. We'll be allowed to, right?*

I don't know, he admitted. *I could see my dad saying it's too risky. Or your new bodyguards might not want you around my brother.*

She cringed at the reminder of exactly how many people she'd have bossing her around once she got home. But now wasn't the time to worry about herself.

Yeah, well . . . they can't keep me away.

He didn't return her smile.

That's not even the worst part, he told her. *The worst part will be when my parents start nagging me and Biana to spend time at Alvar's apartment because "the Council needs to see how he interacts with other people." And if we don't give in, they'll just let him into the house—though I'm sure they'll do that anyway.*

He flung Mr. Snuggles across the room.

"Sorry," he said out loud. "I'm fine—don't worry about the echo."

The echo was only a tiny part of her worries. And she wished she had some magic solution.

The best she could come up with was, "I think you, Biana, and your parents need to sit down and figure out some very specific ground rules for how this is going to work—and I think today is the day to do it, before he moves in. You have some time before sunset. You should go home and lay out everything you can and can't handle: where you're willing to see Alvar and where you're not, under what conditions, how often—all that stuff. And for every compromise you make, demand something in return."

"Like what?"

Sophie considered that. "What about access to your dad's office so you can search it for yourself?"

Fitz leaned back a little. "Huh. That's actually not a bad idea."

Sophie smiled. "You don't need to sound so surprised."

"I'm not. I'm just thinking."

She let him mull it all over for several minutes—even though it felt like an eternity—before she asked, "So . . . does that mean you'll go with Biana? Because you probably shouldn't wait too much longer. You'll want to make sure you get this all ironed out before Alvar gets there."

Fitz closed his eyes. "I really wish you'd stop being right."

"I know what you mean," she said, giving him a few more seconds. Then she asked, "Should we tell Elwin you're leaving?

I'm sure he's going to want to check you one more time before you go."

She was right again.

Elwin also insisted on sending Fitz with a satchel full of elixirs—and while he went over all the instructions, Biana gathered up Fitz's extra clothes and Mr. Snuggles and helped him out of bed and onto his crutches. In less than ten minutes they were ready to go.

"I don't know what you said to him," Biana whispered as Sophie stood and gave her a one-armed hug. "But thank you."

"Anytime," Sophie told her. "Will you be okay?"

"Of course!" And she *almost* sounded convincing.

Then Biana let her go, busying herself with digging out her home crystal as Sophie turned to Fitz, trying to figure out how to say goodbye.

It wasn't like they'd never see each other again. But . . . it felt like an end, somehow.

"So," she mumbled, not sure how to finish that sentence— or what to do with her arms. Or where to stand.

It all felt awkward and weird and wrong—until Fitz dropped his crutches and gently pulled her into a hug.

"I don't want to go," he whispered.

"I don't want you to either," she admitted, hoping her hushed tone hid the thickness in her voice.

She told herself not to pull him tighter so he wouldn't feel how hard her heart was pounding. But she couldn't help leaning closer when she realized his pulse felt just as crazy as hers.

She didn't know what that meant.

But it felt like *something*.

And she could've stood like that for a good long while, but . . . it really wasn't the time for that sort of thing. She wasn't sure when the right time would be—or what would happen when it was.

But for the moment, that was okay.

"Check in when you can," she told him, not wanting to pile on too much pressure.

"I will," he said, clinging to her a second longer before he let go.

Then Biana helped him with his crutches, thankfully not saying a word about their *lengthy* hug as she reached for her brother's hand and held her crystal up to create a path.

Fitz's eyes never left Sophie's as he let Biana lead them forward, offering one last smile before he left.

It was only half a smile.

But she knew it was just for *her*.

And she smiled back as Fitz and Biana stepped into the light and leaped back to Everglen.

TWENTY-SEVEN

FITZ DIDN'T CHECK IN THAT NIGHT.

Sophie hadn't *really* expected him to—or that was what she told herself—since she knew he'd be busy dealing with the return of his nefarious brother.

But she still spent the rest of her day staring at her Imparter, wishing it would light up with his face. Or hoping his crisp, accented voice would flood into her mind and tell her how everything was going—and not *just* because she missed him way more than she should, or because she was worried about how he was handling everything.

It . . . wasn't easy sitting in the same boring cot surrounded by the same boring walls while this huge, monumental thing was happening without her.

"One more night," Elwin kept telling her every time he brought another elixir for her to swallow or coated her arm in another smelly balm.

Around the fourth or fifth treatment, she finally asked, "And then what?"

It was the question she'd been avoiding, not wanting to hear how much recovery she still had ahead.

And it was *not* good news.

More rest.

More elixirs.

Lots more patience.

Plus a *long* list of things her hand and arm weren't going to be doing anytime soon.

He'd even broken it into a timeline—week after week of her *still* not being able to train with the rest of her friends.

She knew she should get up—walk it off—remind herself how far she'd come since she'd entered the Healing Center. But what good was wandering aimlessly through the halls?

Honestly, what good was going home if she was still going to spend most of her time in a different bed staring at different walls and still not actually doing much of anything?

So she sat there, hour after hour, telling herself she wasn't *sulking*, she was *resting* like the good little patient Elwin needed her to be. She'd almost convinced herself it was true, until Keefe marched through the doors to the Healing Center and declared, "Wow, it's like walking into a cloud of sulk in here."

He fanned the air away from his face as he made his way over. "I mean, I figured you'd be feeling a little lost without your Cognate buddy, but trust me: Fitzy isn't worth *this* much angst."

"I'm not pouting about Fitz," Sophie informed him.

"Ah, so you admit you *are* pouting?" he countered, plopping onto the edge of her cot with enough oomph to make the mattress bounce.

She shrugged.

"Hmm. This might be more moping than Krakie can handle—I guess it's a good thing I brought him a friend!" He reached into his cape and pulled out the kraken pin that Sophie had given him to take care of, along with a fresh box of Prattles. "Let's see what we got this time."

He fished out the tiny pouch and uncovered a blue, scale-covered kitten. "A murcat! Gah—that's tricky to name. We already have a Scaley Butt. How about Drifty? Or Sea-Whiskers?"

Sophie sighed. "You don't have to do this."

"If you're talking about being adorable, I really can't help myself."

He said it with a wink *and* a smirk—which wasn't playing fair. But she managed to stop her lips from curving into a smile.

Keefe laughed and reached for her left wrist, carefully pinning Krakie back into place on her makeshift bracelet before adding the murcat next to the kelpie. "Okay, so you have two choices," he told her. "You can tell me what brought on the Foster Funk. *Or* I can guess—and I have some pretty interesting theories."

"So do I," Ro added, snatching the box of Prattles away from Keefe and pouring half the candy into her mouth at once.

"Three seconds to decide," Keefe warned. "Then it's guessing time!"

"It's not a big deal," Sophie told him over the sound of Ro's crunching. "I'm just . . . really sick of being in this bed."

"Okay. Then let's get you out of it! I hear you can do that now!" He hopped back to his feet and offered a hand to help her up. "I promised to show you a secret cafeteria, didn't I? Perfect way to end your Foxfire slumber party!"

It felt a little wrong to go hunting for desserts while Fitz and Biana were trying to figure out how to live with their murdering brother.

But . . . butterblasts did sound pretty good.

"Hang on—*what* are you wearing?" Keefe asked as she threw back her covers, revealing the sparkly slogans on her tunic. "Is that a Bangs Boy reference? Because you know I haven't let him into the Foster Fan Club, right?"

Sophie rolled her eyes. "It's an inside joke—and *Linh* made this for me."

"Yeah, well, it still breaks the fan club rules. As penance, I'm getting you a tunic that says, *Empaths Give Me All the Feels*, and I expect to see you wear it twice as often as Bangs Boy's."

Ro snorted. "Subtle."

"Ridiculous," Sophie corrected.

"I try," Keefe told them as Sophie took his hand and let him pull her slowly to her feet.

"You good?" he asked when she wobbled from the head rush.

No. But she wasn't going to admit that, so she told him, "I'm up."

"You are. It's pretty amazing."

"Isn't it?" Elwin asked as he emerged from his office and helped Sophie strap her arm into a sling. "Bring me back some butterblasts, okay?"

"Done!" Keefe told him, bending his elbow to offer Sophie his arm, and after one brief second, she let him lead her toward the door. "TO THE SECRET CAFETERIA!"

The halls were just as eerie as they'd been the night before, and Sophie tightened her grip on Keefe's arm, trying not to think about shadowflux. But she could still feel that unsettling chill in the air.

It might've been her imagination.

Or it might've meant Tam was there training.

Either way, she let out a relieved breath every time they turned another corner and found the next corridor to be quiet and empty.

"So, you going to tell me what's *really* bothering you?" Keefe asked as he guided her around a wide bend into a hall she actually recognized—the beginning of the Level Three wing.

"I don't know," Sophie told him. "Are *you* going to tell me why you're trying *so* hard to act like everything's normal?"

"What makes you think I'm acting?"

"Uh, the last time I saw you, you'd just found out that your mom had some of your memories shattered. And then you ignored me the next day—and *then* told me you were close to a breakthrough with Tiergan. And now you show up the day after that, don't mention it at all, *and* you're in this, like, Ultra Knight in Shining Armor mode—"

"Aw, you hear that, Ro? Foster thinks I'm her hero!"

"I think you're pretending to be," Sophie corrected, "so I won't notice the shadows under your eyes. Or these."

She reached for his hand and pointed to the faint bruises on his knuckles. "Been punching walls? Or people?"

"The floor, actually," Keefe admitted after a few seconds.

Sophie stopped walking. "Okay, so what'd you learn that has you punching the floor?"

He tilted back his head, staring at the mastodon banners hanging from the amber glass ceiling, which looked mostly gray in the moonlight. "I didn't learn anything. *That's* why I punched the floor. Tiergan helped me find this tiny pocket of hidden memories, and I thought—this is it! But . . . it was all random, useless fragments. A sunset. A couple of trees. A bunch of black fabric. Empty glass vials. Stuff like that. The only useful piece was a pair of green eyes. But they're so blurry we can't even tell if they're from a guy or a girl or a kid or an adult."

"But you know they have to be human eyes," Sophie reminded him.

"Yep. That was my big breakthrough. A couple of blurry human eyes that could belong to literally anyone—plus a whole lot of proof that those memories are probably too smashed up to salvage."

"It's still something," she insisted.

"I guess." His eyes shifted to hers. "So is the fact that you're up out of bed, walking around Foxfire—but it doesn't feel like enough, does it?"

"It doesn't," she agreed, her mind automatically skipping to all the recovery she still had ahead of her.

But she shook those thoughts away.

"It *should*, though," she told him. "It's still a victory."

And if they didn't celebrate those small triumphs, they were going to drive themselves crazy.

So she laced her gloved fingers with his and told him, "Come on. We both deserve some desserts!"

Foxfire's secret "Mentors only" cafeteria turned out to be even more amazing than Sophie had imagined: throne-size chairs surrounding peaceful reflecting pools. Urns blooming with delicate flowers that filled the air with a sweet, spicy perfume. Soft, flickering lighting, and windows that overlooked the glass pyramid in the heart of campus.

And, of course, an entire wall of glass cases filled with all kinds of fancy, colorful confections.

It was kind of like going to a spa, but instead of kale and

cucumber water, there was food people actually wanted to eat.

Even Ro had no complaints, despite the definite presence of sparkles. She sprawled out on one of the chairs and worked her way through an entire tray of ripplefluffs.

"Do I want to know how you found this place?" Sophie wondered as she finished off her third butterblast.

"Of course you do," Keefe told her. "But I never reveal my secrets."

"Even to me?" she asked, not sure where the question came from.

Her cheeks burned as he studied her—and she didn't want to admit that it stung when he said, "Yeah, Foster—even to you."

She shoved another butterblast into her mouth to save herself from having to respond.

But when their eyes met again, his gaze had softened, and he whispered, "At least for now."

The words weren't an invitation. They were an end to the conversation. And since Sophie wasn't sure what they were talking about anymore, she left it at that.

"Thank you," she said as he walked her back to the Healing Center and she tried to make a note of the route so she could find the secret cafeteria again. "Tonight would've been . . . pretty rough if you hadn't stopped by."

"I know," he told her. "For me too."

"Awwwwwww, you guys are SO adorable," Ro jumped in.

"You want to talk about adorable," Keefe snapped back. "I wrote another verse in *The Ballad of Bo and Ro*—and just think! Tomorrow, Foster finally gets to meet your long-lost love!"

"Do *not* share that verse," Ro warned, pretty much guaranteeing that Keefe would be chanting it to her for the rest of the night. But first she told Sophie, "Don't tell him anything about me."

"Why not?" Sophie had to ask.

"Because he doesn't deserve to know."

Keefe leaned closer to Sophie, stage-whispering. "You realize it's now your job to pester Bo for all the details Ro's trying to hide from us."

Ro smirked. "Try it—Bo won't tell you a thing."

"Wanna bet?" Keefe countered.

"Bad idea," Sophie told him. "You've won twice now—that means you're pretty much guaranteed to lose. Especially since this bet relies on me again."

He grinned. "Exactly, Foster. You're always the safe bet."

"Not this time," Ro told him.

"We doing this, then?" Keefe asked her.

Ro folded her arms. "Fine. If I win, I get one guaranteed dare. I can tell you to do anything I want, and you *have* to do it."

Keefe raised one eyebrow. "Deal—but only if I get the same thing if I win."

Ro leaned into his face, flashing a deadly smile. "It's on."

Sophie sighed, laying on the sarcasm nice and thick when she mumbled, "This can only end well."

. . .

Keefe and Ro didn't breathe a word about their new bet to Elwin when they dropped Sophie back at the Healing Center—and Sophie certainly wasn't going to be the one to tell him. He probably wouldn't have to deal with the drama anyway. She'd be out of the Healing Center long before the winner and loser were decided.

And it hit her then.

She really *was* getting out of there.

She really *was* going home.

"Last night," Elwin told her as she worked her way through the latest round of medicine.

"I know—you're almost rid of me! Well . . . until all the house calls."

He grinned and rumpled her hair before handing her Ella. "Get some rest. Tomorrow will be a big day."

Silveny must've sensed the change coming too. That night she filled Sophie's head with dreams of the two of them soaring over snowy mountains, chasing the coming dawn on the brightening horizon. It was peaceful and soothing. But also hopeful. And when the sun rose around them in the dream world, it felt like a new beginning—and maybe it was, because when Sophie opened her sleepy eyes on her last morning in the Healing Center, she was no longer alone.

"Back to your Forkle disguise?" she asked, sitting up to study the bloated, wrinkled figure sitting on the cot across from her. The ruckleberries he must've consumed had made his body swell, stretch, and crinkle, until he looked much more like an elderly human than an elf. And no matter how hard she squinted, she couldn't see any trace of Magnate Leto.

"I have some errands to run," he told her. "So I had to switch things up."

His voice was back to its familiar raspy wheeze, and Sophie knew how silly it was to feel her heart swell at the sound. The elf sitting across from her was technically no different than her slicked-haired principal.

But *this* was the voice—and the face—she'd known all her life. The annoying next-door neighbor who asked too many questions but had turned out to be her protector and creator.

A voice she'd once feared had fallen silent forever.

"Aren't you worried someone will see you?" she had to ask, since his Forkle identity was meant to be much more mysterious. Plus, the Neverseen were supposed to think he was dead.

"He transformed in here," Elwin said behind her, and Sophie turned to find him studying Mr. Forkle through his iridescent spectacles. "I swear, my eyes still don't want to believe what I saw. I think I need to study ruckleberries more. I've clearly been underestimating how potent those little things are."

"But what if people notice the principal is missing?" Sophie asked.

"I'm hoping it will be an uneventful day," Mr. Forkle admitted. "But if anything comes up, Lady Cadence is prepared to cover for me—as is Elwin. It appears having others in on the secret is going to be key, now that it's harder for me to sneak away."

"Why is that, by the way?" Elwin asked as he handed Sophie her morning tray of medicine.

"It's a very long story," Mr. Forkle told him, staring blankly into the distance. "And one I don't have time to share today."

"I take it you're not going to tell me where you're going on these mysterious errands?" Sophie asked.

His lips pulled into a half smile. "And here I thought you'd be happy to have things back to normal."

She closed her eyes, needing a few seconds to let the words sink in.

Back to normal.

That's what this was—even if it would be a new normal for a while.

And she was determined to make the best of it.

But it didn't *really* feel real until she'd chugged down all her medicine and Elwin had flashed a zillion colorful orbs around her arm and given her all kinds of warnings and reminders.

Then he confirmed it. "Yep! Your bones are definitely strong enough to light leap."

"Good," Mr. Forkle said. "Because she'll be making more than one."

"I will?" Sophie asked. "And you really aren't going to tell me where I'm going?"

"Not yet. Dex should be here any minute, and I'll catch

you both up then. In the meantime, you should probably get changed."

He held out a folded tunic and a pair of leggings, both in pale colors without any frills—exactly the way Sophie preferred them—along with a heavy cape and a pair of sturdy boots.

"Your mother brought them by this morning," he explained. "She's *very* eager to have you home. I'm told there will be a feast of epic proportions when we arrive."

Sophie's stomach growled at the thought.

"Need help getting dressed?" Elwin offered, but there was no way that was happening—beyond letting him remove her sling for a few minutes.

"I can handle it," she promised.

And she did.

But . . . it *was* more of a struggle than she wanted it to be.

Her healing arm would only lift so high—only bend at the elbow so much. And her fingers were weak and clumsy. So tying the sash on her tunic?

Pretty much impossible.

"Here," Mr. Forkle said when she emerged from behind her curtain with the ends of her sash tossed around her shoulders like an awkward shawl. He tied a simple bow and she started to step away, but he placed a hand on her shoulder. "Perhaps you'd also like a little help with your hair?"

"*You're* offering to do my hair?" Sophie verified, reaching up to feel the tangled mess.

"I'm an elf of *many* talents," he told her.

Shockingly enough, he wove her hair into the most intricate braid she'd ever seen.

"Do I want to know why you know how to do this?" she asked.

"Of course—but that's a story for another day. For now, we should get that arm back into a sling."

"Yes, we should," Elwin said, slipping the thick silver strap over her head and nestling her arm in the loop of fabric.

"Okay, I'm here," Dex announced a few minutes later, flashing Sophie a quick dimpled grin before turning to Mr. Forkle. "Now tell me where we're going."

"That's all you have to say to Miss Foster?" Mr. Forkle asked. "No comment on the fact that she's finally out of bed and leaving the Healing Center?"

Dex glanced back at Sophie, and she didn't blame him one bit for simply giving her a hasty "Yay—glad you're doing better!" before reeling back toward Mr. Forkle and telling him, "Okay, no more stalling. Tell us where we're going!"

Mr. Forkle smiled. "Somewhere I think you're both going to find very useful."

"That better not be your whole answer," Sophie warned.

"Yeah, and why did I have to ditch Lovise?" Dex added.

"You did?" Sophie asked, realizing Dex's bodyguard wasn't standing in the shadows like she should've been.

"I did," Dex agreed, "and I had to promise to make the

triplets all kinds of pranking elixirs in order to convince them to distract her for me—and I'm pretty sure they're going to bring all of them to Foxfire, so good luck with that."

"I'll make sure the campus is prepared," Mr. Forkle assured him. "And trust me, it's worth the effort. I'm taking you both to meet with one of the most reclusive members of the Black Swan—who happens to not be a fan of goblins. Hence why I asked you to come alone, Mr. Dizznee, and why I'm having us make a detour before I bring Miss Foster home to her abundance of bodyguards. It's time for you two to meet Tinker, our Technopath."

"Okay, this is the coolest place I've ever seen," Dex said as he craned his neck to study the metal-and-glass structure, which couldn't seem to decide if it was a mansion or a machine.

Spinning cogs decorated the sweeping arches and ornate columns that formed the main building, which framed what appeared to be a massive clock tower—except the frosted glass face had five hands instead of two, and five symbols instead of twelve, and none of those symbols were numbers. The markings didn't look like runes, either—too many sharp angles. Sophie had no idea what they were. But the same symbols were also used to mark each of the contraptions attached in a neat row along the very top edge of the tower's roof. The first reminded Sophie of a sundial. The second was probably some sort of weather vane. The third might've been an anemometer, and the fourth was most likely a rain gauge. The last she couldn't begin to guess—all she knew was that it was shiny and spinning very fast.

And then there were the pipes.

So. Many. Pipes.

Gleaming in copper, silver, gold, brass, and steel.

Some jutted from the roof of the main building at varying heights and angles, unleashing curls of thick white steam into the chilly sky. Others snaked down the sides of the tower and tunneled into the dark earth—or crawled into the thicket of evergreens and coiled around the massive trees—or dived into the white-capped river that roared along one side of the structure. But most were crowned with widemouthed funnels and reached out like eager arms toward the misty waterfall that formed a backdrop to the strange scene.

"The waterfall's powering everything, isn't it?" Dex asked, squinting at a brassy funnel that reminded Sophie of a tuba as it swallowed a thick stream of frothy water.

"In part," Mr. Forkle agreed. "From what I understand, Widgetmoor draws energy from earth, air, and water."

"Not fire?" Sophie asked.

"*Never* fire," he confirmed, pointing to the thinnest pipes, which scaled to the tops of the trees. One was low enough for her to see something flat and shiny at the end—a mirror, maybe? Or perhaps a solar panel?

The latter seemed more likely, when Mr. Forkle added,

"Sunlight is the only source of heat that Tinker allows—and only in small doses. She prefers the cold."

She must, if she chose to live where the trees blocked most of the light. The waterfall's mist also made everything damp and shivery—not that Sophie minded. After so many days indoors, it was amazing to feel wind on her skin and to breathe in the scent of pine and wet earth.

"I'm guessing there's a reason she's not a fan of fire," Sophie said, flicking her braid off her shoulder.

"There always is." But whatever the story was, Mr. Forkle didn't share.

Dex wandered to one of the trees, placing his palm against the copper pipe coiling around and around. "The way she connected all of this is amazing."

"I thought you might be impressed," Mr. Forkle said, leaning back to better admire the view. "Widgetmoor feels like stepping into Tinker's brain. It may seem like chaos at first, but everything has a purpose. Nothing is purely aesthetic. And the eccentricity of it only makes it more brilliant."

"Tinker's her code name?" Sophie clarified.

"It started out that way. But it fits her so well that she decided she prefers it. I don't believe she's used her real name in years. Same goes for her disguise, which I've yet to see her without."

Dex frowned. "Does that mean she was already wearing a disguise before she joined the Black Swan?"

"No, it means I wasn't the one to recruit her. Wraith discovered her, but she was reluctant to join our cause without knowing more about us. So she asked him to keep her identity secret and set up a meeting with the rest of the Collective—and she showed up to that meeting in the same disguise she'll be wearing today."

"She still doesn't trust you?" Sophie asked.

"No, we're long past that. The disguise is as much for utility as it is for concealment. You'll see what I mean. But first, you might want to cover your ears. It's about to get *very* loud."

Sophie could only cover her left ear, thanks to her sling, so she tilted her head to press her right ear into her shoulder— and it was a good thing she did, because when all five of the hands on the tower rotated forward, low-pitched bells boomed through the air, loud enough to send pine needles raining around them.

BOOOOOOOOOOONG!

BOOOOOOOOOOONG!

BOOOOOOOOOOONG!

BOOOOOOOOOOONG!

BOOOOOOOOOOONG!

"Is that the time?" Sophie asked when the clearing had fallen silent again—or as silent as it could be. The roar of the water and the whir of the cogs and a thrumming pulse from the tower—all ticking, no tocking—were still a steady hum in her ears.

"To be quite honest, I don't know what the tower is tracking," Mr. Forkle admitted. "I asked Tinker about it once, and she asked me what I wanted it to be and never gave me the real answer—which is something you should prepare yourself for. Tinker considers questions to be far more valuable than answers, so it's rare to get an actual explanation."

Dex snorted. "Huh, I wonder what *that's* like."

"I know," Sophie agreed. "We're so used to everyone telling us everything we want to know the second we want to know it—how will we ever handle that kind of vagueness and mystery?"

Mr. Forkle sighed. "I suppose I walked into that one. What I was *trying* to convey is that Tinker has a very particular way of communicating, and it can take some getting used to. Just try to go with it."

He strode forward, guiding them up a rocky path that was steeper than it looked. Sophie was breathing much harder than she wanted to by the time they reached a massive brushed-steel door with five enormous cogs set deep into the metal: one silver, one gold, one bronze, one copper, and one iron. A coiled steel pipe hung from the chrome ceiling with a contraption mounted to the end that reminded Sophie of a periscope, only it had five different lenses in five different shapes, arranged in a stack from largest to smallest.

Mr. Forkle knocked with five quick raps—Sophie was beginning to wonder if the number held some deeper meaning—and the periscope stretched closer to his face, the lenses lifting and shifting several times before five quick buzzes filled the air.

The gears in the door whirred to life, each spinning at a slightly different speed as the heavy rectangle of metal slid up instead of swinging open, revealing a silver-arched path leading into a wide atrium covered in flowering vines and lacy ferns. Hanging planters dangled from arched points in the cut-glass ceiling, brimming with colorful blooms, and a grassy path wound through the foliage. It was breathtaking and lush, the cold air heady with the scent of jasmine—but it was so . . . *natural*. No sign of anything technical—until something brushed against Sophie's foot. Then she found herself stumbling away from a tiny creature staring up at her—if she could call it a creature.

"Coooooooooooooooooool," Dex breathed. "It's a clockwork rabbit!"

He crouched to study the metal animal, which was all cogs and wires and shiny bits of brass.

The creature tilted its head, studying Dex with marble eyes, and Dex reached out slowly, like he was offering a treat to a frightened cat. The rabbit wiggled its ears a few times, then hopped onto his palm, and Dex stroked the metal plate along its back before turning it over to examine the inner mechanisms.

"The programming on this is like nothing I've ever seen," he said as he ran a finger along the rabbit's foot and watched it flinch, as if the touch had tickled. The rabbit twisted its head, still staring at Dex with unblinking eyes before it leaped out of his hands and landed back on the path with a soft clank.

"There's an owl over there." Sophie pointed to the edge of

one of the planters, where a gleaming chrome owl watched them with huge eyes made from two glowing light bulbs. And over in the corner she spotted a sleek dragon with verdigris scales peeking out from the thick vines. There was also a tiny blue halcyon fluttering near the entrance, with what looked like a music box set into its chest.

"She calls them her *pet projects*," Mr. Forkle explained. "My favorite is the hummingbird—it must be around here somewhere."

He peeled back part of a fern, but only found a pygmy marmoset built from a gold pocket watch.

"I don't understand how she made these," Dex said as he scooped up the tiny monkey and let it wrap its gold-chain tail around his finger.

"You can't see the trick?" a throaty voice asked, and Sophie tried not to gasp when she spotted a red-haired figure emerging from a hatch among the ferns.

Tinker was the tallest elf Sophie had ever seen—and the red curls piled messily on her head only added to her height. But what truly made her striking was the abundance of metal strapped to her hulking frame. A bronze half mask covered the left side of her freckled face, from the top of her forehead to the tip of her pointed chin, leaving only her gray-blue left eye exposed. Her right eye, in contrast, was covered by a round eyepiece that was somehow mounted along her eyebrow, made of five stacked lenses in varying sizes and colors. And a cog-covered earpiece curved along the outer edge of her left ear and dangled down, connecting to a golden choker—similar to the registry pendants they all wore, but with a small silver sphere instead of a crystal bound into the center. Her pants were fitted chain mail, and her shirt was a riveted steel corset, cinching her waist beneath a wide copper tool belt stuffed with hammers and pliers and screwdrivers—plus all kinds of twisted, springy things. Copper bracers around her wrists completed the look, connecting to hinged silver finger guards that covered each of her pointer fingers like metal scales.

Tinker didn't smile as the hatch silently sealed closed. She just stood there, studying them one by one, her gaze lingering on Dex as she repeated, "You can't see the trick?"

Dex's eyebrows scrunched together as he examined the clockwork monkey again.

"No," he eventually admitted. He bent to set the creature on the ground and froze. "Unless it's this."

He lifted the marmoset again and pointed to something in its neck that Sophie couldn't see—just like she couldn't understand any of the Technopathy explanations he rattled off after that. Most of it didn't even sound like words, just gibberish with a bunch of syllables. But she could tell that Tinker was impressed.

Mr. Forkle introduced them. "Tinker, this is Mr. Dizznee and Miss Foster. We appreciate you granting us this rare visit."

Tinker's gaze shifted to the sling supporting Sophie's arm. "They don't know why you brought them here?"

"Not yet. So perhaps we should head to your laboratory. Seems like a more fitting place for that conversation, don't you think?"

Sophie shared a look with Dex—a look that said they both found those words to be uncomfortably ominous. But it didn't stop them from following Tinker through the atrium, to a gilded path that ended in a round silver room with a narrow iron staircase that corkscrewed all the way to the top of the tower.

"Is this a vortinator?" Sophie asked as Tinker motioned for her to go first.

"Do you want it to be?" Tinker countered.

"Not really." Her morning medicine was still sloshing around her stomach—and she only had one good arm, so clinging for dear life while the staircase spun like a tornado wasn't really something she felt like doing with her day.

"It's Tinker's version of one," Mr. Forkle explained. "But I promise you'll find it to be a much gentler experience."

"Want me to go first?" Dex offered when Sophie still hesitated.

She gave him a grateful nod, and he stepped onto the bottom stair, steadying his balance as the staircase sprang to life. But the motion was slow and smooth, just like Mr. Forkle had promised. In fact, when Sophie climbed up behind Dex, she couldn't feel any sign that they were moving. She only knew they were because the crystal skylight grew closer and closer.

"Did you design all of this yourself?" Dex asked, running his hand along the silver wall.

"Don't you work alone?" Tinker wondered.

"Mostly," Dex admitted—which wasn't the answer Sophie had been expecting. She'd always thought of Dex as part of her same team. But then she remembered how often Dex had to stay home, working on gadgets by himself while the rest of their group tackled some other project.

"It's lonely speaking a language few others understand, isn't it?" Tinker asked him.

Dex looked away as he nodded, and Sophie tried to think of something to say. But all thoughts slid out of her head when she caught a glimpse of Tinker's laboratory.

The room was bigger than she'd been imagining, and much, much messier. Each of the long steel tables was piled with gadgets that were still in the process of creation, their gears left exposed, wires tangling in every direction. And the copper floor was covered in screws and nuts and bolts and shards of metal and glass. The air smelled like grease and metal and oil—but not unpleasantly so. It was the scent of a place where hands got dirty and set to work. And all the whirring and humming and ticking gave the space a buzzing energy that made Sophie want to grab the nearest tool and build something.

Dex looked desperate to do the same thing, his eyes staring hungrily at the half-finished gadgets as they followed Tinker deeper into the lab. They had to weave around enormous springs that connected the floor to the ceiling, like columns, and they eventually stopped in front of a cluster of wide-mouthed pipes jutting from the floor, unleashing white swirls into the air that somehow made the room feel colder. Tinker motioned for them to sit at a table that was mostly empty— just two small gray puffs of fur in the middle, along with what looked like an antique jewelry box.

Sophie sank onto the bench, not caring that it was made of frigid metal. Her head was spinning, and she couldn't decide if it was from the cold, the altitude, or the fact that her still-healing body was weaker than she wanted.

Then again, the dizziness could've been triggered by the thousands of gears whirling all around her.

The lab's glass walls were filled with interlocking cogs all spinning in perfect unison, dragging a web of copper wires sideways and slantways and longways until they fed into a circuit in the center of a foggy round window at the far end of the room.

"Are we inside the clock?" Sophie asked, glancing up to find five iron bells dangling from the peaked skylight. "Or whatever it is?"

"It won't chime again until later tonight, in case you're worried," Mr. Forkle assured her. "It only peals five times a day. Though even if we were here for one of them, the sound is strangely muffled."

"That's because of the pillars," Dex explained. "The springs absorb the vibration. And see all those tiny holes?" He pointed to the nearest coil, and Sophie was surprised to notice its texture was more like steel wool. "Those absorb the sound."

Tinker's eyebrow raised. "How long did that take you to puzzle out?"

Dex shrugged. "I don't know—it's pretty obvious, isn't it?"

"I told you his talent was special," Mr. Forkle said.

Tinker nodded, flicking through the different lenses on her eyepiece as she studied Dex closer, making Dex's cheeks flush the same shade as his hair.

He reached for one of the gray puffs resting on the table, like he needed something to fidget with. "It's cool you have tomples. I've always wanted one."

"That thing's alive?" Sophie realized as the puff stirred in his palm.

Dex held the creature out to her. "Yep. Wanna see?"

She'd started to reach for it when he added, "They're kind of like what you'd get if you crossed a hedgehog, a kitten, and a really big cockroach."

Sophie jerked her hand away just in time to avoid the six spindly brown legs that emerged from the fur.

"Okay, that's just wrong," she said, scooting as far as she could from the fluffy bug-of-doom. "Why would you want one of those?"

"Aw, don't listen to her," Dex whispered to the tomple as he set it back on the table. "She doesn't know what cute is— trust me."

He winked and Sophie felt her jaw fall, wondering when they'd reached a point where they could joke about *that*.

"Besides," he added, "tomples feed on dust, so they're awesome to have in labs. I've been asking my dad to get one for Slurps and Burps for years. But he's worried all the alchemy stuff we do could mix with the dust and make the tomple sick. So I'm stuck cleaning all the shelves myself."

The tomple skittered back toward its fluffy friend, and Sophie tried not to squeal like a five-year-old. But she couldn't help it when she noticed a blur of black fur snatch something from the next table over and duck behind one of the larger contraptions.

"Okay, what was *that*?" she asked, only half sure she wanted to know.

"I believe that's Sprocket," Mr. Forkle said as the same clawed black hand reached around a tangle of wires, grabbed what looked like a small circuit board, and yanked it back.

Tinker rushed over and scooped up a black furry creature with a shiny nose and folded ears like a puppy—a gremlin, Sophie realized. And it wasn't letting go of its new treasures, no matter how hard Tinker pulled.

"I can't believe you keep a gremlin around all of this tech," Dex murmured as Sprocket won his tug-of-war and leaped from Tinker's arms, quickly breaking the circuit board into itty-bitty pieces.

"Gremlins love to dismantle things," Mr. Forkle explained to Sophie. "And I've made the same observation, Mr. Dizznee. *Many* times. All Tinker ever tells me is . . ."

"Aren't some challenges worth it?" she finished, reaching into her tool belt and pulling out a tiny metal cube, which she traded with Sprocket for whatever remained of the circuit board. The happy gremlin scurried under the table and immediately set to work prying the cube apart, tossing each piece over its shoulder—which might explain why the floor was so messy. Maybe even why so many of the gadgets looked unfinished.

Sophie wondered how much time Tinker spent redoing what Sprocket had undone.

"It's a way to fill the day, isn't it?" Tinker asked, somehow guessing what Sophie was thinking—and Sophie finally understood what Mr. Forkle meant about her way of communicating.

All questions, no answers.

"It is," Mr. Forkle told Tinker. "But I've found a better way—as you already know."

He turned to Dex. "I haven't brought you to Tinker before, because it allowed you to come at each other's projects with fresh eyes. But I think we're to a point where it would be far more beneficial for you to put your heads together. Lady Iskra is a brilliant Mentor—and you'll still work with her during your Foxfire sessions. But her approach is very traditional, and we both know that traditional isn't where you excel. So I'd love you to start coming here after school and training with Tinker."

"Every day?" Dex asked.

"As often as you can," Mr. Forkle told him.

"Okay, but . . . I'm not going to be able to keep ditching Lovise. She won't fall for the triplets' tricks again."

"Lovise is a goblin?" Tinker confirmed.

"A very loyal goblin," Mr. Forkle clarified. "You can trust her. But I know that will be a challenge, given your past experiences."

Tinker's hands curled into fists, the metal guards covering her pointer fingers making a clinking sound. "Would the goblin be willing to wait outside?"

"I suspect that can be arranged," Mr. Forkle agreed.

Tinker's grip relaxed—slightly. And she dipped her chin in a nod.

"Excellent," Mr. Forkle said. "Then I have your first project."

He reached into his cape pocket and retrieved two clear marble-size spheres, each glinting with tiny colorful jewels set inside—and Sophie's stomach soured as Dex hung his head and looked away.

"Caches?" Tinker asked.

"*Fake* caches," Mr. Forkle corrected. "Or so we've been told. I'd like to verify that information, since it could be a misdirection. But if it's not, I'd like to know how the Neverseen managed to fool us. We might be able to learn something about the identity of their Technopath by studying their handiwork. Plus, we may need to use Kenric's replica if the Council asks Sophie to produce his cache before we recover the real one—"

"You'd give the Council the fake?" Sophie had to ask.

Mr. Forkle nodded. "If we needed to buy ourselves more time, I believe I would. But I'd like to understand exactly how risky that decision would be before I make it. And, quite honestly, I'm also trying to ease my own frustration. I hate to be fooled—and I despise it even more when I can't pinpoint exactly how the trick was achieved. So I'd like to at least know what we missed—particularly because the Neverseen could've made more than one decoy to thwart our next efforts to find the originals."

"Ugh, I hadn't even thought of *that*," Sophie grumbled, choking down the sour taste in her throat.

"Can I see those?" Tinker asked, holding out her hand for the caches.

Mr. Forkle handed them over. "You can keep them for now— but before you get sidetracked, I wanted to discuss another project. One I held off mentioning earlier, because I wanted you to meet Mr. Dizznee and see for yourself that he's both talented and kindhearted. That way you won't be confused by the intention."

"And what intention is that?" Tinker asked.

Mr. Forkle stole a brief glance at Dex and Sophie before he said, "To make weapons."

TWENTY-EIGHT

L ET ME BE CLEAR," MR. FORKLE ADDED, rushing over to Tinker, who was trembling so hard she looked ready to topple over. "I know how you feel about explosives, and I would *never* ask you to make them again. I'm only asking you to help design gadgets that will counteract some of the Neverseen's abilities—and if there's also a way to take out any ogres or dwarves working with them in the process, all the better. But *you* get to decide how you'll approach that challenge. Mr. Dizznee can design the rest on his own."

He helped Tinker lower herself onto the bench, and Sprocket hopped into her lap. She stroked the gremlin's ears as she murmured, "He shouldn't."

The words were hushed and simple—but coming from someone who only spoke in questions, they hit with a thud.

Even Mr. Forkle looked shaken.

"Have you forgotten what happens when you bring that kind of ugliness into the world?" Tinker asked him.

"I know the risks," he promised.

Her focus shifted to Dex as the lenses on her eyepiece rotated. "Do *you*?"

"I do," Dex assured her.

"Then why would you be willing to create such things? Or have you already made them?"

"Mr. Dizznee has made some simple, targeted devices in order to protect himself and his friends," Mr. Forkle answered for him, "and they're part of the reason that Sophie survived this latest attack. But I can assure you, he's not making anything that could cause damage on any sort of large scale—"

"How can you know that?" Tinker interrupted, slamming her fist against the table with a *clang!* that sent the tomples scattering and had Sprocket ducking under the bench. "Why would you think you can control the uncontrollable?"

"We don't," Mr. Forkle admitted. "But this is another reason I'd like you to work with Mr. Dizznee on this project, to offer him wisdom and guidance, and to challenge him to make sure the utmost caution is being taken. You can be the voice of reason."

"Will he listen?" Tinker asked, tapping her metal-guarded finger on the table.

"I will," Dex told her. "I know how messy this stuff can get. One of my gadgets got zapped by a Charger during a standoff in Exile. It was only supposed to set off a shock wave to knock over anyone threatening us, but once it absorbed all that extra energy, I knew it was going to explode—and one of my friends managed to hurl it away. But he got hurt in the process. And I think about that every time I make something new—how quickly everything became so much more dangerous than I wanted it to be, and how it felt to see my friend with this huge wound in his chest, knowing it was my fault, and that if he didn't make it through . . ."

Sophie scooted closer, reaching for his hand.

"Afterward," Dex added quietly, "I wondered if I shouldn't ever make gadgets like that again. But . . . have you faced the Neverseen?"

Tinker shifted her weight. "No."

Another answer that wasn't a question—and it seemed to give Dex confidence. He straightened up as he told her, "I have. And the thing is, they *enjoy* hurting and killing. They're never going to stop—not until they've destroyed everything and taken over. And people like that . . . you can't beat them by playing it safe."

"He's right," Mr. Forkle added softly. "The Neverseen have all but declared war. And war is a messy, horrible thing. It requires crossing lines that probably shouldn't be crossed but *must* be in order to survive. So if someone's willing to step up and handle something that you're not comfortable with, that's good news. Especially if you can offer wisdom to guide them."

Tinker looked away, luring Sprocket back to her lap with another metal cube and trailing her fingers through his shiny fur. "What exactly do you need me to do?"

"Whatever you feel comfortable with," Mr. Forkle told her. "Mr. Dizznee has recently been creating an arsenal of sorts, stored in stashes, and I'd love for you to help him improve on some of those creations, both in their effectiveness and their appearance. I'm hoping that whatever devices you two create can be camouflaged or shrunken. The goal would be for us to have them constantly on hand."

"And when do you want us to begin working on all of this?" Tinker asked.

"Why not today? Mr. Dizznee's already here. Beyond that, I'll leave the schedule up to you—but I'd recommend meeting up as much as possible. I realize you have a number of responsibilities, Mr. Dizznee, between Foxfire and your family's business and your friends. But this needs to be a priority."

"What about the other thing you told me to focus on?" Dex asked. "Helping Sophie protect her . . . newest ability."

"It's okay—Tinker knows Miss Foster is an Enhancer. I've actually asked her to see if she can come up with her own means to control the ability."

"You did?" Dex asked, frowning when Mr. Forkle nodded. "Why?"

"Because I'd rather you focus on this. And, truthfully, I thought the project might need some fresh eyes."

Dex's frown turned to a full-fledged scowl. "It doesn't—I've got it covered."

"Are you sure?" Tinker asked, reaching for the jewelry box in the center of the table. "Would you like to see my solution?"

That threw Dex for a second. "You already made something?"

She dipped her chin and flipped open the gilded lid, filling the room with a tinkling melody that felt familiar even though Sophie couldn't place it. The final note was still ringing as Tinker plucked out four tiny, curved pieces of smooth metal that almost looked like . . .

"Are those supposed to be fingernails?" Sophie asked, imagining all kinds of horrifying application scenarios.

Tinker reached for Sophie's hand. "Why do you assume I would design anything to hurt you?"

Her fingers were ice-cold but careful as she pulled off Sophie's glove and placed one of the metal pieces over Sophie's thumbnail, lining it up before tapping it once and . . .

. . . the metal suctioned perfectly into place.

She repeated the process with a second curl of metal on Sophie's pointer finger. "Can you tap five times like this?" she asked, clicking her fingertips together the way someone would play finger cymbals.

Tap. Tap. Tap. Tap. Tap.

Sophie copied the gesture, and a warm tingle rippled across her skin.

"That's pretty cool," Sophie had to admit.

It got even cooler when she pressed her fingertips against Dex's palm and nothing happened.

No surge of heat sparking between them.

No transfer of energy.

No enhancing.

And when she tapped five times again, cold prickled across her palm, undoing whatever the first taps had done.

Dex sighed and leaned closer, squinting at her silver nails. "It's the same kind of force field *I* used in *my* design. All she did was make hers turn off and on without being removed."

"And camouflaged them quite cleverly," Mr. Forkle noted. "A little metallic polish on the other nails and no one would ever be the wiser—though I still recommend wearing your gloves," he told Sophie. "The Neverseen might grow suspicious if you stop. Plus, it's always wise to have backup, in case technology fails."

"True," Sophie agreed.

She shook her hand as hard as she could to see if the nails would loosen.

They held strong.

Maybe a little *too* strong.

"How am I supposed to take these off?" she asked.

"Why would you need to?" Tinker wondered.

"I don't know. Won't they look weird when my nails grow?"

Tinker tapped the base of each nail twice, and a puff of air loosened the gadgets, allowing Sophie to slide them up or down as needed. All she'd have to do is trim her nails to keep them hidden.

"Is this a better solution than what you were planning?" Tinker asked Dex, with no bravado in her tone. Only curiosity.

But Dex still wouldn't look at her as he nodded. And his sigh was somewhere between a grumble and a harrumph.

"You have a competitive streak, don't you?" Tinker noted.

Sophie and Mr. Forkle both said "yes" while Dex said "no."

"I'm not being *competitive*," he argued. "I'm allowed to be annoyed that I got replaced."

"You weren't *replaced*," Mr. Forkle corrected. "This project, for whatever reason, seemed to be stumping you. So I thought it'd be wise to have someone with a new perspective take a look. Plus, I know you've been busy adjusting the panic switch rings—"

"You have?" Sophie asked.

Dex shrugged. "I'm trying to build a code into them, like 'slide the stone up for one kind of attack, right, left, and down for others.' But I'm not sure how to group it all, since there are so many different threats, and the code has to be simple enough to remember."

"I have some thoughts," Tinker told him, and Dex's jaw tightened, like he was stopping himself from snapping at her.

"Perhaps you could discuss that later," Mr. Forkle suggested, "once Mr. Dizznee has had a bit more time to adjust to collaboration. In the meantime, were you able to come up with anything for those other projects I described?"

Tinker nodded, reaching into the jewelry box and setting two other items on the table in front of Sophie: a plain silver bangle, and a cloak pin shaped like a soaring eagle.

"Is that the Ruewen crest?" Sophie asked, reaching for the pin and comparing it to the one securing her cape. The designs were nearly identical, though hers had touches of color and the new pin was solid silver.

"I sent her a sketch of it," Mr. Forkle explained. "That way it will keep the null better hidden."

Dex peeked over Sophie's shoulder. "You had her build a null? Seriously?"

"What's a null?" Sophie asked when Tinker dipped her chin.

"They block signals," Dex told her. "Or, I guess 'absorb' is a better word."

"Any technological means the Neverseen might have for tracking you will now be halted," Mr. Forkle clarified. "Your parents have swept everything you own with reveldust—and Bo has done several other tests for ogre enzymes. Everything has come back negative. So if the rebels *do* still have a way of monitoring your location, they're most likely using a gadget of some sort—"

"Hidden where?" Sophie asked, glancing at her wrist.

The Neverseen couldn't have implanted something during her kidnapping, could they? Under Brant's burns?

"Relax," Mr. Forkle told her as she scratched at her skin. "This is just a precaution."

"You realize a null is also going to block her registry pendant, right?" Dex jumped in. "And any trackers that Sandor hid in her clothes. Probably my panic switch, too. Why do you think I never suggested anything like that?"

Tinker pointed to the eagle's beak. "What does that do?"

Dex pressed his finger to the tiny point and sighed. "Oh. I guess it lets you approve certain frequencies. I . . . didn't know you could do that."

"Which is why I want Tinker to train you," Mr. Forkle reminded him gently. "There is much for you to learn. But there are also many things you can teach her as well."

Dex gave half a shrug and kept fiddling with the pin's tiny beak.

When it came to pouting, he was a master.

"So as long as I wear that pin, the Neverseen won't be able to track me?" Sophie confirmed.

"They won't be able to track you using technology," Mr. Forkle corrected. "It's still possible there's some other means we're unaware of. But that's why you have an abundance of bodyguards. This is just an extra layer of protection."

"What's the bracelet for?" Sophie asked, reaching for the silver bangle.

"It's an ionic booster, right?" Dex asked Tinker. "Pretty sure that's a bad idea. Elwin won't want you messing with her recovery."

"Who said it was for her injury?" Tinker asked, rifling through her tool belt and pulling out a piece of V-shaped steel with a spring in the center. She handed the contraption to Sophie. "How hard can you squeeze that with your left hand?"

"Apparently not hard at all," Sophie mumbled when she could barely get the spring to compress.

"Don't worry," Mr. Forkle told her, "we're all weak in the hand we don't favor. But since you'll be relying on your left for the next few weeks, I asked Tinker if she could improve your strength. Go ahead and try the bracelet on."

Dex helped Sophie carefully remove her pin-covered cuff, and she tucked it safely in her cape pocket before she slipped on the simple bangle. It slid past her hand, all the way to her elbow, but Tinker tipped her arm forward, making the bracelet settle around her wrist before she pointed to the V-shaped tool. "*Now* how hard can you squeeze?"

"That's crazy!" Sophie said as both ends of the tool crashed together hard enough to make the metal clink. "I don't even have to try." She squeezed it again and again. "I could do this all day!"

"I wouldn't recommend it," Mr. Forkle warned. "Boost or no boost, your muscles are still doing all the work. And if you push too hard, you could tear something—just like if you kept punching with your Sucker Punch, you'd bruise your fingers and throw out your shoulder."

"Why is the bracelet so big, though?" Dex asked as it slid

back down to Sophie's elbow. "Why not make it fit snug around her wrist?"

"Is her hand the only place that needs more strength?" Tinker countered. "Or will her arm and shoulder also require a boost for training?"

"Training?" Sophie repeated, her heart coming to a stop when Mr. Forkle's lips spread into a satisfied smile.

"Yes, Miss Foster," he told her. "That's the real reason I brought you here today. I know how impatient you've been to begin physical training. And with that bracelet, you should be able to."

She could train.

The news whirled around Sophie's head and part of her wanted to sob happy tears and leap across the table and tackle-hug Tinker.

But the practical side of her had to ask: "You don't think training will mess with my recovery?"

"Caution and moderation will be key—as will be Elwin's approval, of course," Mr. Forkle told her. "I'm sure you'll need to limit yourself to simpler exercises and shorter intervals— and obviously you'll only be able to train with your left arm. But honestly, it'll be better for you to become a bit more ambidextrous."

All of that she could live with.

She traced a finger over the precious bracelet and glanced at Tinker. "Thank you."

Tinker's cheek flushed a deep pink, and she looked away as she nodded.

"Well," Mr. Forkle said as he dug out his pathfinder, "I hate to grab these brilliant gadgets and run, but I need to stay on schedule to make my meeting with the Council. Plus, Miss Foster's family is waiting, and I'm sure she's eager to see them."

"Eager" was an understatement.

But first, she had to check with Dex: "You're okay about staying here?"

He glanced around the laboratory. "I guess we'll see how it goes."

Dex helped her trade out her usual Ruewen crest for the new null, and Tinker handed her a silver pillbox that held two more full sets of the nail-shaped gadgets in case anything happened to the first set. And she felt a little like a spy in one of those movies her human dad used to love—fixed up with all kinds of fancy gadgets.

But mostly, she felt *ready*.

"You two have fun," Mr. Forkle told Dex and Tinker as he held his crystal up to the light and offered Sophie his hand. "Come along, Miss Foster. Let's get you home."

The first thing Sophie heard was roaring—loud enough to shake the slowly solidifying ground—followed by an abundance of shouting as Havenfield's sprawling pastures glittered into view.

Sophie gave herself a second to take it all in: the ocean shimmering beyond the property's scenic cliffs, its dark blue waves dappled with glints of warm afternoon sunlight. The wispy branches of Calla's Panakes tree scattering pinkish, purplish, bluish petals across the rolling, grassy hills. And her house, with its crystal walls, golden columns, and gleaming cupola— so much fancier than anywhere she once would've imagined herself living, yet every sparkling inch now felt like home.

So did the next earth-shaking roar. And the next round of shouting. Because one of Sophie's favorite things about Havenfield was the constant adventure.

"I assume that's the gorgodon?" Mr. Forkle said as Sophie turned to follow the flower-lined path that wound past pens of fluffy dinosaurs and loping sasquatches and every other kind of creature imaginable.

"Yep. Sounds like feeding time."

The pasture seemed farther away than Sophie remembered, the path steeper, the sunshine hotter on her skin, and after a few minutes she was fuzzy headed and dripping sweat. But her pace didn't slow. It even increased when she confirmed that one of the voices was Grady's, and she was practically running by the time they rounded the final bend and reached the wide ridge dotted with boulders and windswept trees, where a team of gnomes and dwarves had built the gorgodon's enclosure from arched pieces of steel arranged into a tightly knitted dome.

The pen had a much more cagelike feel than any of the

other Havenfield pastures. But the warps and dents in the metal proved how necessary that added security was, each a souvenir from a moment when the gorgodon had slammed its muscled body against the sides, or struck with its barbed tail, or tried to crunch through the bars with its long, curved fangs.

Sophie always needed a moment to process the sight of the massive beast with its reptilian face, lionlike limbs, and sharply angled wings. And the gorgodon stared right back at her with its slitted yellow eyes—but only for a second. Then it turned back to the half dozen gnomes surrounding the enclosure, snarling at each one before settling on Grady, who stood next to a basket of what looked like purple cantaloupes.

Shards of the same violet fruit littered the ground both inside *and* outside the enclosure, and Grady's gray tunic was splattered with purple pulp. But that didn't stop him from scooping up another melon and shouting, "NOW!"

All six gnomes reached into their pockets and flung tiny black pellets into the cage, peppering the gorgodon's silver feathers.

ROOOOOOOOOOOOOOOOOOAAAAAAAAAAAAAAAR!

As soon as the beast's mouth opened, Grady hurled the purple fruit, sending it sailing between the gorgodon's long fangs and landing on its slimy tongue. The beast tilted its head to roar again, sending the fruit rolling to the back of its throat and forcing it to swallow.

"That's nine!" Grady shouted, pumping his fist. "One more to go!"

The gnomes tossed another batch of black pellets, which were probably seeds to regrow the trampled grass.

ROOOOOOOOOOOOOOOOAAAAAAAAAAAAAAAAAAR!

Grady hurled another purple melon, but the gorgodon was faster, slinging its tail with a perfect strike and showering Grady and several of the gnomes in purple juice.

"Need help?" Sophie called as Grady wiped his face with his soggy sleeve and reached for another piece of fruit.

Grady's head whipped toward the sound of her voice, and before she could blink, he was tossing the purple melon over his shoulder and sprinting to her side, scooping her into a hug that somehow managed to be gentle and crushing—and very, very sticky.

"Sorry," he said, wiping a smear of purple off her arm. "I'm covered in tangourd."

He was. And he smelled like sweat and mud and something strongly peppery. But Sophie didn't care one bit as she wrapped her good arm around him and leaned in.

"I missed you," she whispered into his shoulder.

"Right back at you, kiddo." He bent to kiss her cheek, and she could feel his tears mixing with hers before they both eased back to study each other.

His gaze washed over her sling before settling at the base of her neck, and it took her a second to figure out why he was frowning.

"I still have the Ruewen crest you gave me," she promised,

patting the same cape pocket that held Krakie and his friends. "But Tinker made me this one to block any trackers."

She explained what little she knew about how the null worked, as well as the bangle on her left arm and the silver gadgets covering her nails.

"Sounds like those are all great ideas," Grady said, lifting her wrist to study her new bangle. "But what was that part about starting training?"

"Not without Elwin's approval," Mr. Forkle assured him.

"And *mine*," a squeaky voice added—and Sophie spun toward the sound, wondering how long Sandor had been standing in the shadows of the gorgodon's enclosure without her noticing.

His nose was back to its usual flat shape, and all his cuts and bruises seemed to have healed. He'd also made some additions to his armor: Two wide black belts lined with throwing stars crisscrossed his bare chest, and he had a twisted dagger sheathed on each of his burly arms, all of which made him look decidedly less than huggable—but that didn't stop Sophie from closing the distance between them and wrapping her good arm around his waist.

"Thank you for staying with me," she whispered, leaning into his side and getting a noseful of the musky goblin scent that used to gross her out but now seemed like the best thing in the world.

"Thank you for trusting me," Sandor murmured, his voice thickening as he held her tighter. "I don't deserve it—"

"Yes, you do. I don't deserve to have you risking your life to protect me."

"That's my *honor*," Sandor corrected.

"And mine," another voice said as two child-size arms wrapped around Sophie's waist from behind.

She pivoted into the hug, breathing in the scent of flowers and tree sap and freshly tilled earth, then trailed her hand across Flori's plaited hair.

"I'm so honored to have this chance to keep you safe," Flori told her. "Calla would be so happy."

Sophie stepped back, meeting the tiny gnome's wide gray eyes. Flori's green-toothed smile looked heartbreakingly earnest—and her new outfit made Sophie's heart even heavier. Flori's usual straw-woven dress had been replaced with stiff pants stitched from pieces of bark, and a tunic sewn from dried husks, both of which were probably meant to serve as armor. Mostly they looked scratchy and uncomfortable and like they wouldn't provide nearly enough protection.

"I'm pretty sure Calla would want *you* to stay safe," Sophie whispered.

Flori shook her head. "She would want me to protect the moonlark."

Sophie opened her mouth to argue, but . . . that did sound like Calla.

"Just promise me you'll be careful," she begged, pulling Flori back against her side.

Someone cleared his throat—loudly—and a gruff voice said, "No one told me this assignment would require hugging."

"It doesn't," Flori called over her shoulder. "And even if it did, no one would be hugging *you*."

"Good," the voice snapped back. "*Warriors* do not hug. Or cry. I'm starting to see why the girl needed a proper guard."

Sandor snarled.

"Sophie, meet Bo," Flori said as Sophie craned her neck, trying to follow the voice to the source and not having any luck. "In case you're wondering, yes, he *is* every bit as delightful as he seems."

"Warriors aren't meant to be *delightful*!" Bo growled. "We're meant to be fearsome. And ruthless. And cunning. And merciless."

"And *obedient*," Sandor warned.

"That too," Bo said as he stepped into the sunlight, finally giving Sophie a glimpse of his hulking form. His mottled skin had blended so well with the shadows along a nearby rocky outcropping that he'd been all but invisible until he moved toward her.

He wasn't as huge as King Dimitar, but he had the same apelike shape, with disproportionately long arms, a barrel chest, and squat, muscled legs. He also wore the same metal diaper, but he'd paired it with hammered steel shin guards and a spiked steel plate that curved from the base of his neck to just above his ribs. A brutally barbed sword hung from a steel belt clamped around his waist, along with three saw-edged blades of varying lengths that Sophie hoped she'd never have to see him use.

His face was lumpier than Ro's—more like the other male ogres' Sophie had seen. But there was something a little more refined about his features. A stronger line to his jaw, a deeper gray to his eyes. And paired with the tattoos swirling across his forehead, the pale green stones pierced through his ears, and the darker green stud stuck through the center of his lower lip, Sophie got the distinct impression that Bo might be what other ogres considered handsome.

Even his pointed teeth had a shine as he offered her the barest sliver of a smile and pounded his right fist against his heart.

The gesture was meant to be some sort of greeting, but Sophie was too busy trying to place him among the ogres she'd seen that day in Ravagog. She'd been so focused on sneaking into King Dimitar's mind that she hadn't really looked at the soldiers around him—at least not at their faces.

"You don't remember me, do you?" Bo asked, somehow guessing what she'd been thinking. "I wish I could say the same. It's not easy allying with an enemy."

Sophie's mouth went dry. "We were only—"

"Spare me your explanations," he interrupted. "I'm a Mercadir. I follow the orders of my king. And my king has ordered me to protect you. So I meant no threat"—his eyes flicked to Sandor, who'd drawn his sword—"I only thought we should acknowledge the *challenge* in our situation." His eyes drifted back to Sophie's. "We don't have to be friends. In fact, it's better if we aren't. It will allow me to keep the objectivity your other guards clearly aren't capable of."

Sandor muttered something under his breath, and Sophie had a feeling she was discovering at least one of the reasons Ro was so very anti-Bo.

"All that matters," Bo continued, "is that if you trust me with your life, you won't be disappointed. You'll soon find that you don't need any of these other protectors."

"So you keep claiming," a droll female voice noted from the general direction of a nearby tree. Sophie craned her neck, trying—and failing—to catch a glimpse of her as the voice added, "And yet, we're here to handle threats that involve some from *your* species, aren't we, Bo? Meanwhile *my* people have kept themselves separate from this foolish drama. So I'll have nothing slowing my hand when the time comes."

"Neither will I!" Bo snarled. "I'm looking *very* forward to ending the lives of the fools who dared to think themselves mightier than my king. One in particular."

"Then your hunger for revenge will distract you from your other responsibilities," the female argued. "Either way, it's a liability. Whereas *I'll* be entering each fight without any connection or agenda. No elf, goblin, ogre, or dwarf can say the same. Even you, little gnome—you carry the hate for what these villains tried to do to your species in your heart."

"And you think that makes you more valuable than us?" Bo snapped.

"That, and I'm a better fighter," she said, finally stepping out to face them.

"Sophie, this is Tarina," Grady said, introducing her. Sophie had already guessed, even though the female looked nothing like the other trolls she'd seen.

Tarina was neither tall nor short, neither lean nor muscular—but her averageness ended there. Her greenish hair grew in strands as wide as dreadlocks, but they had a smooth, glossy sheen—the same sheen that coated her blue-green skin, making her look like she'd just stepped out of water. Her huge yellow eyes filled the top half of her face, and her nearly lipless mouth took up most of the lower half, with a small snub nose jutting above it. She stood barefoot and wore only a shaggy gray-green garment that covered her from her shoulders to her knees. Sophie had assumed it was made of fur, but when Tarina drew closer, Sophie realized it was actually made from some sort of moss. And tucked among the thick, scratchy-looking lichen was a strap that hung diagonally across Tarina's body and wrapped around her back, where Sophie could see the edges of a large iron weapon peeking out—some sort of cross between a scythe and an ax, with a sharp point on the end of the pole for stabbing.

"It's okay to stare," Tarina said, her voice taking on a chirpy quality. "Empress Pernille warned me that you're not familiar with my species."

"Sorry," Sophie mumbled, lowering her eyes. "I was just trying to compare you to the other trolls I've seen, and—"

"So you *can* understand me!" Tarina interrupted, and Sophie realized they must've switched to speaking in Trollish. "The empress told me you were fluent, and that your accent was flawless, but I'll admit, I had a hard time believing it. And you can do this with any language, can't you? It's one of those . . . What is it your species calls them? *Special* abilities?"

Sophie nodded. "I'm a Polyglot."

Tarina smiled, flashing unnervingly long white teeth, which matched the curved white claws on her hands and feet. "It's so strange that elves each have different talents. I don't know how you aren't constantly battling with each other over which of you is greater—though I suppose that's what's happening with these enemies, isn't it?"

"Partially," Sophie admitted. "But there's more to it than that."

"There always is," Tarina agreed.

"Is there a reason you're speaking in a language the rest of us can't understand?" Bo demanded to know.

Tarina gave him epic side-eye. "I don't have to explain myself to you, ogre," she said, switching back to the Enlightened Language. "But in *my* world, we take time to understand the perspectives of those we're assigned to protect. That's easier for me to do in my native tongue—and since Sophie's fluent, I'm hoping she doesn't mind humoring me."

"I don't," Sophie agreed, and Tarina smiled and stepped closer—close enough for Sophie to see that there was a word etched into the strap holding her weapon.

Tarina followed her gaze. "Can you read our writing as well?" Her voice sounded chirpier, which probably meant she'd shifted languages again.

Sophie squinted at the letters. "Does that say 'long shot'?"

"It does. We name our weapons as part of our training, and I chose this to remind myself that even when all hope feels lost, I can continue fighting. A sentiment I'm sure you can appreciate—which is rare for your species, isn't it? Elves generally live their glittering lives oblivious to most of this planet's harsh realities. But not you. You also have an incredibly rare worldview from your years living with humans. I'd wager you see things drastically differently than any of us do. And while my people may not be connected to these current problems your world is facing—we're no strangers to war. We know how evil spreads like a virus without any cure. Which is why the empress sent me on this assignment, despite the fact that it requires working alongside those who, another time, another place, would gladly choose to slit my throat. It's also why I'm taking this chance to speak candidly to *you*."

Grady moved to Sophie's side, wrapping an arm around her,

as if he could sense the slight tension knotting her shoulders. "Everything okay?"

"Yep," Sophie said, hoping it was true.

The conversation felt like it was curving, and Sophie couldn't figure out where it was heading. Especially when Tarina added, "We know nothing of this organization you serve—this Black Swan, as you call it—but we know the elvin Council has never fully provided the support my species needs. That's why long ago one of our empresses chose to partner with an elf she trusted instead—someone with the power, intelligence, and determination to stand up for what was right, even when it meant stepping outside the law and forging brave new ground. It's the reason my people still stand strong today. But your world is changing—and therefore *our* world is changing. So we believe the time has come for us to forge another crucial alliance. And Empress Pernille would like to forge that alliance with you."

TWENTY-NINE

OU WANT TO FORM AN ALLIANCE with *me*." Sophie felt the need to clarify, wondering if her brain could've mistranslated a few of Tarina's words. That certainly would've made more sense than anything she'd just heard. "I'm not sure I understand what that means."

"It means that someday you're going to change the world," Tarina told her, "and I'm here to make sure you don't fall before that happens. But I'm also here because my people will likely need your help before all of this is finished. Possibly even sooner than we'd hoped."

"Help with what?" Sophie asked.

"Quite truthfully: We don't know. *That's* why we need you

as our ally. If we could see the path ahead, we could prepare. But all we can say for sure is that these problems will surely spread beyond your shimmering cities. And when they reach my world, we'll need someone to stand with us."

"Okay, but . . . the Black Swan would be a way better—"

"I told you," Tarina interrupted, "we do not know them."

"You don't know me, either," Sophie reminded her. "I've been here for, what? Five minutes? And I spoke to your empress for less than that at the Peace Summit."

"You two may not have spoken much, but she had plenty of time to observe your character. And while you're clearly young and inexperienced, she also found you to be someone who will never stop fighting for what you believe in, regardless of the sacrifices involved or the rules you might have to cast aside, which is the making of an excellent ally. She'd of course planned to wait until you were older before approaching you, but this chance to serve at your side presented itself and couldn't be passed up, not when there have been other shifts as well—signs that these villains might be turning their attention toward my people—"

"Like what?"

"I'll happily discuss them once you prove yourself committed to this alliance—but we're not to that point yet. First I need you to trust me."

Grady pulled Sophie closer, making her wonder if he'd ever learned any Trollish words and was catching snippets of their conversation.

"No one can understand us," Tarina assured her as Sophie studied their rather large audience. "I switched us to an archaic dialect before mentioning anything pertinent. Only someone with your ability could follow."

"That doesn't mean they're not wondering what we're saying," Sophie noted. She was also pretty sure Mr. Forkle would find this suspicious enough to eavesdrop on her thoughts, which would likely be translated for him—but decided it was better not to mention that.

"I'm sure they are," Tarina agreed, flashing a smile with just enough edge to make Bo turn his scowling face away. "But imagine how different it would be if they stumbled upon us discussing this privately, especially given the lengths we would have to go to in order to avoid the other guards. The fact that we're talking so publicly removes any true suspicion and leaves only mild curiosity—and mild curiosity can be misdirected easily enough. I'll handle that in a moment. First, I want to make sure you understand that I'm not asking you to join any plot or scheme with my empress. I'm simply asking you to be someone beyond your Council that we can turn to for help if a need arises."

"What makes you think I'll be able to do anything?" Sophie asked.

"Because you're far more powerful than you realize, both in your talents and in your ability to inspire. The fact that I'm here in a private section of your world, along with an ogre, a goblin, a dwarf, and a gnome—all of whom have sworn to protect you with their lives—proves your value beyond anything you might argue. So do not doubt yourself. And do not doubt my empress's intentions. She would never request something unjust. That's why our other alliance still holds, even to this day."

"An alliance with who?" Sophie asked.

"I can't tell you. Just as I would never give your identity to them. Discretion in these relationships is key to their success."

Sophie fought the urge to sigh—or to reach up and tug on her eyelashes.

"I realize this is a complicated decision, and I'm not asking you to make it right now," Tarina promised. "I simply wanted to plant the seed from the very beginning of our relationship. That way you can have it in your mind as you come to know me. And now it falls on me to convince you that both of our worlds will benefit from this alliance—which is why I want you to know that regardless of what you decide, you have my loyalty and protection."

With that, she turned to Sandor and offered a smile. "Sorry. This is taking far longer than I intended. I've been trying to explain to Sophie why those in my species differ so drastically in appearance from each other, since no one seemed to have explained that to her before. But I fear doing it in my language was a mistake after all and made the subject far more confusing. I think it might be easier for her to understand if I try again in her instinctive language."

Tarina delivered the lie so smoothly that Sophie couldn't decide if she was impressed or unnerved. And when Tarina turned back to her, she continued on without even missing a beat, as though this was what they'd been discussing all along. "As I was trying to say, my people age quite differently than what you're used to—not only following a pattern that you would likely consider a reverse of your aging method, but also because we pass through seven distinct stages throughout the course of our lives, all of which have different physical and mental attributes. As newborns, we're at our strongest physically—but mentally at that stage, we're at our weakest. And as we pass from stage to stage, those conditions slowly flip, with our strength fading and mental capacity enhancing. I happen to be in Stage Four, which is also called our Prime Stage. It's the stage considered to be the most balanced point in our lives, when our mental and physical strength are nearly even. It's why I was chosen for this assignment. But each stage has its advantages and disadvantages. Empress Pernille is Stage Six. The other trolls you've seen were likely Stage Threes or Stage Fives, which is why none of them resembled each other or looked as I do now."

"How fascinating," Bo said, rolling his eyes. "Should we follow this with a lecture on ogre development? Or perhaps the gnome would like to tell us about their life cycles."

Tarina smirked. "If you ever find yourself facing one of our newborns, you might be grateful for this understanding."

"I've faced your soldiers plenty of times."

"I didn't say our *soldiers*—I said our *newborns*. We generally try not to subject anyone to that stage's ferocity. But I might be willing to make an exception for you during the next hatching."

"Hatching?" Sophie asked. "Like . . . from eggs?"

"In a way. Honestly, I can't believe your elvin school hasn't taught you any of these things."

"It's an elite subject," Mr. Forkle explained. "Though you might be right that we should cover the basics earlier than that. Our thought has always been to save that curriculum for those joining the nobility, since they're the ones who may actually interact with your species. But it does seem like an oversight for so many to know so little about a species with whom we share our planet. It also sounds like our information has some gaps. I've never heard of your hatchings either."

"That may be because we're very protective of our newborns—and even more so of those unhatched. But I suppose, since we'll all be spending so much time together, we can consider this to be a learning experience."

She gave Sophie a knowing glance.

In case you're wondering, Mr. Forkle transmitted—and Sophie had to lock her jaw to block a squeal—*I've heard most of your conversation. Sorry to violate your privacy, but when she shifted to her archaic tongue, I had to make sure you weren't being threatened. I won't say much more now, since our conversation might be noticed. But I'm glad she's giving you time to consider—it gives me a chance to do some research. I've never heard any whispers of the trolls having an elvin ally before. So let me do some digging—and try not to let this worry you. I don't think the trolls have an ulterior motive. They sound scared, and I can't blame them, considering the chaos the Neverseen have been causing. I'd like to look into that, as well—make sure there haven't been any concerning incidents that Empress Pernille hasn't shared. In the meantime it's probably best if you don't mention anything about this to your family or friends. I get the impression that the trolls would want this to be an arrangement strictly between you and them.*

That . . . might be a problem, Sophie warned.

Agreed. But we'll address that once we decide if this is even something you should commit to.

Out loud he added, "I believe we have one more guard for you to meet, don't we?"

"We do," Grady said, stomping his foot in a specific pattern against the ground.

Sophie's brain had just put together that he was calling the dwarf, when the soil parted and a molelike creature with brown shaggy fur and a pointed face poked her head out and focused on Sophie through tightly squinted eyes.

Grady introduced them. "Sophie, meet Nubiti. You probably won't see her much, given her sensitivity to sunlight. But she's only a few stomps away if you need her."

"We've developed several codes to communicate various

threats," Sandor added. "I'll teach you the stomping patterns later."

Sophie nodded, turning to the dwarf, trying to think of something better to say than "Hi." But before she could even get that word out, Nubiti flipped back into her hole, kicking her hairy legs and burrowing into the earth, leaving no trace that she'd just been there.

"Bizarre creatures," Bo murmured, raking his teeth over his lip piercing.

"She doesn't have much to say," Grady explained to Sophie. "But I've seen her in action on a few of my assignments with King Enki over the years. She's amazing. As is your whole team," he added, tipping his chin toward each of her guards. "We're still fine-tuning how this is going to work, but we all have the same goal. We want you to know that despite anything the Neverseen have claimed, none of us will let them anywhere near you ever again."

"*Never,*" Sandor agreed. "They thought they were delivering a message. But all they've done is guarantee their failure."

"Anyone else think that's strange?" Tarina jumped in. "Sorry—I don't mean to ruin the pep talk. But I've been trying to understand the Neverseen's motivation, and I keep coming back to the same question: Why stage such a visible attack only to deliver threats, cause temporary injuries, and ask for one small piece of information? They had to know Sophie's security would then be significantly improved, making it nearly impossible to get near her ever again. So why take on that challenge?"

Bo sighed. "I hate to say this—but I agree with the troll."

"They said they wanted me to start cooperating," Sophie told both of them.

"Okay, but . . . you know who cooperates much better than someone you injure and let go?" Tarina asked. "A prisoner who knows you can keep hurting them."

"They've taken Miss Foster hostage before, and it did not end well for them," Mr. Forkle reminded everyone. "And they've lost a number of hideouts already. I doubt they'd want to lose another."

"But they could've stashed her anywhere," Tarina argued. "And it sounded like they had several opportunities to grab Sophie and flee. So there has to be a reason they didn't. They must *want* her to be free."

"Or they wanted me out of commission," Sophie suggested quietly, not wanting to share too much about her troubling theories. "I've lost how many weeks in the Healing Center? And I'm still not fully recovered." She tilted her chin toward her sling—and decided not to mention the echo.

"I suppose that could've made sense if something significant had happened during the time of your recovery," Tarina reasoned. "But nothing has, has it? And here's another thing I don't understand: Why would they *ever* mention that they had some sort of tracker on you? Why volunteer that information, knowing you'd obviously then do everything you could to find and destroy whatever they were using? I don't know these enemies—but they don't seem like the type to make such a foolish mistake. So there has to be a larger goal."

"I'm not saying you're wrong," Mr. Forkle said, reaching up to rub one of his temples. "Or that we shouldn't continue to ponder these questions. But as you said, you do not know the Neverseen. If you did, you'd know that they feed off attention and spectacle to a degree where it truly can be their own folly. For instance: Fintan successfully faked his death. None of us had the slightest suspicion that he was still alive. And his order already relied on cloaks to hide their identities. So he had absolutely no reason to show his face the day he threatened the Council in Eternalia—other than his own vanity. He wanted credit for the feats he'd pulled off. Just like Fintan had no reason to insist that Alvar reveal himself as a traitor. No one had suspected the eldest Vacker of anything at that point—and as a Vanisher, he likely could've kept his ruse going for a good long while and continued to spy on his father and brother and whatever else he'd been doing. And yet, Fintan forced Alvar to reveal himself, for no reason I can think of, other than he wanted to shock us. He wanted us to know that our enemies were everywhere, even in places we might otherwise feel safe. And there is *some* advantage to that. But it's also tremendously reckless—and something I'm hoping to figure out how to exploit someday."

"I suppose," Tarina said, tracing her claws over the letters carved into the strap across her chest. "But I still fear we're missing something."

Sophie didn't argue.

No one did.

Because deep down they all knew that when it came to the Neverseen, they were *always* missing something.

"Are you okay?" Grady asked as Sophie closed her eyes and let out a long, slow breath, trying to stop the monster from stirring up fresh nightmares.

Everything Tarina had raised was terrifying.

But it was also valid.

And she couldn't let the fear set her back.

She was out of the Healing Center now. She needed to start searching for better answers—and she couldn't do that if the echo took control.

And she could start training, she reminded herself, clinging to the words like a lifeline.

Training made the answers less crucial.

Training would make her ready for whatever was happening.

"I'm fine," she said, waiting until the words were true, and giving Grady her most reassuring smile.

Grady didn't look convinced. "I think we should head to the house. Your body's not used to this much activity, so you probably need to get off your feet."

"I agree," Mr. Forkle chimed in. "And I'm afraid this is also when I must leave you. If I don't head to Eternalia soon, the Council will be very annoyed with me." He pulled out his pathfinder and quickly adjusted the crystal. "Oh, and Elwin wanted me to let you know he'll be stopping by after dinner to check Miss Foster's progress and go over her medication regimen."

I'll let you know what the Council's planning for the meeting with Fintan as soon as everything's finalized, he transmitted to Sophie. *And we'll talk more about the trolls once I've investigated. I'm not sure how long either of those tasks will take, so if you don't hear from me for a bit, don't think I've forgotten, okay?*

Sophie nodded, and he waved to the others before stepping into the light and slowly shimmering away.

"Come on, kiddo," Grady said, shaking bits of dried fruit out of his hair and hooking his arm around her. "Let's get you inside—oh, and let's not mention how long you've been home, okay? If Edaline finds out I didn't bring you straight in to see her, she's going to conjure up a pile of mastodon droppings and plop them on my head."

He was teasing, of course. But Edaline actually *had* threatened a manure attack once—and she was definitely a talented enough Conjurer to make it happen.

"Don't you still need to feed the gorgodon one more tangourd?" Sophie reminded him.

"That's right." He turned to the gnomes gathering the pieces of smashed fruit from around the enclosure. "Would you guys mind finishing up without me?"

The gnomes each gave a green thumbs-up and set to work, causing a whole lot more roaring as Grady guided Sophie back down the path, with Sandor glued to her side. The rest of her guards slipped into what must've been a previously agreed-on formation, with Bo taking point, Flori flanking Sophie's opposite side, and Tarina bringing in the rear.

"I hope you're hungry," Grady said when the house came into view. "Edaline made enough treats to feed an entire city."

"I'm starving," Sophie admitted.

Also thirsty.

And sitting down did sound really, *really* good.

A deep ache was settling into every muscle—even ones she didn't know existed—and she was trying not to let it frustrate her. But it was hard not to wish she could fast-forward to the part where she'd be 100 percent back to . . .

All thoughts dropped away when she stepped through the door to Havenfield, into the enormous main room with its elegant white furnishings and gleaming chandeliers. It looked so much homier than it had the day Sophie moved in, even though everything was essentially the same. Maybe it was the dents in the pillows and the footprints on the rugs and all the other tiny signs of life that were now everywhere.

Or maybe it was because it smelled like butter and melting sugar and a million other yummy things that had Sophie's stomach unleashing a growl that could've rivaled the gorgodon's.

Edaline burst through the door from the kitchen to greet

them, and then there was a whole lot more hugging and crying—plus *lots* of questions about how Sophie was feeling. Sophie also mumbled an apology for chasing Edaline away, and Edaline kissed her cheek, promising there were no hard feelings.

"Not to break up the reunion," Sandor interrupted, "but Sophie looks a little pale."

"I just need to sit," Sophie assured everyone.

"It sounds like some food would be good too," Grady added with a wink at Sophie.

Edaline nodded and snapped her fingers, making a round crystal table appear in the center of the room—and the next snap brought Sophie a chair.

Sophie sank onto it gratefully as Edaline continued snapping, bringing in chairs for everyone—including Sophie's bodyguards—along with tray after tray of elvin delicacies: custard bursts and ripplefluffs and pudding puffs and mallowmelt—even butterblasts. There were plenty of savory foods too, of course, and they smelled *delicious*. But Sophie still filled half her plate with desserts, and nobody blamed her.

Even Bo cracked a smile when he had his first bite of mallowmelt—and then helped himself to the rest of the tray.

Tarina took down almost as many ripplefluffs.

They were both sampling their first custard bursts when they jumped to their feet and drew their weapons.

"It's not an intruder," Sandor told them, shaking his head.

"It's the physician—you should've recognized his scent from Sophie's clothes."

"I smell like Elwin?" Sophie asked as a loud knock rattled the door.

"You smell like everyone and everything you've been in contact with," Flori told her as Grady went to let Elwin in—which was a strange thing to realize, even if it also made sense.

"Did you search his bags?" Bo demanded when Elwin shuffled into the room with four overstuffed satchels slung over his shoulders.

"I don't need to," Sandor told him.

Bo snorted. "My king would never be so sloppy with his security."

"Here," Elwin said, setting all four satchels at Bo's feet. "Search away—but don't break anything. Some of that medicine took me all day to brew. And sorry to show up in the middle of dinner," he told Edaline. "I thought you'd be done by now. Want me to come back?"

"Of course not," Edaline assured him, conjuring him a chair next to Sophie's and telling him to help himself.

Elwin was more than happy to help them polish off the rest of the desserts. And when he'd devoured every last crumb, he led Sophie over to the couch and slipped on his iridescent spectacles. "Let's see how you're holding up after such a busy day," he said, snapping his fingers and forming a blue orb around Sophie's head.

Tarina gasped.

"I take it you've never seen a Flasher at work before?" Elwin asked her.

"No," Tarina admitted. "But I've wanted to, ever since I first heard the legends."

"*Legends,*" Bo scoffed. "You're looking at a party trick— nothing more. You want to see something legendary, you should visit our microbiology labs."

"Yes, nothing's more exciting than bacteria," Elwin muttered. "And just so we're clear—my 'party trick' saved your princess's life."

Bo froze. "You treated Romhilda?"

"I did. And I hope I'm around if you ever call her that to her face," Elwin noted, likely remembering how *strongly* Ro felt about people using her full name.

Bo sighed. "Romhilda has a gift for rebelling against tradition. That's why her father sent her here."

"I'm pretty sure he sent her because she's the best," Sophie corrected, not liking his tone.

"I'm sure she loves to claim that," Bo told her. "And there's no denying that she's an incredible warrior. But she's never beaten me—and someday she'll have to accept what that means."

"What does it mean?" Sophie asked.

"Nothing worth sharing."

"How do you know Ro?" Sophie pressed, remembering Keefe and Ro's latest wager. "Did you train together, or . . . ?"

"She's the princess," Bo said simply. "Everyone knows her. And I should begin the nightly patrols."

Sophie couldn't tell if he was trying to dodge her questions. But his vague answer did not bode well for Keefe's chances of another betting victory.

"So . . . how does everything look?" Sophie asked as Elwin shifted to one of those layered light bubbles that showed him the whole spectrum.

"Better than I was expecting," Elwin admitted. "I'd assumed I'd be repairing a bit of damage from all the leaping. But . . . everything looks good. You'll be sore tomorrow, and you definitely need to get some rest. But you haven't set yourself back—and *this*!" He lifted Sophie's left wrist and whistled. "I've seen some crazy gadgets in my day, but this is seriously brilliant. I can see the energy soaking straight into your cells."

Sophie took a slow breath, working up the courage to ask, "So . . . does that mean I can start training tomorrow with my left arm?"

Elwin scratched his chin and adjusted his glasses as he checked her one more time. His expression was impossible to read, and Sophie tried to prepare herself for disappointment.

But he told her, "Yes, I think you're ready."

With Elwin's permission for training secured, Grady and Edaline jumped on board as well.

And Sandor made it official.

Sophie's first lesson would start the next day after her morning round of medicine—which was the only thing everyone could agree on. *Extensive* debate followed over which bodyguard should teach, and what exactly the lessons would be—and Sophie decided to stay out of it, content to sit on the couch and watch Sandor, Bo, and Tarina wave weapons around, trying to outdo each other.

She had a feeling that bodyguard bickering would now be a regular part of her day—and she was good with that. At least they'd all be driving each other as crazy as they'd surely be driving her.

"Not joining in the my-training-is-better-than-your-training fight?" Sophie asked when Flori came to sit beside her.

Flori shook her head. "Most of my defenses cannot be taught to those outside my species. But I have a different request."

"Anything," Sophie told her.

For Calla's niece, the answer was always yes.

Flori's cheeks flushed, and she twirled a strand of hair that had fallen loose from her plaits. "I'm . . . hoping you'll let me sing to you."

"You mean like when Calla would sing to the trees to keep them healthy?" Sophie asked.

"I realize there's a notable difference," Flori assured her. "But . . . I believe we all have a song within us, even if we don't think of it as music. Each life has a rhythm of breaths and heartbeats, and that melody should be drawn on for strength, and comfort, and healing. I know it may sound foolish, but—"

"I think it sounds . . . nice," Sophie promised, wishing she could come up with a better word. The fact that Flori would suggest it felt . . . a little like having Calla back. And Sophie's eyes burned as she whispered, "Thank you."

Flori flashed a green-toothed smile. But it faded when she added, "Your mother also told me about the echoes. And . . . I know nothing of such things. Darkness will always be darkness to me. But I wonder if I could sing them to sleep. If not, perhaps I can soften their tune."

"It's worth a try," Sophie said, her chest warming with a fresh spark of hope as Flori stood and faced her.

The tiny gnome pressed her left hand against Sophie's sling and reached for Sophie's face with her other hand. "May I?" she asked, her fingers hovering just above Sophie's skin.

Sophie nodded, and Flori gently cradled the right side of her head, her fingers shifting back and forth across her temple, like branches swaying in a breeze.

"This is where they hurt you, isn't it?" Flori breathed.

Sophie couldn't seem to push the word "yes" past the massive lump now caught in her throat. So she went with another nod.

"They didn't realize how strong you are," Flori told her. "But I fear you may have forgotten as well. Perhaps I can remind you."

She closed her eyes, swaying softly to some inner rhythm as her delicate voice sang a melody in a language too ancient for Sophie to fully grasp, but somehow she still caught the meaning. The lyrics poured through the air like honey, slowly sinking under Sophie's skin—flooding her heart with warmth and energy, sending it tingling through her veins.

It wasn't a happy song, or a sweet song.

It was deep and rich and poignant.

A song of weathering storms.

An anthem for rising up and growing stronger.

The last note lingered in the air, a fragile, perfect thing neither of them wanted to shatter, and only then did Sophie realize how quiet everyone else had gotten.

She turned to find all eyes not on her—but on Flori. Even Bo stared at the tiny gnome with a hint of wonder. And Tarina was blinking hard enough that she might've been crying—it was hard to tell with the natural gleam to her skin.

Elwin cleared his throat several times before he managed to ask, "Did that help?"

"I'm not sure," Sophie admitted, stretching her weak fingers.

Now that the song had ended, the tingly warmth had faded.

But she did feel . . . energized.

And maybe slightly less achy.

"I think it made a difference," she decided.

"With the echoes?" Edaline asked, hope clinging to every word.

That was much harder to tell—but Sophie needed to know. So even though it was a risk, she closed her eyes and let her mind replay some of the voices that had been haunting her.

And as soon as Gethen's voice rattled through her brain, the monster tried to stir.

"No difference with the echoes," she said, gulping down deep breaths to take back control. "I'm fine," she promised Elwin. "I was careful."

He still insisted on checking her again, just to be sure.

"I must've chosen the wrong song," Flori whispered, mostly to herself. She stared out the windows at the darkening sky. "I'd like to try again."

"Not tonight," Elwin told her.

"No," Flori agreed, her gray eyes focusing on Sophie. "I think this might require a new song to be written. It may take me some time, but . . . when it's ready, will you trust me to try it?"

"Of course," Sophie promised.

And that seemed to settle things.

And not just with Flori's singing.

The bodyguard debate also came to an end, with everyone agreeing that Sophie's first training session would be taught by Sandor and would focus on daggers. The lesson would last one hour and one hour only, and when it was finished, Sophie would hail Elwin to have him come check her.

Assuming there were no setbacks, the next day she'd be allowed to do the same, and if she made it through three days she'd be allowed to extend her training to an hour and fifteen minutes—then to an hour and a half if she made it another three days without problems, and to an hour forty-five if she had three more good days after that.

It was a far cry from the intense eight-hour marathon sessions that Sophie had originally envisioned.

But she wasn't going to complain.

She was just going to squeeze the most she possibly could out of whatever training time they gave her.

Nothing could dampen her mood.

Not the dozens of horrible elixirs she had to choke down.

Or the slightly painful finger stretches Elwin showed her how to do.

Not even when she had to spend seventeen minutes and twenty-nine seconds—yes, she counted—standing at the top of the stairs outside her bedroom while Sandor, Tarina, and Flori performed the most ridiculously exhaustive security sweep in the history of the universe. They checked places no enemy could possibly be hiding, like inside her desk drawers and behind her bookshelves and on top of her bed's fancy canopy. They also inspected every single one of the thousands of flowers woven into her carpet for any trace of a footprint. And when they finally finished, they lowered the shades over her walls of windows and made her promise to stay away from the glass, which felt both unnecessary and unsettling.

But none of it mattered.

She was home.

She could train.

Even better—she could *shower*.

As soon as Sandor gave her the all clear, she nearly sprinted to her bathroom, wrestled her way out of her sling, and prepared to set a new world record for longest, hottest, steamiest shower.

But before she stepped under the colorful streams of water, she worked up the courage to study her reflection. There were no mirrors in the Healing Center, so she hadn't *really* seen herself since the attack. And she'd been imagining . . . bad things. So her knees wobbled with relief when the girl staring back at her didn't look all that battered.

She was a little pale. A little haggard. A little scrawnier than she had been. And her injured arm definitely showed signs that she was still healing: fading bruises and darker blue veins, and the way it didn't hang as straight as her other arm. There were also a few thin white lines along her right hand's knuckles, and she had a feeling they wouldn't be going away.

"But they didn't break me," she said out loud as she stepped under the colorful streams and let the hot water rinse away the grime and tangles.

Showering had always been a way to center herself.

A way to regroup and start again.

"They didn't break me," she said again. "They'll *never* break me."

She wasn't the weak, predictable girl the Neverseen thought she was.

She was Sophie Foster.

She was the moonlark.

And starting tomorrow, she was learning to fight back.

THIRTY

SHOULD YOU BE LYING LIKE THAT?"
Edaline asked when she came to tuck Sophie in.

"Probably not," Sophie admitted. But she couldn't bring herself to shift from her current position: limbs stretched out like a starfish across the top of her humongous bed.

After weeks confined to a narrow cot, she was soaking up *all* the space she could get.

"How about we prop you up and support that arm?" Edaline suggested, which was definitely *not* what Sophie wanted, and Edaline seemed to know that. "Okay, what if I remind you that sitting up will make it easier for you to cuddle with the little friend I brought?"

She held up the tiny cage she'd been hiding behind her back—Iggy's cage—and Sophie relented, slowly pulling herself into a position more like the one she'd been stuck sitting in for days and days as Edaline set the tiny imp free, and he flitted to Sophie's lap.

Iggy's squeaky purr filled the room as he nuzzled against her fingers while she stroked his soft fur—which was not the color Sophie remembered it being.

"I'm assuming Dex was here?" she asked, admiring Iggy's bright yellow fluff, which sparkled like he'd been coated in a thick layer of glitter.

Edaline smiled. "He stopped by yesterday. He wanted it to be your welcome home present—and he seemed pretty excited with how the sparkles turned out. Apparently they glow in the dark."

"Really?" Sophie snapped her fingers to turn off the star-shaped lights dangling from the ceiling, and sure enough, Iggy had a shimmery halo around him—kind of like a lake reflecting moonlight, but thankfully subtle enough that it wouldn't be annoying when she wanted to sleep.

"Dex never fails to amaze," Edaline said as Sophie turned the lights on again and gave Iggy's chubby tummy a good belly rub. "I'm stunned he was able to spend so much time with you today without spoiling the surprise."

"Well, Tinker's place was pretty much a Technopath's dreamland," Sophie told her, realizing she'd need to check on Dex in the morning and find out how working with Tinker had gone.

She'd have to check on Fitz, too, she realized. He still hadn't reached out—which didn't feel like a good sign.

And now that she was thinking about it, she also hadn't heard from Keefe all day.

That probably meant he was up to something she wouldn't like.

"Will you be able to sleep?" Edaline asked, tracing her finger over the worry pucker that had formed between Sophie's eyebrows. "Elwin said you haven't been taking any sedatives, but he gave me some just in case."

She set two bright pink vials on the table beside Sophie's bed.

"Silveny's been keeping my dreams nightmare-free," Sophie promised.

"That's what I hear," Edaline said. "How's she doing?"

"She seems okay. Though I think the pregnancy's starting to make her pretty tired. And she still won't agree to come in for a checkup."

Edaline frowned. "Well . . . I guess we'll just have to keep trying. And remember that lots of animals in the wild have babies without needing our help."

That would've been a whole lot more comforting if Silveny wasn't the only female alicorn left, as far as anyone knew.

What if the reason the species was almost gone was because of complications during birth or something?

"There has to be something we can bribe her with," Sophie decided. "Some treat she won't be able to resist."

"I'll talk to the gnomes," Grady said from her doorway, "see if they have any ideas."

"Good idea," Sophie told him. "Thanks."

"Of course," he said, making his way over just in time to catch a whiff of the toxic burp Iggy had unleashed. He coughed from the stench as he added, "Your mom and I are here for whatever you need—and not just for Silveny."

"We know you've got a lot to adjust to right now, between your recovery and the training," Edaline jumped in.

"And we know it's going to be challenging for you to have so many people following you around, monitoring every little thing you do—and not for the usual reasons someone your age wouldn't be happy about that," Grady told her. "We get that you're not dealing with the usual teenage secrets. You're facing some pretty grown-up problems, kiddo, and you have some pretty major responsibilities, and we understand that some-times that means you can't be as open about what you have going on as we might want you to be."

The way he emphasized certain words made her wonder if this was his subtle way of letting her know that he hadn't been fooled by Tarina's explanation for their Trollish conversation.

But if it was, he didn't say.

He just reached for her good hand and told her, "I realize how tricky it is to be the moonlark, dealing with classified secrets when you have bodyguards shadowing you and parents asking too many questions. And we never want to get in the way—or put you in a position where you feel forced to lie to us. So we want to make you a deal: If you promise to keep *someone* informed about whatever you have going on—and I mean an adult with a little more experience, not just one of your friends—the rest of us, including your bodyguards, will trust you to handle it and try our best not to ask you questions. I'm sure we won't always be able to stop ourselves from trying to figure out what you're up to. But if we start to get in your way, tell us and we'll back off. And know that if you choose to rely on either of us"—he pointed to himself and Edaline—"you don't have to worry that we'll judge you or punish you for anything going on. Our help comes with no strings attached, and it's *always* there if you want it."

"Thank you," Sophie whispered, tightening her grip on his hand. "Sandor seriously agreed to that?"

"I did," Sandor called from the hallway.

"But I thought secrets hinder your ability to protect me," she reminded him.

"They do," he agreed. "But . . . our situation has changed now that I'm not your sole protector. So I'm willing to allow that you might need to be more careful about what you share. But"—he peeked his head through the doorway—"part of the reason that works is because I'm expecting you to hold true to the promise you made back when you were convincing me not to request reassignment. No sneaking away without me."

"Or me," Flori chimed in.

"Or me," Tarina added.

"Or *me*," Bo demanded.

"Wow . . . there are a lot of you out there," Sophie mumbled.

"We'll divide up more once you're asleep," Sandor assured her. "But for now, we're here to keep watch."

Somehow that sounded more like they were there to keep her from leaving.

But she wasn't going anywhere, so it didn't really matter— or at least that's what she tried to tell herself.

"It'll get easier," Edaline said, handing her Ella. "And just so you know, this policy applies to all the normal teenager things too. Tell us as little or as much as you like. But if you need us, we're a safe space."

"Except when it comes to boy stuff," Grady added. "*That* we want to know."

Sophie groaned.

Edaline laughed, leaning in to kiss her cheek. "Now that we've sufficiently embarrassed you, I think it's time to let you rest. If you need anything, you know where to find us."

"Thanks."

They turned off the lights as they left, and Sophie decided to spend a few minutes snuggling with her glowing imp—even if his breath seemed extra stinky.

"Sorry I was gone so long," she told him, scratching behind Iggy's fuzzy ears. "I'll try not to do it again."

The light from his fur made his watery green eyes even brighter than normal—and as he stared intently at her, she wondered if he was trying to let her know he'd missed her. It was hard to tell, since he blasted out a bed-shaking fart a few seconds later that made at least two of her bodyguards cough all the way from the hallway.

And that fart was followed by another fart. And another. And another.

"Ugh—what have they been feeding you?" she asked, gagging as she stumbled out of bed and carried Iggy back to his cage. "Imp bonding time over!"

Iggy's only answer was another fart, and she tossed a blanket over his cage, hoping it would help hold in the stench.

She could've sworn the sound Iggy made was a snicker.

"Need help getting back in bed?" Sandor called through her door.

"I'm good!" she promised. Though it took a lot longer than she wanted to get her arm situated the way it had been before, especially since all she wanted to do was curl up with Ella on her side.

Someday she'd sleep normally again.

But for the moment, she had to take care of herself.

Had to make sure—

Sophie?

For a second, she thought she must've imagined the crisp, accented voice. But it repeated again—louder this time.

SOPHIE?

Fitz? she transmitted back, her heart slamming against her ribs.

IT WORKED! his mind shouted. *I CAN'T BELIEVE I PULLED*

IT OFF! Your blocking makes it WAY harder than connecting with Silveny—did you know that?

She didn't. But it made sense.

How long have you been trying to reach me?

About fifteen minutes. It kinda gave me a headache, but I wanted to check in without anyone being able to eavesdrop, so I just kept searching for the tug and—

Tug? Sophie interrupted.

Yeah. Or maybe "pull" is a better word. I don't know if it's a Cognate thing, or just because your telepathy is so strong, but my thoughts always go straight to you.

Huh, Sophie thought, ordering her brain not to take those words and run wild with them. She knew he didn't mean them the way they sounded.

But her heart refused to get the message and turned all fluttery. And her stomach decided to join in with a few annoying flips.

Sorry I didn't check in earlier, he told her. *Did I wake you?*

No. Iggy's been terrorizing me with toxic farts. I swear he's been saving them up.

He laughed. *Sounds about right. Still glad to be home, though?*

Totally.

Is it weird being there with all the new bodyguards?

Yeah, she admitted, trying to keep her thoughts far away from Tarina, since she'd promised Mr. Forkle she wouldn't tell anyone yet. *But I'm sure it's not as weird as what you're dealing with. How's it going with your brother?*

Ugh. It's been rough. I knew it would be. But it's even worse than I imagined. Alvar's just so . . . happy. Like today. He stopped in the middle of his walk because he HAD to smell all the flowers. And then he got all choked up about how beautiful they were and how amazing it is to smell something that isn't swampy and rancid, and my parents just stood there, eating it up. I swear, if my mom wasn't trying to pretend that she's being objective, she would've run over and given him a hug after the flower thing. And my dad already stopped asking questions. He hit Alvar with, like, three how-could-yous, but Alvar said, "I don't remember," and my dad dropped it. I mean . . . seriously?

I'm sorry, Sophie told him. *That sounds super stressful.*

It is—but don't worry, I'm keeping my temper under control. I almost lost it when they first opened the gates to let Alvar in, but I'd told Biana to kick me to distract me. That got me through—plus a couple of wicked bruises. Word of advice, never let Biana near your shins.

Noted, Sophie said, trying to match his light tone, even though she could tell his was totally forced. *So . . . sounds like you've had to spend some time with Alvar. Does that mean you weren't able to make a deal with your parents?*

No, I was. They just drove a harder bargain than I expected. They made me and Biana promise to cooperate for the next ten days and do whatever they tell us to do. But once the ten days are up, they can't ask us to do anything else, so . . . it's worth it, I guess.

What kind of stuff are they having you do?

So far, just the Council's assignments. They wanted us to share some childhood memories with him to see if it triggered anything. And tomorrow I think we're supposed to play games.

Games?

I know—don't even get me started. That's the brilliant plan from our illustrious Council: Make us play base quest with a murderer. His mind went quiet for a second, and she wondered if he was taking a deep breath. *At least Councillor Oralie will be here to monitor everything tomorrow. Maybe she'll see through his Mr. Perfect act.*

And it's only ten days, Sophie added. *Nine, really, since today is already over.*

Yeah. Kinda sounds like forever, though.

I bet. If you need to talk, I'm here. ANYtime, okay?

Thanks, he thought quietly. *I'm sure I'll take you up on that.*

I hope you do. If you're too tired to reach out like this, I'll always have an Imparter with me.

So will I, he said. *If anything happens—I want to know about it.*

Same with you.

He sighed. *Nothing's going to happen here. Alvar's going to keep up his perfect little act as long as he possibly can—unless I can get him to break.*

How are you going to do that?

Still working on it. But if I have to spend nine more days with him, I'm going to hit him with everything I have.

"You call that a dagger?" Bo asked the next morning, sneering at the weapon Sandor had just handed to Sophie—which was, admittedly, much smaller than she'd been imagining.

The blade was maybe two inches long, and barely wider than a butter knife.

"*This* is a dagger," Bo said, drawing a dark blade as long as his forearm from a sheath hidden somewhere in the back of his armor.

"No, *this* is a dagger," Tarina countered, pulling an even longer silver weapon from somewhere among the tangled threads of her mossy garment, with a blade that spiraled like a corkscrew.

"And *those* are not for beginners," Sandor argued. "Let's also not forget that Sophie is training with her weaker hand."

"But I have Tinker's bracelet," Sophie reminded him.

"Which improves your strength, not your coordination," he corrected. "I'd like you to get through today's lesson without losing any fingers. Besides, any soldier worth the air they're breathing can fight with *any* weapon."

"I'd be more willing to believe you," Sophie noted, "if you weren't holding that."

She pointed to Sandor's dagger, which looked more like half a sword.

Tarina snorted. "I like this girl."

"Fine," Sandor said as he marched back to the satchel he'd brought to the pastures that morning. He returned a few seconds later holding a weapon identical to hers—which looked almost comical in his massive hand. "This blade may be small. But it's just as deadly as any of these other daggers. *Never* underestimate a weapon. I could fight anyone—and win—with this dagger."

"I'd like to see you try," Bo told him.

Sandor didn't blink. "I'd have your surrender in less than three minutes."

Bo's lips curled into a vicious smile. "Prove it."

"Prove it later," Sophie jumped in. "I only get an hour for training, and I'm not wasting it watching you guys play Who's the Better Bodyguard?"

"Correction: I *love* this girl," Tarina informed them.

Sandor tilted his head to study Sophie. "You seem . . . eager."

"Of course I am. I've been stuck in bed for weeks waiting for this, while all my friends trained without me. I have a ton of catching up to do."

"Then I know exactly where to start this lesson." He motioned for her to follow him over to the scarecrowlike dummy that Flori had assembled from lumpy sacks and twisted rags. It didn't have a face, but someone had painted two unnervingly realistic blue eyes across the coarse fabric of the dummy's head.

Sophie froze when she recognized them.

"Who painted those?" she whispered, sucking in a breath to keep the monster from waking. But she could feel the beast stretch its restless legs.

"I did," Sandor told her. "I wanted to make sure these lessons feel *real*."

Mission accomplished.

"I . . . never realized you were such a good artist," she told him, closing her eyes—but the scarecrow's lifelike irises were already burned into her memory.

Gethen's eyes.

"There's a lot you don't know about me," Sandor said, placing a steadying hand on her shoulder. "If this is too much—"

"No!" she interrupted. "I can handle it."

If she couldn't face an imaginary Gethen, how would she ever face the real one again?

"I'm going to trust you to know your limits," Sandor told her, and she nodded, grateful he wasn't going to baby her.

She took another long breath and forced herself to stare back at the dummy until her pulse steadied.

"For the record," Sandor told her, leaning close to whisper, "the next time I see him—he's *mine*."

She wasn't going to argue with that.

"Sooooo," she said, drawing out the word for another calming exhale. "Where do we start?"

"With the most basic element. Before I teach you any fighting techniques, it's important for you to get the feel for what we're really doing here—what actually happens when you utilize a weapon."

"You mean . . . what it's like to kill someone," Sophie clarified, feeling her mouth turn very dry when Sandor nodded.

"It's a different experience with every weapon," he told her. "Daggers are for close-range fights, where every blow comes at tremendous risk. So you need to learn how hard to slash, and which spots to aim for to make it count. Where do *you* think the ideal strike point is?"

"The heart?" Sophie guessed, her voice cracklier than she wanted it to be.

Sandor shook his head. "The heart's important. But the fastest, most effective attack is to the throat."

The world swam behind Sophie's eyes.

"Yes, it's incredibly unpleasant," Sandor told her. "The thing you must remember is that your goal must always be a *quick* end. The longer your enemy lives, the more chances they have to finish you. So if you only have one strike, it's best to aim like this."

He thrust his arm toward the dummy, stopping just short of making contact as he demonstrated the ideal motion—a quick, decisive slash.

No hesitation.

No remorse.

Then he stepped aside.

Her turn.

And it became a lot harder to breathe.

Moving wasn't any easier.

But she let her memory of Umber's cruel laugh carry her forward.

"Wrong," Sandor told her when she'd barely taken a step. "You're forgetting which arm is holding the weapon."

She was.

Even with her right arm strapped in a sling, her brain still defaulted to it.

This was so much harder than she'd thought it would be.

"Okay," she said, squaring her shoulders and tightening her grip on the dagger as she shifted her weight the other way.

In the same motion, she lunged forward, reached up, and slashed her dagger. "Like that?"

"You were supposed to strike the dummy," Sandor noted.

"*You* didn't," she argued.

"That's because I want you to make the first slice. It will feel *very* close to reality."

When he put it like that, she really, really, really didn't want to do it. But that was exactly the kind of weakness the Neverseen were always calling her out on.

So she focused on the painted eyes, channeling her hate and fury into her lunge as she slashed across the dummy's neck, feeling a sickening squish as the blade sank into the cloth—followed by a burst of horrifying red.

The dagger slipped from her grasp and she screamed and stumbled back. But she couldn't stop the splatter from hitting her hand. Her face. Her lips.

Her stomach heaved and she gagged, but somewhere deep in the back of her consciousness, the rational part of her was shouting that something didn't fit.

She'd stabbed a *dummy*.

There *couldn't* be blood.

That realization helped her focus past the bile coating her tongue, picking up a sweet, familiar flavor.

"YOU RIGGED IT WITH LUSHBERRY JUICE?" she shouted as her vision cleared enough to note the look on Sandor's face.

His eyes shone with guilt—but his jaw was set with determination.

"Like I said," he told her, "I made sure these lessons felt real."

"WHY WOULD YOU—"

"Because this isn't a game!" he snapped.

"You think I don't know that?" She pointed to her sling. *"You think I'm doing this for fun?"*

"No. But I think you've lost sight of what you're truly attempting. You're stepping into uncharted territory, both for you and for your species. And you seem to think you'll be able to handle it because you're angry. But emotion won't overrule your instincts—and the battlefield isn't the place to discover that violence is too much for you."

"The battle is coming for me whether I want to fight or not!" Sophie argued.

"I know. I'm not saying you shouldn't be training. But I need you to truly understand the reality of what you're attempting, both so you treat it with the respect and responsibility it requires, and so you're mentally prepared for the ugliness involved with what you're learning. And this was the only way I could think to truly get through to you."

Tarina whistled. "Brutal. But effective."

It was.

Sophie wanted to hate Sandor for it. But . . . she hadn't even managed to hold on to her weapon.

If she'd freaked out like that in the middle of a real fight, she'd probably be dead.

She bent to retrieve the tiny dagger—which didn't look so wimpy anymore—wishing her hand wasn't shaking.

"Are you okay?" Sandor asked, his eyes scanning her from head to toe.

She tried to decide.

The monster was awake now—she could feel that. But it hadn't dragged her under.

And with each deep breath, she forced it to back off.

Maybe it was good to know that—to know her limits actually stretched pretty far.

"I'll be fine," she told him. "I just need a couple of minutes."

Sandor nodded, heading to his satchel and returning with a clean towel. He held it out to her like a white flag. "I'm sorry. I hate having to upset you. But if I don't properly prepare you for the complexities of this new challenge, I'm failing you as your protector. And I won't fail you again. Even if it means making you hate me."

"I don't hate you," she said quietly, wiping the sticky red off her skin, reminding herself it was only juice.

Honestly, she wasn't sure what she was feeling.

Humiliation burned her cheeks. But there was something else—something cold and sour and shuddery.

"You don't think I can do this." She wasn't sure if she was speaking to herself or Sandor at that point.

He answered her anyway. "Wrong. I'm positive you can. I just dread the toll it's going to take on you—and your friends."

"Did they get splattered at the beginning of their training too?" she wondered.

"I don't believe so. But I'll make sure they do. It's essential that you're all physically *and* mentally ready for battle. So plan on further surprises to your own lessons as well."

"More fake blood," Sophie mumbled. "Noted."

"Blood is only part of the horror. Battles have their own sounds. Their own smells. Their own pace. You've experienced pieces of it at times. But I fear someday you'll face it on a much larger, much more overwhelming scale. And while I'll be right there at your side, I do agree that it's best for you to be able to fight back as much as you can. So how about we spend the remaining thirty-six minutes of today's lesson on a skill that should feel a bit more comfortable for you. I promise no more surprises today."

Thirty-six minutes sounded like a *very* long time.

But Sophie let Sandor lead her away from the now red-stained dummy.

"So what are we working on?" she asked, after several long beats of silence.

"This." Sandor spun around and flicked his arm.

The tiny dagger flew out of his hand, blurring through the air and stabbing straight between the dummy's painted eyes.

"The first rule of dagger throwing," Sandor told her, "is: *Never* throw a dagger if you know you're going to need it. That's another reason I gave you such a small weapon to train with. You'll be able to hide several of them in the clothes Flori's designing for you."

Sophie blinked. "Flori's designing clothes for me?"

"With lots of hidden pockets," Sandor agreed. "That way you can always have a few daggers and throwing stars with you— and likely a few of Dex's inventions as well. And you'll need to get in the habit of checking your arsenal and knowing exactly what you're carrying and where to reach it all. That way you'll *know* if you can afford to lose the weapon. If you're down to your last dagger, it's generally best to hold on to it."

"Even if I can take out an enemy?" Sophie asked.

Sandor nodded. "A dagger in hand can cut down *many* enemies. A throw just finishes one—and only if they don't duck or dodge."

"But what if throwing it saves someone?" Sophie countered.

"Then you'll have to decide if their life is worth more than your own," Bo jumped in. "Battles are not for heroics, contrary to what many foolishly believe. They're for *winning*. That must always be your overall goal. If you manage to save anyone in the process, that's a bonus. But your endgame must be *victory*. And the best chance you have of that is by staying alive, because you're far more useful when you're fighting than when you're dead."

Sophie hated every single word of that.

Sandor rested his hand on her shoulder. "There are no easy choices in battle."

"There aren't," Tarina agreed. "That's why our soldiers are trained to fight on instinct. Then there's no looking back and wondering 'what if.' There's simply what happened and who lived."

"I'm . . . not sure my brain can work like that," Sophie admitted.

"Mine doesn't either," Tarina admitted. "At least not anymore. That's why the bulk of my army's ranks are Stage Twos. Those at my stage think too much. Makes us useful for specialized missions like this, but less so for major combat. Battles are surprisingly mindless."

Sophie had no idea how to respond to that.

"We're wasting your training time," Sandor realized. "You should be learning to throw a dagger."

"What's the point, if I'm supposed to hold on to it?" Sophie countered.

"You're supposed to hold on to your *last* weapon," Sandor corrected. "And even then, there may be moments when it's better to let it go. Either way, throwing is still a vital, lifesaving skill to acquire. If you're looking for absolutes or clear black-and-white rules, you won't find them on a battlefield. It's moment by moment. The best you can do is give yourself as many defenses as possible."

He pointed to the target. "Aim for between the eyes."

"Are you going to give me any pointers?" Sophie asked.

"It's all in the wrist," he told her, which wasn't necessarily helpful.

Sophie did her best—but she quickly discovered that daggers were *much* trickier than goblin throwing stars. The slightest error and the weapon didn't just miss the place she'd been aiming for—it bounced harmlessly off the dummy.

Aiming with her left arm was also more challenging than she would've expected, and she completely overcompensated on her first several throws. But by the time her lesson was finished, she'd found a rhythm and could hit *exactly* where Sandor told her to aim every single time.

"Are all elves this quick a study?" Bo wondered when Sophie nailed the dummy between its horrible eyes for the third toss in a row.

"No," Sandor assured him. "Sophie is very special."

"I suspect that's why they call her the moonlark," Tarina said quietly. "Why she's valuable enough to require more guards than even her Councillors. And why it's far better to be on her side."

Her eyes locked with Sophie's, and Sophie could almost feel the words Tarina wasn't saying.

The reminder that the trolls were offering so much more than protection.

"I'm looking forward to tomorrow," Tarina told her. "*I'm* in charge of the lesson."

"Assuming Elwin thinks she's up for more training," Sandor reminded them, studying Sophie from head to toe again. "I know I pushed you pretty hard. On several levels."

He had.

But when Elwin came to check on her, he didn't see any sign of setbacks.

The monster was still stirring, but Sophie had kept it at bay.

"Excellent," Tarina said. "Then tomorrow we'll get to see how brilliantly you and I work together."

"So here's the thing," Keefe said by way of greeting when he hailed Sophie on her Imparter later that evening, while she was sitting on the floor of her bedroom polishing the giant stack of goblin throwing stars that Sandor had given her. "I wanted to stop by today, since I didn't have time yesterday, and I know it makes your imagination shift into mega worry mode when I disappear. But Ro's being a royal pain. She says as soon as I set foot at Havenfield it ends our latest bet, and since I'm assuming you haven't gotten the dirt on Bo-Ro yet, that's not going to be good for me. Any chance you could get on that?"

"I can try again," Sophie told him, cleaning something crusty off one of the blades—which wasn't easy to do with only one hand. "But I doubt it's going to work."

"Not with that attitude! Come on, Foster—you know you're just as curious to hear the saga of Bo and Ro as I am! Time to put those powers of persuasion to use! *Or* you could take a tiny peek inside his head. . . ."

"Uh, you realize if he catches me, I'd end up in an ogre work camp, right?"

"Nah, Ro would never let that happen—especially if you dug out a couple embarrassing Bo secrets to trade with her."

Sophie shook her head, moving on to the next throwing star. "Not happening."

"Fine. Then how about you use that fancy telekinesis of yours to dangle him upside down by his ankles. Maybe threaten him with a few of those weapons you're cleaning until he cracks. Or—"

"Goodbye, Keefe."

"Hang on! You're not going to demand to know what I've been doing the last couple of days?" he asked. "You're slipping, Foster. It *almost* feels like you forgot to worry about me."

She angled her face away from the Imparter because . . . honestly?

Between visiting Tinker and finally coming home and meeting her bodyguards and having Tarina propose an alliance and Sandor's disturbing lesson that morning—plus a long afternoon of trying on different outfits so Flori could take measurements— she hadn't had time to think about a whole lot else.

"I see how it is." Keefe's words were teasing—just like his smile. But his eyes weren't quite as convincing.

Shame burned Sophie's cheeks. "Sorry. It's been a little overwhelming."

He nodded. "I'm sure it has."

"So . . . what *have* you been doing?" she asked, shoving the throwing stars aside. Giving him her full attention.

"Nothing exciting. Mostly just school. Are you *ever* coming back to Foxfire, by the way, or have you decided you're too good for us now that you have your own multispeciesial army?"

"I don't know when the Council will let me come back," she admitted. "They might want me to wait until my arm's not in a sling."

She'd have to ask Magnate Leto the next time she saw him.

And she should probably make some progress on the mountain of assignments that had been piling up while she was stuck in the Healing Center.

But more important: "So that's all you've been doing? Just school? No more memory exercises with Tiergan?"

"Nah. It felt like we went as far as we were going to go, and it led to a whole lot of nowhere. Plus, my dad's keeping me busy with his little Empath lessons."

Her stomach twisted. "How are those going?"

"*Super* fun. It's like, 'Wow—I knew my daddy loved me, but I never realized he was such a big old ball of mush until I got to spend the day soaking up all his fuzzy feelings.'"

"And now the real answer?" Sophie pressed.

Keefe reached up to sweep back his hair—which said a whole lot more than his "It's fine."

Sophie sighed. "Need me to send Krakie to you?"

Half his smile returned. "Nah, he likes you better than me. Everyone does."

"No they don't."

"Oh really? Tell me this: Have *you* heard from the Fitzster since he went home for the happy family reunion?"

Before she could figure out a way to soften her answer, he said, "Exactly. And I get it—why would he hail the best friend who spent a little too much quality time with his creepy brother after running off to join the Neverseen, when he can have a secret Fitzphie convo with his cute little Cognate?"

"Keefe—"

"Relax, I'm just giving you a hard time. It's my greatest joy in life."

It did seem to be.

But their current conversation had also made Sophie feel like a terrible friend. Which was probably why she found herself promising, "I'll get the Bo-Ro story."

"WOO—*now* you're talking! Make sure you push for the really juicy details, too—especially if kissing's involved. Actually, scratch that—I'll need to claw out my brain if I have to picture Ro in a slobbery lip-lock."

"Yeah, let's not go there," Sophie agreed.

"But find out *everything* else. I'm counting on you, Foster."

"I'll do my best."

She was about to click the Imparter off when Keefe asked, "How's Fitz doing?"

She picked up another throwing star, turning it over in her hand. "Pretty much what you'd expect. He and Biana both agreed to play nice for ten days if it means their parents will leave them alone about Alvar after that. But it sounds like it's killing Fitz, having to spend all that time with his brother."

"I bet. I'm starting to think things are never going to be the same in Vacker land."

"I know. Especially if Alvar ends up living there permanently. I think that's why Fitz is so determined to prove it's all an act. He said he's going to use the next nine days to break him—though I guess it's down to eight now."

Keefe blew out a breath. "See, but I don't think Alvar's faking."

"Neither do I," Sophie admitted. "I think . . . without his memories, he's a different person—the person he should've been if something hadn't made him go all creepy."

"Do you really think anything could *make* him that creepy, though?" Keefe wondered. "Or do you think there was something in him that was just waiting to snap?"

"I have no idea."

She also couldn't decide which thought was scarier: that there could be something fundamentally evil in someone that guaranteed they'd turn bad someday, or the idea that any person, under the right circumstances, could end up a villain.

"I guess it all comes down to the reason Alvar switched sides," she decided.

"Yep. I bet if we knew that, we could trigger at least some of his missing memories."

"Too bad Biana's been trying to understand what Alvar meant by 'the Vacker legacy' for months," Sophie grumbled, "and hasn't gotten anywhere."

"I know. I've actually been using the mental exercises Tiergan taught me to dig through my memories of everything Alvar said while I was with the Neverseen, in case I missed any hints. So far, the only thing I can come up with is that he talked about Orem a few times. I mean, it wasn't a big deal—mostly just Vacker gossip about how Orem didn't get along with his mom. But . . . it might be worth seeing what else they can learn about the guy."

"I guess it couldn't hurt," Sophie agreed, even though it felt like a long shot. "I'll mention it the next time Fitz checks in."

"Tell him I said hi," Keefe added. "And . . . try to get some sleep. I know it won't be easy after talking about all of this. But . . . you look pretty tired there, Foster. Everything okay? Need me to leap over there? I will—I don't care if Ro wins the bet."

She had no doubt that he would—and she didn't deserve that kind of dedication.

"I'm good," she promised. "Training is just . . . intense."

"Elwin's letting you train?"

She nodded but didn't have the energy to explain—or to relive that horrible red splatter.

"Hmm," Keefe said, his eyes narrowing as he squinted through the screen to study her. "Sounds like I need to head over there after Daddy's little hugfest tomorrow."

"I'm fine—don't lose your bet. Today was just the first day. It'll be better tomorrow."

Or worse, depending on what Tarina had in mind.

Keefe tore a hand through his hair again. "I can tell there's something you're not telling me right now—but I'm not going to force you to talk about it. If you say you're good, I'll trust you."

She held his stare through the Imparter screen as she told him, "I'm good."

He nodded. "Just remember: the worrying thing you're a master at? I'm pretty good at it too. So . . . don't forget about me, okay?"

There was a rawness to the plea that tugged on Sophie's heart hard enough to drag it into her throat.

"I won't," she promised. "I'll check in tomorrow."

Sophie waited up for Fitz as long as she could. But Sandor's lesson had seriously wiped her out, and her chat with Keefe drained her last bit of energy. She could barely keep her eyes open by the time she decided to call it a day and reach out to Silveny.

Since the monster *still* hadn't fully settled, she was definitely going to need help chasing away any nightmares. But when

Silveny's voice filled her head, the friendly alicorn sounded far less exuberant than usual.

In fact, her greeting sounded downright forced: *Sophie! Friend! Hi!*

What's wrong? Sophie demanded.

Nothing! Nothing! Nothing!

I don't believe you. You sound exhausted.

Tired! Silveny admitted.

Sophie sorted through Silveny's memories, searching for the source of her fatigue. But all the pregnant alicorn had done that day was graze—which seemed like it shouldn't have left her so wiped out.

You NEED to come in for a checkup, Sophie told her—but of course Silveny responded with, *Baby okay! Baby okay!*

I hope that's true, Sophie told her. *But YOU'RE not okay. I really don't think it's normal for you to be this tired.*

Normal! Normal! Normal!

Saying it doesn't make it true. If you don't feel up to coming to me, I can come to you. I promise I'll bring Edaline—not Vika— and she'll do a super-quick exam.

NO! NO! NO! Silveny argued, finding a burst of energy. *NO EXAM! NO VISIT! NO!*

Sophie reached up to rub her temples. *You're really getting ridiculous. You need to let us help you.*

NO HELP! NO HELP! NO HELP!

But—

NO HELP! Silveny interrupted. *JUST! NEED! SLEEP!*

Sophie rubbed her temples a whole lot harder when Silveny turned it into a chant.

JUST! NEED! SLEEP!

JUST! NEED! SLEEP!

JUST! NEED! SLEEP!

FINE! Sophie shouted when she couldn't take it anymore. *Sleep tonight—but I'm checking on you in the morning, and if you're not better . . .*

Better morning! Better morning! Better morning! Silveny promised.

We'll see, Sophie told her.

See. See. See.

Silveny's mental voice faded almost to a whisper, like she'd used up the last dregs of her energy for that final outburst. So when she started to flood Sophie's mind with dreams, Sophie tossed up a mental wall.

Not tonight, Sophie warned. *You need to sleep without having to use any part of your brain for me.*

But Sophie nightmares! Silveny reminded her.

I'll be fine. Sophie grabbed one of the pink elixirs from the table beside her bed and chugged it before she could change her mind. *There. I just took a sedative.*

But—

No, Sophie interrupted. *It's already settled. Now PLEASE get some sleep.*

THIRTY-ONE

SOPHIE! FRIEND! HI! SILVENY SAID THE
next morning, back to her usual energy level—
which was an enormous relief. But it also meant
the poor mama alicorn must've been wearing
herself out trying to help Sophie with her dreams, and that
needed to stop—immediately.

BUT SOPHIE NIGHTMARES! Silveny argued when Sophie
broke the news.

I'll be fine, Sophie assured her. *The sedative worked perfectly.*

She decided not to mention that she'd spent most of the
night dreaming about sparkly pineapples dancing around in
hot pink tutus while wearing giant sunglasses and smiling

at her. She could live with the outlandish imagery if it kept Silveny strong and healthy.

We're still going to check in every night, Sophie added—not making it optional. *And if you try to ignore me, I WILL track you down—and bring Vika with me.*

It wasn't an idle threat. All of Silveny's recent memories kept showing the same rolling seaside hills, which probably meant that was where the alicorns were currently staying. So all Sophie would have to do is jump into the void and picture those grass-covered dunes. Then her teleporting would take her straight to the alicorns.

She was tempted to grab Edaline and do exactly that—but that might freak Silveny out and make her teleport away, which wasn't worth the risk.

So she would save it for a last resort, and hope that she could convince Silveny to see reason and agree to a checkup.

But first, Sophie had to survive Tarina's training session.

Rest as much as you can, she told Silveny as she crawled out of bed, shaking her head to clear away the last of the fruity fog. *I'll reach out again later.*

SOPHIE! TALK! SOON!

The first thing Sophie noticed when she met her bodyguards out in the pastures was that Tarina wasn't wearing her usual mossy garment. Instead she'd squeezed into a slippery black bodysuit that looked like she'd wrapped everything from her neck down in slimy seaweed.

The second thing Sophie noticed was that there was no target. The splattered scarecrow from the day before had disappeared, and Sophie definitely wasn't going to miss it.

She just wasn't sure what that meant for the third thing she spotted: a hefty satchel that Sandor was holding, filled with all the goblin throwing stars she'd spent the previous night polishing.

"Yesterday you proved that you have truly impeccable aim," Tarina said as she shook some sort of blue powder onto her hand. She pressed her palm over her heart, leaving a bold, blue handprint on her bodysuit—then repeated the process to mark her stomach and thigh, then twisted to mark her back as she added, "But yesterday's lesson was also somewhat deceptive. It's incredibly rare in battle to be aiming at a stationary mark. Just like it's rare to be stationary yourself. So today you'll be practicing under much more realistic conditions. Behold your new targets!"

Tarina pointed to the blue handprints, then ran forward a few steps and dropped into a somersault before springing back to her feet with a leap that lifted her several feet off the ground.

Sophie glanced at Sandor. "She doesn't want me to aim at *her*, does she?"

"Unfortunately, she does," Sandor grumbled. "And I renew my objections to this plan!" he told Tarina. "I have a whole system I use to train for moving targets."

"And we both know that no matter how great that system is, it will never fully capture the complexities of aiming at an enemy in motion," Tarina countered. "Real enemies can pivot and leap and duck and dodge and roll." She shifted her body through each movement as she spoke. "The trick is to learn to read body language, and to anticipate how the target will move. None of which can happen with dummies."

"Dummies also can't die if a weapon strikes the wrong place," Bo noted. "The child is good—but she's not as good as you think she is."

"She's better," Tarina insisted. "Which is why I want you moving as well, Sophie. I realize your recovery might limit the amount of running you're able to do. But it's important for you to learn how to aim—and throw—without having to pause. So I need you to keep up with me today for as long as you're physically able. I'll call out which mark I want you to hit at random, and your job is to strike as quickly and accurately as you can."

Sophie ignored the fact that even the *thought* of running made her want to sit down and never get up. Instead she turned back to Sandor. "We're not using throwing stars then, right? We're using splotchers or pebbles or something safer?"

"Wrong!" Tarina informed her. "You need to train with the actual weapons you'll be using in battle, since the weight and motion will be different. Don't worry—my suit will protect me."

Sophie found that *very* hard to believe, particularly since: "It doesn't cover your head."

"Yes, that's the one mark we won't be practicing," Tarina agreed, "for obvious reasons. I've gone for variety instead, targets in slightly less fatal locations that shouldn't be your first choice in a battle. But once I help you master *how* to aim, you'll be able to hit between the eyes without needing to practice that specifically."

"That's not what I meant," Sophie argued. "I meant . . . what if I miss?"

Tarina flashed all of her long white teeth. "I trust you."

"You shouldn't!"

Tarina laughed. "Yes, I should. I'm aware that there are risks. I'm also aware of your talent—and your commitment to keeping everyone safe. It's why you'll make a perfect ally someday."

She said the last part in her chirpy language, so only Sophie could understand.

Sophie replied back the same way. "Making me hurt you isn't going to convince me to form an alliance—it's going to make me think you're insane."

"You won't hurt me, Sophie. You couldn't even if you wanted to. And this isn't about the alliance. It's my job as your bodyguard—and your trainer—to prepare you for battle to the best of my ability. And *this* is the best of my ability. You'll see how well it works if you trust me."

She switched back to the Enlightened Language as she added, "We start on three."

"I don't like this," Sophie said to no one in particular.

"Neither do I," Sandor agreed.

"You don't have to like it," Tarina told them. "But I do expect you to do it, Sophie. And if you don't want to hurt me, I suggest you focus. Your first target is my back."

She counted to three and took off toward the Cliffside gate at the edge of the pastures, glancing over her shoulder to see if Sophie had followed.

Sophie hadn't.

"I'm not joking!" Tarina shouted. "Failure to participate in today's lesson will have serious consequences."

"What kind of consequences?" Sophie asked.

"Best not to find out," Sandor said as he handed Sophie the satchel of throwing stars. "I hope Tarina knows what she's doing."

So did Sophie.

She knew from polishing them the night before that the throwing stars had *very* sharp blades.

But Tarina repeated her command again, warning that it was Sophie's last chance before she'd be punished. So Sophie slung the satchel over her shoulder and took off after her.

Wow, that looks . . . intense, Fitz mentally murmured after he'd reached out telepathically that evening.

Sophie had been far too exhausted to hide any of her recent memories, so he got to watch a vivid replay of her high-stakes training session. And she could feel his mind flinch every time her throws came terrifyingly close to disaster.

But Tarina had been saved each time by her *amazing* reflexes. Sophie had never seen anyone who moved the way Tarina did—as if her bones were made of rubber and could twist and bend and stretch all kinds of impossible ways.

Even Bo's jaw dropped during some of the most harrowing near misses.

Sophie was also pretty sure that the times she'd managed to hit one of the targets were only because Tarina had let her.

Her troll bodyguard was *that* good.

And Sophie suspected that was the point of Tarina's rather daring exercise.

She didn't just want Sophie to trust her.

She wanted Sophie to be impressed.

As if the lesson had been designed to say, *I trust you. You can trust me. And here's why you want to be on my side and have me on yours.*

And if that was Tarina's plan, it . . . kind of worked.

The idea of an alliance felt a whole lot more urgent now that Sophie had a better understanding of the trolls' capabilities.

If creatures that powerful felt they needed an ally among the elves, something big must be happening. And—

Wait—you're forming a secret alliance with the trolls? Fitz interrupted, and Sophie's heart screeched to a stop.

It's okay, he promised. *I'm not going to tell anybody. I know you forgot I was listening—I even tried to tune you out. But I still caught a few details and . . . wow.*

Sophie pinched the bridge of her nose as a headache flared behind her eyes—probably her brain's way of punishing her for being so careless. *I haven't decided what I'm doing. Mr. Forkle wanted to do some research to see if he could figure out why the trolls are asking me now, since timing seems to be a factor. And so far, he hasn't gotten back in touch to let me know what he found.*

So the Black Swan knows? Fitz clarified, flooding her mind with a blast of relief when she confirmed. *Good. I definitely don't think you should make this decision alone.*

I won't. It's been hard enough hiding it from my friends. But Tarina didn't want me to tell anyone, and I figured you have so much going on with Alvar, and we aren't Cognate training right now, and—

Hey, he said, waiting for her thoughts to trail off before he told her, *You don't have to explain. I get why you didn't tell me.*

You do?

Of course. This is huge. Like . . . treason huge.

Treason? Sophie repeated, and all her insides shriveled and twisted.

She hadn't fully considered all the ramifications. But he was right—she was being asked to make an agreement with the leader of another species *without* telling the Council.

If it makes you feel better, Fitz told her, *the Black Swan's done that kind of stuff before. They've had dwarves helping with their cause for a while.*

True. But that doesn't mean King Enki was involved. And Empress Pernille definitely is. Tarina said one of their previous empresses was involved in the other alliance too.

What other alliance?

I don't know. Tarina wouldn't tell me much about it.

And since Sophie had already blown the secret, she went ahead and showed Fitz the replay of the entire conversation.

When the memory finished, he couldn't seem to find any coherent words.

That's how I felt, Sophie admitted. *Part of me still wants to tell her, I'M ONLY FIFTEEN—CAN YOU PLEASE DUMP THIS HUGE RESPONSIBILITY ON SOMEONE WHO ACTUALLY KNOWS WHAT THEY'RE DOING? But . . .*

You're the moonlark, Fitz finished for her.

She sighed. *That's what everybody keeps telling me. At least Tarina gave me time to decide.*

If there's anything I can do to help . . .

Thanks. I might take you up on that—though you have enough to deal with right now.

Eh, I could use a distraction, trust me.

I take it things aren't going any better with your brother?

Nope. I thought I might get him to slip up when I tagged him out in base quest, since he's always been SUCH a sore loser. But he just laughed and told me, "Well played." I swear it's like he's rehearsing all the perfect things to say.

He actually might be. He knows he's going back to that cell if he doesn't convince everyone he's a better person now. But wait—how did you beat him in base quest? Are you off your crutches?

No—I'm just getting better at levitating. I . . . kinda had to after I got tangled in a chandelier my first night home.

Seriously?

Sophie cracked up as she tried to imagine that.

Oh, it was way more humiliating than what you're thinking, he told her, sharing his actual memories of the way the strings of crystals seemed to wrap around him like sparkly tentacles.

How did you even manage to do that? she wondered.

No idea. I was just trying to get upstairs and I launched myself too high, and then my sleeve got caught and I tried to untangle it and next thing I knew Biana was collapsed on the floor in a fit of giggles and my dad was calling for the gnomes. It took five of them to free me. They had to stand on each other's shoulders in a giant gnome stack.

Sophie was laughing so hard that Sandor peeked his head into her room, probably making sure she wasn't losing her mind.

I wish I'd been there, she told Fitz.

Me too. You probably could've floated up there and helped me. My parents were too busy laughing with Biana.

All humor was gone from the last sentence, and there was a distinctly bitter edge to the thought. It reminded Sophie of what Keefe said about Fitz's family being changed forever—which made her realize she hadn't told him about Orem.

It's a long shot, she added after she'd explained everything that Keefe had told her. *But if you have time, it might be worth seeing what you can learn about him.*

I guess. Though I don't see what Orem would have to do with anything.

Well . . . if Luzia's his mom, he would've lived at Everglen, wouldn't he? Sophie wondered.

Yeah, that's probably true.

She could feel his thoughts spinning, but he didn't seem to know where to go with any of them. And neither did she.

I'll see what I can dig up, he told her. *And we could always try to talk to Orem at the Celestial Festival in a few weeks.*

True. If there's anything I can do to help, let me know.

Same. His mind circled back to the Tarina conversation. *And . . . thanks.*

For what?

For trusting me with that huge secret. I know you didn't plan to tell me—but you could've freaked out a lot more than you did when you realized I knew.

I'm actually kind of relieved, she admitted. *It's nice to have someone to talk to.*

I get that. So if you need anything—I'm here.

So am I, she promised.

I know. And . . . I'm really glad you are, because . . . you're the only person I trust.

She sucked in a breath, miraculously managing to last until they'd said good night and their connection was severed before she switched to full-fledged-flutter mode, replaying his words over and over.

You're the only person I trust.

The ONLY person.

And she knew—*knew*—it was something he could say to a close friend.

But it hadn't felt like that.

It felt . . . *significant.*

And for once, she didn't talk herself out of that hope.

Instead, she drifted off to sleep, letting herself dream that he meant something more.

THIRTY-TWO

TIME SHAPED INTO A ROUTINE.

Morning check-ins with Silveny. Evening check-ins with Fitz. Training lessons sandwiched in between—wearing Sophie out both mentally and physically, but never setting her back. She tried hailing Dex a few times, but he was always busy training with Tinker. She tried getting the information Keefe needed, but Bo brought new meaning to the word "evasive." And there were lots of Elwin exams in the mix. Lots of medicine. Lots of tiny improvements—all building to the moment when Elwin decided that Sophie could finally go without her sling.

Her arm felt scrawny and weak, hanging like a foreign object at her side. And she still couldn't do a whole lot with it.

But her reflection in the mirror was back to normal, so she tried to celebrate that victory.

Fitz was freed from his crutches as well, moving with only a slight limp—which Elwin had promised wasn't permanent.

And Fitz and Biana's time playing nice with Alvar slowly wound to an end.

Four days left.

Then three.

Two.

One.

And yet, despite all that time and effort, none of them had much to show for their first ten days home.

Fitz hadn't found any cracks in Alvar's new attitude, and he and Biana hadn't learned anything useful about Orem. Sophie hadn't convinced Silveny to come in for an exam. And Mr. Forkle still hadn't gotten back to her about the trolls— or the meeting with Fintan—so both of those were still in a holding pattern.

The only thing Sophie had managed to do once she could use her right hand again was tackle a big chunk of her makeup Foxfire assignments, despite the fact that her writing looked like a three-year-old's. She could tell a return to school was drawing close on the horizon, and she wanted to be prepared— or as prepared as she could be for the questions she wouldn't be able to answer about where she'd been and what had happened to her. Not to mention the stares and whispers as the world saw the multispeciesial muscle shadowing her every move.

She was trying to imagine what it would be like to step into the glass pyramid for morning orientation when Flori wandered into her bedroom—or Sophie assumed it was Flori. She couldn't see the tiny gnome beyond the mountain of clothes she was carrying.

"Okay," Flori said, dropping the pile on Sophie's bed. "Your new fighting clothes are ready! What do you think?"

There wasn't a single gown in the mix, which automatically earned Sophie's undying devotion. But more important: There were so. Many. Pockets.

Zippered pockets lining each pant leg. Slim pockets hidden inside the waistband. And each tunic was full of secret compartments: under the sash, hidden in the sleeves, tucked under the collars. Plus lots more pockets hidden in the capes. Even the tops of the boots had pockets—and no sign of heels. And the designs were streamlined and simple—the tunics a little shorter to keep them out of the way, the pants stretchier to allow for a wider range of motion. Darker, deeper colors to help her blend in. No jewels. No lace. Nothing decorative—unless it hid a pocket.

It was basically Sophie's dream wardrobe—since jeans and T-shirts weren't really an elvin thing.

And even her Level Four uniforms had been altered to hide as many secrets as they could fit.

"It's all perfect," Sophie promised, ducking into her closet to change into a pair of the new gray pants and a simple navy tunic. No one would be able to tell by looking at her that she could now carry at least twenty different gadgets and weapons with her everywhere she went. But she felt fierce.

"I can make you regular holsters if you want to carry a larger weapon, like a sword," Flori offered when Sophie returned to her bedroom, "and I designed the tunics to fit over a breast-plate, in case you decide you want hidden armor."

"You thought of everything," Sophie told her. "Thank you— I'm sure this was a ton of work."

Flori's cheeks flushed. "Anything to help the moonlark." She scooped up a two-tone gray cape—lighter on the outside, darker on the underside—and helped Sophie clasp it around her shoulders with Tinker's null. "There. Now you're ready to take on the world."

"Uh, I thought this was where all the training was happening— but I guess I'm here for dress-up time?" a familiar voice said from Sophie's doorway.

Sophie spun around to find Marella watching her with folded arms. The blond, pixielike girl was what most would describe as petite—but Marella's feisty attitude was anything but small. Her ice blue eyes narrowed as she studied Sophie, and Sophie tried not to squirm under the scrutiny. Their friendship had always been very on again, off again. And it was highly pos-sible that Sophie's absence over the last few weeks had driven another wedge between them.

"Interesting welcome party you've got downstairs," Marella told her, twisting one of the tiny braids scattered throughout her long, wavy hair. "The troll won't stop asking Tam questions. And the ogre's glaring daggers at Linh. I'm guessing he's realized she's the one who flooded Ravagog."

Sophie blinked. "Tam and Linh are here?"

"Yep. And Wylie. He's busy glaring back at your ogre for glaring at Linh. So there's, like, a fifty-fifty chance we're going to find a scuffle when we head back down. That's why Sandor sent me up to get you."

Sophie headed for the stairs. "What are you guys doing here?"

"I told you—we want in on your training. We'd been meeting at Everglen with Biana and Woltzer, but then that place became a prison. And Lovise was supposed to take over at Dex's house, but he's been off doing Technopath things. So we've been practicing as much as we can at Tam and Linh's place, but we haven't had anyone to teach us, so we're not making a whole lot of progress. I'm sure you can imagine our surprise when we found out you've been getting private lessons and didn't bother to invite us."

She layered on the irritation nice and thick, and Sophie stopped at the top of the stairs, turning to face her. This was the kind of thing they needed to settle as soon as possible.

Sophie was all set to spew out a bunch of excuses about how she was only training for a limited amount of time every day. But . . .

She *could've* arranged for everyone else to train at her house too.

"Sorry," she said instead. "I . . . should've reached out."

Marella nodded. "I know I'm not part of your little core group, but—"

"That wasn't it." Sophie focused on stretching her clumsy, healing fingers. "I've been feeling so behind, knowing you guys were all training while I was stuck in the Healing Center. I guess I wanted to try to catch up."

Marella twisted another braid. "You're not the only one who feels behind, you know. At least you can actually train in your fifty zillion abilities."

The reminder hit home.

Marella had secretly manifested as a Pyrokinetic a few months earlier, and training was technically illegal—though she'd decided to ignore that law to make sure the power didn't get out of control, like it had for Brant. But without another Pyrokinetic to train with, the lessons weren't as helpful as they could be. And if she ever got caught . . .

"I'm *really* sorry," Sophie told her. "I was being selfish. You guys can train here as much as you want."

"You sure your bodyguards will let us? Forkle failed to mention your scary new entourage when he told me you were training. I don't think they like us."

"You've talked to Mr. Forkle?" Sophie asked. "Did he say . . . anything else?"

"Nope. And way to be smooth about whatever it is you don't want to tell me."

"I—"

"Relax. I'm sure I don't want to know. All I want is to train—so if you can convince your daunting defenders to include us in their lessons, that'd be awesome. *And* I'll forgive you for ignoring us if you tell me one thing." She grinned when Sophie nodded. "So all that one-on-one time with Fitz in the Healing Center—anything *happen?*"

Sophie's face burned, and she looked away, mumbling the only answer she could truthfully give. "We're friends."

"Still in denial—got it," Marella said. "You guys seriously need to make it official. It's getting kind of ridiculous. Plus, you're not the only one who'd be happy to snatch that up, you know? So unless there's someone *else . . .*"

Sophie turned to head down the stairs, done with this conversation.

Marella blocked her. "Just promise me you're not going to get all 'I don't know who I love' and spend months angsting about it, 'kay? 'Cause I might have to smack you."

Sophie rolled her eyes. "We'd better get down there before Bo gives Linh the same speech he gave me the first time I met him. I don't think Tam would take it as well as I did."

"There's a Bo and a Ro?" Marella clarified.

"Yep—and if you're looking for gossip, you should focus on them. They have some sort of weird history, but neither of them will tell us what it is. Keefe even made a bet with Ro about it—that's why he's not here. If he comes to Havenfield before I find out the story, Ro gets one unlimited dare."

She was starting to wonder if that'd been Ro's larger plan—to avoid Bo as long as she possibly could.

"Sounds like you've had no problem staying in touch with Keefe," Marella noted as she headed down the stairs. "Why does *that* not surprise me?"

Sophie ignored her, trying to cool her heated cheeks before she had to face the rest of her friends. But she was pretty sure she was still bright red when she reached the main room, where Tarina was in the middle of asking Tam another question—which he looked pretty fidgety about—and Sandor was carefully monitoring the stare-down between Linh, Wylie, and Bo.

"Oh good!" Sophie said, clapping her hands to break the tension and forcing some enthusiasm into her voice. "You guys have met! Does that mean we can skip introductions and get right to discussing a training plan?"

Bo shook his head. "I never agreed to train the girl who wiped out half my city."

Linh didn't cower at the accusation—but she did scoot ever so slightly closer to Wylie. And Wylie moved a little in front of her as Tam crossed the room to stand at his sister's side.

Sophie joined them, standing as tall as she could when she told Bo, "Linh was only there that day because I asked her to be. And if you want to talk about why we had to sneak into Ravagog, I can call Flori down here and she can tell you why her great-great-grandaunt had to sacrifice herself."

Bo locked his jaw.

"Like you said," Sophie told him, "we don't have to be friends. But Linh has risked her life over and over to help protect me. So if she wants training to defend herself, I'm going to find someone willing to help."

"I'll train her," Tarina volunteered, making her way closer. "I'll train them all, if you want." Her eyes shifted to Tam and she told him, "And forgive my earlier enthusiasm. I've heard so many legends about those who control darkness, and I've always wondered how many were true. And you," she said to Wylie. "You're another Flasher, aren't you?"

Wylie frowned. "How did you know?"

"There's a slight aura around you that the physician had as well. I doubt your eyes can see it. My species is particularly sensitive to light."

"Huh," Wylie said, holding up his hand and squinting at it.

Sophie used the opportunity to take a longer look at him, searching for lingering injuries. She hadn't seen Wylie since that horrible day in the desert—so she hadn't had a chance to talk to him after the attack. She cleared her throat and blurted out, "By the way, I never thanked you for saving me that day."

Wylie's gaze dropped to his feet. "It's okay. I never thanked *you* for what you did to protect *me*, so I think we're even."

Sophie stared at her healing hand. "They haven't come after you again?"

He shook his head. "Our new house is well guarded—and pretty impossible to find. But that's also why I've been training. Next time they show up, I'm getting some payback."

"As long as Sophie's home, I'm here and happy to train," Tarina assured him. "Same goes for all of you. We can start today, if you want."

"Actually, I'll be covering their first lesson," Sandor jumped in. "There are a few fundamentals I'd like to begin with."

The glance he gave Sophie immediately conjured memories of splattering red, and she felt more than a little sorry for her friends.

"Would you be willing to prepare the dummy you designed?" Sandor added, directing the question to someone behind Sophie, and she glanced over her shoulder to find Flori standing on the stairs.

But the tiny gnome didn't seem to hear him.

She didn't seem to hear anyone.

She stood frozen, one foot raised like she'd paused in the middle of taking a step. Eyes focused on Tam.

"You okay?" Sophie asked, then had to call Flori's name three times before Flori blinked and nodded.

"Sorry," Flori murmured, swaying softly as she made her way down the rest of the stairs, passing Sophie and heading straight for Tam. "That melody . . . I've felt whispers of it before."

She waved her arms around, and Tam's eyebrows crunched together.

"Am I supposed to know what that means?" he asked.

"I don't," Sophie admitted.

Flori swayed harder, whispering something under her breath.

"What was that?" Sandor asked her.

Flori blinked. "Nothing really. It's just . . . he's carrying a rhythm. Not a sound—more of a pulse. And I've felt it before." She swayed again for a few beats before turning to Sophie. "It's the same pulse you carry in your echoes. But his is much stronger."

"Tam's been training with shadowflux," Sophie remembered. "So maybe that's what you're sensing?"

"Is that bad?" Linh added, sharing a look with her brother.

"No," Flori promised. "It's *very* helpful."

"Where are you going?" Sandor asked as Flori headed for the front door.

"To test a theory. I think I know where to find the song to quiet the echoes."

"Where are we going?" Sophie asked Flori as she followed her away from Havenfield's main pastures—with her friends and bodyguards right behind them. "I thought you said a new song would need to be *written*, not *found*."

"It does," Flori called over her shoulder. "But there's nothing *truly* new in this world. Only new combinations and interpretations. Creation is about building upon what exists and making it your own. And I haven't known where to start. But I think I do now."

"Anyone else *super* confused?" Tam asked.

"Yes!" Linh, Marella, Wylie, Sandor, Bo, and Tarina all said in unison.

Even Sophie was having trouble keeping up. But she told them, "Flori thinks she can heal the shadowflux's echoes the same way she heals the forest. But she has to sing the *right* song."

"And every melody must be connected to something," Flori added quietly. "I think I've figured out this song's roots."

She turned toward the woods that bordered one edge of Havenfield's property, and Sophie realized they were heading for the Grove—a small orchard of bulbous trees where all the gnomes on the property lived.

When the Grove's twisted branches came into view, Flori paused and turned back to Bo. "My people have accepted your presence at Havenfield. But they are not yet ready to accept you near our homes. So I need you to stay here." Her gaze shifted to Tarina. "And it would be better if you stayed back as well. We have no quarrel with the trolls, but there are stories of scattered attacks that make some uneasy."

Bo scowled, but didn't argue. Tarina simply nodded.

Which left only Sophie, Tam, Linh, Marella, Wylie, and Sandor following Flori into the Grove—though Sophie had a feeling Nubiti was trailing them underground—past the rows of swollen, hollow trunks that turned each tree into a tree house of sorts.

Sophie assumed Flori must be leading them to her home, but they wound through the entire gnomish neighborhood, aiming for a shadowy thicket at the end, where the trees were so tightly interwoven that very little sunlight crept in.

Shadows shifted, branches creaked and crackled, and the air turned cold and musky. But Flori's soft humming soothed Sophie's nerves. The melody grew louder with every step until they reached a wide, gnarled tree, and Flori dropped to her knees to examine something tangled around the roots.

Sophie squatted beside her, and the rest of the group formed a half circle around them as Flori trailed her fingers across a wispy vine with dark green pointed leaves and tiny clusters of pearl white buds.

"This is vesperlace," Flori whispered. "It only grows in the darkest parts of the quietest forests—and it only blooms at night, so right now its melody is mostly silent. But I can still feel traces of the same pulse thrumming through the stems that I feel when I listen for your echo. I think it must be the rhythm of darkness. And *that* is where the song must begin."

She closed her eyes, humming again—a lower, more resonant sound with words too soft to catch.

Warmth stirred under Sophie's skin.

It was only the tiniest of prickles—a spark with no kindling to catch hold of. But Flori nodded. "Yes, the song I need lives in everything that thrives in the dark. That's where I must listen."

She folded her legs and nestled into the damp earth, settling in for the rest of the day.

"Do you need me to stay with you?" Sophie offered.

Flori waved her away. "You have far more important uses for your time. Go train. I'll be here, waiting for inspiration."

"So . . . the song is a cure for the echoes?" Fitz verified.

"That's Flori's theory," Sophie agreed. "I guess we won't know for sure until she finds the right melody."

It felt strange talking to him out loud, hearing his crisp accent through her Imparter.

It felt even stranger staring through the screen into his far-too-pretty eyes.

Sophie had talked to Fitz every night since he'd told her she was the only person he trusted. But all of their conversations had been telepathic—which was a very different experience. Technically it was more intimate, with his voice whispering across her consciousness, each thought vulnerable if she didn't remember to guard it. But it was easier in some ways too. She didn't have to worry about flushed cheeks, or quickened breaths, or any other tells that might give away how hard her heart was currently pounding.

But Fitz had been the one to hail her, and she wouldn't ignore him. Plus, she'd been looking for a distraction anyway.

After she'd left Flori alone in the shadowy thicket, Tarina had helped Sandor set up the scarecrowlike dummy for his lesson with Tam, Linh, Marella, and Wylie. Sophie knew it was only a matter of time before there'd be screaming and fake-but-traumatic splattering.

"How long do you think it'll take Flori to finish the song?" Fitz asked.

The hope threaded through the words made her wish she didn't have to tell him, "I have no idea. Flori said she's trying to find where to begin, so I guess it's possible it'll all pour out once she starts. But I have a feeling it's going to be verse by verse. Maybe even lyric by lyric."

Fitz ran a hand down his face, muffling a sigh. "Yeah, you're probably right."

"Why? Is your echo causing problems?" she asked.

"Kind of. It's just . . . it's always *there*. Every time I think it's starting to fade, Alvar spouts some sappy 'look how perfect I am' garbage, or my mom turns all misty eyed and I feel my pulse start to get away from me—and I know how to keep it under control. But . . . I'm getting sick of deep breaths and having to choke back everything I want to say, you know?"

Sophie nodded. "Well . . . at least today's your last day having to be around Alvar, right?"

"It is," he agreed, sounding more tired than relieved. "Starting tomorrow, no one can make me go anywhere near him unless *I* ask to. That's actually why I reached out. Now that I've held up my end of the bargain, I can start calling in some of the other demands I got my parents to agree to. And . . . I need your help for one of them—if you're up for it."

"I'm up for it," Sophie promised.

"I don't know—you might not want to, once you know what it is."

"No, I'm in no matter what," Sophie assured him.

He rewarded her with one of his glorious smiles—which wasn't the reason she'd said it. But it sure was a nice bonus.

Sadly, the smile faded when he told her, "I know we haven't been able to do any Cognate training, so it probably won't be all that different from the other times we've tried, but . . . I *have* to try again. So I demanded another chance to look around Alvar's head—and this time I'm going to hit him with absolutely everything I have. But . . . I can't do that without you. I know it's a lot to ask—"

Sophie shook her head. "It isn't."

She wasn't sure if they'd actually be able to learn anything— but she understood why he needed to try. And so did she, in case she'd been right about her theories—in case the Neverseen had targeted them because of their telepathy.

"You're sure it won't be too hard with your echoes?" he asked.

"I'm sure," Sophie said, holding his stare so he'd see she meant it. "What time do you want me to be there?"

. . .

Sophie barely slept that night, even with the sedative. And by sunrise, she was done tossing and turning.

She told herself she was just trying to stay busy when she spent much longer than normal getting ready, even taking time to line her eyes with gold-flecked eyeliner. Just like she claimed the reason she chose the silky purple tunic that flared at the waist was because it was part of Flori's new fighting wardrobe and *not* because it also happened to look really good on her. She even slipped some goblin throwing stars into the top of her knee-high boots and stuffed a few others into the zipped pockets lining her pants to take full advantage of her battle-ready clothes.

See?

She was just trying to be prepared.

It had absolutely *nothing* to do with seeing a certain teal-eyed boy who'd claimed she was the only person he trusted.

Nope.

And she definitely wasn't thinking about the last time they'd seen each other, when he'd hugged her before leaving the Healing Center.

She was just nervous about searching Alvar's mind.

And really, she should be.

After all, if they couldn't find anything, Fitz would be devastated. And if they *did* find something, it would mean they'd been overlooking the Neverseen's plans for months and months and have some major catching up to do.

That's why her knees were shaking as she made her way up to the fourth floor cupola to use the Leapmaster. It had zero to do with crushes.

And when she got there, she found a whole new reason to feel anxious.

"You're not all coming with me, are you?" she asked Sandor, Bo, Flori, and Tarina, who stood together under the sphere of dangling crystals with their arms crossed.

"That's how this works," Sandor told her. "We go where you go."

"But I'm going to one of the most secure places on the planet—and don't even try to say it isn't! Grizel designed the security. If you all tag along with me, you're basically saying you don't trust her."

Sandor shook his head. "Nice try. Grizel knows that when it comes to your safety, I'm not taking even the slightest risk. So you're bringing all of us with you today." He held out his hand, expecting her to take it.

"I wouldn't fight them on this one, kiddo," Grady said from behind her, and she glanced over her shoulder to find him and Edaline at the top of the stairs. "Be glad your mom and I aren't insisting on joining you too. The last time you went off to meet Fitz, it didn't exactly go well."

"That's because we were in the middle of the desert, not in a super-well-guarded gated estate! Plus, I have this." She pointed to the pin Tinker had made her, which was securing her gold-rimmed cape around her shoulders.

No one looked impressed.

"Fine," Sophie grumbled, trudging over to Sandor and taking his hand.

Flori reached for Sophie's other hand, and as their fingers twined together, Sophie realized . . .

This was the first time since the attack that her right hand had some actual strength.

Not as much as it usually had—and she'd still have to be careful about how much she used it.

But . . . things really were getting back to normal.

"You sure your concentration's up for a leap like this?" Grady asked as Bo and Tarina linked hands with the others. "You're going to have to hold everyone together."

Sophie nodded, feeling a fresh burst of confidence. "Yeah. Don't worry—I've got this."

She called for the Leapmaster to lower the crystal for Everglen, and after one quick breath, she imagined her concentration wrapping around her overprotective group like thick, heavy cloth. When everyone was fully covered—completely in her hold—she smiled at both of her parents. Then she stepped into the Leapmaster's path and let the light carry them away.

Sophie told herself she was running because she didn't want to be late. Not because she was trying to put some distance between herself and her horde of bodyguards—and definitely not because she'd spotted a familiar figure standing next to the glowing bars of Everglen's massive gate.

Apparently, she was lying to herself a lot that day.

And she probably would've been better off walking at a normal pace, because it meant she was sweaty and out of breath by the time she reached Fitz. But that did give her a ready excuse for her red-flushed cheeks when Fitz threw his arms around her, whispering, "Thank you for doing this."

"Of course," she said, smoothing her tunic and cape when he let her go—anything to pretend she didn't notice the way he was looking at her.

"Admiring" might've been a better word.

Fitz Vacker was admiring her.

Or maybe she was reading way too much into it, since his next question was, "How's your arm?"

She held it up to show him, and even though she clearly still needed a little more meat on her new bones, she wasn't lying when she told him, "Pretty good. How about you? How's your leg?"

"Kinda clumsy," he admitted, taking a few steps to show her his subtle limp. "But it's better than crutches."

"I'm sure. Hopefully you won't get tangled in any more chandeliers."

Fitz groaned. "I never should've told you that story."

"But you *did*! And it's officially my favorite!"

His cheeks turned the most adorable shade of pink. "Yeah, well I—"

"You should be closing these gates—not standing there flirting!" Bo snapped, and Sophie decided she was officially Team Ro.

"Glare at me all you want," Bo told her, "but there's no point surrounding a property with fancy glowing bars if you're going to leave the gate wide open while you blush at each other."

"In case you were wondering," Flori told Fitz, "we all think Bo is the worst."

"And I'm happy to keep the path secure if you guys need a few more minutes to *talk*," Tarina added, emphasizing the last word in a way that made Sophie's face feel nuclear.

She backed up, putting more space between herself and Fitz. "If you were wondering what it's like having so many different bodyguards, that about sums it up."

"I guess," he mumbled. "Not that it's much more normal around here."

He pointed to the shadows of a nearby tree, and Grizel seemed to melt out of the darkness, followed by five other goblin warriors.

"The ogre *is* right," Grizel noted, ordering everyone to move deeper into the property so that the gates could clang closed behind them. Her steps were graceful and smooth—not at all like someone recovering from a serious injury, and Sophie hoped that meant Grizel was back to normal.

Both Sandor and Grizel stayed firmly in soldier mode—but for one second when they thought no one was looking, they exchanged a look that made Sophie's heart seriously melt.

"So," Fitz said, clearing his throat. "You ready for this?"

"I think so," Sophie said quietly. "What about you?"

He nodded, offering his arm as he leaned closer and added, "I know it's bad to say this, but . . . I really think we're going to find something today."

Sophie wished she could share that same confidence as she hooked her elbow around his and let him lead her forward, into the heart of Everglen. The path started out familiar, lined with neatly trimmed shrubs and trees in every imaginable color, filling the air with a thick, sweet perfume. But right when the shimmering mansion came into view, they curved the opposite direction, up a series of steep hills that had Sophie's chest heaving by the time they reached an unruly clearing butted against a wall of mossy rock. Scraggly bracken filled most of the space, framing a small, simple structure: a white stone house with a single door, a single window, and a flat roof with dull metal shingles.

It looked like something humans would build, not elves.

No crystal. No jewels. No style of any kind.

Everything about it screamed *temporary*—but whether that was because the current resident was expected to return to his cell or expected to move back with his family was hard to say.

"I'll go first," Grizel informed them, striding toward the door, "and only Fitz, Sophie, and Sandor will be allowed inside with me. The rest of you can spread out and patrol the clearing."

No one argued, and within a few seconds their group had mostly dispersed as Sophie and Fitz joined Grizel, with Sandor right behind them.

"This door can only open for three seconds," Grizel explained as she moved her hand toward a metal panel set into the stone. "Let me know when you're ready."

"Are your parents already inside?" Sophie whispered to Fitz.

He shook his head. "I told them they weren't allowed to be here. But I wouldn't be surprised if Biana's hiding in a corner somewhere."

"Yeah, I've been waiting for her to appear beside us this whole time," Sophie admitted, glancing over her shoulder, half expecting Biana to blink into sight and shout, "I'm right here!"

"Any time now," Grizel nudged.

"Right," Fitz said, taking a quick, deep breath, setting his jaw, and squaring his shoulders.

Sophie tried to do the same, offering Fitz a weak smile to let him know she was ready.

Sandor gripped his sword.

"Okay," Grizel said, pressing her hand against the panel, triggering a loud click as the door swung inward.

They hurried into the house, and the door closed behind them with an unsettling click that echoed off the bare stone walls. The inside was just as boring as the outside: a narrow bed covered in stiff white linens. A small empty table. A lone shelf holding a few worn books. And a single chair facing the only window, where Alvar sat staring out at his rather unimpressive view.

He turned toward them as they entered, his scarred face curling with a smile. "Hello, Sophie. I've been waiting for you."

THIRTY-THREE

OULD YOU LIKE TO SIT?"
Alvar asked when Sophie didn't
respond to his greeting. "I hear
you've been unwell."

He stood and offered her his chair, and Sophie noticed that
he'd put on weight since his Tribunal, already looking a little
less frail. His hair was also trimmed and neatly combed, and his
embroidered tunic looked like it had been tailored just for him.

Other than the gruesome scars, he looked like the Alvar
Sophie first remembered meeting—the charming older
brother home to visit his perfect family.

"She wasn't *unwell*," Fitz snapped. "Your little friends tried to kill her—and you already knew that. Stop pretending like you're so innocent."

"I had nothing to do with that attack," Alvar said calmly.

"This time," Fitz argued. "So sit back down—no one wants your stupid chair."

"Careful," Sophie whispered as Fitz rubbed his chest and took a long breath. "Save your strength for the probe."

"Probe?" Alvar repeated, his smile collapsing with a sigh. "*Another* memory search?"

"Scared?" Fitz countered. "You should be."

Alvar sat down slowly, turning to stare out the window. "Fear has nothing to do with it, little brother. But has it ever occurred to you that I don't *want* to remember?"

"Of course you don't," Fitz agreed. "Remembering means going back to that stinky little cell. And it means we'll have time to stop whatever horrible plan you're a part of."

Alvar shook his head, and when he turned to Sophie his eyes looked pleading, begging her to understand what he was trying to say.

And she did understand. At least a little.

"You don't want to be who you were," she guessed.

Alvar nodded, swallowing several times before he asked, "Have you ever woken up from a nightmare that felt so terrifyingly real, you wanted to cry with relief when you realized it was over and you didn't have to live those horrors?"

Sophie stared at her right hand, shuddering as she remembered the way the bones had shattered. "Not really. My nightmares are all flashbacks of things I've been through."

"And how many are memories that Alvar was a part of?" Fitz asked her. "At least half, right? More?"

"The part of me that did those things is gone," Alvar insisted.

"Yeah, well, the part of you that's left still needs to pay for what you did," Fitz told him.

"I already am—don't you get that?" Alvar asked, raising his voice for the first time. "Do you think I don't see how much pain I've caused? How you and Biana barely look at Mom and Dad because of me being here, and how often I catch them crying after you yell at them? Did you know Councillor Oralie broke down sobbing when she explained what the Neverseen did to Councillor Kenric? She looked at me like . . . I might as well have been the one to burn him alive." He glanced at Sophie as she wrapped her arms around herself. "Do you think it's easy to sit here knowing I helped drag you out of that cave—and then stood there while they tortured you—and that there's nothing I can ever do to make amends? The only worthless thing I have to offer is to let you sit in my uncomfortable chair for a few minutes—and you won't even take me up on it because you hate me that much. Or how about—"

"STOP!" Fitz shouted, stalking over to his brother. "Stop trying to make everyone feel sorry for you!"

"I'm not."

"Yes you are—and you know how I know?" Fitz leaned closer, getting right in his face. "If you were *actually* sorry, you'd volunteer to spend the rest of your life in that horrible cell. Same goes for if you *really* wanted to make sure you never hurt anyone again. But you don't care. All you care about is yourself. And that's how I know that even if you don't recover your memories, someday you'll go back to being that same creepy murderer."

Alvar had no answer.

He just blinked hard and turned back to stare out the window at his unimpressive view.

"Well," Biana said, appearing in the darkest corner. "Looks like this is off to a *great* start."

Grizel's hands curled into fists. "I'm going to strangle Woltzer for letting you sneak away *again*."

"Oh, come on, did you really think I wouldn't be here for this?" Biana asked, raising one eyebrow. "Most of you guys didn't even squeal this time."

She had a point—though that didn't mean Sophie's heart wasn't pounding in her ears.

"How are you feeling?" Biana asked her. "You look . . . really good. Is that a new tunic?"

"It is! Flori made it for me, and it has all these cool pockets for—"

"Can we discuss fashion later?" Sandor interrupted gently. "The less time we spend around the prisoner, the better."

"Right. Sorry. Should we get started?" Sophie asked Fitz.

"Are you going to bother explaining what you're doing to me this time?" Alvar wondered. "Or do I just get to sit here hoping you don't shatter my sanity?"

"You get to sit there," Fitz told him, pressing two fingers against one of Alvar's temples and reaching for Sophie with his other hand.

"I'm assuming we're going gloves off," Sophie verified.

"Are you up for that?" Fitz asked.

She nodded, peeling off her gloves and handing them to Biana, who'd moved to stand between them in case they needed someone to lean on.

"But I'm only making contact with you," Sophie warned Fitz. "I don't think it'd be good to boost Alvar."

"Yeah, definitely not," Fitz agreed.

"Am I supposed to know what you're talking about?" Alvar asked.

They both ignored him, each taking a breath to steady themselves before Sophie laced her fingers with Fitz's, letting the warm energy grow stronger and stronger between them before they stretched out their consciousness and shoved into Alvar's mind.

They started with probing, since they'd never tried that on him before—transmitting any words they could think of that might connect to his time with the Neverseen.

SPY!

LEGACY!

LODESTAR!

NIGHTFALL!

KIDNAP!

ADDLER!

FORBIDDEN CITIES!

MOONLARK!

OREM!

LUZIA!

RAVAGOG!

On and on and on.

Each time, the word shot into Alvar's mind like a lightning bolt.

And each time his fuzzy gray headspace absorbed the energy without so much as a spark.

When they ran out of words, they tried digging deeper into his consciousness. But it was like wading through an endless stack of heavy blankets, each layer more smothering than the last. And there was never anything underneath except more gray fuzz.

Sophie even tried to heal him, wondering if the enhancing would make a difference. But healings only worked when she could find a thread of warmth to follow. And Alvar's mind was much too bland.

"I think you guys need to take a break," Biana warned, her voice sounding very far away. "You're both looking pretty shaky."

Sophie hadn't realized she was trembling—she'd kind of lost track of her body. But she wasn't going to be the one to pull away. She knew how much Fitz needed this.

And the monster wasn't trying to wake.

"I'm fine if you are," she told Fitz.

Alvar moaned, and that seemed to rally Fitz's determination. "Want to do another round of probing?"

She tightened her grip on his hand, sending any energy she could spare.

But their words were seriously scraping bottom.

CLOAK!

CAVE!

SKILL TRAINING!

RUY!

BRANT!

"How is this not working?" Fitz asked, the words practically a growl.

"Because there's nothing left!" Alvar told him, his voice thick and strained. "Just accept it."

Fitz snorted. "I'm sure you'd love that."

"Don't they say the definition of insanity is trying the same thing over and over and expecting a different outcome?" Alvar wondered.

"HOW CAN YOU REMEMBER THAT AND NOT REMEMBER WHY YOU JOINED THE NEVERSEEN?" Fitz screamed. "YOU REALLY THINK—oh."

He staggered back, dropping Sophie's hand and clutching his chest.

"Are you okay?" Sophie asked, grabbing his arms as his knees gave in.

He would've collapsed completely if Biana hadn't caught him by the waist—which made it pretty impossible to believe him when he said, "I'm fine."

"I think he needs some air," Biana warned. "You take him—I'll stay here and keep an eye on things."

Sophie nodded, hooking Fitz's arm around her shoulders and leading him back out to the clearing.

"How's that?" she asked, pointing to a spot in the shade where he could lean against the side of the house.

"I think I need to get away from this place," he admitted. "Can we walk for a bit?"

"You sure you're up for that?"

"Yeah, the echo's calming down. I just need to clear my head."

Sophie glanced at their abundance of bodyguards. "Is that okay with you guys?"

"Stick to the grounds," Grizel told her. "And plan on a few of us trailing behind."

"That's fine," Sophie said, bending her knees to get a better hold on Fitz before leading him out of the clearing. "Where do you want to go?" she asked when the path split ahead.

"Left," he decided. "There's something I want to show you."

THIRTY-FOUR

OW, THIS IS REALLY BEAUTI-
ful," Sophie murmured, spinning in a
slow circle to fully admire the clearing.
The trees looked ancient. Lots of
crackling bark and knobby branches dripping with tendrils of
moss as they formed a wispy canopy. And the long grass was
peppered with swaying wildflowers. But the best part was the
sculptures that seemed to sprout out of the uneven ground—
thin strands of dark metal twisting and spiraling around colorful glass orbs.

"So where exactly are we?" Sophie asked, turning again
and squinting through the trees to where she could see the
halo of Everglen's perimeter fence. Tarina stood in the glow

from the bars, keeping watch from a respectful distance.

Sandor and Grizel had opted to stay at Alvar's apartment—which had definitely surprised Sophie. But she couldn't blame them if they'd wanted some alone time after everything they'd been through. She'd also lost track of Bo and Flori, though she was sure they were out there, along with two other goblins who kept marching slowly around the clearing.

"It doesn't really have a name," Fitz told her, stepping closer and leaning in to whisper, "but this is where the emergency override is. That's what I wanted to show you."

Sophie's eyebrows raised as he led her toward one of the larger statues and pointed to the teal orb supported by intricate swirls of metal. It was the size of a basketball, with silver circles speckling the thick glass.

"*This* is it?" Sophie asked, keeping her voice low.

Fitz nodded, leaning closer again. "I thought you should know how to find it. And . . . I think you should know the code that activates the panel."

"Why?" Sophie whispered.

His lips curled into a small smile, and their eyes locked. "I told you—you're the only one I trust."

She sucked in a breath.

The words sounded even better out loud than they had in her head. And she was pretty sure her heart was going to punch through her ribs any second.

"Is it okay if I transmit the code?" he asked, and she hadn't even finished her nod before her mind filled with his crisp voice.

Scion.

She repeated it to make sure she'd understood.

Yep. And you key it in like this. He placed his palm in the center of the orb and the glass flared with a subtle glow, making each of the silver flecks light up with a tiny letter.

Is it reading your fingerprints? she asked.

Nope, just responding to touch. And there was no rhyme or reason to the letter arrangement, so it took Fitz several seconds to locate the *S-C-I-O-N.* But as soon as he pressed the final letter, the glass orb rotated, revealing the thin seam of a small square.

He tapped the center and the glass swung open like a hinged door, revealing a hidden metal sensor.

That's where you put the DNA to trigger the override, he explained.

And Alvar's DNA no longer works? Sophie verified.

That's what my dad keeps claiming. But that doesn't mean Alvar can't use ours. One good punch and he'd have some of our blood.

Sophie shuddered. *That's why you have guards. And the Warden.*

I know. But I'm trying to be ready for anything. That's why I wanted you to know where the override is, and how it works. I don't know why it might come up, but it's better to be prepared. Do you think you'll be able to find your way here again, if you ever needed to?

I think so, she said, trying to remember which path they'd taken. It hadn't had very many splits to keep track of, but she was feeling turned around. *Are we back near the main gate?*

No, the override is in the opposite corner of the property.

Why? If you're trying to open the gate, wouldn't you want the override to be near it?

I asked my dad the same thing when he first showed it to me, and he said Luzia thought it was better to have it near the back entrance, since that's a lot smaller and easier to move manually.

There's a back entrance?

I didn't know there was one either. We never use it. But it's over there. He pointed toward the spot Tarina had been watching them from a few minutes earlier. She'd moved closer to the clearing now, probably trying to figure out what they were doing. *Luzia hid the button to open it between those two trees right there. And then I guess there's a DNA sensor hidden in the bushes outside to open it from that side—but it's probably all crusty and gross. Honestly, I don't even know if it works. But that's another reason I'm glad my dad posted guards here.*

Me too. Okay, Sophie thought, focusing her photographic memory on recording every detail around her. *I should be able to find my way here if I ever need to, but, uh . . . what good does that actually do? Without your DNA—*

That's why I brought you this, he told her, pulling a tiny vial from the pocket of his navy blue cape, packed with something that looked sorta solid.

Cotton maybe?

I know it's kind of weird, Fitz added, *but it's the only way I could think of to give you a sample.*

Wait—is that . . . is that your DNA? she asked, trying not to grimace.

Actually, it's Biana's DNA. I refused to give you a vial of cotton soaked with my spit.

Sophie appreciated that *immensely*—not that it was much better knowing it was Biana's. But it helped a little.

So I guess that means Biana knows you're doing this, she said, not feeling ready to reach out and take the spit vial yet.

I told her last night—and she wanted me to tell you she swabbed her cheek for the sample right after she brushed her teeth. So it's clean. Well, as clean as it can be—it's still cotton soaked with spit, so . . .

Yeah . . . Sophie had to squirm a little.

She'd never been a fan of the elves' lickable DNA sensors—but this was definitely a new level of yuck.

Though what was the alternative?

Using blood, like Lady Gisela had?

Or fingerprints, like humans did, with sensors that were much easier to fool?

Still, seeing the logic to the system didn't make it any easier to grab the spit vial—but at least she had lots of pocket options.

This was definitely something that screamed *hide it in your boot.*

"Anyway," Fitz said, switching back to verbal conversation as he closed the tiny door on the teal orb and the override spun away. "I guess I should let you head home. You probably have training to do."

She *had* skipped her morning lesson. But . . . "I can stay a little longer—unless you're too wiped from Alvar and want me to go."

He shook his head. "I don't want you to go."

Their eyes met for a second and Sophie commanded her heart *not* to do any flips.

But when it came to Fitz, her heart never listened.

He offered her his arm. "Want to search the grounds and make sure you don't spot any security gaps?"

"Sounds good."

They spent the next several hours wandering the property's perimeter, searching for anything that might be amiss. And Bo and Flori split off to do their own checks. But Tarina stayed with them, and even with her trollish senses on high alert, she couldn't find anything concerning. She even had them circle the entire lake and search several clearings on the other side.

"There really is no trace," she said, scanning the meadow they were standing in.

"No trace of what?" Sophie asked.

"Anything." Tarina spun around to squint at the nearby trees. "There's no trace of anything concerning."

"*Yet*," Fitz added. "I still think there has to be a reason Alvar's here. Or why Luzia gave up this place, or—"

"What do you know about her?" Tarina interrupted.

"Luzia?" Fitz clarified. "Not much. Why?"

"Just curious," Tarina said, turning back to face him. "I'm trying to take full stock of the situation. Because as far as I can tell, everything seems in order. I heard some of the other guards mention that you have a way of tracking your brother's movements. Is that true?"

Fitz nodded. "He has a gadget around his ankle."

"It can even knock him out if he starts to do anything suspicious," Sophie added.

"Smart," Tarina said, mostly to herself. "That should cover everything."

"Let's hope," Sophie mumbled, unable to shake the feeling that they were missing something. "Has your dad let you search his office?"

"Not yet—but that'll be my next demand." He bent to rub the muscles in his healing leg.

"Looks like you need to rest," Sophie noted.

"Probably," he admitted.

"Can you make it back to the house?" The meadow they were in wasn't *that* far away—but there were a few good shade trees if he needed to sit.

"I can make it," he promised. "And hey, then I can show you where I've been hiding out, so my parents couldn't make me do as many Brotherly Bonding Sessions."

Sophie sighed. "I'm so sorry you're dealing with all of this."

"Me too." They set off toward the house, with Tarina trailing several steps behind them. And they were nearly halfway there when Fitz said, "The thing is, though . . . I guess it's only fair. You had to grow up hiding your telepathy and feeling like you didn't belong—and then you had to leave everything behind and start over in a world where people keep trying to kill you. Keefe had to live with his creepy mom and his awful dad manipulating him. Tam and Linh got banished and had to survive all alone for years. Wylie's dad was exiled and his mom faded away right in front of him. Dex has had everyone looking down on him his whole life because his parents are a bad match. I mean . . . when you really think about it, I've had it pretty easy."

"But that doesn't make it any less awful when hard things happen," Sophie reminded him. "You're allowed to feel what you're feeling."

"Not really." Fitz stared at his fingers as he pressed his hand over his heart. "Not until this echo fades away. Until then it's lots of deep breaths and bottling up the rest."

He tried to shrug it off, but it wasn't very convincing.

"Is there anything I can do?" Sophie offered.

He reached for her hand. "You're here."

That . . . was an *amazing* answer. And Sophie was very glad she was wearing gloves, so he couldn't feel the way her palms were sweating as they drew closer to Everglen's shimmering mansion. It was more of a castle than a home, with its crystal turrets and gables—a perfect, pretty place that screamed *privilege* with every glittering wall.

Sophie had spent several nights there over the years—had even been invited to live there when Grady and Edaline were struggling with her adoption. But she hadn't realized how little of Everglen she'd actually seen until Fitz led her under a vine-draped arch on the right side of the house and into a small courtyard she'd never noticed before. Smooth marble stepping stones brought them to a single gleaming door made of braided silver, with the Vacker crest emblazoned across the handle.

Fitz eased the door open silently—like they were sneaking in—as he motioned for Sophie to follow him into a room that was *way* bigger than what she'd been expecting. The space could easily fit hundreds of people and still have room to spare—though they'd have nowhere to sit. There wasn't a single piece of furniture anywhere.

But the sparseness did nothing to dull the overall opulence. The walls were a combination of crystal and mahogany panels, broken up with teal curtains made from thick velvet. And the floor was made of gold stamped with an elaborate swirling pattern. Massive chandeliers dangled from the cathedral-height ceiling, casting flecks of rainbow over everything.

"What is this place?" Sophie whispered, tiptoeing over to a giant portrait of the five Vackers hanging above a fireplace big enough for her to stand in.

"The reception hall," Fitz said, as if that was the most normal thing in the world.

She couldn't help giggling. "Your house has a *reception hall*. Of course it does."

He grinned. "It's not *that* weird. Lots of houses have them."

"Mine doesn't."

"It used to. What do you think your bedroom used to be?"

Sophie's jaw fell open.

She'd never thought about it before—her bedroom was just sort of there when she moved in. But it made sense, given how huge her room was. There was also the fact that Jolie had used a different bedroom down on the second floor—which was beautiful, but also wasn't nearly as huge or fancy as Sophie's room was. And Dex had told her one time that Grady and Edaline used to be known for throwing huge parties but stopped after they lost Jolie.

Fitz laughed. "I just blew your mind, didn't I?"

"A little," she admitted, turning to study the room again. "Do you guys use this place very often?"

She wasn't sure how she'd feel if the Vackers had been hosting tons of parties without inviting her.

Fitz shook his head. "We used it a few years ago. And I'm sure my mom's planning on using it again in a couple of years."

"What happens in a couple of years?" Sophie asked.

His cheeks flushed redder than she'd ever seen, and his eyes dropped to his shuffling feet.

Which was how Sophie guessed his answer, even before he said, "Winnowing Galas."

THIRTY-FIVE

FITZ MEANT *HIS* WINNOWING GALAS—
but he didn't say that.

Still . . .

Not saying it didn't make it any less true.

He'd already registered for the match.

He'd already turned in his match packet.

And even though he'd talked about waiting longer than usual to pick up his first list, sooner or later he would do it. And if Sophie hadn't registered . . .

"I just made things awkward, didn't I?" Fitz asked, his eyes fixed firmly on his boots.

Sophie tried to clear the squeak out of her voice. "Of course not. It's not like it's a secret. Obviously you're going to have Winnowing Galas someday."

She just *so* wasn't ready to think about it.

But he'd said "a couple of years," so . . . there was that.

She glanced over her shoulder, hoping to find a bodyguard who could help her change the subject. But Tarina must've been waiting outside, and the others still hadn't caught up with them.

Honestly, what was the point of having *five* bodyguards if they weren't around to save her from another miserable match-making conversation?

"So, you guys had the galas for Alvar already?" she asked, trying to at least steer the conversation toward less dangerous territory.

"Yeah." He reached up and ran a hand through his hair. "Alvar had two. One when he first entered the elite levels, and another after he graduated."

She turned to study the hall again, trying to picture it full of fancy elves in their fanciest clothes. "What were the galas like?"

"I don't really know," Fitz admitted. "I wasn't invited—though I did sneak into the second one and steal some cake. But my dad caught me after, like, five minutes."

"Why weren't you invited?"

"Winnowing Galas are restricted to the people on your match list and their parents."

Sophie frowned. "So . . . you don't get to have any of your friends there?"

There was a beat of silence before he said, "Not unless they're one of my matches."

Which made sense, Sophie supposed.

Winnowing Galas weren't just pretty parties. They were a way to start scratching names off your list—or circling them.

"So . . . you could technically end up throwing a party for an entire room full of strangers," Sophie realized.

Fitz nodded. "I mean, usually you at least know *of* them—either you've seen them at Foxfire, or your parents know each other, or something. And in some ways that might make it easier? My mom said she was friends with *everyone* at hers and it was super awkward. And I can kinda see how it would be, since . . . how do you choose who to talk to first? I think that's why they came up with the dance cards as a tradition. Then people just sign up whenever and you work your way down the card."

"You have to dance with a *hundred* people?" Sophie had to ask. Her feet hurt just thinking about it.

"Nah, not everyone signs up for a dance. And some won't even come to the gala."

"Why not?"

He shrugged. "Maybe they already know who they like. Or maybe they just know they're not interested in you. Or maybe they registered but they're not looking for a relationship yet.

There are actually lots of reasons someone might skip. That's why registering isn't *as* big of a deal as you keep thinking it is—but don't worry, I'm *not* trying to have that conversation again. Just know that it's usually more like half that show up."

"Huh," Sophie mumbled. "I guess that makes sense."

But she had a feeling it wouldn't be like that for Fitz.

He was a *Vacker*.

It was like . . . being matched with a prince.

A really, really *cute* prince.

She was pretty sure everyone on his list would be bragging about it.

And that was the thing she hadn't really let herself think about, because she was too busy trying to decide if she wanted to register.

If she *did*—if she set aside all her reservations—what were the odds of her ending up on his list?

What matchmaker would say, *Let's pair our golden boy with the weird girl with the freaky brown eyes who grew up with humans and will never fully fit into our world?*

Her gaze drifted back to the enormous Vacker family portrait, which must've been painted somewhat recently.

Between their poses and their jewels, they . . . looked like royalty.

The prettiest of all the pretty people, with their perfect posture and perfect hair and perfect clothes.

And she didn't fit.

"What's wrong?" Fitz asked, stepping closer.

She blinked to cool her burning eyes. "Just trying to figure out when this was painted."

"A couple of months after you healed my dad. My mom said we needed to commemorate that we were all still together. Aaaaaand then we found out about Alvar." His hands curled into fists. "He looks smug, doesn't he? I bet it's because he was sneaking into my dad's office during the breaks to snoop around."

That was definitely possible.

And Sophie tried to compare Alvar's cool, painted expression against the scarred, emotional guy she'd seen that morning.

But her eyes kept shifting back to the portrait of Fitz, and the longer she looked, the more she wondered how she could've let her silly crush go on and on without putting a stop to it.

How could she have ever fooled herself into thinking she had a chance?

"Seriously, what's wrong?" Fitz asked, stepping in front of her. "You look like you're ready to cry."

She shook her head, knowing if she tried to speak right then she *would* cry—and that would be a thousand times worse than the day she threw up on him.

"Is it Alvar?" he asked. "Did he say something?"

She shook her head again, sucking in a deep breath.

His eyes widened. "Is it your echo?"

She wished it was. The monster was so much easier to resist than the crushing regret and humiliation trying to bury her.

"No," she managed to force out. "I just . . ."

"What?" he begged when she didn't go on. He took her hand, gently twining his fingers with hers. "Please tell me. You can tell me *anything*."

Not this.

She knew that now.

There was only one way this ended.

Which meant it was time to get over her crush—once and for all—and be his friend for real.

Leave the rest for the perfect matches that would someday be filling this shimmering hall and adding their names to his dance card.

Accept that she would never be one of them.

He looked away, chewing his lower lip hard enough that it almost looked painful before he turned back to her and said, "I want it to be you."

The words seemed to burst out of him, and then they just hung there—these strange, impossible things that wouldn't compute.

Fitz seemed just as stunned by them as she was.

"I wasn't reading your mind—in case that's what you're wondering," he said, running a hand down his face.

A hand that was shaking.

"I wouldn't do that without your permission. Especially for this."

"This," Sophie repeated, noticing the hand holding hers was shaking too.

And his cheeks . . . they were flushed.

And he'd said . . .

He'd said . . .

"I want it to be you."

It took her a second to realize he'd said it again. And he looked less startled this time—more . . . relieved as he took a step closer, leaving very little space between them.

"I'm sorry," he whispered. "I've been trying not to say that, because it's not fair. But . . . I couldn't let you stand there looking like . . . like you do when someone gives you a compliment and you don't believe it. I'm trying not to pressure you, Sophie. I know you're not sure about any of this." He used his shaky arm to gesture around the room. "But . . . I'm so tired of trying to hide the fact that the only name I want to see on my lists is . . . yours."

She sucked in a sharp breath, nearly choking on it thanks to the way her heart had crammed itself into her throat.

He couldn't have just said that.

It had to be a misunderstanding.

Or a daydream.

Or . . . or . . . anything.

But he was leaning closer, leaving barely a breath between them.

And his eyes.

She couldn't deny what she saw in them.

It gave her the courage to blurt out, "I've liked you since the day I met you."

She'd thought he'd given her perfect smiles before. But the one right then?

Amazing.

And it only grew bigger when she bumbled out, "And you know I don't just mean 'like,' right? I mean *like*. Like, *like*, like."

UGH—WHY WAS SHE SO BAD AT THIS?

Fitz laughed and took her other hand, holding on in a way that felt different from all the other times they'd held hands before—like he was never going to let her go again. Which miraculously stopped her from saying "like" anymore.

It might've stopped her from ever talking again. Especially when she realized his eyes were now focused on her lips.

"Sooooo . . ." He dragged out the word. "What do we do now?"

Sophie had ideas.

Lots of ideas.

But then Fitz dropped her hands and clutched his chest, blowing out a breath.

"Oh no—is it your echo?" she gasped, reaching for him in case he needed help regaining his balance.

"I'm fine," he promised through another slow exhale. "Better than fine."

He glanced down to his heart, where she hadn't realized her hand now rested.

And they were standing even closer.

So, so close.

They'd barely have to move, if they wanted to . . .

But Sophie couldn't seem to find the courage to close that last bit of space. Because this was Fitz, and it was everything, and . . . what if she was bad at it? The only other time she'd done it hadn't exactly gone well. And if she had to see that kind of disappointment in his eyes, she—

"I have a new goal," Fitz said quietly, interrupting her downward mental spiral. "I'm going to get you to trust me."

Her eyes met his. "I do trust you."

"Then trust this." He reached up and cupped her cheek, and her triumphant heartbeat drowned out everything as her brain screamed, *HE'S GOING TO KISS ME!*

But right before their lips met, she realized hers wasn't the only voice shouting in her head. And she stumbled back as pure terror stabbed into her brain, along with a transmission that made everything inside her freeze solid.

Silveny begging, *SOPHIE! HELP! PAIN!*

THIRTY-SIX

ORRY!" SOPHIE SAID, FEELING LIKE her heart was ripping in half when she saw the shock and hurt on Fitz's face—but she'd have to deal with that later. "I have to go—Silveny's in pain and begging for help."

That was all the explanation she had time for as she sprinted for the reception hall's door, transmitting, *WHERE ARE YOU?*

Silveny filled Sophie's head with the same beach scenery she'd shown her several times before. *HELP! PAIN! HURRY!*

I'M ON MY WAY! Sophie promised, crashing into Tarina as she raced into the courtyard.

Tarina grabbed her shoulders, both to steady her and to stop her. "What's going on?"

"I have to go," Sophie said, thrashing to break free. "Silveny's in trouble."

Tarina tightened her hold. "Who's Silveny?"

"I don't have time to explain! Where's the nearest cliff?" she asked Fitz as he caught up with them.

"You're going to teleport?" he asked.

She nodded, hoping there was something closer than the bluffs they'd used the last time she teleported away from Everglen. She couldn't afford to go running through the forest.

"I can levitate us high enough," Fitz offered.

"You're sure?"

When he promised he was, Sophie told him, "Let's go."

"Not without me." Tarina released one of Sophie's shoulders and grabbed Fitz's arm in the same motion.

"Fine," Sophie told her. "But we have to go *now*."

Fitz wrapped his other arm around Sophie's waist, and she let herself lean on him, soaking up his steady strength. For one second their eyes met, and Sophie released a relieved breath when she saw his hurt had been replaced with pure determination.

"Let's go find her," he said, floating them off the ground fast enough to leave Sophie's stomach far behind.

"How high do you need?" he shouted over the wind.

"As high as you can go."

"Why?" Tarina kicked her legs nervously as the scenery grew smaller and smaller. "Why aren't we just doing that light leaping thing?"

"Because I don't have a crystal with a facet leading where we're going," Sophie explained. "And this should be high enough, Fitz." The air was much thinner and colder, and Everglen looked like a doll's house. "Drop us."

"*DROP US?*" Tarina repeated.

"It'll be fine," Sophie told her. "Just hang on to me."

Fitz hugged Sophie tighter, and Tarina's grip on her hand turned crushing as he counted to three and let them plummet.

Tarina unleashed a colorful array of Trollish words as the ground drew closer and closer—but Sophie tuned her out, focusing on the warmth gathering in her mind and the adrenaline pumping through her veins.

Right before they would've splattered all over the courtyard, she blasted the burning energy out of her brain, splitting the air with a thunderous crack and dropping them into darkness.

"For the record, I'm not a fan of teleporting," Tarina said, her voice hoarse and shaky as they drifted through the nothingness of the void.

"Almost over," Fitz promised.

Sophie closed her eyes, concentrating on the beachy images that Silveny had sent her. But as the scene shifted into focus, she changed her mind, switching to mental images of Havenfield.

Thunder clapped again, sending them tumbling into the familiar pastures.

"What the—?" Grady shouted as Tarina yelled more colorful words.

"Is this where we're supposed to be?" Fitz asked.

Sophie ignored them, stumbling to her feet and shouting, "Where's Edaline?"

"Right here," Edaline called out behind her, racing over from Verdi's pasture. "What's wrong?"

"I don't know." Sophie had to fight the sudden overwhelming urge to collapse into Edaline's arms and sob as she told her, "Silveny's in pain."

"Is it the ba—" Edaline started to ask, but Sophie cut her off, not wanting to give voice to that particular fear.

"I don't know. We were teleporting to help her when I realized I don't have medicine or bandages or . . . I have no idea what I'm going to need, but it didn't seem like a good idea to go there empty-handed."

"Give me one minute to gather what we need," Edaline said, taking off for the shed where they kept the supplies for all the animals.

"Meet us at the gate," Sophie called after her, deciding they should save Fitz's energy. Plus, she'd teleported off Havenfield's cliffs many times.

They ran toward the high metal fence that blocked the steep drop to the rocky shore.

"Please tell me you're not going to make us jump," Tarina begged as Sophie licked the DNA sensor on the lock.

"You don't have to come with us," Sophie reminded her.

"Protecting you is my responsibility," Tarina argued. "Now more than ever."

"Yeah, where are Sandor and Bo?" Grady asked as Sophie pulled the gates open. "And Flori? And Grizel?"

"Back at Everglen," Fitz told him.

"They weren't with us when Silveny's transmission came through," Sophie added. "And I couldn't waste time trying to find them. Will you hail Alden and tell him what's going on so they don't panic?"

Grady pulled an Imparter from his pocket and quickly passed along what little information he had as Edaline joined them, carrying an overstuffed satchel.

"Ready?" Sophie asked, holding out her hands.

Grady grabbed one first. "I'm going with you. You could be teleporting into an attack."

That was another thing that Sophie had been trying very hard not to think about. But she found herself checking her pockets, feeling for the throwing stars she'd tucked away before she'd left that morning. "Okay, we go on three."

Fitz took her other hand as Edaline reached for Grady. And Tarina grumbled more Trollish curses as she grabbed ahold of Edaline.

"Hang on tight," Sophie warned, counting off quickly before dragging them over the edge and causing a wide range of shrieks.

They fell and fell and fell, until Sophie had enough energy

to crack the sky again and launch them back into the void.

Please don't let us be too late, she thought, sending the plea into the darkness before she concentrated on the images that Silveny had given her. Fitz tightened his grip on her hand and she clung to him like a lifeline as the void split, dropping them onto a stretch of grass-covered dunes.

"SILVENY—WHERE ARE YOU?" Sophie screamed, squinting through the bright sunlight and finding only empty shoreline.

For several horrible seconds the only sound was the salty wind. But then . . .

Frantic whinnying, somewhere in the distance.

Tarina drew her weapon and charged toward the cries with Grady hot on her heels. Edaline was a few steps behind, but Sophie kept tripping over the long grass and the shifting sand. And Fitz was struggling with his limp.

"Here," he said, scooping her into his arms and levitating them over the dunes.

It probably should've felt strange letting him hold her like that after what had almost happened between them, but all Sophie could think about were the whinnies growing louder and louder. And when they crested the tallest hill, they got their first glimpse of a small, private cove where Greyfell was stamping his hooves and flapping his wings.

Silveny lay collapsed on her side, her wings spread limply behind her.

"NO!" Sophie yelled, leaping out of Fitz's arms as she channeled every drop of energy she had left and ran flat out.

"I don't . . . see . . . any blood," Edaline said through panting breaths, keeping pace right behind her.

Sophie didn't either.

But Silveny also wasn't getting up. And her mane looked tangled. And her usually shimmering fur had somehow dulled.

HELP! PAIN! HURRY! Silveny begged.

What's happening? Sophie transmitted as she closed the last distance between them.

PAIN! PAIN! PAIN!

Sophie took a quick glance at Silveny's body, trying to find a wound or a twisted limb. But other than her swollen belly, everything looked normal.

Which left only the bigger worry—the fear Sophie had been trying so hard not to acknowledge.

Is it the baby?

Silveny lifted her head, letting out a weak snuffle as her gold-flecked brown eyes focused on Sophie—and the fear and heartache in that stare shredded Sophie's insides.

Edaline dropped to her knees, running her hands over Silveny's belly, which really was *huge* now that Sophie was closer to it. And when Silveny's muscles contracted, Edaline's eyes met Sophie's. "Silveny's in labor."

THIRTY-SEVEN

LABOR IS GOOD NEWS, RIGHT?" FITZ asked, glancing between Sophie and Edaline. "That's what's supposed to happen?"

"Not yet," Sophie said, counting off the weeks in her head.

She didn't know the exact number, but she knew they were still *way* off from what Silveny had estimated for her due date.

Unless Silveny had been wrong—which *was* possible.

It wasn't like Silveny had ever had a baby before, or had any alicorn friends to tell her what to expect. And the elves had never cared for a pregnant alicorn either, so the whole thing could've been a miscalculation.

But Silveny's eyes locked with Sophie's again, and the panic that flooded Sophie's head was so real and sharp it felt like daggers.

Baby early. Baby early, Silveny transmitted.

Sophie swallowed hard. "She says it's too soon. I don't know how she knows, but she seems pretty sure."

Greyfell unleashed a terrified whinny.

"Then we're going to need Vika's help," Edaline told her. "And we're not going to be able to take Silveny to her."

Sophie jumped to her feet. "I'll bring Vika here."

Grady pulled out his pathfinder, spinning the crystal. "I don't think I have Sterling Gables on this."

"That's fine—I've been there before. I can teleport."

"Want me to levitate us again?" Fitz offered, reaching for Sophie's hand.

Sophie nodded, holding on tight as Tarina heaved a dramatic sigh and took Sophie's other hand.

"Just what I was hoping for—more teleporting," Tarina grumbled.

"You could stay here," Sophie reminded her.

Tarina shook her head. "I go where you go."

Sophie glanced at her parents. "Will you be okay without us?"

"We'll do our best," Edaline promised as Silveny let out another strained snuffle and her muscles contracted again. "But hurry."

Trampling hooves and startled cries echoed around them as Sophie, Fitz, and Tarina dropped out of the void in front of a crystal-and-silver mansion, surrounded by pastures filled with unicorns.

"What's the meaning of this?" a sharp voice demanded, and Tarina leaped into a battle stance, shielding Sophie behind her as a dark-haired elf stalked toward them holding a shovel out like a weapon.

"It's fine—it's just Timkin," Sophie told Tarina, peeking around her shoulder. "Where's Vika?"

"Why do you want to know?" he demanded, his eyes fixed on Tarina.

"We need her help," Fitz told him. "Silveny's in labor."

"What?" a startled voice gasped from the direction of the house. And Sophie spun around to find a tall, gangly girl staring at her from the doorway.

Stina.

Sophie's former nemesis—who she still didn't necessarily *like.*

But none of that mattered.

"Silveny's in labor," Sophie repeated. "We need your mom—now."

Stina nodded, her mass of dark curls shaking as she shouted into her house, "MOM—THE ALICORN'S IN LABOR!" then motioned for Sophie to follow her as she jogged toward a barn-like structure tucked among two of the larger pastures.

"How far apart are the contractions?" Stina asked when Sophie caught up to her.

"I don't know," Sophie admitted. "I don't think Edaline timed them."

"So Silveny's at Havenfield?"

"No, I brought Grady and Edaline to her. She's at some beach that she and Greyfell have been hiding out at."

"Ugh, so we're going to need *everything*," Stina grumbled, picking up her pace and ducking into the barn. "And just so I'm clear," she said, leaning closer to whisper, "that's a troll, right?"

"She's one of my new bodyguards," Sophie agreed.

Stina blew out a breath, tossing several curls off her forehead. "Okay. I don't know why I'm surprised anymore. Come on." She headed for a series of cabinets lining the far wall and started handing out supplies for everyone to carry: metal basins and casks of water and stacks of towels and blankets, satchels of medicine, plus several tongslike contraptions—and Sophie really didn't want to think about how they'd be used.

"Don't forget gloves," Vika called from behind them, and Sophie turned to find Stina's mom pulling her dark wavy hair into a ponytail. "How far apart are the contractions?" she asked, not bothering with a greeting.

"She doesn't know," Stina answered for Sophie. "The alicorn's in the middle of a beach. Grady and Edaline are with her. And unless I'm remembering wrong, the baby's coming early."

"Yes, this is *very* early," Vika agreed.

Both mother and daughter shared a look that was much too grim for Sophie's liking before Vika shot Tarina a wary glance and moved to inspect the supplies. She added a few other balms and poultices to what Stina had already gathered and rested her hands on her narrow hips, surveying what was left in the cabinets. "Well, I guess this'll have to do."

"How do we get to the beach?" Stina asked.

"You're coming too?" Sophie asked.

"My daughter's been assisting with births all of her life," Vika agreed, which sounded like kind of a gross way to grow up, if Sophie was honest, but she wasn't about to turn down help—even if that help came from Stina Heks.

Sophie turned to Fitz. "Are you going to be able to levitate with all of us *and* all of these supplies?"

"Why would he need to?" Vika wondered.

"Because it's the only way I can teleport us where we need to go," Sophie told her. "Unless you have a cliff we can jump off."

Vika paled. "No. No cliffs."

Fitz ran a hand down his face. "I'll make it work."

He didn't sound very confident, though. And Sophie wasn't sure if her enhancing would help boost a skill. "I'll help lift some of it," she told him. "My levitating's not *that* shaky."

"We do make a pretty good team," Fitz said, and Sophie had to give him a tiny smile.

"I can handle it," Timkin said behind them. "Levitation was one of my strengths at Exillium."

Sophie glanced at Fitz, wishing they were trusting people she actually liked. But they'd lost enough time.

"Okay," she said. "Let's go."

. . .

Under different circumstances, Sophie might've enjoyed how much the Hekses flailed and screamed when she made them plummet into the void—or the way they landed in a heap among the grassy dunes.

But she was too focused on the agonized whinnies slicing through the ocean air—which were so much louder than they'd been before Sophie and Fitz left. And she couldn't stop thinking about the look that Vika and Stina had shared when they'd been talking about how early it was for Silveny to be in labor.

There hadn't just been worry in their eyes.

There'd been *dread*.

It was the kind of look that people gave each other when they already knew what was going to happen and didn't want to break the bad news yet.

"We're over here!" Edaline called. "Hurry!"

They ran as fast as they could.

But it didn't feel fast enough when they reached the cove and saw how much Silveny's condition had escalated. She was thrashing and kicking now, flapping her wings and rocking her head as Edaline fought to hold her down and Grady struggled to calm Greyfell, who was bucking and screeching.

Sophie's eyes blurred and her knees gave in, but Fitz was there to catch her, pulling her against him and whispering, "It's okay."

But it wasn't.

And the fact that her heart didn't give even the slightest

flutter said a lot about how numb she was feeling. So did the fact that she didn't blush when Stina called out, "Snuggle later, Fitzphie! Right now I need you to help me set up the birthing area."

But it did snap Sophie out of her daze long enough for her to see that Vika was now helping Edaline pin Silveny, and Timkin and Tarina were helping drag Greyfell back while Stina scrambled to spread the blankets over the sand.

Stina shouted for Sophie and Fitz to fill the basins with water from the casks and mix in different poultices. And when that was done, their job was to soak towels in the thick liquids and wring them out, so they'd be damp and cool without being too drippy. Sophie's right hand held up better than she would've expected. But still, about halfway through, her healing fingers started to ache. And Fitz must've noticed because he had them switch to an assembly line system, so all she had to do was dunk and pass.

She would've hugged him for it, but they couldn't lose those precious seconds.

By the time they'd finished, the adults had managed to haul Silveny into place, and Stina draped some of the towels over her pregnant belly. Vika soaked another towel in some sort of thick, clear syrup and wrapped it around Silveny's face, finally getting her to still. She even managed to wrap another around Greyfell, and Grady and Timkin eased Greyfell to the ground as he seemed to fall asleep.

"Was that a sedative?" Sophie asked.

"More of a calming agent," Vika told her. "Paired with sensory deprivation. Silveny's also responding to the poultice on her abdomen, which is dulling the pain of her contractions." She reached up to wipe sweat off her forehead before turning to Edaline. "Have you timed them?"

Edaline nodded. "They seem to be about five minutes apart."

"Well . . . I suppose that's the first bit of good news," Vika said, pulling on elbow-length gloves. "Gives us a little more time to figure this out."

"Maybe not," Edaline said, glancing at Grady with a dread-filled look that was much too similar to the one Stina and Vika had shared back at Sterling Gables.

"What does that mean?" Sophie demanded.

"I don't know yet," Edaline told her. "I haven't been able to do a full exam."

"But," Sophie prompted her to finish.

Edaline wrung her hands, *"But* . . . I might know why Silveny's in labor this early. And why she's refused to come in for exams—but I want Vika to confirm it before we put it out there."

"You're referring to how distended Silveny is," Vika noted.

"I am," Edaline agreed. "And . . . I'm very much hoping you'll prove me wrong."

"So am I," Vika told her.

Sophie's legs started to wobble—but Fitz was right there to

keep her steady as she asked, "Will someone please tell me what you're talking about?"

"Give me five minutes," Vika said, slipping on a pair of glasses similar to the spectacles Elwin always wore and dropping to her knees at Silveny's side.

Vika slid her hands under the towels and rubbed gently over Silveny's baby bulge, feeling every inch before Stina handed her a corded contraption. Vika pressed one end to Silveny's abdomen and the other to her ear, listening in several different places. The final part of the exam involved Silveny's tail region and was *much* more personal—and Sophie was pretty sure she was going to need to bleach her eyeballs after watching.

But nothing was as awful as the grim looks that Vika, Stina, and Edaline all shared as Vika pulled off her gloves.

"What is it?" Sophie whispered, and Fitz wrapped his arms tighter around her.

Vika sighed, tilting her head back to stare at the sky. "Unfortunately, it's what I feared the moment you told me Silveny was in early labor. Her body is trying to expel the babies because it can no longer support them."

The words were so awful, it took Sophie a second to realize, "Babies—*plural?*"

Edaline nodded. "Twins."

THIRTY-EIGHT

TWINS," SOPHIE REPEATED, STARING at Silveny's huge baby bulge and wondering how long the stubborn alicorn had been keeping that secret from her.

Then again, maybe she'd also been giving Sophie hints.

Silveny always told her, *BABY OKAY! BABY OKAY!* And since Silveny usually repeated everything in threes, that had probably been deliberate.

But . . . why not just come out and say it?

And why refuse exams when she had double the lives at stake?

Sophie voiced the questions out loud as Vika ran her hands slowly across Silveny's abdomen again.

"Instincts are powerful things," she said quietly. "Silveny likely knew carrying both babies to term was a foolish decision."

"If this is about that stupid, judgy attitude elves have toward multiple births—" Sophie started, but Vika held up her hand.

"It isn't. It's a simple fact of nature. Equines rarely survive multiple births."

"*Rarely,*" Sophie noted. "So sometimes it works out?"

"There are *always* exceptions," Vika agreed. "But I don't think you realize how slim the odds are. In all the generations that my family's spent breeding unicorns, we've only had two multiple births survive—and in one of those cases the mother didn't make it. And before you go claiming that alicorns are a different species and might fare better, remember why we're here. The babies are coming—and it's far too early for them to be viable on their own. Silveny's body is telling us that it simply cannot handle this."

Fitz tightened his hold on Sophie again, but she didn't want to be comforted anymore. She needed to think—move—plan.

Find a solution.

"What about incubators?" she asked, pulling away from Fitz to pace. "Couldn't we put the babies—"

"If they were several weeks older, yes," Vika cut in. "But given how early it is in the pregnancy and the vitals I'm detecting for the babies, unfortunately, they're not going to make it."

"So we don't even try?" Sophie snapped back.

"Of course we will. I'll do everything in my power. But there are certain rules in nature that cannot be cheated. You need to prepare yourself for today to be a very hard day."

Tears burned Sophie's eyes and she blinked them back. "And there's no way we can just . . . stop the labor?"

"Not when the contractions are already five minutes apart," Vika told her.

"But even if you'd gotten us here earlier," Stina added quietly, "I doubt it would've helped. See how low the babies have dropped?" She pointed to Silveny's stomach. "I bet Silveny's been having contractions for several days. So . . . don't blame yourself. It's not your fault."

That was the nicest, most considerate thing that Stina had ever said to her. And it nearly broke Sophie apart.

If *Stina* was trying to comfort her . . .

"Hey," Fitz said, stepping closer and offering his shoulder, not seeming to care at all that she'd just pushed him away.

Sophie sank against him, tears soaking his cape as she clung as tightly to him as he clung to her.

"There's seriously nothing you can do?" Fitz asked, his voice shaky with tears of his own. "What if we bring Elwin here, or Livvy, or—"

"You can bring as many physicians as you want," Vika interrupted. "They'll all tell you the same thing. We're going to lose these babies—heartbreaking and devastating as that is. And we can't let that break our focus. We still have a victory to claim today. We've arrived with enough time to save Silveny—and that is incredibly fortunate. I don't think you realize how often we lose the mother in these kinds of situations. And the babies are also well positioned, so we should even be able to preserve her ability to conceive—which is far better than I imagined when I realized we'd be facing this challenge. So let's try to focus on that—on pulling Silveny through this and giving her a second chance at being a mother someday. It means we'll also have another chance to reset the Timeline to Extinction."

"Extinction?" Tarina repeated, crouching to study Silveny. "So these are the creatures I've heard reports of."

"The last of their kind," Timkin agreed.

Tarina scratched her chin. "Then these aren't normal babies. . . ."

"No," Vika murmured. "A lot of hopes have been resting on them. But . . . as long as nothing goes terribly wrong today, the alicorns will have another chance."

"They may not want it," Sophie warned, glancing at Grady and Edaline, who seemed to be very interested in the way she was all wrapped up in Fitz. And she couldn't bring herself to care. "You guys know what it's like to lose a child. Silveny and Greyfell are about to lose two."

"It will be brutal," Edaline agreed, moving closer, trailing gentle fingers through Sophie's hair. "This kind of grief . . . There are no words for it. But Silveny is *strong*. She couldn't have survived so long on her own if she wasn't. And she has Greyfell. And *you*. And all of us. She has a whole world ready to do whatever she needs to get through. So it will be hard, and it will likely take time, but . . . she won't let this loss break her."

Sophie wanted to believe her.

But *she* felt broken, and she wasn't even the one about to lose two babies.

"There might be another option," Tarina said, her voice soft and chirpy.

Sophie stumbled away from everyone to face her. "What do you mean?"

Tarina leaned closer. "I can't answer that question unless you agree to our alliance—and I promise I'm not saying that to force your hand. The information I'd have to share beyond what I've just said . . . I can't share it unless you've sworn to protect it. And even then, it leaves my people vulnerable in ways you wouldn't be able to imagine. So I need your word that you're with us—*truly* with us. Otherwise I can't take that risk."

"Should we be concerned that they're speaking in a language we can't understand?" Timkin asked, making Sophie realize Tarina had shifted them to Trollish.

"They do that sometimes," Grady told him, with a casualness that didn't match the knowing glance he aimed at Sophie.

And Timkin didn't look convinced.

But Sophie would worry about that later.

"If I agree to your alliance, what exactly do I get?" she asked Tarina in her language.

Tarina glanced at Silveny, studying her for a long second before she told Sophie, "If we act quickly enough, my people and I can save these babies."

"How?" Sophie demanded, trying to fight the hope that was already sparking to life inside her. She was still speaking in Trollish, but Sophie felt the need to lower her voice when she continued, "*How* can you save Silveny's babies?"

Tarina sighed. "I told you, I can't share that information until you agree to an alliance."

"And how am I supposed to believe you if you won't give me any proof?" Sophie argued. "You heard why Vika thinks it's hopeless. What can you do that she can't?"

"*Many* things," Tarina promised.

Sophie shook her head. "You have to do better than that. You're asking me to commit treason—"

"No, I'm asking you to promise you'll be there for my people should we ever need your help—like you were there for the gnomes when the ogres and Neverseen came after them."

"I didn't have an alliance with the gnomes when I did that," Sophie reminded her. "It was just the right thing to do."

"And I'm sure that's how you'll feel about any favors we might ask. We do not take advantage of our allies or call on them unless it is absolutely necessary. My empress simply likes to be prepared—likes to know that she has made whatever arrangements she can to keep her people safe. She's also happy to repay any loyalty shown to her—which is why I know she'd allow me to make this offer. But I'm still going out on a limb by making it without asking for permission—and I'm taking that risk because I realize that time is of the utmost in this situation—and that applies to you as well. If you waver too long on this decision, I won't be able to help save these babies. But I also can't go any further without securing your commitment. So think fast, Sophie."

"How do I even agree?" Sophie wondered. "Am I supposed to take some sort of oath? Sign my name in blood?"

"You're supposed to give me your word. I know you wouldn't make that kind of promise without meaning it. Otherwise we wouldn't be having this conversation. You would've just agreed, taken what you wanted, and backed out later. But that's not who you are—and it's not who we are either. If you make us this commitment, we will do all we can to honor it from our end. Not just in this instance."

Sophie looked away, noting the mix of curious and suspicious faces watching them *very* closely—especially Fitz, who looked like he'd guessed at least part of what they were saying.

"You guys okay?" Grady asked.

Sophie nodded. "I'm just . . . asking Tarina about trollish medicine to see if they have anything that might help."

Edaline straightened. "Do they?"

"I'm trying to think," Tarina told her, shifting back to Trollish before she told Sophie, "Brilliant cover. You've now laid the groundwork for the story we would need to craft should you accept my help. And not to add pressure to you—but there are a number of steps we'll have to take, and the alicorn is already beginning to stir again."

Sophie's gaze darted back to Silveny, and her stomach twisted when she saw that Tarina was right. Silveny was making tiny movements—mostly leg twitches and tail flicks. But it was only a matter of time before she'd be thrashing again. Sophie had seen enough human movies and TV shows to know how messy and painful birth could be. And to think that at the end of it, instead of getting to nuzzle her new babies, Silveny would have to face the overwhelming grief of knowing they were gone . . .

"You're *sure* you can save them?" she whispered in Trollish.

Tarina sighed. "I suppose it wouldn't be fair of me to make a *guarantee*, since what I'm offering has obviously never been tested on anything beyond my own species. But it *should* work. And it's the best chance you have."

The only chance.

And didn't Silveny deserve it?

The Council might even agree, given how much they cared about the Timeline to Extinction—not that Sophie could tell them what she was doing.

She wished Mr. Forkle was there to weigh in with his opinions—or that he'd at least gotten back to her with the results of his research.

This was all happening too fast.

She couldn't do it on her own.

And maybe she didn't have to.

Her focus shifted back to Fitz, who now had a deep crinkle between his eyebrows. She could tell he *wasn't* telepathically eavesdropping—but he clearly wanted to be.

Trust me, she transmitted to him, before glancing back at Tarina. "The thing you need to understand," she said in Trollish, "is that it wasn't just me who saved the gnomes that day in Ravagog. So if you want an alliance with me, you're going to need to let me be open about it with my friends. I'm not saying I'll spill every single secret. But I don't work alone. And I can't commit to something that requires me to lie to everyone."

Tarina let out a heavy breath, smoothing the thick green strands of her hair. "I suppose we can leave that mostly to your judgment—with the understanding that we'll need to establish some boundaries once we're not so pressed for time."

Sophie nodded.

"Was that an agreement?" Tarina asked. "Because I'm going to need something a bit clearer than that."

Sophie swallowed hard, keeping her eyes on Silveny to remind herself why she was doing this. "Okay, we have an alliance. Now tell me how we save Silveny's babies."

"Perhaps we should go somewhere with a bit less of an audience," Tarina suggested, her eyes flicking to Timkin, who'd gone from looking suspicious to looking seriously concerned.

When Sophie nodded, Tarina switched back to the Enlightened Language and said, "We're going to take a quick walk so I can contact my empress."

Edaline sucked in a breath. "Does that mean you've thought of something that might help?"

"It's possible," Tarina agreed. "And I realize time is of the essence, so if there's anything you can do to slow the progress of the alicorn's labor—do it. We'll be back in a few minutes."

Sophie could feel everyone's stunned stares trying to hold her there like mental tractor beams. But no one argued as Tarina led her down the beach, their feet kicking up sand as they tried to hurry without seeming frantic—even though Sophie had never felt so impatient.

She managed to wait until they'd rounded a bend and left Silveny's cove for a wider, rockier stretch of shoreline. Then she reeled on Tarina and whisper-hissed, "Okay, what's the plan?"

"It's best if we continue in my language, just to be safe," Tarina warned, and the chirpiness of the words made it clear she'd already switched. "I wouldn't be surprised if we have a few eavesdroppers. Your boyfriend in particular."

"He's not my boyfr—" Sophie started to tell her, but she cut herself off when she realized that might not actually be true.

Fitz had almost kissed her.

And he'd told her he wanted to find her name on his match lists.

And she'd told him she'd liked him forever.

And he'd been so helpful and amazing ever since.

But . . . none of that actually meant they were dating.

She wasn't even sure if she was *ready* to date Fitz, knowing it would cause all kinds of changes—new rules from her parents, possible drama among their friends.

But that definitely wasn't what she should be thinking about at the moment. So she shoved all those complicated new worries into another mental box she'd deal with later and asked again in Tarina's language, "How do we save Silveny's babies?"

Tarina turned to watch the dark waves crashing against the shore. "This is likely going to sound very strange. But remember when I told you that those in my species are *hatched* when they're born and you assumed I meant hatching from eggs?"

Sophie nodded. "You made it sound like eggs weren't really a part of it."

"They're not," Tarina agreed. "At least not the way you might be picturing them. Our young do not develop inside any sort of shell, like birds or reptiles. Instead the process is much closer to marsupials. And what I mean by that is, our babies are born at an incredibly early stage—but instead of moving to a pouch to develop, they're implanted into a hive, where they can finish developing and grow to a proper size."

"A hive," Sophie repeated, her mind immediately conjuring up images of giant beehives filled with thousands of unborn trolls thrashing around inside honeycomb shells waiting to burst into the world as violent newborns—and she *really* hoped her brain was wrong. "So . . . you're thinking we'd put Silveny's babies into the hive and let them finish growing in there?"

Tarina nodded. "The hive should be able to provide them with everything they need to reach viability."

"Okay, so . . . how do we do that?" Sophie wondered. "We can't move Silveny—"

"No, we'll need to retrieve two of our transport pods."

"Transport pods." Sophie knew she needed to stop repeating everything Tarina was saying like a parrot. But her brain seemed to require that extra second to process.

"Think of them like portable wombs," Tarina told her. "Something our scientists invented in order to ensure that every baby reached the hive with enough time to be safely implanted with the rest of the colony. Before them, we used to lose a few babies every year. It's strange how nature sometimes isn't enough, don't you think? Strange that we have to invent ways to survive something that should be automatic—like what's happening with your alicorn. You would think her body wouldn't have become pregnant with twins unless it could support them. But . . . sometimes nature needs a little help."

Sophie couldn't think of what to say to any of that, so she went with a nod—and tried her best not to look thoroughly grossed out. It wasn't fair to be bothered by something just because it was different from what she considered normal. But it wasn't easy when Tarina was using words like "pods" and "colony" and "implanted"—all of which sounded like something straight out of human science fiction and made her think of aliens or giant bugs.

"If it helps," Tarina told her, "I had a similar reaction the first time I learned that some creatures have bellies that stretch and bulge as the baby develops fully inside them, and then the mother has to push the baby out through a process that looks rather slimy and painful."

When she put it that way, it definitely didn't sound a whole lot better.

"I think I'm never having kids," Sophie decided.

Tarina laughed. "I'm pretty sure we all feel that way at some point."

"Probably," Sophie said, shaking her head to clear away the biological horror show going on in her brain.

It didn't matter how weird it all sounded.

It only mattered that it *worked*.

"Okay, so . . . two questions," Sophie told Tarina. "Where do we get the pods? And why was this such a big secret that I had to swear to an alliance before you'd tell me? Isn't a lot of what you just explained something I'll be taught in school someday?"

"Well, I doubt your mentors will get quite as specific. But . . . the answer to both questions is related. Our birthing process is not a secret. But the location of our hive definitely is, and that's where we keep the transport pods. And bringing you there also requires me to reveal something that's *beyond* classified. Something I doubt our empress ever planned on sharing. That's why this is such a risk. The only way to help you means . . . revealing the identity of our other elvin ally since the hive is at their property."

Sophie felt her eyes stretch wide.

Tarina nodded. "I figured that might be your reaction. And I won't waste time making you renew your promise for secrecy.

I'm trusting you to keep your word. I also won't waste time sharing the whole lengthy history. All you really need to know is that several thousand years ago, our hive was raided by ogres. We managed to fight them off and maintain control of our lands. But in that one night, we lost an entire generation." She lowered her head, giving those ancient losses a moment of silence. "And after we'd buried our dead, we realized how vulnerable we were. The ogres knew what our hive looked like now. They'd never stop until they found it again. And while our empress considered turning to your Council for protection, she'd already seen how little help they gave the gnomes after the ogres stole their homeland. And she feared her people would fare as poorly. She'd also seen the brilliant illusions that were hiding your cities in plain sight. And she realized that was what we needed—that extra layer of clever camouflage to keep our hive secret. So instead of speaking with your Councillors, she approached the elf who was directly responsible for concealing your world."

Sophie grabbed her arm, feeling like the earth had just tilted sharply. "Please tell me you're not talking about Vespera."

She couldn't breathe again until Tarina told her, "No. My empress allied with the elf who actually implemented the illusions, since she was the one we'd need in order to veil our hive."

The earth tilted the other way as Sophie realized there was only one person Tarina could mean—the name Tarina confirmed a second later.

Luzia Vacker.

THIRTY-NINE

ARE YOU TELLING ME YOUR HIVE
is at Everglen?" Sophie asked, tightening
her grip on Tarina and trying to keep her
knees from collapsing.

But Tarina shook her head. And Sophie could breathe again.
Until Tarina added, "That's where it used to be."

Then everything was back to spinning.

And Sophie had to fight very hard not to scream when she
said, "You didn't think you should mention this when we were
there a few hours ago, searching for security risks because a
member of the Neverseen is now living at the property?"

"I didn't," Tarina agreed—sounding annoyingly calm—
"because I wasn't authorized to share that information. I'm still

technically not authorized to do so, but you've at least agreed to an alliance. And I'm counting on my empress to understand why I've taken this leap. More important, though: Everglen no longer matters. The hive had to be moved several decades ago, when we needed more space."

Well.

That solved the mystery of why Luzia left Everglen and gave it to Alden.

But if the old hive was gone, why suggest he install the fence?

"Is there something valuable in the abandoned hive—something the Neverseen might want to get their hands on?" Sophie wondered.

Tarina shook her head. "It would be nothing more than an empty nest—though I believe it was destroyed."

"You *believe*," Sophie emphasized.

"Yes, Sophie. Not every detail about everything gets shared with me. But I searched for the hive today while we were at Everglen. It used to be near the lake. And I couldn't find a single trace of it."

The words should've made Sophie feel better.

But she didn't like coincidences. And it felt *very* coincidental knowing that Alvar was back at Everglen under somewhat suspicious circumstances while Vespera was now free—especially since it wasn't that big of a stretch to think that Vespera might've known about Luzia's alliance, or at least suspected it. Luzia likely used illusions that Vespera designed to hide the hive.

Sophie also didn't love knowing that the whole time Tarina had been helping search Everglen, she'd had her own secret agenda—or that she hid that agenda so perfectly.

Tarina was smooth.

Maybe a little too smooth.

"We need to tell the Council," Sophie decided. "Just to be safe. I bet it would get them to move Alvar."

Tarina grabbed her wrist, like she was afraid Sophie was going to race straight to Eternalia. "You can't do that, Sophie. Not only would you be breaching the alliance you just made with me—but you'd be dragging Luzia into all kinds of trouble. *And* you'd be endangering the lives of thousands of unhatched babies—all to address some minor worry that you have no evidence to support."

Sophie sighed. "Fine. Then we need to at least tell Grizel—"

"Absolutely not!" Tarina interrupted. "No goblin is allowed to know anything about our hives."

"You can trust Grizel."

"No—*you* can trust her," Tarina corrected. "The goblins have always cooperated peacefully with your people. My people have not had that luxury. Instead, we've endured a long history of attacks. And I don't think you realize the larger significance of our hive. Remember: Our deadliest soldiers are our newborns and Stage Ones. So wiping them out before they hatch doesn't just destroy a generation and crush the lives of the families waiting for them—it decimates our army for several years to come."

"But we can't just ignore this," Sophie argued. "You've never dealt with the Neverseen before—you don't know how they work. Things like this . . . These are the things you look back on and regret. Someone has to find that hive—or whatever's left of it—and make sure there's nothing there we need to worry about."

"I can do it," Fitz offered, rising from where he'd been crouching among the long grass.

Tarina's eyes narrowed. "How can you understand us?"

"I can't," Fitz admitted, glancing nervously at Sophie. "I swear I wasn't planning on sneaking into your mind. I was just trying to stay close, to make sure nothing weird was happening. But then Tarina grabbed your wrist, and your voices got louder, and . . . I had to make sure you were okay—and then I heard Luzia's name and . . ."

"Elvin mind tricks," Tarina muttered.

It's okay, Sophie transmitted to Fitz. *I would've done the same thing.*

Really? he asked, a hint of a smile curling his lips.

It turned into a real grin when Sophie admitted, *I'm glad you're here.*

Out loud she added, "And I was already planning on telling Fitz about all of this—I warned you I wasn't going to hide things from my friends. And the hive was at *his* house. Protected by someone in *his* family—and his brother may be part of some plan centered around it."

"There's no plan!" Tarina insisted, tugging on her thick green hair. "The hive was destroyed when we moved to a newer, bigger location."

"I hope you're right," Fitz told her. "But I'm still going to check. And since it sounds like you don't know exactly where it was, I'll make Luzia tell me."

Tarina grumbled something through a sigh. "Fine. But you must complete the search when no one can see you—especially the goblins on the property."

"I can do that," Fitz agreed.

"I hope you guys just figured out something good," Stina shouted over to them, making them all flinch as she jogged closer, "because Silveny's contractions are down to three and a half minutes apart."

Sophie's heart stopped. "How much time does that give us?"

"Not a lot—so if you're planning something, you'd better get on it."

"She's right," Tarina agreed. "We can deal with everything else later. Right now we need to get those transport pods."

"What does that mean?" Stina asked.

"It means the babies still have a chance," Sophie told her, grabbing Fitz's hand when he offered it to her. "So do *anything* you can to slow the contractions. We'll be back as fast as we can."

Tarina reached for Sophie's other hand and Fitz floated them into the sky as Stina shouted, "Where are you going?"

"I don't know," Sophie called back before glancing at Fitz. "I don't suppose you know where Luzia lives now?" she asked him quietly.

"I've seen pictures of Dawnheath," he said. "Will that be enough if you search my memories?"

"It'll have to be," Sophie told him, slipping into his mind.

He led her right to the images she needed, and as she committed them to memory he promised her, *We're going to make this work, Sophie. Whatever it takes.*

I hope so.

And because it was true, she found herself telling him again, *I'm really glad you're here.*

Me too, he said with a smile that made everything a little better. *Thanks for trusting me.*

Their eyes held for a second, and his were full of all the words there wasn't time for.

Then he let them fall into the void.

"What if Luzia's not home?" Sophie murmured, shielding her face from the glare of the enormous fence, which was twice as high as Everglen's and three times as bright. So bright, in fact, that she couldn't see anything past the glow from the metal bars.

They'd been standing outside the property's entrance for

a little more than two minutes—time they couldn't afford to waste. But the gates were locked, and as far as Sophie could tell, there wasn't a doorbell or an intercom, or any other means of letting Luzia know they were there.

"I'm sure she's on her way," Tarina said with a confidence that didn't match how tightly she gripped the handle of her weapon, or the way she kept glancing over her shoulder to check some creak or crackle from the overgrown forest behind them.

The tangled trees were blanketed in thick green moss, and the squashy ground was dotted with mushrooms, like something out of a movie—but the kind of movie where the characters were being hunted by something lurking in the misty shadows.

Fitz must've been feeling the same way, because he scooted closer to Sophie, holding tight to her gloved hand as he called out, "Luzia—it's Fitz Vacker. Please let us in."

The call bounced off the trees but triggered no response, and Sophie was starting to wonder how hard it would be to scale the fence—or what would happen if they tried to levitate over it—when a soft click had them stumbling back as the gates swung slowly outward, and a silhouetted figure stalked toward them.

"What is the meaning of this?" Luzia demanded, her annoyed tone twisting Sophie's stomach into knots.

They didn't have time to win Luzia over.

They needed her to cooperate immediately.

Which meant Sophie had to get right to the point.

"The alicorn went into early labor," she told Luzia, not bothering to mask the fear in her voice. "She's having twins, and we're told the babies aren't going to survive unless we move them somewhere they can finish developing."

Luzia paused midstep, her form still a shadowed shape against the blinding light. "And why are you coming to me?"

"Because they know about the hive," Tarina said boldly. "I offered to let them use two of our transport pods so they can implant the newborn alicorns and let them finish developing as though they're part of the colony."

Luzia backed away. "I don't know what you're—"

"Yes, you do," Sophie interrupted.

"It's okay," Tarina assured Luzia. "The girl is an ally. The empress recruited her specifically."

"And the boy?" Luzia countered, tilting her head toward Fitz.

"He . . . was part of the girl's deal," Tarina admitted. "She doesn't work alone."

Luzia turned to Sophie. "Someday you'll understand how foolish that is."

"Maybe," Sophie said, not willing to lose focus. "But right now we're trying to save two unborn alicorns—and you *know* how important those babies are. So if I have to shove past you to get to that hive, I will. The contractions are only three and a half minutes apart. We need those pods *now*."

"Such authority for someone so young," Luzia said. "And yet

you speak without wisdom." She strode forward enough that she finally moved past the gates' glare, becoming fully visible. And Luzia was every bit as striking as Sophie remembered from the Tribunal—maybe even more so with her black hair pulled back into a sleek ponytail, drawing more attention to her pointed ears. Her bronze skin shimmered with flecks of gold, which matched her severely cut golden tunic, and with her knee-high golden boots, she'd gone from Egyptian goddess to Amazonian warrior. Which made it all the more terrifying when she folded her well-toned arms and told Sophie, "You cannot put the alicorns into the hive."

"With all due respect," Tarina countered, stalking a few steps closer, "you don't get to make that decision. We rely on you for secrecy—but the hive belongs to *my* people."

"It does," Luzia agreed. "So it's surprising that *I* have to be the one to remind *you* that the eclipse is coming."

"What does that have to do with anything?" Fitz demanded.

"It means . . . there will be a mass hatching," Tarina said quietly.

Luzia nodded. "I assume you don't need me to explain why it would be far too dangerous to have the alicorns trapped in the hive, surrounded by hundreds of wild newborns."

Even Sophie could understand that—and the realization felt like a deathblow.

Tears spilled down her cheeks as she said, "So . . . we can't save them."

Fitz pulled Sophie against him.

"I'm sorry," Tarina whispered. "The timing's just . . . off."

Luzia studied each of them in turn. Then she rolled her eyes. "I always forget how melodramatic the young are. How easily defeated. It's what's ruining our world, if you ask me. Someday you'll have the perspective to not crumble at the first hint of disappointment—to see the next step without needing someone to explain it."

"Does that mean there's still a way to save the babies?" Sophie asked, willing to overlook the insults—willing to overlook *anything*—if Luzia could give her that.

"It depends on how much time we have. I can arrange for a private hive to be set up specifically for the alicorns," Luzia told her. "But the construction obviously must be done by trolls. And I only have two staying on the property."

"Can you help?" Fitz asked Tarina.

Tarina shook her head. "I can't leave Sophie's side. Plus, you'll need someone who knows how to utilize our transport pods to get the babies settled and stable."

"How long can they stay in the transport pods?" Sophie wondered.

"Usually no more than a couple of hours," Tarina warned. "Possibly less, since the alicorns will likely be larger than our younglings and burn through the nutrition and oxygen faster."

"And how long does it take to set up a hive?" Fitz asked.

"Longer than that," Luzia told him.

"Then work faster," Sophie told her. "Call for backup. Do whatever you have to do. This could be our only chance to reset the Timeline to Extinction. It's up to us to find a way to make it work."

"Finally—a bit of gumption," Luzia noted, studying Sophie through narrowed eyes. "Perhaps there's hope for the future yet."

"There won't be if we keep wasting time," Fitz reminded them.

"Indeed." Luzia motioned for them to follow her. "I'll show you where to retrieve the transport pods—but you *cannot* tell anyone that I'm helping with this."

"They won't," Tarina promised, with a warning look at Sophie and Fitz. "All I'll be telling the others is that I have permission from my empress to place the babies into one of our hives, and that for security purposes, I cannot give them the location."

"*Do* you have permission from your empress for this?" Luzia asked.

"I don't need it," Tarina told her, which wasn't really an answer.

But Luzia let it go. "Well, then if you want to save these babies, I suggest we get to work. Follow me."

"*This* is the hive?" Sophie asked, backing away from the towering briar patch blocking a thin opening in the side of a jagged cliff. Even the smallest thorns were bigger than her head and packed so tightly together that Sophie couldn't see a way through that wouldn't involve getting impaled.

The entrance itself was also so narrow that even if Sophie turned sideways, she wasn't sure how she'd squeeze inside. But there were no other gaps in the rock—and the cliff ended at a slimy-looking lake that stretched for miles.

Honestly, Luzia's new property was a *huge* step down from Everglen.

"Don't believe everything your eyes are telling you," Luzia told her. "The hive is protected by numerous illusions, and I don't have time to walk you through it, so I'm counting on you to figure it out. Once you have the alicorns sealed safely inside the transport pods, find somewhere private and hail me. I'll make sure I carry an Imparter."

With that, she raced back the way they'd come, down the bumpy path that wound into the forest.

"Think that means the briars aren't really there?" Fitz reached out to touch the nearest thorn—and whipped his hand back when it drew a drop of blood.

"Do you know the trick?" Sophie asked Tarina.

Tarina shook her head, touching a different thorn and getting pricked as well. "I've only visited the hive through my world, where it isn't camouflaged."

Sophie sighed, wishing she could grab the nearest rock and throw it as hard as she could. But that wouldn't help the situation. Neither would chasing down Luzia and forcing her to give them better instructions, since it *was* more important for Luzia to focus on building the new hive.

"Okay," Sophie said quietly, trying to think through what Luzia had told them. "She told us not to believe our eyes. So what about our other senses?"

Something did seem off about where they were standing—but she couldn't put her finger on it because everything looked normal.

It felt normal too.

A dry breeze kept making the briars crackle—which sounded right.

And the lake . . .

"Wait—the lake isn't rippling from the wind," Sophie realized.

And now that she thought about it, the air should've had a sour, musty smell from all that icky, stagnant water.

"The lake must not be real," she decided, moving to the edge and tapping the water with her toe.

She'd expected to find solid ground, but . . . wetness soaked through the fabric of her boot.

But the lake didn't ripple, so . . . maybe she was still right? There was only one way to really know for sure.

"If I fall in," she told Fitz and Tarina, "you're not allowed to laugh."

"I would never," Fitz assured her. "I'll even give you my cape to dry off."

His smile was so sweet. And it was such . . . such a *boyfriend* thing to offer . . . that Sophie couldn't help blushing when she smiled back.

But now *so* wasn't the time.

Fitz seemed to get that too as they both turned back to the lake-that-might-not-be-a-lake, and Sophie wished the water didn't look so thick and green, like a lake of snot. But if that's what it took to help Silveny . . .

"All right, here goes nothing," she said, preparing for a slimy splash as she raised her foot over the lake, stepped down, and . . .

Found solid ground underneath a couple inches of water.

The next step had the same result. And the next.

"That looks super weird," Fitz told her.

"I know—I keep having to remind myself I'm not in the middle of a disgusting lake."

At least she hoped she wasn't. She couldn't tell where the water was coming from. But it was shallow, at least. And after a few more steps, the air around her seemed to shimmer, and it was like passing through some sort of veil. One second she was standing in a sea of sludge. The next she was walking through a shimmery reflecting pool surrounding a humongous tree that hadn't been there before. And as she splashed closer, she realized the arched hole in the trunk created a path that led down into the muddy soil, weaving around the ancient roots and disappearing underground.

"I think I found it!" she shouted. "I know trees are usually gnomish things, but—"

"Gnomes aren't the only ones who rely on the sturdiness of the forest," Tarina said right behind her, startling Sophie so badly she nearly fell over.

Fitz caught her shoulders. "Sorry. We followed you when you disappeared, and I thought you might have heard us splashing. But sound is kind of weird here."

It was.

The air seemed to swallow their voices, which must've been another part of the illusion keeping the hive hidden.

"We should hurry," Tarina told them, heading for the path. "We usually keep the transport pods toward the back of the hive, so we still have some walking ahead of us."

Of course they did.

Because nothing could *ever* be quick or easy—even when lives were on the line.

"Anything we should know before we go down there?" Fitz asked.

"Yes," Tarina told him. "Don't touch anything."

That turned out to be an easy rule to follow.

The hive was made of a gloopy, sticky mud coated in stinky bioluminescent fungus that filled the massive cavern with a subtle blue-green glow. And the walls were long rows of stacked compartments—kind of like a honeycomb. Each cubby was sealed off with a thick, slimy membrane. And inside?

It truly was like something out of science fiction.

The unhatched troll babies floated in some sort of green jelly that reminded Sophie of the aloe vera gel her human parents used to smear on her sunburns, only filled with tiny bubbles that had a soft white glow. And even with their bodies half curled, the baby trolls towered over Tarina, their muscles bulging and lined with dark veins.

Some of them moved, stretching against their barriers and making the membranes drip milky fluid onto the stone floor. Others had their eyes open, staring at nothing—or maybe staring at everything. Sophie didn't want to know which. All she knew was that it felt like the beasts could burst free any second, and she was *very* glad Silveny's babies would be kept somewhere else.

"Is it me, or is it super stuffy down here?" Fitz asked, tugging on the neckline of his tunic and fanning his face.

"Our babies thrive in heat," Tarina explained. "The solution they're developing in is kept at one hundred and fifty degrees— much too hot for your fragile elvin bodies."

"Will that be too hot for the alicorns?" Sophie wondered.

"We'll likely have to adjust. It generally matches the mother's body temperature, so we'll need to take a reading of Silveny's. And here we are." She pointed to a wall of shelves filled with what looked like glass clamshells the size of beach balls.

"Will those be big enough?" Sophie worried, trying to imagine what size Silveny's babies would be.

"The material they're made from can expand. But we may have to get creative with how we position them. I suspect this whole process is going to be an exercise in problem solving—but we'll make it work." Tarina handed Sophie and Fitz each a transport pod to carry as she filled a satchel with metal flasks from a different shelf.

"You okay?" Fitz asked as Sophie struggled to adjust her grip on the pod. "Is that too much for your arm?"

"No, it's actually lighter than I expected," Sophie told him, wondering what the pod was made of. "What about you—how's your leg?"

"I'm fine."

Sophie hoped that was true, because they still had more walking ahead. They were closer to the troll exit than Luzia's house at that point, but it still took them several endless minutes before they emerged back into daylight and caught a glimpse of the trollish world.

All Sophie really had time to see were two bluffs connected by a web of intricate bridges. Then Fitz was launching them into the sky, and Sophie plunged them into the void.

"IT'S ABOUT TIME!" Stina screamed as they tumbled across the grassy dunes, and she dragged them to their feet before they'd even stopped rolling. "I don't know where you've been or what you're planning, but you'd better explain it fast. The first baby is already crowning."

FORTY

SOPHIE LEARNED MORE ABOUT BIRTH that day than she'd ever really wanted to know. For instance, she learned that "crowning" meant one of the babies' heads was starting to emerge—which was something she definitely wished she could unsee.

She also learned it was much better to stay near Silveny's face, where she could stroke her mane and rub her velvety nose and not have to think about what was happening around her tail region. And she could do her best to keep Silveny calm as Vika made a lot of very gag-worthy splashing sounds that had Fitz turning incredibly green.

"Looks like we have a baby girl," Vika announced a few seconds later. "And she's alive. For now."

Silveny locked eyes with Sophie, and her desperate voice poured into Sophie's head, along with a mix of joy and sadness that twisted Sophie's heart into knots.

SOPHIE PROMISE! BABY OKAY! BABY OKAY!

Sophie wished she could give Silveny the assurance she knew the terrified mama alicorn needed. But she told her, *I promise, we're doing everything we can.*

And they were.

Tarina had already prepared the transport pods, filling them with a mix of water and fluids from the flasks she'd brought with her. And she attached a series of suction-cup-style tubes to baby alicorn number one and lowered her into the warm goo, where her tiny limbs did seem to relax.

"Here you go, Mama," Tarina said, bringing the pod over to Silveny's face and giving her a chance for one quick nuzzle. "That's your baby's scent, so you'll recognize her if she gets stronger and we can bring her back to you."

Silveny let out a snuffly whinny—somewhere between elation and devastation—and rubbed her nose against her daughter's tiny head with a look of absolute devotion. The baby didn't open her eyes or make a sound, but she nudged her nose against her mama. Sophie felt tears trickle down her cheeks as Silveny begged again, *SOPHIE PROMISE! BABY OKAY! BABY OKAY!*

More tears poured down as Tarina carried the pod over to Greyfell, letting the papa alicorn endure the same emotional roller coaster as he nuzzled his tiny daughter for the first time. The floating newborn looked so small and helpless, all knobby knees and fuzzy fur and tucked-in wings. And her head didn't have a full horn yet—more of a pointy nubbin peeking out of the strands of her short mane. She also wasn't as silvery as her mama—more of a mix of white, yellow, and pearl—and Sophie decided she looked like she'd been dipped in moonlight.

And something stirred inside Sophie as she watched Tarina seal the pod tight—a kind of absolute determination that had her promising Silveny and Greyfell that they would see that tiny baby again. If Luzia couldn't get a new hive built in time, then Sophie would stand guard inside the troll hive and fight off all the newborns. She didn't care what it took—that little moon-dipped alicorn was going to *live*.

And so was her brother, who arrived a minute later and let out the world's tiniest nicker. He had blue tips on his wings just like his daddy.

Tarina tucked him safely in his pod and gave Silveny and Greyfell each another heartbreaking nuzzle with their son. Then she sealed him in tight and set him next to his sister.

Everyone gathered around the pods to watch the sweet babies float in their temporary wombs—except Vika and Edaline, who were busy doing some final slurpy-sounding things to finish up the whole birth process. And Sophie stayed with Silveny, stroking her nose and transmitting that her babies were okay over and over until Vika draped a fresh towel over Silveny's face and said it was time for the tired mama to sleep.

"She'll be okay?" Sophie had to ask as Silveny's body stilled.

Vika nodded. "There were zero complications. So far, at least." Her eyes shifted to the baby pods. "So . . . what now?"

"Now I have a call to make," Sophie said, pulling out her Imparter and sneaking off to a secluded section of the beach to hail Luzia Vacker.

"Did both babies survive the delivery?" Luzia asked the second her face filled the screen.

"They did." Sophie's voice choked as she said it—who knew watching life come into the world was this overwhelming? "And Silveny seems to be doing pretty good too. How's the hive coming?"

"Faster than expected. I found an existing structure that served our needs, so we didn't have to start from scratch. The trolls are treating the walls now and preparing the membranes. Shouldn't be much longer, barring some sort of disaster."

Fresh tears welled in Sophie's eyes. "That's . . . really good news."

"I wouldn't get my hopes up yet," Luzia warned. "The babies still have to survive the implanting. Some trolls don't even make it through that, and it's their natural way of developing. You're dealing with dozens of guesses and estimates and—"

"I know," Sophie interrupted. "I know the odds are still against us, but . . . we're going to beat them. We *have* to. When you see these little babies—"

"I'm sure they're very cute," Luzia cut in. "Just remember: Nature has no problem being cruel."

"Well . . . today we're going to make it play nice," Sophie decided. "I don't care what it takes. So when do I bring the transport pods to you?"

"Not yet. I still need to figure out what to do for security. And I'm not sure how you'll find where we are."

"You're not at Dawnheath?"

"No." The word had a bitter laugh attached to it. "That would be disastrous. You'll have to inform the Council about everything that's happened, and I can't have them asking why I'm involved, or wanting access to my property to visit their precious alicorns. This can't connect to me in any way—do you understand?"

Sophie nodded, even if she didn't totally get why Luzia's alliance with the trolls needed to be secret. All she'd done was set up a safe place for them to have their babies—wasn't that a *good* thing?

Unless she'd done other stuff that Sophie didn't know about . . .

"So where are you?" she asked, deciding she'd worry about Luzia Vacker's secrets later, once Silveny's babies were safe.

"It doesn't have a name—and it won't be on any pathfinders or Leapmasters. That's why I'm not sure how you'll get to me. It's an old abandoned tower I thought of when I realized it'd be better to keep the babies closer to the sky, so they're in their natural environment when they hatch."

"Then hold your Imparter up to the tower and show me what it looks like," Sophie told her. "That's all I'll need to teleport there."

"Really?" Luzia asked, her eyebrows lifting as she pulled her Imparter back and swung it to face a weathered, vine-wrapped tower surrounded by mountains. "Is that enough?"

"It should be." Sophie closed her eyes, testing to make sure her memory had recorded the image perfectly. "I'll be right there."

"Wait!" Luzia's face appeared across the screen again. "It's not safe yet. I still need to figure out how to keep the hive hidden. The cloaking cannot look like my handiwork, so we're going to need someone talented enough to follow a set of instructions I leave for them for some very different kinds of illusions—and they can't be anyone I know."

"I'm sure I can find someone," Sophie assured her.

"Yes, that's right. You don't work alone."

"I don't," Sophie agreed, ignoring the judgment in Luzia's tone.

"Is that why you felt the need to drag my nephew—well, my great-great-great-great-you-get-the-point-nephew—into your hastily thought-out alliance?"

"I didn't *drag* him in. And he didn't actually make them any promises. But I did warn Tarina that I wasn't going to keep secrets from my friends."

"You sound very proud of yourself for that."

"I am," Sophie agreed. "I had to learn the hard way that trying to do everything by myself doesn't go well."

"Neither does involving the people you care about in agreements you cannot possibly understand."

"All I've agreed to is to be someone the trolls can come to if they need help," Sophie argued. "And since you agreed to the same thing, I don't really get why you're giving me a lecture."

"Hindsight, Sophie. It comes with lots of regret."

Sophie's chest tightened. "You're saying you regret your alliance with the trolls."

Luzia sighed and looked away. "I'm saying I regret parts of it—though I suspect we all regret parts of every major decision we make. We choose the best we can, based on whatever information we're given. And then . . . we have to live with it."

"Well," Sophie said, swallowing back the sourness on her tongue, "I can live with it if it saves these alicorn babies. And Tarina—"

"Tarina won't be your problem. It's the empress who'll bring you the real challenge. And it won't happen right away. That's how it sneaks up on you."

"What does?"

"Who knows? But something always comes up. Just remember that sharing this planet with other intelligent species means that everything is far more complicated than it seems. And while I'm counting on you to keep your word and not let anyone know of my involvement . . . if you find yourself in a bind, you know where to find me."

"Okay," Sophie said slowly.

She wasn't sure what they were talking about anymore. But it was giving her a stomachache.

"Anyway," Luzia said, breaking the silence, "none of that matters at the moment. Right now, I need you to bring me two elves who can implement the illusions we're going to need to prevent the new hive from being discovered. It's going to require two very specific abilities."

"Which abilities?" Sophie asked.

"A Flasher and a Shade."

FORTY-ONE

JUST SO I'M CLEAR," TAM SAID, TUGGING HIS bangs over his eyes. "You need me to teleport with you to the middle of nowhere and use my ability to follow a list of instructions written by some mystery person in order to camouflage a tower, so you can implant the newborn alicorns into some sort of troll-baby hive?"

"Well, first we have to find Wylie, because I guess we need him for this too," Sophie corrected. "But otherwise . . . yeah. And we don't have a lot of time. The babies are safe for now, but we don't know how long they'll last in the pods—"

"Or how long it's going to take to implant them," Tarina added.

Or if the implanting will work, Sophie thought—but she didn't say that.

Fitz must've guessed that she was thinking it, though, because he scooted closer. And Sophie let herself lean against him.

She wasn't totally sure how to act around him anymore—especially now that they were with some of their friends. But she was tired. And emotionally wrung out. And *really* glad that Fitz had insisted on going with her when she'd borrowed Grady's pathfinder to leap to Tiergan's house.

Someday, she wanted to take a longer look around the home of her telepathy Mentor and see if she could learn a bit more about him. But at the moment, her brain could barely process the fact that he seemed to live on his own private island.

Tam whistled. "And to think, when I left Exillium, I thought my life was maybe going to be a little more normal."

"Is that a yes?" Sophie pressed.

Tam nodded.

"I can take you to Wylie's new place," Linh offered, pulling a pendant out from under her tunic.

"Actually, it'd probably be better if we just borrow that crystal," Sophie admitted. "I don't know if it'll be bad to show up at the hive with extra people."

Linh pouted. "But . . . I want to see the baby alicorns."

"They're not there yet," Sophie reminded her. "And I promise I'll bring you to them as soon as I can, okay?"

Linh sighed but agreed, ordering Tam to be careful as she handed him her necklace.

"Yay, we're light leaping again!" Tarina said when they stepped into the path.

But a few minutes later—after Wylie agreed to join them—they were back to teleporting. And Wylie seemed to hate the process even more than Tarina did.

To be fair, it'd been one of Sophie's rougher landings—though that wasn't totally her fault. The image Luzia had shown her of the tower had left out the rather key detail that it rested on the edge of a lush forest, and their momentum as they exited the void sent them toppling into the trees.

She'd have to make sure things went much smoother when it was time to bring the baby alicorns there.

On the outside the tower looked like a picture-perfect ruin, complete with crumbling walls and mossy stones and overgrown vines. But inside it was all sticky mud and bioluminescence and slimy membranes. The trolls were in the process of making the goopy green mixture the babies would be floating in, and that was apparently the last step before the hive would be ready for implantation. Which meant Tam and Wylie needed to get to work following the instructions Luzia had left for them on a rolled scroll tucked into the handle of the tower's door.

"You're really not going to tell us who wrote these?" Wylie asked as he scanned the surprisingly long list of steps.

"I can't," Sophie told him. "And if anyone asks, you have to make it seem like you and Tam came up with the illusions yourself."

"I doubt Lady Zillah will believe that," Tam warned. "Half this stuff I don't even understand."

"But you can do it?" Fitz asked.

Tam skimmed the list again. "Yeah, it's just a lot of 'send shadows here and here and here.' I don't get *how* that's going to create some powerful illusion, but . . . I guess we'll find out."

The first several steps seemed to center on shooting alternating beams of shadows and light at a series of small mirrors that Luzia must've placed before she left. Some dotted the perimeter of the tower, but most were scattered throughout the forest, dangling from trees, leaning against mossy rocks, and tucked among the thick ferns.

"You two wait here," Tarina told Sophie and Fitz, pointing to a fallen log in a shadowy clearing. "I want to do a quick patrol of the forest. I don't like how thick it is. Limits my visibility."

Sophie wasn't a fan either. There were too many scraggly, creaking branches. Too many places to hide. Too many twisted shapes playing tricks on her eyes.

She had to force herself to stay still as she sat next to Fitz on the mossy log. But her skin kept prickling and she couldn't help glancing over her shoulder every few minutes. And the longer they sat there, the more her senses seemed to heighten, until every tiny rustle or crackle morphed into proof that they weren't alone.

"This place is giving me the creeps," Fitz whispered.

"Me too." And Sophie wasn't sure if she was relieved or extra worried now that she knew Fitz was picking up on the same unsettling vibe. "I keep telling myself I'm just being paranoid because this is our first time since the attack being somewhere that doesn't have a billion goblins marching around. But . . . it feels like someone's watching us, doesn't it?"

"It does," Fitz whispered back.

"Tarina would've found them by now, though, wouldn't she?" Sophie asked, trying to stay rational.

"You'd think," Fitz agreed.

But Tarina had been gone a pretty long time.

And Sophie had no idea how strong trollish senses were—not that it necessarily mattered. Grizel and Sandor hadn't detected the Neverseen that day in the desert.

Or Tarina could be the presence that she and Fitz were both feeling.

Or it could be Nubiti. Sophie wasn't sure how closely her dwarven bodyguard was tailing her, but . . . maybe she surfaced from time to time to check on certain things.

She'd almost convinced herself it was all her imagination running wild—after all, how would anyone know where to find her? She was wearing Tinker's null. And she'd gotten rid of the pendant with the tracker. And they were at some nameless ruin they'd never been to before.

But then a twig snapped nearby, loud enough to make her heart skip several beats.

"Think that was an animal?" Fitz whispered.

"No idea." But if it was, it was *big*—so that wasn't necessarily a good thing.

She glanced at Tam and Wylie, who stood closer to the forest's edge, oblivious to everything except the swirling beams of light and shadow shooting out of their hands.

And that's when she realized—*Wylie* was with them.

She unzipped a couple of the pockets on her pants and removed two goblin throwing stars, handing one to Fitz and gripping the other with her left hand, reminding herself that Tinker's bracelet would boost her throw if it came to that.

Did you see something? Fitz transmitted.

No, but I want to be ready. And it felt good holding the weapon, knowing that this time she wouldn't hesitate to use it—and that her aim was really, really good. *I'm worried the Neverseen might be coming after Wylie.*

Fitz's eyes widened. *You think?*

I honestly don't know. But it makes enough sense that I don't want to risk it.

So what do we do?

She chewed her lip as she considered their options, glancing again at Tam and Wylie. *I think we should split up. You keep watch from over there*—she pointed to a patch of ferns about a hundred feet away that were thick enough to hide him—*and I'll stay here. That way we cover them from both sides, and Ruy can't trap us in the same force field.*

I guess that makes sense, Fitz admitted. *But I don't like it.*

Sophie didn't either.

It's only a hundred feet, she reminded both of them. *And here—take these.* She removed the two goblin throwing stars she'd hidden in her boots and handed them to Fitz. *I still have a few more, don't worry.*

Fitz nodded grimly, tucking the extras into his cape before he turned to head where she'd pointed. But after a step he spun back and threw his arms around her, hugging her much tighter than he usually did. *Stay safe, okay?*

You too, she told him, watching him sneak away and wondering how she was supposed to defend herself now that her knees had turned into jelly.

Get it together, she mentally chided, shaking her left shoulder to loosen it and making sure Tinker's bangle rested against her left wrist as she scanned the shadows.

There was one patch dead ahead that felt darker than the others. And she took a silent step closer, wondering if investigating was a smart move or something she'd really regret.

Another step.

Another.

Only a few left.

And then . . . glaring light flared behind her.

Wylie and Tam both let out startled gasps and Sophie spun around, feeling her mouth drop open when she saw how the light and shadows shooting between them had formed a sort of expanding portal, revealing a bridge of weathered white wood stretching over an endless chasm.

But that couldn't be, could it?

Where was the tower?

And then she realized: It must be the illusion Luzia designed.

Now anyone trying to find the alicorns would see a long bridge that looked very uninviting instead of the tower hiding them, and—

A branch creaked again—much, *much* too close—and Sophie whipped around, flinging her throwing star toward the sound.

SHHHHHHICK!

Someone yelped, and more branches crunched. Sophie charged forward, hurdling a fallen log as she leaped to find . . .

Tarina.

With her back pressed tightly to the ground, her eyes wide as she stared up at Sophie.

"Guess it's a good thing I know how to dodge," she said, sounding genuinely shaken as she pulled herself to her feet and pointed to the slice in her mossy garment—right across her chest.

Sophie leaned closer, not breathing again until she confirmed that there was no blood. "I'm sorry! I . . . I guess I need to wait to see my target before I throw."

Tarina brushed the dirt off her shoulders. "That definitely helps. But sometimes it's not possible, so it's important to try to keep track of where your friends are. Though I suppose I should've remembered that you're armed and been clearer that it was me approaching."

"So it was you this whole time?" Fitz asked as he rushed over to join them.

"What was?" Tarina countered. "And why weren't you two sitting where I told you?"

"Because we kept hearing creepy sounds!" Fitz told her.

Sophie reached for him, needing something to lean on again. Between the adrenaline and the reality of what could've happened if Tarina didn't have such fast reflexes . . .

"It felt like someone was watching us," she whispered to Tarina. "That was you, right?"

Tarina frowned. "I haven't been close—but I'd know if someone had been here. I . . ."

Her voice trailed off as her eyes focused on a tree several feet away.

She stalked closer, examining a broken branch, before looking down and sucking in a breath.

It took Sophie a second to spot what Tarina was seeing through the shadows.

Footprints.

Elvin footprints.

FORTY-TWO

I T COULD'VE BEEN LUZIA," FITZ SAID FOR what had to be the tenth time, repeating the conclusion that Tarina had come to.

And it did make sense. Luzia might've secretly stuck around to make sure Tam and Wylie pulled off her illusions without any problems. There was also no way to tell exactly how fresh the footprints were, so they could've been made earlier, when Luzia was figuring out where to place all of her mirrors.

Sophie had hailed Luzia to verify either theory, but Luzia didn't answer—which didn't mean anything, but . . . Sophie didn't like it. And the monster in her mind was wide awake now. Stalking her thoughts. Trying to stir up trouble. But she fought back the haunting voices with lots of deep breaths. And by leaning again on Fitz.

She was very aware of Wylie and Tam watching them, but Fitz didn't seem to care one bit. And that was good, because his shoulder was quickly becoming her favorite place in the whole world.

They stood as a group on the other side of the illusion, watching the trolls make their final preparations to the tower.

"What if it's not safe for the babies?" Sophie whispered.

"I can have my empress post guards here," Tarina offered.

It wasn't a bad idea. But Sophie couldn't help thinking about Luzia's vague warnings about the trollish empress and decided, "I want Sandor to sweep the forest as well. And Flori. And Bo. And Nubiti, if she hasn't already. And I want it to happen before we bring the babies here."

"Sounds like we have lots of teleporting to do," Tarina noted with surprisingly little whining.

And the next few hours were an exhausting blur.

By the time Tam and Wylie had leaped home—and Sophie, Fitz, and Tarina had brought Sandor, Flori, and Bo to patrol the tower—Edaline was hailing Sophie on her Imparter, warning that the babies needed to be implanted *soon*.

So they had to rush back to the beach to figure out how to safely transport the tiny, much paler alicorns. Which meant bringing Vika and Stina to help, and Timkin to boost Fitz's levitation. Grady and Edaline offered to come along too, but someone needed to help Silveny and Greyfell and bring them somewhere they could rest and recover.

They made Sophie promise to keep them updated—and to return to Havenfield as soon as everything was finished—and then it was back to the tower again, where the trolls took one look at the babies and insisted they be implanted *right* then.

Even watching it with her own eyes, Sophie couldn't begin to describe the implanting. All she knew was that there were lots of squishy tubes and an abundance of slime. And the last step apparently required them to stop the babies' hearts for some terrifying but necessary reason, and they all got to spend an endless moment holding their breath and waiting to see if the pulses would return.

Three seconds ticked by.

Five.

Ten.

And then the tower was filled with the soft flutter of two steady alicorn heartbeats.

"WE DID IT!" Fitz shouted, grabbing Sophie and spinning her around.

And for that one moment Sophie didn't care about the monster in her mind or her alliance with the trolls or what might be hiding in the shadows or how much trouble she was going to be in with Sandor for running off.

She didn't even care how closely Stina was watching as

she held on tight to Fitz and let him keep spinning and spinning her.

Because she could finally stretch out her consciousness and transmit with every bit of remaining mental energy, *BABY OKAY! BABY OKAY!*

FORTY-THREE

KAY, THAT MIGHT BE THE SWEET-est thing I've ever seen," Sophie murmured as she watched Silveny and Greyfell sleep in her favorite pasture at Havenfield—the one that caught just the right breeze and always ended up blanketed in petals from Calla's Panakes tree. Greyfell had his legs tucked underneath him and one wing draped protectively over Silveny, who lay on her side with her head resting against Greyfell's chest.

"I know," Fitz said quietly. "I never knew horses could snuggle."

He moved a little closer and Sophie had a feeling he was going to put his arm around her again—and she was all for that. But then his gaze drifted to Grady and his arm stayed noticeably by his side.

Grady had been watching them *very* closely since they'd gotten back from the new alicorn-baby hive—though "glaring" might've been a better word for it. And Edaline had been giving Sophie a lot of raised eyebrows and sappy smiles.

Parents.

"Do you think the alicorns will be safe here?" Sophie asked them, hoping a distraction would tone down the humiliation. Plus, it was a valid question. She'd had to move Silveny to the Sanctuary after the last time she'd lived at Havenfield—and even that hadn't been secure enough to keep the Neverseen from coming after her.

"They're free to go anytime they want," Edaline reminded her. "But I have a feeling they'll stay until the babies leave the hive—and they're probably going to want you to take them there as soon as Silveny's feeling up to it."

"But there's nothing for them to see," Sophie noted. "The tower's too narrow for them to go inside—and even if they could, all they'd see is their babies floating in a bunch of green goo."

"That may be," Edaline told her, "but, speaking as a mother, I promise, you won't be able to keep Silveny away from that tower."

"Yeah, probably not," Sophie begrudgingly agreed.

She'd already checked Silveny's dreams, to make sure the

worn-out mama wasn't haunted by nightmares from the stressful labor—and all she'd found was an endless replay of the moment Silveny had gotten to nuzzle her new son and daughter.

"Did Sandor say how much longer he'll be at the hive?" Grady asked.

"I wish," Sophie admitted. "But I'm guessing it'll be at least a few more hours."

Sandor and Tarina were both waiting for new goblin and troll guards to arrive, so Sandor had asked Bo and Flori to get Sophie back to Havenfield safely—which meant she'd already endured two lectures on why she should've taken a few seconds to find them before she ran off. But Sophie was certain that Sandor would have a *lot* more to say on the matter once he got home.

Sophie was tired just thinking about it.

"*Well*," Grady said, "I'm sure you two are both ready to get some rest, so . . ." His eyes narrowed at Fitz, all but kicking him off the property.

Edaline shook her head at him. "Don't be ridiculous. It's barely past sunset. And I'm sure they have *lots* to talk about."

And then, as if she wasn't being horrifyingly obvious enough, she gave Sophie another eyebrow raise and hooked her arm around Grady's, dragging him toward the house.

"Is it possible to die from embarrassment?" Sophie wondered as Grady grumbled a bunch of *loud* protests about how he'd rather stay out in the pastures.

Fitz laughed. "If you think they're bad, wait until my parents find out about us."

And there it was—the word that changed everything.

Us.

That was all it took for them to suddenly be . . . a thing.

And Sophie couldn't decide if she wanted to spin cartwheels or bury her face in her hands to hide her flushing cheeks.

"In case that sounded wrong," Fitz added quickly, "they're going to be *super* excited. Though Biana's probably going to follow me around saying *I told you so* a lot, so prepare yourself for that."

"She is?" Sophie asked. "You talked to her about . . . about this?"

For some reason, she couldn't throw out the "us" word as easily as Fitz had. But he didn't seem to notice.

"Yeah, she's been teasing me about it for a while—nagging me to stop wimping out and confess already. She tried to convince me to get you crush cuffs for a finals gift when you finished Level Three, but I didn't want to pressure you like that." He stepped closer, reaching for her hands and sounding so adorably shy as he told her, "But . . . if you want some, I'd go get them in a heartbeat."

"Wow," Sophie breathed. "That's . . ."

She couldn't find the words to finish that sentence.

To have him saying these things—after years of wishing and hoping and dreaming and . . .

It was . . . *unreal*.

And part of her wanted to grab him and kiss him silly.

But another part wanted to cry—and for some reason that wimpy part of her was winning.

"Hey," Fitz said, gently tilting up her chin so he could study her. "You okay?"

Her nod might've been the world's most unconvincing nod. And she waited for Fitz to freak out. She deserved that. He was being so sweet and honest and perfect, and she was . . .

What was she?

Scared, maybe?

And nervous.

And excited.

And not totally believing that any of this was real, and waiting for it to all turn out to be some huge misunderstanding.

And—

"Is this too much right now?" Fitz whispered. "I know it's been a *crazy* day, so . . . we can wait."

Sophie shook her head.

Waiting would only make it worse. Then there'd be even more pressure to say all the right things just like Fitz was.

And she wanted to.

Just like she wanted to go back to that moment in Everglen's reception hall, before Silveny interrupted them, when it all felt so exciting and incredible and not quite so real.

Real wasn't *bad*.

But it was . . . *complicated*.

It was parents and friends getting involved.

And the whole school knowing.

And . . . and crush cuffs. Which meant being "hopefuls." Which meant . . .

"Okay," Fitz said, blowing out a breath, "I think I know what's going on."

He led Sophie over to the Panakes tree, waiting for her to sit in the soft grass before he sat down across from her—mostly giving her space.

But their knees touched.

And Sophie's entire world narrowed to that tiny point of contact, everything fluttering so wildly that she couldn't meet his eyes. So she leaned back against the braided bark of Calla's tree and watched the wispy branches dance around them on a soft night breeze that smelled like flowers and the ocean and was laced with the faintest whisper of a sweet melody.

As far as romantic settings went, it was pretty much perfect— especially since this was where they'd already had a couple of other "moments."

And Sophie realized then . . .

Those really had been *moments*.

She hadn't been misreading the situation.

She'd just been too scared to believe it.

And now . . . she was terrified.

"So," Fitz said, watching her fidget with some of the fallen

blossoms. "Do you want to say it? Or do you want me to guess? Or do you want me to drop it and we'll just sit here and stare at the stars?" He glanced over his shoulder and pointed to the sky, which had faded to a peaceful swirl of purple and blue, brushed with flecks of twinkling glitter. "Anything's fine, Sophie. Seriously." He reached for her hand, gently tangling her gloved fingers with his. "I told you my new goal is to get you to trust me. And I mean it. I know this is hard for you. It's hard for me, too—but in a different way. I'm only worried you're going to laugh or—"

"I would *never* laugh," Sophie interrupted. "I *do* like you, Fitz. You . . . have no idea how much."

His smile shone in the dim light.

"I might have some idea," he said, reaching up to tuck a strand of her hair behind her ear—and Sophie couldn't help leaning into his hand. "So why don't you just tell me what's really going on in here," he added, tapping her temple as he made the request.

Sophie swallowed, fighting to find her voice. The most she could manage was a whisper. "I'm thinking . . . I want all of this to be real so badly, but . . . I can't really control that. Even if I register for the match . . ."

Fitz nodded. "I figured that's what you might be thinking." His fingers trailed gently across her cheek, triggering so many tingles she almost missed it when he said, "You don't have to worry about that, Sophie. There's no way we won't be matched."

It was really hard not to laugh. "How can you say that?"

"How can I not?"

"Oh please, let's . . . let's be realistic. You're this . . . golden child from this golden family, and I'm—"

"The most powerful elf our world has ever seen," he finished for her. "I know you don't see yourself that way—it's one of the things I like about you. You could be the most arrogant, obnoxious person ever, and you're not. But sometimes I wish you saw yourself a *little* clearer, so you'd actually believe me when I tell you this." He waited patiently for her to meet his eyes. "You're brilliant and talented and beautiful and—are you crying?"

"Sorry," she said as his thumb brushed away the tears she hadn't been able to blink back in time. "Sorry."

"Don't apologize!"

"Why? I'm being ridiculous. It's just . . . no one's ever said anything like that to me before."

And to have it coming from him . . .

He brushed another tear away, and she pretty much melted against his hand. "I'm glad I got to be the first to do it," he whispered, leaning close enough for his breath to tickle her damp cheek. "And I'm going to keep doing it until I make you believe me, okay? I mean it. I'm not giving up until you realize how awesome it's all going to be. And until then . . . we're good."

"We're good," Sophie repeated, the words like a splash of cold water.

"I don't mean it like a bad thing. I mean . . . we wait to do

FORTY-FOUR

GRADY AND EDALINE TRIED TO pretend that they hadn't been waiting for Sophie when she found them standing by the stairs after she'd finally said good night to Fitz. Just like they tried to pretend that they were simply making sure she didn't need help when they stopped by her room *three* times as she got ready for bed.

The fourth time Edaline came alone, and Sophie knew she was in for it.

"Let me make this easy, okay?" Edaline said, leaning against the door frame, either giving Sophie space or blocking her escape—it was hard to tell. "I trust you, Sophie. So you don't *have* to talk to me about how scared you were for Silveny and her this for real until you're ready. Until I can tell you I think you're amazing and it doesn't make you cry."

"I might always cry about that," she warned him.

He laughed softly. "Fine. Then until they're only happy tears. Okay? No pressure. No time limit. You set the pace and I'll just . . . follow your lead. But I'll be right here whenever you're ready—well, not *right* here because that'd get a little creepy. But . . . you know what I mean, right?"

She did, actually.

And it was . . . perfect.

All the panic had melted away.

"So," he said slowly, "we're good?"

"I think so," she said, still worrying she was about to lose something special.

But Fitz shook his head, like he knew what she was thinking, and whispered, "Just trust me, Sophie."

He leaned even closer and her heart became very aware that he might kiss her.

And she would've let him—and had *zero* regrets.

But when he closed his eyes, his lips only brushed her cheek, and he whispered, "Trust me," again.

And even though it wasn't everything . . .

It was a *real* beginning.

And for now, that was more than enough.

babies. Or about what happened with Alvar at Everglen. Just like you don't have to tell me what you said to Tarina to convince her to help, or where you guys went to get those transport pods. And we *definitely* don't have to discuss what's going on with you and Fitz. *But.* I'm your mom, so I have to at least make sure you know that if you *need* to talk about any of it, you can. I won't get upset. I'll even try my best to not make it embarrassing. And . . . you never know—I might be able to help. So . . . offer's on the table."

"Thanks," Sophie mumbled.

They stared at each other for a beat. Then Edaline nodded and turned to go. But she'd only taken one step before she glanced over her shoulder. "While I'm being honest, I should probably confess to peeking out the window a few times tonight while you and Fitz were having your very sweet moment."

Sophie groaned and covered her face with her hands. "I thought you said you wouldn't make this embarrassing."

"I said I'd *try*. Plus, there's nothing embarrassing about the way he was looking at you, Sophie. That boy is *smitten*. You know that, right?"

Sophie groaned louder. But after a second, she had to peek through her fingers and ask, "You really think so?" Which was a mistake, because the next thing she knew Edaline was plopping down next to her on the bed, settling in for a long heart-to-heart.

"Oh, stop trying to hide under the covers," Edaline said, grabbing Sophie's blankets before she could pull them over her head. "You asked the question. And yes, I think he's smitten.

He has been for a while. And I know he's always been special to you—don't even try to deny it. So . . . I'm glad you guys are finally figuring that out. Just try to be prepared for the fact that dating changes things, and—"

"We're not dating," Sophie interrupted.

Edaline's eyebrows raised.

"We're not. We're . . . waiting. Until it doesn't feel so scary."

"See?" Edaline said, leaning in to kiss her cheek "And *that* is why I trust you. You've always been such a smart girl, Sophie. And you've always been so good at staying true to yourself, despite the tremendous pressure you're under. I hope you hold fast to that and never feel pressured to be anything other than *you*." She reached for Sophie's healing hand, checking each of her knuckles—which were slightly swollen from all the strain—as she added, "And I hope you know how proud we are of how you handled everything with Silveny today. Those babies are alive because of you."

Sophie reached for Ella with her other hand. "I just hope they make it. I mean . . . they're safe right now, but there are still so many things that could go wrong."

"I know. But no matter what happens, you gave them the best possible chance you could. Be proud of that. Be proud of every choice you made today, even if you discover consequences later. And know that Grady and I are here to support you through whatever lies ahead."

"As am I," Sandor said from the doorway. "Though that's

difficult for me to do when you vanish without me. But"—he held up his hands to silence her explanation—"I realize I must accept the role I played in that decision. I chose to rely on your other bodyguards to keep you safe for a few hours. And that's exactly what Tarina did, even if it turned out to include much more adventure than I'd anticipated. So I can't fault any of you. But from now on, count on me not letting you out of my sight."

Sophie nodded. "How's the security at the hive?"

"Good. Tarina volunteered to stay the night to make sure the patrols are running smoothly. And none of them know what they're protecting, because we're trying to keep rumors to a minimum. So we stationed them all on the other side of the illusion. They think they're guarding the bridge."

"Smart," Sophie told him. "Thank you."

"Sure." He moved to his usual post, just outside her door, and it felt like proof that life was shifting back to normal.

"I should let you rest," Edaline told her, handing Sophie a vial of pink sedative. "Tomorrow will be another exhausting day."

"It will?" Sophie asked, not sure why she was surprised.

Edaline nodded. "Grady had to contact the Council and tell them what was happening. They'll be here first thing in the morning to have you answer some questions."

Sophie sighed and knocked back her elixir. "Of course."

When the Council said "first thing in the morning"—they meant it. The sun was barely beginning to warm the sky when

Sandor, Grady, and Bo led Sophie into the pastures, where all twelve Councillors were lined up around Silveny and Greyfell's enclosure.

Thankfully, both alicorns were still sleeping, too exhausted to notice their audience, who'd shown up in all their jewels and finery, likely trying to intimidate Sophie—though Oralie and Bronte gave her grateful smiles.

Lots of questions followed, many of which made it clear that the Council suspected another elf had been involved in her visit to the troll's hive—had *long* suspected it, in fact. But Sophie refused to give Luzia away and stuck with short, simple answers.

Councillor Emery sighed. "You're not going to make this easy, are you?"

"I'm pretty sure that's my job," Sophie countered.

"As the moonlark?" Councillor Alina asked with a notable scoff in her voice.

Sophie smiled sweetly at her. "As a teenager."

Bo made a choked sound that might've been a laugh.

Then the Council demanded to see the baby alicorns, and Sophie found it particularly enjoyable when she got to drag them, as well as Sandor and Bo, off a cliff. She may have even waited a second longer than necessary before she split the sky and plunged them into the void. And the landing might've intentionally been a little bumpy.

"First order of business," Councillor Alina said, shaking

bits of grass out of her now disheveled hair. "We're making a crystal to light leap to this place."

"Agreed," Councillor Emery said, his usually rich voice hoarse from all the screaming. "I've already noted the coordinates. And don't worry, Miss Foster, we'll only make one."

"Which *I'll* be in charge of," Bronte added.

They had to take turns filing into the hive to inspect the babies, and no one seemed to know what to make of the tiny alicorns floating in the thick green goo. But Tarina assured them that everything was going well, and that as long as nothing changed, they'd have happy, healthy babies hatching in a few weeks.

"Weeks?" Sophie repeated, counting in her head. "I think Silveny was supposed to be pregnant for longer than that."

"That won't matter," Tarina assured her. "I suspect they'll progress faster in the hives. Especially with the coming eclipse."

"What does the eclipse have to do with anything?" Councillor Terik wondered, beating Sophie to the question.

"Eclipses trigger hatchings," Tarina said, as if that were self-explanatory. "Though I suppose it's possible the effect won't be the same for another species. But you'll want to prepare for it just in case. The morning after the eclipse, you'll likely have two healthy alicorn babies on your hands."

Silveny and Greyfell were awake by the time Sophie leaped back to Havenfield with Sandor, Bo, and Tarina. And even though the recovering mama was too weak to stand up, she still managed to blast Sophie's brain with an abundance of *loud* transmissions.

SOPHIE! HI! BABY OKAY? BABY OKAY? VISIT! VISIT! VISIT!

I'll take you to see them as soon as you're strong enough, Sophie promised. *But you know you're not up for that yet. They're doing great, though.*

She shared her memories of the floating babies, and Silveny's mind clung to the images of their tiny sleeping faces. But the longer Silveny looked, the more Sophie's head felt like it might burst from the love and happiness and worry and sadness and loneliness and relief that was swelling inside her.

I know you miss them, she said gently.

MISS! MISS! MISS!

With each repetition, Silveny's sorrow seemed to deepen.

Hey, it's okay, Sophie promised. *You'll see them soon.*

And even though she didn't want to get Silveny's hopes up too high, she told her what Tarina had said about the eclipse. But Silveny didn't seem as excited as she'd expected her to be.

WEEKS? WEEKS? WEEKS?

I guess that probably sounds like a really long time to you, huh? Sophie realized. *But it's less than it would've been if you carried all the way to your due date. And I'm sure it'll go faster than you're thinking.*

Silveny and Greyfell shared a look. Then they both hung their heads.

Aw, none of that, Sophie told them, trying to think of a way to cheer them up.

Flying wasn't possible until Silveny was stronger. And the swizzlespice she brought over barely got a reaction.

Come on, there must be something that would make you happy, Sophie insisted.

Which of course brought on a lot of *VISIT BABY! VISIT BABY!* even though Silveny seemed to realize she couldn't handle teleporting yet. And the overwrought mama's mood seemed to spiral ever downward.

And then Sophie had an idea. *What about—*

KEEFE! KEEFE! KEEFE! Silveny transmitted, with a blast of joy so strong it nearly knocked Sophie over. And Sophie assumed Silveny must've seen what she'd been thinking before she'd had a chance to finish saying it.

Until Keefe said right behind her, "I hear I missed all the excitement."

"You're here?" Sophie asked, spinning around and catching a quick glimpse of the epic Bo-Ro glarefest going on before shifting her focus to Keefe. "Does that mean you lost the bet?"

"It does! And I'm sure I'm going to regret all of my life choices when Ro figures out her dare, *but* . . . sometimes you win, and . . ." He shrugged, adding a smirk that felt a little forced. "I mean, the thing is—if you and Fitz are visiting troll-baby hives without me, I am *definitely* losing at life, you know?

Plus, I knew Silveny was here, so of course she was going to be craving some quality Keefe time, isn't that right, Glitter Butt?"

KEEFE! KEEFE! KEEFE!

"See? She needs me. Can I go into the enclosure?"

"As long as Silveny doesn't mind," Sophie agreed.

A fresh round of *KEEFE! KEEFE! KEEFE!* made it clear Silveny was a big fan of that idea.

Sophie followed Keefe through the gate, stopping to stroke Greyfell's neck as Keefe crouched near Silveny and trailed his fingers gently down her velvet-soft nose. "Hey there, pretty mama," he said as she nuzzled his hand. "Should I call you Mama Glitter Butt now?"

Mama Glitter Butt! Mama Glitter Butt!

But the sadness had crept back into Silveny's thoughts.

Keefe scooted closer, holding her face with both hands as he looked into her eyes. "Don't be sad. *Nothing* bad is going to happen to those babies—not on Foster's watch. So you just rest up, okay? It'll all be better soon."

Soon! Soon! Soon! Silveny said with even less enthusiasm.

"Hmm. Feels like my brilliant pep talk isn't doing its job—so how about we play Name That Baby Alicorn? Otherwise I'm going to call them Sparkle Tushie Number One and Number Two. Actually, I'm probably going to call them that anyway—but I might *occasionally* go with something more official, as long as Mama and Papa pick something that pleases me."

Silveny didn't seem to understand anything he was saying, so Sophie did her best to explain telepathically.

Name baby? Name baby? Silveny asked, glancing at Greyfell.

"I don't think they've picked anything yet," Sophie told Keefe.

He clapped his hands. "Perfect! It's a girl and a boy, right? So how about Keeferina and the Keefster?"

"Keeferina?" Sophie had to ask.

Even Silveny looked like she was wincing.

"Or Keefette. Or Keefelle. Or Keefiana. Honestly, I thought you'd fight me harder on the Keefster."

"How about nothing with Keefe?" Sophie suggested.

"See, but there really is no better name, is there?" He glanced at Silveny, who definitely did not chant any Keefes. "Fine. Your loss. How about an homage to the Mysterious Miss F instead? We could have a little Sophie and a little Foster—though now that I'm saying that out loud, I'm realizing how confusing that would get. What's your middle name, again? Something with an *E*?"

"Elizabeth," Sophie confirmed. "What's yours?"

"It's 'Nope'—as in nope, we're *so* not going there."

"Why not?" Ro asked, momentarily breaking the Bo-Ro glarefest.

"Because I have enough humiliation in my immediate future, thanks to you," he told her.

"Yeah, I think you're going to have to tell me now," Sophie insisted.

"See, but I'm too busy naming alicorn babies. They're silver, right? So how about Sterling and Argent?"

"*Argent?*" Sophie repeated.

"Yeah, wow, I'm pretty bad at this. You might want to help, or I'm going back to Keeferina."

Sophie pictured the babies' tiny faces. "What about Luna for the girl? It means 'moon,' and she kinda looked like she was dipped in moonlight."

"Wow, look at you with the fancy logic!" Keefe teased, but Sophie could barely hear him as Silveny tried out the name in her mind.

Luna. Luna! LUNA!

"Huh," Sophie said, "I think she likes it."

"Yeah, I think she does," Keefe agreed, petting Silveny's nose again. "*And* this means we can still have a little Keefster!"

Silveny gave him some major alicorn side-eye.

"*Fine.* No Keefster—though you're missing out." He went back to thinking. "What about Wynn? Because we all know the little guy is going to be made of win!"

"I actually like Wynn," Sophie admitted, glancing at Silveny as she turned the name over in her mind.

Wynn. Wynn! WYNN!

Keefe smirked. "Feels like it's Wynn for the win!"

"Wynn and Luna," Sophie said. "I like it."

So did Silveny and Greyfell, who kept repeating both names over and over as Greyfell settled next to Silveny for more alicorn snuggling. And Sophie shot Keefe a grateful smile as they made their way out of the pasture.

"Thanks," she whispered. "You really got Silveny out of her funk."

"That's what I'm here for. To de-funk all the . . . You know what? I'm actually not sure where I'm going with that sentence."

Sophie wasn't either—which wasn't like him. His jokes were always so instant and effortless. And there was a strange, twitchy energy to the way he was moving, like someone who'd guzzled way too much caffeine.

Or someone who was nervous.

"So how did you know the alicorns were here?" she asked, leading him to the shade of Calla's Panakes tree.

Keefe didn't sit down beside her. Instead he stayed standing, kicking up fallen petals and shifting his weight from leg to leg. "Oh. I stopped by Everglen this morning. Figured it was time to be a good best friend and see how Fitzy was holding up, you know? And, um . . . he filled me in on . . . everything."

"Oh really?" Sophie asked, internally cringing at what those little pauses probably meant.

The one thing she and Fitz had forgotten to discuss was how much they were going to tell anyone about . . . whatever it was that was going on with them—not that it mattered with Keefe.

Empaths.

"And *there's* the mood shift," Keefe said quietly.

Sophie bit her lip, deciding denial was the only way to survive this. "I have no idea what you mean."

"Yeah, I figured you'd say that." He reached up, tearing a hand through his hair. "Okay. I know you don't want to do this—and trust me, it's the *last* thing I want to do. But . . . Fitz is my best friend. And you're . . . you. And no matter what . . . I don't want to ruin that. So . . . I figured you should know that I *know*, okay? I *know* something's changed."

Sophie took a steadying breath. "I don't—"

"Come on, Foster," Keefe interrupted with a sigh. "You know you can't lie to me. So yeah, maybe nothing's changed *officially* since I'm pretty sure Fitz would've bragged about it endlessly. But I can feel it. Right here." He pressed his hand against his heart. And for a second his features got all pinched and strained. "So I just wanted to say: You don't have to act like it's a secret. Because it's not. It never really has been, honestly. I've been waiting for you guys to figure it out for years. I'm pretty sure our whole group has, between all the blushing and the cute little gifts and the 'look at us, aren't we the cutest Cognates ever?' and the 'let's stare into each other's eyes and do some trust exercises,' and the 'teal is my favorite color in the whole world but no one realizes why.'"

He'd said the last few parts with such a spot-on impression of her voice that Sophie crossed her arms and scooted away from him. "Wow. Okay. Not sure why you're being such a jerk about it, but . . ."

Keefe dropped his gaze to the ground, kicking up lots more fallen petals. "You're right. I'm sorry. Those were just . . . bad jokes. I don't know why I made them." He swiped a hand through his hair again, letting out a long, slow sigh. "What I'm *trying* to say is . . . I knew this was coming. So . . . congrats! And as long as you guys don't expect me to start playing chaperone—and keep all Fitzphie smooching and snuggling far, far away—then . . . it doesn't have to be weird, okay?"

"Really?" Ro cut in. "*That's* what you want to tell her?"

"Yes," Keefe said through gritted teeth.

Ro snorted. "Maybe I should use my dare—"

"Don't," Keefe snapped, turning to face her. "Even you're not *that* mean."

"Are you sure?" Bo countered.

Ro drew a dagger from her breastplate and aimed it at him. "Give me one reason to use this. I'm *begging* you."

"I feel exactly the same way," Bo told her, drawing his sword.

And with that, Flori, Tarina, and Sandor all appeared from wherever they'd been lurking among the shadows.

"Oh, relax," Bo growled at them. "The princess and I won't be sparring anytime soon. We have to wait for that. Though I'm still hoping she'll change her mind, since she knows what will happen."

"I do," Ro agreed. "You'll finally realize that the only reason I've never beaten you is because I've been saving my best tricks for when it counts."

"Has it ever occurred to you that I'm doing the same thing?" Bo countered. "*And* I've still beaten you every single time?"

"Ugh, would you guys just admit you're in love with each other already?" Keefe told them. "If Fitzphie can do it, anyone can!"

Bo and Ro aimed their weapons at him—and Sophie was tempted to grab a throwing star and join in.

"Trust me, boy, if love were any part of this, it would make things *very* easy," Bo snarled at him.

"Don't," Ro commanded.

Bo ignored her. "You want to know what's going on between me and the princess? Ask her father—he's the one who arranged our marriage. Performed the ceremony himself, and gave us *these*."

He pointed to the tattoos on their foreheads, which actually **did kinda match.**

"So wait," Sophie said, trying to process. "You guys are *married*."

Ro gritted her teeth. "It's not what you're thinking."

"Uh, I'm thinking you're Mr. and Mrs. Bo-Ro," Keefe cut in.

Ro waved her dagger at him. "Don't make me hurt you— and you know I'm not talking about using this blade to do it." Keefe's **mouth snapped shut as she added, "Yes, we're married. But it's all just a formality. My father's foolish plan to protect** his two strongest warriors."

"Protecting *me* had nothing to do with this," Bo argued.

"Dimitar came to me personally—begged me to cooperate as a personal favor. Said it was the only way he could think of to prevent his headstrong daughter from getting herself killed in the final spar."

Ro's eyes flashed with betrayal and hate.

"Uh . . . final spar?" Keefe asked. "I think we're going to need a little more explanation."

Bo's glare had Keefe stumbling back a step. "In our world, our supreme leader isn't chosen by birth or inheritance. They're chosen by victory. And whenever the current ruler steps aside—or perishes—all of the top warriors who wish to take over must spar to the death. Whoever's left standing becomes the new king or queen, thereby earning the respect of the people and eliminating all possible usurpers."

"I suppose that's one way to do it," Tarina said, mostly under her breath.

"And my king knows that Romhilda can't—"

"IT'S RO!" she shouted, whipping her dagger at his head.

Bo knocked it away with his sword—along with the next dagger. And the one after that.

"You're proving your father's point! He knows if we spar, I *will* end you. But as my wife, there's no need for you to compete. You can be queen by *my* victory—and give our world the *two* strongest fighters as leaders."

"Or you can be king by *my* victory," Ro countered, "which is why *I* agreed to the arrangement. Then you'll still be alive to handle the army since I find soldiers annoying. And I'll rule the people."

"Aw, isn't this the most romantic thing you've ever heard?" Keefe asked Sophie. "Really hits you in the feels. A love story for the ages."

"I told you," Bo growled. "Love has no part in this. And it's far better that way. A king needs a clear head and unbiased judgment. Love only gets in the way. And if you don't believe me, why don't you ask Ro about Cadfael?"

"Cadfael," Sophie repeated, needing a second to place the name. "You mean the guy who's probably the leader of all the ogres who defected to the Neverseen?"

"That would be him. Ro didn't tell you?" Bo asked with the most vicious smile Sophie had ever seen. "He's her ex-boyfriend."

To say Sandor was unhappy that Ro had a personal connection to the enemy was an understatement—especially since she'd had plenty of chances to reveal that information. And no matter how many times Ro insisted that she'd have zero problem ending Cadfael's life—and that she'd only kept their relationship secret because she knew it would distract everyone with foolish conclusions—Sandor kept right on muttering "compromised" under his breath.

"Compromised?" Ro eventually snapped. "You want to talk about compromised? What happens if you have to decide between saving your little girlfriend, or saving one of us? And you"—she pointed at Keefe—"what happens the next time you face your mom? Is there any way you'd follow an order to stand down—even if there was a good reason to do exactly that? Just like we know your Vanisher friend is desperate to get her invisible little hands on Vespera after what happened in that creepy mirrored place. And her brother will take any excuse to smash his brother's face in, even if it ends up being the wrong call. Even you"—her eyes shifted to Sophie—"I'm betting their Shade is going to be your number one target, after all you've gone through with those echoes. Or maybe you'll want the Telepath for the threats he made during the attack. Or revenge on Keefe's mom for the mess you've seen in his memories. Actually, you're a bad example, since you have good reasons to hate *everybody*—and you're also always trying to save everybody, so you're going to be a mess of conflicted decisions. My point is, the idea of 'no biases in battle' is a myth. We all have them. Especially when there are this many enemies."

"*Too* many," Sophie mumbled under her breath. They seriously had *way* too many enemies.

Sandor sighed and rubbed his forehead. "All of that may be true, but I'm sure you can still see my dilemma."

"Fine—you want me to prove my loyalty?" Ro countered. "Let me run the next training session. I'll teach everyone the easiest ways to cut down one of my kind."

Bo cleared his throat. "I don't think that's wise."

"Of course you don't," Ro snapped back. "Because you don't actually care about this assignment. You're just here to cause drama until I agree to give my father whatever he wants to make him reassign you. And I'm sure that's what you're hoping for too, so you can get out of sparkle town. But guess what, hubby? I'm done giving either of you what you want. You get to be stuck here with me until you're ready to claw your eyes out from all the glitter. And you can watch me do everything in my power to prepare these kids for the battles coming their way, because like it or not, *they* are the only ones who are going to clean up this mess."

"See, I was with you right up until you called us kids," Keefe told her, and it was a miracle Ro didn't launch a dagger at his head.

Instead, she straightened up and said to no one in particular, "If you're done questioning my loyalty, and you've soaked up enough of my personal drama, follow me and I'll teach you something that will save your life."

She stalked deeper into the pastures, and Sophie and Keefe shared a look before they turned to follow her. And the rest of the afternoon was filled with learning where all of the ogres' pressure points were. They weren't always where Sophie would've expected—they were in the back of the elbow, and the underside of their nose, and between their pointer and middle fingers.

"You really won't get in trouble for teaching us this stuff?" Sophie had to ask when Ro showed them an opening in the way the ogres swung their swords, which left a moment where their elbow was particularly vulnerable.

"Please, if an elf with a few hours of training can take us down, we deserve to die," Ro countered. "But Cadfael won't expect you to know it. And I want to see the look on his face when that costs him a few of his grunts."

So she made them practice the punches and stabs and thrusts that would inflict the most pain over and over and over, until Sophie and Keefe were both sweaty and out of breath and dead on their feet.

"You should probably take a break," Keefe said as he watched Sophie study her right hand. She'd trained mostly with her left, but her knuckles were still swollen from the day before.

"Yeah, I need to check on Silveny anyway." She turned to head toward the alicorns' pasture. But she'd only made it a few steps before Keefe ran to catch up with her.

"Hey, Foster?" he said, stepping in front of her to block the path. "I'm . . . really sorry about earlier. I never should've said the stuff I said. What I meant to say is . . . I'm really happy for you—and Fitz. You guys are perfect for each other."

Sophie's face burned. So did her eyes. And she couldn't decide if the tangled emotions clawing up her throat were proof that she definitely wasn't ready for things with Fitz to be public—or because she still couldn't imagine people using the word "perfect" to describe the two of them together. But she told Keefe, "Thanks."

He tore his hands through his hair again, looking like he was changing his mind about his next words several times before he said, "So . . . you don't hate me?"

Sophie rolled her eyes. "Ugh, how many times do I have to tell you—I'm never going to hate you!"

His smile looked tired. "Well. I guess that's good enough. For now."

Mr. Forkle stopped by that evening, and once Grady and Edaline had gone upstairs—and Sandor had led the other bodyguards outside for patrols—Sophie decided to tell him everything.

Well, everything except the mushy Fitz stuff, because . . . *no*.

But she told him about the alliance she'd made with Tarina, even though she knew he'd probably be upset that she didn't wait to find out what he learned through his research. And she told him about Luzia, because the Black Swan needed to know there'd once been a troll hive at Everglen. Plus, she wanted someone else to hear what Luzia had implied about the challenges of working with the empress.

"Do you think I made a mistake agreeing to the alliance?" she whispered when Mr. Forkle rose from his spot on the couch and paced to the windows overlooking Havenfield's pastures.

"I *think*," he said slowly, "that you made the best possible decision under the given circumstances. Which is all any of us would ever ask."

Breathing became a little easier. But Sophie still felt the need to add, "What if the trolls want something I can't give?"

"Well, if it helps, I haven't found anything troubling about Empress Pernille in my research. But if Luzia turns out to be right, then you'll make the best possible decision whenever the time comes. Life is a series of hard choices, Miss Foster. The most you can do is face them one at a time."

"Does that mean you're not mad at me for making the deal without checking with you?"

"Of course I'm not. If you'd delayed, I'd be staring at two devastated alicorns right now, and their babies would've been lost." He stared at his swollen, wrinkled hands, twisting the thick fingers together. "The truth is, now that there's only one of me, I'm falling further and further behind in my responsibilities, and the Black Swan is suffering. We've been all but useless to you these last several weeks—myself especially. I still haven't even finished arranging your meeting with Fintan—though I'm getting close. But the good news is, you're growing more confident with each passing day. And I know I speak for the entire Collective when I say that we trust your judgment. I'm also grateful you've been willing to confide in me about all of this. Perhaps it's proof that you're ready to take on even greater responsibility in the order."

Sophie sat up straighter. "Like what?"

"I'm not sure yet." He gazed blankly into the distance for several seconds before his focus shifted back to the pastures.

"You realize as soon as Silveny's able, she's going to head straight to her babies. I'm sure she's already plucked images of the tower from your mind so she'll be ready to teleport."

"Is that bad?"

"It depends on how high Luzia's illusions stretch into the sky. Would you be willing to take me there to check?"

"Now?"

"Unless you're too tired—"

"I'm fine. But I need to clear it with Sandor. If I disappear again, he might handcuff himself to my wrist."

Mr. Forkle smiled. "I could see him doing that."

Not surprisingly, all of her bodyguards insisted on joining them. And Grady and Edaline asked to tag along. So it turned out to be quite a large group that jumped off Havenfield's moonlit cliffs. And Sophie was glad to have the company when she saw how eerie the tower's clearing looked at night, with all the shifting shadows. The hive itself also felt even more alien now that the only light was coming from the glowing green fluid surrounding the tube-covered babies.

"Hey, Luna," she whispered, wishing the tiny alicorn would blink or stir or do *something* to prove that she really was okay.

But Luna stayed fast asleep.

So did Wynn.

"Did I miss when you named them?" Edaline asked.

"Yeah, Keefe brought it up today—and be glad Silveny didn't go with Keeferina and the Keefster."

Grady sighed. "That boy."

"He's quite the character," Mr. Forkle agreed, heading outside to study Luzia's illusion. "It's a brilliant design," he murmured, squatting to examine a few of the carefully placed mirrors.

"Then why are you frowning?" Sophie wondered aloud.

"Well, for one thing, the masking on the sky is quite thin, so it does seem like it'd be safer for Silveny and Greyfell to keep their distance—which won't be easy to convince them to do."

"And the other thing?" Sophie pressed.

"I'm not sure if it counts as a *thing*, but . . . using mirrors for camouflage this way . . . that's the method Vespera developed." *And I realize Luzia already admitted at Alvar's Tribunal that she used Vespera's methods,* he added telepathically. *But it does make me wonder how much contact the two actually had. I think it might be time to pay Luzia a visit.*

Won't that make it pretty obvious that I told you about her?

Probably—but don't look so nervous. Luzia's no fool. I'm sure she's assuming you're going to tell someone in our order. And she knows the Black Swan has no problem hiding things from the Council, so she doesn't have any reason to be worried. I'm honestly surprised she never reached out to us before—especially when she was helping the trolls relocate their hive to Dawnheath. That had to have been a tremendous endeavor.

Do you think it's weird that she had Alden install the gate around Everglen after she moved out? I mean . . . if the hive's destroyed, why would he need it? And why didn't she have that kind of security when she lived there?

I can see why that might feel significant. But it's important to remember that our world hasn't always been so tumultuous. Up until a few decades ago, things truly were peaceful enough that she wouldn't have needed that level of security. I also suspect that adding the fence to Everglen was her way of normalizing the one she added at Dawnheath, as well as a means of protecting any lingering evidence that might remain of the hive. You said Mr. Vacker's going to be searching for it?

Sophie nodded, realizing she should check in with Fitz to see if he found anything.

Cue all the flutters.

Keep me posted, Mr. Forkle told her, standing and pulling out his pathfinder. *I'll be Magnate Leto again starting tomorrow. Hail me anytime. Or stop by my office on Monday.*

Monday?

He smiled. *Yes, Miss Foster. Your arm has recovered nicely, and I don't want you falling too far behind on your studies. So I think it's time for you and Mr. Vacker to return to Foxfire.*

School was the *last* thing Sophie felt like adding to her to-do list. But apparently it wasn't optional. So Monday morning she found herself dressed in one of the Level Four uniforms that Flori had added secret pockets to, trying to decide which was making her palms sweatier: knowing she was about to walk onto campus trailed by her multispeciesial entourage, or knowing she was about to face a million awkward decisions about how to act around Fitz in such a public place—with Keefe watching.

And the day was every bit as disastrous as she'd imagined. Like when she stepped into the glass pyramid for morning orientation and the entire room went pin-drop silent. Or how Bo kept growling, "What are you staring at?" to everyone they passed in the halls. Or lunch, when Sophie chose to sit between Keefe and Dex because she was worried it'd look too suspicious if she sat next to Fitz, and when she'd met his beautiful eyes, he'd looked . . . super hurt. Add in the fact that she hadn't caught up on all of her missed assignments—and the fact that her writing was still mostly illegible—and it was almost a relief when she got called into the Healing Center on her way to study hall. Guzzling gross elixirs would be way easier than trying to figure out how to apologize to Fitz without the rest of their friends noticing.

But when she got to the Healing Center, Fitz was there, leaning against the cot he'd been stuck in for all those weeks. And he wouldn't meet her eyes.

"I think we should wait in the hall and keep an eye on anyone approaching," Grizel told Sandor and the other guards, which didn't sound that suspicious until she shot Sophie a look that seemed to say *good luck* as she herded everyone back out the door, leaving Sophie and Fitz alone.

Sophie glanced over her shoulder, noting that Elwin was in

his office as she moved to Fitz's side, careful to keep a couple of inches between them. "I'm sorry. I *wanted* to sit next to you. It just felt like that would start a bunch of gossip—which is silly, I know. It's not like we never sit together. I'm . . . really bad at this."

Fitz sighed. "It's not your fault. I thought we'd have a couple more weeks to figure stuff out before we had to be back here."

"So did I." She hesitated a beat and reached for his hand, letting out a relieved breath when he didn't pull away. "I know I'm overthinking everything. I just . . ."

"I know." He trailed his thumb over the back of her hand, causing a zillion tingles. "I'm sorry too. I'd just been looking forward to sitting next to you all day."

Oh wow.

It was amazing she didn't melt into a puddle of goo right there.

She might have, if she hadn't caught a glimpse of Elwin heading toward them. And she was trying to decide what to do about the fact that she was still holding Fitz's hand, when Fitz made the decision for her, giving her fingers a reassuring squeeze before gently letting go.

"Just like old times," Elwin announced, setting down the trays of medicine he'd been carrying. "But first, let's see how you're doing."

He flashed several colorful orbs around Sophie's arm, not looking happy about her knuckles swelling. And Fitz apparently had some similar swelling in his bad leg.

"Well, I can't say I'm surprised, since I heard about the crazy day you guys had with those alicorn babies. That's why I called you in—well, that, and Lady Zillah is wondering about your echoes. Do they still stir?"

Fitz nodded, rubbing his chest. "I'm good most of the time, but big mood swings get me."

"Pretty much the same for me," Sophie agreed. "And I still take sedatives every night to avoid nightmares."

Elwin reached up to muss his hair. "Well, I know this is going to sound risky, but Lady Zillah said it might help if she knew exactly how many seconds it takes before the echoes react. So do you think you could each take turns thinking about one of your triggers so I can time it? I'll be right here to help with anything you need."

Sophie and Fitz shared a look before Fitz hopped up on the cot and sat leaning against the wall. And Sophie had a feeling he let himself think about Alvar, because in about ten seconds he was clutching his chest and gulping down breaths.

Sophie's reaction took a little longer.

She started with Gethen's taunts, letting his horrible voice flood her mind—and she could feel the monster lift its head. But the beast didn't get up, staying put through each of the other haunting voices that Sophie let join the punishing chorus. Until she dredged up the one she'd buried the deepest.

Sophie, please—stop!

The second her sister's terrified voice rang through her mind, the monster was thrashing and kicking—and so was she.

"It's okay," Fitz told her, taking her hand again. "Just breathe."

She was trying. But the monster fought back, clawing and scraping against her consciousness.

"Breathe with me," Fitz told her, setting the rhythm—and she clung to his hand like an anchor as she let their breaths fall in sync.

Slowly, steadily, the beast skulked back to the shadows.

"The good news," Elwin said, sounding a bit shaken as he flashed an orb of light around her, "is that I don't see any damage. So you are getting stronger. And hopefully these readings will help Lady Zillah find an answer."

Sophie hoped so too.

But until then, she had to stay far, far away from that memory—even if it killed her to be so close to the truth and leave it buried.

"You okay?" Fitz asked as she chugged her medicine with trembling hands.

She nodded.

But she must not have been very convincing, because Fitz checked on her again before she went to bed that night.

Are you sure the sedative will be enough to keep the nightmares away? he asked.

I think so. Especially since Flori sang a little bit of her new song to me. She only has one verse right now, but . . . it's crazy how the melody makes everything warm and tingly. It does seem like it might be the solution, once she figures out the rest of the verses.

Does she know how long it'll be?

No. But she said she works on it every night while we sleep. So hopefully soon.

By the end of that first week back at Foxfire, Sophie's life had fallen into a new pattern with school in the mornings followed by training in the afternoons with any friends who gathered at Havenfield.

Fitz always went home to Everglen, hoping to find some trace of the old troll hive. But every night he'd check in telepathically—and even though he never had any news to report, all those conversations really helped things feel less strange and scary between them.

They sat next to each other every day during lunch, and if their friends noticed, they didn't bring it up.

Even Biana.

Even *Keefe*—though he wasn't around very much. He landed in lunch detention on day two for some random prank he never bothered to explain. And his father was still insisting on having their private Empath lessons, so he had to rush home every day as soon as Foxfire ended.

And Tam had to leave Havenfield by sunset for his shadow-flux lessons with Lady Zillah.

And Dex still spent most of his time with Tinker. But he'd stop by when he had completed creations to deliver, like their newly enhanced panic switches—which could now send a quick voice recording of what they were facing—and these fancy new gadgets that reminded Sophie of a twenty-sided die and unleashed a cloud of mist meant to scatter someone's concentration.

Flori spent her days making everyone new clothes so they'd all have plenty of pockets to tuck things away in, and her nights wandering the forest in search of song lyrics. So Sandor, Tarina, and Bo took turns training Sophie, Linh, Marella, Biana, and Wylie—though the rest of them could train much longer than Sophie's arm would let her. But whenever she had to stop early, she spent the extra time keeping Silveny and Greyfell company.

The anxious alicorns had *not* been happy when Sophie warned them that visiting their babies might give away their location. But they didn't argue. Silveny seemed to realize that all the months she'd spent ignoring Sophie's advice had nearly cost the babies their lives, and she was determined not to make the same mistake again—even if it was breaking her heart to stay away from them.

Sophie tried to keep Silveny's spirits up by passing along the updates Tarina got every morning from the trolls who were keeping an eye on the babies. But there wasn't a whole lot of actual news to share. Luna and Wynn were stable, but progressing slower than expected. In fact, by the end of the second week, the trolls were convinced the babies wouldn't be hatching during the coming eclipse. Which made sense, considering how much time should have been left in Silveny's pregnancy.

But Silveny was devastated.

And after three days of watching her mope around her pasture, ignoring food and treats and everyone, Sophie tried a new tactic.

Fly with me? she asked, pointing at the sky.

Fly? Silveny repeated, not sounding nearly as excited as Sophie wanted.

But Sophie kept pushing, sending memories of all the times they'd flown together, and reminding Silveny of how long it'd been. And when that *still* didn't convince her, Sophie played her secret weapon.

Please? she asked. *It might help me have better dreams tonight.*

Help Sophie? Silveny said, her mind turning over the words until they shifted from a question to an answer. *Help Sophie! Help Sophie! Help Sophie!*

"What are you doing?" Linh asked as Sophie pulled her hair back into a ponytail and headed for the enclosure. "Are you guys going to fly?"

"That's the plan," Sophie agreed, and Linh let out a giddy squeal.

"Can I come too? I'm *so* over battle training. And Tam just left. And . . . okay, I just really really really want to fly with the pretty, sparkly horses!"

Sophie laughed and glanced at Greyfell, transmitting Linh's request. He sized Linh up for a second, then lowered into a crouch—his way of saying *sure, climb aboard*—causing a whole lot more squealing as Linh sprinted into the pasture and practically leaped onto Greyfell's muscled back.

And Silveny seemed much more excited by the idea as she bent to let Sophie climb on.

Thanks, Mama Glitter Butt, Sophie told her, wrapping her arms around Silveny's neck as Silveny flapped her enormous wings, launching them airborne.

They didn't fly far, just circled the pastures as the sky shifted from twilight to glittering night. A full moon lit up the sky, bouncing off the clouds as they dipped and dove and swooped through the sea of stars. And the higher they flew, the more Silveny's heart seemed to lift, until she sounded much more like her usual self.

SOPHIE! FRIEND! FLY!

Fly! Sophie agreed.

And they did. For hours and hours until they all felt ready for a good night's sleep.

But Grady was waiting for them when they landed. And he had a note from Mr. Forkle, which had Sophie wide awake again.

There were no clues or mysteries like in the messages the Black Swan used to leave her. Just a simple, clear instruction:

Prepare yourself. The Council has finalized your meeting with Fintan. At the end of the week, I'll be bringing you and Fitz to his cell.

FORTY-FIVE

OU DON'T HAVE TO BE NERVOUS,"
Fitz said, reaching for Sophie's wrist to stop
her before she could tug out any more itchy
eyelashes.

"I'm trying not to be," she promised.

After all, they'd been preparing for this moment all week.

They'd worked through hours and hours of trust exercises—
which were surprisingly easy, now that all the crush stuff was
out in the open between them. And they'd rehearsed different
conversation tactics over and over again.

But . . . this was *Fintan*.

Every time Sophie thought his name, she could hear her

human parents' voices in her mind, explaining all the reasons she should *never* play with fire.

And yet, here she was, stepping right back into Fintan's game.

She pushed her long sleeves up to her elbows, wishing Mr. Forkle would hurry. He was a few minutes late—and since he'd told them to dress as warmly as possible, it was getting pretty miserable waiting outside. But when they'd tried waiting *inside*, they'd had to deal with Edaline's sappy smiles and Grady's glaring, so standing in the sun in heavy clothes was a worthwhile sacrifice.

Still, Sophie wished she'd chosen something that breathed a little better than her layered gray tunic and velvet cape—plus black pants and boots and gloves and a knitted cap she still wasn't sure if she should've let Vertina talk her into. Fitz had called it cute, but . . . it had a sparkly pom-pom on the top.

"Okay," he said, leading her into the shade—which did help a little. "I was going to save this for later, but I think you need a distraction."

"Uh . . . what kind of distraction?" she asked, very aware that they were back under the swaying branches of Calla's Panakes tree.

Fitz's lips curled into a shy smile. "I realized it'd been a while since I gave you a present. So I snuck over to Atlantis this morning and . . ." He reached into the pocket of his burgundy cape and pulled out a small silver box. "I *really* hope you don't hate it. Biana's always telling me I have the worst taste in gifts—but . . . I figured it'd be weird letting my sister shop for my . . . for you."

Sophie didn't miss that tiny slip.

But . . . had he been about to call her his 'girlfriend'?

Or his 'hopeful'?

Because there was a *big* difference.

In fact, even with all their Cognate training, they'd still never addressed the questions that sat between them like a giant, gaping chasm.

Was she going to register for the match?

And if she didn't . . . ?

"Here," Fitz said, handing her the box.

The size and shape screamed *jewelry*—and Sophie's stomach felt extra flippy as she lifted the lid and . . .

"Oh wow."

"Do you hate it?" he whispered, sounding genuinely worried as she traced her fingers over the shimmering teal pendant.

It was shaped like a heart.

She shook her head, trying to find something to say that wouldn't be embarrassingly mushy. "It's . . . beautiful."

Fitz beamed. "Here, I'll help you put it on."

He stepped behind her and swept her hair aside, and she was pretty sure she didn't breathe the entire time he tied the silk cord around her neck.

They didn't have a mirror, but she could tell the pendant

hung just below her collarbone, where everyone would see it—and probably know exactly what it meant.

But . . . that was good, wasn't it?

That was—

Someone cleared his throat, and Sophie whipped around to find Mr. Forkle giving them a raised-eyebrow look that had Fitz's cheeks flushing adorably red.

"Sorry I'm late," Mr. Forkle told them. "It ended up being much more difficult to switch identities today than I expected."

Sophie frowned. "Wait—if Fintan sees you like that, he'll know you're still alive."

"Which is why I won't let him see me unless I decide I want to. *This*"—he gestured to his swollen face—"is a backup plan, in case we need to regain the upper hand in the conversation. A way to shock some of the bravado out of him."

"And you're sure we shouldn't be joining you?" Tarina asked as she stepped out of the shadows with Bo and Flori.

Sandor and Grizel were the only guards that the Council had approved for the visit—and even they weren't allowed inside the actual prison.

Mr. Forkle nodded. "The Council's decision is final. They wouldn't even give me a permanent crystal, for fear I might try to copy it. They're being *very* cautious. So it will just be the five of us. And we'll be leaping there with this." He held up a smooth stone with a single fleck of glitter glinting in the center and waved for Sophie, Fitz, Sandor, and Grizel to gather around him.

Sweat was dripping down his face—probably from the thick tunic he was wearing, along with two layers of capes. But it might've also been a hint of nerves.

His hand even trembled as Sophie reached for it, and she realized . . .

This would be the first time he'd face one of his brother's killers.

"You okay?" she asked him.

He nodded. "But let's make today count."

"H-how ar-are y-y-you n-not sh-sh-shivering?" Fitz asked Sophie as they trudged through the knee-deep snow. The cave they were aiming for was only a few hundred yards away, but given the way their legs kept sinking in, it was quite the epic trudge.

"Keefe helped me practice body temperature regulation," Sophie explained, wishing she'd thought to use the skill when she'd been sweating at Havenfield. "The trick is to focus on friction, like where your clothes rub your skin or where your toes scrape the sides of your boots. That's all generating little bursts of heat your mind can amplify."

"Huh." Fitz's eyebrows crunched together—and so did Mr. Forkle's—like they were each attempting to apply the tactic. But neither seemed to have much success as they shivered through the final paces to the icicle-crusted cave, which looked like a giant mouth jutting out of the frozen earth, eager to devour them with jagged teeth.

"If the cold gets to be too much, I'm sure they have extra cloaks tucked away somewhere," Mr. Forkle told Sandor and Grizel as they moved to join the other, much warmer-dressed goblin guards lined up like sentinels on each side of the arched entrance.

"We'll be fine," Sandor said, shooting Sophie a look that seemed to say, *Be careful—and hurry.*

She nodded, watching Mr. Forkle and Fitz disappear into the prison. But she needed a second before she could follow.

Caves always triggered their own special flashbacks and nightmares, thanks to her kidnapping. So she inhaled a few long breaths to let the monster know *she* was still in control, before she took a cautious step forward, out of the wind and into the cavern.

She'd planned to catch right up with the others, but the cave's floor was solid ice, so she had to tread slowly to keep from slipping. Plus, her eyes needed time to adjust to the dim blue light radiating from bioluminescent spheres dangling from the arched ceiling. Her breath clouded in front of her and she focused on the burn in her tired leg muscles as she followed a path that wound down into the frozen earth.

Soon everything was ice—the walls, the floor, the ceiling. No heat. No kindling, except the clothes they were wearing—which might actually be a problem.

"Should we be wearing something fire resistant, like we did in Oblivimyre?" Sophie whisper-hissed, wondering why she hadn't thought to ask before.

"No," Mr. Forkle called back to her, his voice bouncing off the walls and making some of the ice crackle. "Fintan cannot spark a flame here—you truly can trust that. And dressing this way shows him how inconsequential he's become—how your only concern today was for your own comfort. Trust me, that will eat at him more than you could ever imagine."

"I guess," Sophie mumbled as the path curved so sharply that she lost sight of everyone. But when she rounded the bend, she found Fitz waiting for her.

He offered his arm. "Sorry, I shouldn't have gone ahead without you."

"I was fine," she assured him. But she was glad to have someone to lean on when the floor angled sharply downhill a few curves later.

"Think it'd be easier to plop down and slide the rest of the way?" Fitz asked.

"No," Mr. Forkle called back to him.

"I'm more worried about what it's going to be like climbing back out of here," Sophie admitted.

Fitz groaned. "I wasn't even thinking about that."

On and on the path stretched, until Sophie was starting to feel pretty tempted by Fitz's treat-the-prison-like-a-frozen-waterslide plan. But then it curved again and widened into a frozen bubble of a room, with a narrow walkway surrounding a smaller, inner ice bubble. And sitting inside on a lone block of ice was a sickeningly familiar blond elf with pointed Ancient ears.

"Fintan," Fitz whispered, and Sophie jumped in front of Mr. Forkle, fanning out the sides of her cape and trying to shield him as much as she could.

"Relax, Miss Foster," Mr. Forkle told her. "*We* can hear and view him from all sides. But the bubble is reflective on his side—everywhere except the point right there." He gestured to where two throne-size chairs carved from clear ice had been set up outside the bubble, facing straight at Fintan. "I'm told there's a sensor in the floor that activates once you're seated, allowing Fintan to hear you. So don't sit until you're ready. And remember: *He* called this meeting, so let *him* carry the conversation. Never forget that every word he says may be a lie to manipulate you. Do *not* react. Do not volunteer *any* information. And if you need to communicate with each other, do it telepathically. Also: Be very careful about when and how you attempt to enter his mind. Fintan may not be a Telepath, but he's been defending his thoughts for millennia."

It was the same instructions they'd gone over *many* times. But it was still good to have the reminder as Sophie and Fitz made their way toward the icy thrones.

Fintan's sky blue eyes watched their every move as they sat down, and Sophie felt the monster stir inside her, eager to tear into all of her worst Fintan nightmares. But she met Fintan's gaze head-on—and maybe it was the dim lighting, or the dirty-dishwater color of his wrinkled robe, but he looked older than she remembered.

Haggard.

Not that it stopped him from twisting his slender features into a chilly smile. "Miss Foster. Mr. Vacker. How nice of you to finally join me."

They each took a calming breath as they nodded.

"Oh, let me guess. You're planning to follow the whole let-the-prisoner-do-all-the-talking approach? I think you're forgetting that I practically invented that strategy back when I was young and naive and serving the wrong side. Much like you are now." He paused, like he'd expected to earn a rise from them. "Very well. I guess you'd prefer we simply stare at each other?"

"We'd *prefer* you to tell us why you asked us to come here," Fitz countered.

"Well, I couldn't exactly come to see you, now could I? So welcome to my humble home!" He waved his hands around his frozen bubble, drawing more attention to the sparseness of it. Save for the block of ice he sat on—and three others stacked behind him—the space was empty. Sophie also noticed how thin the fabric of his crumpled robe looked. Definitely not something that would provide much escape from the cold. His lips even had a faint blue tinge as he said, "Tell me, Sophie, does it make you happy to see the cold reality of my conditions? Have you been picturing me bathed in luxury, idling my days away while feasting on delicacies and celebrating my glorious accomplishments?"

Sophie shrugged, refusing to admit how close he was to some of her imaginings.

"Enough with the silence!" He stomped his feet against the icy floor—hard enough to cause a few hairline cracks. "You've wasted too much time already."

"We've barely been here five minutes," Fitz corrected.

"And how many weeks have passed since I extended the invitation?" Fintan argued. "I expected you to be far more eager."

"Well," Sophie told him, crossing her arms, "I guess we're not as predictable as you thought."

He gritted his teeth. "You're picking a *very* bad time to play games."

"*We're* playing games?" Fitz snapped.

"Of course you are. You think I don't realize you're sitting there trying to keep me distracted so I won't notice that someone's trying to slip into my mind—and not doing a very good job, I might add, so I'm guessing it's you," he said to Fitz. "You think I didn't plan on you coming here with all sorts of ridiculous plans for how to steal my memories? I can assure you—you won't learn anything that way. Not even you, Sophie. But if you want to know what I'm thinking, all you need to do is ask."

"Right," Fitz scoffed. "So you can feed us a bunch of lies?"

"Actually"—he leaned back as far as he could on his block of ice, like he was attempting to get more comfortable yet looking anything but—"today I'm prepared to offer some vital truth."

Sophie laughed. "You expect us to believe that?"

"No. But I expect you to believe that I invited you here

because I want something from you. Surely you've already assumed that much. Just like I can assume you'll never give it to me for free. So . . . I'm willing to offer a trade—and it's the deal of the century for you, because I happen to have some valuable information about what you'll soon be facing." He studied their faces, clicking his tongue. "Such jaded skepticism from elves so young. Though I suppose I can't truly blame you, given how many times you've lost—and *whom* you've lost."

Part of Sophie wanted Mr. Forkle to step forward right then and shout, "DO YOU MEAN ME?"

But they didn't need anything so drastic. Not when she could turn to Fitz and say, "I told you this would be pointless."

And Fitz could nod and start to stand.

"Oh, are we to the part where you pretend to walk away?" Fintan asked.

"No, we're to the part where we *actually* walk away," Sophie told him, leaning closer to the curve of ice separating them. "You want to know why we took so long to come here? Because we've realized that You. Don't. Matter. Vespera would've amended all of her plans the second you were arrested. And Gisela's running things now anyway."

"Trust me—Vespera won't let anyone *run* her. And certain parts of her plans *can't* change—not unless she wants to wait for the next Celestial Festival."

Fitz sat back down.

Fintan smirked. "Looks like I finally have your attention."

Should we shove into his mind now? Fitz transmitted. *Whatever he wants to tell us has to be close to the surface.*

And I'm sure it'll be mixed with a bunch of lies, so we won't be able to tell what's actually important, Sophie warned. *I think it's better to keep him talking, at least until—*

"Ooh, looks like I've even got you conferring telepathically," Fintan said, tilting his head to study them. "And since I'm assuming you're discussing some foolish plan to infiltrate my memories, let me remind you: You've *never* learned anything from me that way—and I can assure you, that's not going to change today. And thanks to how long you stalled this meeting, you're just a week shy of the festival. So how about you try playing it smart from now on and do things my way?"

"What's your way?" Fitz demanded.

"A simple barter. You agree to give me what I want. I tell you what you need. And since I'm sure you're about to claim that you can't trust me—I'll prove that you can. I'll give you each one free question. No time to strategize, though. Just blurt out what's on your mind in three . . . two . . ."

"What's the Neverseen's plan for my brother?" Fitz asked, shooting Sophie an apologetic glance.

In all their practice, they'd agreed to wait until Fintan brought up Alvar.

Fintan smiled. "I figured that would be your question. And the truth is, your brother's not capable of fulfilling any grand purpose. He lacks the talent for any complicated assignment.

He couldn't even recognize that Sophie was an elf when he was staring right at her, remember? His one true value—aside from his willingness to follow orders—was his connection to your family. And he lost that the day I made him reveal his identity." He stared at his hands, picking at his nails. "In hindsight, I suppose I was far too hasty that day. Just as I was far too hasty when I revealed my own escape and survival. I tried to speed the timeline along and it cost me—and it cost your brother even more because he'd never been much use in the first place. *That's* why we're both where we are. But while Vespera was right with her estimation of your brother's worth, she's wrong about mine. She thinks it's safe to leave me here, shivering away, because I don't know what she's up to. But I do."

The words had a strange ring of truth to them.

Sophie knew how foolish that was to admit—even to herself.

This was Fintan.

It was a game.

But . . . everything he'd said synced with several thoughts she'd had as well.

"And what about you, Sophie?" Fintan asked, the gleam in his eyes making it clear he knew he was getting to her. "You missed my countdown to ask a question of your own. But I know how hard this is for you, given the things you and I have gone through together. So I'll give you one more chance. One question—one answer, in three . . . two . . ."

"What was Keefe's mom having him do in the memories

she erased?" she blurted out, hoping she was making the right decision.

She probably should've asked for the location of the real caches.

Actually, she probably should've stayed quiet.

But for some reason, when he'd started counting down, Keefe's devastated face had popped into her mind, from the day he'd told her that Tiergan's mental exercises had been a dead end. And the question just sort of tumbled out.

Fintan's eyebrows lifted, proof that she'd surprised him, too. But he shook his head. "*That* is not a single answer. The boy did many things. Served many purposes."

Sophie blew out a breath. "Okay, then tell me why she sent him to London to deliver a message to a house with a green door."

His eyebrows shot up higher. "That memory wasn't meant to be recovered."

Sophie shrugged. "Well, it was."

One of his eyes twitched, and he picked at his nails for several long seconds before he told her, "Truthfully? I don't have all the details on that. Some projects Gisela kept to herself. All I know is that she was hoping to recruit someone and it didn't work out."

"A human?" Sophie pressed.

Fintan nodded. And he looked so reluctant to do it that Sophie had to believe it was the truth—or a shade of it at least.

"So," he said, straightening up, "now that I've sufficiently proven myself, we're to the part where you agree to give me what I want."

"And what's that?" Fitz asked, before Sophie could decide if they should end the conversation. They'd already gotten more than she expected. They should leave while they were ahead.

But then Fintan said, "There was a new girl with you the day I was arrested. Caprise Redek's daughter. And she's another Pyrokinetic—don't bother lying. I could tell."

Sophie swallowed, trying to find her voice after her mouth dried up on her. "*She* has nothing to do with this."

"If that were true, she wouldn't have been with you that day in Nightfall—but that's not why I'm bringing her up." He leaned closer, and all the smugness dripped out of his expression, leaving something that almost looked sincere. "The girl needs training—*real* training. From someone who shares her ability—and not those fools the Council has under surveillance. They've spent so long suppressing their fire that it's all but burned out their minds. The same thing will happen to the girl. Or she'll unleash herself on the world like Brant—"

"You trained Brant," Sophie reminded him.

"I did. And my training was never the issue. The mistake was bringing him into my cause. I didn't realize how much the distractions would affect him—or myself for that matter."

"Is this the part where you try to convince us you're just a poor, misunderstood villain?" Sophie asked.

His eye twitched again. "In a way, I suppose it is. The simple fact is, I joined the Neverseen because the Council was wrong about my ability, and it was time to undo the damage they were causing."

"And you thought the best way to do that was burning people alive?" Fitz argued.

"Hindsight," Fintan said as Sophie shuddered. "I allied with too many others—too many enemies with their own plans and agendas—and all those distractions led me down paths I never intended to follow, thinking everything was connected. But it wasn't. I can see that now. Just as I can see there's no coming back for me. This"—he waved his arms around the ice bubble—"is where I will end. And I can live with that. But I can't live with knowing another child—another Pyrokinetic— is going to become everything we fear simply because we're too prejudiced to give her a chance. I don't even have to be around flame to teach her. I just need someone to bring her here. And I know she's your friend—"

"Exactly," Sophie interrupted. "She's our *friend*. We're not bargaining with her life—"

"But you will be, if you refuse my offer. You'll be deciding her future for her. Don't make that mistake. Don't be as small-minded as everyone else. For once, be the force for change that your creators designed you to be. Your friend *needs* training—"

"Not with a murderer," Sophie snapped back.

"Yes, actually. With someone who knows firsthand how easily the power can drag you under. Someone who understands the struggle, knows the temptations, knows the—"

"If your intentions are so noble," Fitz cut in, "why hold Vespera's plans hostage?"

"Exactly," Sophie added. "If you want to prove we can trust you—prove it for *real*. Help us stop whatever's happening at the Celestial Festival. Otherwise you're admitting this is all a big head game to get your way. And I'm done playing."

Fintan sighed, watching the puff of white breath slowly dissipate in the frigid air before he closed his eyes. "The truth is, I . . . don't have *that* much more to offer. Vespera kept her plan vague. But I know she was fixated on Luzia Vacker—something about stolen ideas. And she was livid when she found out our world has an entire celebration centered around the talents of Luzia's son. She called it a farce. Told us she was going to show everyone the truth behind the Vacker legacy. And it's been a countdown to the Celestial Festival ever since. She even got our ogres involved. But that's all I can tell you. So . . . I guess it's your call. You can trust me and cancel the festival—or better yet, make it a trap and take your chance to finally get ahead. You have a week to figure it out. And when that week is over— when you've seen that I'm not lying to you—bring me the girl and let me train her."

FORTY-SIX

WE SHOULD CANCEL THE festival!" Sophie couldn't tell who shouted it that time. Her house had been crammed with so many people yelling at each other for so many hours that she couldn't keep track of it all anymore.

As soon as they'd arrived back at Havenfield, Mr. Forkle had hailed the rest of the Black Swan's Collective, *and* all twelve Councillors, *and* Alden, *and* Luzia, *and* Orem Vacker—*and* gathered Grady and Edaline and all of Sophie's bodyguards.

And while he'd been doing that, Sophie had hailed all of her friends and told them to hurry over as well—everyone except Marella. Since the Council had to be involved, it was smarter to keep Marella—and anything to do with pyrokinesis—out of this. Mr. Forkle had even decided not to share that Fintan had made any demands, knowing it would raise too many questions.

Once they figured out what to do about the festival, Sophie was going to tell Marella everything and let her decide what role she wanted to play. But she was starting to think that was never going to happen—especially when someone chimed in with yet another "We *can't* cancel the festival!" and the debate circled back around.

The argument fell into two camps.

Camp A—aka Camp *We Should Cancel the Festival*—kept pointing out that if they didn't cancel, they'd be putting thousands of lives in danger and giving the Neverseen a chance for another very public victory.

And Camp B—the *We Can't Cancel the Festival* Crew—had a varied list of arguments that ranged from "We don't even know if Fintan's telling the truth" to "This could be our chance to finally arrest the Neverseen," plus a dash of "If we cancel the festival, we're telling our people we have no confidence in our ability to protect them."

As for who belonged in each camp—it changed moment by moment.

Even Sophie went back and forth, wishing there were a way to trap the Neverseen without risking any lives.

The only thing she knew for certain was that Luzia was being *very* quiet. So when the argument rose to yet another shouting crescendo, Sophie used the distraction to weave her way over to where Luzia stood gazing out at the alicorn pasture.

"Don't you think it's time to tell us the truth about your connection to Vespera?" she asked Luzia under her breath.

Luzia rolled her eyes. "I *have* told you the truth—just like I told your puffy leader the truth when he showed up at my house and asked me about things you weren't authorized to share."

"I—"

Luzia held up her hand. "Yes, I know. You don't work alone. But *I* do. Which is why I kept my contact with Vespera limited to discussing her designs for shielding our cities—and her designs *required* a Flasher to implement them, so claiming they were stolen would be ludicrous."

"Then why is she fixated on you?" Sophie countered.

"How would I know? She's clearly unstable—though quite honestly, I'm not convinced that she *is* fixated on me. The word of a murderous Pyrokinetic is hardly reliable. Particularly since Fintan and I have a history." Luzia glanced over her shoulder, probably making sure no one was listening, and Sophie found herself staring at Luzia's pointed ears, wondering how small the world must've been all those thousands of years ago. Apparently it was fairly small, since Luzia added, "One of the five Pyrokinetics who died during Fintan's ill-advised Everblaze lesson was a close friend of mine. So I was one of the louder advocates of banning the ability. Perhaps this is Fintan's way of settling that score. Tying my name in with whatever horrors he and Vespera have worked up, trying to drag me down with them, using claims so vague it's impossible for me to concretely defend myself."

Sophie sighed.

She was getting very tired of having the people she didn't trust make so much sense—especially since they were contradicting each other.

But she still had questions. "What's the Vacker legacy?"

"How am I supposed to know?" Luzia argued. "A legacy is rarely one thing. And it's generally defined by those outside looking in, rather than those living it. That's like me asking you what the moonlark's legacy is."

Fair points.

"Fine. How do you think Vespera would define it?" Sophie asked her.

Luzia shrugged. "Your guess is as good as mine. You're asking me to speculate on how a disgraced fugitive I barely know would define my family's contributions to this world. The most I can say is she probably doesn't like us. Criminals tend to despise those on the side of the law."

"*Are* you on the side of the law?" Sophie asked. "Or are you on your own side?"

"I could ask you the same question, couldn't I?" Luzia leaned in closer. "Tell me, Sophie: How many things are you hiding from the Council right now? I'd wager it's even more than I am."

Another very valid point.

So valid that Sophie was almost ready to concede and turn her attention back to the still ongoing argument when she realized . . .

"What about the hatching?" she whispered. "It happens on the eclipse, right?"

"Technically the morning after," Luzia corrected. "But the eclipse always triggers it. Why?"

"Because the Celestial Festival is always on the eclipse too."

Luzia shook her head. "That's a coincidence."

"I don't like coincidences."

"Neither do I. But that doesn't mean they don't happen. My son doesn't know what you—and now your *order*, thanks to you—know about my properties, and he's the one who instituted the traditions that grew into the festival."

"You never told Orem?"

"I never told *anyone*. Like I keep saying: I work *alone*. And I'm done with this conversation—but here's some food for thought before I go. The hatching never takes place anywhere near the festival. And this year it's farther away than ever—which is another coincidence. The Prism Peaks simply have an excellent view of the eclipse's totality."

"The Prism Peaks?" Sophie repeated.

Luzia raised one eyebrow. "That's the festival's location—or it will be if they don't cancel it. Perhaps you should be paying better attention."

With that she turned and shoved her way into the crowd of arguing adults, crossing to the other side of the room. And only then did Sophie notice that Keefe had subtly positioned himself on Luzia's other side at some point during their conversation.

She scooted closer to him. "I don't suppose you managed to get a reading on her while we were talking, did you?"

"I tried. But it's kinda hard without physical contact," Keefe admitted. "I could tell she's worried, though—*really* worried, if I felt it in the air. But I couldn't tell why. She could be nervous for Orem's safety at the festival. Or nervous that her name's wrapped up in this. Or it could have to do with whatever you guys were whispering about. I couldn't hear much, but it sounded like there's some stuff you haven't shared with the group."

"A little. I'll catch you guys all up as soon as this craziness is over." She pointed to the ongoing argument, which seemed to have escalated between Wraith and Councillor Alina—and looked especially bizarre as Alina shouted at a floating, bodiless cloak. "And by the way," she added quietly, "there's something you and I need to talk about too."

"Oh?" His eyes darted to the necklace Fitz had given her, and Sophie had to resist the urge to cover the sparkly teal heart with her palm.

"Not *that*," she whispered, wishing her face didn't feel so warm. "It's something else. Just don't leave when the others do, okay?"

Keefe nodded, his lips flicking with the slightest hint of a smirk. "Don't worry, Foster. I'm not going anywhere."

. . .

A ridiculous number of hours later, just as the sun started to brighten the dawn sky, the arguing masses finally reached a consensus.

They weren't going to let the Neverseen spoil their beloved tradition.

Canceling the festival would be giving in to fear—*and* passing up an opportunity to get ahead of their enemies. So they were going to stand strong, up their security, and set a trap instead.

It felt like the right decision.

But it was also a risk. And Sophie wished there was a way to warn everyone that the festival might be more dangerous than they realized.

"I know what you're thinking," Mr. Forkle said, his eyes on her even though his voice was raised enough to address the whole room. "And it's good that you're feeling that responsibility. We all should. It's our job now to come up with a plan that will protect every single innocent person at the festival. We'll have to be more thorough and prepared than we ever have been before."

"And more clever," Councillor Emery added, his rich voice raspy from the endless debating. "If we're setting a trap for the Neverseen, we can't have our security giving us away."

"And the trap needs to *work*," Bronte emphasized. "We can't blow this chance."

Mr. Forkle nodded. "Which is why we're going to need everyone's full support and cooperation. Yours especially," he said, pointing to Orem, Luzia, Tam, and Wylie. "Illusion is going to be key to hiding our defenses."

The four of them agreed. And that seemed to settle things for the night—if night was even the right word anymore. Mr. Forkle promised to contact everyone after they'd had a chance to rest, assuring them that he'd figure out when and where they could start working on their plans for the trap and the security. They had six days to figure it out, and it was going to be a massive multispeciesial endeavor like nothing they'd ever attempted before.

Honestly, it was pretty amazing watching the Black Swan and the Council work so closely together. Sophie hoped it was proof that this time they'd get it right. Otherwise . . .

Nope.

It was better not to let failure be an option.

This time, the Neverseen were going to lose.

The adults dispersed after that, but Sophie asked her friends to stay, taking a few minutes to tell them about Fintan's demand for Marella, and everything she hadn't already shared about Luzia and the troll hives. She could tell Tarina wasn't happy with her for that. But Sophie—unlike Luzia—*didn't* work alone.

"I don't know if any of the Luzia stuff's important," she said when she'd finished. "But I wanted to make sure you guys all knew about it, in case it is."

All of her friends nodded.

"Can I go with you when you talk to Marella tomorrow?" Biana asked. "Or, I guess I should say 'today.'"

"We should all go, shouldn't we?" Fitz said.

Biana shook her head. "Not if we're going to her house. Her mom can't handle a crowd like that."

Caprise Redek struggled with her emotions thanks to a traumatic brain injury she'd suffered years earlier. And the fact that Biana had thought of that—and Sophie hadn't gotten that far yet—made it clear how smart it would be to have Biana with her.

"Hail me when you wake up and we'll figure out when to head over," Sophie told Biana.

"And let us know how it goes," Dex told both of them.

Sophie promised she would, and with that, her friends started leaping back to their houses. But Keefe hung back with Ro, just like she'd asked him to.

So did Fitz. And he looked a little confused when he realized Keefe wasn't leaving.

I asked him to stay so I could tell him what Fintan said about his memories, Sophie explained telepathically.

Want me to stay too? Fitz offered.

Sophie chewed her lip. *I think it'll be better if it's just him and me. Why?*

"Uh, fun as it is being here for a Fitzphie starefest," Keefe interrupted, "you don't really need me for that, so . . ."

"Sorry," Sophie told him, "I was just . . . saying goodbye to Fitz."

Which sounded like more of a dismissal than she meant it to.

Sorry, she transmitted to Fitz, wondering why this felt so unnecessarily complicated. *I know Keefe's your best friend—and I know we were both searching his memories. But I just . . . I think he'll take it easier if it comes from me.*

But we didn't really learn anything big, Fitz reminded her.

Exactly. That's why I'm worried. This is probably the most he's going to learn about that memory and it isn't much, so—

"Seriously, I'll just go," Keefe told them. "You guys carry on with all the staring and the mega mood swings."

Fitz sighed. "No, it's fine. I'm going."

Ro muttered something that sounded a little like "about time," but they all ignored her.

Thank you, Sophie transmitted to Fitz.

He nodded, stepping closer and pulling her into a hug—a hug that lasted longer than Sophie expected. Long enough that she finally had to pull away, hoping her face wasn't super red.

"Hail me when you're back from Marella's, okay?" Fitz asked, reaching up to tuck her hair behind her ear.

"I will," Sophie promised.

His fingers lingered on her cheek a few seconds longer. Then he raised his home crystal up to the light and leaped away.

Keefe whistled, tearing his hands through his hair. "Wow, so that's how it's going to be now, huh? I mean, I appreciate you skipping the whole goodbye-smoochy-smoochy thing, but—"

"Ugh, we don't do that yet," Sophie corrected—and then instantly regretted it.

Keefe raised one eyebrow. "Does that mean—"

"I have some news about your mom," she jumped in, going for an immediate subject change.

And it worked a little too well. All the blood seemed to drain from Keefe's face, and he squared his shoulders like he was bracing for impact.

"Well . . . I guess 'news' is the wrong word," Sophie hedged. "Maybe 'update' is better? Or . . . 'clarification'?"

Ugh, why was this so hard?

She blew out a breath and plunged ahead. "Fintan let Fitz and me each ask one question when he was trying to prove that we could trust him. So I asked him about the shattered memory you recovered—"

"You did?" Keefe interrupted.

"Well, first I tried asking about all your missing memories, but Fintan called me out for being too broad. So I asked about the damaged memory we found. And he confirmed that you weren't supposed to get that one back."

Keefe closed his eyes. "Anything else?"

"A little. He said your mom kept certain projects to herself, so he didn't know very much about them. But he did tell me that your mom sent you to that house in London to try to recruit someone for something—and yes, she was trying to recruit a human. Fintan said it didn't work out. And . . . that's all he told me. I know that's not much to go on, but . . ."

"Hey, it's more than I had," he said quietly.

His legs were wobbling at that point, and he stumbled over to the staircase and sank onto the bottom step.

Sophie sat beside him, reaching for his hand. "Are you okay?"

He stared at their tangled fingers. "Yeah."

The silence stretched and stretched, until Sophie had to break it. "I'm sorry it's not more."

"Uh, you *so* don't need to apologize. I mean . . . you had *one* question you could ask Fintan, and you used it to ask about my memory. That's . . ."

He looked away, blinking hard.

It looked like he was fighting back tears, but Sophie could tell he didn't want her to see them. Even Ro had stepped back, standing quietly in the corner. Giving them space.

So Sophie just squeezed his hand a little tighter, letting him cling to her if he needed to.

"Thank you for thinking about me," he whispered. "No one does that."

"Lots of people care about you, Keefe," Sophie gently corrected.

He sighed. "I guess, but . . ."

"But what?" she asked when he didn't finish.

He turned to study her for a long second before he shook his head. "But I should let you get some sleep. Sounds like we have a big day ahead of us."

"So this is where Marella lives," Sophie said mostly to herself as she studied the sprawling structure. The domed roofs at varying heights and the bougainvillea draping the walls reminded her a little of pictures she'd seen of the Greek isles. But all the crystal and silver made it look much more elvin.

"You've never been here?" Biana asked.

Sophie shook her head.

And for some reason—probably because Marella always looked a little disheveled—she'd been imagining the Redek house to be a bit more chaotic. Maybe even a little run-down. But everything was immaculate. Neat rows of perfectly trimmed hedges. Vibrant flower beds without a single weed. A square reflecting pool that was so glassy, it looked like a mirror of the sky. Even the silver railings lining the house's numerous balconies gleamed like they'd just been polished—though Sophie couldn't look at them without wondering which was the balcony that Marella's mom had fallen off when she injured herself.

They all looked *very* high up. And the ground beneath them did *not* look soft. So it was pretty amazing that Caprise had survived.

"Are you guys just going to stand there all day?" Marella asked, making Sophie and Biana jump. They'd both been so busy studying the property that they hadn't heard Marella open the front door. "Or are you going to tell me what was so urgent that we *had* to meet here?"

Sophie had planned to have this conversation at Havenfield, but Mr. Forkle had decided that her house would be the least suspicious place for everyone to work on the festival's security, since it would look like they were combining their efforts to protect the newly returned alicorns. So half the Council had already been back in the main room by the time Sophie'd headed downstairs for breakfast, and the rest would be arriving soon.

"Where's a good place to talk?" she asked Marella.

Marella glanced over her shoulder, tugging on one of her braids before she stepped forward and closed the door. "It's probably better to stay out here right now. My mom's having a rough day."

"Sorry," Biana told her, and Sophie wished she could think of something useful to add as she followed Marella over to a huge stone fire pit on the far side of the house, surrounded by golden beanbag chairs.

"These are made from flareadon fur," Marella explained as she sank into one and motioned for Sophie and Biana to do the same. "That way they're fire resistant. My dad built this place after I manifested. Figured it might be good for me to have somewhere I could practice without it looking too suspicious *and* without burning the house down."

"Smart," Biana said, glancing at Sophie with a look that seemed to say, *How do you want to do this?*

Sophie cleared her throat—but before she could get a word out, Marella told her, "Whatever it is, don't try to sugarcoat it, okay? I'm guessing by the shadows under your eyes that it's something big. So let's just get it over with."

Sophie nodded. "Okay. It's . . . about Fintan."

She went on to repeat everything Fintan had told her about why Marella needed to train with him, making sure she didn't add any of her own thoughts or worries into the conversation. This needed to be Marella's decision, since she would be the one taking the risk either way, whether she chose to train with the enemy or chose to ignore his warnings about her ability.

Marella leaned forward when Sophie finished, holding her hands over the fire pit and sparking tiny tendrils of blue flame over each of her fingers. "Would the Council even allow me to train?"

"I don't know," Sophie told her. "I'm not sure if we'd tell them. Technically, I've seen where the prison is now, so I could teleport there anytime, with or without anyone's permission."

"Would the guards let you in, though?" Biana wondered.

"I guess that's a good point," Sophie admitted. "Well . . . I'm sure we could come up with some other excuse for why we're visiting. That way you could still keep your ability secret if you want."

"I don't *want* any of this," Marella muttered.

The flames hovering over her fingers turned white hot and Biana dragged her beanbag closer, placing a hand on Marella's arm. "This probably isn't much help, but . . . we're here for you, okay? I know we haven't always done a good job of showing that. But we *are*. You need us to break you into that prison for training? We'll make it happen."

"Exactly," Sophie agreed. "I mean, we broke into Exile. How hard could it be?"

The flames over Marella's hands cooled back to blue, and her lips pulled into a smile. "You guys should see the looks on your bodyguards' faces right now. It's like a contest to see who can give the evilest glare—though your guard doesn't really look surprised, Biana."

"I'm sure he isn't," Biana said, smiling over her shoulder at poor Woltzer.

"The only reason I'm not dragging you all back to Havenfield," Sandor told them, "is because I'm assuming this is hyperbole to show your loyalty."

"Maybe, maybe not," Biana told him, tossing her hair.

"Obviously there's a lot to figure out," Sophie jumped in, before Sandor could shift into overprotective mode. "And there's no hurry for you to decide," she told Marella. "We just wanted to tell you what Fintan said as soon as we could so you wouldn't think we were hiding it from you. But you can think about it for as long as—"

"I have to do it," Marella interrupted, letting the flames over her hands swell bigger and bigger, until it looked like she was about to lose control. Then she curled her fingers, snuffing the fire out with a thin curl of smoke. "I *have* to train with Fintan. I know there will be risks, but . . . he's right about this power. It isn't just that flames call to me. It's like they're *in* me. This constant inferno in my head, begging me to let it take control."

Sophie tried to hide her shudder, but Marella still noticed.

And instead of looking hurt or angry—like she had every right to—she looked . . . scared.

"I'm fine," she said, twisting one of her braids around her finger. "It's just . . . I can see how I might *not* be fine after a few years of this, if that makes sense. That's why I have to train. I'd rather not turn into some creepy pyromaniac, you know?"

Sophie and Biana both tried to smile at the joke.

"So . . . yeah," Marella said, twisting her braid tighter. "How soon do you think I'll be able to start training?"

"I'll talk to Mr. Forkle as soon as I can get him away from the Council," Sophie promised. "But I think we might need to get through the Celestial Festival first."

She caught Marella up about Fintan's other warnings.

"That's fine," Marella told her. "It's only six days."

And it hit Sophie then.

They were only *six days* from their next standoff with the Neverseen.

Six.

Days.

The monster liked that. It stretched its legs and sharpened its claws, eager to dig up every flashback from all the other times she'd battled her enemies—and lost.

But we have six days to prepare! she tried to remind herself. *It won't be like the other times.*

Six days wasn't much, though.

The Neverseen had been preparing for way, *way* longer.

"Hey," Marella said, snapping her fingers in front of Sophie's face to drag her out of her panic. "You still with us?"

"Yeah," Sophie said, sucking in a slow breath and shaking her head to clear it. "I was just . . . thinking about how much there is to do."

"We have lots of help this time," Biana reminded her.

"I know. But with the Neverseen . . . we're always missing something. There's always some trick we don't see until it's too late and—"

"About that," Marella cut in. "I know you're probably going to tell me I should sit this one out because the festival's so public. But . . . you might need me. I won't use my ability unless I have to, but it's probably smart to have the option."

Sophie wanted to argue.

But she stopped herself.

Because the truth was . . .

They were going to need all the help they could get.

Six days became five days.

Then four.

And by the time they were down to three, it felt like the monster was stalking every thought Sophie had. Even the sedatives couldn't fully put the beast to rest, and shadows lurked among the glitter and sparkles in her dreams—along with a haunting voice, wholly her own this time, whispering over and over, *What are we missing? What are we missing? What are we missing?*

She hated letting the adults handle all the preparations, but she didn't have the kind of power and resources that they did. So she spent her days training with her friends and bodyguards, pushing her still-healing body as hard as she could without reinjuring anything. And every night she made Mr. Forkle walk her through how the plan was coming together.

The good news was, the security for the festival seemed solid. Every guard they could spare was already being secretly transported to the festival grounds at the base of the Prism Peaks and hidden behind different illusions that Luzia, Orem, Tam, Wylie, and any other Flashers and Shades the Council trusted were carefully preparing. That way the amount of soldiers would *look* the same as previous years—but they'd have a secret army ready and waiting. Dwarves would also be lurking underground, and several gnomes had volunteered to take up positions in any nearby trees. King Dimitar also sent a dozen soldiers to serve under Bo's command, and Bo had taken a temporary leave from guarding Sophie to hide at the festival site, in case Cadfael and the other deserters showed up like Fintan had implied.

But the true genius to the strategy was the other illusions that Luzia had designed to camouflage all the Neverseen's biggest targets. The "Councillors" that the audience would be staring at would actually be a projection of the real Council, who would be hidden behind one of the larger groups of soldiers and "broadcasting" everything they said. Orem would be doing the same for his presentation. And anyone who saw Sophie or her friends, family, and bodyguards milling about the audience would actually be seeing projected doppelgängers set up specifically near the hidden guards like bait in a trap. In reality, they'd be patrolling the crowd in disguise, searching for signs of the Neverseen.

It was a whole new level of artful duplicity, and everyone was incredibly proud of how smoothly it was coming together.

But it didn't silence Sophie's haunting whisper.

What are we missing? What are we missing? What are we missing?

And with two days to go, she figured out what it was.

"What if we're wrong?" she asked, trying not to fidget as she stood in front of Fitz, Keefe, Biana, Dex, Linh, and Marella, who'd all gathered under Calla's Panakes tree after she'd hailed them for an emergency meeting. Wylie and Tam were with Orem and Luzia, strengthening the illusions at the Prism Peaks. And the adults were still using Havenfield's main room for their continued planning.

"What if we're wrong about what?" Fitz asked.

Sophie took a steadying breath to keep the monster calm. "I mean, what if Fintan was lying? It's not like the other stuff he told us was all that earth-shattering. The festival warning was the only thing concrete—and what if that was his plan?"

"I thought we already decided we couldn't ignore the warning, just in case," Dex reminded her. "Wasn't that why we had to listen to everyone argue all night?"

"Right," Sophie agreed. "But once we decided to take it seriously, it's like we forgot that if Fintan lied about this, it was probably to keep us distracted so we'd be completely caught off guard by anything else. So the question is, where else are we vulnerable?"

"Everglen," Fitz said immediately. "Alvar will still be there. And my dad sent half the guards to the festival."

"That still leaves the other half," Biana reminded him. "And the gate. And the Warden on his ankle. And the fact that he has no memories. I think we're covered."

Sophie nodded slowly. "You still have guards posted at the override, right?"

"Yes," Fitz said, running a hand down his face. "But I don't like that Alvar will be alone there without us. Maybe I should stay home and keep an eye on him."

"Or you could take this," Dex said, pulling the Warden's bracelet off his wrist and handing it to Fitz. "That way you can help out at the festival *and* keep an eye on Alvar's movements. You know the property better than I do, so that probably makes more sense. You'll know right away if he's going anywhere or doing anything weird. And if he starts to, just hit that button and drop him."

"Or I *could* drop him now and leave him unconscious for the whole thing," Fitz suggested.

"You could," Mr. Forkle said behind them. "But then you'd be as bad as our enemies."

Fitz looked like he could live with that.

"I understand the inclination, Mr. Vacker," Mr. Forkle said. "I truly do. But punishing someone because you expect them to commit a crime will always be unjust. The second your brother does anything inappropriate—*if* he does anything inappropriate—you have my full permission to push that button. But until then, let's not lose sight of who we are."

Fitz muttered something Sophie couldn't understand as he slipped the bracelet onto his wrist. But he dropped the subject.

"I'm assuming this little gathering involves a lot of stressing and worrying?" Mr. Forkle noted, turning his attention to Sophie.

"We're just trying to think through all the plan Bs, in case we're wrong about plan A," she explained. "We still have two days to prepare—might as well be thorough."

"I suppose. But try not to let yourselves lose focus. The Neverseen like grandstanding and sending the messages through dramatic public displays. The festival makes sense."

It did.

But knowing that didn't silence that haunting question.

What are we missing? What are we missing? What are we missing?

And the day of the festival, Sophie finally remembered the other event happening during the eclipse.

"Do you think this could have anything to do with your hatching?" she asked Tarina. "Maybe the Neverseen are planning a raid on your hive."

Tarina snorted. "If they are, they've *foolishly* misjudged our species. That hive will be one of the most dangerous places in the world tomorrow morning, full of untamed, bloodthirsty newborns."

Sophie shivered. "Okay, but . . . that's the morning. What about tonight?"

"Some newborns will hatch early. And all it takes is one—trust me. In fact, you should almost hope your enemies have miscalculated so greatly. They would all be shredded to pieces in minutes."

Sophie shivered harder, deciding to take Tarina at her word.

"The only hatching you should be worried about is the alicorn babies," Tarina added, and Sophie's heart stumbled a beat.

"I thought the caretakers at the hive said they won't be hatching tomorrow," Sophie reminded her. "Silveny's had me ask you every day."

"Yes," Tarina agreed. "The membranes haven't thinned like they have at the other hive. But this is new for us, and we will all be very busy tonight. So if you're determined to be prepared, you might want to consider moving the alicorn parents to the hive, since they have a way of reaching out to you telepathically. Then they could call for help if they need it."

That . . . was a really good idea.

The Collective agreed. And the Council even offered to light leap the alicorns there so that there was no risk that they'd be seen. And it definitely wasn't hard to convince Silveny and Greyfell to teleport over to their babies.

But before they left, Silveny called Sophie over to her pasture. Sophie hadn't told either of the alicorns about what might happen that night at the festival, but Silveny must've plucked the worries from Sophie's mind, because she nuzzled her nose into Sophie's neck and asked, *SOPHIE SAFE?*

I'll try, Sophie promised.

NO TRY! Silveny told her. *SAFE! SAFE! SAFE!*

She flooded Sophie with such an overwhelming burst of confidence that she tingled from head to toe. And Sophie tried to cling to the feeling as she watched the alicorns crack the sunset-streaked sky and teleport away. But it faded when she made her way back inside and found Fitz, Keefe, Dex, Tam, Biana, Marella, Wylie, and Linh busy arming themselves with throwing stars and daggers and the gadgets that Dex and Tinker had made. And the last wisps vanished when Flori shuffled in with a basket of Panakes blossoms and ordered everyone to fill their pockets with as many flowers as they could.

Reality sank in then, along with the stomach-twisting realization that if things went wrong that night, there would be pain.

And blood.

And maybe worse.

"Everyone, gather around," Magnate Leto called, clapping his hands as he strode into the room. He'd chosen to switch identities to prevent the Neverseen from realizing he was still alive. And it was his job to bring them to the festival, along with their various guards.

Everyone else was already at the Prism Peaks, in position.

Already in danger.

"We must be ready to leave in the next few minutes," Magnate Leto said as he handed them each a heavy hooded cloak to hide their faces. They'd be wearing different colors, different styles, and should blend right in with the rest of the crowd, since it was cold where they were heading. "I know this certainly isn't your first time taking a risk like this, but I want you to know how much I admire the bravery of each and every one of you. I wish I could guarantee that everything will go perfectly. But that's rarely how it works. So stick to the plan. But also stick together. And trust your instincts. If something feels wrong, it probably is. We've prepared as best as we can, but the real work still comes down to each of us in the moment. Be smart. Be careful. Rely on each other. And with any luck, we'll be celebrating a victory tonight!"

Everyone let out a cheer—almost a battle cry—as they all locked hands.

But Sophie could feel the trembles in their grips.

And she felt just as shaky as they stepped into the path and let the light carry them away to face their enemies once again.

FORTY-SEVEN

A HUGE RED MOON FILLED THE dark sky as Sophie and her friends arrived at the Celestial Festival. A blood moon, as humans sometimes called it, and it seemed fitting, given the circumstances—not that anyone in the crowd appeared to be sharing Sophie's sense of dread.

The mood felt just as joyous as it had the last time Sophie attended the festival—maybe even more so, since everything was set against a much more vibrant backdrop. The Prism Peaks must've gotten their name from the unusual striations running along the jagged mountains—wide, arcing bands of red, blue, green, and white that were vivid enough to be distinct even in the moonlight. Beyond that, the star-flecked sky stretched like a glittering canvas, ready for Orem's show to begin. And while peo-ple waited, they set up midnight picnics and tossed tiny sparkling firecrackers, showering the scene with glints of colorful light.

No one was paying any attention to Sophie's group—they were too distracted by all the sights and conversations—but she still pulled her hood up over her head to hide her face. Her friends all did the same, and they blended in perfectly with the rest of the bundled-up crowd around them—which would've been reassuring, except . . . the Neverseen could also count on the same camouflage.

All right, Magnate Leto transmitted, making all of them jump. *We should get moving. The earlier we spot the enemy, the sooner we'll be able to take control of the situation. It's probably best if you break into groups so you can cover more ground—but don't wander too far. Remember that the rest of the Collective—and several more members of our order—will be searching other areas. It's about being thorough and questioning any detail that feels off. I also want you to meet back here at our base point every thirty min-utes in case we need to adjust our strategy.* He pointed to a blanket a few feet away, piled with pillows and overstuffed baskets.

"Aw, you brought snacks!" Keefe said.

Actually, that was Edaline. Magnate Leto nudged his chin toward the fringes of the crowd, and it took Sophie several seconds to find her mom shrouded in a lavender cloak, with Grady next to her in pale blue.

The nervous smiles they gave her when their eyes met

seemed to say, *Please be careful.* And Sophie hoped her responding nod told them to do the same.

No one goes off alone, no matter the circumstances, Magnate Leto continued. *Especially you, Miss Vacker. Vanish if you wish, but stay near some of your friends. And if any of you see anything suspicious, set off one of these.* He passed around a sack filled with what looked like tiny silver marbles, and they each grabbed a handful. *The Council distributed them to everyone, so they won't be suspicious, but yours are the only ones that flash purple, so we'll be able to—*

Purple sparks crackled at his feet, making him stumble back.

"What?" Keefe asked. "Someone needed to make sure they work, right?" He set off another one with a smirk. "Yep, I think we're good."

Magnate Leto breathed a long-suffering sigh.

But Sophie was grateful for the bit of levity. It sent the monster skittering to the back of her mind.

"So, who's going with whom?" Linh asked, careful to keep her voice hushed.

"I dunno," Keefe whispered back, "but I call 'not it' for Team Fitzphie."

Actually, Sophie transmitted to everyone, trying not to feel stung by that, *I think Fitz and I should split up, since we can communicate with each other telepathically.*

I agree, Magnate Leto confirmed. *In fact, it might be better to stick with only two groups—that way you're all in contact.*

Fitz did not look happy about that arrangement. Especially

when Keefe announced, "Well then, looks like we're bringing back Team Foster-Keefe! Who's with us?"

Tam was the first to join.

"What?" he asked when he saw everyone's shocked expressions. "Sophie's always the biggest target, right? And I'm the only one who can break through force fields. Plus, I can use some of the stuff Lady Zillah taught me if Umber comes after her."

Somehow that sounded equal parts touching and terrifying.

"I'll go with them too," Marella decided, "since I don't have a bodyguard and Sophie has, like, fifty."

"Only two right now," Sophie quietly corrected.

Bo was hidden away with the new ogres. Flori was somewhere in the scattered trees with the other gnomes. And Nubiti was underground with the other dwarves. So she only had Sandor and Tarina, and they'd be giving her a much wider berth—like all the bodyguards would be doing with their charges—to avoid drawing any attention away from the projected decoys.

But it still probably made sense to spread out their backup. So Biana and Dex went with Fitz—that way their group would have Grizel, Woltzer, and Lovise trailing behind. And Sophie's group had Sandor, Tarina, and Ro—along with Wylie, who moved to stand with them when Linh went over to Fitz.

Okay, Magnate Leto transmitted. *One group goes one way, one group goes the other, and you circle back here every half hour. Keep in touch as needed. And remember, you're not just looking for black cloaks. Gethen, Vespera, and Lady Gisela may go without their dis-*

guises tonight, since we already know their identities. We also know they have a Guster working with them, so if you feel any strange winds, set off a purple flash immediately. Same goes for any shifting shadows that could mean Umber's around. Or any flashes that might be Ruy's force fields.

"Anyone else think we have too many enemies?" Marella muttered under her breath.

They all nodded.

But if things go according to plan, Magnate Leto added, *by the end of the night we may reduce that number significantly. Maybe even completely.*

And so the search began. And it was . . .

. . . kind of boring.

Sophie knew that was a strange way to feel while hunting for the villains who'd beaten and broken her so badly that she was *still* recovering.

But . . .

All they were doing was walking. And scanning faces. And squinting at shadows. And listening to the wind. Which was both tedious and totally unproductive.

The thirty minutes felt like thirty hours before they were circling back to their friends and learning that the other group had an equally unexciting search. And Sophie knew that was technically good news, since no villains meant no danger. But . . . if the Neverseen didn't show, it also meant all their planning was a waste—and that Fintan had tricked them again.

"I'm starting to think it'd be easier if I just ran onto the stage and shouted, 'Hey, Mom, we know you're here! Come out, come out wherever you are!'" Keefe grumbled as they headed into round two of walk-scan-squint-listen duty.

"But you're not going to, right?" Wylie seemed to need Keefe to verify.

Keefe shrugged. "Ask me again when we we're on round three of this."

Loud fanfare drowned out Wylie's reply, and all twelve Councillors shimmered onto the stage amid cheers and whistles and applause from the excited crowd—or that's what it looked like, at least.

"I may not trust Luzia," Keefe whispered as Councillor Emery launched into his welcome speech, "but she sure can pull off an amazing illusion. I mean . . . I *know* that's not actually them standing up there, and my brain's still like, *yes it is.*"

"Mine too," Sophie admitted, wondering if maybe that was *why* it was so hard to trust Luzia.

Luzia could hide *anything* she wanted.

"Is it bad that the festival's starting?" Marella asked when applause erupted again and the Councillors appeared to glitter away. Orem's projection took their place, and the cheers were so loud, Marella practically had to shout when she added, "Shouldn't we have found them by now?"

"Not necessarily," Wylie told her. "I'd think the Neverseen would want to wait for Orem's performance to be in full swing.

That way when they interrupt, they'll already have everyone's attention."

"I guess." But Marella didn't sound convinced.

And honestly, neither was Sophie.

The haunting voice was back—and the doubt had gone from question to conclusion: *We're missing something. We're missing something. We're missing something.*

The voice got a whole lot louder when Orem started painting the sky with streaks of color and bursts of shimmer and sparkle. The audience was so focused on the spectacle that they were completely oblivious to their surroundings.

Perfect, easy targets.

But Sophie still couldn't find anything suspicious. Everything was exactly as it should be—until Fitz's voice filled her head.

Alvar's moving.

What do you mean by "moving"? she asked.

I've been tracking him all night, and he's been sitting in his apartment. And now he's walking around.

Okay. Well. That's not that weird, she tried to remind him. *He's probably just going for a walk after sitting for so long, or—*

Or he's trying to escape, Fitz argued. *I'm sure he's noticed that there are fewer guards on the property tonight—and he knows we're not home. AND he waited until the festival started, probably assuming we'd all be too distracted watching Orem do his thing to pay attention to the Warden.*

But he still can't get past the gate, Sophie reminded him.

Maybe he thinks he can.

Is he even near the gate?

Not yet—and I think I should hit the button before he is.

Sophie bit her lip. *I get why you're worried, but . . . maybe wait a LITTLE longer—just to be sure.*

Why do I have to be sure? It's ALVAR—and it's not like hitting the button is going to kill him.

No. But . . . it sounds pretty painful. And . . . it just doesn't seem like something you should do without having a good reason.

I have a good reason!

"What's going on?" Keefe whispered to Sophie. "Your mood's spiking all over the place."

She rubbed her temples. "Fitz is freaking out because Alvar's tracker shows he's moving around Everglen, and he thinks that means Alvar's trying to escape—but . . . Alvar's not even near the gate. And . . . I just don't see him being that foolish. He knows how much security is in place. And he knows the Council—and his parents—are totally on his side right now, so I don't see why he'd take that risk. But Fitz wants to take him out with the Warden, and . . . maybe I'm a wimp, but . . . I think he should wait a little longer—at least until we have more proof."

"You're not a wimp," Keefe told her. "Fitz is zap-happy."

"He is," she agreed, relieved someone understood why she was hesitating.

But when she told Fitz that Keefe also thought he should wait, Fitz's mental voice sharpened.

Well THAT'S convenient.

What is? she asked.

Keefe siding with you. I wonder why he'd do that?

Uh . . . because he agrees that Alvar should at least be near the gate before we punish him for trying to escape, Sophie argued, sighing when Fitz's mind went silent. *I'm not saying you're wrong,* she added, putting a little extra energy behind the words in case he was trying to block her. *I'm saying . . . wait until you're sure.*

I'm sure.

Sophie rubbed her temples harder. *Well . . . I guess it's your call. But . . . at least wait until we're all together.*

Why?

I don't know. She was mostly stalling, hoping a few deep breaths would make him a little more reasonable, but she flung out a quick *In case it messes with your echo. It's kind of an emotional thing, you know? And it'll only take, like, two extra minutes to meet up, and . . . I want to be there for you.*

A beat of silence and then . . .

Fine.

The word had a definite edge.

Please don't be mad at me, Sophie begged.

I'm not, he promised. *I'm just frustrated. Now Alvar's moving back the other way, and I can't figure out what he's doing.*

Which seemed like a pretty good reason to *not* zap him, but she decided not to point that out. *Just get to the base point. We'll figure it out together.*

Yeah, see you soon.

And Fitz looked so genuinely relieved when she got there a few minutes later that her heart did a tiny flip—until he shoved his wrist under her nose and pointed to the narrow silver screen that Dex had built into the Warden's band. "See that flashing dot? That's Alvar. And see that glowing line? That's the back gate. Look how close they are—and getting closer every second."

"His heart rate's elevated too," Dex added, pointing to a blinking red light next to the screen.

Biana looked as pale as Sophie felt as she stared at the screen, watching the flashing dot creep closer to the glowing line.

"Okay," Sophie said, reaching for Fitz's free hand—as much to steady him as she was trying to steady herself. "If you think you should press the button, then—"

"I do," Fitz said before she could finish.

Click!

"Was something supposed to happen?" Biana whispered when the tiny lights kept flashing.

"Yeah, the cuff should've glowed green and the screen should've gone blank," Dex said as Fitz pressed the switch again and again. "I don't understand. I tested it a billion times." He placed his hand over the bracelet. "The tech feels fine."

But when he pressed the button himself, nothing happened.

"Could Alvar have done something to the part around his ankle?" Keefe asked.

Before Dex could answer, Fitz let out a frustrated growl and yanked the bracelet off his wrist, flinging it into the darkness as hard as he could.

"Why'd you do that?" Dex snapped. "I could've made some adjustments."

"We don't have time. We need to get to Everglen *now*." Fitz turned to Sophie, grabbing her hands. "You can teleport us there, right? Even with the gates?"

She'd done it before. But . . .

"I have to think," she told him. Because teleporting would take them right to where Alvar was—but with everyone's eyes on the sky, the crowd would definitely notice the teenagers levitating toward the stars and then plummeting back down. Not to mention the booming thunderclap when she split open the void.

They'd also be abandoning their assignments—and if the Neverseen snuck in because they weren't there to do their job . . .

"We don't have time to think!" Fitz said, loud enough to turn several heads. "We have to go. *Please*—if he gets away . . ."

It was the crack in his voice that won Sophie over.

"I'm going too," Biana informed them, wrapping her arm around her brother.

"Pretty sure we all are, right?" Keefe asked, hooking his arm with Sophie's.

"I know *I* am," Sandor said, stepping out of the shadows with Tarina and Grizel. Ro was right behind him—and so were Lovise and Woltzer—and before Sophie could blink, all her friends and bodyguards had linked into a tight circle and Fitz was floating them off the ground.

She managed to transmit what was happening to Magnate Leto as they climbed higher and higher, causing a number of gasps and cheers from the crowd—who hopefully thought it was all part of the show when Fitz sent them crashing back down and Sophie dropped them into the void.

She'd only gotten a vague glimpse of Everglen's back gate, so she pictured the clearing for the override instead, tearing open the darkness and landing them among the swirling metal statues with their reflective orbs.

Fitz was on his feet immediately, charging toward the fence's pale glow—the only real light, other than the eerie red moon—and Sophie chased after him, opening her mind and trying to track Alvar's thoughts.

But she didn't need to.

Alvar was standing a few feet back from the glowing bars, gazing into the darkness beyond.

Before he even registered their presence, Fitz tackled him—hard.

"What are you doing?" Alvar shouted as he flailed and thrashed to get Fitz off him.

"THOUGHT YOU COULD ESCAPE?" Fitz asked, pinning Alvar's shoulders.

"Of course not!"

"LIAR!" Fitz slammed Alvar into the ground again. And this

time Alvar fought back, thrusting his knee into Fitz's stomach and kicking free with his other leg—but he'd barely rolled to his side before Fitz jumped him again and punched him in the face. "WHAT'D YOU DO TO THE WARDEN?"

"Nothing!" Alvar promised, and the red streaming from his nose glinted in the moonlight as he lifted his head and his wild eyes met Sophie's. "Please—I don't know what you're talking about!"

Fitz punched him again, hitting Alvar in the mouth with a horrible crunch.

"Shouldn't we do something?" Sophie asked, turning to her friends, who were all hanging back a step, looking dazed.

"Maybe we should—" Biana started to say.

But a choking sound cut her off, and when Sophie turned back to the fight, Fitz had his arm pressed against Alvar's throat, cutting off his air supply.

"TELL ME WHAT YOU WERE DOING OUT HERE!" he demanded.

Alvar wheezed. "Heard . . . noises."

"WHAT KIND OF NOISES?!"

"Hey," Keefe said, stepping forward and grabbing Fitz's shoulder. "He can't talk if he's unconscious."

"And you're bleeding," Biana added, leaning on Dex as she pointed a shaky hand at Fitz's dripping knuckles.

When neither of them seemed to get through to him, Sophie stepped closer, whispering in Fitz's ear, "You have to be careful of your echo."

She was honestly amazed he hadn't collapsed from it already.

He must've been a little surprised too, because he reached for his chest like he needed to check, and Alvar rolled to his side, hacking and coughing and spitting out some of the red staining his teeth.

"Here," Sophie said, tearing off a strip of fabric from her sleeve, reaching for Fitz's hand and carefully wrapping his bleeding knuckles.

"Ready to tell us what's going on?" Keefe asked, crouching in front of Alvar.

"I have no idea," Alvar promised. "I heard noises outside the fence and—"

"What kind of noises?" Grizel interrupted.

Alvar wiped his mouth with his sleeve. "Crashes mostly. But some sounded like voices."

"Right," Fitz muttered, wincing as Sophie tightened the knot on his bandage to give the wounds some compression. "And let me guess—you want us to run out there and check? Did you use that trick on the guards? Is that why they're not here?"

Alvar shook his head, his desperate eyes flicking from face to face before lingering on his sister. "The guards heard the noises too. They told me to stay here while they searched the forest. That's what I was doing when Fitz assaulted me—"

"Assaulted," Fitz muttered.

"Look at me, Fitz!" Alvar snapped, pointing to his face. Even in the dim light, Sophie could see that his lip was split and his nose looked swollen. "I get it—you hate me. But I'm telling you the truth. I left my apartment because I heard noises. And I haven't touched my ankle tracker, if that's what you meant." He turned back to Biana. "Please—you *have* to believe me."

If he was lying, he was the best liar Sophie had ever seen.

Biana looked convinced, especially when Keefe told them, "He's telling the truth. I'd be able to tell if he wasn't."

Fitz snorted. "Right—like you could tell with your mom?"

Which was a *super*-low blow.

But Keefe let it go. "There's an easy enough way to know for sure. We'll ask the guards when they get back—see if they tell us the same story."

"They will," Alvar assured them. "I'm sure they'll be back any second."

But seconds turned into minutes. And when enough time had piled up, Keefe had to block Fitz from lunging for Alvar again.

"You did something to them, didn't you?" Fitz demanded. "They should be back by now!"

"There's a lot of ground to cover out there," Alvar argued. "They're probably just being thorough. Please." His eyes darted from his sister to Sophie. "I swear—I didn't do *anything* to them."

"He didn't," a voice agreed from the shadows beyond the gate—a voice that made the monster roar so loud, it nearly knocked her over. "I did."

A force field flared with the final words, momentarily whiting out the world. And when Sophie's eyes adjusted, she found herself staring at a scene straight out of her nightmares: a massive glowing dome on the other side of Everglen's fence, with four elves inside.

Gethen.

Two black-cloaked figures.

And Vespera.

FORTY-EIGHT

I KNEW IT!" FITZ YELLED, LUNGING FOR Alvar again as Sophie reached for one of her daggers— and the rest of her friends and bodyguards drew weapons of their own.

"You know *nothing*," Gethen assured Fitz, turning to the cloaked figure on his right. "And let's make sure this doesn't take any longer than necessary."

"Spread out!" Sophie warned—but she was too late. The figure had to be Ruy, and he extended his arms, trapping their whole group inside a force field.

"Don't!" Sandor shouted as Tarina swung her scythelike weapon at the wall of white energy, and Grizel barely pulled Tarina back before she electrocuted herself.

"How sweet," Gethen said. "Goblins cooperating with a troll—I doubt that'll last much longer."

"It'll last longer than you will," Wylie snapped, thrusting his arms forward and blasting a blue beam into the force field.

"Still using the same tricks?" Ruy asked, waving his hands and thickening the shield until the world turned blurry, like Vaseline smeared over glass. "You should try practicing sometime. It does wonders."

"It does," Dex agreed, tossing a handful of shiny brass gadgets that . . .

. . . bounced harmlessly off the shield.

Ruy cracked up as Dex met the same frustrating result with a handful of copper spheres. "Anyone else?"

"Yes!" Tam said, shoving his palms forward and launching a bolt of whirling shadows at the force field. The darkness sank into the white light and fanned out like fissures—and a second bolt made the black lines spread, like cracks in glass.

"So you're the Shade I've heard so much about," the other cloaked figure said, flicking her wrist and drawing all of Tam's shadows over to her—and oh, how the monster loved the sound of Umber's voice.

It brought Sophie to her knees, the world spinning, fading, slipping . . .

"Easy, Foster," Keefe said, dropping to the ground beside her, peeling off one of her gloves and tangling her fingers with his. Soft blue breezes flitted through her mind, and he whispered,

"Breathe," as he pulled off her other glove to give her double the energy. "Just breathe."

"Looks like our last visit left an even bigger impression on the moonlark than I'd hoped," Gethen noted. "Well done, Umber."

Sophie set her jaw, wanting to snap back with something clever and fierce.

But she didn't feel clever or fierce.

She felt like a clueless, weak fool who'd missed the Neverseen's plan yet again. And now she couldn't even stand strong as she faced them.

"You've got this," Keefe told her, sending more breezes into her mind as he helped her back to her feet.

"So this was never about the festival," Wylie said through gritted teeth as he combined his blue light with Tam's next blast of shadows.

"I wouldn't say that," Gethen told him. "The festival just isn't involved the way Fintan assumed it would be—and really, he should've known better. If he wants to ruin our plans, it's going to take a whole lot more than tattling on us to the Black Swan."

"So Fintan isn't a part of this?" Marella asked as Umber unraveled all the progress Wylie and Tam had made on the force field.

Gethen tilted his head to study her. "I'd heard there was another new recruit. Gisela's right—the moonlark's greatest talent does seem to be convincing people to risk their lives for her misguided cause."

"And where is Mommy Dearest tonight?" Keefe asked. "Aren't you getting a little tired of doing all her dirty work for her? Or has there been another mutiny?"

"No mutiny," Gethen assured him. "We're all working together rather well, now that Fintan isn't around to disrupt things."

"Then where is she?" Keefe countered.

Gethen smiled. "At the festival."

Panic flared with the words—but so did a fresh swell of confidence as Sophie reminded herself how thoroughly prepared the Collective and the Council were for whatever Keefe's mom might be planning.

"I wouldn't smile yet, Sophie," Gethen told her. "You truly have no idea what's going on."

"Then why don't you tell us?" she suggested, glad her voice was working again. "I'm assuming that's why you're holding us here."

"Actually, I don't want to spoil the surprise," he said smoothly. "It'll be so much more fun watching you discover it for yourselves."

"Is that why you're being so quiet?" Biana asked Vespera, and Sophie noticed that Biana had thrown back the sides of her cape to reveal her arms. The pale scars that Vespera had given her looked slightly brighter in the moonlight, but Biana definitely wasn't ashamed—and her steps were steady as she stalked to the edge of their force field.

Vespera flashed one of her flat, emotionless smiles and strode closer to Biana, smoothing the front of her ridiculous gown. The gold bodice hung loose on Vespera's frail frame, and the skirt flared so wide that Sophie wouldn't have been surprised if there were hoops sewn into it. Between the dress and the fabric headpiece that Vespera had also worn the last time they saw her—which wrapped her dark hair in a net of jeweled chains to block elvin abilities—Vespera looked like she'd thought they'd be heading to a ball, not standing around in a dark forest, ready for . . . whatever this was.

"I must say, I thought you'd have made a bit more progress on your force field by now," Gethen said, directing the comment to Tam. "I heard you'd been training."

"I have been," Tam snapped back, weaving his shadows with the purple rays that Wylie had started blasting. He slashed the beam at the force field, cutting straight through the white energy like butter.

"Foolish," Umber said, clicking her tongue as she waved her arm and unraveled Tam's shadows. "Polluting your power with light when you should be thriving on the darkness."

She hissed words Sophie couldn't understand—words that made the monster howl—and thick, unnatural black poured from her fingertips, twisting into an arrow.

"Why do you look so afraid?" Umber asked Tam as he stumbled back from the shadowflux. "*This* is your true strength. It's time for you to embrace that."

Sophie cried out as Umber hurled the arrow, and it zipped through the force field, aimed perfectly at Biana's head. But Tam snarled something before the darkness hit, and the arrow vaporized into a thick black mist.

"Now *that's* more like it," Umber told him. "*That* I can work with."

"Good," Gethen said. "Then we should move this along."

"Aren't you forgetting something?" Fitz asked, shoving Alvar forward. He'd bound Alvar's hands behind his back with strips of his cloak and had a dagger pointed at Alvar's side to keep him from fighting. "You trapped your accomplice with us."

"What makes you think we want him?" Gethen asked.

"Why else would you be here?" Fitz countered. "You need him to do something for you—either here or at the festival."

Gethen tilted his head. "What if I told you that you were right?"

"What?" Biana asked, the word mostly a gasp.

But Gethen kept his eyes on Fitz. "What if I told you that your brother is the key to everything we're planning tonight—"

"I'M NOT!" Alvar shouted.

Gethen clicked his tongue. "So he says. But you know better, don't you, Fitz? You've known all along that something didn't add up—and no one would listen to you, would they? How frustrating that must've been. Even Sophie hasn't believed you, has she? And we all know how much you rely on her. All this time, you were right. Is that what you want to hear?"

"This sounds like a game," Keefe warned as Fitz's arm

shook, forcing him to adjust his grip on the dagger. At some point he'd lost the bandage Sophie had made for him, and his hand looked slippery and red.

"No game," Gethen insisted, stepping closer, the light from the force field making his stare more piercing as it bored into Fitz. "Just a simple question. If I'm telling the truth—if Alvar's the key—then how are you going to stop him from fulfilling his role?"

"I'M NOT PLAYING A ROLE!" Alvar screamed.

"He's good, isn't he?" Gethen asked.

"He's not pretending," Sophie assured Fitz. "Alvar still doesn't have any of his memories—I just checked."

"Doesn't matter," Gethen argued, keeping his eyes locked on Fitz. "You know how we work. You know how carefully we plan things. You think we can't pull the strings to make what we need happen, with or without Alvar knowing?"

"I'll never help you!" Alvar swore.

"You already have. You met us out here, didn't you? And that made your brother and all his friends rush over." Gethen smiled as Fitz sucked in a breath. "I bet you had to drag everyone here, didn't you, Fitz? And even now—as we're talking—they still refuse to see what you do, don't they? Look at your sister."

Fitz did, and Biana looked . . . torn—her eyes mostly on the knife in Fitz's bleeding hand.

"So the question is," Gethen continued, "what are you going to do about it, Fitz? How do *you* stop the inevitable, when no one else will?"

Fitz straightened up. "I'll knock Alvar out."

"That's all?" Gethen sighed dramatically. "Don't you think we would've thought of that? Don't you realize that everything you've done up until now has been completely predictable—except one thing. Only *one*: that dagger in your hand. I didn't think you had it in you—but there you are, holding a permanent solution to the threat you're facing. But will you have the courage to use it?"

"Okay, this is *definitely* a game," Keefe warned as Fitz adjusted his grip on the weapon again.

"To what end?" Umber countered.

That's what Sophie was trying to figure out—and not making any progress.

But Keefe was right—this was a game. And Sophie was pretty sure they were losing, if Fitz's shaking was any indication, or the fact that Biana looked ready to vomit.

Careful of your echo, she transmitted to Fitz, taking a cautious step closer to him. *That might be their plan—to make you collapse under all this stress and emotion so Alvar can get away.*

Fitz's eyes darted to hers, and he took another long, slow breath, lowering his dagger ever so slightly.

Gethen glared at Sophie. "Whatever you think you've figured out, I can assure you, you're wrong." His gaze shifted to Alvar. "Perhaps I'm trying to see if we recruited the wrong Vacker. Or perhaps I simply want everyone to know that you had a choice tonight." He focused on Fitz again as he said it. "*You* have a chance, right now, to take control of this situation—a chance to eliminate the threat before it becomes anything more. It's the only way to stop what's coming next, I promise you. So the question is, will you take it? Or will you live with the regret of knowing you could've prevented everything coming next? And there are big things coming, Fitz. Bigger than you can imagine. Much, much bigger than what's already been done." He raised his sword, showing everyone how the blade was stained red. "Told you I'd find another use for it eventually," he said to Sophie. "I do hope those guards weren't friends of yours."

Bile burned Sophie's throat and tears stung her eyes as all the goblins let out a primal roar.

Gethen smiled wider. "So, Fitz. What's it going to be?"

"Don't," Sophie said as Fitz raised the dagger again. "He's manipulating you."

"Probably," Fitz admitted. "But . . . what if it's not the way you think? What if this is their way of preparing their minds for what they're about to do? Think about it—if they warn us and we ignore it, then they don't have to feel guilty about whatever horrible things they do. Then it's *our* fault, and they don't have to worry about their sanity."

"But what about *your* sanity?" she countered, glancing at her friends for help.

Keefe stepped up. "Yeah, uh, you realize they're trying to get you to *kill* Alvar, right?"

"*Of course I do!*" Fitz snapped, turning to Biana. "But he's a *murderer.*"

"I know," Biana whispered, leaning on Tam and Dex for support. "But . . . you're not."

"And I'm not that person anymore!" Alvar swore.

"I DON'T BELIEVE YOU!" Fitz knocked Alvar down to his knees.

"DON'T!" Biana shouted. "Don't let them break you the way they broke him."

"There has to be another way," Linh added.

"And if there isn't?" Fitz asked, tears gleaming in his eyes. "Can you live with yourselves if someone else dies tonight?"

"Yes," Tam said immediately. "Because we're not responsible for what *they* do. Only what *we* do."

"How noble," Gethen scoffed. "I wonder, though, if others will agree. Or if they'll look back on this moment—after everything else unfolds—and see it as proof that the moonlark and her friends are too weak to do what needs to be done, even when the opportunity is handed to them."

Fitz sucked in a shaky breath, staring at the dagger in his hand—not with fear, but determination.

"Please, Fitz," Sophie begged. "I get it—I get why you think you have to do this. But this isn't who we are."

"Isn't it?" he argued. "Why have we been training, then? Why are we carrying weapons if we aren't going to use them? I thought we were fighting back!"

"But this isn't fighting back," she corrected. "This is preemptive murder."

"She's right," Biana said, tears streaming down her pale cheeks. "Whatever happens, we'll deal with it—but not this. This will break you—that's what they want."

Fitz stared at her for a long second, then at each of his friends, before his gaze settled on Sophie. "If I let him go," he whispered, "we're going to regret it."

"Maybe," she admitted. "But if you kill him, we'll regret it more. Even you."

Please, she transmitted. *Don't let them do this to you. It'll ruin you, and . . . I don't want to lose you.*

He sighed, and for a long second she couldn't tell what he was going to do.

Then he lowered the dagger.

"I told you," Vespera said, stalking closer to Gethen. "They will always make the wrong decision. They will always choose weakness. And now it is time for them to pay the consequences."

Alvar groaned and slumped to the ground.

"What's wrong?" Sophie asked.

Before he could answer, the world went black—and the monster roared.

But this time, the darkness didn't last.

This time Tam was there, shredding Umber's shadows as fast as she could form them.

And Wylie was blasting the force field with searing blue light over and over.

This time we win, Sophie thought as their glowing cage unraveled.

She grabbed a throwing star and lined up her aim as Tam launched a bolt of shadows toward the Neverseen's shield and . . .

Everything blinked away.

"I don't understand," Linh said as Wylie sent up a flare, illuminating nothing but grass and trees.

"I think I do," Sophie murmured. She wobbled on her feet, and Keefe rushed over to steady her. "I think . . . that was an illusion—like the Councillors were at the festival."

"She's right!" Wylie blasted light toward a mirror hidden among the foliage, and the beam refracted off a dozen others.

"So they were never here?" Marella asked as Biana said, "Um, guys."

"They have to be close," Keefe reminded them. "Otherwise Umber and Ruy couldn't have been able to make those force fields and shadows—*those* were real."

"He's right," Ro said, sniffing the air. "I can smell a faint trail going this way!"

"Guys!" Biana shouted as the goblins charged after Ro. "We have another problem."

"What?" Sophie asked, not sure how much more her brain could handle.

Biana's eyes locked with Fitz's, and her stare was pure, painful dread as she admitted, "Alvar's gone."

FORTY-NINE

E CAN'T BE FAR," KEEFE SAID AS
Tarina made a quick sweep of the clearing and
Fitz shouted all kinds of furious things that
Sophie tried her best to ignore.

She focused on opening up her mind and feeling for any
trace of Alvar's thoughts—but there was too much mental
chaos drowning everything out.

"He can't light leap with the Warden," Dex reminded them.

Fitz barked a bitter laugh. "Your Warden is junk! If it worked,
Alvar would be unconscious right now."

"Yeah, what's going on with your gadgets?" Biana asked
quietly.

"I don't know," Dex admitted. "I *swear* they worked when I

tested them. It's like . . . something's interfering somehow—almost like . . . ohhhhhhh."

"What?" Fitz demanded as Dex mumbled a string of words none of them could understand.

Dex swallowed hard, looking genuinely sorry as he pointed to Sophie's cloak pin. "It must be the null. I bet it's blocking the tech around you."

Sophie's heart stopped. "But . . . the bracelet was still getting Alvar's signal—and I've been able to use my Imparter."

"Receiving's different than sending—and Imparters utilize a whole other kind of frequency." Dex pressed his fist into his head, muttering to himself about how he should've thought of that.

"But—" Sophie tried to argue.

"We don't have time for this," Wylie warned. "Just get rid of the pin and let's go find Alvar—and the Neverseen."

"He's right," Tam, Linh, and Marella all agreed.

So did Tarina, who yanked the null off Sophie's cloak when she saw how hard Sophie's hands were shaking.

Dex dismantled it faster than a gremlin. "That was definitely the problem."

Sophie's eyes burned from the disgust on Fitz's face—and she knew what he had to be thinking: If she hadn't talked him into meeting up with her before he pressed the Warden's button, none of this would be happening.

"Hey," Keefe said, reaching for her hand and filling her head with another calming breeze.

She hadn't noticed that she still wasn't wearing her gloves, and part of her wondered if she should tap her fingers to turn on Tinker's fingernail gadgets.

But what if those caused some other huge, unexpected problem?

"The good news," Dex said, "is this means the Warden's still working. So Alvar has to be on the property."

"Yeah, and I'm sure he's busy helping the Neverseen do whatever creepy thing they came here to do—just like Gethen said he would." Fitz punched the air, sending red splattering from his wounded fist.

"Or . . . maybe Alvar's just scared of you," Linh suggested. "You did come pretty close to killing him. Maybe he figured he should disappear until everything calmed down."

"It's possible," Marella agreed. "Just because he's gone doesn't mean he's helping the enemy. He seemed pretty against that."

He *had*. But . . . that was before something happened that no one else seemed to have noticed. And Sophie was tempted to leave it that way—tempted to keep everyone in the dark until she knew for sure, since it was only going to make Fitz hate her more than he already did.

But if she was right, her friends needed to know what they were dealing with. So she forced herself to blurt out, "I think Alvar might've gotten his memories back."

Biana wrapped her arms around herself. "You mean when he collapsed and groaned like that?"

Sophie nodded.

"What was the trigger?" Fitz asked, and it was the calm in his voice that got her, like he'd moved beyond rage to a scary sort of numb.

"I can only guess," she told him quietly. "But . . . it might've been the sound of Vespera's voice. That'd explain why she stayed silent up until then—which seemed super weird—and why Alvar reacted as soon as he heard it."

"That makes sense," Wylie agreed. "And it's pretty smart, actually, since it's something they knew Alvar wouldn't hear until they wanted his memories to come back."

Fitz's laugh was dark and cold—followed by a sharp intake of breath. And he rubbed his chest as his eyes focused on Sophie. "If he hurts someone, it's on—"

"He won't," Keefe jumped in, saving Sophie from finding out if Fitz had been planning to end that sentence with "you" or "us." "You're tracking him, right, Foster?"

"Trying to," she said, choking down a huge lump in her throat as she stretched out her consciousness again.

"You can do that while you move, right?" Keefe asked, turning to the others when she nodded. "Good. Then I say we follow where Ro led the rest, since he might be heading the same way. And if we need to change course, let us know, okay, Foster?"

She nodded again, and Keefe reached for her hand. "Relax. You've got this," he promised, sending one more soothing breeze into her head before he took off running.

Everyone followed, racing down the path, which grew darker and darker the farther they moved away from the glowing gate—until they could only see a few feet in front of them.

Sophie fought to keep up, but the mental multitasking slowed her down. And she soon found herself running next to Fitz at the back of their group, since he was still dealing with his healing leg.

He didn't say anything.

Didn't even look at her.

And she couldn't blame him, after everything that had happened.

It also wasn't the time to talk things out, so she let her regret fuel her determination as she pushed her consciousness farther and farther and farther, until . . .

"I found him!" she called. "And we're heading the right way!"

"Great," Fitz snorted. "So he went right to the Neverseen."

"I know," Sophie said quietly. "I'm—"

"You realize where we're going, right?" he interrupted. "This path goes straight to the main gate."

Sophie's stomach twisted.

"His DNA won't open it, though," Biana reminded them. "Plus, maybe . . ."

"Maybe what?" Fitz pressed.

Biana sighed. "Maybe he's not cooperating as much as you think he is. Just because he got his memories back doesn't mean—"

"You need to stop thinking like that, *right now*," Fitz interrupted. "I mean it—if he was with us on this, he wouldn't have run off—"

"But—"

"NO!" Fitz snapped. "If you're still deluding yourself into thinking he's on our side, you might as well hang back right here, because you're going to turn this into a bigger mess than it already is."

Sophie couldn't help wondering if he really meant the words for her—especially since a tiny part of her had to agree with what Biana was saying.

But that wasn't what mattered at the moment.

They could figure out what side Alvar was on once they caught up with him. For now, they needed to start working together again. So she closed her eyes for a beat—which wasn't a smart thing to do when running, but she could barely see through the darkness anyway. And it made it easier to whisper to him, "I'm sorry, Fitz."

For several long seconds the only sounds were gasping breaths and pounding feet as their whole group seemed to wait for Fitz's response. And just when Sophie thought he wasn't going to acknowledge her, he said, "I don't blame *you*."

There wasn't a whole lot of warmth in his voice.

But it was progress.

And it would have to be enough for the moment, because the path was curving again, and when they rounded the bend they spotted a halo of light up ahead.

"That's from the gate, right?" Dex asked.

Sophie hoped so. But . . . it had a whitish hue.

"Fan out," Keefe said under his breath. "We need to make Ruy trap us one by one. Hopefully that'll buy us a little time."

"Ruy should be our prime target," Wylie added as they all reached for weapons. "He's their safety net."

Sophie knew he was right, and she told herself to aim for black cloaks as she grabbed a throwing star. But as soon as she burst into the clearing, all she could see was Alvar standing over by the gate's control panel, and . . . she let her weapon fly, holding her breath as it arced perfectly toward the panel, hopefully hard enough to damage the sensor and . . .

. . . it sparked off of a new force field that sprang up around Alvar.

Another force field trapped her a second later, and she threw herself backward to avoid crashing into the shocking energy.

Only then did she take stock of her situation, and . . . it wasn't good news.

Her friends and Tarina were all snared under glowing domes of their own—she didn't know how Ruy could work so fast—and Sandor, Grizel, Woltzer, Ro, and Lovise were trapped under another, looking scratched and bruised.

Meanwhile, Gethen, Ruy, Vespera, and Umber were completely unscathed as they stood in the safety of their own shield, waiting just outside the gate.

And Alvar . . . he wasn't standing by the panel empty-handed.

He was holding a bloody scrap of fabric that Sophie took a second to recognize.

Fitz's missing bandage.

Covered in plenty of his DNA.

Which . . . seemed like a pretty clear statement of which side Alvar had chosen.

His timid, mournful expression was also gone, replaced with his old familiar arrogance. As if someone had flipped a switch and the old Alvar was back—just like that.

"You made it in time for the main event," Vespera said when her eyes locked with Sophie's.

"And you'll be staying *right* there," Ruy added, flashing fresh layers to the force fields that Tam, Wylie, and Dex were already attacking.

"So go ahead, Alvar," Gethen called. "We all know how much you've gone through to get to this moment. Time to fulfill your assignment—"

"Hang on," Keefe interrupted, turning to Alvar. "You seriously allowed them to erase your memories, torture you, drug you, abandon you, almost kill you—*and* let you rot for months in a miserable prison cell—all in hopes that the Council would move you back to Everglen so you could . . . open a gate?"

"It was not about the task," Vespera answered for Alvar. "It was about proving his value."

"By opening a gate," Keefe insisted. "That's . . . the *dumbest* thing I've ever heard in my life."

Sophie had to agree.

But Alvar held his head high, holding his same arrogant expression, and even Biana looked like she was starting to accept that the old Alvar had fully returned.

More important, though: Keefe's stalling had given Wylie, Tam, and Dex a chance to make progress on dismantling the force fields holding them. So Sophie asked Gethen, "Nobody could think of an easier way to get into Everglen? I can think of five off the top of my head."

"And they all take, like, two minutes, right?" Keefe asked her.

"Probably less," Sophie corrected.

Vespera shrugged, knocking one of her golden sleeves off her shoulder. "If someone is willing to jump through ridiculous hoops to prove their loyalty, who am I to stop them? Alvar created the plan himself."

Keefe turned back to the eldest Vacker. "So, wait. *You* said, 'Hey, I know! Why don't you slice me up with a shamkniv—'"

"*That* was his punishment for the problem he created," Vespera corrected, "which I was very generous to allow him a chance to redeem himself for."

"Sure," Keefe agreed, rolling his eyes. "Full body torture seems like a totally reasonable punishment for . . . What was the problem again? A locked gate?"

"It was not *any* locked gate," Vespera argued. "It was a locked gate that he *would have had* ready access to, had he kept his identity hidden the way Ruy and Umber did, rather than following Fintan's foolish lead. So I told him that I did not care how he fixed it, just that he did by the night of the festival."

"What does the festival have to do with anything?" Biana asked.

"You'll see soon enough," Gethen told her. "And we're wasting too much time. Go ahead, Alvar."

"SERIOUSLY?" Sophie shouted as Alvar reached for the gate's sensor. Even if he had chosen his side—maybe she could change his mind. "After all the times you swore you'd never go back to their cause, even if you got your memories back. All the times you swore you wanted to make them pay for the scars they carved into you. All the horrors they let you suffer through—you're just going to fall right back into the role they want you to play."

"Never underestimate the power of a total-memory flashback," Gethen told her. "It's the perfect mental reset."

"Okay, *that's* the dumbest thing *I've* ever heard," Sophie said, keeping her focus on Alvar. "This is crazy. You're not some robot that needs resetting. You're a person with a brain and . . . and feelings. And you know this is wrong. I *know* you know it—even if you don't want to admit it. Just like I know you don't want to go back to being that creepy person everyone hated."

Alvar tilted his chin higher, but she could see the tremble in his jaw—a tiny crack in his facade. Proof that this truly wasn't over as long as the gate wasn't open.

She leaned closer, holding his stare as she added, "The Council gave you a second chance—and you haven't blown it yet. You could stop this right now and prove you really are the better person you've been claiming to be. Think about the life you could have—how happy you could be. Think about how happy you would make your family."

And that was the moment she lost him.

"You want to talk about my *family*?" he snapped, his features angling into hard lines. "And I don't mean the brother who would've been happy to murder me about ten minutes ago—though that was eye-opening. And I don't mean the sister who would've stood by and let him do it while shedding a few pretty tears, either. I don't even mean the parents who've only been so supportive recently because they know they all but phased me out of their lives the moment they chose to have more children. No, that's only the beginning of the glorious *Vacker legacy*—and *that's* why I did this. Tonight, I finally get to show everyone who the Vackers truly are—and my bratty little brother and sister get to watch."

"Alvar asked that his reward for fulfilling this assignment be that I allow you to join us for the big reveal," Vespera told Sophie and her friends. "And I will keep my word, so long as you stay on your best behavior. Your goblins will be staying here—as will your ogre. But I will allow the troll to come with you, since I am curious to see her reaction as well. And if I detect *anything* untoward, I will let Umber show you exactly how much pain she can trigger with shadowflux—and trust me, you cannot even begin to fathom it. Understood?"

She waited for each of them to nod before she told Alvar, "Let us in."

Alvar bowed his head, and Sophie's heart turned heavier and heavier as he smeared Fitz's blood on the sensor and the gates swung slowly inward, letting Gethen, Vespera, Ruy, and Umber stride smoothly into the property.

"And just in case you're still thinking you'll find a way to be heroes," Gethen added, "allow me to introduce your escorts for this journey into the Vacker family history."

He whistled through his teeth and the earth rumbled softly, sending all the goblins leaping to their feet.

Sophie braced for an army of dwarves, but when the ground opened up, four of the biggest, scariest ogres she'd ever seen marched toward them, licking their pointed black teeth.

FIFTY

ELL, IF IT ISN'T OUR MIGHTY
princess—cowering with a bunch of
worthless goblins!" the tallest ogre of
the four said as he circled the force
field that Ro, Sandor, Grizel, Lovise, and Woltzer were currently trapped in. "Seems fitting, doesn't it?"

The other three ogres grunted and jeered.

They each wore spiked metal diapers, spiked shin guards,
and spiked forearm bracers—but the ogre harassing Ro had
two swords instead of one, both strapped across his massive
back in crisscrossed sheaths. Swirls of tattoos decorated his
chest, and his head had a thin shock of slicked white hair.

Ro studied her painted claws, not bothering to look at him

as she said, "I don't know, Cadfael. It seems much more fitting that you let the Neverseen call for you like you're their little pet. Do you do tricks for them if they toss you a treat? Is that what today is?"

Cadfael raised one of his eyebrows—which was pierced with four silver spikes. "You want to talk about pets? I hear you spend your days serving at the heels of some scrawny, worthless brat." He glanced over his shoulder at Sophie and her friends. "It's the one in the middle, isn't it? He keeps glaring at me." He swaggered over, and Sophie found herself feeling grateful for the force fields around them when Cadfael stepped right in front of Keefe. "Oh yeah, it's definitely this one. Look at the way his little hands are all curled up like he wants to punch me."

"Actually, I was thinking more about cutting off that ruby," Keefe told him, pointing to a large stone pierced through the skin on Cadfael's stomach, right above the dip of his spiked metal diaper. "I could keep it with the jewel I sliced out of Dimitar's ear when I beat him at sparring. *And* I'd be doing you a favor, 'cause, dude, that is *not* a good look."

Bad idea to anger the scary ogre, Sophie transmitted.

See, and I think it sounds like a whole lot of fun, Keefe countered.

He didn't even blink when Cadfael drew a dagger from a sheath hidden in one of his bracers and said, "I bet Ro likes that smart mouth of yours. So maybe I should cut out your tongue."

Keefe smirked. "I'm pretty sure she'd thank you for that."

"I would," Ro agreed.

Cadfael gritted his teeth. "Then maybe I should gut him, so you have to crawl home to Daddy—or your pathetic husband."

"No gutting today," Gethen cut in as Sophie's stomach turned all kinds of sour. "We have a different message to send."

"And if you want your payment, I suggest you cooperate," Vespera added to Cadfael.

"Oh, so you *are* getting a treat!" Ro said, standing up and clapping her hands. "Tell me, Cad—what's the going rate for treason these days?"

"Anything I want." He sheathed his dagger and turned back to face her. "That's the beauty of setting my own rules. But have fun sulking with your goblins."

"Are we ready?" Ruy asked.

Vespera turned back to Sophie. "Since you have all started arming yourselves, I expect you to empty your pockets before we go. Same goes for you, troll."

Sophie's chest tightened with each weapon she was forced to toss aside. But she managed to keep one dagger and a couple of throwing stars in the hidden pockets in her boots—and she hoped her friends were able to do the same.

Before she could transmit to check, their force fields blinked away, leaving the clearing much darker as the ogres herded them into a clump.

This is good, Fitz transmitted, nudging his way closer to Sophie while the Neverseen were busy searching Tarina for any weapons she might still be concealing. *It's going to be even darker once we're away from the glow of the gates. So if we stay close, we might be able to teleport away before they notice what we're doing.*

But we can't abandon Sandor and the others, Sophie reminded him. *Plus, I don't think we can leave until we know what the Neverseen are really up to. We need to figure out a plan. Is it . . . is it okay if I hold your hand? Only because enhancing should make it easier for us to form a mental link with everyone. Not for . . . anything else.*

He reached for her, and she could feel the rough scabs crusting his wounded knuckles as their fingers tangled together. *You don't have to ask to do this.*

Sophie looked away, her eyes burning as much as her cheeks. *I just . . . figured I should make sure, after . . .*

Fitz sighed. *It's a bad day, but . . . I meant what I said—I don't blame you. You couldn't have known about the null. And I wouldn't have backed down on Alvar if I didn't realize you were right.*

She risked a glance at him, surprised at how calm he looked.

I know, he said, reminding her that he could hear what she was thinking. *In a weird way, it's like . . . things finally make sense. Alvar's exactly who I thought he was. The Neverseen are trying to pull off some elaborate plan. So now it's just time to do what we always do and focus on stopping them.*

Sophie nodded, knowing there was probably more they needed to say—but he was right about focusing. *We need to figure out how to get our bodyguards back,* she transmitted, and Fitz used the energy pouring from her fingertips to send the message to all their friends—who did an impressive job of *not* flinching as her voice filled their heads.

Already on it, Biana told them—which made everyone realize Biana was missing. *I'm fine,* she promised. *No one saw me sneak away, and I'm just bringing Sandor one of Dex's gadgets so he can take out their force field. I'll be back in a second.*

It was actually eighteen seconds before Biana made it safely back to their group—and Sophie was pretty sure each second shaved a year off her life.

Why isn't the force field flashing? Dex asked.

Because they have to wait to use it until Ruy's gone, Biana reminded him, *otherwise Ruy will just trap them again. So I put it right next to the force field—close enough that if they dig, the shift in the soil should make it roll into the wall of energy. And I asked them to hang back for a few minutes once they're free.*

Why? the rest of their friends wondered.

Sophie understood, even before Biana said, *Because I want to see what the Vacker legacy is—don't you?* And Sophie agreed.

It had to be something huge if Alvar was willing to go through so much to expose it—and if his memories of it made him revert back to his old self so fully.

"*Now* are we ready?" Umber asked as Gethen shoved Tarina back into Sophie's group.

"We are," Vespera said, turning to Alvar, who nodded and led them away from the gates.

Into the dark.

Soon, the only light came from the eerie red moon, which was slowly shifting back to silver as the eclipse progressed.

"So are you going to tell us where we're going?" Keefe asked. "Or do you want us to guess? My money's on Fitz's room, since the amount of hair products in there is kind of a legacy."

"We're not going to the house," Gethen told him.

"What about the lake?" Tarina asked.

"No," Vespera said, which ruled out Sophie's theory that this had something to do with the destroyed troll hive.

But it had to be about Luzia.

She was the original owner of the property.

And she was way too good at hiding things.

Sophie kept her eyes on the shadows, squinting at the scenery, trying to recognize anything. *I think they're taking us to the override,* she transmitted.

That's what I'm thinking too, Fitz said.

What's the override? Marella asked.

It's a way to shut down the fence around the property, Biana explained.

Okay, Wylie thought slowly, *if that's their plan, why didn't they just have Alvar do that instead of opening the gate?*

That was a very good question.

And no one had an answer.

So they concentrated on coming up with a survival plan.

If this gets ugly, we're going to need a way of taking the ogres out fast, Sophie told them. *Linh—can you call the water in the lake?*

It's pretty far away, Linh admitted. *But I bet I could if you enhanced me.*

But a wave isn't going to do much good if Ruy's around, Biana warned them. *He'll just shield everyone.*

What about that light-shadow thing that made Ruy flee the last attack—do you know how to re-create that? Dex asked Tam and Wylie.

I wasn't there, Tam reminded him. *So I can only guess what Umber did—and shadowflux is pretty unstable, so if I'm wrong, there's no way to know what problems it might cause.*

Well . . . we'll call that our backup plan, Fitz decided. *Anyone got any other ideas?*

I can always start some fires, Marella thought quietly. *But there's a pretty good chance I'll burn your house down.*

Another backup plan, Fitz told her. *What else?*

I could try transmitting to Magnate Leto, Sophie suggested. *See if he can send over any help. But . . . they might be dealing with their own mess, since I told him where we were going and he hasn't sent anyone to check on us.*

Yeah, and we know my mom's there, Keefe added. *So . . . that's not good.*

I'm sure it's not, Fitz agreed.

But worrying about that wasn't going to help anything.

I have a feeling the only way out of this is to fight, Sophie thought quietly. *We wait for Sandor and the others to catch up, and then we use whatever weapons and training we have and hope we catch them by surprise.*

And if it gets too ugly, Fitz added, *we hit them with waves and fire and whatever that shadow-light reaction is.*

There's also my sloppy inflicting, Sophie noted, *which might work on the ogres. They aren't wearing headpieces—but I might take you guys out too, so . . .*

So we have a lot of messy plans that cause a lot of problems, Marella finished for her. *But . . . I guess it's better than nothing.*

And sadly, that was all the planning they had time for. The path was getting brighter as they drew closer to the glowing fence, and the next bend they rounded brought them back to the clearing with the override.

"Have you figured it out yet?" Vespera asked, waving her arms at all the swirling metal statues.

"You want us to turn off Everglen's fence?" Sophie guessed.

"No, I want you to see beyond what your eyes tell you," Vespera corrected, tilting her face toward the moon. "Long ago, I realized the best place to hide things was in plain sight. And I shared my theories with someone I respected—someone who has since been using that knowledge to put a veil over everyone's eyes for the last several millennia, while I've wasted away in Lumenaria for similar crimes. So now it's time to shatter those illusions."

With a swish of her golden gown, Vespera reached for the mirrored orb in one of the tallest statues, lifted it from the coils of metal, and hurled it at the ground. And as the glass splintered into a million pieces, the world around them flickered away, revealing a hidden section of the clearing that stretched into the space that used to look like a wall of dark trees.

Now there was a large grassy knoll bathed in the moonlight—and pressed into the side was a round silver door, like they'd found some sort of futuristic hobbit hole.

Even Alvar looked shocked by the revelation.

But no one was as stunned as Tarina. "It can't be," she whispered, stumbling forward and running her hand across the smooth metal.

"I assure you, it is," Vespera told her.

"What is it?" Biana asked.

Tarina leaned closer, sniffing the earth around the curve of the door. "It's . . . a hive."

Sophie frowned. "I thought your hives were connected to trees."

"They don't have to be," Tarina told her, still sniffing the ground. "All we actually need is a suitable space. But this . . . shouldn't be here."

"No," Vespera agreed. "It shouldn't. And yet, here it is."

"So this is the old hive, then?" Fitz asked. "That's why I couldn't find it?"

Tarina shook her head, and her voice cracked as she said, "No, this is something else."

"It is indeed." The smile on Vespera's lips glowed in the dim light, and it looked like there was actually some emotion behind it.

But it was a cold, vindictive kind of glee that had Sophie

pulling her cloak tighter around herself and checking to make sure the few weapons she'd held on to were easily within reach.

"How did you know about this place?" Fitz asked, directing the question to Alvar, who was making a slow circle around the shadowy mound, still looking a little dazed—like maybe he'd only heard that something was hidden there but had never actually seen it.

Vespera answered for him. "He learned from the same person who told me: Orem."

"But . . . Luzia said Orem didn't know about the hives or her connection to the trolls," Sophie argued.

"Yes, Luzia says many things, does she not?" Vespera said quietly. "It gets very hard to determine when she is fooling you and when she is fooling herself. Perhaps she truly believes that she kept the secret from her son. Perhaps she is simply so used to her deceptions that they now feel as though they are fact. Either way, Orem asked me about his mother's secret project long ago, thinking I surely must have been involved. And that was when I realized that Luzia had stolen ideas far beyond the illusions I had given her to play with and was now dealing with things she neither understood nor fully appreciated. But before I could confront her, I was arrested—and I have long suspected that she may have been the reason behind that. A desperate attempt at keeping all of this hidden. And so it has been, for all those long years. *I* have been disgraced—removed from history because I was willing to make the changes our world needs but does not yet wish to accept. And Luzia has been celebrated, her family name becoming the epitome of glory and excellence. But not any longer. It is high time for the world to see the reality. And to see that this hive—"

"Is still active," Tarina interrupted, holding up a clump of grass she'd torn from the ground. "It's sealed from this side, as it would've been if it were abandoned. But someone on the other side—*my* side—must still be using it. I can feel the energy pulsing through the earth. But I've never heard of this place—and I've never seen a hive fused with metal. It's so . . . unnatural."

Vespera raised one eyebrow. "Did you really believe your empresses would not have secrets of their own?"

"Not like this. Our hives are celebrated. They would never be kept hidden."

"Oh, I believe you will find that there is much to keep hidden here," Vespera said with another gleeful smile. "Unseal the entrance, Alvar."

"NO!" Tarina lunged to grab his arm—only to find herself dragged back by Cadfael.

"You don't give the orders, little troll," he said as Tarina twisted and thrashed.

"And *you* don't understand," she snarled back. "That is an *active* hive! And look at the sky." She pointed to the moon, where the last of the red was slowly slipping away as the eclipse finished its cycle. Her eyes locked with Sophie's, and Sophie tasted bile when Tarina added, "You don't know what stirs in there."

"But that is exactly what the world needs to find out," Vespera insisted, waving Alvar forward. He frowned at the silver door, searching for a latch.

"I'm serious!" Tarina shouted. "If any newborns have hatched, you cannot unleash them."

Cadfael tightened his grip as she tried to break free again. "You're really so scared of your own kin?"

"Newborns have no kin," Tarina told him. "No reason. Not even any self-preservation. Just insatiable hunger and unfathomable strength. They are my kind in our most primal, animalistic stage, and we keep them locked away until the worst of their bloodlust sates."

"*These* will not be normal newborns," Vespera assured her. "Luzia and your empress have been experimenting—trying to infuse that power and strength into a being with more cunning reason."

Tarina shuddered. "If that is true, then . . . then that is all the more reason to keep them sealed away. If their *experiments* had been successful, I would've heard of their triumph."

"Well, then it's time for the world to see their failings. Unseal the hive!" Vespera ordered again.

Alvar pointed to the metal. "How? There's no handle—no latch."

"Ugh, you really are worthless," Umber said, shoving him aside and sending shadows skittering across the door, brushing away the light layer by layer and revealing a panel that must've been hidden by another of Luzia's illusions.

Sophie let out a relieved breath. "That will need Luzia's DNA!"

"Exactly," Vespera said, holding up a vial that looked a lot like the one that Fitz had given Sophie for the override. "And Orem happily provided some."

"You have no idea how much you're going to regret this," Tarina warned as Vespera handed the vial to Alvar.

"I assure you, I am beyond regret," Vespera said. "Go ahead, Alvar. Show us your family's legacy."

Alvar stepped toward the panel, and Sophie couldn't help wondering if such enormous stakes had ever come down to a vial of spit. But then the panel was flashing green—the light almost glaring in the dark clearing—and there was a rushing sound, like an air lock unsealing. Rotten, sour fumes slammed against their senses, making them gag and cough as the door swung slowly open, and Sophie palmed one of her only throwing stars as they stared into the space beyond.

The round, sunken room had several metal stairways leading down, lit by the orange glow from some sort of technical panel in the center. And the drippy walls were lined with twelve hexagonal cubbies, like a single strip of honeycomb. Most were covered in a thick, slimy white film that blocked any glimpse of what brewed in the amber-colored goo beyond. But not all of them.

"Think those three were always empty?" Keefe said, voicing

the question that Sophie hadn't wanted to ask as she searched every shadow for signs of life.

There weren't many places to hide.

And as the seconds dragged on, Sophie's pulse slowly began to steady—until she caught a flicker of motion on the edge of her peripheral vision.

"Did you see that?" she whispered, squinting at the darkest corner of the room.

None of her friends nodded.

But the motion flickered again—and this time *everyone* saw them.

Three pairs of glowing orange eyes.

"SEAL THE HIVE!" Tarina commanded—and this time Umber listened, grabbing the door and swinging it closed as fast as she could.

But the newborns were faster, their massive bodies a blur of slimy muscle and ragged claws as they slammed against the door hard enough to rip it off its hinges, sending the huge circle of metal crashing down on top of Umber.

Then the beasts were free, trampling into the clearing and raising their heads to sniff out their new surroundings as everyone scrambled back and reached for weapons. Moonlight glinted off their wet skin, giving them a slippery blue-gray tint, and Sophie caught a glimpse of hippo-size fanged teeth as one of the newborns charged one of Cadfael's soldiers.

The ogre's sword clanged uselessly off the beast's thick skin, and the two went tumbling out of the clearing, rolling farther and farther, until all Sophie could see was the faint outline of their thrashing limbs in the darkness. The grunts and growls grew more feral—more brutal—until they cut off with an ear-splitting screech and a horrific crunch. Slurping sounds followed, and Sophie turned away, not wanting to see the newborn as it began to feed.

She focused on other sounds—a tangle of snarls and growls—and caught a glimpse of Tarina on the opposite edge of the clearing, wrestling one of the beasts with her bare hands.

The third newborn was stalking back and forth around Umber, who was still buried under the heavy door. A glowing force field kept Umber safe, and the beast kept shocking itself again and again, trying to tear its way through the white energy. And Sophie couldn't understand why it was so relentless, until she saw the red staining the ground.

She couldn't see enough of Umber's body to tell how badly she was injured. But . . . Umber wasn't moving. And she'd lost a lot of blood.

If Gethen, Vespera, and Ruy cared about their fallen Shade, they didn't show it as they stood under their own force field, which was positioned much closer to where Tarina and the newborn were waging their battle.

And there was no sign of Alvar anywhere—but Sophie couldn't blame him for hiding.

"Stay back!" Tarina shouted when Sophie and her friends

ran over to help her. She kicked at the newborn's stocky legs, trying to knock it off-balance—but the newborn was much too strong. The beast twisted free, leaping for Sophie's throat—and Tarina grabbed its feet and dragged it back to her. "I mean it," she grunted, barely dodging its snapping teeth. "Light leap—teleport—whatever you need to do. Just get out of here and head somewhere safe!"

Sophie was tempted. This fight was beyond anything they'd trained for. But . . .

"What about you?" she asked as the newborn raked its claws across Tarina's face.

"I'm not leaving until this hive is sealed again," Tarina gritted out, thick red lines streaming down her cheeks.

"How do we do that?" Dex asked. "It doesn't even have a door anymore."

"I'm not sure yet," Tarina admitted, grabbing the newborn's giant fangs and wrenching them away from her neck. "But that's *my* problem. *My* people made these beasts."

"Luzia helped," Biana argued.

"She might've helped with some of the others. But not with this batch," Tarina insisted. "The hive was sealed on your side."

"Yeah, until my brother and his creepy friends opened it," Fitz reminded her. "And now they're hiding under their little shield like cowards."

"This is not our fight," Vespera said. "And this is not your fight either. If you had any sense of survival, you would flee."

That settled it for Sophie. "I'm not going anywhere," she told her friends. "But if you guys want to leave—"

"I'm staying," Keefe interrupted, and Dex, Tam, Linh, and Wylie agreed.

Marella hesitated a second before she added, "Pretty sure you guys are going to need to fight these things with fire, so I'm in."

"Me too," Biana added.

Fitz nodded. "Today I'm starting a new Vacker legacy!"

"A legacy of fools who get themselves slaughtered while trying to be heroes," Gethen noted.

"Seriously," Ruy added. "You guys haven't even noticed that one of the newborns ran off already, heading who knows where."

They all whipped around, squinting through the darkness beyond the clearing, to where Sophie had last heard the newborn feasting on the fallen ogre—and found nothing but silence and shadows.

"The other ogres must've gone after it," Linh said—and she was probably right. Cadfael and his remaining soldiers were nowhere to be seen either.

"Just to be safe," Wylie added, "we need to make sure we're each focusing on different directions. This clearing is *big*, and this property is even bigger, so if we divide up where we're keeping lookout—"

"You can watch the beast as it devours you," Ruy finished for him. "Genius plan!"

"You're right!" Tam snapped. "It's way smarter to send them after *you*." He whispered something in a dark shadowy language, and a spiral of shadowflux blasted out of his palms, slamming into the Neverseen's force field so hard that the glowing energy exploded in a shower of sparks.

Ruy raised his arms to form another, but Tam was faster, binding Ruy's wrists in unnaturally black shadows that seeped under his skin, turning his fingers as dark as the shadowflux itself. And when Ruy waved his blackened hands . . .

Nothing.

Not even a flicker of power.

"Interesting," Gethen said. "You've trained far harder than I realized."

"I have," Tam snarled—though Sophie could tell by the pitch of his voice that he was a little stunned by what he'd just pulled off. "And now you can fight like the rest of us! We'll see how long you last!"

The beast attacking Umber's shield seemed eager to take on that challenge, pivoting toward the three newly exposed members of the Neverseen and charging full speed ahead.

"I told you, this is not our fight," Vespera said, grabbing hold of Ruy as Gethen raised a crystal up to the moonlight. None of them so much as looked Umber's way as they left their injured Shade behind to save themselves.

The newborn roared and pivoted again, lunging for Tam, like it held him responsible for its lost prey.

Linh slammed it with a blast of water, but the beast shook itself dry and kept right on charging.

"Flame time?" Marella asked.

"Not unless we can herd them all a *lot* closer," Sophie told her, reaching for one of her throwing stars. She checked her aim twice before letting the star fly and . . .

. . . nailed the beast right in one of its orange eyes—hard.

The newborn went down even harder, clawing at its injured face—and its agonized wails caught the *other* newborn's attention. With a rage-filled screech, the final newborn shoved Tarina aside and raced after Sophie with furious speed.

Sophie flung a throwing star at its head—her *last* throwing star—but it ducked the strike easily, leaving her with only a tiny dagger left in her arsenal. She hurled that, too, remembering Sandor's lecture about the importance of holding on to at least one weapon only *after* the beast dodged that blade and she had zero options left—except to turn and flee.

"HEY, NEWBIE, OVER HERE! I'LL BE WAY MORE FUN TO EAT!!!" Keefe shouted—but the newborn stayed fixated on Sophie as she sprinted away from the glow of the one remaining force field, hoping to lose the beast in the darkness beyond.

She channeled every single drop of energy into her sprint, knowing she'd never be fast enough to outrun the bloodthirsty beast, but hoping she could at least lure it far enough away from her friends that they'd have time to seal the hive and flee to safety. Her muscles burned and her lungs screamed for air, but still she kept pushing, pushing, pushing, barreling through the darkness with no idea where she was going, turning down any path she spotted. But no matter which way she went, she could still hear the newborn gaining on her—and it was so much more terrifying than the mental monster she'd been battling for so many weeks. Until finally, the beast was close enough to leap. She braced for impact, hoping it would finish her quickly and—

—a mass of gray tackled the newborn away, both creatures tumbling into the trees with a snarl and a screech.

"That was close!" Ro shouted, and Sophie spun around, squinting through the shadows until she picked out the shapes of Ro and three goblins running toward her down a moonlit path. The light was too dim to see that it was Grizel, Lovise, and Woltzer until they were much closer. And Sophie was glad they were safe—and grateful for the backup—but . . .

She hated knowing that all the crunching and snarling in the trees was happening to *Sandor*. And if he ended up like that ogre . . .

"Aim for its eyes!" she shouted. "That's the only place they seem to be vulnerable."

"Actually, it's better to rip out their teeth and stab them with the fangs," Cadfael informed her as he crawled silently out of a gap in the ground and held up a huge bloody tooth in his badly shredded hand. "Apparently the only thing that can kill them is themselves."

"It's fine," Ro said as Sophie stumbled back. "He's on our side—for now, at least."

"I'm on whatever side is ending these beasts," Cadfael agreed.

Sophie nodded, wondering if the fact that Cadfael was alone meant the other ogres were . . .

Probably better not to think about it. Especially with all the grunting and screeching still going on in the trees.

Cadfael didn't look so great. His swords were gone, as were both of his shin guards. And he had deep gouges running down each of his legs.

"Did you kill the newborn you went after?" she asked.

He nodded grimly, staring at the bloody fang in his hand. "I've never fought anything like that—and I've fought many trolls in my day. Whatever the trolls are doing in that hive violates *all* of the treaties."

Sophie was sure it did. But they'd have to deal with that after they got the hive sealed up again.

"Should someone go help Sandor?" she had to ask as a gut-wrenching screech rang through the air, followed by a series of gruesome cracks.

"He's got this," Grizel insisted, and Sophie tried to tell herself that if Grizel wasn't worried, she shouldn't be either.

But she didn't *really* breathe again until Sandor shouted, "Another one down!"

He stumbled out of the tree line a minute later, holding out his arm—which looked like it had been chewed up and spit out a few times—and showing off the two newborn fangs in his palm.

"Cadfael said there were only three newborns," Grizel said as she took a fang from Sandor. "So only one more to go, right?"

"Yeah," Sophie said. "And I already took out one of its eyes."

"Then let's finish this." Sandor ordered her to stay behind him as they charged toward the clearing, and Sophie was surprised to realize how far she'd run in her desperate sprint. It took several excruciating minutes to make it back to the hive. And when they got there . . .

"So much for only one left," Cadfael muttered.

Sophie could only nod and count.

One newborn grappling with Tarina.

One newborn screeching at Marella as she waved it back with her flaming hands.

One newborn trapped in a bubble of water by Linh—and it didn't seem to be drowning.

One newborn that Wylie kept blasting with bolts of light.

Four, total—and none of them had a damaged eye. So there might actually be five.

And the entrance to the hive was still wide open. More could hatch any second—though Tam was over there doing something with inky black shadows, so hopefully that meant he was working on an actual plan.

"THERE YOU ARE!" Keefe shouted, racing over from a different path—and nearly knocking Sophie over with his hug. "Sorry," he said as she fumbled to regain her balance. "I was just starting to think . . . I mean . . . I knew you could handle yourself . . . but . . ."

His voice cracked, and he squeezed her even tighter.

She hugged him back, feeling like she could breathe for the first time in a while. "It's okay—I'm fine. How's everyone else?"

"Still fighting," he promised. "But . . . it's been pretty rough in there since the new batch attacked." He ended their hug and stepped back—and Sophie noticed bits of red splattered across his neck and cheek. "Please tell me those fangs you're holding mean you've found a way to kill these beasts," he begged the bodyguards.

"We have," Cadfael answered for them—and if Keefe was surprised to see the ogre with their group, he didn't show it.

"Does the injured one still breathe?" Sandor asked.

Keefe nodded. "I've been trying to find it. But it's hard to follow the trail in the dark."

"On it," Ro said, pointing to a patch of shadows between two gnarled trees and telling Keefe, "Wait there."

"You too," Sandor told Sophie, waving Grizel, Woltzer, and Lovise forward. Cadfael joined them as well. "We'll call for you when everything's clear."

"You're sure you don't need our help?" Sophie had to ask, even though she was totally good sitting back and letting the bodyguards take over. Some problems screamed *Let the big muscly warriors handle this*—and killer mutant newborn trolls was definitely one of them.

Sandor assured her they'd be fine, and Sophie slumped against one of the trees, trying not to let herself feel too relieved. This was far from over, and there were so many things that could still go wrong.

"Have you guys figured out a plan for sealing the hive?" she asked. "Is that what Tam's doing over there?"

"I think so," Keefe told her. "But I've been newborn hunting for the last few minutes—and looking for you. So I don't know if anything's changed since Tam dismantled the force field and they pulled the door off Umber's body."

"Body?" Sophie repeated, standing up straight again. "She's . . . dead?"

He squirmed a little as he nodded. "It looked like she died pretty quickly—which I guess makes sense, between the door falling on her and the newborns trampling on top of it. But . . . yeah. She's definitely gone."

Sophie wrapped her arms around herself, trying to figure out what to do with that information.

"I know," Keefe said, scooting closer, letting her lean on him. "I don't know what to feel either. I mean . . . after what she did to you—and what she did today—she deserved it. But . . . it was weird to see her all crushed like that."

Sophie squeezed her eyes shut, trying not to picture it. But she could feel bile rising up her throat anyway.

Time for a quick subject change.

"Think we should go down there and try to get the door back

on the hive?" she asked. "I know Sandor and Ro told us to wait here, but every second we leave the hive open, more newborns could hatch."

"Not necessarily."

"What do you mean?"

He chewed his lip. "I should probably let Fitz be the one to explain."

The name pinched her heart, jolting her awake.

Keefe had said everyone was still fighting, but when she checked the clearing again, she realized Fitz and Biana were missing—and she kind of hated herself for not realizing that sooner.

"They're safe," Keefe promised. "It's just . . . kind of complicated."

"Complicated," Sophie repeated, hating how ominous that sounded. Injuries could be complicated. Especially serious ones.

"They're safe," Keefe assured her again. "They're just . . . in the hive—which isn't as scary as it sounds."

"Uh—there are still *five* unhatched newborns in there, ready to hatch any second!" Sophie argued.

"Actually, there aren't. It's still the middle of the night. They won't hatch until the morning."

"Maybe that's what Tarina *says*, but since *seven* of them have already hatched, I'm thinking—"

"Only three," Keefe corrected. "*Three* hatched early. The other four were freed."

"Freed." She knew she needed to stop repeating what he said—but it'd been a long day and her brain was having trouble computing.

Keefe blew out a breath. "Okay, I'll give you the short version and let Fitz fill in the details. It turns out . . . Alvar snuck into the hive while we were fighting and slashed four more membranes."

"Alvar's still here?" She'd assumed he'd been the first to flee when everything turned scary and deadly—though maybe that was foolish, since the Warden wouldn't let him leave the property.

"Sorta. Like I said . . . it's *complicated*. I'll take you to Fitz as soon as we get the all clear, and then it'll make a lot more sense—I swear."

Sophie really wasn't in the mood to wait—but Keefe wouldn't tell her anything else. So when Cadfael finally finished off the last newborn, she all but sprinted into the clearing, trying not to look at all the carnage as she ran. But she still caught a glimpse of Umber's mangled body, half pressed into the ground outside the hive.

Umber's hood still mostly covered her face—but the part she could see was so misshapen that she had a feeling the skull had been crushed so badly that they'd never be able to figure out what she looked like.

Not that it mattered anyway.

Umber was dead.

Like, *really* dead—definitely no coming back from what happened.

One enemy down.

It should've made her feel better, but . . . mostly she just wanted to vomit.

"Disgusting, isn't it?" Cadfael asked, and Sophie jumped, wondering how long he'd been standing there.

She had to clear her throat several times to get her voice to work. "Well, it's a dead body. . . ."

He shook his head. "That's not what I meant. They left her here. With all the power and tricks they have. They just left her here to rot. One of their own. It's disgusting. I'm not leaving here without my soldiers—even if there's not much left of them."

Sophie was tempted to point out that when a band of ogres attacked Havenfield, they'd left bodies behind as well.

But maybe Cadfael hadn't been a part of that.

"These are the people you're choosing to serve, Cad," Ro said as she joined them.

"I'm not *serving* anyone," he snapped. "I pick and choose my assignments."

Ro crossed her arms. "How's that working out for you?"

He gritted his teeth, flashing all the jagged points, but said nothing as he stalked away.

Ro followed, and for a second Sophie thought she was alone, until she realized Keefe was standing quietly beside her—

which reminded her where she was supposed to be heading.

"Maybe you should get a little fresh air before you go inside the hive," he suggested. "'Cause if you're this queasy now, it's only going to get worse."

He had a point. She could already smell the rancid stench waiting for her inside—and she definitely wasn't looking forward to seeing that drippy honeycomb of milky-membraned cubbies now that she knew exactly what was growing in that amber-colored goo.

But . . . Fitz and Biana were waiting in there—and she needed to know why.

"I'll be fine," she promised, heading for the door.

"I'll be right here," Keefe told her, offering a weak smile as she peered inside, half expecting to spot more blinking orange eyes.

But the hive looked mostly like she remembered it—just with more empty cubbies. And two familiar figures standing off to the side with their backs facing away from her.

When nothing jumped out to murder her, she took one last breath of somewhat fresh-smelling air before she forced her legs to carry her into the hot, stinky hive. Her footsteps clanged down the metal stairs and were somehow even louder as she crossed the floor, but Fitz and Biana didn't respond. They didn't even acknowledge her when she stopped right behind them, peering over their shoulders and trying to figure out why the cubby they were staring at had captured their attention.

It was a little different than the others—filled with a thicker, darker orange goo that didn't have any glowing bubbles mixed in to illuminate it. And instead of a milky membrane, the cubby was sealed by a sheet of smooth glass.

Sophie squinted and squinted and squinted, and she was one step away from admitting that she had *no* idea what she was looking at.

And then . . . the shadows parted and she spotted a face—and not one of the monstrous newborn beasts she'd been expecting.

That might've been easier than looking at the still, floating form of Alvar.

His eyes were closed, his expression so calm that he almost looked like he was sleeping.

But no one could sleep in thick orange goo—at least not for long.

"I wasn't planning to kill him this time," Fitz whispered, making Sophie jump. "I was just trying to trap him, so he couldn't get away or let out any more newborns. And Biana had shoved him into that cubby, so I started hitting buttons on the panel to see if there was a way to lock him in and . . . next thing I knew, the glass lowered and the goop started pouring in and . . ."

Biana shuddered.

Fitz swallowed hard, blinking several times before he turned to Sophie, his eyes absolutely unreadable. "Is it wrong that I'm not sorry?"

Sophie needed a second before she could answer. "No. Not

after what he did. And . . . he had lots of chances."

Fitz nodded and went back to staring at the floating body.

What if I told you I stopped pressing buttons? he transmitted quietly.

I . . . don't know what that means, Sophie admitted.

There was a moment, as the cubby was filling. Alvar was pounding on the glass, shouting things. And . . . I looked at the panel and realized one of the buttons probably opened up a drain. And I stopped *pressing things.*

Sophie's mouth went dry with the confession, and her insides twisted all kinds of horrible ways. But . . . she knew what he needed.

She tapped her fingernails to trigger Tinker's gadgets and gently twined her fingers with his scabbed hand, struggling to think of something to say. The best she could come up with was something Mr. Forkle had told her:

Life is a series of hard choices.

It didn't sound very comforting. But Fitz tangled his fingers with hers and she tried to stand there with him, supporting him any way she could.

But every time the shadows shifted and she caught another glimpse of Alvar's lifeless face, the walls closed in and her chest tightened and finally she had to drop his hand, mumbling about needing air as she stumbled for the exit.

And Keefe was right where she'd left him—right where he'd said he'd be—his arms stretched out and ready to catch her, like he'd known she'd be dizzy and heaving by the time she finally fled.

He didn't say a word as he led her over to another cluster of trees, one that was far enough away that she couldn't see or smell anything from that horrible place. He helped her lower herself to the grass, and she tapped her fingers to bring back her enhancing as he sat down beside her, holding her hands and filling her mind with soothing breezes.

"You okay?" he asked when her breathing steadied.

"I think so," she whispered. "Just . . . kind of in shock."

He nodded. "Sounds about right."

"Pretty sure we all are," Dex said quietly as he made his way over, followed by Linh, Marella, and Wylie.

"I have a feeling we're going to have to drag them out of there when it's time to seal the hive," Tam added as he joined them.

Sophie blinked. Right. They had to seal the hive.

With Alvar in there.

Now she understood what Keefe meant by "complicated."

"How much longer do we have before we have to seal it?" Sophie whispered, barely getting the words past her dry throat.

"Tarina said we could give them another hour," Tam said. "But not much more than that."

"I hailed Alden and Della," Keefe added quietly. "In case they wanted to . . . you know . . . I think they're going to try to rush over as soon as they can break free from all the chaos at the festival—and don't worry," Keefe added, sending another calming breeze into Sophie's head, "he said everyone's safe over there. It sounded like something big went down with my mom, but no one was hurt."

No one was hurt.

Sophie clung to the words, repeating them over and over in her head, reminding herself how incredibly lucky they'd been. Once again they'd miscalculated the Neverseen's plans—and hadn't been nearly as ready as they should've been. And yet: *No one was hurt.*

The Neverseen couldn't say the same. They'd lost *two* members. Maybe that made this a turning point in their ongoing game. The first time the other players truly slipped.

After all, the Neverseen had *also* miscalculated—scrambling almost as much as she and her friends had. *And* they'd ended up fleeing like cowards after losing two of their members.

Maybe they—

"Care to share any of the thoughts behind this sudden burst of confidence I'm picking up on, Foster?" Keefe asked, jolting her out of her interior monologue. "I'm pretty sure we could all use that kind of boost after what we just lived through."

She supposed he had a point.

But before she could get more than a few words out, Silveny's voice crashed into her head, shouting, *SOPHIE! KEEFE! TAM! HELP! HURRY!*

FIFTY-ONE

SILVENY ASKED FOR *ME*?" TAM MUR-
mured. *"Why?"*

"No idea," Sophie admitted, trying to remember if Tam and Silveny had ever spent any actual
time together. "All I know is, she keeps transmitting it over and
over: '*SOPHIE! KEEFE! TAM! HELP! HURRY!*'"

"Do you think the babies are hatching?" Dex asked.

Sophie reached up to rub her temples. "They're not supposed to be. But I can't think of anything else Silveny would
need."

Not unless she let her mind imagine all kinds of terrifying
things—and she was trying very hard not to do that. There had
to be a logical explanation.

Silveny wouldn't drag her into danger without any warning.

"But why would she want Keefe and my brother there, if this is about the babies?" Linh wondered.

"Uh, she wants *me* there because she knows I'm awesome at everything," Keefe jumped in, "and she's bringing in Bangs Boy because she clearly needs to rethink her life choices."

He smirked as he said it, but it looked super forced, and Sophie knew he was only trying to ease her rising panic.

"We're wasting too much time," she realized. "Silveny wouldn't push for help like this if it wasn't important, so we need to go—now. Ro, since you're right here, will you be our designated bodyguard?"

Ro raised one eyebrow. "I think what you *meant* to say is that since I'm the most powerful, amazing bodyguard you've ever met, you desperately need my protection during this risky endeavor you're about to embark on with your friends."

"Right," Sophie mumbled. "That."

"Deep breaths, Foster," Keefe said with a quick glare at the ogre princess. "We made it through everything else tonight— we'll make it through this."

Sophie nodded blankly. "Okay, can someone please find Sandor and Tarina and tell them what's happening?"

Linh promised she would—pulling her brother in for a hug and making him swear he'd be extra careful. Then Sophie was tapping her fingers to make sure she blocked her enhancing, and she reached for Keefe's and Tam's hands. As soon as

Ro completed the circle, Tam launched them off the ground faster and smoother than Fitz ever had, thanks to his years at Exillium, leaving them hovering so high up, it looked like they could touch the moon.

The eclipse had completed its cycle, and it should've felt like proof that they were past anything the Neverseen had planned for that evening. But it mostly reminded Sophie that this endless night *still* wasn't over. So when they crashed into the void, Sophie decided to set them down in the forest beyond the illusions that kept the alicorns' hive hidden—that way she could check in with the guards and make sure there was nothing they needed to know before heading in.

But the guards were nowhere to be found.

"If the alicorns *are* hatching, the caretakers at the hive might've called the guards over to help," Keefe suggested—which sorta made sense. Except . . . the guards weren't supposed to know the hive existed.

The forest also felt much too dark and quiet.

And Silveny's transmissions had reached a whole new decibel.

"I don't know what's going on," Sophie whispered as they reached the edge of the illusion—the point where their next step would take them into whatever reality was waiting for them over at the hive. "But . . . I'm getting a bad feeling. So promise me— no matter what happens—we'll stick together, okay?"

Tam and Keefe eyed each other for a second before they nodded.

Ro drew her sword.

"All right," Sophie murmured. "Here goes."

She reached for Keefe's and Tam's hands again, taking a long breath to shove the monster somewhere she could manage it. Then together, they stepped through the illusion. It looked like they were tumbling off a cliff, but in reality, their feet touched down on the same solid ground they'd been standing on before, and the light and shadows rippled around them, revealing the alicorns' tower silhouetted against the dark sky.

Silveny and Greyfell stood outside with their wings flared wide, and Silveny's transmissions screeched to a halt as her eyes locked with Sophie's. Silence swelled inside Sophie's mind, along with a choking wave of regret and something that felt like desperation as both alicorns lowered their wings to reveal a female standing between them.

Keefe's mom.

SORRY! Silveny transmitted as Keefe's grip went slack from shock. *BABY DANGER! BABY DANGER!*

Sophie had no doubt of that.

It's fine! she promised the guilty alicorn. *Whatever this is, we'll figure it out.*

Out loud, she asked, "What do you want?"

Lady Gisela reached up to smooth a strand of her blond hair into her beaded headpiece—which she'd probably worn to block Sophie's abilities—and it took Sophie a second to realize why that gesture felt so significant. For months and months, ever since Fintan had tortured her and locked her away in an ogre prison, Keefe's mom had hidden her face behind the hood of her black cloak. But now she stood boldly uncovered before them. And there was no sign of the brutal scars that Sophie had been imagining. Instead, her pale skin looked sort of . . . stretched—like the human women Sophie sometimes saw growing up who'd had too much plastic surgery.

"You all look as tired as I feel," Lady Gisela said, her ice blue eyes lingering on her son. "So let's get right down to this, shall we?"

"Yes, let's," Ro agreed, whipping a dagger at Lady Gisela's head.

Keefe's mom sighed, looking gloriously bored as she reached up and snatched the dagger out of the air, mere inches from the tip of her nose. "Guess that means it's my turn," she said, raising her other hand, which held a familiar silver-nozzled weapon.

She aimed for Greyfell's face, pulling the trigger in the same smooth motion and shooting the male alicorn right between the eyes.

Whinnies and screams pierced Sophie's eardrums, and her knees threatened to give out as she imagined bullets and blood—but some tiny part of her brain reminded her that she'd seen that weapon before. And when she managed to focus, she found that the splatter covering Greyfell's shimmering fur was blue, not red—and instead of an oozing wound, he had a congealed blue blob sinking into his skin.

"You remember how soporidine works, don't you?" Keefe's mom asked as black veins bulged across Greyfell's body, and the mighty male alicorn collapsed. She said something else after that, but Sophie couldn't hear it over her pounding heart and the roaring monster and Silveny's panicked transmissions—until Lady Gisela shifted her weapon to Silveny and shot her just below her shimmering horn.

The mama alicorn crumpled like a piece of paper, and the only thing that stopped Sophie from doing the same was Keefe, who wrapped his arm around her waist as his other hand pressed his palm against hers. After a few seconds, Sophie remembered to tap her fingers to bring back her enhancing, and her mind flooded with calming breezes.

"Well done, Keefe," Lady Gisela told him. "You've always been the best at keeping Sophie together during these stressful situations. That's why I had Silveny ask for you when I made her send those transmissions. I need the moonlark to focus—you with me, Sophie?" She waited for Sophie to nod before she added, "Good. Now. As I was trying to say, I know it's been a while since you've seen us use soporidine. We have to conserve our supply, after all. So just to make sure we're all on the same page: The dose I just gave your precious alicorns is half of what I gave Ro in Atlantis. Which means we have a little time to chat before things become fatal—but not *too* much, so I'd recommend keeping your interruptions to yourself. The sooner we settle things, the sooner I can give you this."

She dropped Ro's dagger, letting the blade sink point-first into the ground, so that she could reach into her pocket and retrieve two vials, each containing an orange blob. "*This* is the antidote that Silveny and Greyfell need. And I wouldn't do that if I were you," she warned, pointing her silver weapon at Ro's chest and freezing the ogre princess midlunge. "Another fun fact about soporidine: Your body reacts more harshly to it every time you're exposed. So considering how close you came to dying last time, I'd recommend spending the rest of this conversation right where you are. Same goes for whatever you're doing with those shadows, Tam." Her eyes flicked to the Shade. "There's no reason for you to bring pain upon yourself. How about we make a deal instead?"

Sophie stood up straighter. "We'll never give you the baby alicorns."

"Yes, I figured you might say that, considering our location. The good news is, I don't want them. My plans now go *far* beyond trying to blackmail the Council with the Timeline to Extinction."

"Then why are we here?" Keefe demanded.

His mom smiled. "Just because I don't personally want the babies doesn't make them any less valuable. I knew the second Umber followed you here that it would be a crucial bargaining chip. Mind you, I'd been planning to use it for something else, but . . . circumstances change."

"When did Umber follow us here?" Sophie asked—then

shivered when her brain dredged up the answer. "Wait—was she that presence Fitz and I felt in the forest?"

Lady Gisela nodded. "Umber can track your echoes—or . . . she *could*. Before . . ." She heaved a heavy sigh. "So much talent, wasted by such a senseless accident."

"It wasn't an accident," Sophie argued. "Tarina warned her not to open that door."

"Yes, I saw."

"How?" Keefe asked. "I thought you were at the festival."

"I was. You still haven't pieced it together?" She laughed at their blank stares. "Well, I suppose you have been a bit busy tonight. But I thought for sure you would've realized that the reason Vespera kept talking about showing the world was because everything that happened at Everglen was broadcast at the festival—that way *everyone* got to see the truth about what Luzia Vacker has been doing. *And* they got to see proof that no matter how brave and determined the moonlark and her friends may be, they're still no match for those with true power."

"Really?" Keefe asked. "Seems to me like they got to see you guys unleash something you didn't understand, then cower under a force field for a bit and finally flee without even recovering the body of your fallen friend. I'm sure everyone was super impressed."

Lady Gisela's eyes darkened. "I'll admit—certain things didn't go as smoothly as I'd hoped. That's the problem with letting

Vespera arrange the plan. She overcomplicates everything. Leaves room for costly mistakes. I much prefer to keep things simple. Like what we're here for right now: a simple exchange. I have what you want"—she waved the vials of antidote—"and you have what I need."

"And what's that?" Sophie demanded.

"Yes, I suppose we should get to that, shouldn't we? After all, there's no telling what kind of damage the soporidine is doing to your alicorns. Every minute we waste—"

"Then tell us already!" Keefe snapped.

"Isn't it obvious?" Her eyes shifted to Tam. "I'm sure you've been wondering why I brought *you* here. And the simple truth is, I need a new Shade."

Tam snorted. "So, what, you're here to kidnap me?"

"No. Kidnappings never work—we learned that the hard way with Sophie. I'm here to recruit you—*officially*. We started the process months ago, after you made such an impression on us in Atlantis. Why do you think I sent Umber to attack Sophie and Fitz with shadowflux?" She grinned when Sophie flinched. "I knew their injuries would inspire you to finally start training in the power—and I must say, it worked out even better than I anticipated. I saw you in action tonight. *Very* impressive. Still lacking Umber's experience, but we should be able to get you up to speed in time—assuming we get started right away. Which is why I'm here."

She jingled the vials of antidote again, and Sophie had to

laugh. "You think you're the only one with the antidote to sopori-dine? Fintan gave us a stash months ago."

"I'm sure he did. But hasn't that photographic memory of yours noticed that both the soporidine I used and the antidote I'm offering are different colors than the ones I used on the princess? We made dozens of variations, and you need *this* type to save your sparkly winged friends. They won't survive with-out it. And if that's not enough motivation for you, let's not forget that I could march into that hive right now and shoot soporidine into the gel the babies are developing in. How long do you think they'd last? One hour? Two? Who knows if the cure could even undo the damage?"

"UGH—DO YOU HEAR YOURSELF RIGHT NOW?" Keefe shouted. "HOW CAN YOU BE THIS CREEPY?"

"I never said I *want* these things to happen, Keefe," she said calmly. "I'm very much hoping it doesn't come to that. But it's not up to me. It's up to him." Her eyes focused back on Tam, who'd gone ghostly pale. "Oh, relax, it's not nearly as traumatic as you're thinking. All I'm asking right now is for you to give us a chance. Come with me. See what our cause *truly* is. As long as you don't make any trouble, you'll be perfectly safe."

"You'll also be their prisoner," Keefe jumped in. "You think they'll just let you go home after that? You think they won't make more threats? Today it's the alicorns—but what about tomorrow? Who will they go after next?"

"That's easy," Lady Gisela said, tucking another strand of

hair into her hairpiece. "We'll go after Linh. We're already set up for it. If I give the word, chaos could rain down on your twin within a matter of hours. Is that really what you want?"

Tam wobbled like he'd been punched in the gut, and Sophie tightened her grip on his hand.

We'll NEVER let that happen, she transmitted.

"I'm sure Sophie's trying to assure you right now that she can protect Linh," Lady Gisela guessed. "But you and I both know she can't make that guarantee. She'll try her best—but you've seen how often her 'best' simply isn't enough. Are you willing to risk that for your sister? After all you and Linh have been through together?"

Don't listen to her, Sophie begged. *She's just trying to get in your head.*

"I know this isn't easy to hear," Lady Gisela added. "Especially with all the myths and misconceptions about my order, and all the ways other leaders have stepped in and botched things. Sometimes I wish I had Sophie's talent for recruitment. One pretty smile and she has friends lining up to risk their lives."

"I've never *recruited* anyone!" Sophie practically growled.

"Are you sure? From what I hear, you dragged both Tam and Linh into the Black Swan after you saw how powerful they were at Exillium—and kudos to you for having such a sharp eye for talent. But tell me this, Tam, were you *eager* to swear fealty to the order after Sophie brought you to them? Or did you have reservations?"

Tam didn't answer, but his silence said enough.

"You hesitated, didn't you?" Lady Gisela pressed. "Because you could see that something didn't add up. And I'd wager the only real reason you came around was to keep Linh happy. How is this, if you *really* think about it, all that different from that?"

Keefe snorted a laugh. "Are you serious right now? You're threatening Linh's life and claiming it's the same thing as Linh getting over her trust issues faster? See what she does, Tam? See how she plays with your head?"

"There's no game this time," his mom insisted. "I'm simply right. If you hear us out, I guarantee you'll realize that *we* are the only ones with an actual solution to the problems in this world, and that you've been wasting your talent serving the wrong side. I can show you more proof than you can possibly imagine. But right now, I don't have that kind of time— and neither do you." She pointed to the sky, which was slowly brightening with the coming dawn, then back to Silveny and Greyfell. "Look how the poison is spreading."

Sophie choked back a gag when she saw the intricate web of black veins covering both unconscious alicorns.

"They need this," Lady Gisela pressed, holding up the vials of antidote again. "And you can give it to them with a simple yes."

"Please tell me you're not actually considering this," Keefe begged when Tam tugged on his bangs.

"Do I have a choice?" Tam snapped back.

"Yes," Sophie promised. "You *do*. There's *always* a choice."

"But that doesn't mean it's a good choice," Lady Gisela countered. "Remember what's at stake here. Not just for Silveny and Greyfell."

Tam's voice filled Sophie's head, and she glanced down to find his shadow crossing hers so he could shadow-whisper just to her, "I . . . think I have to go with her. If I don't—and something happens to Linh . . ."

And what if something happens to you? Sophie transmitted back.

"I can handle myself," his shadow voice insisted. "If I can survive my parents—and years of Exillium—I can find a way to navigate through whatever this is. And who knows, if I play nice for a while, maybe I can learn something useful about their plan."

That sounds a lot like what Keefe thought when he ran off to join the Neverseen—and you saw how well that worked out for him, Sophie reminded him.

"Yeah . . . but he still made it back." His shadow edged closer, his voice turning more urgent. "And I don't really care about me. I care about Linh—if I go with them now, you'll have more time to figure out how to *really* protect her. *And* you'll save Silveny and Greyfell."

"Don't do it," Keefe pleaded, probably feeling Tam's mood shift.

"I have to," Tam said, pulling his hand free from Sophie and stepping closer to Lady Gisela. "But I want your word that if I do, you'll leave my sister alone."

"Of course, Tam. As long as you cooperate." She held out the vials of antidote. "Do we have a deal? And keep in mind that if you say yes, it's effective immediately. No goodbyes. No looking back. No one has time for that. And absolutely no contact with anyone until you've had a chance to experience our side and train in our methods—and that goes for your friends as well. If they try to rescue you, none of you will like what happens."

"Uh, if you needed proof that this is a BAD IDEA," Keefe said, "I'm pretty sure that covers it."

"No, that simply acknowledges that the transition will be bumpy," Lady Gisela insisted. "It's all only temporary. The day will come when you'll finally understand what we're truly working toward and fully commit to our cause—and when that day comes, you'll have every freedom you could possibly want. In the meantime, you can take comfort in knowing that every day you play nice, you're keeping your lovely sister safe."

"Bad idea," Keefe repeated as Tam reached for the vials.

But Tam still grabbed them, and Sophie couldn't watch, couldn't believe this was happening, couldn't even look at him as he passed the antidote along to her. But she still nodded when he said, "Keep an eye on Linh. Tell her I'll be back as soon as I can."

Keefe shook his head. "You just made the biggest mistake of your life. I know. I've made it."

"Yeah, well, I'm not you," Tam snapped back as he crossed over to Lady Gisela's side.

"That's very true," Lady Gisela said, hooking her arm through his. "And I think it's important you remember that—in case you think you're starting a new game right now, and that you'll be able to flip sides the way my son foolishly tried to do. He may speak poorly of his experience with my order and think he escaped just in time. But he has no idea why he's still alive." She turned to Keefe, and her expression softened, the resemblance between them becoming much stronger. "I love my son. I will always hold out hope for him. And that gives him a certain level of privilege and protection—one you will never be able to rely on. You're talented and I very much hope this works out. But until you prove yourself? You're expendable."

With that, she raised her weapon and clocked Tam hard on the side of the head, knocking him out as she held a crystal up to the light and leaped away.

FIFTY-TWO

SOPHIE HAD NEVER SEEN KEEFE QUITE so speechless before. And she didn't have many words either. But she scraped together the voice to tell him, "You can't blame yourself for this."

He didn't look convinced.

But he reached for her, pulling her into a shaky hug. And they both clung to each other until they had the strength to move again.

Then it was time to focus—time to make Tam's sacrifice count. So they set to work, scraping any extra soporidine off of Silveny's and Greyfell's fur and smearing the antidote on instead.

While they waited, Ro went to make sure Wynn and Luna

were okay, and thankfully both babies were safely floating in their goo-filled cubbies.

A few minutes later—after a vivid sunrise washed away the last wisps of that very long, very dark night—Silveny and Greyfell were awake. Both alicorns were emotionally overwhelmed, of course, and Silveny flooded Sophie's mind with guilty apologies. But Sophie kept assuring her: *You did what you had to do.*

Just like Tam had—hard as that was for Sophie to accept.

This time . . . Lady Gisela beat them.

Sophie had replayed their standoff outside the hive over and over, trying to find a way she could've steered the situation toward a better ending. But she always wound up at the same place, with Tam sacrificing his freedom in order to keep the alicorns and his sister safe.

So now she needed to figure out where they went from here.

Planning a rescue would only put Tam and Linh in more danger, and possibly others as well. But were they really supposed to leave Tam alone with the Neverseen—being trained, tested, and force-fed propaganda in hopes that he'd eventually join their ranks for real?

"Yes."

The answer, surprisingly, came from Linh, who was wiping away the last of her tears.

Linh had been waiting under Calla's Panakes with Sandor, Dex, Wylie, and Marella when Sophie and Keefe brought Silveny and Greyfell back to Havenfield. Ro had stayed behind to guard the babies. And things had naturally been a bit of an emotional roller coaster when everyone realized that Tam was missing. But once they switched from *reacting* to *planning*, Linh had turned determined.

"Tam can take care of himself," she said, gathering all of her spilled tears and forming them into a tiny floating heart. "He doesn't need us trying to save him. If we really want to help, we need to take down the Neverseen—that's the only way we'll ever be free of them."

She was right, of course.

The question was, *"How?"*

All they had were the same dead ends that had gotten them nowhere for months and months, like the missing starstone, the mystery of what happened to Wylie's mom, Keefe's damaged memories, and the key to the Archetype. The real caches were also out there somewhere, if they could figure out how to find them. And Lady Gisela had made it clear that the Neverseen were still planning something for their soporidine—something that may or may not require the help of a Shade.

But that still felt like a whole lot of nothing.

So did Marella's offer to see if she could learn anything from Fintan during their training.

Fintan *had* been right that something was going to happen at the Celestial Festival. But he clearly had a lot of gaps in his knowledge.

Plus, the Council would be watching those lessons *very*

closely. They'd seen Marella use her ability against the newborns—most of their world had, in fact. And since it had been such a spectacle, and Marella had kept herself well under control, the Council agreed to give training a chance—which was actually a pretty huge change for the Lost Cities.

And it was only the beginning.

The Council had also promised *lots* more announcements in the days ahead, as they figured out what to do about Luzia and Orem and the trolls. In the meantime, they'd stationed guards outside the hive at Everglen, even though Tarina had sealed it before she left to speak with her empress.

"What'd they do about Alvar?" Sophie had to ask, cringing as her mind dredged up the gruesome memory of his lifeless face, floating in—

"That's right," Dex said, dragging her mind away from the horrifying flashback. "You weren't there for that part."

"Which part?" she asked, not liking the way all her friends shared a very strange look.

Marella was the one who finally told her. "After you guys left, Tarina cleared Fitz and Biana out so she could make some final preparations for the hive. But then Alden and Della got there and . . . and wanted to see the body. So they went in and . . . the cubby was empty."

"Empty," Sophie repeated, struggling to find some other meaning for the word.

Marella nodded. "The glass was broken, and half the goop

had spilled onto the floor. But . . . Alvar was in there for, like, an hour without air—and Tarina said the liquid pours in super hot, so I don't see how—"

"Survival instincts," Keefe interrupted, swiping a hand down his face before his eyes met Sophie's. "Breathing control and body temperature regulation."

Sophie wanted to kick something.

Alvar excelled at both skills. And he was a Vanisher, so he could've turned invisible once he was free and snuck out the door.

"So . . . he's still alive," she murmured, needing to say it to make her brain believe it.

"We think so," Dex admitted.

"And Fitz *freaked*," Marella added. "So . . . you should probably check on your boyfriend."

Sophie couldn't tell if Marella was teasing or not. But either way, the word sat there, daring her to deny it.

She didn't.

But she didn't confirm it either.

Because now was absolutely not the time.

She did take Marella's advice, though, and reached out telepathically to Fitz as soon as she crawled into bed—once she'd survived Sandor's *"Seriously—no more running off!"* lecture and answered Grady's and Edaline's ten thousand questions about Tam and the alicorns and everything that happened at Everglen.

And Fitz sounded . . . *bleak*—especially after she caught him up about Tam.

So . . . we thought we took out Alvar, but we didn't, he thought bitterly. *And it doesn't matter that they lost Umber because they stole Tam. AND they humiliated my family—made it look like my parents have been hiding mutant troll experiments the whole time they've lived here. Apparently there's going to be a Tribunal about it.*

Sophie couldn't think of anything to say except *I'm sorry.*

She could almost hear him sigh before he told her, *No, I'M sorry. I shouldn't make this about me. And . . . I know there were a bunch of times yesterday when I was a total jerk and—*

Don't, she interrupted. *It was a* horrible *day. No one handles situations like that perfectly. But we got through it, and now . . . we just keep going.*

Yeah. He sounded even less excited than she felt. *Will you be able to sleep?*

Probably not, she admitted, even though she needed to. She'd been awake so long, she couldn't remember the last time she slept.

Me neither, Fitz told her. *If you need me, I'm here, okay?*

So am I, she promised, severing their connection and wishing her brain had an off switch so she could stop wondering when they'd see Alvar again or where Lady Gisela brought Tam, or imagining bloodthirsty newborns lurking in every shadow, ready to jump out and—

"You're still awake," a soft voice said from her doorway, and

Sophie turned to find Flori, holding four small potted plants. "I figured you might have trouble finding rest after everything you lived through. So I wondered if you might be willing to let me test my new song on your echoes."

"You finished it?"

Flori smiled as she nodded, padding over to the bed and placing one plant next to each pole of her bed's canopy. One held a sprig of vesperlace. The others were plants Sophie didn't recognize, but Flori called them dimmetines, respitillis, and hushspurs. "These are from the four places where I drew inspiration for the verses—and I only found the hushspurs because of the festival. They trailed up the trunks of the trees we chose to hide in, and halfway through the night they changed their tune. I don't know if they sensed the coming danger or if they simply wanted to show me what they could do, but that was the piece I needed. May I?"

"Should I sit up, or . . . ?" Sophie asked.

"No, just close your eyes." Flori's gentle fingers brushed Sophie's cheek as her fragile voice hummed a slow, sweet melody—a rhythm that felt like a pulse as Flori breathed out soft lyrics in that ancient earthy language.

The first verse was a celebration of night—a ballad of dancing shadows and creeping mist and all the tiny, soothing shifts that let the world slip into restful slumber.

But as the lyrics carried on, they curved to an ode to darkness itself. A reminder that there was purpose and power, even in the blackest places. Even to the shadows within herself.

The anger.

And doubts.

And sadness.

The memories that were too painful to replay.

All rang with vulnerability *and* strength.

And with each new beat—each new pulse—the monster changed shape. Until it wasn't a monster at all. Just something else that lived inside her. Something she could embrace. And when Sophie gave her mind over to the shadows, the shadows welcomed her in.

And she slept as the echoes faded away.

Sophie woke to the heady perfume of exotic flowers, and when she opened her eyes, her canopy was wrapped in the delicate vines from the four plants Flori had brought for her, which had tripled in size thanks to Flori's song.

She could've lain there breathing it in all day.

But there was too much to do.

Starting with a visit to Everglen.

She'd brought Flori over, hoping the new song would quiet Fitz's echoes the same way it silenced hers. But they both got a little sidetracked by the chaos.

Sophie had assumed there would be cleanup and changes to the Vacker estate's security after everything that happened. But she never expected to see the massive gates come tumbling down.

"The Council has decided that it's best we send the message that there are no secrets here," Alden explained when he spotted Sophie staring at the fallen metal panels. "And they are probably wise."

"Will it be safe, though?" Sophie had to ask. "Especially with . . ."

She stopped herself from mentioning Alvar.

"Don't worry—there will be *plenty* of security," Alden promised. "It just won't be as showy. And right now, it's better we draw a little less attention."

Alvar's apartment was also gone.

And the hive was being buried.

She decided not to ask what they did with the bodies. Instead she asked, "Are you okay?"

Alden sighed, turning to watch the gnomes tear down another panel of glowing bars. "It's not easy realizing you've been played for a fool. Or that someone you love . . . doesn't deserve that sentiment. It was agonizing enough watching what all of you went through that night, knowing there was nothing I could do to help—Gisela made that clear with plenty of threats. But . . . watching Alvar. Seeing the moment the flashback hit. And he stopped being the son I'd just started to believe I was getting back, and instead became the monster I never wanted to believe he truly was. Well . . . let's just say that's going to stay with me. Just as I'm sure everything else that happened here is going to stay with lots of people for years to come. It's going to be quite a legacy to live down. But change . . . is what our world needs. I suspect my family won't be the only one experiencing a few growing pains."

No, probably not.

Though "growing pains" was putting it somewhat mildly.

Thanks to the *very* public Tribunal of Luzia over the next few days—and the more private investigations into Orem's, Alden's, and Della's involvement as well—there seemed to be a never-ending stream of gossip about "the Vacker legacy."

Fitz and Biana bore it well, but Sophie could tell it was eating at them.

So it seemed especially timely when they heard from the caretakers at the alicorns' hive that the babies' membranes were thinning.

The next day became a constant baby watch, with Sophie and her friends—and Silveny and Greyfell—camped outside the hive. And while it definitely wasn't a place with happy memories, Sophie found herself periodically wandering back to the last place she'd seen Tam.

She needed the reminder that even though she and her friends weren't going to tear apart the world to find him and risk putting him in more danger—that they could *never* forget that Tam was gone, and never stop looking for ways to take down their enemies.

A very tentative plan was already starting to come together— but they were determined to be patient. The Neverseen pulled off their victories by being meticulous and calculating. If she and her friends were going to beat them, they needed to do the same.

In the meantime, Linh had made all of them promise that they would still try to find joy in the small victories, because that's what Tam would want them to do. Like the moment several long hours later when two very gangly, very slimy alicorn babies burst through the gooey walls of their hive and stumbled into the world to nuzzle against their overjoyed parents.

There were so many tears and hugs and shouts of "BABY OKAY!" to echo Silveny's transmissions that Sophie thought her heart—and head—might explode from the sheer joy of it. Even Fitz was laughing—something he didn't do very much these days. And when Sophie went over to join him, he pulled her into a hug and spun her around, just like he had the day they'd first implanted the babies.

"You guys are good together," Biana said later, appearing beside Sophie in Havenfield's pastures, where the happy alicorn family had decided to stay. "And no, I'm not talking about the alicorns, so don't try to play that game. I'm talking about the thing you and I have been very noticeably *not* talking about since it happened, and I think it's high time we acknowledge it, don't you?"

"Probably," Sophie admitted, fighting the sudden urge to tug on all her eyelashes. "Though there's not really anything to acknowledge right now."

"Yeah, that's what I hear. Why is that, by the way? I thought you'd be, like, running out to get crush cuffs first thing, once you finally stopped being oblivious and realized how long my brother's liked you."

"How long *has* he liked me?" Sophie asked—blurting out the question before she could stop it. "Never mind. Forget I asked. I don't want to put you in the middle."

"I guess it's probably good if we draw that line now, before you guys get to the super-mushy stage," Biana agreed. But she leaned in and whispered, "I know for sure he's had a crush since we were all together in Alluveterre."

"Really?" Sophie was *dying* to ask for more details. But she left it at that, going with a more important question. "You don't mind?"

"Nope. Like I said, you guys are good together. And I'm not the only one who sees that. You seriously need to stop worrying so much about the match. You're *perfect* for each other. You'll see."

Sophie still had her doubts. But . . . strangely enough, she was also starting to want to find out. Maybe it was selfish of her to think about something like that when Linh was having to live every day worrying about her brother, and Tam was off who knew where being stuck doing who knew what.

Or . . . maybe that was *why* she was more tempted than she'd been before. Maybe what was going on with Tam was also a good reminder of how quickly the game could change and something super important could be taken away. And maybe it was better to make sure there could never be any regrets—never be something she'd look back at and think, *If only I hadn't been so afraid.*

The thought nestled into her brain, buzzing around for a couple more days. Until one morning over breakfast, she found herself saying, "If I wanted to register for the match, how do I do it? Is there a process, or . . . ?"

She had to stop there.

Edaline looked like she wanted to grab her and hug her, while Grady looked like he wanted to haul her upstairs and lock her in her room, and she was definitely regretting bringing it up.

But Edaline also told her, "All you have to do is say the word, and we'll take you over straightaway."

Sophie had walked every street in Atlantis during the desperate days she'd spent trying to rescue her human parents. But somehow she'd never noticed the shimmering crystal tower that straddled one of the widest, most bustling canals.

Half of the structure stood on one side of the dark water and half on the other, angling toward each other and merging to form a massive twisted spire. It wasn't the tallest building on the street, or the fanciest. But it was definitely the most intimidating—probably because of the round silver medallion set into the center of the arch, embossed with a very specific symbol: a giant *M* shaped from two strands of DNA.

The official seal of the matchmakers.

"You okay?" Edaline asked, reaching for Sophie's shaky hand as their carriage driver jerked the reins, making the eurypterid slow to a stop.

Sophie nodded, squinting at the runes surrounding the matchmakers' seal. "What do those say?"

"Progress, Prosperity, Permanence, and Proliferation," Grady told her. "The goals of every match."

Sophie sighed. "Well, *that's* romantic."

"It's not *as* bad as it sounds," Edaline promised. "But you *don't* have to do this."

"I know."

But the thing was . . . she kind of did.

I want it to be you.

That's what Fitz had told her.

And . . . she wanted it to be him, too—wanted them to be *together*, and enjoy whatever time they had before the next epic battle with the Neverseen.

She didn't need a list to make that happen—and she'd definitely gone around and around for several more days after she'd asked Edaline about the process. But she'd decided to stop letting the fact that she'd been raised differently hold her back. So she climbed out of the silver carriage, miraculously managing not to trip over all her layers of tulle and silk.

She'd worn the frilliest, fanciest gown in her closet, figuring she might as well go all in. And it didn't hurt that the fabric was the most perfect shade of shimmering teal.

"Okay," Edaline said, hooking an arm around Sophie as Grady did the same on her other side. "Let's get you registered!"

Sophie could've sworn she'd heard Grady mumble, "Here we go again" under his breath as they headed up the path—but it was hard to tell with the way her pulse was thrumming in her ears. The walk was probably only twenty steps, but it felt like they'd journeyed for miles by the time they reached the pair of enormous silver doors stamped with the matchmakers' seal.

"Whenever you're ready," Edaline told her, hanging back a step with Grady.

Leaving it up to her.

Sophie closed her eyes, remembering the feel of Fitz's lips on her cheek when he'd whispered, *Just trust me.*

And she reminded herself of the promise she'd made Linh—to seize the small victories.

It was *definitely* a victory when she pulled open the doors and stepped into an empty white foyer lit by an enormous crystal chandelier. Her heels clicked across the pale floor—which bore a glittering mosaic of the matchmakers' symbol—as she headed for a curved, sweeping staircase that took her up and over, to the center of the canal. By the time she reached the final step, she was seriously regretting her wardrobe choices—until she got a look at the glass room she'd entered and caught a glimpse of the crowd.

The room was a sea of throne-size chairs filled with perfect, beautiful people in perfect, beautiful clothes, flashing perfect, beautiful smiles. One boy even winked as Sophie scanned the room trying to figure out where she was supposed to go.

"Just take a seat anywhere you want," Edaline explained. "Your registry pendant let them know you were here the second you walked through the door. They'll come to us when it's our turn."

Sophie nodded, choosing three seats in one of the shadowy corners—but it didn't stop people from noticing her. She was even *more* recognizable, thanks to the Neverseen's show at the festival. So she got to spend the next hour discovering that she'd rather fight bloodthirsty trolls or be attacked with shadowflux than sit in a frilly dress pretending she didn't notice that people were whispering about her.

And boy, were they whispering.

Every few seconds it was *Sophie Foster, Sophie Foster, Sophie Foster.*

"Sophie Foster?" a female with very thick bangs and very red lips asked.

"Yes," Sophie squeaked—then cleared her throat and tried again. "Yeah, that's me."

The female nodded, giving Sophie a quick once-over before her turquoise eyes locked with Sophie's brown ones. Her expression stayed neutral. But a tiny pucker formed between her arched brows as she said, "I'm Ceri. And I'm here to collect you."

"Great," Sophie said, willing her feet not to trip as she stood.

"You're not coming?" she asked Grady and Edaline when she realized they were still sitting.

Grady shook his head. "From here on out, you're on your own, kiddo." He smiled as he said it, but there was something sad in his tone, and she found herself bending to hug each of her parents before she followed Ceri down a glass hall lined with dozens of identical silver doors.

"I never realized there were this many matchmakers," Sophie said, mostly to break the awkward silence.

"There aren't." Ceri led Sophie to the very last door and pressed her palm on a black panel in the center, triggering a soft beep before the door slid open, revealing a small, square room with mirrored walls. She didn't follow Sophie in, telling her to take a seat in the room's only chair and that someone would be with her shortly.

Which meant Sophie quickly discovered that it was even worse sitting all alone in a cold little room with only her panicked thoughts and an infinite number of reflections of herself for company.

She reached for Fitz's necklace, tracing her thumb over and over the glittering heart to remind herself why she was doing this. And when that didn't help, she finally surrendered and tugged out an itchy eyelash.

Three more had been flicked away—one even wished on, because she'd hit *that* low—before one of the mirrored walls split open and two females entered the room. One had dark skin, full lips, and naturally textured hair, and the other was shorter, freckled, and blond—and yet something about them seemed identical. Sophie assumed it was their matching white gowns and the fact that they both clutched a small square of glass to their chests. But when they both sat on the stools that rose out of the floor, she realized their movements were perfectly in sync—every step, every smile, every flick of their wrists or hair. Even every blink.

It was seriously eerie.

"Miss Foster," the blond female said, and Sophie was relieved they didn't talk in sync as well. "I'm Brisa."

"And I'm Juji," the other female added. "Sorry to keep you waiting."

"No problem," Sophie assured them. "You guys are busy today."

"We always are," Brisa agreed.

"So let's keep this moving. We've already reviewed your records," Juji told her, "and we need to verify a few things before we proceed."

Sophie nodded and they both tapped their screens, making them light up.

"Your listed birthplace is San Diego," Juji noted. "That's not in the Lost Cities."

"Yes," Sophie agreed. "It's a human—Forbidden—city. It's . . . kind of a long story."

"So I've heard," Brisa said, tilting her head to study Sophie.

"I've only been told bits and pieces, but it sounds fascinating. I imagine we'll need the full story by the time we get to your packets. Should provide an interesting challenge."

"I'm quite excited, actually," Juji agreed. "We never get anything new around here."

"Oh, well, great." Sophie wondered if it would be weird to say, *How about you throw Fitz Vacker on the list and see what happens?*

They tapped their screens again.

"Now, under family, it shows that you were born to humans originally named Will and Emma Foster," Juji noted.

Sophie nodded, fighting off a pang of sadness.

"And obviously you've been adopted by Lord and Lady Ruewen," Brisa added.

Lord and Lady?

Sophie never thought of Grady and Edaline with titles—but they were accurate, so she nodded again.

"But it looks like no one's filled in your genetic parents," Brisa said, tapping the screen a few more times. "What names should I put in?"

"Oh." Sophie fidgeted in her chair. "Funny thing, but . . . I don't know."

Juji frowned. "You don't know who your biological parents are?"

"No. No one's ever told me. I've tried to guess a few times, but I've always been wrong."

"Can't you just ask the people who made you? The"—Brisa squinted at her screen—"Black Swan?"

"I have. But they said I'm not allowed to know—some sort of privacy thing for the donors, I guess. It's super weird, but . . ." She shrugged.

Juji and Brisa shared a long look before Juji said, "Okay. Let's see what happens."

They both tapped several buttons on their screens and leaned back.

"It's processing," Brisa explained. "Should be just a minute."

But it wasn't.

It wasn't two minutes either.

Or three.

By four, Sophie's back was drenched with sweat and she was having to sit on her hands to spare her eyelashes.

By five, even Juji and Brisa were getting fidgety. But they kept right on smiling, until their screens made a soft beeping sound and flashed red.

Red was rarely good.

"Is something wrong?" Sophie had to ask.

Juji and Brisa shared a look, before they both held up their screens to let her read the result herself.

. . . . .. •. ... . •. . .... •.. •. . . . .•

Acknowledgments

Well. I'm pretty sure you're all plotting revenge after that ending—and I can't say I blame you. It's definitely my evilest collection of game changers yet. And I know it probably feels like I'm trying to torment you—but, honestly, this book was a *huge* labor of love. I have never poured so much of myself into anything in my life. So thank you for reading, and for sticking with me (and Sophie), and for forgiving me for leaving you with all those unanswered questions while I write the next book. I promise I'll make book eight worth waiting for!

There's a reason I dedicated this book to my awesome team at Simon & Schuster. *Flashback* truly wouldn't exist without all the wonderful people who worked so many long hours—even weekends and holidays—to get this book edited, copyedited, proofread, formatted, and ready for the printer in time. It seriously feels like I have my own publishing army, and I'm so honored to work with such amazing people, including Liesa Abrams Mignogna—my long-suffering editor—and Katherine Devendorf, Adam Smith, Rebecca Vitkus, Elizabeth Mims, Stacey Sakal, Karin Paprocki, Mike Rosamilia, Jon Anderson, Mara Anastas, Chriscynethia Ford, Jodie Hockensmith, Lauren Hoffman, Caitlin Sweeny, Alissa Nigro, Anna Jarzab, Nicole Russo, Jessica Smith, Bernadette Flinn, Steve Scott, Michelle Fadlalla, Jenn Rothkin, Ian Reilly, Christina Pecorale,

Victor Iannone, and the entire sales team. And Jason Chan always earns my eternal gratitude for drawing the Best. Covers. Ever.

I'd also be lost without my amazing agent, Laura Rennert (and everyone else at Andrea Brown Literary and Taryn Fagerness Agency). And I think I need to hug Cécile Pournin, Mathilde Tamae-Bouhon, and everyone at Lumen Editions for all they endured in order to get this book translated for French readers.

I never would've made it through this impossible schedule if it hadn't been for the brainstorming sessions, pep talks, and steady support of Faith Hochhalter, Sara McClung, Victoria Morris, Kari Olson, C. J. Redwine, and Sarah Wylie. And if I didn't have so many fabulous teachers, librarians, and booksellers supporting the series, I wouldn't get to have this job.

Lastly, I have to end by thanking my family. Mom and Dad, thank you for all the lunches you brought over and all the incoherent, sleep-deprived phone calls you endured (and all the other things you did—there were so many)! I'm hoping next year won't be so hectic, but even if it is, I know I can always count on you. Love you!

The following is a bonus scene of sorts—a moment between Alden, Ro, and Keefe that technically happened before the first page of *Flashback*, but that couldn't be included in the book because the Keeper books are always limited to Sophie's point of view. So think of this as my present to you guys (especially to Team Keefe). Something I wrote to show you that important conversation, since it gets mentioned a few times in the story. And to give you some fun, additional insights into our favorite Lord Hunkyhair! Happy reading!

THE TALK

L ORD ALDEN," LORD CASSIUS SAID, dipping his head in what could barely count as a bow before he stepped aside to let Alden enter the Shores of Solace—aka his used-to-be-secret-even-though-no-one-actually-wanted-to-go-there-with-him beach house. "I thought the Council ordered all of you Vackers to be at Tribunal Hall today for the big verdict. It's all I've heard about for days. People do so love a good scandal—and this is one of the best our world has seen in ages."

"The sentencing isn't until this afternoon," Alden explained, ignoring the rest of Cassius's jab as he made his way toward a room with mother-of-pearl walls. His teal eyes looked far from impressed as they skimmed over the fancy furniture and enormous ocean-view windows—but his gaze softened when he focused on the blond boy sprawled across one of the couches. "I was hoping I'd find you here."

Keefe pulled himself to his feet, making sure to brush all the crumbs from the butterblast he'd snacked on for breakfast onto the otherwise pristine floor. "Is everything okay?"

Alden nodded. "But I'd love a quick word with you, if you don't mind. Perhaps somewhere a bit more private?"

"Or I can lock Lord Nosypants in a closet," Ro offered, striding out of a shadowy corner and flashing a pointy-tooth grin.

How the pink-haired, heavily armed ogre princess could make people forget she was in the room was one of life's great mysteries.

"Let's save that fun for later," Keefe decided, leading Alden to the one place at his father's house where he felt like he could breathe: a wide outdoor patio facing a glittering black sand beach. Cushioned swings swayed in the salty wind, and Alden sank onto one of them, watching the turquoise waves crash against the shore long enough for Keefe's brain to put together a pretty extensive list of scary things that might be happening.

Clearly Foster's ever-worrying ways were rubbing off on him.

"Sooo . . . ," he said, dragging out the word as he plopped onto the swing next to Alden. "What's going on?"

"Nothing bad," Alden assured him. "I'm just hoping you'll be willing to attend the Tribunal today."

Ro groaned. "*Noooooooooo!* Then *I* have to go, and everyone's going to be all smug and sparkly and give boring speeches about how brilliant they are—and I'm not even allowed to stab anybody!"

Keefe ignored her. "I thought it was family only."

"It was. But I've convinced the Council to make an exception, because Fitz is going to need a friend today."

Yeah, that was kind of an understatement. Keefe was pretty sure Fitz was going to go into rage-monster mode if the Council gave Alvar anything less than a life sentence. And if Alden felt the need to bring in reinforcements . . .

Keefe slumped back against the cushions. "Does that mean you know—"

"What I know," Alden interrupted, "is that I'm doing everything in my power to get my family through this."

Which wasn't really an answer.

"The thing is," he added quietly, "my son is far more likely to listen to you than he is to me. Especially under the circumstances."

"Okay, but if you're looking for a voice of wisdom, you'd be better off asking someone who's a bit more . . . shall we say, responsible?" Keefe felt the need to point out.

"I agree. Which is why I've arranged clearance for Sophie to attend as well."

"Perfect!" Ro jumped in. "Then you don't need us!"

"Actually, *that's* why I do." Alden's eyes dropped to his

hands, his fingers twisting the edge of his embroidered cape. "You and I both know, Keefe, that my son doesn't necessarily excel at controlling his temper. And . . . I don't think either of us wants to see him channel any of that anger toward Sophie. So if you're there—"

"Hang on." Ro made a time-out gesture. "Are you seriously asking Keefe to be the punching bag during your pretty boy's little temper tantrums?"

"Of course not! I'm asking an *Empath* to watch for moments when his *best friend* is getting close to losing control of his emotions, and to keep him from saying or doing anything he'll later regret."

"Or you could just leave our pretty little blond girl out of this one," Ro reminded him.

"No, I can't. Fitz . . . needs her." His eyes shifted to Keefe, and there was something tentative about his expression.

Something *nervous.*

"He needs her," he repeated **gently**, taking a long breath before he added, "I think you know that. And . . . I suspect you know how Sophie feels too."

Unfortunately, Keefe did—and he was always trying hard not to think about it, because it made him want to punch things.

"Hate to break it to you guys," Ro informed them, "but Blondie doesn't know *what* she feels."

"Perhaps not," Alden conceded. "But that mostly has to do

with the fact that my son has yet to make things clear. Once he does . . ."

He didn't finish the sentence, but he didn't need to. Keefe was well aware of all the miserable mushiness he had ahead.

The hand-holding.

And cuddling.

And . . .

Ugh, if he had to watch them kiss, he was going to vomit all over his boots.

Alden placed his hand softly over Keefe's, waiting for Keefe to meet his eyes before he told him, "I realize that all of this is . . . *complicated* for you, given how you feel about—"

"I'm just gonna stop you right there," Keefe cut in, pulling his hand away and jumping off the swing. He paced to the far end of the patio, relieved that his legs pulled it off with some swagger. "Leave the feelings-reading to us Empaths, okay? 'Cause you're wrong. Like, super, super wrong."

"No, I'm not."

Keefe was dying to ask him how he could be so sure—and if that meant Fitz had figured it out too. But that would mean admitting it, and the only way he was going to get through this was to deny, deny, deny.

Alden sighed. "Sorry. I know this conversation is difficult—and I'm not trying to meddle—"

"Um, I'm pretty sure this is the definition of meddling," Ro argued.

"No, it's the definition of caring." Alden stood and made his way closer, wrapping an arm around Keefe's shoulders. "You may not be my genetic son," he said quietly, "but I've long considered you part of my family."

Keefe had to remind himself to breathe.

Part of him wanted to pull away and run. The other part wanted to lean back and see what it felt like to not have to stand on his own. But he was pretty sure that either way, he'd end up getting hurt.

So he just stood there, stiff and silent, watching the frothy water smooth the dark sand into a shiny, blank canvas.

It wasn't fair that the beach got so many do-overs.

"I've never told anyone this," Alden murmured, "but long before I met Della, there was . . . another. Someone I was convinced was my perfect match—and the matchmakers agreed. But, as it turned out, she . . . preferred a close friend of mine." He let the words hang there for a beat before he added, "So I'm no stranger to your situation, Keefe."

"There's no situation," Keefe insisted.

"Maybe there isn't. But I'm going to pass on some wisdom to you anyway. I'm a father. It's what I do. And don't worry, I'm not about to give you a long speech on how someday you'll find your true match like I did—though *you will*." He pulled Keefe slightly closer, giving his shoulder a gentle squeeze. "The wisdom I want to give you is simply this: If you really care about them . . . let them be happy."

Let them be happy.

Those words made Keefe want to vomit even more than the idea of Fitzphie smoochfests.

"I know," Alden said gently. "Believe me, I understand exactly how heartbreaking that is to hear. But take it from someone who ended up losing two valuable friendships. There's only one way this ends—"

"Uh, no there isn't!" Ro snapped. "We're talking about teenagers! Stop acting like any of this is a done deal." She waited for Keefe to meet her eyes before she added, "It *isn't*."

Alden sighed. "I suppose only time will tell. But that doesn't change where we are today. *Today*, Sophie and Fitz are both going to need your help. So the question is, are you willing to be their friend?"

Keefe opened his mouth to answer, but Alden shook his head, drawing Keefe into a hug before he stepped away.

"That's all I came here to say," he said, pulling his pathfinder out of his cape's inner pocket. "I hope I'll see you at Tribunal Hall in a few hours. But I'll leave that up to you. Think about what I've said, okay?"

Keefe managed a shaky nod as Alden held the crystal up to the sunlight and glittered away.

"That guy's got a lot of nerve," Ro grumbled. "You know what that was, right? He's trying to get you to back off so he can keep his spoiled son happy—and he's totally using your daddy issues to make you play along!" She held out her arm, pretending she was wrapping it around an imaginary person's shoulders. "*I've long considered you part of my family*—what a stinking load of garbage! He's just trying to get rid of the competition. So what you need to do now is—"

"I'm going to the Tribunal," Keefe interrupted.

Ro rolled her eyes. "Of *course* you are. That's what you do—sabotage yourself over and over because it's easier than putting yourself out there!"

"I'm not sabotaging anything! Sophie's not some prize that Fitz and I get to fight over. She's a person. And she has her own feelings—and no one knows those feelings better than I do!"

Ro blinked, and he realized he'd shouted that super loud.

Loud enough that he was pretty sure his father had heard every word.

But it didn't matter.

Lord Cassius wasn't the type to go for a heart-to-heart.

Keefe's hands curled into fists and he sucked in a deep, slow breath before he said, "I'm going to the Tribunal. Because two of my friends are going to be there. And they're going to need me. You can whine about it all you want. Or you can stay here. . . ."

"Oh, I'm going," Ro warned. "And there will be an *abundance* of whining."

"Bring it on," Keefe muttered, heading for his room to get changed. He tried to slam the door in Ro's face, but the ogre princess had annoyingly fast reflexes and managed to block it with her elbow.

She sighed. "Fine. I'll leave you to your sulking. But just . . . promise me something, okay? Don't give up."

"I'm not," Keefe said.

And he meant it.

He *wasn't* giving up.

He was just . . . waiting.

Being the best friend he could be.

Trying not to wreck anything.

And hoping, hoping, hoping that someday things would change.

Read on for a peek at Sophie's next adventure in
Keeper of the Lost Cities, Book Eight: LEGACY

BEFORE SOPHIE COULD CHANGE HER mind, she plopped down on her enormous canopied bed and stared at the crystal stars dangling from her ceiling, watching them sparkle in the bright afternoon sunlight as she gathered her mental strength. The warm energy churned inside her mind, humming as it grew stronger and stronger and stronger. And when she could feel it buzzing against the backs of her eyes, she shoved it out of her head, along with the loudest call she could muster.

TAM—CAN YOU HEAR ME? IT'S SOPHIE!

She repeated the words over and over, imagining the force like thick syrup pouring across the sky in every direction—

covering the world. And as her consciousness spread, she closed her eyes and tried to feel for . . .

Actually, she wasn't sure.

She hadn't communicated telepathically with Tam very often, so she didn't know how to recognize his thoughts the way she could with Fitz and Keefe.

TAM! PLEASE, I NEED TO TALK TO YOU!

A headache prickled the edge of her consciousness, but she gave herself several long, slow breaths and timed her next transmissions with each exhale, keeping the message shorter to save her energy.

Tam.

Tam!

TAM!

Still nothing—and she could feel her concentration draining to the dregs.

If Fitz were there, he could've given her a mental boost, the way he always did when they worked together. But she'd let her silly matchmaking worries keep him away. She had to stop that—had to figure out how to keep things balanced and—

Sophie?

The voice was a ghost in the shadows—cold and whispery.

TAM!

Yeah. But I shouldn't be talking to you like this. It's way too dangerous.

I know, but—

There's no "but," Tam interrupted, and the feel of his thoughts shifted with the words, like the darkness was crystalizing into ice. *Gethen checks my memories constantly.*

Sophie's heart screeched to a stop.

She'd forgotten that the Neverseen's only Telepath had been in the Black Swan's custody when Keefe had been living with the enemy. So they hadn't had to worry about anyone discovering their conversations unless someone caught them in the act and somehow figured out what was happening.

They also hadn't had to worry about Keefe unwittingly revealing anything he wasn't supposed to.

Has Gethen probed your mind? she asked, trying to keep the transmission as quiet as possible.

Of course. That was the first thing he did.

Bile burned Sophie's throat.

Probing was a type of deep mental search that could uncover pretty much anything when performed by a skilled Telepath.

And Tam knew all of their secrets.

All.

Of.

Them.

So if Gethen had probed his mind . . .

Then the Neverseen now knew that Sophie was an Enhancer. And that Mr. Forkle was still technically alive—and that Magnate Leto and Sir Astin were two of his alter egos. And that Granite and Squall—two other members of the Black Swan's

Collective—were Sir Tiergan and Juline Dizznee. And they knew every single lead that Sophie and her friends had uncovered— and everything they *didn't* know as well, like how to open Councillor Kenric's cache if they ever got their hands on the real one again. And how little Sophie had learned, from healing Prentice's mind and from searching Wylie's memories, about what had happened the day Wylie's mom died.

This is so bad, she thought, reaching up to rub her temples.

Did Tam know where they'd hidden her human family after they'd rescued them from Nightfall?

And how much did he know about the security at Havenfield?

Were Silveny, Greyfell, and the babies still safe there?

I'm sorry, Tam's mind murmured, and the frigidness of his voice thawed a little. *I tried to block him, but . . . Gethen's too powerful.*

He was.

Sophie had faced off against him several times, and it had never gone well—and she was a Telepath with an impenetrable mind.

It's not your fault, she promised, wanting to punch herself for not figuring this out earlier. If she had, they could've started taking precautions from the moment Tam had left.

Actually, she should've thought of it before he turned himself over. Maybe he wouldn't have gone if he'd known how much he was going to compromise the Black Swan in the process. After all, Tam had been to some of the Black Swan's hideouts. He knew the oath they made when they swore fealty, and what weapons and fighting techniques Sophie and her friends had been practicing during their battle training, and—

Yeah, Tam thought, interrupting her ever-spiraling panic. *Now you get why I can't talk. He's going to know everything you tell me, and he's already learned enough.*

Okay. She took a deep breath, reminding herself that she couldn't change what had already happened.

Time to focus on damage control.

You can still tell ME something, she reminded him. *Even if they know you told me, they'll have to change their plans—and that'll buy us some time.*

His thoughts froze again. *Uh, you think they tell me anything important?*

There must be something. Maybe some clue to where you are, like a landmark you recognized?

Nope. I'm in a cave. All I've seen are rocks.

What color are they?

They're rocks, Sophie. There's nothing special about them.

Are you sure it's a cave and not somewhere underground?

Underground might mean he was close to Loamnore.

I don't know. All I can tell is that it's dark and stuffy.

So it's hot? Like . . . maybe you're in a desert?

I seriously have no idea. The Neverseen are smart. They're not going to let me learn anything that would give their hideout away.

His mental voice stayed soft and whispery, but there was a sharpness to his thoughts that Sophie had never experienced. It felt like each word was a shard of darkness, slicing into her head.

But she wasn't going to let him scare her away. *Have you met any other members of the order?*

A couple—but they wear cloaks and use code names, and barely say two words to me when we train, so I can't tell you anything about them.

Wait—you're training with them? Does that mean there's another Shade?

No. I don't know what these guys can do. Or maybe they're female. I can't tell. Lady Gisela keeps me alone in a corner, practicing from Umber's journals.

A shiver rippled down Sophie's spine. *Umber had journals?*

Lots of them. And I have to work through all of her exercises.

Well . . . *that* was terrifying.

What kind of exercises? Sophie asked—and when he hesitated, she added, *Shadowflux training, right?*

Obviously.

The response bothered her more than a single word should—but it was the icy confidence behind it.

The Tam she knew had been reluctant to train in the dark element. Almost afraid of its strange power. And now he sounded . . . proud.

You need to be careful, she warned him. *You don't know how*

Umber's training will affect you. She was one of the creepiest people I've ever met.

The bones in her hand throbbed, remembering the way Umber had shattered them one by one.

I AM being careful, Tam assured her. *But the training is unavoidable.*

Then tell me what they're having you do so I can figure out what they're planning and get you out of there. You're already going to be in trouble for talking to me, right? Why not make it worth it?

Uh, because they can make their punishments WAY worse.

Don't worry—Linh's safe.

You can't know that for sure. And even if you're right, they have plenty of ways they can punish ME.

Sophie was certain they did. And she hated putting him in that position. But leaving him with the Neverseen was feeling beyond scary. She had to find a way to get him out of there, before they made him do something terrifying.

Please, she begged. *You know what's at stake—especially if you're studying Umber's journals.*

I DO know what's at stake. My sister's LIFE.

The coldness wrapping each thought sank all the way to her bones. *We'll protect her.*

Yeah. I've seen how well that protection works. I can't take that risk.

So . . . what? You'll just do whatever creepy things the Neverseen tell you to do and hang the consequences?

I don't know.

That's not good enough!

Well, it's going to have to be!

Sophie locked her jaw to stop her teeth from chattering. *I can already feel a change in you, Tam. Just from your mind. I think Umber's training is affecting you.*

I can handle it.

You know Keefe said the same thing, right? Sophie asked.

She'd hoped that would knock some sense into him, given the strange animosity between the two boys. But Tam's thoughts were frozen claws as he said, *I guess I get where he was coming from now.*

Tam—

No—just stop! You're making everything worse. Leave me alone. His thoughts stirred like an artic flurry.

I can't do that.

Well, you're going to have to. If you try reaching out to me again, I'll run straight to Gethen so he can hear everything you say. I can't put Linh at risk.

Meanwhile you're putting Linh's safety ahead of everyone else's— do you really think she wants you to do that?

I don't care. I'm her twin. Protecting her is my job. And I think you're forgetting that I also saved Silveny and Greyfell—and their babies—by agreeing to cooperate.

I could've saved them another way.

How? I'm sure you've spent the last couple of weeks replaying what happened over and over—can you honestly tell me you've thought of anything else that would've cured them in time?

She hadn't.

But she couldn't admit that.

You've seen the kind of cruelty the Neverseen are capable of, Tam. You really want to be a part of that?

The mental flurry picked up speed, hurling each word at her. *I don't have a choice!*

There's always a choice!

Well, right now, I'm choosing to be done with this conversation.

Tam—

No, it's time for you to leave me alone, Sophie. Get out of my head—or I'll make you go away.

Tam, please—

The flurry spun into a hurricane—a black storm crashing into her brain. And Tam's booming voice was thunder amid the tempest.

I'M SORRY—I DIDN'T MEAN ANY OF THAT. I HAD TO PUT ON A GOOD SHOW SO GETHEN WON'T GET SUSPICIOUS WHEN HE CHECKS MY MEMORIES LATER. AND I NEEDED TIME TO GATHER THE SHADOWFLUX I'M USING TO SHROUD THIS THOUGHT, SO HE CAN'T HEAR ANYTHING I'M SAYING. HE'LL PROBABLY STILL BE ABLE TO SEE THAT I SENT SOMETHING, SO I CAN'T TELL YOU MUCH—AND YOU CAN'T REACH OUT TO ME LIKE THIS AGAIN. IT'S WAY TOO DANGEROUS FOR

*EVERYONE. JUST . . . TRUST ME TO HANDLE THIS. I
HAVE THINGS UNDER CONTROL—OR I WILL, IF YOU
DO ONE FAVOR FOR ME. I NEED YOU TO KEEP KEEFE
AWAY UNTIL THIS IS OVER. IF YOU CAN'T CONVINCE
HIM TO COOPERATE, MAKE UP A FAKE PROJECT TO
DISTRACT HIM. OR LOCK HIM UP SOMEWHERE IF YOU
HAVE TO. I DON'T CARE. JUST DON'T LET HIM GET
NEAR THE NEVERSEEN—AND DEFINITELY DON'T LET
HIM GET NEAR ME.*

Why not? Sophie asked, struggling to pick his words out of
the frozen chaos. Her heart was pounding as hard as her head,
drowning out everything with the *thump! thump! thump!*

But she still managed to catch when Tam said, *BECAUSE
HIS MOM ORDERED ME TO KILL HIM.*

Lose yourself in the world of the *New York Times* bestselling UNWANTEDS series!

"The Hunger Games meets Harry Potter."
—*KIRKUS REVIEWS*, ON *THE UNWANTEDS*